Archaeologist and anthropologist **Steven Erikson** is the bestselling author of the genre-defining The Malazan Book of the Fallen, a multi-volume epic fantasy that has been hailed a masterwork of the imagination and one of the top ten fantasy series of all time. The first novel in the series, *Gardens of the Moon*, was shortlisted for the World Fantasy Award. He has also written several novellas set in the same world. *Forge of Darkness* is the first Kharkanas novel and takes readers back to the origins of the Malazan world. *Fall of Light* continues this epic tale. A lifelong science fiction reader, he has also written fiction affectionately parodying a long-running SF television series and *Rejoice*, a novel of first contact. *The God is Not Willing* is the opening chapter in a new sequence – The Tales of Witness – and is set in the world of the Malazan Empire, ten years after the events recounted in *The Crippled God*.

Steven Erikson lives in Victoria, Canada. To find out more, visit www.steven-erikson.org – and you can also find him on Facebook: Steven Erikson – Author

Acclaim for Steven Erikson's
THE MALAZAN BOOK OF THE FALLEN

'Erikson is an extraordinary writer . . . my advice to anyone
who might listen to me is: treat yourself'
STEPHEN R. DONALDSON

'Give me the evocation of a rich, complex and yet ultimately
unknowable other world, with a compelling suggestion of intricate
history and mythology and lore. Give me mystery amid the grand
narrative . . . Give me a world in which every sea hides a crumbled
Atlantis, every ruin has a tale to tell, every broken blade is a silent
legacy of struggles unknown. Give me, in other words, the fantasy
work of Steven Erikson . . . a master of lost and forgotten
epochs, a weaver of ancient epics'
SALON.COM

'I stand slack-jawed in awe of *The Malazan Book of the Fallen*.
This masterwork of the imagination may be the high
watermark of epic fantasy'
GLEN COOK

'The most masterful piece of fiction I have ever read. It has
single-handedly changed everything we thought we knew about
fantasy literature and redefined what is possible'
SF SITE

'Rare is the writer who so fluidly combines a sense of mythic power
and depth of world with fully realized characters and thrilling action,
but Steven Erikson manages it spectacularly'
MICHAEL A. STACKPOLE

'Erikson's magnum opus, *The Malazan Book of the Fallen*,
sits in pole position as the very best and most ambitious
epic fantasy saga ever written'
PAT'S FANTASY HOTLIST

'This is true myth in the making, a drawing upon fantasy to recreate
histories and legends as rich as any found within our culture'
INTERZONE

'Arguably the best fantasy series ever written. This is of course
subject to personal opinion . . . but few can deny that the quality
and ambition of the ten books that make up *The Malazan
Book of the Fallen* are unmatched within the genre'
FANTASY BOOK REVIEW

By Steven Erikson

The Malazan Book of the Fallen
GARDENS OF THE MOON
DEADHOUSE GATES
MEMORIES OF ICE
HOUSE OF CHAINS
MIDNIGHT TIDES
THE BONEHUNTERS
REAPER'S GALE
TOLL THE HOUNDS
DUST OF DREAMS
THE CRIPPLED GOD

THE FIRST COLLECTED TALES OF
BAUCHELAIN AND KORBAL BROACH
THE SECOND COLLECTED TALES OF
BAUCHELAIN AND KORBAL BROACH

The Kharkanas Trilogy
FORGE OF DARKNESS
FALL OF LIGHT

The Tales of Witness
THE GOD IS NOT WILLING

Other fiction
THIS RIVER AWAKENS
THE DEVIL DELIVERED AND OTHER
TALES
WILLFUL CHILD

*For more information on Steven Erikson and his books,
see his website at www.steven-erikson.org*

Gardens of the Moon
A Tale of the
Malazan Book of the Fallen

STEVEN ERIKSON

PENGUIN BOOKS

TRANSWORLD PUBLISHERS
Penguin Random House, One Embassy Gardens,
8 Viaduct Gardens, London SW11 7BW
www.penguin.co.uk

Transworld is part of the Penguin Random House group of companies
whose addresses can be found at global.penguinrandomhouse.com

First published in Great Britain in 1999 by Bantam Press
an imprint of Transworld Publishers
Bantam edition published 2000
Penguin paperback edition published 2024

A CIP catalogue record for this book
is available from the British Library.

ISBN
9781804995518 (B format)

Typeset in Goudy by Falcon Oast Graphic Art Ltd.
Printed and bound in Great Britain by Clays Ltd, Elcograf S.p.A.

The authorized representative in the EEA is Penguin Random House Ireland,
Morrison Chambers, 32 Nassau Street, Dublin D02 YH68.

Penguin Random House is committed to a sustainable future
for our business, our readers and our planet. This book is made
from Forest Stewardship Council® certified paper.

This novel is dedicated to I. C. Esslemont

worlds to conquer worlds to share

Acknowledgements

No novel is ever written in isolation. The author wishes to thank the following for their support over the years: Clare Thomas, Bowen, Mark Paxton-MacRae, David Keck, Courtney, Ryan, Chris and Rick, Mireille Theriacelt, Dennis Valdron, Keith Addison, Susan, David and Harriet, Clare and David Thomas Jr, Chris Rodell, Patrick Carroll, Kate Peach, Peter Knowlson, Rune, Kent and Val and the kids, my tireless agent Patrick Walsh, and Simon Taylor, one terrific editor.

Contents

Contents

GENABACKIS:
The Malazan Campaign ca. 1160 Burn's Sleep

PANNION DOMIN
✦ PREVIOUS FREE CITIES
✗ BATTLES
◌ MALAZAN OCCUPATION

SCALE
0   50   100 leagues

HUDD SEA

TOBLAI TUNDRA

Malyn Sea

NORTHWIND TUNDRA

Hoop
R. Gan   Horan
Caniss   Evino

TARTHEN RANGE

FREE CITY PLAIN

Genabaris
Prospect   Mottyntaeas
GRINNING FATE RANGE   Bettrys   Genalle
Nathilog   Mott   Blued
L. Blued   Owndos   Cajate
Ayjhan   Graz   Greydog   Ostann   R. Searr
BLACKDOG   Bodd   Abor   Sogena   Apple
FOREST   Yenys   One Eye Cat   ONE EYE RANGE   Tulips
TISANNIS PLAIN   Crest Bay
Bear   OLD KING   R. Toe   Crest
The   PLATEAU   HARBINGER
REACH   Patch   Cat   Cruk   PENINSULA
Oach   Glead   R. Letor   Anklos   Stand
MISTRAL   RHIVI PLAIN   Lead Sea   FALL
PLATEAU   LEAD STEPPES   SEPHAL   Taph   ISLE
MOUNTAINS
Greenwater   Rhivi   BHEDERIN
Lake   Trail   PLATEAU   BARGHAST
MORANTH   RANGE
FOREST   Pale   TAHLYN   The
CLOUD   MOUNTAINS   DIVIDE
FOREST
Mengal   MORANTH
MOUNTAINS
Dhavran   Lake Azur   Saltoan   Capustan
Gredfallan   GADROBI   Lest
Kurl   HILLS   R. Catlin   VISION MTNS.   Setta
DARUJHISTAN   Maurik
R. Maiten   CINNAMON   Coral
DWELLING   WASTES   Coral Bay
PLAIN   GODS WALK   R. Stem   RUST
MOUNTAINS   OCEAN
Bastion   Sarn   Pilgrim
Kel Tor   Lake
Heath   Outlook
PALAT
FOREST
PLAIN of LAMATATH   R. Heath

N

Callows

The Twins

NG

To Morn   To Elingarth

MENINGALLE OCEAN

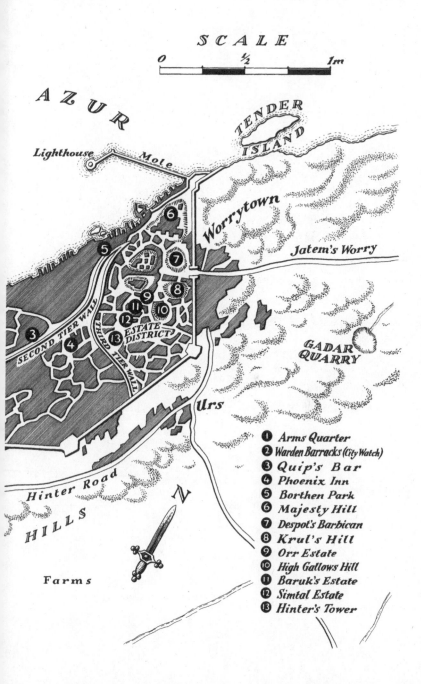

SCALE

0   ½   1m

AZUR

Lighthouse Mole

TENDER ISLAND

Worrytown

Jatem's Worry

Second Tier Wall

Third Tier Wall

ESTATE DISTRICT

Urs

GADAR QUARRY

Hinter Road

HILLS

Farms

N

① Arms Quarter
② Warden Barracks (City Watch)
③ Quip's Bar
④ Phoenix Inn
⑤ Borthen Park
⑥ Majesty Hill
⑦ Despot's Barbican
⑧ Krul's Hill
⑨ Orr Estate
⑩ High Gallows Hill
⑪ Baruk's Estate
⑫ Simtal Estate
⑬ Hinter's Tower

DRAMATIS PERSONAE

The Malazan Empire

Onearm's Host

Tattersail, Cadre Sorceress, 2nd Army, a reader of the Deck of Dragons
Hairlock, Cadre Mage, 2nd Army, an unpleasant rival of Tayschrenn
Calot, Cadre Mage, 2nd Army, Tattersail's lover
Toc the Younger, scout, 2nd Army, a Claw agent badly scarred at the Siege of Pale

The Bridgeburners

Sergeant Whiskeyjack, 9th Squad, past commander of the 2nd Army
Corporal Kalam, 9th Squad, an ex-Claw from Seven Cities
Quick Ben, 9th Squad, a Seven Cities Mage
Sorry, 9th Squad, a deadly killer in the guise of a young girl
Hedge, 9th Squad, a sapper
Fiddler, 9th Squad, a sapper
Trotts, 9th Squad, a Barghast warrior
Mallet, 9th Squad, the squad healer
Sergeant Antsy, 7th Squad
Picker, 7th Squad

The Imperial Command

Ganoes Stabro Paran, a noble-born officer in the Malazan Empire

Dujek Onearm, High Fist, Malazan Armies, Genabackis Campaign
Tayschrenn, High Mage to the Empress
Bellurdan, High Mage to the Empress
Nightchill, High Sorceress to the Empress
A'Karonys, High Mage to the Empress
Lorn, Adjunct to the Empress
Topper, Commander of the Claw
Empress Laseen, Ruler of the Malazan Empire

House Paran (Unta)

Tavore, Ganoes' sister (middle-child)
Felisin, Ganoes' youngest sister
Gamet, House Guard and veteran

In the Emperor's Time

Emperor Kellanved, the founder of the Empire, assassinated by Laseen
Dancer, the Emperor's chief adviser, assassinated by Laseen
Surly, Laseen's old name when Commander of the Claw
Dassem Ultor, the First Sword of Empire, killed outside Y'ghatan, Seven Cities
Toc (the Elder), disappeared in Laseen's purges of the Old Guard

In Darujhistan

The Phoenix Inn Regulars

Kruppe, a man of false modesty

Crokus Younghand, a young thief
Rallick Nom, an assassin in the Guild
Murillio, a courtier
Coll, a drunk
Meese, a regular
Irilta, a regular
Scurve, the barman
Sulty, a serving woman
Chert, an unlucky bully

The T'orrud Cabal

Baruk, a High Alchemist
Derudan, a Witch of Tennes
Mammot, a High Priest of D'riss and eminent scholar, uncle
to Crokus
Travale, a pious soldier of the Cabal
Tholis, a High Mage
Parald, a High Mage

The Council

Turban Orr, a powerful councilman and Simtal's lover
Lim, an ally of Turban Orr
Simtal, Lady of Simtal Estate
Estraysian D'Arle, a rival of Turban Orr
Challice D'Arle, his daughter

The Guild of Assassins

Vorcan, Mistress of the Guild (also known as the Master of
Assassins)
Ocelot, Rallick Nom's Clan Leader

Talo Krafar, an assassin of Jurrig Denatte's Clan
Krute of Talient, an agent of the Guild

Also in the city

The Eel, a rumoured master-spy
Circle Breaker, an agent of the Eel
Vildrom, a city guard
Captain Stillis, Captain of Guard, Simtal Estate

Further players

The Tiste Andii

Anomander Rake, Lord of Moon's Spawn, Son of Darkness, Knight of Darkness
Serrat, second-in-command to Rake
Korlat, a night-hunter and blood-kin to Serrat
Orfantal, a night-hunter
Horult, a night-hunter

The T'lan Imass

Logros, Commander of the T'lan Imass Clans serving the Malazan Empire
Onos T'oolan, a clanless warrior
Pran Chole, a Bonecaster (shaman) of the Kron T'lan Imass
Kig Aven, a Clan Leader

Others

Crone, a Great Raven and servant to Anomander Rake
Silanah, an Eleint and companion to Anomander Rake

Raest, a Jaghut Tyrant
K'rul, an Elder God, the Maker of Paths
Caladan Brood, the warlord, opposing the Malazan armies in the North Campaign
Kallor, Brood's second-in-command
Prince K'azz D'Avore, Commander of the Crimson Guard
Jorrick Sharplance, a Crimson Guard officer
Cowl, a High Mage in the Crimson Guard
Corporal Blues, Sixth Blade of the Crimson Guard
Fingers, Sixth Blade of the Crimson Guard
The Hound Baran, a Hound of Shadow
The Hound Blind, a Hound of Shadow
The Hound Gear, a Hound of Shadow
The Hound Rood, a Hound of Shadow
The Hound Shan, a Hound of Shadow
The Hound Doan, a Hound of Shadow
The Hound Ganrod, a Hound of Shadow
Shadowthrone/Ammanas, Ruler of the Warren of Shadow

The Rope/Cotillion, Companion of Shadowthrone and Patron of Assassins
Icarium, Builder of the Wheel of Ages in Darujhistan
Mappo, Icarium's companion
The Pannion Seer, a Prophet Tyrant ruling the Pannion Domin

Gardens of the Moon

Now these ashes have grown cold, we open the old book.
These oil-stained pages recount the tales of the Fallen,
a frayed empire, words without warmth. The hearth
has ebbed, its gleam and life's sparks are but memories
against dimming eyes – what cast my mind, what hue my
thoughts as I open the Book of the Fallen
and breathe deep the scent of history?
Listen, then, to these words carried on that breath.
These tales are the tales of us all, again yet again.
We are history relived and that is all, without end that is all.

The Emperor is dead!
So too his right hand – now cold, now severed!
But mark these dying shadows,
twinned and flowing bloody and beaten,
down and away from mortal sight . . .
From sceptre's rule dismissed,
from gild candelabra the light now fled,
from a hearth ringed in hard jewels,
seven years this warmth has bled . . .

The Emperor is dead.
So too his master'd companion, the rope cut clean.
But mark this burgeoning return –
faltering dark, the tattered shroud –
embracing children in Empire's dying light.
Hear now the dirge faint reprised,
before the sun's fall, this day spills red
on buckled earth, and in obsidian eyes
vengeance chimes seven times . . .

Call to Shadow (I.i. 1–18)
Felisin (b.1146)

Prologue

Prologue

1154th Year of Burn's Sleep
96th Year of the Malazan Empire
The Last Year of Emperor Kellanved's Reign

The stains of rust seemed to map blood seas on the black, pocked surface of Mock's Vane. A century old, it squatted on the point of an old pike that had been bolted to the outer top of the Hold's wall. Monstrous and mis-shapen, it had been cold-hammered into the form of a winged demon, teeth bared in a leering grin, and was tugged and buffeted in squealing protest with every gust of wind.

The winds were contrary the day columns of smoke rose over the Mouse Quarter of Malaz City. The Vane's silence announced the sudden falling-off of the sea breeze that came clambering over the ragged walls of Mock's Hold, then it creaked back into life as the hot, spark-scattered and smoke-filled breath of the Mouse Quarter reached across the city to sweep the promontory's heights.

Ganoes Stabro Paran of the House of Paran stood on tiptoe to see over the merlon. Behind him rose Mock's Hold, once capital of the Empire but now, since the mainland had been conquered, relegated once more to a Fist's holding. To his left rose the pike and its wayward trophy.

For Ganoes, the ancient fortification overlooking the city was too familiar to be of interest. This visit was his third in as many years; he'd long ago explored the courtyard with its heaved cobblestones, the Old Keep – now a stable, its upper floor home to pigeons and swallows and bats – and the citadel where even now his father negotiated the island export tithe with the harbour officials. In the last instance, of course, a goodly portion was out of bounds, even for a son of a noble house; for it was in the citadel that the Fist had his residence, and in the inner chambers that such affairs of the Empire as concerned this island were conducted.

Mock's Hold forgotten behind him, Ganoes' attention was on the tattered city below, and the riots that ran through its poorest quarter. Mock's Hold stood atop a cliff. The higher land of the Pinnacle was reached by a switchback staircase carved into the limestone of the cliff wall. The drop to the city below was eighty armspans or more, with the Hold's battered wall adding still another six. The Mouse was at the city's inland edge, an uneven spreading of hovels and overgrown tiers cut in half by the silt-heavy river that crawled towards the harbour. With most of Malaz City between Ganoes' position and the riots, it was hard to make out any detail, beyond the growing pillars of black smoke.

It was midday, but the flash and thundering concussion of magery made the air seem dark and heavy.

Armour clanking, a soldier appeared along the wall near him. The man leaned vambraced forearms on the battlement, the scabbard of his longsword scraping against the stones. 'Glad for your pure blood, eh?' he asked, grey eyes on the smouldering city below.

The boy studied the soldier. He already knew the complete regimental accoutrements of the Imperial Army, and the man at his side was a commander in the Third – one of the Emperor's own, an élite. On his dark grey shoulder-cloak was a silver brooch: a bridge of stone, lit by ruby flames. A *Bridgeburner*.

High-ranking soldiers and officials of the Empire commonly passed through Mock's Hold. The island of Malaz remained a vital port of call, especially now that the Korel wars to the south had begun. Ganoes had brushed shoulders with more than his share, here and in the capital, Unta.

'Is it true, then?' Ganoes asked boldly.

'Is what true?'

'The First Sword of Empire. Dassem Ultor. We heard in the capital before we left. He's dead. Is it true? Is Dassem dead?'

The man seemed to flinch, his gaze unwavering on the

Mouse. 'Such is war,' he muttered, under his breath, as if the words were not meant for anyone else's ears.

'You're with the Third. I thought the Third was with him, in Seven Cities. At Y'Ghatan—'

'Hood's Breath, they're still looking for his body in the still-hot rubble of that damned city, and here you are, a merchant's son three thousand leagues from Seven Cities with information only a few are supposed to possess.' He still did not turn. 'I know not your sources, but take my advice and keep what you know to yourself.'

Ganoes shrugged. 'It's said he betrayed a god.'

Finally the man faced him. His face was scarred, and something that might have been a burn marred his jaw and left cheek. For all that, he looked young for a commander. 'Heed the lesson there, son.'

'What lesson?'

'Every decision you make can change the world. The best life is the one the gods don't notice. You want to live free, boy, live quietly.'

'I want to be a soldier. A hero.'

'You'll grow out of it.'

Mock's Vane squealed as a wayward gust from the harbour cleared the grainy smoke. Ganoes could now smell rotting fish and the waterfront's stink of humanity.

Another Bridgeburner, this one with a broken, scorched fiddle strapped to his back, came up to the commander. He was wiry and if anything younger – only a few years older than Ganoes himself, who was twelve. Strange pockmarks covered his face and the backs of his hands, and his armour was a mixture of foreign accoutrements over a threadbare, stained uniform. A shortsword hung in a cracked wooden scabbard at his hip. He leaned against the merlon beside the other man with the ease of long familiarity.

'It's a bad smell when sorcerers panic,' the newcomer

5

said. 'They're losing control down there. Hardly the need for a whole cadre of mages, just to sniff out a few wax-witches.'

The commander sighed. 'Thought to wait to see if they'd rein themselves in.'

The soldier grunted. 'They are all new, untested. This could scar some of them for ever. Besides,' he added, 'more than a few down there are following someone else's orders.'

'A suspicion, no more.'

'The proof's right there,' the other man said. 'In the Mouse.'

'Perhaps.'

'You're too protective,' the man said. 'Surly says it's your greatest weakness.'

'Surly's the Emperor's concern, not mine.'

A second grunt answered that. 'Maybe all of us before too long.'

The commander was silent, slowly turning to study his companion.

The man shrugged. 'Just a feeling. She's taking a new name, you know. Laseen.'

'Laseen?'

'Napan word. Means—'

'I know what it means.'

'Hope the Emperor does, too.'

Ganoes said, 'It means Thronemaster.'

The two looked down at him.

The wind shifted again, making the iron demon groan on its perch – a smell of cool stone from the Hold itself. 'My tutor's Napan,' Ganoes explained.

A new voice spoke behind them, a woman's, imperious and cold. 'Commander.'

Both soldiers turned, but without haste. The commander said to his companion, 'The new company needs help down there. Send Dujek and a wing, and get some sappers to contain the fires – wouldn't do to have the whole city burn.'

6

The soldier nodded, marched away, sparing the woman not a single glance.

She stood with two bodyguards near the portal in the citadel's square tower. Her dusky blue skin marked her as Napan, but she was otherwise plain, wearing a salt-stained grey robe, her mousy hair cut short like a soldier's, her features thin and unmemorable. It was, however, her bodyguards that sent a shiver through Ganoes. They flanked her: tall, swathed in black, hands hidden in sleeves, hoods shadowing their faces. Ganoes had never seen a Claw before, but he instinctively knew these creatures to be acolytes of the cult. Which meant the woman was . . .

The commander said, 'It's your mess, Surly. Seems I'll have to clean it up.'

Ganoes was shocked at the absence of fear – the near-contempt in the soldier's voice. Surly had created the Claw, making it a power rivalled only by the Emperor himself.

'That is no longer my name, Commander.'

The man grimaced. 'So I've heard. You must be feeling confident in the Emperor's absence. He's not the only one who remembers you as nothing more than a serving-wench down in the Old Quarter. I take it the gratitude's washed off long since.'

The woman's face betrayed no change of expression to mark if the man's words had stung. 'The command was a simple one,' she said. 'It seems your new officers are unable to cope with the task.'

'It's got out of hand,' the commander said. 'They're unseasoned—'

'Not my concern,' she snapped. 'Nor am I particularly disappointed. Loss of control delivers its own lessons to those who oppose us.'

'Oppose? A handful of minor witches selling their meagre talents – to what sinister end? Finding the coraval schools on the shoals in the bay. Hood's Breath, woman, hardly a threat to the Empire.'

'Unsanctioned. Defiant of the new laws—'

'*Your* laws, Surly. They won't work, and when the Emperor returns he'll quash your prohibition of sorcery, you can be certain of that.'

The woman smiled coldly. 'You'll be pleased to know that the Tower's signalled the approach of the transports for your new recruits. We'll not miss you or your restless, seditious soldiers, Commander.'

Without another word, or a single glance spared for the boy standing beside the commander, she swung about and, flanked by her silent bodyguards, re-entered the citadel.

Ganoes and the commander returned their attention to the riot in the Mouse. Flames were visible, climbing through the smoke.

'One day I'll be a soldier,' Ganoes said.

The man grunted. 'Only if you fail at all else, son. Taking up the sword is the last act of desperate men. Mark my words and find yourself a more worthy dream.'

Ganoes scowled. 'You're not like the other soldiers I've talked to. You sound more like my father.'

'But I'm not your father,' the man growled.

'The world,' Ganoes said, 'doesn't need another wine merchant.'

The commander's eyes narrowed, gauging. He opened his mouth to make the obvious reply, then shut it again.

Ganoes Paran looked back down at the burning quarter, pleased with himself. *Even a boy, Commander, can make a point.*

Mock's Vane swung once more. Hot smoke rolled over the wall, engulfing them. A reek of burning cloth, scorched paint and stone, and now of something sweet. 'An abattoir's caught fire,' Ganoes said. 'Pigs.'

The commander grimaced. After a long moment he sighed and leaned back down on the merlon. 'As you say, boy, as you say.'

8

BOOK ONE

PALE

. . . In the eighth year the Free Cities of Genabackis established contracts with a number of mercenary armies to oppose the Imperium's advance; prominent among these were the Crimson Guard, under the command of Prince K'azz D'Avore (see Volumes III & V); and the Tiste Andii regiments of Moon's Spawn, under the command of Caladan Brood and others.

The forces of the Malazan Empire, commanded by High Fist Dujek Onearm, consisted in that year of the 2nd, 5th and 6th Armies, as well as legions of Moranth.

In retrospect two observations can be made. The first is that the Moranth alliance of 1156 marked a fundamental change in the science of warfare for the Malazan Imperium, which would prove efficacious in the short term. The second observation worth noting is that the involvement of the sorcerous Tiste Andii of Moon's Spawn represented the beginning of the continent's Sorcery Enfilade, with devastating consequences.

In the Year of Burn's Sleep 1163, the Siege of Pale ended with a now legendary sorcerous conflagration . . .

Imperial Campaigns 1158–1194
Volume IV, Genabackis
Imrygyn Tallobant (b.1151)

CHAPTER ONE

The old stones of this road
have rung with iron
black-shod hoofs and drums
where I saw him walking
up from the sea between the hills soaked red
in sunset he came, a boy among the echoes
sons and brothers all in ranks
of warrior ghosts he came to pass
where I sat on the worn final
league-stone at day's end –
his stride spoke loud all I needed
know of him on this road of stone –
the boy walks
another soldier, another one
bright heart not yet cooled
to hard iron

Mother's Lament
Anonymous

1161st Year of Burn's Sleep
103rd Year of the Malazan Empire
7th Year of Empress Laseen's Rule

'**P**rod and pull,' the old woman was saying, ''tis the way of the Empress, as like the gods themselves.' She leaned to one side and spat, then brought a soiled cloth to her wrinkled lips. 'Three husbands and two sons I saw off to war.'

The fishergirl's eyes shone as she watched the column of mounted soldiers thunder past, and she only half listened to the hag standing beside her. The girl's breath had risen to the pace of the magnificent horses. She felt her face burning, a flush that had nothing to do with the heat. The day was dying, the sun's red smear over the trees on her right, and the sea's sighing against her face had grown cool.

'That was in the days of the Emperor,' the hag continued. 'Hood roast the bastard's soul on a spit. But look on, lass. Laseen scatters bones with the best of them. Heh, she started with *his*, didn't she, now?'

The fishergirl nodded faintly. As befitted the lowborn, they waited by the roadside, the old woman burdened beneath a rough sack filled with turnips, the girl with a heavy basket balanced on her head. Every minute or so the old woman shifted the sack from one bony shoulder to the other. With the riders crowding them on the road and the ditch behind them a steep drop to broken rocks, she had no place to put down the sack.

'Scatters bones, I said. Bones of husbands, bones of sons, bones of wives and bones of daughters. All the same to her. All the same to the Empire.' The old woman spat a second time. 'Three husbands and two sons, ten coin apiece a year. Five of ten's fifty. Fifty coin a year's cold company, lass. Cold in winter, cold in bed.'

The fishergirl wiped dust from her forehead. Her bright eyes darted among the soldiers passing before her. The young men atop their high-backed saddles held expressions stern and fixed straight ahead. The few women who rode among them sat tall and somehow fiercer than the men. The sunset cast red glints from their helms, flashing so that the girl's eyes stung and her vision blurred.

'You're the fisherman's daughter,' the old woman said. 'I seen you afore on the road, and down on the strand. Seen you and your dad at market. Missing an arm, ain't he? More bones for her collection is likely, eh?' She made a chopping motion with one hand, then nodded. 'Mine's the first house on the track. I use the coin to buy candles. Five candles I burn every night, five candles to keep old Rigga company. It's a tired house, full of tired things and me one of them, lass. What you got in the basket there?'

Slowly the fishergirl realized that a question had been asked of her. She pulled her attention from the soldiers and smiled down at the old woman. 'I'm sorry,' she said, 'the horses are so loud.'

Rigga raised her voice. 'I asked what you got in your basket, lass?'

'Twine. Enough for three nets. We need to get one ready for tomorrow. Dadda lost his last one – something in the deep waters took it and a whole catch, too. Ilgrand Lender wants the money he loaned us and we need a catch tomorrow. A good one.' She smiled again and swept her gaze back to the soldiers. 'Isn't it wonderful?' she breathed.

Rigga's hand shot out and snagged the girl's thick black hair, yanked it hard.

The girl cried out. The basket on her head lurched, then slid down on to one shoulder. She grabbed frantically for it but it was too heavy. The basket struck the ground and split apart. 'Aaai!' the girl gasped, attempting to kneel. But Rigga pulled and snapped her head around.

'You listen to me, lass!' The old woman's sour breath hissed

13

against the girl's face. 'The Empire's been grinding this land down for a hundred years. You was born in it. I wasn't. When I was your age Itko Kan was a country. We flew a banner and it was ours. We were free, lass.'

The girl was sickened by Rigga's breath. She squeezed shut her eyes.

'Mark this truth, child, else the Cloak of Lies blinds you for ever.' Rigga's voice took on a droning cadence, and all at once the girl stiffened. *Rigga, Riggalai the Seer, the wax-witch who trapped souls in candles and burned them. Souls devoured in flame*— Rigga's words carried the chilling tone of prophecy. 'Mark this truth. I am the last to speak to you. You are the last to hear me. Thus are we linked, you and I, beyond all else.'

Rigga's fingers snagged tighter in the girl's hair. 'Across the sea the Empress has driven her knife into virgin soil. The blood now comes in a tide and it'll sweep you under, child, if you're not careful. They'll put a sword in your hand, they'll give you a fine horse, and they'll send you across that sea. But a shadow will embrace your soul. Now, listen! Bury this deep! Rigga will preserve you because we are linked, you and I. But it is all I can do, understand? Look to the Lord spawned in Darkness; his is the hand that shall free you, though he'll know it not—'

'What's this?' a voice bellowed.

Rigga swung to face the road. An outrider had slowed his mount. The Seer released the girl's hair.

The girl staggered back a step. A rock on the road's edge turned underfoot and she fell. When she looked up the outrider had trotted past. Another thundered up in his wake.

'Leave the pretty one alone, hag,' this one growled, and as he rode by he leaned in his saddle and swung an open, gauntleted hand. The iron-scaled glove cracked against Rigga's head, spinning her around. She toppled.

The fishergirl screamed as Rigga landed heavily across her thighs. A thread of crimson spit spattered her face.

14

Whimpering, the girl pushed herself back across the gravel, then used her feet to shove away Rigga's body. She climbed to her knees.

Something within Rigga's prophecy seemed lodged in the girl's head, heavy as a stone and hidden from light. She found she could not retrieve a single word the Seer had said. She reached out and grasped Rigga's woollen shawl. Carefully, she rolled the old woman over. Blood covered one side of Rigga's head, running down behind the ear. More blood smeared her lined chin and stained her mouth. The eyes stared sightlessly.

The fishergirl pulled back, unable to catch her breath. Desperate, she looked about. The column of soldiers had passed, leaving nothing but dust and the distant tremble of hoofs. Rigga's bag of turnips had spilled on to the road. Among the trampled vegetables lay five tallow candles. The girl managed a ragged lungful of dusty air. Wiping her nose, she looked to her own basket.

'Never mind the candles,' she mumbled, in a thick, odd voice. 'They're gone, aren't they, now? Just a scattering of bones. Never mind.' She crawled towards the bundles of twine that had fallen from the breached basket, and when she spoke again her voice was young, normal. 'We need the twine. We'll work all night and get one ready. Dadda's waiting. He's right at the door, he's looking up the track, he's waiting to see me.'

She stopped, a shiver running through her. The sun's light was almost gone. An unseasonal chill bled from the shadows, which now flowed like water across the road.

'Here it comes, then,' the girl grated softly, in a voice that wasn't her own.

A soft-gloved hand fell on her shoulder. She ducked down, cowering.

'Easy, girl,' said a man's voice. 'It's over. Nothing to be done for her now.'

The fishergirl looked up. A man swathed in black leaned over

15

her, his face obscured beneath a hood's shadow. 'But he hit her,' the girl said, in a child's voice. 'And we have nets to tie, me and Dadda—'

'Let's get you on your feet,' the man said, moving his long-fingered hands down under her arms. He straightened, lifting her effortlessly. Her sandalled feet dangled in the air before he set her down.

Now she saw a second man, shorter, also clothed in black. This one stood on the road and was turned away, his gaze in the direction the soldiers had gone. He spoke, his voice reed-thin. 'Wasn't much of a life,' he said, not turning to face her. 'A minor talent, long since dried up of the Gift. Oh, she might have managed one more, but we'll never know, will we?'

The fishergirl stumbled over to Rigga's bag and picked up a candle. She straightened, her eyes suddenly hard, then deliberately spat on to the road.

The shorter man's head snapped towards her. Within the hood it seemed the shadows played alone.

The girl shrank back a step. 'It was a good life,' she whispered. 'She had these candles, you see. Five of them. Five for—'

'Necromancy,' the short man cut in.

The taller man, still at her side, said softly, 'I see them, child. I understand what they mean.'

The other man snorted. 'The witch harboured five frail, weak souls. Nothing grand.' He cocked his head. 'I can hear them now. Calling for her.'

Tears filled the girl's eyes. A wordless anguish seemed to well up from that black stone in her mind. She wiped her cheeks. 'Where did you come from?' she asked abruptly. 'We didn't see you on the road.'

The man beside her half turned to the gravel track. 'On the other side,' he said, a smile in his tone. 'Waiting, just like you.'

The other giggled. 'On the other side indeed.' He

16

faced down the road again and raised his arms.

The girl drew in a sharp breath as darkness descended. A loud, tearing sound filled the air for a second, then the darkness dissipated and the girl's eyes widened.

Seven massive Hounds now sat around the man in the road. The eyes of these beasts glowed yellow, and all were turned in the same direction as the man himself.

She heard him hiss, 'Eager, are we? Then go!'

Silently, the Hounds bolted down the road.

Their master turned and said to the man beside her, 'Something to gnaw on Laseen's mind.' He giggled again.

'Must you complicate things?' the other answered wearily.

The short man stiffened. 'They are within sight of the column.' He cocked his head. From up the road came the scream of horses. He sighed. 'You've reached a decision, Cotillion?'

The other grunted amusedly. 'Using my name, Ammanas, means you've just decided for me. We can hardly leave her here now, can we?'

'Of course we can, old friend. Just not breathing.'

Cotillion looked down on the girl. 'No,' he said quietly, 'she'll do.'

The fishergirl bit her lip. Still clutching Rigga's candle, she took another step back, her wide eyes darting from one man to the other.

'Pity,' Ammanas said.

Cotillion seemed to nod, then he cleared his throat and said, 'It'll take time.'

An amused note entered Ammanas's reply. 'And have we time? True vengeance needs the slow, careful stalking of the victim. Have you forgotten the pain she once delivered us? Laseen's back is against the wall already. She might fall without our help. Where would be the satisfaction in that?'

Cotillion's response was cool and dry. 'You've always

17

underestimated the Empress. Hence our present circumstances . . . No.' He gestured at the fishergirl. 'We'll need this one. Laseen's raised the ire of Moon's Spawn, and that's a hornet's nest if ever there was one. The timing is perfect.'

Faintly, above the screaming horses, came the shrieks of men and women, a sound that pierced the girl's heart. Her eyes darted to Rigga's motionless form on the roadside, then back to Ammanas, who now approached her. She thought to run but her legs had weakened to a helpless trembling. He came close and seemed to study her, even though the shadows within his hood remained impenetrable.

'A fishergirl?' he asked, in a kindly tone.

She nodded.

'Have you a name?'

'Enough!' Cotillion growled. 'She's not some mouse under your paw, Ammanas. Besides, I've chosen her and I will choose her name as well.'

Ammanas stepped back. 'Pity,' he said again.

The girl raised imploring hands. 'Please,' she begged Cotillion, 'I've done nothing! My father's a poor man, but he'll pay you all he can. He needs me, and the twine – he's waiting right now!' She felt herself go wet between her legs and quickly sat down on the ground. 'I've done nothing!' Shame rose through her and she put her hands in her lap. 'Please.'

'I've no choice any more, child,' Cotillion said. 'After all, you know our names.'

'I've never heard them before!' the girl cried.

The man sighed. 'With what's happening up the road right now, well, you'd be questioned. Unpleasantly. There are those who know our names.'

'You see, lass,' Ammanas added, suppressing a giggle, 'we're not supposed to be here. There are names, and then there are *names*.' He swung to Cotillion and said, in a chilling voice, 'Her father must be dealt with. My Hounds?'

18

'No,' Cotillion said. 'He lives.'

'Then how?'

'I suspect,' Cotillion said, 'greed will suffice, once the slate is wiped clean.' Sarcasm filled his next words. 'I'm sure you can manage the sorcery in that, can't you?'

Ammanas giggled. 'Beware of shadows bearing gifts.'

Cotillion faced the girl again. He lifted his arms out to the sides. The shadows that held his features in darkness now flowed out around his body.

Ammanas spoke, and to the girl his words seemed to come from a great distance. 'She's ideal. The Empress could never track her down, could never even so much as guess.' He raised his voice. 'It's not so bad a thing, lass, to be the pawn of a god.'

'Prod and pull,' the fishergirl said quickly.

Cotillion hesitated at her strange comment, then he shrugged. The shadows whirled out to engulf the girl. With their cold touch her mind fell away, down into darkness. Her last fleeting sensation was of the soft wax of the candle in her right hand, and how it seemed to well up between the fingers of her clenched fist.

The captain shifted in his saddle and glanced at the woman riding beside him. 'We've closed the road on both sides, Adjunct. Moved the local traffic inland. So far, no word's leaked.' He wiped sweat from his brow and winced. The hot woollen cap beneath his helm had rubbed his forehead raw.

'Something wrong, Captain?'

He shook his head, squinting up the road. 'Helmet's loose. Had more hair the last time I wore it.'

The Adjunct to the Empress did not reply.

The mid-morning sun made the road's white, dusty surface almost blinding. The captain felt sweat running down his body, and the mail of his helm's lobster tail kept nipping the hairs on his neck. Already his lower back ached. It had been years since

19

he'd last ridden a horse, and the roll was slow in coming. With every saddle-bounce he felt vertebrae crunch.

It had been a long time since somebody's title had been enough to straighten him up. But this was the Adjunct to the Empress, Laseen's personal servant, an extension of her Imperial will. The last thing the captain wanted was to show his misery to this young, dangerous woman.

Up ahead the road began its long, winding ascent. A salty wind blew from their left, whistling through the newly budding trees lining that side of the road. By mid-afternoon, that wind would breathe hot as a baker's oven, carrying with it the stench of the mudflats. And the sun's heat would bring something else as well. The captain hoped to be back in Kan by then.

He tried not to think about the place they rode towards. Leave that to the Adjunct. In his years of service to the Empire, he'd seen enough to know when to shut everything down inside his skull. This was one of those times.

The Adjunct spoke. 'You've been stationed here long, Captain?'

'Aye,' the man growled.

The woman waited, then asked, 'How long?'

He hesitated. 'Thirteen years, Adjunct.'

'You fought for the Emperor, then,' she said.

'Aye.'

'And survived the purge.'

The captain threw her a look. If she felt his gaze, she gave no indication. Her eyes remained on the road ahead; she rolled easily in the saddle, the scabbarded longsword hitched high under her left arm – ready for mounted battle. Her hair was either cut short or drawn up under her helm. Her figure was lithe enough, the captain mused.

'Finished?' she asked. 'I was asking about the purges commanded by Empress Laseen following her predecessor's untimely death.'

20

The captain gritted his teeth, ducked his chin to draw up the helm's strap – he hadn't had time to shave and the buckle was chafing. 'Not everyone was killed, Adjunct. The people of Itko Kan aren't exactly excitable. None of those riots and mass executions that hit other parts of the Empire. We all just sat tight and waited.'

'I take it,' the Adjunct said, with a slight smile, 'you're not noble-born, Captain.'

He grunted. 'If I'd been noble-born, I wouldn't have survived, even here in Itko Kan. We both know that. Her orders were specific, and even the droll Kanese didn't dare disobey the Empress.' He scowled. 'No, up through the ranks, Adjunct.'

'Your last engagement?'

'Wickan Plains.'

They rode on in silence for a time, passing the occasional soldier stationed on the road. Off to their left the trees fell away to ragged heather, and the sea beyond showed its white-capped expanse. The Adjunct spoke. 'This area you've contained, how many of your guard have you deployed to patrol it?'

'Eleven hundred,' the captain replied.

Her head turned at this, her cool gaze tightening beneath the rim of her helm.

The captain studied her expression. 'The carnage stretches half a league from the sea, Adjunct, and a quarter-league inland.'

The woman said nothing.

They approached the summit. A score of soldiers had gathered there, and others waited along the slope's rise. All had turned to watch them.

'Prepare yourself, Adjunct.'

The woman studied the faces lining the roadside. She knew these to be hardened men and women, veterans of the siege of

21

Li Heng and the Wickan Wars out on the north plains. But something had been clawed into their eyes that had left them raw and exposed. They looked upon her with a yearning that she found disturbing, as if they hungered for answers. She fought the urge to speak to them as she passed, to offer whatever comforting words she could. Such gifts were not hers to give, however, nor had they ever been. In this she was much the same as the Empress.

From beyond the summit she heard the cries of gulls and crows, a sound that rose into a high-pitched roar as they reached the rise. Ignoring the soldiers on either side, the Adjunct moved her horse forward. The captain followed. They came to the crest and looked down. The road dipped here for perhaps a fifth of a league, climbing again at the far end to a promontory.

Thousands of gulls and crows covered the ground, spilling over into the ditches and among the low, rough heather and gorse. Beneath this churning sea of black and white the ground was a uniform red. Here and there rose the ribbed humps of horses, and from among the squalling birds came the glint of iron.

The captain reached up and unstrapped his helm. He lifted it slowly from his head, then set it down over his saddle horn. 'Adjunct . . .'

'I am named Lorn,' the woman said softly.

'One hundred and seventy-five men and women. Two hundred and ten horses. The Nineteenth Regiment of the Itko Kanese Eighth Cavalry.' The captain's throat tightened briefly. He looked at Lorn. 'Dead.' His horse shied under him as it caught an updraught. He closed savagely on the reins and the animal stilled, nostrils wide and ears back, muscles trembling under him. The Adjunct's stallion made no move. 'All had their weapons bared. All fought whatever enemy attacked them. But the dead are all ours.'

22

'You've checked the beach below?' Lorn asked, still staring down on the road.

'No signs of a landing,' the captain replied. 'No tracks any-where, neither seaward nor inland. There are more dead than these, Adjunct. Farmers, peasants, fisherfolk, travellers on the road. All of them torn apart, limbs scattered – children, live-stock, dogs.' He stopped abruptly and turned away. 'Over four hundred dead,' he grated. 'We're not certain of the exact count.'

'Of course,' Lorn said, her tone devoid of feeling. 'No witnesses?'

'None.'

A man was riding towards them on the road below, leaning close to his horse's ear as he talked the frightened animal through the carnage. Birds rose in shrieking complaint in front of him, settling again once he had passed.

'Who is that?' the Adjunct asked.

The captain grunted. 'Lieutenant Ganoes Paran. He's new to my command. From Unta.'

Lorn's eyes narrowed on the young man. He'd reached the edge of the depression, stopping to relay orders to the work crews. He leaned back in his saddle then and glanced in their direction. 'Paran. From House Paran?'

'Aye, gold in his veins and all that.'

'Call him up here.'

The captain gestured and the lieutenant kicked his mount's flanks. Moments later he reined in beside the captain and saluted.

The man and his horse were covered from head to toe in blood and bits of flesh. Flies and wasps buzzed hungrily around them. Lorn saw in Lieutenant Paran's face none of the youth that rightly belonged there. For all that, it was an easy face to rest eyes upon.

'You checked the other side, Lieutenant?' the captain asked.

23

Paran nodded. 'Yes, sir. There's a small fishing settlement down from the promontory. A dozen or so huts. Bodies in all but two. Most of the barques look to be in, though there's one empty mooring pole.'

Lorn cut in. 'Lieutenant, describe the empty huts.'

He batted at a threatening wasp before answering. 'One was at the top of the strand, just off the trail from the road. We think it belonged to an old woman we found dead on the road, about half a league south of here.'

'Why?'

'Adjunct, the hut's contents were that of an old woman. Also, she seemed in the habit of burning candles. Tallow candles, in fact. The old woman on the road had a sack full of turnips and a handful of tallow candles. Tallow's expensive here, Adjunct.'

Lorn asked, 'How many times have you ridden through this battlefield, Lieutenant?'

'Enough to be getting used to it, Adjunct.' He grimaced.

'And the second empty hut?'

'A man and a girl, we think. The hut's close to the tidemark, opposite the empty mooring pole.'

'No sign of them?'

'None, Adjunct. Of course, we're still finding bodies, along the road, out in the fields.'

'But not on the beach.'

'No.'

The Adjunct frowned, aware that both men were watching her. 'Captain, what kind of weapons killed your soldiers?'

The captain hesitated, then turned a glare on the lieutenant. 'You've been crawling around down there, Paran, let's hear your opinion.'

Paran's answering smile was tight. 'Yes, sir. Natural weapons.'

The captain felt a sinking feeling in his stomach. He'd hoped he'd been wrong.

24

'What do you mean,' Lorn asked, 'natural weapons?'

'Teeth, mostly. Very big, very sharp ones.'

The captain cleared his throat, then said, 'There haven't been wolves in Itko Kan for a hundred years. In any case, no carcasses around—'

'If it was wolves,' Paran said, turning to eye the basin, 'they were as big as mules. No tracks, Adjunct. Not even a tuft of hair.'

'Not wolves, then,' Lorn said.

Paran shrugged.

The Adjunct drew a deep breath, held it, then let it out in a slow sigh. 'I want to see this fishing village.'

The captain made ready to don his helmet, but the Adjunct shook her head. 'Lieutenant Paran will suffice, Captain. I suggest you take personal command of your guard in the meantime. The dead must be removed as quickly as possible. All evidence of the massacre is to be erased.'

'Understood, Adjunct,' the captain said, hoping he'd kept the relief out of his voice.

Lorn turned to the young noble. 'Well, Lieutenant?'

He nodded and clucked his horse into motion.

It was when the birds scattered from their path that the Adjunct found herself envying the captain. Before her the roused carrion-eaters exposed a carpet of armour, broken bones and meat. The air was hot, turgid and cloying. She saw soldiers, still helmed, their heads crushed by what must have been huge, terribly powerful jaws. She saw torn mail, crumpled shields, and limbs that had been ripped from bodies. Lorn managed only a few moments of careful examination of the scene around them before she fixed her gaze on the promontory ahead, unable to encompass the magnitude of the slaughter. Her stallion, bred of the finest lines of Seven Cities stock, a warhorse trained in the blood for generations, had lost its proud, unyielding strut,

25

and now picked its way carefully along the road.

Lorn realized she needed a distraction, and sought it in conversation. 'Lieutenant, have you received your commission yet?'

'No, Adjunct. I expect to be stationed in the capital.'

She raised an eyebrow. 'Indeed. And how will you manage that?'

Paran squinted ahead, a tight smile on his lips. 'It will be arranged.'

'I see.' Lorn fell silent. 'The nobles have refrained from seeking military commissions, kept their heads low for a long time, haven't they?'

'Since the first days of the Empire. The Emperor held no love for us. Whereas Empress Laseen's concerns seem to lie elsewhere.'

Lorn eyed the young man. 'I see you like taking risks, Lieutenant,' she said. 'Unless your presumption extends to goading the Adjunct to the Empress. Are you that confident of your blood's invincibility?'

'Since when is speaking the truth presumptuous?'

'You *are* young, aren't you?'

This seemed to sting Paran. A flush rose in his smooth-shaven cheeks. 'Adjunct, for the past seven hours I have been knee-deep in torn flesh and spilled blood. I've been fighting crows and gulls for bodies – do you know what these birds are doing here? Precisely? They're tearing off strips of meat and fighting over them; they're getting fat on eyeballs and tongues, livers and hearts. In their frantic greed they fling the meat around ...' He paused, visibly regaining control over himself as he straightened in his saddle. 'I'm not young any more, Adjunct. As for presumption, I honestly couldn't care less. Truth can't be danced around, not out here, not now, not ever again.'

They reached the far slope. Off to the left a narrow track led down towards the sea. Paran gestured to it, then angled his horse forward.

Lorn followed, her thoughtful expression holding on the lieutenant's broad back, before she turned her attention to the route they took. The path was narrow, skirting the promontory's bluff. Off to the left the trail's edge dropped away to rocks sixty feet below. The tide was out, the waves breaking on a reef a few hundred yards offshore. Pools filled the black bedrock's cracks and basins, dully reflecting an overcast sky.

They came to a bend, and beyond and below stretched a crescent-shaped beach. Above it, at the promontory's foot, lay a broad, grassy shelf on which squatted a dozen huts.

The Adjunct swung her gaze seaward. The barques rested on their low flanks beside their mooring poles. The air above the beach and the tidal flat was empty – not a bird in sight.

She halted her mount. A moment later Paran glanced back at her then did the same. He watched her as she removed her helmet and shook out her long, auburn hair. It was wet and stringy with sweat. The lieutenant rode back to her side, a questioning look in his eyes.

'Lieutenant Paran, your words were well spoken.' She breathed in the salty air, then met his gaze. 'You won't be stationed in Unta, I'm afraid. You will be taking your orders from me as a commissioned officer on my staff.'

His eyes slowly narrowed. 'What happened to those soldiers, Adjunct?'

She didn't answer immediately, leaning back on her saddle and scanning the distant sea. 'Someone's been here,' she said. 'A sorcerer of great power. Something's happened, and we're being diverted from discovering it.'

Paran's mouth dropped open. 'Killing four hundred people was a diversion?'

'If that man and his daughter had been out fishing, they'd have come in with the tide.'

27

'But—'

'You won't find their bodies, Lieutenant.'

Paran was puzzled. 'Now what?'

She glanced at him, then swung her horse around. 'We go back.'

'That's it?' He stared after her as she directed her mount back up the trail, then rode to catch up. 'Wait a minute, Adjunct,' he said, as he came alongside.

She gave him a warning look.

Paran shook his head. 'No. If I'm now on your staff, I have to know more about what's going on.'

She placed her helmet back on and cinched tight the strap under her chin. Her long hair dangled in tattered ropes down over her Imperial cape. 'Very well. As you know, Lieutenant, I'm no mage—'

'No,' Paran cut in, with a cold grin, 'you just hunt them down and kill them.'

'Don't interrupt me again. As I was saying, I am anathema to sorcery. That means, Lieutenant, that, even though I'm not a practitioner, I have a relationship with magic. Of sorts. We know each other, if you will. I know the patterns of sorcery, and I know the patterns of the minds that use it. We were meant to conclude that the slaughter was thorough, and random. It was neither. There's a path here, and we have to find it.'

Slowly Paran nodded.

'Your first task, Lieutenant, is to ride to the market town – what's its name again?'

'Gerrom.'

'Yes, Gerrom. They'll know this fishing village, since that's where the catch is sold. Ask around, find out which fisher family consisted of a father and daughter. Get me their names, and their descriptions. Use the militia if the locals are recalcitrant.'

28

'They won't be,' Paran said. 'The Kanese are co-operative folk.'

They reached the top of the trail and stopped at the road. Below, wagons rocked among the bodies, the oxen braying and stamping their blood-soaked hoofs. Soldiers shouted in the press, while overhead wheeled thousands of birds. The scene stank of panic. At the far end stood the captain, his helmet hanging from its strap in one hand.

The Adjunct stared down on the scene with hard eyes. 'For their sake,' she said, 'I hope you're right, Lieutenant.'

As he watched the two riders approach, something told the captain that his days of ease in Itko Kan were numbered. His helmet felt heavy in his hand. He eyed Paran. That thin-blooded bastard had it made. *A hundred strings pulling him every step of the way to some cushy posting in some peaceful city.*

He saw Lorn studying him as they came to the crest. 'Captain, I have a request for you.'

The captain grunted. *Request, hell. The Empress has to check her slippers every morning to make sure this one isn't already in them.* 'Of course, Adjunct.'

The woman dismounted, as did Paran. The lieutenant's expression was impassive. Was that arrogance, or had the Adjunct given him something to think about?

'Captain,' Lorn began, 'I understand there's a recruiting drive under way in Kan. Do you pull in people from outside the city?'

'To join? Sure, more of them than anyone else. City folk got too much to give up. Besides, they get the bad news first. Most of the peasants don't know everything's gone to hell on Genabackis. A lot of them figure city folk whine too much anyway. May I ask why?'

'You may.' Lorn turned to watch the soldiers cleaning up the road. 'I need a list of recent recruits. Within the last two days.

Forget the ones born in the city, just the outlying ones. And only the women and/or old men.'

The captain grunted again. 'Should be a short list, Adjunct.'

'I hope so, Captain.'

'You figured out what's behind all this?'

Still following the activity on the road below, Lorn said, 'No idea.'

Yes, the captain thought, and I'm the Emperor reincarnated. 'Too bad,' he muttered.

'Oh.' The Adjunct faced him. 'Lieutenant Paran is now on my staff. I trust you'll make the necessary adjustments.'

'As you wish, Adjunct. I love paperwork.'

That earned him a slight smile. Then it was gone. 'Lieutenant Paran will be leaving now.'

The captain looked at the young noble and smiled, letting the smile say everything. Working for the Adjunct was like being the worm on the hook. The Adjunct was the hook, and at the other end of the line was the Empress. Let him squirm.

A sour expression flitted across Paran's face. 'Yes, Adjunct.' He climbed back into the saddle, saluted, then rode off down the road.

The captain watched him leave, then said, 'Anything else, Adjunct?'

'Yes.'

Her tone brought him around.

'I would like to hear a soldier's opinion of the nobility's present inroads on the Imperial command structure.'

The captain stared hard at her. 'It ain't pretty, Adjunct.'

'Go on.'

The captain talked.

It was the eighth day of recruiting and Staff Sergeant Aragan sat bleary-eyed behind his desk as yet another whelp was prodded forward by the corporal. They'd had some luck here in

Kan. Fishing's best in the backwaters, Kan's Fist had said. All they get around here is stories. Stories don't make you bleed. Stories don't make you go hungry, don't give you sore feet. When you're young and smelling of pigshit and convinced there ain't a weapon in all the damn world that's going to hurt you, all stories do is make you want to be part of them.

The old woman was right. As usual. These people had been under the boot so long they actually liked it. Well, Aragan thought, the education begins here.

It had been a bad day, with the local captain roaring off with three companies and leaving not one solid rumour in their wake about what was going on. And if that wasn't bad enough, Laseen's Adjunct arrived from Unta not ten minutes later, using one of those eerie magical Warrens to get here. Though he'd never seen her, just her name on the hot, dry wind was enough to give him the shakes. Mage killer, the scorpion in the Imperial pocket.

Aragan scowled down at the writing tablet and waited until the corporal cleared his throat. Then he looked up.

The recruit standing before him took the staff sergeant aback. He opened his mouth, on his tongue a lashing tirade designed to send the young ones scampering. A second later he shut it again, the words unspoken. Kan's Fist had made her instructions abundantly clear: if they had two arms, two legs and a head, take them. The Genabackis campaign was a mess. Fresh bodies were needed.

He grinned at the girl. She matched the Fist's description perfectly. Still. 'All right, lass, you understand you're in line to join the Malazan Marines, right?'

The girl nodded, her gaze steady and cool and fixed on Aragan.

The recruiter's expression tightened. *Damn, she can't be more than twelve or thirteen. If this was my daughter . . .*

What's got her eyes looking so bloody old? The last time he'd

31

seen anything like them had been outside Mott Forest, on Genabackis – he'd been marching through farmland hit by five years' drought and a war twice as long. Those old eyes were brought by hunger, or death. He scowled. 'What's your name, girl?'

'Am I in, then?' she asked quietly.

Aragan nodded, a sudden headache pounding against the inside of his skull. 'You'll get your assignment in a week's time, unless you got a preference.'

'Genabackan campaign,' the girl answered immediately. 'Under the command of High Fist Dujek Onearm. Onearm's Host.'

Aragan blinked. 'I'll make a note,' he said softly. 'Your name, soldier?'

'Sorry. My name is Sorry.'

Aragan jotted the name down on his tablet. 'Dismissed, soldier. The corporal will tell you where to go.' He looked up as she was near the door. 'And wash all that mud off your feet.' Aragan continued writing for a moment, then stopped. It hadn't rained in weeks. And the mud around here was half-way between green and grey, not dark red. He tossed down the stylus and massaged his temples. *Well, at least the headache's fading.*

Gerrom was a league and a half inland along the Old Kan Road, a pre-Empire thoroughfare rarely used since the Imperial raised coast road had been constructed. The traffic on it these days was mostly on foot, local farmers and fishers with their goods. Of them only unravelled and torn bundles of clothing, broken baskets and trampled vegetables littering the track remained to give evidence of their passage. A lame mule, the last sentinel overseeing the refuse of an exodus, stood dumbly nearby, ankle-deep in a rice paddy. It spared Paran a single forlorn glance as he rode past.

The detritus looked to be no more than a day old, the fruits and green-leaved vegetables only now beginning to rot in the afternoon heat.

His horse carrying him at a slow walk, Paran watched as the first outbuildings of the small trader town came into view through the dusty haze. No one moved between the shabby mudbrick houses; no dogs came out to challenge him, and the only cart in sight leaned on a single wheel. To add to the uncanny scene, the air was still, empty of birdsong. Paran loosened the sword in its scabbard.

As he neared the outbuildings he halted his mount. The exodus had been swift, a panicked flight. Yet he saw no bodies, no signs of violence beyond the haste evident in those leaving. He drew a deep breath, slowly released it, then clicked his horse forward. The main street was in effect the town's only street, leading at its far end to a T intersection marked by a single two-storey stone building: the Imperial Constabulary. Its tin-backed shutters were closed, its heavy banded door shut. As he approached Paran held his eyes on the building.

He dismounted before it, tying his mare to the hitching rail then looking back up the street. No movement. Unsheathing his blade, Paran swung back to the Constabulary door.

A soft, steady sound from within stopped him, too low to be heard from any distance but now, as he stood before the huge door, he could hear a liquid murmuring that raised the hairs on his neck. Paran reached out with his sword and set its point under the latch. He lifted the iron handle upward until it disengaged, then pushed open the door.

Movement rippled in the gloom within, a flap and soft thumping of air carrying to Paran the redolent stench of putrifying flesh. Breathing hard and with a mouth dry as old cotton, he waited for his eyes to adjust.

He stared into the Constabulary's outer room, and it was a mass of movement, a chilling soft sussuration of throats giving

33

voice. The chamber was filled with black pigeons cooing in icy calm. Uniformed human shapes lay in their midst, stretched haphazardly across the floor amid droppings and drifting black down. Sweat and death clung to the air thick as gauze.

He took a step inside. The pigeons rustled but otherwise ignored him. None made for the open doorway.

Swollen faces with coin-dull eyes stared up from the shadows; the faces were blue, as of men suffocated. Paran looked down at one of the soldiers. 'Not a healthy thing,' he muttered, 'wearing these uniforms these days.'

A conjuring of birds to keep mocking vigil. Dark humour's not to my liking any more, I think. He shook himself, walked across the room. The pigeons tracked away from his boots, clucking. The door to the captain's office was ajar. Musty light bled through the shuttered windows' uneven joins. Sheathing his sword, Paran entered the office. The captain still sat in his chair, his face bloated and bruised in shades of blue, green and grey.

Paran swept damp feathers from the desktop, rummaged through the scroll work. The papyrus sheets fell apart under his touch, the leaves rotten and oily between his fingers.

A thorough eliminating of the trail.

He turned away, walked swiftly back through the outer room until he stepped into the warm light. He closed the Constabulary door as, no doubt, the villagers had.

The dark bloom of sorcery was a stain few cared to examine too closely. It had a way of spreading.

Paran untethered his mare, climbed into the saddle and rode from the abandoned town. He did not look back.

The sun sat heavy and bloated amid a smear of crimson cloud on the horizon. Paran fought to keep his eyes open. It had been a long day. *A horrific day.* The land around him, once familiar and safe, had become something else, a place stirred with the dark currents of sorcery. He was not looking forward to a night camped in the open.

His mount plodded onward, head down, as dusk slowly enveloped them. Pulled by the weary chains of his thoughts, Paran tried to make sense of what had happened since morning.

Snatched out from the shadow of that sour-faced, laconic captain and the garrison at Kan, the lieutenant had seen his prospects begin a quick rise. Aide to the Adjunct was an advancement in his career he could not have even imagined a week ago. Despite the profession he had chosen, his father and his sisters were bound to be impressed, perhaps even awed, by his achievement. Like so many other noble-born sons and daughters, he'd long since set his sights on the Imperial military, hungry for prestige and bored with the complacent, static attitudes of the noble class in general. Paran wanted something more challenging than co-ordinating shipments of wine, or overseeing the breeding of horses.

Nor was he among the first to enlist, thus easing the way for entrance into officer training and selective postings. It had just been ill-luck that saw him sent to Kan, where a veteran garrison had been licking its wounds for nigh on six years. There'd been little respect for an untested lieutenant, and even less for a noble-born.

Paran suspected that that had changed since the slaughter on the road. He'd handled it better than many of those veterans, helped in no small part by the superb breeding of his horse. More, to prove to them all his cool, detached professionalism, he'd volunteered to lead the inspection detail.

He'd done well, although the detail had proved . . . difficult. He'd heard screaming while crawling around among the bodies, coming from somewhere inside his own head. His eyes had fixed on details, oddities – the peculiar twist of this body, the inexplicable smile on that dead soldier's face – but what had proved hardest was what had been done to the horses. Crusted foam-filled nostrils and mouths – the signs of terror – and the wounds were terrible, huge and devastating. Bile and faeces stained the once-proud mounts, and over everything was a glittering carpet of blood and slivers of red flesh. He had nearly wept for those horses.

He shifted uneasily on the saddle, feeling a clamminess come to his hands where they rested on the ornate horn. He'd held on to his confidence through the whole episode; yet now, as his thoughts returned to that horrid scene, it was as if something that had always been solid in his mind now stuttered, shied, threatening his balance; the faint contempt he'd shown for those veterans in his troop, kneeling helpless on the roadside racked by dry-heaves, returned to him now with a ghoulish cast. And the echo that came from the Constabulary at Gerrom, arriving like a late blow to his already bruised and battered soul, rose once again to pluck at the defensive numbness still holding him in check.

Paran straightened with an effort. He'd told the Adjunct his youth was gone. He'd told her other things as well, fearless, uncaring, lacking all the caution his father had instilled in him when it came to the many faces of the Empire.

From a great distance in his mind came old, old words: *live quietly*. He'd rejected that notion then; he rejected it still. The Adjunct, however, had noticed him. He wondered now, for the first time, if he was right to feel pride. That hard-bitten commander of so many years ago, on the walls of Mock's Hold, would have spat at Paran's feet, with contempt, had he now stood before him. The boy was a boy no longer, but a man. *Should've heeded my words, son. Now look at you.*

His mare pulled up suddenly, hoofs thumping confusedly on the rutted road. Paran reached for his weapon as he looked uneasily around in the gloom. The track ran through rice paddies, the nearest shacks of the peasants on a parallel ridge a hundred paces from the road. Yet a figure now blocked the road.

A cold breath swirled lazily past, pinning back the mare's ears and widening her nostrils as she flinched.

The figure – a man by his height – was swathed in shades of green: cloaked, hooded, wearing a faded tunic and linen leggings above green-dyed leather boots. A single long-knife, the weapon of choice among Seven Cities warriors, was slung through a thin belt. The man's hands, faintly grey in the afternoon light, glittered with rings, rings on every finger, above and below the knuckles. He raised one now, holding up a clay jug.

'Thirsty, Lieutenant?' The man's voice was soft, the tone strangely melodic.

'Have I business with you?' Paran asked, his hand remaining on the grip of his longsword.

The man smiled, pulling back his hood. His face was long, the skin a lighter shade of grey, the eyes dark and strangely angled. He looked to be in his early thirties, though his hair was white. 'The Adjunct asked of me a favour,' he said. 'She grows impatient for your report. I am to escort you ... with haste.' He shook the jug. 'But first, a repast. I have a veritable feast secreted in my pockets – far better fare than a browbeaten Kanese village can offer. Join me, here on the roadside. We can amuse ourselves in conversation and idle watching of peasants toiling endlessly. I am named Topper.'

'I know that name,' Paran said.

'Well, you should,' Topper replied. 'I am he, alas. The blood of a Tiste Andii races in my veins, seeking escape, no doubt, from its more common human stream. Mine was the hand that took the life of Unta's royal line, king, queen, sons and daughters.'

'And cousins, second cousins, third—'

'Expunging all hope, indeed. Such was my duty as a Claw of unsurpassed skill. But you have failed in answering my question.'

'Which was?'

'Thirsty?'

Scowling, Paran dismounted. 'I thought you said the Adjunct wished for haste.'

'Hasten we shall, Lieutenant, once we've filled our bellies, and conversed in civil fashion.'

'Your reputation puts civility far down your list of skills, Claw.'

'It's a most cherished trait of mine that sees far too little opportunity for exercise these fell days, Lieutenant. Surely you'd grant me some of your precious time, since I'm to be your escort?'

'Whatever arrangement you made with the Adjunct is between you and her,' Paran said, approaching. 'I owe you nothing, Topper. Except enmity.'

The Claw squatted, removing wrapped packages from his pockets, followed by two crystal goblets. He uncorked the jug. 'Ancient wounds. I was led to understand you've taken a different path, leaving behind the dull, jostling ranks of the nobility.' He poured, filling the goblets with amber-coloured wine. 'You are now one with the body of Empire, Lieutenant. It commands you. You respond unquestioningly to its will. You are a small part of a muscle in that body. No more. No less. The time for old grudges is long past. So,' he set down the jug and handed Paran a goblet, 'we now salute new beginnings, Ganoes Paran, lieutenant and aide to Adjunct Lorn.'

Scowling, Paran accepted the goblet.

The two drank.

Topper smiled, producing a silk handkerchief to dab against his lips. 'There now, that wasn't so difficult, was it? May I call you by your chosen name?'

'Paran will do. And you? What title does the commander of the Claw hold?'

Topper smiled again. 'Laseen still commands the Claw. I

38

assist her. In this way I too am an aide of sorts. You may call me by my chosen name, of course. I'm not one for maintaining formalities beyond a reasonable point in an acquaintance.'

Paran sat down on the muddy road. 'And we've passed that point?'

'Indeed.'

'How do you decide?'

'Ah, well.' Topper began unwrapping his packages, revealing cheese, fistbread, fruit and berries. 'I make acquaintances in one of two ways. You've seen the second of those.'

'And the first?'

'No time for proper introductions in those instances, alas.'

Wearily Paran unstrapped and removed his helm. 'Do you wish to hear what I found in Gerrom?' he asked, running a hand through his black hair.

Topper shrugged. 'If you've the need.'

'Perhaps I'd better await my audience with the Adjunct.'

The Claw smiled. 'You have begun to learn, Paran. Never be too easy with the knowledge you possess. Words are like coin – it pays to hoard.'

'Until you die on a bed of gold,' Paran said.

'Hungry? I hate eating alone.'

Paran accepted a chunk of fistbread. 'So, was the Adjunct truly impatient, or are you here for other reasons?'

With a smile, the Claw rose. 'Alas, genteel conversation is done. Our way opens.' He faced the road.

Paran turned to see a curtain in the air tear open on the road, spilling dull yellow light. *A Warren, the secret paths of sorcery.* 'Hood's Breath.' He sighed, fighting off a sudden chill. Within he could see a greyish pathway, humped on either side by low mounded walls and vaulted overhead by impenetrable ochre-hued mist. The air swept past into the portal like a drawn breath, revealing the pathway to be of ash as invisible currents stirred and raised spinning dust-devils.

'You will have to get used to this,' Topper said.

Paran collected his mare's reins and slung his helm on the saddlehorn. 'Lead on,' he said.

The Claw cast him a quick appraising glance, then strode into the Warren.

Paran followed. The portalway closed behind them, in its place a continuation of the path. Itko Kan had vanished, and with it all signs of life. The world they had entered was barren, deathly. The banked mounds lining the trail proved to be more ash. The air was gritty, tasting of metal.

'Welcome to the Imperial Warren,' Topper said, with a hint of mockery.

'Pleasant.'

'Carved by force out of . . . what was here before. Has such an effort ever been achieved before? Only the gods can say.'

They began walking.

'I take it, then,' Paran said, 'that no god claims this Warren. By this, you cheat the tolls, the gatekeepers, the guardians on unseen bridges, and all the others said to dwell in the Warrens in service to their immortal masters.'

Topper grunted. 'You imagine the Warrens as crowded as that? Well, the beliefs of the ignorant are ever entertaining. You shall be good company on this short journey, I think.'

Paran fell silent. The horizons beyond the banked heaps of ash were close, a vague blending of ochre sky and grey-black ground. Sweat trickled under his mail hauberk. His mare snorted heavily.

'In case you were wondering,' Topper said, after a time, 'the Adjunct is now in Unta. We will use this Warren to cross the distance – three hundred leagues in only a few short hours. Some think the Empire has grown too large, some even think their remote provinces are beyond the Empress Laseen's reach. As you have just learned, Paran, such beliefs are held by fools.'

The mare snorted again.

'I've shamed you into silence, then? I do apologize, Lieutenant, for mocking your ignorance—'

'It's a risk you'll have to live with,' Paran said.

The next thousand paces of silence belonged to Topper.

No shifting of light marked the passing of hours. A number of times they came upon places where the ash embankments had been disturbed, as if by the passage of something large, shambling; and wide, slithery trails led off into the gloom. In one such place they found a dark encrusted stain and the scatter of chain links like coins in the dust. Topper examined the scene closely while Paran watched.

Hardly the secure road he'd have me believe. There're strangers here, and they're not friendly.

He was not surprised to find Topper increasing their pace thereafter. A short while later they came to a stone archway. It had been recently constructed, and Paran recognized the basalt as Untan, from the Imperial quarries outside the capital. The walls of his family's estate were of the same grey-black glittering stone. At the centre of the arch, high over their heads, was carved a taloned hand holding a crystal globe: the Malazan Imperial sigil.

Beyond the arch was darkness.

Paran cleared his throat. 'We have arrived?'

Topper spun to him. 'You answer civility with arrogance, Lieutenant. You'd do well to shed the noble hauteur.'

Smiling, Paran gestured. 'Lead on, escort.'

In a whirl of cloak Topper stepped through the arch and vanished.

The mare bucked as Paran pulled her closer to the arch, head tossing. He tried to soothe her but it was no use. Finally, he climbed into the saddle and gathered up the reins. He straightened the horse, then drove hard his spurs into her flanks. She bolted, leaped into the void.

41

Light and colours exploded outward, engulfing them. The mare's hoofs landed with a crunching thump, scattering something that might be gravel in all directions. Paran halted his horse, blinking as he took in the scene around them. A vast chamber, its ceiling glittering with beaten gold, its walls lined with tapestries, and a score of armoured guards closing in on all sides.

Alarmed, the mare sidestepped to send Topper sprawling. A hoof lashed out after him, missing by a handspan. More gravel crunched – only it was not gravel, Paran saw, but mosaic stones. Topper rolled to his feet with a curse, his eyes flashing as he glared at the lieutenant.

The guardsmen seemed to respond to some unspoken order, slowly withdrawing to their positions along the walls. Paran swung his attention from Topper. Before him was a raised dais surmounted by a throne of twisted bone. In the throne sat the Empress.

Silence fell in the chamber except for the crunch of semi-precious gems beneath the mare's hoofs. Grimacing, Paran dismounted, warily eyeing the woman seated on the throne.

Laseen had changed little since the only other time he'd been this close to her; plain and unadorned, her hair short and fair above the blue tint of her unmemorable features. Her brown eyes regarded him narrowly.

Paran adjusted his sword-belt, clasped his hands and bowed from the waist. 'Empress.'

'I see,' Laseen drawled, 'that you did not heed the commander's advice of seven years ago.'

He blinked in surprise.

She continued, 'Of course, he did not heed the advice given him, either. I wonder what god tossed you two together on that parapet – I would do service to acknowledge its sense of humour. Did you imagine the Imperial Arch would exit in the stables, Lieutenant?'

42

'My horse was reluctant to make the passage, Empress.'

'With good reason.'

Paran smiled. 'Unlike me, she's of a breed known for its intelligence. Please accept my humblest apologies.'

'Topper will see you to the Adjunct.' She gestured, and a guardsman came forward to collect the mare's reins.

Paran bowed again then faced the Claw with a smile.

Topper led him to a side door.

'You fool!' he snapped, as the door was closed soundly behind them. He strode quickly down the narrow hallway. Paran made no effort to keep pace, forcing the Claw to wait at the far end where a set of stairs wound upward. Topper's expression was dark with fury. 'What was that about a parapet? You've met her before – when?'

'Since she declined to explain I can only follow her example,' Paran said. He eyed the saddle-backed stairs. 'This would be the West Tower, then. The Tower of Dust—'

'To the top floor. The Adjunct awaits you in her chambers – there's no other doors so you won't get lost, just keep on until you reach the top.'

Paran nodded and began climbing.

The door to the tower's top room was ajar. Paran rapped a knuckle against it and stepped inside. The Adjunct was seated at a bench at the far end, her back to a wide window. Its shutters were thrown open, revealing the red glint of sunrise. She was getting dressed. Paran halted, embarrassed.

'I'm not one for modesty,' the Adjunct said. 'Enter and close the door behind you.'

Paran did as he was bidden. He looked around. Faded tapestries lined the walls. Ragged furs covered the stone tiles of the floor. The furniture – what little there was – was old, Napan in style and thus artless.

The Adjunct rose to shrug into her leather armour. Her hair

43

shimmered in the red light. 'You look exhausted, Lieutenant. Please, sit.'

He looked around, found a chair and slumped gratefully into it. 'The trail's been thoroughly obscured, Adjunct. The only people left in Gerrom aren't likely to talk.'

She fastened the last of the clasps. 'Unless I were to send a necromancer.'

He grunted. 'Tales of pigeons – I think the possibility was foreseen.'

She regarded him with a raised brow.

'Pardon, Adjunct. It seems that death's heralds were . . . birds.'

'And were we to glance through the eyes of the dead soldiers, we would see little else. Pigeons, you said?'

He nodded.

'Curious.' She fell silent.

He watched her for a moment longer. 'Was I bait, Adjunct?'

'No.'

'And Topper's timely arrival?'

'Convenience.'

He fell silent. When he closed his eyes his head spun. He'd not realized how weary he'd become. It was a moment before he understood that she was speaking to him. He shook himself, straightened.

The Adjunct stood before him. 'Sleep later, not now, Lieutenant. I was informing you of your future. It would be well if you paid attention. You completed your task as instructed. Indeed, you have proved yourself highly . . . resilient. To all outward appearances, I am done with you, Lieutenant. You will be returned to the Officer Corps here in Unta. What will follow will be a number of postings, completing your official training. As for your time in Itko Kan, nothing unusual occurred there, do you understand me?'

'Yes.'

'Good.'

'And what of what really happened there, Adjunct? Do we abandon pursuit? Do we resign ourselves to never knowing exactly what happened, or why? Or is it simply me who is to be abandoned?'

'Lieutenant, this is a trail we must not follow too closely, but follow it we shall, and you will be central to the effort. I have assumed – perhaps in error – that you would wish to see it through, to be witness when the time for vengeance finally arrives. Was I wrong? Perhaps you've seen enough and seek only a return to normality.'

He closed his eyes. 'Adjunct, I would be there when the time came.'

She was silent and he knew without opening his eyes that she was studying him, gauging his worth. He was beyond unease and beyond caring. He'd stated his desire; the decision was hers.

'We proceed slowly. Your reassignment will take effect in a few days' time. In the meanwhile, go home to your father's estate. Get some rest.'

He opened his eyes and rose to his feet. As he reached the doorway she spoke again. 'Lieutenant, I trust you won't repeat the scene in the Hall of the Throne.'

'I doubt I'd earn as many laughs the second time around, Adjunct.'

As he reached the stairs he heard what might have been a cough from the room behind him. It was hard to imagine that it could have been anything else.

As he led his horse through the streets of Unta he felt numb inside. The familiar sights, the teeming, interminable crowds, the voices and clash of languages all struck Paran as something strange, something altered, not before his eyes but in that unknowable place between his eyes and his thoughts. The change was his alone, and it made him feel shorn, outcast.

Yet the place was the same: the scenes before him were as they always had been and even in watching it pass by all around him, nothing had changed. It was the gift of noble blood that kept the world at a distance, to be observed from a position unsullied, unjostled by the commonry. *Gift . . . and curse.*

Now, however, Paran walked among them without the family guards. The power of blood was gone, and all he possessed by way of armour was the uniform he now wore. Not a craftsman, not a hawker, not a merchant, but a soldier. A weapon of the Empire, and the Empire had those in the tens of thousands.

He passed through Toll Ramp Gate and made his way along Marble Slope Road, where the first merchant estates appeared, pushed back from the cobbled street, half hidden by courtyard walls. The foliage of gardens joined their lively colours with brightly painted walls; the crowds diminished and private guards were visible outside arching gates. The sweltering air lost its reek of sewage and rotting food, slipping cooler across unseen fountains and carrying into the avenue the fragrance of blossoms.

Smells of childhood.

The estates spread out as he led his horse deeper into the Noble District. Breathing-space purchased by history and ancient coin. The Empire seemed to melt away, a distant, mundane concern. Here, families traced their lines back seven centuries to those tribal horsemen who had first come to this land from the east. In blood and fire, as was always the way, they had conquered and subdued the cousins of the Kanese who'd built villages along this coast. From warrior horsemen to horsebreeders to merchants of wine, beer and cloth. An ancient nobility of the blade, now a nobility of hoarded gold, trade agreements, subtle manoeuvrings and hidden corruptions in gilded rooms and oil-lit corridors.

Paran had imagined himself acquiring trappings that closed a circle, a return to the blade from which his family had emerged, strong and savage, all those centuries ago. For his choice, his father had condemned him.

He came to a familiar postern, a single high door along one side wall and facing an alley that in another part of the city would be a wide street. There was no guard here, just a thin bell-chain, which he pulled twice.

Alone in the alley, Paran waited.

A bar clanked on the other side, a voice growled a curse as the door swung back on protesting hinges.

Paran found himself staring down at an unfamiliar face. The man was old, scarred and wearing much-mended chain-mail that ended raggedly around his knees. His pot-helm was uneven with hammered-out dents, yet polished bright.

The man eyed Paran up and down with watery grey eyes, then grunted, 'The tapestry lives.'

'Excuse me?'

The guardsman swung the door wide. 'Older now, of course, but it's all the same by the lines. Good artist, to capture the way of standing, the expression and all. Welcome home, Ganoes.'

Paran led his horse through the narrow doorway. The path was between two outbuildings of the estate, showing sky overhead.

'I don't know you, soldier,' Paran said. 'But it seems my portrait has been well studied by the guards. Is it now a throw-rug in your barracks?'

'Something like that.'

'What is your name?'

'Gamet,' the guard answered, as he followed behind the horse after shutting and locking the door. 'In service to your father these last three years.'

'And before that, Gamet?'

47

'Not a question asked.'

They came to the courtyard. Paran paused to study the guardsman. 'My father's usually thorough in researching the histories of those entering his employ.'

Gamet grinned, revealing a full set of white teeth. 'Oh, that he did. And here I am. Guess it weren't too dishonourable.'

'You're a veteran.'

'Here, sir, I'll take your horse.'

Paran passed over the reins. He swung about and looked round the courtyard. It seemed smaller than he remembered. The old well, made by the nameless people who'd lived here before even the Kanese, looked ready to crumble into a heap of dust. No craftsman would reset those ancient carved stones, fearing the curse of awakened ghosts. Under the estate house itself were similarly unmortared stones in the deepest reaches, the many rooms and tunnels too bent, twisted and uneven to use.

Servants and groundskeepers moved back and forth in the yard. None had yet noticed Paran's arrival.

Gamet cleared his throat. 'Your father and mother aren't here.'

He nodded. There'd be foals to care for at Emalau, the country estate.

'Your sisters are, though,' Gamet continued. 'I'll have the house servants freshen up your room.'

'It's been left as it was, then?'

Gamet grinned again. 'Well, clear out the extra furniture and casks, then. Storage space at a premium, you know . . .'

'As always.' Paran sighed and, without another word, made his way to the house entrance.

The feast hall echoed to Paran's boots as he strode to the long dining table. Cats bolted across the floor, scattering at his approach. He unclasped his travelling cloak, tossed it across the back of a chair, then sat at a longbench and leaned his back against the panelled wall. He closed his eyes.

A few minutes passed, then a woman's voice spoke. 'I thought you were in Itko Kan.'

He opened his eyes. His sister Tavore, a year younger than him, stood close to the head of the table, one hand on the back of their father's chair. She was as plain as ever, a slash of bloodless lines comprising her features, her reddish hair trimmed shorter than was the style. She was taller than the last time he'd seen her, nearly his own height, no longer the awkward child. Her expression revealed nothing as she studied him.

'Reassignment,' Paran said.

'To here? We would have heard.'

Ah, yes, you would have, wouldn't you? All the sly whisperings among the connected families.

'Unplanned,' he conceded, 'but done nevertheless. Not stationed here in Unta, though. My visit is only a few days.'

'Have you been promoted?'

He smiled. 'Is the investment about to reap coin? Reluctant as it was, we still must think in terms of potential influence, mustn't we?'

'Managing this family's position is no longer your responsibility, brother.'

'Ah, it's yours now, then? Has Father withdrawn from the daily chores?'

'Slowly. His health is failing. Had you asked, even in Itko Kan . . .'

He sighed. 'Still making up for me, Tavore? Assuming the burden of my failings? I hardly left here on a carpet of petals, you may recall. In any case, I always assumed the house affairs would fall into capable hands . . .'

Her pale eyes narrowed, but pride silenced the obvious question.

He asked, 'And how is Felisin?'

'At her studies. She's not heard of your return. She will be very excited, then crushed to hear of the shortness of your visit.'

'Is she your rival now, Tavore?'

His sister snorted, turning away. 'Felisin? She's too soft for this world, brother. For any world, I think. She's not changed. She'll be happy to see you.'

He watched her stiff back as she left the hall.

He smelled of sweat – his own and the mare's – travel and grime, and of something else as well . . . *Old blood and old fear.* Paran looked around. *Much smaller than I remembered.*

CHAPTER TWO

With the coming of the Moranth
the tide turned.
And like ships in a harbour
the Free Cities were swept under
Imperial seas.
The war entered its twelfth year,
the Year of the Shattered Moon
and its sudden spawn
of deathly rain and
black-winged promise.
Two cities remained to contest
the Malazan onslaught.
One stalwart, proud banners
beneath Dark's powerful wing.
The other divided –
– without an army,
bereft of allies –
The strong city fell first.

Call to Shadow
Felisin (b.1146)

51

1163rd Year of Burn's Sleep (two years later)
105th Year of the Malazan Empire
9th Year of Empress Laseen's Rule

Through the pallor of smoke ravens wheeled. Their calls raised a shrill chorus above the cries of wounded and dying soldiers. The stench of seared flesh hung unmoving in the haze.

On the third hill overlooking the fallen city of Pale, Tattersail stood alone. Scattered around the sorceress the curled remains of burnt armour – greaves, breastplates, helms and weapons – lay heaped in piles. An hour earlier there had been men and women wearing that armour, but of them there was no sign. The silence within those empty shells rang like a dirge in Tattersail's head.

Her arms were crossed, tight against her chest. The burgundy cloak with its silver emblem betokening her command of the 2nd Army's wizard cadre now hung from her round shoulders stained and scorched. Her oval, fleshy face, usually parading an expression of cherubic humour, was etched with deep-shadowed lines, leaving her cheeks flaccid and pale.

For all the smells and sounds surrounding Tattersail, she found herself listening to a deeper silence. In some ways it came from the empty armour surrounding her, an absence that was in itself an accusation. But there was another source of the silence. The sorcery that had been unleashed here today had been enough to fray the fabric between the worlds. Whatever dwelt beyond, in the Warrens of Chaos, felt close enough to reach out and touch.

She'd thought her emotions spent, used up by the terror she had just been through, but as she watched the tight ranks of a legion of Moranth Black marching into the city a frost of hatred slipped over her heavy-lidded eyes.

Allies. They're claiming their hour of blood. At the end of that hour there would be a score thousand fewer survivors among the citizens of Pale. The long savage history between the neighbouring peoples was about to have the scales of retribution balanced. By the sword. *Shedunul's mercy, hasn't there been enough?*

A dozen fires raged unchecked through the city. The siege was over, finally, after three long years. But Tattersail knew that there was more to come. Something hid, and waited, in the silence. So she would wait as well. The deaths of this day deserved that much from her – after all, she had failed in all the other ways that mattered.

On the plain below, the bodies of Malazan soldiers covered the ground, a rumpled carpet of dead. Limbs jutted upward here and there, ravens perching on them like overlords. Soldiers who had survived the slaughter wandered in a daze among the bodies, seeking fallen comrades. Tattersail's eyes followed them achingly.

'They're coming,' said a voice, a dozen feet to her left. Slowly she turned. The wizard Hairlock lay sprawled on the burnt armour, the pate of his shaved skull reflecting the dull sky. A wave of sorcery had destroyed him from the hips down. Pink, mud-spattered entrails billowed out from under his ribcage, webbed by drying fluids. A faint penumbra of sorcery revealed his efforts at staying alive.

'Thought you were dead,' Tattersail muttered.

'Felt lucky today.'

'You don't look it.'

Hairlock's grunt released a gout of dark thick blood from below his heart. 'They're coming,' he said. 'See them yet?'

She swung her attention to the slope, her pale eyes narrowing. Four soldiers approached. 'Who are they?'

The wizard didn't answer.

Tattersail faced him again and found his hard gaze fixed on

her, intent in the way a dying person achieves in those last moments. 'Thought you'd take a wave through the gut, huh? Well, I suppose that's one way to get shipped out of here.'

His reply surprised her. 'The tough façade ill fits you, 'Sail. Always has.' He frowned and blinked rapidly, fighting off darkness, she supposed. 'There's always the risk of knowing too much. Be glad I spared you.' He smiled, unveiling red-stained teeth. 'Think nice thoughts. The flesh fades.'

She eyed him steadily, wondering at his sudden ... *humanity*. Maybe dying did away with the usual games, the pretences of the living dance. Maybe she just wasn't prepared to see the mortal man in Hairlock finally showing itself. Tattersail prised her arms from the dreadful, aching hug she had wrapped around herself, and sighed shakily. 'You're right. It's not the time for façades, is it? I never liked you, Hairlock, but I'd never question your courage – I never will.' She studied him critically, a part of her astonished that the horror of his wound didn't so much as make her flinch. 'I don't think even Tayschrenn's arts are enough to save you, Hairlock.'

Something cunning flashed in his eyes and he barked a pained laugh. 'Dear girl,' he gasped, 'your naïvety never fails to charm me.'

'Of course,' she snapped, stung at falling for his sudden ingenuousness. 'One last joke on me, just for old times' sake.'

'You misunderstand—'

'Are you so certain? You're saying it isn't over yet. Your hatred of our High Mage is fierce enough to let you slip Hood's cold grasp, is that it? Vengeance from beyond the grave?'

'You must know me by now. I always arrange a back door.'

'You can't even crawl. How do you plan on getting to it?'

The wizard licked his cracked lips. 'Part of the deal,' he said softly. 'The door comes to me. Comes even as we speak.'

Unease coiled around her insides. Behind her, Tattersail heard the crunch of armour and the rattle of iron, the sound arriving like a cold wind. She turned to see the four soldiers appear on the summit. Three men, one woman, mud-smeared and crimson-streaked, their faces almost bone-white. The sorceress found her eyes drawn to the woman, who hung back like an unwelcome afterthought as the three men approached. The girl was young, pretty as an icicle and looking as warm to the touch. *Something wrong there. Careful.*

The man in the lead – a sergeant by the torque on his arm – came up to Tattersail. Set deep in a lined, exhausted face, his dark grey eyes searched hers dispassionately. 'This one?' he asked, turning to the tall, thin black-skinned man who came up beside him.

This man shook his head. 'No, the one we want is over there,' he said. Though he spoke Malazan, his harsh accent was Seven Cities.

The third and last man, also black, slipped past on the sergeant's left and for all his girth seemed to glide forward, his eyes on Hairlock. His ignoring Tattersail made her feel somehow slighted. She considered a well-chosen word or two as he stepped around her, but the effort seemed suddenly too much.

'Well,' she said to the sergeant, 'if you're the burial detail, you're early. He's not dead yet. Of course,' she continued, 'you're not the burial detail. I know that. Hairlock's made some kind of deal – he's thinking he can survive with half a body.'

The sergeant's lips grew taut beneath his grizzled, wiry beard. 'What's your point, Sorceress?'

The black man beside the sergeant glanced back at the young girl still standing a dozen paces behind them. He seemed to shiver, but his lean face was expressionless as he turned back and offered Tattersail an enigmatic shrug before moving past her.

She shuddered involuntarily as power buffeted her senses. She drew a sharp breath. *He's a mage.* Tattersail tracked the man as he joined his comrade at Hairlock's side, striving to see

55

through the muck and blood covering his uniform. 'Who are you people?'

'Ninth squad, the Second.'

'Ninth?' The breath hissed from her teeth. 'You're Bridgeburners.' Her eyes narrowed on the battered sergeant. 'The Ninth. That makes you Whiskeyjack.'

He seemed to flinch.

Tattersail found her mouth dry. She cleared her throat. 'I've heard of you, of course. I've heard the—'

'Doesn't matter,' he interrupted, his voice grating. 'Old stories grow like weeds.'

She rubbed at her face, feeling grime gather under her nails. *Bridgeburners.* They'd been the old Emperor's élite, his favourites, but since Laseen's bloody coup nine years ago they'd been pushed hard into every rat's nest in sight. Almost a decade of this had cut them down to a single, undermanned division. Among them, names had emerged. The survivors, mostly squad sergeants, names that pushed their way into the Malazan armies on Genabackis, and beyond. Names, spicing the already sweeping legend of Onearm's Host. *Detoran, Antsy, Spindle, Whiskeyjack.* Names heavy with glory and bitter with the cynicism that every army feeds on. They carried with them like an emblazoned standard the madness of this unending campaign.

Sergeant Whiskeyjack was studying the wreckage on the hill. Tattersail watched him piece together what had happened. A muscle in his cheek twitched. He looked at her with new understanding, a hint of softening behind his grey eyes that almost broke Tattersail then and there. 'Are you the last left in the cadre?' he asked.

She looked away, feeling brittle. 'The last left standing. It wasn't skill, either. Just lucky.'

If he heard her bitterness he gave no sign, falling silent as he watched his two Seven Cities soldiers crouching low over Hairlock.

Tattersail licked her lips, shifted uneasily. She glanced over to the two soldiers. A quiet conversation was under way. She heard Hairlock laugh, the sound a soft jolt that made her wince. 'The tall one,' she said. 'He's a mage, isn't he?'

Whiskeyjack grunted, then said, 'His name's Quick Ben.'

'Not the one he was born with.'

'No.'

She rolled her shoulders against the weight of her cloak, momentarily easing the dull pain in her lower back. 'I should know him, Sergeant. That kind of power gets noticed. He's no novice.'

'No,' Whiskeyjack replied. 'He isn't.'

She felt herself getting angry. 'I want an explanation. What's happening here?'

Whiskeyjack grimaced. 'Not much, by the looks of it.' He raised his voice. 'Quick Ben!'

The mage looked over. 'Some last-minute negotiations, Sergeant,' he said, flashing a white grin.

'Hood's Breath.' Tattersail sighed, turning away. The girl, she saw, still stood at the hill's crest and seemed to be studying the Moranth columns passing into the city. As if sensing Tattersail's attention, her head snapped around. Her expression startled the sorceress. Tattersail pulled her eyes away. 'Is this what's left of your squad, Sergeant? Two desert marauders and a blood-hungry recruit?'

Whiskeyjack's tone was flat: 'I have seven left.'

'This morning?'

'Fifteen.'

Something's wrong here. Feeling a need to say something, she said, 'Better than most.' She cursed silently as the blood drained from the sergeant's face. 'Still,' she added, 'I'm sure they were good men, the ones you lost.'

'Good at dying,' he said.

The brutality of his words shocked her. Mentally reeling,

she squeezed shut her eyes, fighting back tears of bewilderment and frustration. *Too much has happened. I'm not ready for this. I'm not ready for Whiskeyjack, a man buckling under his own legend, a man who's climbed more than one mountain of the dead in service to the Empire.*

The Bridgeburners hadn't shown themselves much over the past three years. Since the siege began, they'd been assigned the task of undermining Pale's massive, ancient walls. That order had come straight from the capital, and it was either a cruel joke or the product of appalling ignorance: the whole valley was a glacial dump, a rock pile plugging a crevice that reached so far underground even Tattersail's mages had trouble finding its bottom. *They've been underground three years running. When was the last time they saw the sun?*

Tattersail stiffened suddenly. 'Sergeant.' She opened her eyes to him. 'You've been in your tunnels since this morning?'

With sinking understanding, she watched anguish flit across the man's face. 'What tunnels?' he said softly, then moved to stride past her.

She reached out and closed her hand on his arm. A shock seemed to run through him. 'Whiskeyjack,' she whispered, 'you've guessed as much. About – about me, about what happened here on this hill, all these soldiers.' She hesitated, then said, 'Failure's something we share. I'm sorry.'

He pulled away, eyes averted. 'Don't be, Sorceress.' He met her gaze. 'Regret's not something we can afford.'

She watched him walk to his soldiers.

A young woman's voice spoke directly behind Tattersail. 'We numbered fourteen hundred this morning, Sorceress.'

Tattersail turned. At this close range, she saw that the girl couldn't be more than fifteen years old. The exception was her eyes, which held the dull glint of weathered onyx – they looked ancient, every emotion eroded away into extinction. 'And now?'

The girl's shrug was almost careless. 'Thirty, maybe thirty-five. Four of the five tunnels fell in completely. We were in the fifth and dug our way out. Fiddler and Hedge are working on the others, but they figure everybody else's been buried for good. They tried to round up some help.' A cold, knowing smile spread across her mud-streaked face. 'But your master, the High Mage, stopped them.'

'Tayschrenn did what? Why?'

The girl frowned, as if disappointed. Then she simply walked away, stopping at the hill's crest and facing the city again.

Tattersail stared after her. The girl had thrown that last statement at her as if hunting for some particular response. *Complicity?* In any case, a clean miss. *Tayschrenn's not making any friends. Good.* The day had been a disaster, and the blame fell squarely at the High Mage's feet. She stared at Pale, then lifted her gaze to the smoke-filled sky above it.

That massive, looming shape she had greeted every morning for the last three years was indeed gone. She still had trouble believing it, despite the evidence of her eyes. 'You warned us,' she whispered to the empty sky, as the memories of the morning returned. 'You warned us, didn't you?'

She'd been sleeping with Calot the past four months: a little diversionary pleasure to ease the boredom of a siege that wasn't going anywhere. At least, that was how she explained to herself their unprofessional conduct. It was more than that, of course, much more. But being honest with herself had never been one of Tattersail's strengths.

The magical summons, when it came, awakened her before Calot. The mage's small but well-proportioned body was snug in the many soft pillows of her flesh. She opened her eyes to find him clinging to her like a child. Then he, too, sensed the calling and awoke to her smile.

59

'Hairlock?' he asked, shivering as he climbed out from under the blankets.

Tattersail grimaced. 'Who else? The man never sleeps.'

'What now, I wonder?' He stood, looking around for his tunic.

She was watching him. He was so thin, making them an odd combination. Through the faint dawn light seeping through the canvas tent walls, the sharp, bony angles of his body looked soft, almost child-like. For a man a century old, he carried it well. 'Hairlock's been running errands for Dujek,' she said. 'It's probably just an update.'

Calot grunted as he pulled on his boots. 'That's what you get for taking command of the cadre, 'Sail. Anyway, it was easier saluting Nedurian, let me tell you. Whenever I look at you, I just want to—'

'Stick to business, Calot,' Tattersail said, meaning it with humour though it came out with enough of an edge to make Calot glance at her sharply.

'Something up?' he asked quietly, the old frown finding its familiar lines on his high forehead.

Thought I'd got rid of those. Tattersail sighed. 'Can't tell, except that Hairlock's contacted both of us. If it was just a report, you'd still be snoring.'

In growing tension they finished dressing in silence. Less than an hour later Calot would be incinerated beneath a wave of blue fire, and ravens would be answering Tattersail's despairing scream. But, for the moment, the two mages were readying themselves for an unscheduled gathering at High Fist Dujek Onearm's command tent.

In the muddy path beyond Calot's tent, soldiers of the last watch huddled around braziers filled with burning horse dung, holding out hands to the heat. Few walked the pathways, the hour still too early. Row upon row of grey tents climbed the hills overlooking the plain that surrounded the city of Pale.

Regimental standards ruffled sullenly in a faint breeze – the wind had turned since last night, carrying to Tattersail the stench of the latrine trenches. Overhead the remaining handful of stars dimmed into insignificance in the lightening sky. The world seemed almost peaceful.

Drawing her cloak against the chill, Tattersail paused outside the tent and turned to study the enormous mountain hanging suspended a quarter-mile above the city of Pale. She scanned the battered face of Moon's Spawn – its name for as long as she could remember. Ragged as a blackened tooth, the basalt fortress was home to the most powerful enemy the Malazan Empire had ever faced. High above the earth, Moon's Spawn could not be breached by siege. Even Laseen's own undead army, the T'lan Imass, who travelled as easily as dust on the wind, were unable, or unwilling, to penetrate its magical defences.

Pale's wizards had found a powerful ally. Tattersail recalled that the Empire had locked horns with the Moon's mysterious lord once before, in the days of the Emperor. Things had threatened to get ugly, but then Moon's Spawn withdrew from the game. No one still living knew why – just one of the thousand secrets the Emperor took with him to his watery grave.

The Moon's reappearance here on Genabackis had been a surprise. And this time, there was no last-minute reprieve. A half-dozen legions of the sorcerous Tiste Andii descended from Moon's Spawn, and under the command of a warlord named Caladan Brood they joined forces with the Crimson Guard mercenaries. Together, the two armies proceeded to drive back the Malaz 5th Army, which had been pushing eastward along the northern edge of Rhivi Plain. For the past four years the battered 5th had been bogged down in Blackdog Forest, forcing them to make a stand against Brood and the Crimson Guard. It was a stand fast becoming a death sentence.

But, clearly, Caladan Brood and the Tiste Andii weren't the only inhabitants of Moon's Spawn. An unseen lord remained in command of the fortress, bringing it here and sealing a pact with Pale's formidable wizards.

Tattersail's cadre had little hope of magically challenging such opposition. So the siege had ground to a halt, with the exception of the Bridgeburners who never relaxed their stubborn efforts to undermine the city's ancient walls.

Stay, she prayed to Moon's Spawn. *Turn your face endlessly, and keep the smell of blood, the screams of the dying from settling on this land. Wait for us to blink first.*

Calot waited beside her. He said nothing, understanding the ritual this had become. It was one of the many reasons why Tattersail loved the man. As a friend, of course. Nothing serious, nothing frightening in the love for a friend.

'I sense impatience in Hairlock,' Calot murmured beside her.

She sighed. 'I do, too. That's why I'm reluctant.'

'I know, but we can't dally too long, 'Sail.' He grinned mischievously. 'Bad form.'

'Hmmm, can't have them jumping to conclusions, can we?'

'They wouldn't have to jump very far. Anyway,' his smile faltered slightly, 'let's get going.'

A few minutes later they arrived at the command tent. The lone marine standing guard at the flap seemed nervous as he saluted the two mages. Tattersail paused and searched his eyes. 'Seventh Regiment?'

Avoiding her gaze, the guard nodded. 'Yes, Sorceress. Third Squad.'

'Thought you looked familiar. Give my regards to Sergeant Rusty.' She stepped closer. 'Something in the air, soldier?'

He blinked. 'High in the air, Sorceress. High as they come.'

Tattersail glanced at Calot, who had paused at the tent flap.

Calot puffed out his cheeks, making a comical face. 'Thought I smelled him.'

She winced at this confirmation. The guard, she saw, was sweating under his iron helmet. 'Thanks for the warning, soldier.'

'Always an even trade, Sorceress.' The man snapped a second salute, this one sharper, and in its way more personal. *Years and years of this. Insisting I'm family to them, one of the 2nd Army – the oldest intact force, one of the Emperor's own. Always an even trade, Sorceress. Save our skins, we'll save yours. Family, after all. Why, then, do I always feel so estranged from them?* Tattersail returned the salute.

They entered the command tent. She sensed immediately the presence of power, what Calot called *smell*. It made his eyes water. It gave her a migraine headache. This particular emanation was a power she knew well, and it was anathema to her own. Which made the headaches all the worse.

Inside the tent, lanterns cast a dim smoky light on the dozen or so wooden chairs in the first compartment. A camp-table off to one side held a tin pitcher of watered wine and six tarnished cups that glistened with droplets of condensation.

Calot muttered beside her, 'Hood's Breath, 'Sail, I hate this.'

As her eyes adjusted to the gloom, Tattersail saw, through the opening that led into the tent's second compartment, a familiar robed figure. He leaned with long-fingered hands on Dujek's map-table. His magenta cloak rippled like water though he remained motionless. 'Oh, really now,' Tattersail whispered.

'Just my thought,' Calot said, wiping his eyes.

'Do you think,' she said, as they took their seats, 'it's a studied pose?'

Calot grinned. 'Absolutely. Laseen's High Mage couldn't read a battle map if his life depended on it.'

'So long as our lives don't depend on it.'

A voice spoke from a chair near them, 'Today we work.'

Tattersail scowled at the preternatural darkness enwreathing the chair. 'You're as bad as Tayschrenn, Hairlock. And be glad I didn't decide to sit in that chair.'

Dully, a row of yellow teeth appeared, then the rest of the mage took shape as Hairlock relinquished the spell. Beads of sweat marked the man's flat, scarred brow and shaved pate – nothing unusual there: Hairlock would sweat in an ice-pit. He held his head at an angle, achieving in his expression something like smug detachment combined with contempt. He fixed his small dark eyes on Tattersail. 'You remember work, don't you?' His smile broadened, further flattening his mashed, misaligned nose. 'It's what you were doing before you started rolling in the sack with dear Calot here. Before you went *soft*.'

Tattersail drew breath for a retort, but was interrupted by Calot's slow, easy drawl. 'Lonely, Hairlock? Should I tell you that the camp-followers demand double the coin from you?' He waved a hand, as if clearing away unsavoury thoughts. 'The simple fact is, Dujek chose Tattersail to command the cadre after Nedurian's untimely demise at Mott Wood. You may not like it, but that's just too bad. It's the price you pay for ambivalence.'

Hairlock reached down and brushed a speck of dirt from his satin slippers, which had, improbably, escaped unmarred the muddy streets outside. 'Blind faith, dear comrades, is for fools—'

He was interrupted by the tent flap swishing aside. High Fist Dujek Onearm entered, the soap of his morning shave still clotting the hair in his ears, the smell of cinnamon water wafting after him.

Over the years, Tattersail had come to attach much to that aroma. Security, stability, *sanity*. Dujek Onearm represented all those things, and not just to her but to the army that fought for him. As he stopped now in the centre of the room and surveyed the three mages, she leaned back slightly and, from under heavy lids, studied the High Fist. Three years of enforced passivity in this siege seemed to have acted like a tonic on the ageing man. He looked more like fifty rather than his seventy-nine years. His grey eyes remained sharp and unyielding in his tanned, lean face. He stood straight, which made him seem taller than his five and a half feet, wearing simple, unadorned leathers, stained as much by sweat as by the Imperial magenta dye. The stump of his left arm, just below the shoulder, was wrapped in leather strips. His hairy chalk-white calves were visible between the sharkskin straps of the Napan sandals.

Calot withdrew a handkerchief from his sleeve and tossed it to Dujek.

The High Mage snagged it. 'Again? Damn that barber,' he growled, wiping the soap from his jaw and ears. 'I swear he does it on purpose.' He balled the handkerchief and flung it on to Calot's lap. 'Now, we're all here. Good. Regular business first. Hairlock, you finished jawing with the boys below?'

Hairlock stifled a yawn. 'Some sapper named Fiddler took me in, showed me around.' He paused to pluck lint from his brocaded sleeve, then met Dujek's eyes. 'Give them six or seven years and they might have reached the city walls by then.'

'It's pointless,' Tattersail said, 'which is what I put in my report.' She squinted up at Dujek. 'Assuming it ever made it to the Imperial Court.'

'Camel's still swimming,' Calot said.

Dujek grunted – as close as he ever got to laughing. 'All right, cadre, listen carefully. Two things.' A faint scowl crossed his scarred features. 'One, the Empress has sent a Claw. They're in the city, hunting down Pale's wizards.'

A chill danced up Tattersail's spine. No one liked having the Claws around. Those Imperial assassins – Laseen's favoured

65

weapon – kept their poisoned daggers sharp for anyone and everyone, Malazans included.

It seemed Calot was thinking the same thing, for he sat up sharply. 'If they're here for any other reason . . .'

'They'll have to come through me first,' Dujek said, his lone hand reaching down to rest on the pommel of his longsword.

He has an audience, there in the other room. He's telling the man commanding the Claw how things stand. Shedunul bless him.

Hairlock spoke. 'They'll go to ground. They're wizards, not idiots.'

It was a moment before Tattersail understood the man's comment. *Oh, right. Pale's wizards.*

Dujek glanced down at Hairlock, gauging, then he nodded. 'Two, we're attacking Moon's Spawn today.'

In the other compartment, High Mage Tayschrenn turned at these words and approached slowly. Within his hood a broad smile creased his dark face, a momentary cracking of seamless features. The smile passed quickly, the ageless skin becoming smooth once again. 'Hello, my colleagues,' he said, droll and menacing all at once.

Hairlock snorted. 'Keep the melodrama to a minimum, Tayschrenn, and we'll all be happier.'

Ignoring Hairlock's comment, the High Mage continued, 'The Empress has lost her patience with Moon's Spawn—'

Dujek cocked his head and interrupted, his voice softly grating. 'The Empress is scared enough to hit first and hit hard. Tell it plain, Magicker. This is your front line you're talking to here. Show some respect, dammit.'

The High Mage shrugged. 'Of course, High Fist.' He faced the cadre. 'Your group, myself and three other High Mages will strike Moon's Spawn within the hour. The North Campaign has drawn most of the edifice's inhabitants away. We believe that the Moon's lord is alone. For almost three years his mere presence has been enough to hold us in check. This

66

morning, my colleagues, we will test this lord's mettle.'

'And hope to hell he's been bluffing all this time,' Dujek added, a scowl deepening the lines on his forehead. 'Any questions?'

'How soon can I get a transfer?' Calot asked.

Tattersail cleared her throat. 'What do we know about the Lord of Moon's Spawn?'

'Scant little, I'm afraid,' Tayschrenn said, his eyes veiled. 'A Tiste Andii, for certain. An archmage.'

Hairlock leaned forward and deliberately spat at the floor in front of Tayschrenn. 'Tiste Andii, High Mage? I think we can be a little more specific than that, don't you?'

Tattersail's migraine worsened. She realized she was holding her breath, slowly forced it out as she gauged Tayschrenn's reaction – to the man's words and to the traditional Seven Cities challenge.

'An archmage,' Tayschrenn repeated. 'Perhaps *the* Archmage of the Tiste Andii. Dear Hairlock,' he added, his voice lowering a notch, 'your primitive tribal gestures remain quaint, if somewhat tasteless.'

Hairlock bared his teeth. 'The Tiste Andii are Mother Dark's first children. You've felt the tremors through the Warrens of Sorcery, Tayschrenn. So have I. Ask Dujek about the reports coming down from the North Campaign. Elder magic – Kurald Galain. The Lord of Moon's Spawn is the Master Archmage – you know his name as well as I do.'

'I know nothing of the sort,' the High Mage snapped, losing his calm at last. 'Perhaps you'd care to enlighten us, Hairlock, and then I can begin inquiries as to your sources.'

'Ahh!' Hairlock bolted forward in his chair, an eager malice in his taut face. 'A threat from the High Mage. Now we're getting somewhere. Answer me this, then. Why only three other High Mages? We've hardly been thinned out that badly. More, why didn't we do this two years ago?'

67

Whatever was building between Hairlock and Tayschrenn was interrupted by Dujek, who growled wordlessly, then said, 'We're desperate, mage. The North Campaign has gone sour. The Fifth is damn near gone, and won't be getting any reinforcements until next spring. The point is, the Moon's lord could have his army back any day now. I don't want to have to send you up against an army of Tiste Andii, and I sure as hell don't want the Second having to show two fronts with a relieving force coming down on them. Bad tactics, and whoever this Caladan Brood is, he's shown himself adept at making us pay for our mistakes.'

'Caladan Brood,' Calot murmured. 'I swear I've heard that name somewhere before. Odd that I've never given it much thought.'

Tattersail's eyes narrowed on Tayschrenn. Calot was right: the name of the man commanding the Tiste Andii alongside the Crimson Guard *did* sound familiar – but in an old way, echoing ancient legends, perhaps, or some epic poem.

The High Mage met her gaze, flat and calculating. 'The need,' he said, turning to the others, 'for justifications has passed. The Empress has commanded, and we must obey.'

Hairlock snorted a second time. 'Speaking of twisting arms,' he sat back, still smiling contemptuously at Tayschrenn, 'remember how we played cat and mouse at Aren? This plan has your stink on it. You've been itching for a chance like this for a long time.' His grin turned savage. 'Who, then, are the other three High Mages? Let me guess—'

'Enough!' Tayschrenn stepped close to Hairlock, who went very still, eyes glittering.

The lanterns had dimmed. Calot used the handkerchief in his lap to wipe tears from his cheeks.

Power, oh, damn, my head feels ready to crack wide open.

'Very well,' Hairlock whispered, 'let's lay it out on the table. I'm sure the High Fist will appreciate you putting all his suspicions in the proper order. Make it plain, old friend.'

Tattersail glanced at Dujek. The commander's face had closed up, his sharp eyes narrow and fixed on Tayschrenn. He was doing some hard thinking.

Calot leaned against her. 'What the hell's going on, 'Sail?'

'No idea,' she whispered, 'but it's heating up nicely.' Though she'd made her comment light, her mind was whirling around a cold knot of fear. Hairlock had been with the Empire longer than she had – or Calot. He'd been among the sorcerers who'd fought against the Malazans in Seven Cities, before Aren fell and the Holy Falah'd were scattered, before he'd been given the choice of death or service to the new masters. He'd joined the 2nd's cadre at Pan'potsun – like Dujek himself he'd been there, with the Emperor's old guard, when the first vipers of usurpation had stirred, the day the Empire's First Sword was betrayed and brutally murdered. Hairlock *knew* something. But what?

'All right,' Dujek drawled, 'we've got work to do. Let's get at it.'

Tattersail sighed. Old Onearm's way with words. She swung a look on the man. She knew him well, not as a friend – Dujek didn't make friends – but as the best military mind left in the Empire. If, as Hairlock had just implied, the High Fist was being betrayed by someone, somewhere, and if Tayschrenn was part of it . . . *we're a bent bough*, Calot had once said of Onearm's Host, *and beware the Empire when it breaks. Seven Cities' soldiery, the closeted ghosts of the conquered but unconquerable . . .*

Tayschrenn gestured to her and to the other mages. Tattersail rose, as did Calot. Hairlock remained seated, eyes closed as if asleep.

Calot said to Dujek, 'About that transfer.'

'Later,' the High Fist grunted. 'Paperwork's a nightmare when you've only got one arm.' He surveyed his cadre and was about to add something but Calot spoke first.

69

'Anomandaris.'

Hairlock's eyes snapped open, found Tayschrenn with bright pleasure. 'Ahhh,' he said, into the silence following Calot's single pronouncement. 'Of course. Three more High Mages? Only three?'

Tattersail stared at Dujek's pale, still face. 'The poem,' she said quietly. 'I remember now.

'Caladan Brood, the menhired one,
winter-bearing, barrowed and sorrowless . . .'

Calot picked up the next lines.

'. . . in a tomb bereaved of words,
and in his hands that have crushed anvils—'

Tattersail continued,

'the hammer of his song –
he lives asleep, so give silent warning
to all – wake him not.
Wake him not.'

Everyone in the compartment was staring at Tattersail now as her last words fell away. 'He's awake, it seems,' she said, her mouth dry. '"Anomandaris", the epic poem by Fisher Keltath.'

'The poem's not about Caladan Brood,' Dujek said, frowning.

'No,' she agreed. 'It's mostly about his companion.'

Hairlock climbed slowly to his feet. He stepped close to Tayschrenn. 'Anomander Rake, Lord of the Tiste Andii, who are the souls of Starless Night. Rake, the Mane of Chaos. That's who the Moon's lord is, and you're pitting four High Mages and a single cadre against him.'

70

Tayschrenn's smooth face held the faintest sheen of sweat now. 'The Tiste Andii,' he said, in an even voice, 'are not like us. To you they may seem unpredictable, but they aren't. Just different. They have no cause of their own. They simply move from one human drama to the next. Do you actually think Anomander Rake will stay and fight?'

'Has Caladan Brood backed away?' Hairlock snapped.

'He is not Tiste Andii, Hairlock. He's human – some say with Barghast blood, but none the less he shares nothing of Elder blood, or its ways.'

Tattersail said, 'You're counting on Rake betraying Pale's wizards – betraying the pact made between them.'

'The risk is not as overreaching as it may seem,' the High Mage said. 'Bellurdan has done the research in Genabaris, Sorceress. Some new scrolls of *Gothos' Folly* were discovered in a mountain fastness beyond Blackdog Forest. Among the writings are discussions of the Tiste Andii, and other peoples from the Elder Age. And remember, Moon's Spawn has retreated from a direct confrontation with the Empire before.'

The waves of fear sweeping through Tattersail made her knees weak. She sat down again, heavily enough to make the camp chair creak. 'You've condemned us to death,' she said, 'if your gamble proves wrong. Not just us, High Mage, all of Onearm's Host.'

Tayschrenn swung round slowly, putting his back to Hairlock and the others. 'Empress Laseen's orders,' he said, without turning. 'Our colleagues come by Warren. When they arrive, I will detail the positioning. That is all.' He strode into the map room, resumed his original stance.

Dujek seemed to have aged in front of Tattersail's eyes. Swiftly she slid her glance from him, too anguished to meet the abandonment in his eyes, and the suspicion curdling beneath its surface. *Coward – that's what you are, woman. A coward.*

71

Finally the High Fist cleared his throat. 'Prepare your Warrens, cadre. As usual, always an even trade.'

Give the High Mage credit, Tattersail thought. There was Tayschrenn, standing on the first hill, almost inside the Moon's shadow. They had arrayed themselves into three groups, each taking a hilltop on the plain outside Pale's walls. The cadre's was most distant, Tayschrenn's the closest. On the centre hill stood the three other High Mages. Tattersail knew them all. Nightchill, raven-haired, tall, imperious and with a cruel streak the old Emperor used to drool over. At her side her life-long companion, Bellurdan, skull-crusher, a Thelomen giant who would test his prodigious strength against the Moon's portal, should it come to that. And A'Karonys, fire-wielder, short and round, his burning staff taller than a spear.

The 2nd and 6th Armies had formed ranks on the plain, weapons bared and awaiting the call to march on the city when the time came. Seven thousand veterans and four thousand recruits. The Black Moranth legions lined the ridge to the west a quarter-mile distant.

No wind stirred the midday air. Biting midges roved in visible clouds through the soldiers waiting below. The sky was overcast, the cloud cover thin but absolute.

Tattersail stood on the hill's crest, sweat running down under her clothing, and watched the soldiers on the plain before facing her meagre cadre. At full strength, six mages should have been arrayed behind her, but there were only two. Off to one side Hairlock waited, wrapped in the dark grey rain-cloak that was his battle attire – looking smug.

Calot nudged Tattersail and jerked his head towards Hairlock. 'What's he so happy about?'

'Hairlock,' Tattersail called. The man swung his head. 'Were you right about the three High Mages?'

He smiled, then turned away again.

'I hate it when he's hiding something,' Calot said.

The sorceress grunted. 'He's added something up, all right. What's so particular about Nightchill, Bellurdan and A'Karonys? Why did Tayschrenn pick them and how did Hairlock know he'd pick them?'

'Questions, questions.' Calot sighed. 'All three are old hands at this kind of stuff. Back in the days of the Emperor they each commanded a company of Adepts – when the Empire had enough mages in the ranks to form actual companies. A'Karonys climbed through the ranks in the Falari Campaign, and Bellurdan and Nightchill were from before even then – came down from Fenn on the Quon mainland during the unification wars.'

'All old hands,' Tattersail mused, 'as you said. None have been active lately, have they? Their last campaign was Seven Cities—'

'Where A'Karonys took a beating in the Pan'potsun Wastes—'

'He was left hanging – the Emperor had just been assassinated. Everything was chaotic. The T'lan Imass refused to acknowledge the new Empress, marched themselves off into the Jhag Odhan.'

'Rumour has it they're back, at half-strength – whatever they ran into out there wasn't pleasant.'

Tattersail nodded. 'Nightchill and Bellurdan were told to report to Nathilog, left sitting on their hands for the past six, seven years—'

'Until Tayschrenn sent the Thelomen off to Genabaris, to study a pile of ancient scrolls, of all things.'

'I'm frightened,' Tattersail admitted. 'Very frightened. Did you see Dujek's face? He *knew* something – a realization, and it hit him like a dagger in the back.'

'Time to work,' Hairlock called.

Calot and Tattersail swung around.

A shiver ran through her. Moon's Spawn had been revolving steadily for the last three years. It had just stopped. Near its very top, on the side facing them, was a small ledge, and a shadowed recess had appeared. A portal. No movement showed yet. 'He knows,' she whispered.

'And he isn't running,' Calot added.

Down on the first hill, High Mage Tayschrenn rose and lifted his arms out to the sides. A wave of golden flame spanned his hands, then rolled upward, growing as it raced towards Moon's Spawn. The spell crashed against the black rock, sending chunks hurtling out, then down. A rain of death descended into the city of Pale, and among the Malazan legions waiting in the plain.

'It's begun,' Calot breathed.

Silence answered Tayschrenn's first attack, save for the faint scatter of rubble on the city's tiled rooftops and the distant cries of wounded soldiers on the plain. Everyone's eyes were trained upward.

The reply was not what anyone expected.

A black cloud enshrouded Moon's Spawn, followed by faint shrieking. A moment later the cloud spread out, fragmenting, and Tattersail realized what she was seeing.

Ravens.

Thousands upon thousands of Great Ravens. They must have nested among the crags and pocks in the Moon's surface. Their shrieks grew more defined, a caterwaul of outrage. They wheeled out from the Moon, their fifteen-foot wingspans catching the wind and lifting them high above the city and plain.

Fear lurched into terror in Tattersail's heart.

Hairlock barked a laugh and whirled to them. 'These are the Moon's messengers, colleagues!' Madness glittered in his eyes. 'These carrion birds!' He flung back his cloak and raised his arms. 'Imagine a lord who's kept thirty thousand Great Ravens well fed!'

A figure had appeared on the ledge before the portal, its arms upraised, long silver hair blowing from its head.

Mane of Chaos. Anomander Rake. Lord of the black-skinned Tiste Andii, who has looked down on a hundred thousand winters, who has tasted the blood of dragons, who leads the last of his kind, seated in the Throne of Sorrow and a kingdom tragic and fey – a kingdom with no land to call its own.

Anomander Rake looked tiny against the backdrop of his edifice, almost insubstantial at this distance. The illusion was about to be shattered. She gasped as the aura of his power bloomed outward – *to see it at such a distance* . . . 'Channel your Warrens,' Tattersail commanded, her voice cracking. 'Now!'

Even as Rake gathered his power, twin balls of blue fire raced upward from the centre hill. They struck the Moon near its base and rocked it. Tayschrenn launched another wave of gilden flames, crashing with amber spume and red-tongued smoke.

The Moon's lord responded. A black, writhing wave rolled down to the first hill. The High Mage was buffeted to his knees deflecting it, the hilltop around him blighted as the necrous power rolled down the slopes, engulfing nearby ranks of soldiers. Tattersail watched as a midnight flash swallowed the hapless men, followed by a thump that thundered through the earth. When the flash dissipated, the soldiers lay in rotting heaps, mown down like stalks of grain.

Kurald Galain sorcery. Elder magic, the Breath of Chaos.

Her breaths coming fast and tight in her chest, Tattersail felt her Thyr Warren flow into her. She shaped it, muttering chain-words under her breath, then unleashed the power. Calot followed, drawing from his Mockra Warren. Hairlock surrounded himself in his own mysterious source, and the cadre entered the fray.

Everything narrowed down for Tattersail from then on, yet a part of her mind remained distant, held on a leash of terror, observing with a kind of muffled vision all that happened around her.

The world became a living nightmare, as sorcery flew upward to batter Moon's Spawn, and sorcery rained downward, indiscriminate and devastating. Earth rose skyward in thundering columns. Rocks ripped through men like hot stones through snow. A downpour of ash descended to cover the living and dead alike. The sky dimmed to pallid rose, the sun a coppery disc behind the haze.

She saw a wave sweep past Hairlock's defences, cutting him in half. His howl was more rage than pain, instantly muted as virulent power washed over Tattersail and she found her own defences assailed by the sorcery's cold, screaming will as it sought to destroy her. She reeled back, brought up short by Calot as he added his Mockra power to bolster her faltering parries. Then the assault passed, sweeping on and down the hill to their left.

Tattersail had fallen to her knees. Calot stood over her, chaining words of power around her, his face turned away from Moon's Spawn, fixed on something or someone down below on the plain. His eyes were wide with terror.

Too late Tattersail understood what was happening. Calot was defending her at his own expense. A final act, even as he watched his own death erupt around him. A blast of bright fire engulfed him. Abruptly the net of protection over Tattersail vanished. A wash of crackling heat from where Calot had stood sent her tumbling to one side. She felt more than heard her own shriek, and her sense of distance closed in then, a layer of mental defence obliterated.

Spitting dirt and ashes, Tattersail climbed to her feet and fought on, no longer launching attacks, just struggling to remain alive. Somewhere in the back of her head a voice was screaming, urgent, panicked. *Calot had faced the plain not Moon's Spawn – he'd faced right! Hairlock had been struck from the plain!*

She watched as a Kenryll'ah demon arose beneath Nightchill. Laughing shrilly, the towering, gaunt creature tore Nightchill limb from limb. It had begun feeding by the time Bellurdan arrived. The Thelomen bellowed as the demon raked its knife-like talons against his chest. Ignoring the wounds and the blood that sprayed from them, he closed his hands around the demon's head and crushed it.

A'Karonys unleashed gouts of flame from the staff in his hands until Moon's Spawn almost disappeared inside a ball of fire. Then ethereal wings of ice closed around the short, fat wizard, freezing him where he stood. An instant later he was crushed to dust.

Magic rained in an endless storm around Tayschrenn, where he still knelt on the withered, blackened hilltop. But every wave directed his way he shunted aside, wreaking devastation among the soldiers cowering on the plain. Through the carnage filling the air, through the ash and shrill-tongued ravens, through the raining rocks and the screams of the wounded and dying, through the blood-chilling shrieks of demons flinging themselves into ranks of soldiery – through it all sounded the steady thunder of the High Mage's onslaught. Enormous cliffs, sheared from the Moon's face and raging with flame and trailing columns of black smoke, fell down into the city of Pale, transforming the city into its own cauldron of death and chaos.

Her ears numbed and body throbbing as if her flesh itself gasped for breath, Tattersail was slow to grasp that the sorcery had ceased. Even the voice shrieking in the back of her mind had fallen silent. She raised bleary eyes to see Moon's Spawn, billowing smoke and ablaze in a dozen places on its ravaged mien, moving away, pulling back. Then it was past the city, unsteady in its revolutions and leaning to one side. Moon's Spawn headed south, towards the distant Tahlyn Mountains.

She looked around, vaguely recalling that a company of

soldiers had sought refuge on the blasted summit. Then something had hit her, taking all she had left to resist it. Now, nothing was left of the company but their armour. *Always an even trade, Sorceress.* She fought against a sob, then swung her attention to the first hill.

Tayschrenn was down, but alive. A half-dozen marines scampered up the hillside to gather around the High Mage. A minute later they carried him away.

Bellurdan, most of his clothing burned away and his flesh scorched red, remained on the centre hill, collecting Nightchill's scattered limbs and raising his voice in a mournful wail. The sight, in all its horror and pathos, struck Tattersail's heart like a hammer on an anvil. Quickly she turned away. 'Damn you, Tayschrenn.'

Pale had fallen. The price was Onearm's Host and four mages. Only now were the Black Moranth legions moving in. Tattersail's jaw clenched, her lips drawing from their fullness into a thin white line. Something tugged at her memory, and she felt a growing certainty that this scene was not yet played out.

The sorceress waited.

The Warrens of Magic dwelt in the beyond. Find the gate and nudge it open a crack. What leaks out is yours to shape. With these words a young woman set out on the path to sorcery. Open yourself to the Warren that comes to you – that finds you. Draw forth its power – as much as your body and soul are capable of containing – but remember, when the body fails, the gate closes.

Tattersail's limbs ached. She felt as though someone had been beating her with clubs for the past two hours. The last thing she had expected was that bitter taste on her tongue that said something nasty and ugly had come to the hilltop. Such warnings seldom came to a practitioner unless the gate was open, a Warren unveiled and bristling with power. She'd heard tales from other sorcerers, and she'd read mouldy scrolls that touched on moments like these, when the power arrived groaning and deadly, and each time, it was said, a *god* had stepped on to the mortal ground.

If she could have driven the nail of immortal presence in this place, however, it would have to be Hood, the God of Death. Yet her instincts said no. She didn't believe a god had arrived, but *something else had*. What frustrated the sorceress was that she couldn't decide who among the people surrounding her was the dangerous one. Something kept drawing her gaze back to the young girl. But the child seemed only half there most of the time.

The voices behind her finally drew her attention. Sergeant Whiskeyjack stood over Quick Ben and the other soldier, both of whom still knelt at Hairlock's side. Quick Ben clutched an oblong object, wrapped in hides, and was looking up at his sergeant as if awaiting approval.

There was tension between the two men. Frowning, Tattersail walked over. 'What are you doing?' she asked Quick Ben, her eyes on the object in the wizard's almost feminine hands. He seemed not to have heard, his eyes on the sergeant.

Whiskeyjack shot her a glance. 'Go ahead, Quick,' he growled, then strode off to stand at the hill's edge, facing west – towards the Moranth Mountains.

Quick Ben's fine, ascetic features tightened. He nodded at his companion. 'Get ready, Kalam.'

The soldier named Kalam leaned back on his haunches, his hands in his sleeves. The position seemed an odd response to Quick Ben's request, but the mage seemed satisfied. Tattersail watched as he laid one of his thin, spidery hands on Hairlock's trembling, blood-splashed chest. He whispered a few chaining words and closed his eyes.

'That sounded like Denul,' Tattersail said, glancing at Kalam, who remained motionless in his crouch. 'But not quite,' she added slowly. 'He's twisted it somehow.' She fell silent then, seeing something in Kalam that reminded her of a snake waiting to strike. *Wouldn't take much to set him off, I think. Just a few more ill-timed words, a careless move towards Quick Ben or Hairlock.* The man was big, bearish, but she remembered his dangerous glide past her. *Snake indeed, the man's a killer, a soldier who's reached the next level in the art of murder. Not just a job any more, this man likes it.* She wondered then if it wasn't this energy, this quiet promise of menace, that swept over her with the flavour of sexual tension. Tattersail sighed. *A day for perversity.*

Quick Ben had resumed his chaining words, this time over the object, which he now set down beside Hairlock. She watched as enwreathing power enveloped the wrapped object, watched in growing apprehension as the mage traced his long fingers along the hide's seams. The energy trickled from him with absolute control. He was her superior in the lore. He had opened a Warren she didn't even recognize.

'Who are you people?' she whispered, stepping back.

Hairlock's eyes snapped open, clear of pain and shock. His gaze found Tattersail and the stained smile came easily to his broken lips. 'Lost arts, 'Sail. What you're about to see hasn't been done in a thousand years.' His face darkened then and the smile faded. Something burned in his eyes. 'Think back, woman! Calot and I. When we went down. What did you see? Did you feel something? Something odd? Come on, think! Look at me! See my wound, see how I'm lying! Which direction was I facing when that wave hit?'

She saw the fire in his eyes, of anger mingled with triumph. 'I'm not sure,' she said slowly. 'Something, yes.' That detached, reasoning part of her mind that had laboured with her throughout the battle, that had screamed in her mind at Calot's death, screamed in answer to the waves of sorcery – *to the fact that they had come from the plain*. Her eyes narrowed on

80

Hairlock. 'Anomander Rake never bothered to aim. He was being indiscriminate. Those waves of power were *aimed*, weren't they? Coming at us from the wrong side.' She was trembling. 'But why? Why would Tayschrenn do that?'

Hairlock reached up one mangled hand and clutched Quick Ben's cloak. 'Use her, Mage. I'll take the chance.'

Tattersail's thoughts raced. Hairlock had been sent down into the tunnels by Dujek. And Whiskeyjack and his squad had been down there. A deal had been struck. 'Hairlock, what's happening here?' she demanded, fear clenching the muscles of her neck and shoulders. 'What do you mean, "use" me?'

'You're not blind, woman!'

'Quiet,' Quick Ben said. He laid down the object on the wizard's ravaged chest, positioning it carefully so that it was centred lengthways along Hairlock's breastbone. The top end reached to just under the man's chin, the bottom end extending a few inches beyond what was left of his torso. Webs of black energy spun incessantly over the hide's mottled surface.

Quick Ben passed a hand over the object and the web spread outward. The glittering black threads traced a chaotic pattern that insinuated Hairlock's entire body, over flesh and through it, the pattern ever changing, the changes coming faster and faster. Hairlock jerked, his eyes bulging, then fell back. A breath escaped his lungs in a slow, steady hiss. When it ceased with a wet gurgle, he did not draw another.

Quick Ben sat back on his haunches and glanced over at Whiskeyjack. The sergeant was now facing them, his expression unreadable.

Tattersail wiped sweat from her brow with a grimy sleeve. 'It didn't work, then. You failed to do whatever it was you were trying to do.'

Quick Ben climbed to his feet. Kalam picked up the wrapped object and stepped close to Tattersail. The assassin's eyes were dark, penetrating as they searched her face.

Quick Ben spoke. 'Hold on to it, Sorceress. Take it back to your tent and unwrap it there. Above all, don't let Tayschrenn see it.'

Tattersail scowled. 'What? Just like that?' Her gaze fell on the object. 'I don't even know what I'd be accepting. Whatever it is, I don't like it.'

The girl spoke directly behind her in a voice that was sharp and accusing. 'I don't know what you've done, Wizard. I felt you keeping me away. That was unkind.'

Tattersail faced the girl, then glanced back at Quick Ben. *What is all this?* The black man's expression was glacial, but she saw a flicker around his eyes. Looked like fear.

Whiskeyjack rounded on the girl at her words. 'You got something to say about all this, recruit?' His tone was tight.

The girl's dark eyes slid to her sergeant. She shrugged, then walked away.

Kalam offered the object to Tattersail. 'Answers,' he said quietly, in a north Seven Cities accent, melodic and round. 'We all need answers, Sorceress. The High Mage killed your comrades. Look at us, we're all that's left of the Bridgeburners. Answers aren't easily . . . attained. Will you pay the price?'

With a final glance at Hairlock's lifeless body – so brutally torn apart – and the lifeless stare of his eyes, she accepted the object. It felt light in her hands. Whatever was within the hide cocoon was slight in size; parts of it moved and against her grip she felt knobs and shafts of something hard. She stared at the assassin's bearish face. 'I want,' she said slowly, 'to see Tayschrenn get what he deserves.'

'Then we're in agreement,' Kalam said, smiling. 'This is where it starts.'

Tattersail felt her stomach jump at that smile. *Woman, what's got into you?* She sighed. 'Done.' As she turned away to descend the slope and make her way back to the main camp, she caught the girl's eye. A chill rippled through her. The sorceress stopped. 'You, recruit,' she called. 'What's your name?'

The girl smiled as if at a private joke. 'Sorry.'

Tattersail grunted. It figured. She tucked the package under an arm and staggered down the slope.

Sergeant Whiskeyjack kicked at a helmet and watched as it tumbled and bounced down the hillside. He spun and glared at Quick Ben. 'It's done?'

The wizard's eyes darted to Sorry, then he nodded.

'You will draw unwarranted attention on our squad,' the young girl told Whiskeyjack. 'High Mage Tayschrenn will notice.'

The sergeant raised an eyebrow. 'Unwarranted attention? What the hell does that mean?'

Sorry made no reply.

Whiskeyjack bit back sharp words. What had Fiddler called her? *An uncanny bitch.* He'd said it to her face and she'd just stared him down with those dead, stony eyes. As much as he hated to admit it, Whiskeyjack shared the sapper's crude assessment. What made things even more disturbing, this fifteen-year-old girl had Quick Ben scared half out of his wits, and the wizard didn't want to talk about it. What had the Empire sent him?

His gaze swung back to Tattersail. She was crossing the killing field below. The ravens rose screaming from her path, and remained circling overhead, their caws uneasy and frightened. The sergeant felt Kalam's solid presence at his side.

'Hood's Breath,' Whiskeyjack muttered. 'That sorceress seems an unholy terror as far as those birds are concerned.'

'Not her,' Kalam said. 'It's what she's carrying.'

Whiskeyjack scratched his beard, his eyes narrowing. 'This stinks. You sure it's necessary?'

Kalam shrugged.

'Whiskeyjack,' Quick Ben said, behind them, 'they *kept* us in the tunnels. Do you think the High Mage couldn't have guessed what would happen?'

The sergeant faced his wizard. A dozen paces beyond stood Sorry, well within hearing range. Whiskeyjack scowled at her, but said nothing.

After a moment of heavy silence, the sergeant turned his attention to the city. The last of the Moranth legions was marching beneath the West Gate's arch. Columns of black smoke rose from behind the battered, scarred walls. He knew something of the history of grim enmity between the Moranth and the citizens of the once Free City of Pale. Contested trade routes, two mercantile powers at each other's throat. And Pale won more often than not. At long last it seemed that the black-armoured warriors from beyond the western mountains, whose faces remained hidden behind the chitinous visors on their helms and who spoke in clicks and buzzes, were evening the score. Faintly, beyond the cries of carrion birds, came the wail of men, women and children dying beneath the sword.

'Sounds like the Empress is keeping her word with the Moranth,' Quick Ben said quietly. 'An hour of slaughter. I didn't think Dujek—'

'Dujek knows his orders,' Whiskeyjack cut in. 'And there's a High Mage taloned on his shoulder.'

'An hour,' Kalam repeated. 'Then we clean up the mess.'

'Not our squad,' Whiskeyjack said. 'We've received new orders.'

The two men stared at their sergeant.

'And you still need convincing?' Quick Ben demanded. 'They're driving us into the ground. They mean to—'

'Enough!' Whiskeyjack barked. 'Not now. Kalam, find Fiddler. We need resupply from the Moranth. Round up the rest, Quick, and take Sorry with you. Join me outside the High Fist's tent in an hour.'

'And you?' Quick Ben asked. 'What are you going to do?'

The sergeant heard an ill-concealed yearning in the wizard's voice. The man needed a direction, or maybe confirmation that they were doing the right thing. *A little late for that.* Even so, Whiskeyjack felt a pang of regret – he couldn't give what Quick Ben wanted the most. He couldn't tell him that things would turn out for the best. He sank down on his haunches, his eyes on Pale. 'What am I going to do? I'm going to do some thinking, Quick Ben. I've been listening to you and Kalam, to Mallet and Fiddler, even Trotts has been jawing in my ear. Well, now it's my turn. So leave me be, Wizard, and take that damn girl with you.'

Quick Ben flinched, seeming to withdraw. Something in Whiskeyjack's words had made him very unhappy – or maybe everything.

The sergeant was too tired to worry about it. He had their new assignment to think over. Had he been a religious man, Whiskeyjack would have let blood in Hood's Bowl, calling upon the shades of his ancestors. As much as he hated to admit it, he shared the feeling among his squad: someone in the Empire wanted the Bridgeburners dead.

Pale was behind them now, the nightmare nothing but the taste of ashes in his mouth. Ahead lay their next destination: the legendary city of Darujhistan. Whiskeyjack had a premonition that a new nightmare was about to begin.

Down in the camp just beyond the last crest of denuded hills, horse-drawn carts loaded with wounded soldiers crowded the narrow aisles between the tent rows. All the precise order of the Malazan encampment had disintegrated, and the air was febrile with soldiers screaming their pain, giving voice to horror.

Tattersail threaded her way around the dazed survivors, stepping across puddles of blood in the wagon-ruts, her eyes lingering on an obscene pile of amputated limbs outside the cutter tents. From the massive sprawl of the camp followers' slum of tents and shelters came a wailing dirge – a broken chorus of thousands of voices, the sound a chilling reminder that war was always a thing of grief.

In some military headquarters back in the Empire's capital of Unta, three thousand leagues distant, an anonymous aide would paint a red stroke across the 2nd Army on the active list, and then write in fine script beside it: *Pale, late winter, the 1163rd Year of Burn's Sleep.* Thus would the death of nine thousand men and women be noted. And then forgotten.

Tattersail grimaced. *Some of us won't forget.* The Bridgeburners harboured some frightening suspicions. The thought of challenging Tayschrenn in a direct confrontation appealed to her sense of outrage and – if the High Mage *had* killed Calot – her feeling of betrayal. But she knew that her emotions had a way of running away with her. A sorcery duel with the Empire's High Mage would buy her a quick passage to Hood's Gate. Self-righteous wrath had planted more corpses in the ground than an empire could lay claim to, and as Calot used to say: Shake your fist all you want but dead is dead.

She'd witnessed all too many scenes of death since she'd first joined the ranks of the Malazan Empire, but at least they couldn't be laid squarely at her feet. That was the difference, and it had been enough for a long time. *Not as I once was. I've spent twenty years washing the blood from my hands.* Right now, however, the scene that rose again and again behind her eyes was the empty armour on the hilltop, and it gnawed at her heart. Those men and women had been running to *her*, looking for protection against the horrors of the plain below. It had been a desperate act, a fatal one, but she understood it. Tayschrenn didn't care about them, but she did. She was one of their own. In past battles they'd fought like rabid dogs to keep enemy legions from killing her. This time, it was a mage war. *Her* territory. Favours were traded in the 2nd. It's what kept everyone alive, and it was what had made the 2nd a legion of legend. Those soldiers had expectations, and they had the right to them. They'd come to her for salvation. And they died for it.

And if I had sacrificed myself then? Cast my Warren's defences on to them instead of shielding my own hide? She'd been surviving on instinct back then, and her instincts had had nothing to do with altruism. Those kind of people didn't live long in war.

Being alive, Tattersail concluded as she approached her tent, isn't the same as feeling good about it. She entered her tent and closed the flap behind her, then stood surveying her worldly possessions. Scant few, after two hundred and nineteen years of life. The oak chest containing her book of Thyr sorcery remained sealed by warding spells; the small collection of alchemical devices lay scattered on the tabletop beside her cot, like a child's toys abandoned in mid-game.

Amid the clutter sat her Deck of Dragons. Her gaze lingered on the reading cards before continuing its round. Everything looked different now, as if the chest, the alchemy, and her clothes all belonged to someone else: someone younger, someone still possessing a shred of vanity. Only the Deck – the Fatid – called out to her like an old friend.

Tattersail walked over to stand before it. With an absent gesture she set down the package given her by Kalam, then pulled out a stool from under the table. Sitting down, she reached for the Deck. She hesitated.

It had been months. Something had kept her away. Maybe Calot's death could have been foretold, and maybe that suspicion had been pacing in the darkness of her thoughts all this time. Pain and fear had been shaping her soul all her life, but her time with Calot had been another kind of shaping, something light, happy, pleasantly floating. She'd called it mere diversion.

'How's that for wilful denial?' She heard the bitterness in her tone and hated herself for it. Her old demons were back, laughing at the death of her illusions. *You refused the Deck once before, the night before Mock's throat was opened, the night before Dancer and the man who would one day rule an Empire stole into your master's – your lover's – Hold. Would you deny that a pattern exists, woman?*

Her vision blurry with memories she'd thought buried for ever, she looked down at the Deck, blinking rapidly. 'Do I want you to talk to me, old friend? Do I need your reminders, your wry confirmation that faith is for fools?'

A motion caught the corner of her eye. Whatever was inside the bound hide had moved. Lumps rose here and there, pushing against the seams. Tattersail stared. Then, her breath catching, she reached to it and set it in front of her. She withdrew a small dagger from her belt and began to cut the seams. The object within went still, as if awaiting the result of her efforts. She peeled back a sliced flap of hide.

' 'Sail,' said a familiar voice.

Her eyes widened as a wooden marionette, wearing bright yellow silk clothing, climbed out of the bag. Painted on its round face were features she recognized.

'Hairlock.'

'Good to see you again,' the marionette said, rising to its feet. It wobbled and held out artfully carved hands to regain balance. 'And the soul did shift,' he said, doffing his floppy hat and managing an unsteady bow.

Soul shifting. 'But that's been lost for centuries. Not even Tayschrenn—' She stopped, pursing her lips. Her thoughts raced.

'Later,' Hairlock said. He took a few steps, then bent his head forward to study his new body. 'Well,' he sighed, 'one mustn't quibble, must one?' He looked up and fixed painted eyes on the sorceress. 'You have to go to my tent before the thought occurs to Tayschrenn. I need my Book. You're part of this now. There's no turning back.'

'Part of what?'

Hairlock made no reply, having broken his uncanny stare. He lowered himself down to his knees. 'Thought I smelled a Deck,' he said.

Sweat ran in cold rivulets under Tattersail's arms. Hairlock had made her uneasy at the best of times, *but this* . . . She could smell her own fear. That he'd swung his gaze from her made her grateful for small mercies. This was Elder Magic, Kurald Galain, if the legends were true, and it was deadly, vicious, raw and primal. The Bridgeburners had a reputation for being a mean crowd, but to walk the Warrens closest to Chaos was pure madness. Or desperation.

Almost of its own accord, her Thyr Warren opened and a surge of power filled her weary body. Her eyes snapped to the Deck.

Hairlock must have sensed it. 'Tattersail,' he whispered, amusement in his tone. 'Come. The Fatid calls to you. Read what is to be read.'

Profoundly disturbed by her own answering flush of excitement, Tattersail reluctantly reached for the Deck of Dragons. She saw her hand tremble as it closed on it. She shuffled slowly, feeling the chill of the lacquered wooden cards seep into her fingers and then her arms. 'I feel a storm raging in them already,' she said, trimming the Deck and setting it down on the tabletop.

Hairlock's answering laugh was eager and mean. 'First House sets the course. Quickly!'

She turned over the top card. Her breath caught. 'Knight of Dark.'

Hairlock sighed. 'The Lord of Night rules this game. Of course.'

Tattersail studied the painted figure. The face remained blurred as it always did; the Knight was naked, his skin jet black. From the hips up he was human, heavily muscled, holding aloft a black two-handed sword that trailed smoky, ethereal chains drifting off into the background's empty darkness. His lower body was draconian, its armoured scales black, paling to grey at the belly. As always, she saw something new, something she had never seen before that pertained to the moment. There was a shape suspended in the darkness above the Knight's head: she could only detect it on the edge of her vision, a vague hint that vanished when she focused on the place itself. *Of course, you never give up the truth so easily, do you?*

'Second card,' Hairlock urged, crouching close to the playing field inscribed on the tabletop.

She flipped the second card. 'Oponn.' The two-faced Jester of Chance.

'Hood's Curse on their meddling ways,' Hairlock growled.

The Lady held the upright position, her male twin's bemused stare upside down at the card's foot. Thus the thread of luck that pulled back rather than pushed forward – the thread of success. The Lady's expression seemed soft, almost tender, a new facet marking how things now balanced. A second heretofore unseen detail caught Tattersail's intense study. Where the Lord's right hand reached up to touch the Lady's left a tiny silver disc spanned the space between them. The sorceress leaned forward, squinting. A coin, and on the face a male head. She blinked. No, female. Then male, then female. She sat back suddenly. The coin was spinning.

'Next!' Hairlock demanded. 'You are too slow!'

Tattersail saw that the marionette was paying no attention to the card Oponn, and had in fact probably given it only sufficient notice to identify it. She drew a deep breath. Hairlock and the Bridgeburners were tied up in this, she knew that instinctively, but her own role was as yet undecided. With these two cards, she already knew more than they did. It still wasn't much, but it might be enough to keep her alive in what was to come. She released her breath all at once, reached forward and slammed a palm down on the Deck.

Hairlock jumped, then whirled to her. 'You hold on this?' he raged. 'You hold on the Fool? The second card? Absurd! Play on, woman!'

'No,' Tattersail replied, sweeping the two cards into her hands and returning them to the Deck. 'I've chosen to hold. And there's nothing you can do about it.' She rose.

'Bitch! I can kill you in the blink of an eye! Here and now!'

'Fine,' Tattersail said. 'A good excuse for missing Tayschrenn's debriefing. By all means proceed, Hairlock.' Crossing her arms, she waited.

The marionette snarled. 'No,' he said. 'I have need of you. And you despise Tayschrenn even more than I.' He cocked his head, reconsidering his last words, then barked a laugh. 'Thus I am assured there will be no betrayal.'

Tattersail thought about that. 'You are right,' she said. She turned and walked to the tent flap. Her hand closed on the rough canvas, then she stopped. 'Hairlock, how well can you hear?'

'Well enough,' the marionette growled behind her.

'Do you hear anything, then?' *A spinning coin?*

'Camp sounds, is all. Why, what do you hear?'

Tattersail smiled. Without answering she pulled aside the tent flap and went outside. As she headed towards the command tent, a strange hope sang through her.

She'd never held Oponn as an ally. Calling on luck in anything was sheer idiocy. The first House she had placed, Darkness, touched her hand ice-cold, loud with the crashing waves of violence and power run amok – and yet an odd flavour there, something like salvation. The Knight could be

91

enemy or ally, or more likely neither. Just out there, unpredictable, self-absorbed. But Oponn rode the warrior's shadow, leaving House Dark tottering on the edge, suspended in a place between night and day. More than anything else, it had been Oponn's spinning coin that had demanded her choice to hold.

Hairlock heard nothing. *Wonderful.*

Even now, as she approached the command tent, the faint sound continued in her head, as it would for some time, she believed. The coin spun, and spun. Oponn whirled two faces to the cosmos, but it was the Lady's bet. *Spin on, silver. Spin on.*

CHAPTER THREE

Thelomen Tartheno Toblakai . . .
find the names of a people
so reluctant to fade
into oblivion . . .
Their legend rots
my cynical cast and blights
my eyes with bright glory . . .
'Cross not the loyal cage
embracing their unassailable heart . . .

. . . Cross not these stolid menhirs,
ever loyal to the earth.'
Thelomen Tartheno Toblakai . . .
Still standing, these towering pillars
mar the gelid scape
of my mind . . .

Gothos' Folly (II.iv)
Gothos (b.?)

The imperial trireme carved the deep-sea troughs like a relentless axe-blade, sails stretched and spars creaking under the steady wind. Captain Ganoes Paran remained in his cabin. He had long since grown tired of scanning the eastern horizon for the first sighting of land. It would come, and it would come soon.

He leaned against the sloping wall opposite his bunk, watching the lanterns sway and idly tossing his dagger into the lone table's centre pole, which was now studded with countless tiny holes.

A cool musty brush of air swept across his face and he turned to see Topper emerge from the Imperial Warren. It had been two years since he'd last seen the Claw Master. 'Hood's Breath, man,' Paran said, 'can't you find another colour of cloth? This perverse love of green must surely be curable.'

The tall half-blood Tiste Andii seemed to be wearing the same clothes as the last time Paran had seen him: green wool, green leather. Only the countless rings spearing his long fingers showed any splash of contrary colour. The Claw Master had arrived in a sour mood and Paran's opening words had not improved it. 'You imagine I enjoy such journeys, Captain? Seeking out a ship on the ocean is a challenge of sorcery few could manage.'

'Makes you a reliable messenger, then,' Paran muttered.

'I see you've made no effort to improve on courtesy, Captain – I admit I understand nothing of the Adjunct's faith in you.'

'Don't lose sleep over it, Topper. Now you've found me, what is the message?'

The man scowled. 'She's with the Bridgeburners. Outside Pale.'

'The siege continues? How old is your information?'

'Less than a week, which is as long as I've been hunting you. In any case,' he continued, 'the deadlock is about to be broken.'

Paran grunted. Then he frowned. 'Which squad?'

'You know them all?'

'Yes,' Paran asserted.

Topper's scowl deepened, then he raised a hand and began examining his rings. 'Whiskeyjack's. She's one of his recruits.'

Paran closed his eyes. It should not have surprised him. *The gods are playing with me. Question is, which gods? Oh, Whiskeyjack. You once commanded an army, back when Laseen was named Surly, back when you could have listened to your companion, when you could have made a choice. You could've stopped Surly. Hell, perhaps you could have stopped me. But now you command a squad, just a squad, and she's the Empress. And me? I'm a fool who followed his dream, and now all I desire is its end.* He opened his eyes and regarded Topper. 'Whiskeyjack. The War of Seven Cities: through the breach at Aren, the Holy Desert Raraku, Pan'potsun, Nathilog . . .'

'All in the Emperor's time, Paran.'

'So,' Paran said, 'I'm to take command of Whiskeyjack's squad. The mission will take us to Darujhistan, to the city of cities.'

'Your recruit is showing her powers,' Topper said, grimacing. 'She's corrupted the Bridgeburners, possibly even Dujek Onearm and the entire Second and Third Armies on Genabackis.'

'You can't be serious. Besides, my concern is with the recruit. With her. Only her. The Adjunct agrees we've waited long enough. Now you're telling me we've waited too long? I can't believe Dujek's about to become a renegade – not Dujek. Not Whiskeyjack either.'

'You are to proceed as planned, but I have been instructed to remind you that secrecy is paramount, now more than ever. An agent of the Claw will contact you once you reach Pale. Trust no one else. Your recruit's found her weapon, and with it she means to strike at the heart of the Empire. Failure cannot be considered.' Topper's odd eyes glinted. 'If you now feel unequal to the task . . .'

Paran studied the man standing before him. *If it's as*

bad as you describe, why not send in a hand of Claw assassins?

The man sighed, as if he'd somehow heard Paran's silent question. 'A god is using her, Captain. She won't die easily. The plan for dealing with her has required . . . adjustments. Expansion, in fact. Additional threats must be taken care of, but these are threads already woven. Do as you have been commanded. All risk must be removed if we are to take Darujhistan, and the Empress wants Darujhistan. She also feels it is time for Dujek Onearm to be . . .' he smiled '. . . disarmed.'

'Why?'

'He has a following. It's still held that the Emperor had old Onearm in mind as his heir.'

Paran snorted. 'The Emperor planned to rule for ever, Topper. This suspicion of Laseen's is plain ridiculous and persists only because it justifies her paranoia.'

'Captain,' Topper said quietly, 'greater men than you have died for less. The Empress expects obedience of her servants, and demands loyalty.'

'Any reasonable ruler would have the expectation and the demand the other way round.'

Topper's mouth thinned to a pale line. 'Assume command of the squad, stay close to the recruit but otherwise do nothing to make her suspicious of you. Once in place you are to wait. Understood?'

Paran looked away, his gaze finding the porthole. Beyond was blue sky. *There were too many omissions, half-truths and outright lies in this . . . this chaotic mess. How will I play it, when the time comes? The recruit must die. At least that much is certain. But the rest? Whiskeyjack, I remember you, you stood tall then, and in my dreams I never imagined this growing nightmare. Will I have your blood on my hands when all this is done?* At the very heart of things, he realized, he no longer knew who was the ultimate betrayer in all this, if a betrayer there must be. Was the Empire the Empress? Or was it something else, a legacy, an ambition, a vision at the far end of peace and wealth for all? Or was it a beast that could not cease devouring? Darujhistan – the greatest city in the world. Would it come to the Empire in flames? Was there wisdom in opening its gates? Within the troubled borders of the Malazan Empire, people lived in such peace as their ancestors had never imagined; and if not for the Claw, for the endless wars in distant lands, there would be freedom as well. Had this been the Emperor's dream at the very beginning? Did it matter any more?

'Are my instructions understood, Captain?'

He glanced over at the man and waved a hand. 'Well enough.'

Snarling, Topper spread wide his arms. The Imperial Warren yawned behind him. He stepped back and was gone.

Paran leaned forward, his head in his hands.

It was the Season of Currents and in the port city of Genabaris the heavy Malazan transports rocked and twisted, straining at their ropes like massive beasts. The piers, unused to such gargantuan craft moored alongside them, creaked ominously with every wayward, savage pull on the bollards.

Crates and cloth-wrapped bundles crowded the yards, supplies fresh in from the Seven Cities and destined for the front lines. Supply clerks clambered over them like monkeys, hunting sigils of identification and chattering to each other over the heads of dockmen and soldiers.

The agent leaned against a crate at the foot of the pier, his burly arms crossed and his small, narrow eyes fixed on the officer sitting on a bundle some thirty yards further down the pier. Neither had moved in the last hour.

The agent was having a hard time convincing himself that this was the man he'd been sent to retrieve. He looked awfully young, and as green as the rancid water of this bay. His uniform still bore its maker's chalk lines, and the leather grip of his longsword showed not a single sweat-stain. He had the stink of nobility about him like a perfumed cloud. And for the past hour he'd just been sitting there, hands in lap, shoulders hunched, watching like some stupid cow the frenzied activity swirling around him. Though he ranked captain, not a single soldier even bothered to salute him – the stink wasn't subtle.

The Adjunct must have been knocked on her head during that last assassination attempt on the Empress. It was the only possible explanation for this farce of a man rating the kind of service the agent was about to deliver. *In person, yet*. These days, he concluded sourly, the whole show was being run by idiots.

With a loud sigh, the agent pushed himself upright and sauntered over to the officer.

The man didn't even know he had company until the agent stepped in front of him, then he looked up.

The agent did some quick rethinking. Something in this man's gaze was dangerous. There was a glitter there, buried deep, that made the man's eyes seem older than the rest of his face. 'Name?' The agent's question was a strained grunt.

'Took your time about it,' the captain said, rising.

A *tall bastard, too*. The agent scowled. He hated tall bastards. 'Who're you waiting for, Captain?'

The man looked up the pier. 'The waiting's over. Let's walk. I'll just take it on faith you know where we're going.' He reached down and retrieved a duffel bag, then took the lead.

The agent moved up beside the captain. 'Fine,' he growled. 'Be that way.' They left the pier and the agent turned them up the first street on the right. 'A Green Quorl came in last night. You'll be taken directly to Cloud Forest, and from there a Black will take you into Pale.'

The captain gave the agent a blank stare.

'You never heard of Quorls?'

'No. I assume they're a means of transportation. Why else

would I be removed from a ship a thousand leagues distant from Pale?'

'The Moranth use them, and we're using the Moranth.' The agent scowled to himself. 'Using them a lot, these days. The Green do most of the courier stuff, and moving people around like you and me, but the Black are stationed in Pale, and the different clans don't like to mix. The Moranth are made up of a bunch of clans, got colours for names, and wear them too. Nobody gets confused that way.'

'And I'm to ride with a Green, on a Quorl?'

'You got it, Captain.'

They headed up a narrow street. Malazan guards milled around every crossing, hands on their weapons.

The captain returned a salute from one such squad. 'Having trouble with insurrections?' he asked.

'Insurrections, yeah. Trouble, no.'

'Let's see if I understand you correctly.' The captain's tone was stiff. 'Instead of delivering me by ship to a point nearest Pale, I'm to ride overland with a bunch of half-human bar-barians who smell like grasshoppers and dress like them, too. And this way, no one will notice, especially since it'll take us a year to get to Pale and by then everything will have gone all to hell. Correct so far?'

Grinning, the agent shook his head. Despite his hatred for tall men or, rather, men taller than himself, he felt his guard going down. At least this one talked straight – and, for a noble, that was pretty impressive. Maybe Lorn still had the old stuff after all. 'You said overland? Well, hell, yes, Captain. Way overland.' He stopped at a nondescript doorway and turned to the man. 'Quorls, you see, they fly. They got wings. Four in fact. And you can see right through every one of them, and if you're of a mind you can poke your finger through one of those wings. Only don't do it when you're a quarter-mile up, right? 'Cause it may be a long way down but it'll seem awfully fast at the time. You hear me, Captain?' He opened the door. Beyond rose a staircase.

The man's face had lost its colour. 'So much for intelligence reports,' he muttered.

The agent's grin widened. 'We see them before you do. Life's on a need-to-know. Remember that, Captain . . .?'

The man's smile was the only answer he gave.

They entered and closed the door behind them.

A young marine intercepted Tattersail as she made her way across the compound in what was now Empire headquarters in Pale. The boy's face had bewilderment written all over it, and he opened his mouth a few times before any words came out.

'Sorceress?'

She stopped. The thought of having Tayschrenn wait a little longer appealed to her. 'What is it, soldier?'

The marine stole a glance over one shoulder, then said, 'The guards, Sorceress. They've got something of a problem. They sent me to—'

'Who? Which guards? Take me to them.'

'Yes, Sorceress.'

She followed the marine around the nearest corner of the main building, where the compound wall ran close, creating a narrow passage running the building's length. At the far end knelt a figure, his bare head bowed. Beside him was a large, lumpy burlap sack, covered in brown stains. Clouds of flies swarmed around both the man and the sack.

The marine halted and turned to the sorceress. 'He still hasn't moved. The guards keep getting sick when they patrol through here.'

Tattersail stared at the huddled man, a sudden welling of tears behind her eyes. Ignoring the marine, she strode into the aisle. The stench hit her like a wall. Damn, she thought, he's been here since the battle. Five days. The sorceress came closer. Though Bellurdan knelt, his head came near to her own height. The Thelomen High Mage still wore what was left of his battle garb, the ragged strips of fur scorched and torn, the rough weave of fragments of tunic stained with blood. As she arrived to stop before him, she saw that his neck and face were covered in burn blisters, and most of his hair was gone.

'You look terrible, Bellurdan,' she said.

The giant's head slowly turned. Red-rimmed eyes focused on her face. 'Ah,' he rumbled. 'Tattersail.' His exhausted smile cracked the charred flesh of one cheek. The wound gaped red and dry.

That smile almost broke her down. 'You need healing, old friend.' Her gaze flicked to the burlap sack. Its surface crawled with flies. 'Come on. Nightchill would bite your head off if she could see you now.' She felt a trembling steal into her, but grimly pressed on. 'We'll take care of her, Bellurdan. You and me. But we'll need our strength to do that.'

The Thelomen shook his head slowly. 'I choose this, Tattersail. The scars without are the scars within.' He drew a deep breath. 'I will survive these wounds. And I alone will raise my love's barrow. But the time is not yet right.' He laid a massive hand on the sack. 'Tayschrenn has given me leave to do this. Will you do the same?'

Tattersail was shocked to feel the surge of anger rising up in her. 'Tayschrenn gave you leave, did he?' To her own ears her voice sounded brutal, a harsh grating of sarcasm. She saw Bellurdan flinch and seem to withdraw, and a part of her wanted to wail, to throw her arms around the giant and weep, but rage possessed her. 'That bastard killed Nightchill, Bellurdan! The Moon's lord had neither the time nor the inclination to raise demons. Think about it! Tayschrenn had the time to prepare—'

'No!' The Thelomen's voice thundered down the aisle. He surged to his feet and Tattersail stepped back. The giant looked ready to tear down the walls, a desperate fire in his eyes. His hands closed into fists. Then his glare fixed on her. He seemed to freeze. All at once his shoulders slumped, his hands opened, and his eyes dimmed. 'No,' he said again, this time in a tone filled with sorrow. 'Tayschrenn is our protector. As he has always been, Tattersail. Remember the very beginning? The Emperor was mad, but Tayschrenn stood at his side. He shaped the Empire's dream and so opposed the Emperor's nightmare. We underestimated the Lord of Moon's Spawn, that is all.'

Tattersail stared up at Bellurdan's ravaged face. The memory of Hairlock's torn body returned to her. There was an echo there, but she couldn't quite catch it. 'I remember the beginning,' she said softly, doing some searching of her own. The memories remained sharp, but whatever thread there was that connected then to now still eluded her. She wanted desperately to talk to Quick Ben, but she had seen nothing of the Bridgeburners since the day of the battle. They'd left her with Hairlock, and that puppet scared her more and more with every passing day. Particularly now that he'd found a grudge to hold on to – the scene with the Deck of Dragons still smarted – and he worked it by keeping her in the dark. 'The Emperor had a knack for gathering the right people around him,' she continued. 'But he wasn't a fool. He knew the betrayal would come from that group. What made us the right people was our power. I remember, Bellurdan.' She shook her head. 'The Emperor's gone, but the power's still here.'

Tattersail's breath caught. 'And that's it,' she said, half to herself. 'Tayschrenn's the thread.'

'The Emperor was insane,' Bellurdan said. 'Else he would have protected himself better.'

Tattersail frowned at that. The Thelomen had a point. Like she'd just said, that old man wasn't a fool. So what had happened? 'I'm sorry. We must talk later. The High Mage has summoned me. Bellurdan, will we talk later?'

The giant nodded. 'As you wish. Soon I will depart to raise Nightchill's barrow. Far out on the Rhivi Plain, I think.'

Tattersail glanced back up the aisle. The marine still stood there, shifting from one foot to the other. 'Bellurdan, would you mind if I cast a sealing spell on her remains?'

His eyes clouded and he looked down at the sack. 'The guards are unhappy, it's true.' He thought for a moment, then said, 'Yes, Tattersail. You may do that.'

'It smells bad from here to the throne,' Kalam said, his scarred face twisted with worry. He sat crouched on his haunches, absently scratching the lines of a web on the ground with his dagger, then looked up at his sergeant.

Whiskeyjack eyed Pale's stained walls, the muscles of his jaw bunching beneath his beard. 'The last time I stood on this hill,' he said, his gaze narrowing, 'it was crowded with armour. And a mage and a half.' He was silent for a time, then he sighed. 'Go on, Corporal.'

Kalam nodded. 'I pulled some old threads,' he said, squinting against the harsh morning light. 'Somebody high up has us marked. Could be the court itself, or maybe the nobility – there's rumours they're back at it behind the scenes.' He grimaced. 'And now we've got some new captain from Unta eager to get our throats cut. Four captains in the last three years, not one worth his weight in salt.'

Quick Ben stood ten feet away, at the hill's crest, his arms crossed. He now spoke. 'You heard the plan. Come on, Whiskeyjack. That man slid straight out of the palace and into our laps on a stream of—'

'Quiet,' Whiskeyjack muttered. 'I'm thinking.'

Kalam and Quick Ben exchanged glances.

A long minute passed. On the road below troop wagons rattled in the ruts leading into the city. Remnants of the 5th and 6th Armies, already battered, almost broken, by Caladan Brood and the Crimson Guard. Whiskeyjack shook his head. The only force intact was the Moranth, and they seemed determined to field only the Black regiments, using the Green for lifts and drops – and where the hell was the Gold he'd been hearing so much about? *Damn those unhuman bastards anyway.* Pale's gutters still ran red from their hour of retribution. Once the burial shifts were through, there'd be a few more hills outside the city's walls. Big ones.

There would be nothing to mark thirteen hundred dead Bridgeburners, though. The worms didn't need to travel far to feast on those bodies. What chilled the sergeant to his bones was the fact that, apart from the few survivors, nobody had made a serious effort to save them. Some low-ranking officer had delivered Tayschrenn's commiserations on those lost in the line of duty, then had unloaded a wagonload of tripe about heroism and sacrifice. His audience of thirty-nine stone-faced soldiers had looked on without a word. The officer was found dead in his room two hours later, expertly garotted. The mood was bad – nobody in the regiment would have even thought of something so ugly five years ago. But now they didn't blink at the news.

Garotte – sounds like Claw work. Kalam had suggested it was a set-up, an elaborate frame to discredit what was left of the Bridgeburners. Whiskeyjack was sceptical.

He tried to clear his thoughts. If there was a pattern it would be a simple one, simple enough to pass by unnoticed. But exhaustion seeped in like a thick haze behind his eyes. He took a deep lungful of the morning air. 'The new recruit?' he asked.

Kalam rose from his haunches with a grunt. A faraway and long-ago look entered his eyes. 'Maybe,' he said finally. 'Pretty young for a Claw, though.'

'I never believed in pure evil before Sorry showed up,' Quick Ben said. 'But you're right, she's awfully young. How long are they trained before they're sent out?'

Kalam shrugged uneasily. 'Fifteen years minimum. Mind you, they get them young. Five or six.'

'Could be magery involved, making her look younger than she is,' Quick Ben said. 'High-level stuff, but within Tayschrenn's abilities.'

'Seems too obvious,' Whiskeyjack muttered. 'Call it bad upbringing.'

Quick Ben snorted. 'Don't tell me you believe that, Whiskeyjack.'

The sergeant's face tightened. 'The subject's closed on Sorry. And don't tell me what I think, Wizard.' He faced Kalam. 'All right. You think the Empire's into killing its own these days. You think Laseen's cleaning her house, maybe? Or someone close to her? Getting rid of certain people. Fine. Tell me why.'

'The old guard,' Kalam replied immediately. 'Everyone still loyal to the Emperor's memory.'

'Doesn't wash,' Whiskeyjack said. 'We're all dying off anyway. We don't need Laseen's help. Apart from Dujek there's not a man in this army here who even knows the Emperor's name, and nobody'd give a damn in any case. He's dead. Long live the Empress.'

'She ain't got the patience to wait it out,' Quick Ben said.

Kalam nodded agreement. 'She's losing momentum as it is. Things used to be better – it's that memory she wants dead.'

'Hairlock's our snake in the hole,' Quick Ben said with a sharp nod. 'It'll work, Whiskeyjack. I know what I'm doing on this one.'

'We do it the way the Emperor would have,' Kalam added. 'We turn the game. We do our own house-cleaning.'

Whiskeyjack raised a hand. 'All right. Now be quiet. You're both sounding too damn rehearsed.' He paused. 'It's a theory. A complicated one. Who's in the know and who isn't?' He scowled at Quick Ben's expression. 'Right, that's Hairlock's task. But what happens when you come face to face with someone big, powerful and mean?'

'Like Tayschrenn?' The wizard grinned.

'Right. I'm sure you've got an answer. Let's see if I can work it out myself. You look for someone even nastier. You make a deal and you set things up, and if we're quick enough we'll come out smelling of roses. Am I close, Wizard?'

Kalam snorted his amusement.

Quick Ben looked away. 'Back in the Seven Cities, before the Empire showed up—'

'Back in the Seven Cities is back in the Seven Cities,' Whiskeyjack said. 'Hell, I led the company chasing you across the desert, remember? I know how you work, Quick. And I know you're damn good at this. But I also recall that you were the only one of your cabal to come out alive back then. And this time?'

The wizard seemed hurt by Whiskeyjack's words. His lips thinned to a straight line.

The sergeant sighed. 'All right. We go with it. Start things rolling. And pull that sorceress all the way in. We'll need her if Hairlock breaks his chains.'

'And Sorry?' Kalam asked.

Whiskeyjack hesitated. He knew the question behind that question. Quick Ben was the squad's brains, but Kalam was their killer. Both made him uneasy with their single-minded devotion to their respective talents. 'Leave her alone,' he said at last. 'For now.'

Kalam and Quick Ben sighed, sharing a grin behind their sergeant's back.

'Just don't get cocky,' Whiskeyjack said drily.

The grins faded.

The sergeant's gaze returned to the wagons entering the city. Two riders approached. 'All right,' he said. 'Mount up. Here comes our reception committee.' The riders were from his squad, Fiddler and Sorry.

'You think the new captain's arrived?' Kalam asked, as he

106

climbed into his saddle. His roan mare turned her head and snapped at him. He growled in return. A moment later the two long-time companions settled down into their mutual mistrust.

Whiskeyjack looked on, amused. 'Probably. Let's head down to them. Anybody up on the wall watching us might be getting antsy.' Then his humour fell away. They had, indeed, just turned the game. And the timing couldn't have been worse. He knew the full extent of their next mission, and in that he knew more than either Quick Ben or Kalam. There was no point in complicating things even further, though. *They'll find out soon enough.*

Tattersail stood half a dozen feet behind High Mage Tayschrenn. The Malazan banners snapped in the wind, the spars creaking above the smoke-stained turret, but here in the shelter of the wall the air was calm. On the western horizon across from her rose the Moranth Mountains, reaching a mangled arm northward to Genabaris. As the range swept southward it joined the Tahlyn in a jagged line stretching a thousand leagues into the east. Off to her right lay the flat yellow-grassed Rhivi Plain.

Tayschrenn leaned on a merlon looking down on the wagons rolling into the city. From below rose the groans of oxen and shouting soldiers. The High Mage hadn't moved or said a word in some minutes. Off to his left waited a small wood table, its surface scarred and pitted and crowded with runes cut deep into the oak. Peculiar dark stains blotted the surface here and there.

Knots of tension throbbed in Tattersail's shoulders. Meeting Bellurdan had shaken her, and she didn't feel up to what was to come.

'Bridgeburners,' the High Mage muttered.

Startled, the sorceress frowned, then stepped up to stand beside Tayschrenn. Descending from a hill off to the right, a

107

hill she knew intimately, rode a party of soldiers. Even from this distance she recognized four of them: Quick Ben, Kalam, Whiskeyjack and that recruit, Sorry. The fifth rider was a short, wiry man, who had sapper written all over him. 'Oh?' she said, feigning lack of interest.

'Whiskeyjack's squad,' Tayschrenn said. He turned his full gaze on the sorceress. 'The same squad you spoke with immediately following the Moon's retreat.' The High Mage smiled, then clapped Tattersail's shoulder. 'Come. I require a Reading. Let's begin.' He walked over to stand before the table. 'Oponn's strands are twisting a peculiar maze, the influence snares me again and again.' He turned his back to the wall and sat down on a crenel, then looked up. 'Tattersail,' he said soberly, 'in matters of Empire, I am the servant of the Empress.'

Tattersail recalled their argument at the debriefing. Nothing had been resolved. 'Perhaps I should take my complaints to her, then.'

Tayschrenn's brows rose. 'I take that as sarcastic.'

'You do?'

The High Mage said, stiffly, 'I do, and be thankful for it, woman.'

Tattersail pulled out her Deck and held it against her stomach, running her fingers over the top card. Cool, a feeling of great weight and darkness. She set the Deck in the table's centre, then lowered her bulk slowly into a kneeling position. Her gaze locked with Tayschrenn's. 'Shall we begin?'

'Tell me of the Spinning Coin.'

Tattersail's breath caught. She could not move.

'First card,' Tayschrenn commanded.

With an effort she expelled the air from her lungs in a hissing sigh. Damn him, she thought. An echo of laughter sounded in her head, and she realized that someone, something, had opened the way. An Ascendant was reaching through her, its presence cool and amused, almost fickle. Her eyes shut of their own accord, and she reached for the first card. She flipped it almost haphazardly to her right. Eyes still closed, she felt herself smile. 'An unaligned card: Orb. Judgement and true sight.' The second card she tossed to the left side of the field. 'Virgin, High House Death. Here scarred and blindfolded, with blood on her hands.'

Faintly, as if from a great distance away, came the sound of horses, thundering closer, now beneath her, as if the earth had swallowed them. Then the sound rose anew, behind her. She felt herself nod. *The recruit.* 'The blood on her hands is not her own, the crime not its own. The cloth against her eyes is wet.'

She slapped the third card immediately in front of her. Behind her lids an image formed. It left her cold and frightened. 'Assassin, High House Shadow. The Rope, a count of knots unending, the Patron of Assassins is in this game.' For a moment she thought she heard the howling of Hounds. She laid a hand on the fourth card and felt a thrill of recognition ripple through her, followed by something like false modesty. 'Oponn, Lady's head high, Lord's low.' She picked it up and set it down opposite Tayschrenn.

There's your block. She smiled to herself. *Chew on it awhile, High Mage. The Lady regards you with disgust.* Tattersail knew he must be burning with questions, but he wouldn't speak them. There was too much power behind this opening. Had he sensed the Ascendant's presence? She wondered if it scared him.

'The Coin,' she heard herself say, 'spins on, High Mage. Its face looks upon many, a handful perhaps, and here is their card.' She set the fifth card to Oponn's right, edges touching. 'Another unaligned card: Crown. Wisdom and justice, as it is upright. Around it a fair city's walls, lit by flames of gas, blue and green.' She pondered. 'Yes, Darujhistan, the last Free City.'

The way closed, the Ascendant withdrawing as if bored. Tattersail's eyes opened, an unexpected warmth comforting her weary body. 'Into Oponn's maze,' she said, amused at the truth hidden in that statement. 'I can take it no further, High Mage.'

Tayschrenn's breath gusted out and he leaned back. 'You've gone far past what I've managed, Sorceress.' His face was drawn as he looked at her. 'I'm impressed with your source, though not pleased with its message.' He frowned, planting his elbows on his knees and steepling his long-fingered hands before his face. 'This Spinning Coin, ever echoing. There's the Jester's humour in this shaping – even now I feel we are being misled. Death's Virgin, a likely deceit.'

It was now Tattersail's turn to be impressed. The High Mage was an Adept, then. Had he, too, heard the laughter punctuating the laying of the field? She hoped not. 'You might be right,' she said. 'The Virgin's face is ever changing – it could be anyone. Can't say the same for Oponn, or the Rope's.' She nodded. 'A very possible deception,' she said, pleased to be conversing with an equal – a truth that made her grimace inwardly. *It's always better when hatred and outrage stay pure, uncompromised.*

'I would hear your thoughts,' Tayschrenn said.

Tattersail started, shied from the High Mage's steady gaze. She began collecting the cards. Would it hurt to offer some explanation? *If anything, it will leave him even more rattled than he already is.* 'Deception is the Patron Assassin's forte. I sensed nothing of his presumed master, Shadowthrone himself. Makes me suspect the Rope is on his own here. Beware the Assassin, High Mage, if anything his games are even more subtle than Shadowthrone's. And while Oponn plays their own version, it remains the same game, and that game is being played out in our world. The Twins of Luck have no control in Shadow's Realm, and Shadow is a Warren known for slipping its boundaries. For breaking the rules.'

'True enough,' Tayschrenn said, rising to his feet with a grunt. 'The birth of that bastard realm has ever troubled me.'

'It's young yet,' Tattersail said. She picked up her Deck and returned it to the pocket inside her cloak. 'Its final shaping is still centuries away, and it may never happen. Recall other new Houses that ended up dying a quick death.'

'This one stinks of too much power.' Tayschrenn returned to his study of the Moranth Mountains. 'My gratitude,' he said, as Tattersail went to the steps leading down into the city, 'is worth something, I hope. In any case, Sorceress, you have it.'

Tattersail hesitated at the landing, then began the descent. He'd be less magnanimous if he found out that she had just misled him. She could guess the Virgin's identity. Her thoughts travelled back to the moment of the Virgin's appearance. The horses she had heard, passing beneath, hadn't been an illusion. Whiskeyjack's squad had just entered the city, through the gate below. And among them rode Sorry. Coincidence? Maybe, but she didn't think so. The Spinning Coin had faintly wobbled at that instant, then its ringing returned. Though she heard it in her mind day and night, it had become almost second nature, and Tattersail found she had to concentrate to find it. But she'd caught the nudge, felt the pitch change and sensed a brief instant of uncertainty.

Death's Virgin, and the Assassin of High House Shadow. There was a connection there, somehow, and it bothered Oponn. Obviously, everything remained in a flux. 'Terrific,' she muttered, as she reached the bottom of the staircase.

She saw the young marine who had approached her earlier. He stood in a line of recruits in the centre of the compound. No commanding officer was in sight. Tattersail called the boy over.

'Yes, Sorceress?' he asked, as he arrived to stand at attention in front of her.

'What are you all standing around for, soldier?'

'We're about to be issued our weapons. The staff sergeant's

111

gone to bring the wagon round.'

Tattersail nodded. 'I have a task for you. I'll see that you get your weapons – but not the tinny ones your friends are about to receive. If a superior officer questions your absence, refer him to me.'

'Yes, Sorceress.'

A pang of regret hit Tattersail upon meeting the boy's bright, eager gaze. Chances were, he'd be dead within a few months. The Empire had many crimes staining its banner, but this was the worst of them. She sighed. 'Deliver, in person, this message to Sergeant Whiskeyjack, Bridgeburners. The fat lady with the spells wants to talk. You have it, soldier?'

The boy blanched.

'Let's hear it.'

The marine repeated the message in a deadpan tone.

Tattersail smiled. 'Very good. Now run along, and don't forget to get an answer from him. I'll be in my quarters.'

Captain Paran swung around for a last look at the Black Moranth. The squad had just reached the plateau's crest. He watched until they disappeared from view, then shifted his gaze back to the city in the east.

From this distance, with the wide, flat plain in between, Pale seemed peaceful enough, although the ground outside the walls was studded with black basaltic rubble and the memory of smoke and fire clung to the air. Along the wall scaffolding rose in places, tiny figures crowding the frameworks. They appeared to be rebuilding huge gaps in the stonework. From the north gate a sluggish stream of wagons wound out towards the hills, the air above them filled with crows. Along the edge of those hills ran a line of mounds too regular to be natural.

He'd heard the rumours, here and there. Five dead mages, two of them High Mages. The 2nd's losses enough to fire speculation that it would be merged with the 5th and the 6th to form a new regiment. And Moon's Spawn had retreated south, across the Tahlyn Mountains to Lake Azur, trailing smoke, drifting and leaning to one side like a spent thunderhead. But one tale reached into the captain's thoughts deeper than all the rest: the Bridgeburners were gone. Some stories said killed to a man; others insisted that a few squads had made it out of the tunnels before the collapse.

Paran was frustrated. He'd been among Moranth for days. The uncanny warriors hardly ever spoke, and when they did it was to each other in that incomprehensible tongue of theirs. All of his information was out of date, and that put him in an unfamiliar position. Mind you, he thought, since Genabaris it had been one unfamiliar situation after another.

So here he was, on the waiting end of things once again. He readjusted his duffel bag and was preparing for a long wait when he saw a horseman top the far plateau's crest. The man had an extra mount with him, and he rode straight for the captain.

He sighed. Dealing with the Claw always grated. They were so damn smug. With the exception of that man in Genabaris, none seemed to like him much. It had been a long time since he'd known someone he could call a friend. Over two years, in fact.

The rider arrived. Seeing him up close, Paran took an involuntary step back. Half the man's face had been burned away. A patch covered the right eye and the man held his head at an odd angle. The man flashed a ghastly grin, then dismounted.

'You're the one, huh?' he asked in a rasping voice.

'Is it true about the Bridgeburners?' Paran demanded. 'Wiped out?'

'More or less. Five squads left, or thereabouts. About forty in all.' His left eye squinted and he reached up to adjust his

113

battered helmet. 'Didn't know where you'd be heading before. Do now. You're Whiskeyjack's new captain, huh?'

'Sergeant Whiskeyjack is known to you?' Paran scowled. This Claw wasn't like the others. Whatever thinking they did about him they kept to themselves, and he preferred it that way.

The man climbed back into his saddle. 'Let's ride. We can talk on the way.'

Paran went to the other horse and tied his bag to the saddle, which was of the Seven Cities style, high-backed and with a hinged horn that folded forward – he'd seen several like this on this continent. It was a detail he'd already filed away. Natives from the Seven Cities had a predisposition for making trouble, and this whole Genabackan Campaign had been a foul-up from the very start. *No coincidence, that.* Most of the 2nd, 5th and 6th Armies had been recruited from the Seven Cities subcontinent.

He mounted and they settled into a steady canter across the plateau.

The Claw talked. 'Sergeant Whiskeyjack's got a lot of followers around here. Acts like he don't know it. You got to remember something that's been damn near forgotten back in Malaz – Whiskeyjack once commanded his own company . . .'

Paran's head snapped around. That fact had been thoroughly stripped from the annals. As far as Empire history was concerned, it had never happened.

'. . . back in the days when Dassem Ultor ran the military,' the Claw continued blithely. 'It was Whiskeyjack's Seventh Company that ran down the Seven Cities' mage cabal out in the Pan'potsun Wastes. He ended the war then and there. Of course, everything went to hell after that, what with Hood taking Ultor's daughter. And not long after that, when Ultor died, all his men were pulled down fast. That's when the bureaucrats swallowed up the Army. Damn jackals. And they've been sniping at each other ever since and to hell with the campaigns.' The Claw sat forward, pushing the saddlehorn down, and spat past his horse's left ear.

Paran shivered, seeing that gesture. In the old days it had announced the beginning of tribal war among the Seven Cities. Now, it had become the symbol of the Malaz 2nd Army. 'Are you suggesting,' he cut in, 'that the story you've just told me is commonplace?'

'Not in detail,' the Claw admitted. 'But some old veterans in the Second fought with Ultor, not just in Seven Cities but as far back as Falar.'

Paran thought for a time. The man riding beside him, though a Claw, was also 2nd Army. And he'd been through a lot with them. It made for an interesting perspective. He glanced at the man and saw him grinning. 'What's so funny?'

The man shrugged. 'The Bridgeburners are a little hot, these days. They're getting chaff for recruits and that makes it look like they're about to be disbanded. You talk with whoever it is you talk with back in Malaz, you tell them they'd end up with a mutiny on their hands, they start messing with the Bridgeburners. That's in every report I send but no one seems to listen to me.' His grin broadened. 'Maybe they think I've been turned or something, eh?'

Paran shrugged. 'You were called in to meet me, weren't you?'

The Claw laughed. 'You've really been out of touch, haven't you? They called me in because I'm the last Active in the Second. And as for the Fifth and Sixth – forget it. Brood's Tiste Andii could pick out a Claw from a thousand paces. None of them left, either. My own Claw Master was garotted two days back – that's something else, ain't it? You, I inherited, Captain. Once we hit the city, I send you on your way, and that's probably the last we'll ever see of each other. You deliver your mission details as Captain of the Ninth Squad, they either

115

laugh in your face or they stick a knife in your eye – it's even betting what they'll do. Too bad, but there it is.'

Up ahead loomed the gates of Pale.

'One more thing,' the Claw said, his eyes on the merlons above the gate, 'just a bone I'll throw you in case Oponn's smiling on you. The High Mage Tayschrenn's running things here. Dujek's not happy, especially considering what happened with Moon's Spawn. It's a bad situation between them, but the High Mage is relying on his being in close and constant communication with the Empress, and that's what's keeping him on top. A warning, then. Dujek's soldiers will follow him . . . *anywhere*. And that goes for the Fifth and Sixth Armies, too. What's been gathered here is a storm waiting to break.'

Paran stared at the man. Topper had explained the situation, but Paran had dismissed the man's assessment – it had seemed too much like a scenario devised to justify the Empress filling the gallows. *Not a tangle I want to get involved in. Leave me to complete my single task – I desire no more than that.*

As they passed into the gate's shadow, the Claw spoke again. 'By the by, Tayschrenn just watched us arrive. Any chance he knows you, Captain?'

'No.' I hope not, he added silently.

As they trotted into the city proper and a wall of sound rose to meet them, Paran's eyes glazed slightly. Pale was a madhouse, buildings on all sides gutted by fire, the streets, despite being cobble-heaved in places and dented in others, were packed with people, carts, braying animals and marines. He wondered if he should start measuring his life in minutes. Taking command of a squad that had gone through four captains in three years, then delivering a mission that no sane soldier would consider, coupled with a brewing firestorm of a large-scale insurrection possibly headed by the Empire's finest military commander, against a High Mage who looked to be carving his own rather big niche in the world – all of this had

116

Paran feeling somewhat dismayed.

He was jolted by a heavy slap on his back. The Claw had moved his horse close and now he leaned over.

'Out of your depth, Captain? Don't worry, every damn person here's out of their depth. Some know it, some don't. It's the ones who don't you got to worry about. Start with what's right in front of you and forget the rest for now. It'll show up in its own time. Find any marine and ask direction to the Bridgeburners. That's the easy part.'

Paran nodded.

The Claw hesitated, then leaned closer. 'I've been thinking, Captain. It's a hunch, mind you, but I think you're here to do some good. No, don't bother answering. Only, if you get into trouble, you get word to Toc the Younger, that's me. I'm in the Messenger Corps, outrider class, the Second. All right?'

Paran nodded again. 'Thank you,' he said, just as a loud crash sounded behind them, followed by a chorus of angry voices. Neither rider turned.

'What's that you said, Captain?'

Paran smiled. 'Better head off. Keep your cover – in case something happens to me. I'll find myself a guide, by the book.'

'Sure thing, Captain.' Toc the Younger waved, then swung his mount down a side-street. Moments later Paran lost sight of him. He drew a deep breath, then cast his gaze about, searching for a likely soldier.

Paran knew that his early years in the noble courts of his homeland had prepared him well for the kind of deception Adjunct Lorn demanded of him. In the past two years, however, he had begun to recognize more clearly what he was becoming. That brash, honest youth who had spoken with the Empress's Adjunct that day on the Itko Kanese coast now gnawed at him. He'd dropped right into Lorn's lap like a lump of unshaped clay. And she had proceeded to do what she did best.

117

What frightened Paran most, these days, was that he had grown used to being used. He'd been someone else so many times that he saw a thousand faces, heard a thousand voices, all at war with his own. When he thought of himself, of that young noble-born man with the overblown faith in honesty and integrity, the vision that came to him now was of something cold, hard and dark. It hid in the deepest shadows of his mind, and it watched. No contemplation, no judgement, just icy, clinical observation.

He didn't think that that young man would see the light of day again. He would just shrink further back, swallowed by darkness, then disappear, leaving no trace.

And Paran wondered if he even cared any more.

He marched into the barracks that had once housed Pale's Noble Guard. One old veteran lounged on a nearby cot, her rag-wrapped feet jutting over the end. The mattress had been stripped away and tossed into a corner; the woman lay on the flat boards, her hands behind her head.

Paran's gaze held on her briefly, then travelled down the ward. With the lone exception of the veteran marine, the place was empty. He returned his attention to her. 'Corporal, is it?'

The woman didn't move. 'Yeah, what?'

'I take it,' he said drily, 'that the chain of command has thoroughly disintegrated around here.'

Her eyes opened and managed a lazy sweep of the officer standing before her. 'Probably,' she said, then closed her eyes again. 'You looking for somebody or what?'

'I'm looking for the Ninth Squad, Corporal.'

'Why? They in trouble again?'

Paran smiled to himself. 'Are you the average Bridgeburner, Corporal?'

'All the average ones are dead,' she said.

'Who's your commander?' Paran asked.

118

'Antsy, but he's not here.'

'I can see that.' The captain waited, then sighed. 'Well, where is this Antsy?'

'Try Knobb's Inn, up the street. The last I seen of him he was losing his shirt to Hedge. Antsy's a card-player, right, only not a good one.' She began picking at a tooth at the back of her mouth.

Paran's brows rose. 'Your commander gambles with his men?'

'Antsy's a sergeant,' the woman explained. 'Our captain's dead. Anyway, Hedge is not in our squad.'

'Oh, and what squad is he with?'

The woman grinned, swallowing whatever her finger had dislodged. 'The Ninth.'

'What's your name, Corporal?'

'Picker, what's yours?'

'Captain Paran.'

Picker shot up into a sitting position, her eyes wide. 'Oh, you're the new captain who's yet to pull a sword, eh?'

Paran grinned. 'That's right.'

'You got any idea of the odds on you right now? It doesn't look good.'

'What do you mean?'

She smiled a broad smile. 'The way I pick it,' she said, leaning back down and closing her eyes again, 'the first blood you see on your hands is gonna be your own, Captain Paran. Go back to Quon Tali where it's safe. Go on, the Empress needs her feet licked.'

'They're clean enough,' Paran said. He was not sure how to deal with this situation. Part of him wanted to draw his sword and cut Picker in half. Another wanted to laugh, and that one had an edge of hysteria to it.

Behind him the outer door banged open and heavy footsteps sounded on the floorboards. Paran turned. A red-faced sergeant, his face dominated by an enormous handlebar moustache, stormed into the room. Ignoring Paran, he strode up beside Picker's cot and glowered down at her.

'Dammit, Picker, you told me Hedge was having a bad run, and now that bow-legged turd's cleaned me out!'

'Hedge *is* having a bad run,' Picker said. 'But yours is worse. You never asked me about that, did you? Antsy, meet Captain Paran, the Ninth's new officer.'

The sergeant swung around and stared. 'Hood's Breath,' he muttered, then faced Picker again.

'I'm looking for Whiskeyjack, Sergeant,' Paran said softly.

Something in the captain's tone brought Antsy around. He opened his mouth, then shut it when his eyes caught Paran's steady gaze. 'Some kid delivered a message. Whiskeyjack trooped out. A few of his people are at Knobb's.'

'Thank you, Sergeant.' Paran walked stiffly from the room.

Antsy let out a long breath and glanced at Picker.

'Two days,' she pronounced, 'then somebody does him. Old Rockface has already laid twenty to that.'

Antsy's expression tightened. 'Something tells me that'd be a damned shame.'

Paran entered Knobb's Inn and stopped just inside the doorway. The place was packed with soldiers, their voices a jumbled roar. Only a few showed on their uniforms the flame emblem of the Bridgeburners. The rest were 2nd Army.

At a large table beneath an overhanging walkway that fronted rooms on the first floor half a dozen Bridgeburners sat playing cards. A wide-shouldered man whose black hair was braided into a pony-tail and knotted with charms and fetishes sat with his back to the room, dealing out the cards with infinite patience. Even through the high-tide roar, Paran could hear the man's monotone counting. The others at the table deluged the dealer with curses, to little effect.

'Barghast,' Paran murmured, his gaze on the dealer. 'Only one in the Bridgeburners. That's the Ninth, then.' He took a deep breath, then plunged into the crowd.

By the time he arrived behind the Barghast his fine cloak was drenched with sour ale and bitter wine, and sweat cast a shine on his forehead. The Barghast, he saw, had just finished the deal and was setting down the deck in the table's centre, revealing as he did so the endless blue woad tattooing on his bared arm, the spiral patterns marred here and there by white scars.

'Is this the Ninth?' Paran asked loudly.

The man opposite the Barghast glanced up, his weathered face the same colour as his leather cap, then returned his attention to his cards. 'You Captain Paran?'

'I am. And you, soldier?'

'Hedge.' He nodded at the heavy man seated to his right. 'That's Mallet, the squad's healer. And the Barghast's name is Trotts, and it ain't because he likes jogging.' He jerked his head to his left. 'The rest don't matter – they're Second Army and lousy players to boot. Take a seat, Captain. Whiskeyjack and the rest been called out for the time being. Should be back soon.'

Paran found an empty chair and pulled it up between Mallet and Trotts.

Hedge growled, 'Hey, Trotts, you gonna call this game or what?'

Releasing a long breath, Paran turned to Mallet. 'Tell me, Healer, what's the average life expectancy for an officer in the Bridgeburners?'

A grunt escaped Hedge's lips. 'Before or after Moon's Spawn?'

Mallet's heavy brows rose slightly as he answered the captain. 'Maybe two campaigns. Depends on a lot of things. Balls ain't enough, but it helps. And that means forgetting everything you

121

learned and jumping into your sergeant's lap like a babe. You listen to him, you might make it.'

Hedge thumped the table. 'Wake up, Trotts! What are we playing here?'

The Barghast scowled. 'I'm thinking,' he rumbled.

Paran leaned back and unhitched his belt.

Trotts decided on a game, to the groans of Hedge, Mallet and the three 2nd Army soldiers, since it was the game Trotts always decided on.

Mallet spoke. 'Captain, you've been hearing things about the Bridgeburners, right?'

Paran nodded. 'Most officers are terrified of the Bridgeburners. Word is, the mortality rate's so high because half the captains end up with a dagger in their back.'

He paused, and was about to continue when he noticed the sudden silence. The game had stopped, and all eyes had fixed on him. Sweat broke out under Paran's clothing. 'And from what I've seen so far,' he pressed on, 'I'm likely to believe that rumour. But I'll tell you something – all of you – if I die with a knife in my back, it'd better be because I earned it. Otherwise, I will be severely disappointed.' He hitched his belt and rose. 'Tell the sergeant I'll be in the barracks. I'd like to speak with him before we're officially mustered.'

Hedge gave a slow nod. 'Will do, Captain.' The man hesitated. 'Uh, Captain? Care to sit in on the game?'

Paran shook his head. 'Thanks, no.' A grin tugged the corner of his mouth. 'Bad practice, an officer taking his enlisted men's money.'

'Now there's a challenge you'd better back up some time,' Hedge said, his eyes brightening.

'I'll think about it,' Paran replied, as he left the table. Pushing through the crowd, he felt a growing sense of something that caught him completely off-guard: insignificance. A lot of arrogance had been drilled into him, from his days as a

122

boy among the nobility through to his time at the academy. That arrogance now cowered in some corner of his brain, shocked silent and numb.

He had known that well before he'd met the Adjunct: his path into and through the officer training corps of the Marine Academy had been an easy procession marked by winks and nods. But the Empire's wars were fought here, thousands of leagues away, and here, Paran realized, nobody cared one whit about court influences and mutually favourable deals. Those short-cuts swelled his chances of dying, and dying fast. If not for the Adjunct, he'd have been totally unprepared to take command.

Paran grimaced as he pushed open the tavern door and stepped out into the street. It was no wonder the old Emperor's armies had so easily devoured the feudal kingdoms in his path on the road to Empire. He was suddenly glad of the stains marring his uniform – he no longer looked out of place.

He strode into the alley leading to the barracks' side entrance. The way lay in shadow beneath high-walled buildings and the faded canopies that hung over sagging balconies. Pale was a dying city. He knew enough of its history to recognize the bleached tints of long-lost glory. True, it had commanded enough power to forge an alliance with Moon's Spawn, but the captain suspected that that had had more to do with the Moon's lord's sense of expedience than to any kind of mutual recognition of power. The local gentry made much of finery and pomp, but their props looked tired and worn. He wondered how alike he and his kind were with these droopy citizens—

A sound behind him, the faintest scuff, made him turn. A shadow-wrapped figure closed on him. Paran cried out, snatching at his sword. An icy wind washed over him as the figure moved in. The captain backpedalled, seeing the glint of blades in each hand. He twisted to one side, his sword half-way out of

123

the scabbard. His attacker's left hand darted up. Paran jerked his head back, throwing his shoulder forward to block a blade that never arrived. Instead, the long dagger slid like fire into his chest. A second blade sank into his side even as blood gushed up inside to fill his mouth. Coughing and groaning, Paran reeled, careened off a wall, then slid down with one hand grasping futilely at the damp stones, his fingernails gouging tracks through the mould.

A blackness closed around his thoughts which seemed to involve only a deep, heartfelt regret. Faintly, a ringing sound came to his ears, as if something small and metallic was skittering across a hard surface. The sound remained, of something spinning, and the darkness encroached no further.

'Sloppy,' a man said in a thin voice. 'I am surprised.' The accent was familiar, pulling him to a childhood memory, his father dealing with Dal Honese traders.

The answer came from directly above Paran. 'Keeping an eye on me?' Another accent he recognized, Kanese, and the voice seemed to come from a girl, or a child, yet he knew it was the voice of his killer.

'Coincidence,' the other replied, then giggled. 'Someone – something, I should say – has entered our Warren. Uninvited. My Hounds hunt.'

'I don't believe in coincidences.'

Again came the giggle. 'Nor do I. Two years ago we began a game of our own. A simple settling of old scores. It seems we have stumbled into a wholly different game here in Pale.'

'Whose?'

'I shall have that answer soon enough.'

'Don't get distracted, Ammanas. Laseen remains our target, and the collapse of the Empire she rules but never earned.'

'I have, as always, supreme confidence in you, Cotillion.'

'I must be getting back,' the girl said, moving away.

'Of course. So this is the man Lorn sent to find you?'

124

'I believe so. This should draw her into the fray, in any case.'
'And this is desirable?'

The conversation faded as the two speakers walked away leaving, as the only sound in Paran's head, that whirring hum, as if a coin was spinning, endlessly spinning.

CHAPTER FOUR

They were of a kind, then
the histories writ large
in tattooed tracery
the tales a tracking
of old wounds
but something glowed hard
in their eyes – those
flame-gnawed arches,
that vanishing span,
they are their own past
each in turn destined
to fall in line
on the quiet wayside
beside the river
they refuse to name . . .

The Bridgeburners (IV.i)
Toc the Younger (b.1141)

Tattersail glared at Whiskeyjack. 'Hairlock is insane,' she
pronounced. 'That edge to him was always there, but
he's chewed holes in his own Warrens and he's tasting

Chaos. Worse yet, it's making him more powerful, more dangerous.'

They had gathered in Tattersail's quarters, which consisted of an outer room – where they now sat – and a bedroom with the rare luxury of a solid wood door. The past occupants had hastily stripped the place of anything valuable and portable, leaving behind only the larger pieces of furniture. Tattersail sat at the table, along with Whiskeyjack, Quick Ben and Kalam, and the sapper named Fiddler. The air in the room had grown hot, stifling.

'Of course he's insane,' Quick Ben replied, looking at his sergeant, whose face remained impassive. The wizard hastily added, 'But that's to be expected. Fener's tail, lady, he's got the body of a puppet! Of course that's twisted him.'

'How twisted?' Whiskeyjack asked his wizard. 'He's supposed to be watching our backs, isn't he?'

Kalam said, 'Quick's got him under control. Hairlock's back-tracking, working through the maze – he'll find out who in the Empire wants us dead.'

'The danger,' Quick Ben added, rounding on Tattersail, 'is his being detected. He needs to slip through the Warrens the unconventional way – the regular paths are all trip-wired.'

Tattersail mulled over that point, then nodded. 'Tayschrenn would find him, or at least catch wind that someone's sniffing around. But Hairlock's using the power of Chaos, the paths that lie *between* Warrens, and that's unhealthy – not just for him, but for all of us.'

'Why all of us?' Whiskeyjack asked.

Quick Ben answered, 'It weakens the Warrens, frays the fabric, which in turns allows Hairlock to break into them at will . . . and out again. But we have no choice. We have to give Hairlock his rope. For now.'

The sorceress sighed, massaging her brow. 'Tayschrenn's the one you're looking for. I've already told you—'

'That's not good enough,' Quick Ben cut in. 'How many agents is he using? What are the details of the plan – what the hell *is* the plan? Is all this on Laseen's orders, or is the High Mage eyeing the throne for himself? We need to know, dammit!'

'All right, all right,' Tattersail said. 'So Hairlock unravels the whole thing for you – then what? Do you intend to try to kill Tayschrenn and everyone else involved? Are you counting on my help in that?' She looked from one face to the next. Each revealed nothing. Anger flared and she rose. 'I know,' she said stiffly, 'that Tayschrenn probably murdered A'Karonys, Nightchill, and my cadre. He probably knew your tunnels would collapse around you, and he might well have decided that Dujek's Second was a threat that needed culling. But if you think I'm going to help you without knowing what you're planning, you're mistaken. There's more to all this than you're willing to tell me. If it was just your survival at stake, why don't you just desert? I doubt Dujek would chase you down. Unless, of course, Tayschrenn's suspicions about Onearm and the Second are grounded in truth – you've plans for a mutiny, proclaiming Dujek Emperor and marching off to Genabaris.' She paused, looking from one man to the next. 'Has Tayschrenn simply anticipated you, thereby fouling up your plans? Am I being pulled into a conspiracy? If I am, then I have to know its eventual goals. I have that right, don't I?'

Whiskeyjack grunted, then reached for the jug of wine standing on the table. He refilled everyone's cup.

Quick Ben let out a long breath, then rubbed the back of his neck. 'Tattersail,' he said quietly, 'we're not going to challenge Tayschrenn directly. That would be suicide. No, we'll cut away his support, carefully, with precision, then we arrange his . . . *fall from grace*. Assuming the Empress is not involved. But we need to know more, we need those answers before we can decide our options. You don't have to get any more involved than you already are. In fact, it's safer that way. Hairlock wants you to protect *his* back, failing every other option. Chances are, that won't be necessary.' He looked up and gave her a strained smile. 'Leave Tayschrenn to me and Kalam.'

All very well, but you didn't answer me. Tattersail looked at the other black-skinned man, her eyes narrowing. 'You were a Claw once, weren't you?'

Kalam shrugged.

'I thought no one could leave – alive.'

He shrugged again.

The sapper, Fiddler, growled something incomprehensible and rose from his chair. He began pacing, his bandied legs carrying him from one wall to the next, like a fox in a pit. No one paid him any further attention.

Whiskeyjack handed a cup to Tattersail. 'Stay with us in this, Sorceress. Quick Ben doesn't usually foul things . . . too badly.' He made a sour face. 'I admit, I'm not completely convinced either, but I've learned to trust him. You can take that for whatever it's worth.'

Tattersail took a deep draught of wine. She wiped her lips. 'Your squad's heading to Darujhistan tonight. Covert, which means I won't be able to communicate with you if the situation turns bad.'

'Tayschrenn would detect the usual ways,' Quick Ben said. 'Hairlock's our only unbreachable link – you reach us through him, Tattersail.'

Whiskeyjack eyed the sorceress. 'Back to Hairlock. You don't trust him.'

'No.'

The sergeant fell silent, his gaze fixed on the tabletop. His impassive expression fell away, revealing a war of emotions.

He keeps his world bottled up, but the pressure's building. She wondered what would happen when everything broke loose inside him.

The two Seven Cities men waited, eyes on their sergeant. Only Fiddler continued his preoccupied pacing. The sapper's mismatched uniform still carried the stains of the tunnels. Someone else's blood had splashed thickly on the front of his tunic – as if a friend had died in his arms. Poorly healed blisters showed under the uneven bristle of his cheeks and jaw, and his lank red hair hung haphazardly beneath his leather helmet.

A long minute passed, then the sergeant nodded sharply to himself. His hard eyes still fixed on the tabletop, he said, 'All right, Sorceress. We'll give you this. Quick Ben, tell her about Sorry.'

Tattersail's brows rose. She crossed her arms and faced the wizard.

Quick Ben looked none too pleased. He shifted uneasily and cast a hopeful glance at Kalam, but the big man looked away.

Whiskeyjack growled, 'Now, Wizard.'

Quick Ben met Tattersail's steady gaze with an almost child-like expression – fear, guilt and chagrin flitted across his fine features. 'You remember her?'

She barked a harsh laugh. 'Not an easy one to forget. An odd . . . sense . . . about her. Dangerous.' She thought about revealing what she'd learned during her Fatid with Tayschrenn. *Virgin of Death*. But something held her back. No, she corrected herself, not just something – *I still don't trust them*. 'You suspect she's in the service of someone else?'

The wizard's face was ashen. He cleared his throat. 'She was recruited two years ago in Itko Kan, one of the usual sweeps across the Empire's heartland.'

Kalam's voice rumbled beside her. 'Something ugly happened there at around the same time. It's been buried pretty deep, but the Adjunct became involved, and a Claw came in her wake and silenced damn near everyone in the city guard who might have talked. I made use of old sources, scrounged up some odd details.'

130

'Odd,' Quick Ben said, 'and revealing, if you know what you're looking for.'

Tattersail smiled to herself. These two men had a way of talking in tandem. She returned her attention to the wizard, who continued.

'Seems a company of cavalry hit some hard luck. No survivors. As for what they ran into, it had something to do with—'

'Dogs,' Kalam finished without missing a beat.

The sorceress frowned at the assassin.

'Put it together,' Quick Ben said, drawing her attention once again. 'Adjunct Lorn is Laseen's personal mage-killer. Her arrival on the scene suggests sorcery was involved in the massacre. High sorcery.' The wizard's gaze narrowed on Tattersail and he waited.

She swallowed another mouthful of wine. *The Fatid showed me. Dogs and sorcery.* Into her mind returned the image of the Rope as she had seen it in the reading. *High House Shadow, ruled by Shadowthrone and the Rope, and in their service –* 'The Seven Hounds of Shadow.' She looked to Whiskeyjack but the sergeant's eyes remained downcast, his expression blank as stone.

'Good,' Quick Ben snapped, somewhat impatiently. 'The Hounds hunted. That's our guess, but it's a good one. The Nineteenth Regiment of the Eighth Cavalry were all killed, even their horses. A league's worth of coastline settlements needed repopulating.'

'Fine.' Tattersail sighed. 'But what does this have to do with Sorry?'

The wizard turned away and Kalam spoke. 'Hairlock's going to follow more than just one trail, Sorceress. We're pretty sure Sorry is somehow involved with House Shadow . . .'

'It certainly seems,' Tattersail said, 'that since its arrival in the Deck and the opening of its Warren, Shadow's path crosses the Empire's far too often to be accidental. Why should the Warren between Light and Dark display such ... obsession with the Malazan Empire?'

Kalam's gaze was veiled. 'Odd, isn't it? After all, the Warren only appeared following the Emperor's assassination at Laseen's hand. Shadowthrone and his companion the Patron of Assassins – Cotillion – were unheard of before Kellanved and Dancer's deaths. It also seems that whatever ... disagreement there is between House Shadow and Empress Laseen is, uhm, personal ...'

Tattersail closed her eyes. *Dammit, it's that obvious, isn't it?* 'Quick Ben,' she said, 'hasn't there always been an accessible Warren of Shadow? Rashan, the Warren of Illusions?'

'Rashan is a false Warren, Sorceress. A shadow of what it claims to represent, if you'll excuse my wording. It is itself an illusion. The gods alone know where it came from, or who created it in the first place, or even why. But the true Warren of Shadow has been closed, inaccessible for millennia, until the 1154th year of Burn's Sleep, nine years ago. The earliest writings of House Shadow seemed to indicate that its throne was occupied by a Tiste Edur—'

'Tiste Edur?' Tattersail interrupted. 'Who were they?'

The wizard shrugged. 'Cousins of the Tiste Andii? I don't know, Sorceress.'

You don't know? Actually, it seems you know a hell of a lot.

Quick Ben shrugged to punctuate his last words, then he added, 'In any case, we believe Sorry is connected with House Shadow.'

Whiskeyjack startled everyone by surging to his feet. 'I'm not convinced,' he said, throwing Quick Ben a glare that told Tattersail there had been countless arguments over this issue. 'Sorry likes killing, and having her around is like having spiders down your shirt. I know all that, I can see it and feel it the same as any of you. It doesn't mean she's some kind of demon.' He turned to face Kalam. 'She kills like you do, Kalam. You've both got ice in your veins. So what? I look at you and I see a man because that's what men are capable of – I don't hunt for excuses because I don't like to think that that's how nasty we can get. We look at Sorry and we see reflections of ourselves. Hood take it, if we don't like what we see.'

He sat down just as abruptly as he had risen, and reached for the wine jug. When he continued his voice had dropped a notch. 'That is my opinion, anyway. I'm no expert on demons but I've seen enough mortal men and women *act* like demons, given the need. My squad's wizard is scared witless by a fifteen-year-old girl. My assassin slips a knife into his palm whenever she's within twenty paces of him.' He met Tattersail's eyes. 'So, Hairlock has two missions instead of one, and if you think Quick Ben and Kalam are correct in their suspicions you can walk from all this – I know how things go when gods step into the fray.' The lines around his eyes tightened momentarily, a replaying of memories. 'I know,' he whispered.

Tattersail slowly let out her breath, which she had been holding since the sergeant first rose to his feet. His needs were clear to her now: he wanted Sorry to be just human, just a girl twisted hard by a hard world. Because that was something he understood, something he could deal with. 'Back in Seven Cities,' she said quietly, 'the story goes that the Emperor's First Sword – his commander of his armies – Dassem Ultor, had accepted a god's offer. Hood made Dassem his Knight of Death. Then something happened, something went . . . wrong. And Dassem renounced the title, swore a vow of vengeance against Hood – against the Lord of Death himself. All at once other Ascendants started meddling, manipulating events. It all culminated with Dassem's murder, then the Emperor's assassination, and blood in the streets, temples at war, sorceries unleashed.' She paused, seeing the memories of those times reflected in Whiskeyjack's face. 'You were there.' *And you don't*

133

want it to happen again, here and now. You think if you can deny that Sorry serves Shadow your conviction will be enough to shape reality. You need to believe that to save your sanity, because there are some things in life that you can go through only once. Oh, Whiskeyjack, I can't ease your burden. You see, I think Quick Ben and Kalam are right. 'If Shadow has claimed the girl, the trail will be evident – Hairlock will find it.'

'Do you walk away from this?' the sergeant asked.

Tattersail smiled. 'The only death I fear is dying ignorant. No, is my answer.' *Brave words, woman. These people have a way of bringing out the best – or maybe the worst – in me.*

Something glittered in Whiskeyjack's eyes, and he nodded. 'So that's that,' he said gruffly. He leaned back. 'What's on your mind, Fiddler?' he asked the sapper, who was still pacing behind him.

'Got a bad feeling,' the man muttered. 'Something's wrong. Not here, though, but close by. It's just—' He stopped, cocking his head, then he sighed, resuming his uneasy walk. 'Not sure, not sure.'

Tattersail's eyes followed the wiry little man. A natural talent? Something working on pure instinct? Very rare. 'I think you should listen to him,' she said.

Whiskeyjack gave her a pained look.

Kalam grinned, a network of lines crinkling around his dark eyes. 'Fiddler saved our lives in the tunnel,' he explained. 'One of his *bad feelings*.'

Tattersail leaned back in her chair and crossed her arms. She asked, 'So where is Sorry right now?'

Fiddler whirled, his eyes widening on the sorceress. His mouth opened, then snapped shut again.

The other three surged to their feet, chairs toppling backwards.

'We've got to get going,' Fiddler grated. 'There's a knife out there, and it's got blood on it.'

Whiskeyjack checked his longsword. 'Kalam, out front twenty paces.' He faced Tattersail as the assassin slipped out. 'We lost her a couple of hours ago. Happens a lot between missions.' His face looked drawn. 'There may be no connection with this bloodied knife.'

A blossoming of power filled the room and Tattersail spun to face Quick Ben. The wizard had accessed his Warren. The sorcery bled a strange, swirling flavour that she could not recognize, and it frightened her with its intensity. She met the black man's shining eyes. 'I should know you,' she whispered. 'There's not enough true masters in this world for me to not know you. Who are you, Quick Ben?'

Whiskeyjack interjected, 'Everyone ready?'

The wizard's only answer to Tattersail was a shrug. To Whiskeyjack he said, 'Ready.'

The sergeant strode to the door. 'Take care, Sorceress.'

A moment later they were gone. Tattersail righted the chairs, then refilled her goblet with wine. *High House Shadow, and a knife in the dark. A new game's begun, or the old one's just turned.*

Paran opened his eyes to bright, hot sunlight, but the sky above him was . . . wrong. He saw no sun; the yellow glare was sharp yet sourceless. Heat gusted down on him with oppressive weight.

A moaning sound filled the air, not wind because there was no wind. He tried to think, tried to recall his last memories, but the past was blank, torn away, and only fragments remained: a ship's cabin, the thunk of his dagger as he flung it again and again against a wooden post; a man with rings, hair of white, grinning sardonically.

He rolled to one side, seeking the source of the moaning sound. A dozen paces away on the flat plain that was neither grass nor earth rose an arched gateway leading to—

135

Nothing. I've seen such gates before. None so large, I think, as this one. None looking quite like this . . . this thing. Twisted, upright yet from his position sideways, the gate was not, he realized, made of stone. *Bodies, naked human figures. Carved likenesses? No . . . oh, no.* The figures moved, groaned, slowly writhed in place. Flesh blackened, as if stained with peat, eyes closed and mouths open with faint, endless moans.

Paran climbed to his feet, staggered as a wave of dizziness ran through him, then fell once again to the ground.

'Something like indecision,' a voice said coolly.

Blinking, Paran rolled on to his back. Above him stood a young man and woman – twins. The man wore loose silk clothing, white and gold; his thin face was pale, expressionless. His twin was wrapped in a shimmering purple cape, her blonde hair casting reddish glints.

It was the man who'd spoken. He smiled without humour down at Paran. 'We've long admired your . . .' His eyes widened.

'Sword,' the woman finished, a smirk in her tone.

'Far more subtle than, say, a coin, don't you think?' The man's smile turned mocking. 'Most,' he said, swinging his head to study the ghastly edifice of the gate, 'don't pause here. It's said there was a cult, once, in the habit of drowning victims in bogs . . . I imagine Hood finds them aesthetically pleasing.'

'Hardly surprising,' the woman drawled, 'that Death has no taste.'

Paran tried to sit up, but his limbs refused the command. He dropped his head back, feeling the strange loam yield to its weight. 'What has happened?' he rasped.

'You were murdered,' the man said lightly.

Paran closed his eyes. 'Why, then, have I not passed through Hood's Gate, if that is what it is?'

'We're meddling,' the woman said.

Oponn, the Twins of Chance. And my sword, my untested blade purchased years ago, with a name I chose so capriciously— 'What does Oponn want from me?'

'Only this stumbling, ignorant thing you call your life, dear boy. The trouble with Ascendants is that they try to rig every game. Of course, *we* delight in . . . uncertainty.'

A distant howl stroked the air.

'Oops,' the man said. 'Come to make certain of things, I'd say. We'd best leave, sister. Sorry, Captain, but it seems you'll pass through that Gate after all.'

'Maybe,' the woman said.

Her brother rounded on her. 'We agreed! No confrontation! Confrontation's messy. Unpleasant. I despise discomfiting scenes! Besides, the ones who come don't play fair.'

'Then neither do we,' the sister snapped. She turned to the gate, raised her voice, 'Lord of Death! We would speak with you! Hood!'

Paran rolled his head, watched as a bent, limping figure emerged from the Gate. Wearing rags, the figure slowly approached. Paran squinted – an old woman, a child with drool on its chin, a deformed young girl, a stunted, broken Trell, a desiccated Tiste Andii—

'Oh, make up your mind!' the sister said.

The apparition cocked a death's head, the grin of its teeth stained muddy yellow. 'You have chosen,' it said in quavering voice, 'unimaginatively.'

'You are not Hood.' The brother scowled.

Bones shifted under creaking skin. 'The lord is busy.'

'Busy? We do not take kindly to insults,' the sister said.

The apparition cackled, then stopped abruptly. 'How unfortunate. A mellifluous, deep-throated laugh would be more to my liking. Ah well, in answer: nor does my lord appreciate your interruption of this natural passage of a soul.'

'Murdered at the hand of a god,' the sister said. 'That makes him fair game.'

137

The creature grunted, shuffled close to look down at Paran. The eye sockets glimmered faintly, as if old pearls hid within the shadows. 'What, Oponn,' it asked, as it studied Paran, 'do you wish of my lord?'

'Nothing from me,' the brother said, turning away.

'Sister?'

'Even for the gods,' she replied, 'death awaits, an uncertainty hiding deep within them.' She paused. 'Make them uncertain.'

The creature cackled again, and again cut it short. 'Reciprocity.'

'Of course,' the sister responded. 'I'll look for another, a death premature. Meaningless, even.'

The apparition was silent, then the head creaked in a nod. 'In this mortal's shadow, of course.'

'Agreed.'

'My shadow?' Paran asked. 'What does that mean, precisely?'

'Much sorrow, alas,' the apparition said. 'Someone close to you shall walk through Death's Gates . . . in your place.'

'No. Take me instead, I beg of you.'

'Be quiet!' snapped the apparition. 'Pathos makes me ill.'

The howl reverberated again, much closer this time.

'We'd best leave,' the brother said.

The apparition opened its jaws as if to laugh, then clacked them shut. 'No,' it muttered, 'not again.' It hobbled back to the Gate, pausing once to turn back and wave.

The sister rolled her eyes.

'Time to leave,' the brother repeated uneasily.

'Yes, yes,' his sister said, eyeing Paran.

The captain sighed, looking away. 'No final riddles, if you please.' When he looked back Oponn was gone. Once again he tried to sit up. Once again he failed.

A new presence arrived, filling the air with tension, a smell of threat.

Sighing, Paran craned his head around. He saw a pair of Hounds – massive hulking creatures, dark, tongues lolling as they sat, watching him. *These are what killed the company in Itko Kan. These are the cursed, horrifying beasts.* Both Hounds froze, heads hunching towards him, as if seeing the hatred in his eyes. Paran felt his heart go cold at their avid attention. He was slow to realize he had bared his teeth.

A stain of shadow separated the two Hounds, the stain vaguely man-shaped and translucent. The shadow spoke. 'The one Lorn sent. I would have thought someone of . . . ability. Though, it must be said, you died well.'

'Evidently not,' Paran said.

'Ah, yes,' the shadow said, 'and so it falls to me to complete the task. Busy hours, these.'

Paran thought of Oponn's conversation with Hood's servant. *Uncertainty. If a god fears anything . . .* 'The day you die, Shadowthrone,' he said quietly, 'I will be waiting for you on the other side of that gate. With a smile. Gods *can* die, can't they?'

Something crackled in the portalway of the gate. Shadowthrone and the Hounds flinched.

Paran continued, wondering at his own courage, to bait these Ascendants. *Always despised authority, didn't I?* 'Half-way between life and death – this promise costs me nothing, you see.'

'Liar, the only Warren that can touch you now is—'

'Death,' Paran said. 'Of course,' he added, 'someone else . . . interceded, and was certain to leave long before you and your too-loud Hounds arrived.'

The King of High House Shadow edged forward. 'Who? What does it plan? Who opposes us?'

'Find your own answers, Shadowthrone. You do understand, don't you, that if you send me on my way now, your . . . opposition will seek other means? Knowing nothing of who their

139

next tool is, how will you sniff out their next move? You'll be left darting at shadows.'

'Easier to follow you,' the god conceded. 'I must speak with my companion—'

'As you like,' Paran interrupted. 'I wish I could stand . . .'

The god rasped laughter. 'If you stand, you walk. One way only. You have a reprieve – and if Hood comes to gather you to your feet, the guiding hand is his, not ours. Excellent. And if you live, so shall my shadow follow you.'

Paran grunted. 'My shadow's a crowded place, these days.' His eyes fell once again on the Hounds. The creatures watched him still, their eyes faint coals. *I'll have you yet.* As if fanned by his silent promise, the red glows sharpened.

The god resumed speaking, but the world had darkened around Paran, fading, dwindling, until the voice was gone, and with it all awareness but the faint, renewed spinning of a coin.

An unknown span of time passed in which Paran wandered through memories he had thought long lost – his days as a child clinging to his mother's dress and taking his first, tottering steps; the nights of storm when he raced down the chill hallway to his parents' bedroom, tiny feet slapping on the cold stone; holding the hands of his two sisters as they stood waiting on the hard cobbles of the courtyard – waiting, waiting for someone. The images seemed to lurch sideways in his head. His mother's dress? No, an old woman in the service of the household. Not his parents' bedroom, but those of the servants; and there, in the courtyard with his sisters, they'd stood half the morning, awaiting the arrival of their mother and father, two people they barely knew.

In his mind scenes replayed themselves, moments of mysterious import, hidden significance, pieces of a puzzle he couldn't recognize, shaped by hands not his own and with a purpose he couldn't fathom. A tremor of fear travelled the length of his thoughts as he sensed that something – someone – was busy reordering the formative events of his life, turning them on end and casting them into the present new shadows. Somehow, the guiding hand . . . *played*. With him, with his life.

It seemed an odd kind of death—

Voices reached him.

'Aw, hell.' A face bent close to Paran's own, looked into his open blank eyes. The face was Picker's. 'He didn't stand a chance,' she said.

Sergeant Antsy spoke from a few feet away. 'Nobody in the Ninth would've done him like this,' he said. 'Not right here in the city.'

Picker reached out and touched the chest wound, her fingers surprisingly soft on his torn flesh. 'This isn't Kalam's work.'

'You all right here?' Antsy asked. 'I'm going to get Hedge and Mallet, and whoever else has shown up.'

'Go ahead,' Picker replied, seeking and finding the second wound, eight inches below the first. 'This one came later, right-handed and weak.'

A very odd death indeed, Paran thought. What held him here? Had there been another . . . place? A place of heat, searing yellow light? And voices, figures faint, indistinct, there beneath the arch of . . . of crowds strangely held in place, eyes closed, mouths open. A chorus of the dead . . . Had he gone somewhere only to return to these real voices, these real hands on his flesh? How could he see through the empty glass of his eyes, or feel the woman's gentle touch on his body? And what of the pain, rising as from a great depth like a leviathan?

Picker withdrew her hands and rested her elbows on her thighs as she crouched before Paran. 'Now, how come you're still bleeding, Captain? Those knife wounds are at least an hour old.'

The pain reached the surface. Paran felt his gummy lips

141

split. The hinges of his jaw cracked and he drew in a savage gasp. Then screamed.

Picker bolted backwards, her sword appearing in her hand as if from nowhere as she backed to the alley's far wall. 'Shedenul's mercy!'

Boots pounded on the cobbles off to her right and her head whipped around. 'Healer! The bastard's alive!'

The third bell after midnight tolled sonorously through the city of Pale, echoing down streets emptied by the curfew. A light rain had begun, casting the night sky with a murky gold hue. In front of the large, rambling estate, two blocks from the old palace, that had become part of the 2nd's quarters, two marines wrapped in black raincapes stood guard outside the main gate.

'Damned miserable night, ain't it?' one said, shivering.

The other shifted his pike to his left shoulder and hawked a mouthful of phlegm into the gutter. 'You just guessing, mind,' he said, wagging his head. 'Any other brilliant insights you feel ready to toss my way, you just speak up, hear?'

'What did I do?' the first man demanded, hurt.

The second soldier stiffened. 'Hush, someone coming up the street.'

The guards waited tensely, hands on their weapons. A figure crossed from the opposite side and stepped into the torchlight.

'Halt,' the second guard growled. 'Advance slowly, and you'd better have business here.'

The man took a step closer. 'Kalam, Bridgeburners, the Ninth,' he said quietly.

The marines remained wary, but the Bridgeburner kept his distance, his dark face glistening in the rain. 'What's your business here?' the second guard asked.

Kalam grunted and glanced back down the street. 'We didn't expect to be coming back. As for our business, well, it's

142

better that Tayschrenn don't know about it. You with me, soldier?'

The marine grinned and spat a second time into the gutter. 'Kalam – you'd be Whiskeyjack's corporal.' There was a new tone of respect in his voice. 'Whatever you want you've got.'

'Damned right,' the other soldier growled. 'I was at Nathilog, sir. You want us blinded by the rain for the next hour or so, you just say the word.'

'We're bringing in a body,' Kalam said. 'But this never happened on your shift.'

'Hood's Gate, no,' the second marine said. 'Peaceful as the Seventh Dawn.'

From down the street came the sounds of a number of men approaching. Kalam waved them forward, then slipped inside as the first guard unlocked the gate. 'What do you figure they're up to?' he asked, after Kalam had disappeared.

The other shrugged. 'Hope it'll stick something hard and sharp up Tayschrenn, Hood take the treacherous murderer. And, knowing them Bridgeburners, that's exactly what they'll do.' He fell silent as the group arrived. Two men carried a third man between them. The second soldier's eyes widened as he saw the rank of the unconscious man, and the blood staining the front of his baldric. 'Oponn's luck,' he hissed to the Bridgeburner nearest him, a man wearing a tarnished leather cap. 'The pull not the push,' he added.

The Bridgeburner threw him a sharp look. 'You see a woman come after us you get out of her way, you hear me?'

'A woman? Who?'

'She's in the Ninth, and she might be thirsty for blood,' the man replied, as he and his comrade dragged the captain through the gate. 'Forget security,' he said, over his shoulder. 'Just stay alive if you can.'

The two marines stared at each other after the men had

143

passed. After a moment the first soldier reached to close the gate. The other man stopped him.

'Leave it open,' he muttered. 'Let's find some shadows, close but not too close.'

'Hell of a night,' the first marine said.

'You got a thing about stating the obvious, haven't you?' the other said, as he moved away from the gate.

The first man shrugged helplessly, then hurried to follow.

Tattersail stared long and hard at the card centred on the field she had laid down. She had chosen a spiral pattern, working her way through the entire Deck of Dragons and arriving with a final card, which could mark either an apex or an epiphany depending on how it placed itself.

The spiral had become a pit, a tunnel downward, and at its root, seeming distant and shadow-hazed, waited the image of a Hound. She sensed an immediacy to this reading. High House Shadow had become involved, a challenge to Oponn's command of the game. Her eyes were drawn to the first card she had placed, at the spiral's very beginning. The Mason of High House Death held a minor position among the overall rankings, but now the figure etched on the wood seemed to have risen to an eminent placing. Brother to the Soldier of the same House, the Mason's image was that of a lean, greying man clothed in faded leathers. His massive, vein-roped hands held stone-cutting tools and around him rose roughly dressed menhirs. Tattersail found she could make out faint glyphs on the stones, a language unfamiliar to her but reminiscent of Seven Cities' script. In the House of Death the Mason was the builder of barrows, the placer of stones, a promise of death not to one or a few but to many. The language on the menhirs delivered a message not intended for her: the Mason had carved those words for himself, and time had worn the edges – even the man himself appeared starkly weathered, his face latticed with cracks, his silvered beard thin and tangled. The role had been assumed by a man who'd once worked in stone, but no longer.

The sorceress was having difficulty understanding this field. The patterns she saw startled her: it was as if a whole new game had begun, with players stepping on to the scene at every turn. Midway through the spiral was High House Dark's Knight, its placement counterpoint to both the beginning and the end. As with the last time the Deck had unveiled this draconian figure, something hovered in the inky sky behind the Knight, as elusive as ever, at times seeming like a dark stain on her own eyes.

The Knight's sword reached a black, smoky streak towards the Hound at the spiral's apex, and in this instance she knew its meaning. The future held a clash between the Knight and High House Shadow. The thought both frightened Tattersail and left her feeling relieved – it would be a confrontation. There would be no alliance between the Houses. It was a rare thing to see such a clear and direct link between two Houses: the potential for devastation left her cold with worry. Blood spilled on such a high level of power cast aftershocks down through the world. Inevitably, people would be hurt. And this thought brought her round back to the Mason of High House Death. Tattersail's heart thudded heavy in her chest. She blinked sweat from her eyes and managed a few deep breaths.

'Blood,' she murmured, 'ever flows downward.' *The Mason's shaping a barrow – after all, he is Death's servant – and he will touch me directly. That barrow . . . is it mine? Do I back out? Abandon the Bridgeburners to their fate, flee from Tayschrenn, from the Empire?*

An ancient memory flooded her thoughts, which she had repressed for almost two centuries. The image shook her. Once again she walked the muddy streets of the village where she had been born, a child bearing the Talent, a child who had seen the horsemen of war sweeping down into their sheltered lives. A child who had run away from the knowledge, telling no one, and the night came, a night of screams and death.

Guilt rose within her, its spectre visage hauntingly familiar. After all these years its face still held the power to shatter her world, making hollow those things she needed solid, rattling her illusion of security with a shame almost two hundred years old.

The image sank once again into its viscid pool, but it left her changed. There would be no running away this time. Her eyes returned one last time to the Hound. The beast's eyes seemed to burn with yellow fire, boring into her as if seeking to brand her soul.

She stiffened in her chair as a cold presence washed over her from behind. Slowly, Tattersail turned.

'Sorry for not giving you warning,' Quick Ben said, emerging from the swirling cloud of his Warren. It held a strange, spicy scent. 'Company's coming,' he said, seeming distracted. 'I've called Hairlock. He comes by Warren.'

Tattersail shivered as a wave of premonition brushed her spine. She faced the Deck again and began to collect the cards.

'The situation's just become a lot more complicated,' the wizard said behind her.

The sorceress paused, giving herself a small, tight smile. 'Really?' she murmured.

The wind flung rain against Whiskeyjack's face. Faintly through the dark night the fourth bell clanged. The sergeant pulled his raincape tighter and wearily shifted his stance. The view from the rooftop of the palace's east turret was mostly obscured by sheets of rain. 'You've been chewing on something for days,' he said, to the man beside him. 'Let's hear it, soldier.'

Fiddler wiped the rain from his eyes and squinted into the

east. 'Not much to tell you, Sarge,' he said gruffly. 'Just feelings. That sorceress, for one.'

'Tattersail?'

'Yeah.' Metal clinked as the sapper unstrapped his sword belt. 'Hate this damned thing,' he muttered.

Whiskeyjack watched as the man tossed the belt and scabbarded shortsword to the rooftop's pebbled surface behind them. 'Just don't forget it like you did last time,' the sergeant said, hiding a grin.

Fiddler winced. 'Make one mistake and nobody lets you forget it.'

Whiskeyjack made no reply, though his shoulders shook with laughter.

'Hood's Bones,' Fiddler went on, 'I ain't no fighter. Not like that, anyway. Was born in an alley in Malaz City, learned the stone-cutting trade breaking into barrows up on the plain behind Mock's Hold.' He glanced up at his sergeant. 'You used to be a stone-cutter, too. Just like me. Only I'm no fast learner in soldiering like you was. It was the ranks or the mines for me – sometimes I think I went and made the wrong choice.'

Whiskeyjack's amusement died as a pang followed Fiddler's words. Learn what? he wondered. *How to kill people? How to send them off to die in some foreign land?* 'What's your feeling on Tattersail?' the sergeant asked curtly.

'Scared,' the sapper responded. 'She's got some old demons riding her, is my guess, and they're closing in.'

Whiskeyjack grunted. 'It's rare you'll find a mage with a pleasant past,' he said. 'Story goes she wasn't recruited, she was on the run. Then she messed up with her first posting.'

'It's bad timing her going all soft on us now.'

'She's lost her cadre. She's been betrayed. Without the Empire, what's she got to hold on to?' *What has any of us got?*

'It's like she's ready to cry, right on the edge, every single minute. I'm thinking she's lost her backbone, Sarge. If

147

Tayschrenn puts her under his thumb, she's liable to squeal.'

'I think you've underestimated the sorceress, Fiddler,' Whiskeyjack said. 'She's a survivor – and loyal. It's not common news, but she's been offered the title of High Mage more than once and she won't accept. It doesn't show, but a head-to-head between her and Tayschrenn would be a close thing. She's a Master of her Warren, and you don't acquire that with a weak spine.'

Fiddler whistled softly, leaned his arms on the parapet. 'I stand corrected.'

'Anything else, Sapper?'

'Just one,' Fiddler replied, deadpan.

Whiskeyjack stiffened. He knew what that tone implied. 'Go on.'

'Something's about to be unleashed tonight, Sergeant.' Fiddler swung round, his eyes glittering in the darkness. 'It's going to be messy.'

Both men turned at the thumping of the roof's trap-door. High Fist Dujek Onearm emerged, the light from the room below a broken beacon rising around him. He cleared the ladder's last rung and stepped on to the roof. 'Give me a hand with this damn door here,' he called to the two men.

They strode over, their boots crunching on the gravel scatter. 'Any word on Captain Paran, High Fist?' Whiskeyjack asked, as Fiddler crouched over the trap-door and, with a grunt, levered it back into place.

'None,' Dujek said. 'He's disappeared. Then again so has that killer of yours, Kalam.'

Whiskeyjack shook his head. 'I know where he is, and where he's been all night. Hedge and Mallet were the last to see the captain, leaving Knob's Inn, and then he just seems to vanish. High Fist, we didn't kill this Captain Paran.'

'Don't quibble with words,' Dujek muttered. 'Damn it, Fiddler, is that your sword lying over there? In a *puddle*?'

Breath hissed between Fiddler's teeth and he hurried over to the weapon.

'The man's a hopeless legend,' Dujek said. 'Shedenul bless his hide.' He paused, seeming to reorder his thoughts. 'OK, perish the thought, then. You didn't kill Paran. So where is he?'

'We're looking,' Whiskeyjack said tonelessly.

The High Fist sighed. 'All right. Understood. You want to know who else might be wanting Paran dead, and that means explaining who sent him. Well, he's Adjunct Lorn's man, has been for some time. He's not Claw, though. He's a bloody noble's son from Unta.'

Fiddler had donned his weapon and now stood twenty paces away at the roof's edge, hands on his hips. *A good man. They're all good, dammit.* Whiskeyjack blinked the rain from his eyes. 'From the capital? Could be someone in those circles. Nobody likes the old noble families, not even the nobles themselves.'

'It's possible,' Dujek conceded, without much conviction. 'In any case, he's to command your squad, and not for just this mission. The assignment's permanent.'

Whiskeyjack asked, 'Is the Darujhistan infiltration his own idea?'

The High Fist replied, 'No, but whose it is is anybody's guess. Maybe the Adjunct, maybe the Empress herself. So what all that means is we're sending you in anyway.' He scowled briefly. 'I'm to relay the final details to you.' He faced the sergeant. 'Assuming Paran is gone for good.'

'May I speak freely, High Fist?'

Dujek barked a laugh. 'You think I don't know it, Whiskeyjack? The plan stinks. A tactical nightmare—'

'I don't agree.'

'What?'

'I think it will do just as it was intended to do,' the sergeant said dully, his gaze at first on the lightening eastern horizon, then on the soldier standing at the roof's edge. *Because it is intended to get us all killed.*

The High Fist studied the sergeant's face, then he said, 'Come with me.' He led Whiskeyjack over to where Fiddler stood. The sapper gave them a nod. A moment later all three stood looking down on the city. Pale's ill-lit streets wound between the rough blocks of buildings that seemed unwilling to yield the night; behind curtains of rain their squatting silhouettes appeared to shiver before the coming dawn.

After a while, Dujek said quietly, 'Damned lonely out here, isn't it?'

Fiddler grunted. 'That it is, sir.'

Whiskeyjack closed his eyes. Whatever was happening thousands of leagues away was being played out here. Such was Empire, and it always would be, no matter the place or the people. They were all instruments blind to the hands shaping them. The sergeant had faced that truth long ago. It had galled him then and it galled him now. The only relief, these days, seemed to come with exhaustion.

'There's pressure,' the High Fist continued slowly, 'to disband the Bridgeburners. I've already received the order to merge the Second with the Fifth and Sixth. We'll stand as the Fifth, near full complement. The tides are bringing new waters to our shore, gentlemen, and they smell bitter.' He hesitated, then said, 'If you and your squad come out of Darujhistan alive, Sergeant, you have my permission just to walk.'

Whiskeyjack's head snapped around and Fiddler stiffened.

Dujek nodded. 'You heard me. And as for the rest of the Bridgeburners, well, rest easy that I'll take care of them.' The High Fist glanced eastward, baring his teeth in a humourless grin. 'They're pushing me. But there's no way in hell they're going to leave me with no room to manoeuvre. I've got ten thousand soldiers I owe a lot to—'

'Excuse me, sir,' Fiddler cut in, 'there's ten thousand

soldiers saying they're the ones owing. You say the word and—'

'Quiet,' Dujek warned.

'Yes, sir.'

Whiskeyjack remained silent, his thoughts a whirling maelstrom. Desertion. That word rang in his head like a dirge. And Fiddler's assertion was, he felt, a true one. If High Fist Dujek decided it was time to make a move, the last place Whiskeyjack wanted to be was on the run hundreds of leagues away from the centre of things. He was too close to Dujek and, though they strove to hide it, the history between them ever churned beneath the surface. There'd been a time when Dujek had called *him* 'sir', and though Whiskeyjack held no grudges he knew that Dujek still had trouble accepting the change of fortunes. If the time came, Whiskeyjack intended to be at Onearm's side.

'High Fist,' he said at last, aware that both men had been waiting for him to speak, 'there's still a few Bridgeburners left. Fewer hands on the sword. But the sword's still sharp. It's not our style to make life easy for those who oppose us – whoever they happen to be. To just quietly walk away . . .' The sergeant sighed. 'Well, that'd suit them, wouldn't it? While there's a hand on the sword, a single hand, the Bridgeburners won't back down. It settles on honour, I guess.'

'I hear you,' Dujek said. Then he grunted. 'Well, here they come.'

Whiskeyjack looked up, followed the High Fist's gaze into the eastern sky.

Quick Ben cocked his head, then hissed through his teeth. 'The Hounds have caught his trail,' he said.

Kalam cursed vehemently, surging to his feet.

Sitting on the bed, Tattersail frowned bleary-eyed at the bearish man as he paced, his footsteps on the floorboards barely raising a creak. Big as he was, Kalam seemed to glide, giving the scene an almost surreal feel, with the wizard cross-legged and hovering a few inches off the wooden floor in the room's centre.

Tattersail realized she was exhausted. Too much was happening, and it was happening all at once. She shook herself mentally and returned her attention to Quick Ben.

The wizard was linked to Hairlock, and the marionette had been on someone's – *something's* – trail, which led down into the Warren of Shadow. Hairlock had reached the very gates of the Shadow Realm, and then he had gone beyond.

For a time Quick Ben had lost contact with the puppet, and those long minutes of silence had left everyone's nerves in tatters. When Hairlock's presence returned to the wizard he no longer moved alone.

'He's coming out,' Quick Ben announced. 'Shifting Warrens. With Oponn's luck he'll lose the Hounds.'

Tattersail winced at the wizard's casual use of the Fool's name. With so many currents swirling so close beneath the surface it might well call unwelcome attention to them.

Weariness hung heavy in the room like bitter incense, redolent with sweat and tension. After his last words Quick Ben had bowed his head. Tattersail knew his mind now travelled the Warrens, clinging to Hairlock's shoulder with an unbreakable grip.

Kalam's pacing brought him before the sorceress. He stopped and faced her. 'What about Tayschrenn?' he asked gruffly, his hands twitching.

'He knows something has happened. He's hunting, but the quarry eludes him.' She smiled up at the assassin. 'I feel him moving cautiously. Very cautiously. For all he knows, the quarry might be a rabbit, or a wolf.'

Kalam's expression remained grim. 'Or a Hound,' he muttered, then resumed his pacing.

Tattersail stared at him. Was this what Hairlock was doing?

Drawing a Hound after him? Were they all leading Tayschrenn into a deadly ambush? 'I trust not,' she said, her eyes hardening on the assassin. 'That would be foolish.'

Kalam ignored her, pointedly avoiding her gaze.

Tattersail rose. 'Not foolish. Insane. Do you realize what could be unleashed here? Some believe the Hounds are more ancient than the Shadow Realm itself. But it's not just them – power draws power. If one Ascendant parts the fabric here and now, others will come, smelling blood. Come the dawn every mortal in this city could be dead.'

'Easy, lady,' Kalam said. 'Nobody wants a Hound loosed in the city. I spoke from fear.' He still would not look at her.

The assassin's admission startled Tattersail. It was shame that kept his eyes from her. Fear was an admission of weakness. 'For Hood's Sake,' she sighed, 'I've been sitting on a pillow for the past two hours.'

That caught him. He stopped, faced her, then laughed.

It was a deep, smooth laugh, and it pleased her immensely.

The bedroom door opened and Mallet entered the room, his round face shiny and flushed. The healer glanced briefly at Quick Ben, then walked to Tattersail, where he crouched down in front of her. 'By all rights,' he said quietly, 'Captain Paran should be in an Officer's Hole with five feet of mud on his pretty face.' He nodded to Kalam, who had joined them. 'The first wound was fatal, up under his heart. A professional thrust,' he added, with a meaningful look at the assassin. 'The second would have done him more slowly, but no less certain.'

Kalam grimaced. 'So he should be dead. He isn't. Which means?'

'Intervention,' Tattersail answered, a queasy feeling settling in her stomach. Her heavy-lidded gaze fixed on Mallet. 'Your Denul skills proved sufficient?'

The healer quirked a smile. 'It was easy. I had help.' He explained, 'The wounds were already closing, the damage

153

already mended. I quickened it some, but that's all. There's been a deep trauma, both body and mind. By all rights it should be weeks before he recovers physically. And that alone could be a problem.'

'What do you mean?' Tattersail asked.

Kalam strode to the table, retrieved a jug of wine and three clay cups. He rejoined them and began pouring as Mallet said, 'Healing should never be separated between the flesh and the sense of the flesh. It's hard to explain. The Denul Warrens involve every aspect of healing, since damage, when it occurs, does so on all levels. Shock is the scar that bridges the gap between the body and the mind.'

'All and well,' Kalam growled, handing the healer a cup. 'What about Paran?'

Mallet took a long draught and wiped at his mouth. 'Whatever force interceded cared for nothing but healing the flesh. He may well be on his feet in a day or two, but the shock needs time to heal.'

'You couldn't do it?' Tattersail asked.

He shook his head. 'All such things are intertwined. Whatever interceded severed those connections. How many shocks, traumatic events, has Paran received in his lifetime? Which scar am I to trace? I may well do more damage in my ignorance.'

Tattersail thought about the young man they had dragged into her room an hour earlier. After his scream in the alley, announcing to Picker that he still lived, he had fallen into unconsciousness. All that she knew of Paran was that he was a noble's son; that he'd come from Unta, and that he was the squad's new officer on their mission in Darujhistan.

'In any case,' Mallet said, draining his cup, 'Hedge is keeping an eye on him. He may come to any minute, but there's no telling what state his mind will be in.' The healer grinned at Kalam. 'Hedge has taken a liking to

154

the brat.' His grin broadened as the assassin cursed.

Tattersail raised an eyebrow.

Seeing her expression, Mallet explained, 'Hedge also adopts stray dogs – and other, uh, needy creatures.' He glanced at Kalam, who had resumed pacing. 'And he can get stubborn about it, too.'

The corporal growled wordlessly.

Tattersail smiled. The smile faded as her thoughts returned to Captain Paran. 'He's going to be used,' she pronounced, flatly. 'Like a sword.'

Mallet sobered with her words. 'There's nothing of mercy in the healing, only calculation.'

Quick Ben's voice startled them all. 'The attempt on his life came from Shadow.'

There was silence in the room.

Tattersail sighed. Before, it had been just a suspicion. She saw Mallet and Kalam exchange glances, and guessed at what passed between them. Wherever Sorry was, when she returned to the fold there would be some hard questions. And Tattersail now knew – with certainty – that the girl belonged to Shadow.

'And that means,' Quick Ben resumed blithely, 'that who-ever interceded on Paran's behalf is now in direct opposition with the Realm of Shadow.' His head turned, dark eyes fixing on the sorceress. 'We'll need to know what Paran knows, whenever he comes around. Only—'

'We won't be here,' Kalam finished.

'As if Hairlock wasn't enough,' Tattersail muttered, 'now you want me nursing this captain of yours.'

Quick Ben rose, brushing the dust from his leather leggings. 'Hairlock will be gone for some time. Those Hounds are stubborn. It may be a while before he can shake them. Or, if the worst comes to the worst,' the wizard grinned darkly, 'he'll turn on them and give the Shadow Lord something to think about.'

155

Kalam said to Mallet, 'Gather up Hedge. We've got to move.'

Quick Ben's last comment left Tattersail cold. She grimaced at the ashen taste in her mouth, and watched in silence as the squad prepared to leave. They had a mission ahead of them, one that would take them right into the heart of Darujhistan. That city was the next on the Empire's list, the last Free City, the continent's lone gem worthy enough to covet. The squad would infiltrate, prepare the way. They'd be entirely on their own. In a strange way, Tattersail almost envied the isolation they were about to enter. Almost, but not quite. She feared they would all die.

The Mason's Barrow returned to her thoughts as if raised by her own fears. It was, she realized, big enough to hold them all.

With dawn a blade-thin crimson streak at their backs, the Black Moranth, crouching on the high saddles of their Quorl mounts, glittered like diamonds slick with blood. Whiskeyjack, Fiddler and the High Fist watched the dozen fliers approach. Overhead the rain had lessened, and around the nearby rooftops smudges of grey mist sank down to scuff stone and tile.

'Where's your squad, Sergeant?' Dujek asked.

Whiskeyjack nodded at Fiddler, who turned and headed back to the trap-door. 'They'll be here,' the sergeant answered.

The sparkling, skin-thin wings of the Quorl, four to each creature, seemed to flip for the briefest of moments, and as one the twelve Moranth descended towards the turret's rooftop. The sharp whirring sound of the wings was punctuated by the clicked commands of the Moranth riders as they called out to each other. They swept over the heads of the two men with a bare five feet to spare, and without ceremony landed behind them.

Fiddler had disappeared into the room below. Dujek, his hand on his hip, glared at the Moranth for a moment before

156

grumbling something inaudible and making his way to the trap-door.

Whiskeyjack walked up to the nearest Moranth. A black chitin visor covered the soldier's face, and it turned towards the sergeant in silent regard. 'There was one among you,' Whiskeyjack said, 'one-handed. He was five times marked for valour. Does he still live?'

The Black Moranth did not reply.

The sergeant shrugged and turned his attention to the Quorls. Though he had ridden their backs before, they continued to fascinate him. The winged creatures balanced on four thin legs emerging from beneath the saddles. They waited on the rooftop with wings splayed out and quivering fast enough to create a haze of water droplets suspended around them. Their long, oddly segmented tails jutted straight out behind them, multi-hued and twenty feet in length. Whiskeyjack's nostrils twitched as the now familiar acrid scent reached him. The nearest Quorl's enormous, wedge-shaped head was dominated by faceted eyes and articulating mandibles. Two additional limbs – arms, he supposed – were tucked underneath. As he stared the Quorl's head swivelled until its left eye faced him squarely.

The sergeant continued staring, wondering what the Quorl was seeing, wondering what it was thinking – if it thought at all. Curious, he gave the Quorl a nod.

The head cocked, then turned away. Whiskeyjack's eyes widened to see the tip of the Quorl's tail curl up briefly. It was the first time he had seen such a motion.

The alliance between the Moranth and the Empire had changed the face of Imperial war. The Malazan tactics here on Genabackis had twisted into a new shape, one increasingly dependent on transport by air of both soldiers and supplies. Such dependency was dangerous, as far as Whiskeyjack was concerned. *We know so little about these Moranth – no one has ever seen their cities in the forest. I can't even tell their sex.* Most scholars held that they were true humans, but there was no way to tell – the Moranth collected their own dead from the battlefields. There would be trouble in the Empire if the Moranth ever exercised a thirst for power. From what he had heard, however, the various colour factions among them marked an ever-changing hierarchy, and the rivalry and competition remained at a fanatical pitch.

High Fist Dujek marched back to Whiskeyjack's side, his hard expression softened slightly with relief. From the trap-door, voices rose in argument. 'They've arrived,' Dujek said. 'Giving your new recruit an earful about something – and don't tell me what because I don't want to know.'

Whiskeyjack's momentary relief was shattered by what he only now realized was the secret hope that Sorry had deserted. So his men had found her after all, or she had found them. Either way, his veterans did not sound happy to see her. He couldn't blame them. Had she tried to kill Paran? That seemed to be the suspicion of Quick Ben and Kalam.

Kalam was doing most of the bellowing, putting more into his role as corporal than was warranted, and Dujek's searching glance at Whiskeyjack was enough to push him towards the trap-door. He came to the edge and glared down into the room below. Everyone was there, standing in a menacing circle around Sorry, who leaned against the ladder as if bored by the whole proceedings.

'Quiet!' Whiskeyjack roared down. 'Check your supplies and get up here, now!' He watched them scamper, then gave a satisfied nod and returned to where the High Fist waited.

Dujek was rubbing the stump of his left arm, frowning distractedly. 'Damn this weather,' he muttered.

'Mallet could ease that,' Whiskeyjack said.

'Not necessary,' Dujek replied. 'I'm just getting old.' He scratched his jaw. 'All of your heavy supplies have been

158

delivered to the drop point. Ready to fly, Sergeant?'

Whiskeyjack eyed the ridged second saddles on the Quorl where they rose up at the back of the thorax like cowls, then nodded sharply.

They watched as the squad members emerged from the square doorway, each wearing a raincape and burdened with a heavy pack. Fiddler and Hedge were engaged in a whispering argument, the latter casting a glare back at Trotts who'd trodden on his heel. The Barghast had attached his entire collection of charms, trinkets and trophies to various parts of his burly body, looking like a bedecked leadwood tree during the Kanese Fête of the Scorpions. Barghast were known for their odd sense of humour. Quick Ben and Kalam flanked Sorry, both men glowering and on edge, while Sorry, ignoring everyone, slowly made her way to the waiting Quorls. Her satchel was no bigger than a bedroll, and the raincape she wore was more like a cloak – not standard issue – reaching down to her ankles. She'd raised the hood. Despite the dawn's burgeoning light her face remained in shadow. *This is all I have left.* Whiskeyjack sighed.

Dujek asked quietly, 'How is she doing, Sergeant?'

'Still breathing,' Whiskeyjack replied stonily.

The High Fist slowly shook his head. 'So damn young these days . . .'

A memory returned to Whiskeyjack as he considered Dujek's words. On a brief attachment to the 5th, away from the siege at Pale, in the midst of the Mott Campaign, Sorry had joined them from the new troops arriving at Nathilog. He'd watched her put a knife to three local mercenaries they'd taken prisoner in Greydog – ostensibly to glean information but, he recalled with a shudder, it had been nothing like that. Not an act of expedience. He had stared aghast, horrified, as Sorry set to work on their loins. He remembered meeting Kalam's gaze, and the desperate gesture that sent the black man surging forward, knives bared. Kalam had pushed past Sorry and with three quick motions had laid open the men's throats. And then came the moment that still twisted Whiskeyjack's heart. In their last, frothing words, the mercenaries had *blessed* Kalam.

Sorry had merely sheathed her weapon, then walked away.

Though the woman had been with the squad for two years, still his men called her a recruit, and they would probably do so until the day they died. There was a meaning there, and Whiskeyjack understood it well. Recruits were not Bridge-burners. The stripping away of that label was an earned thing, a recognition brought by deeds. Sorry was a recruit because the thought of having her inextricably enfolded within the Bridgeburners burned like a hot knife in the throat of everyone in his squad. And that was something to which the sergeant himself was not immune.

As all of this flashed through Whiskeyjack's thoughts, his usually impassive expression failed him. In his head, he replied: Young? No, you can forgive the young, you can answer their simple needs, and you can look in their eyes and find enough there that is recognizable. But her? No. Best to avoid those eyes, in which there was nothing that was young – nothing at all.

'Let's get you moving,' Dujek growled. 'Mount everyone up.' The High Fist turned to say a few last words to the sergeant, but what he saw in Whiskeyjack's face killed those words in his throat.

Two muted thunderclaps sounded in the city as the east spread its crimson cloak skyward, the first report followed scant minutes later by the second. The last of the night's tears churned down gunnels and swirled along street gutters. Muddy puddles filled potholes, reflecting the thinning clouds over-head with an opaque cast. Among the narrow crooked alleys of Pale's Krael Quarter, the chill and damp of the night clung to the dark spaces with tenacity. Here, the mould-laden bricks and worn cobbles had swallowed the second thunderclap, leaving no echo to challenge the patter of water droplets.

Down one aisle, winding south along the outer wall, loped a dog the size of a mule. Its massive head was slung low forward in front of the broad, bunched muscles of its shoulders. That it had seen a night without rain was marked by its dusty, dry, mottled grey and black fur. The animal's muzzle was speckled with grey, and its eyes glowed amber.

The Hound, marked Seventh among Shadowthrone's servants and called Gear, hunted. The quarry was elusive, cunning, and swift in its flight. Yet Gear felt close. He knew that it was no human he tracked – no mortal man or woman could have escaped his jaws for so long. Even more astonishing, Gear had yet to catch a glimpse of the quarry. But it had trespassed, with impunity it had entered the Shadow Realm, trailing Shadowthrone himself and strumming all the webs Gear's lord had spun. The only answer to such an affront was death.

Soon, the Hound knew, *he* would be the hunted one, and if those hunters came in numbers and in strength Gear would be hard pressed to continue his search. There were those within the city who had felt the savage partings of the fabric. And less than a minute after passing through the Warren's gate Gear's hackles had stiffened, telling him of nearby magic's burgeoning. Thus far the Hound had eluded detection, but that would not last.

He moved silent and cautiously through the maze of shanties and lean-tos crouching against the city wall, ignoring the occasional denizen come out to taste the dawn's rain-cleansed air. He stepped over the beggars sprawled in his path. Local dogs and ratters gave him one glance then slunk away, ears flattened and tail sweeping the muddy ground.

As Gear rounded the corner of a sunken stone house the

161

morning breeze brought his head round. He paused, eyes searching down the street opposite him. Mist drifted here and there, and the first carts of the lesser merchants were being pulled out by figures wrapped warm against the chill – the Hound was running out of time.

Gear's eyes travelled down the length of the street, focusing on a large, walled estate at the far end. Four soldiers lounged before its gate, watching passers-by with little interest and talking among themselves. Gear's head lifted, his study finding a shuttered window on the estate's second floor.

Anticipation and pleasure surged through the Hound. He had found the trail's end. Lowering his head again, he moved, his gaze unwavering on the four guards.

The shift had ended. As the new marines approached they both noticed that the gate was unlocked, ajar.

'What's this?' one asked, eyeing the two drawn faces of the soldiers who stood against the wall.

'It's been that kind of night,' the elder responded. 'The kind where you don't ask questions.'

The two new men exchanged glances, then the one who had spoken gave the older man a nod and a grin. 'I know the kind. Well, get on, then. Your cots are waiting.'

The older man shifted his pike and seemed to sag. His gaze flicked to his partner, but the young man had his attention on something up the street. 'I'd guess it's too late now,' the older man said to the newcomers, 'meaning it won't happen and so it don't matter, but if a woman shows up, a Bridgeburner, you let her through and keep your eyes on the walls.'

'Look at that dog,' the younger soldier said.

'We hear you,' said the new man. 'Life in the Second—'

'Look at that dog,' the young marine repeated.

The others turned to look up the street. The old guard stared, his eyes widening, then he hissed a curse and fumbled

162

with his pike. None of the others managed even that much before the Hound was upon them.

Sleepless, Tattersail lay flat on her back on the bed in the outer room. Her exhaustion had reached a point where even sleep eluded her so she stared at the ceiling, her thoughts wandering in a disordered review of the past seven days. Despite her initial anger at being embroiled in the Bridgeburners' schemes, she had to acknowledge the excitement she felt.

The desire to collect her possessions and open a Warren, away from the Empire, away from Hairlock's madness and hunger, away from the field of an endless war, now seemed an ancient one, born of a desperation she no longer felt.

But it was more than just a renewed sense of humanity that compelled her to stay to see it through – the Bridgeburners, after all, had shown again and again that they could take care of their own affairs. No, she wanted to see Tayschrenn *pulled down*. It was a truth that frightened her. Hunger for vengeance poisoned the soul. And it was likely that she would have to wait a long time to see Tayschrenn's just demise. She wondered if, having fed on that poison for so long, she might not end up viewing the world with Hairlock's shining bright mad eyes.

'Too much,' she muttered. 'Too much all at once.'

A sound at the door startled her. She sat up. 'Oh,' she said, scowling, 'you've returned.'

'Safe and sound,' Hairlock said. 'Sorry to disappoint you, 'Sail.' The marionette waved one tiny, gloved hand and the door behind him closed, its latch falling into place. 'Much feared, these Hounds of Shadow,' he said, sauntering into the room's centre and pirouetting once before sitting down, legs splayed and arms hanging limp. He sniggered. 'But in the end nothing more than glorified mutts, stupid and slow and sniffing at every tree. Finding naught of sly Hairlock.'

Tattersail leaned back and closed her eyes. 'Quick Ben was displeased by your sloppiness.'

'Fool!' Hairlock spat. 'I leave him to his watching, I leave him convinced that such knowledge has power over me while I go where I choose. He eagerly lays claim to commanding me, a foolishness I give him now, to make my vengeance sweeter.'

She had heard it all before and knew he was working on her, seeking to weaken her resolve. Unfortunately he was succeeding in part, for she felt doubt. Maybe Hairlock was telling the truth: maybe Quick Ben had already lost him, yet remained ignorant of the fact. 'Keep your vengeance for the man who stole your legs and then your body,' Tattersail said drily. 'Tayschrenn still mocks you.'

'He'll pay first!' Hairlock shrieked. Then he hunched down, gripping his sides. 'One thing at a time,' he whispered.

From the compound beyond the window came the first screams.

Tattersail bolted upright as Hairlock shouted: 'Found! I mustn't be seen, woman!'

The marionette leaped to his feet and scurried to his box against the far wall. 'Destroy the Hound – you've no choice!' Scrambling, he opened the box and climbed inside. The lid thudded into place and the nimbus of a protective spell suffused it.

Tattersail stood by the bed, hesitating. Wood shattered below and the building shook. Men shrieked, weapons clanged. The sorceress pushed herself upright, terror seeping into her limbs like molten lead. *Destroy a Hound of Shadow?* Heavy thumps rattled the window, as of bodies being flung aside on the floor below, then the thumps reached the foot of the stairs, and the screaming stopped. From the compound she heard soldiers shouting.

Tattersail drew on her Thyr Warren. Power swept into her and pushed aside the paralysing fear. She straightened, all exhaustion gone, and swung her gaze on the door. Wood creaked, then the timber panel exploded inwards, as if flung from a catapult, and was instantly buffeted aside by Tattersail's magical shield. The twin impacts shattered it, flinging shards and splinters against the ceiling and walls. Glass broke behind her, the window's shutters springing open. An icy wind roiled into the room.

The Hound appeared, its eyes yellow flames, the muscles of its high shoulders taut, rippling under its skin. The creature's power swept like a wave over Tattersail and she drew a sharp breath. The Hound was *old*, older than anything she had ever encountered. It paused in the doorway, sniffing the air, blood dripping from its black lips. Then its gaze fixed on the iron-bound box against the wall to Tattersail's left. The beast stepped forward.

'No,' she said.

The Hound froze. Its massive head swung slow and measured to her, as if it was noticing her for the first time. Its lips peeled back to reveal the luminescent gleam of canines the length of a man's thumb.

Damn you, Hairlock! I need your help! Please!

A white strip flashed above the Hound's eyes as the lids snapped back. It charged.

The attack was so swift that Tattersail was unable to raise her hands before the beast was upon her, surging through her outer magic as if it was no more than a brisk wind. Her closest defences, a layering of High Wards, met the Hound's charge like a stone wall. She felt cracks streak outwards, deep fissures reaching through to her arms and chest with a snapping sound immediately replaced by spurting blood. This, and the Hound's momentum, flung her back through the air. The wards at her back cushioned the blow as she hit the wall beside the window. Mortar puffed into the air around her, and fragments of crushed brick scattered across the floor.

165

The Hound had fallen to its knees. Shaking its head, it regained its feet, snorted, then attacked again.

Tattersail, her wits rocked by the first charge, weakly lifted one blood-streaked arm before her face, unable to do anything else.

As the Hound sprang into the air, jaws open and reaching for her head, a wave of grey light struck the beast in the side, throwing it into the bed to Tattersail's right. Wood crunched. With a grunt the Hound was up again, wheeling this time to face Hairlock, who stood perched atop his box, glistening with sweat and arms raised. 'Oh, yes, Gear,' he shrilled. 'I'm your quarry!'

Tattersail slumped, then leaned to one side and vomited on the floor. A chaotic Warren swirled in the room, a miasma that churned into her like riotous pestilence. It radiated from Hairlock in visible pulses of grainy grey shot through with black.

The Hound eyed Hairlock, its sides heaving. It was as if it was trying to dispel the waves of power from its brain. A low growl rumbled in its chest – its first sound. The wide head sagged.

Tattersail stared, then understanding struck a hammer blow to her chest. 'Hound!' she screamed. 'He's reaching for your soul! Escape! *Get out of here!*'

The beast's growl deepened, but it did not move.

None of the three noticed the door to the inner bedroom opening off to the left, or the halting appearance of Captain Paran, wrapped in the colourless woollen blanket that covered him down to his ankles. Pale and drawn, the man moved forward, a blank cast to his eyes, which were fixed on the Hound. As the invisible battle of wills continued between Gear and Hairlock, Paran stepped closer.

The movement caught Tattersail's eye. She opened her mouth to shout a warning, but Paran moved first. The blanket parted to reveal a longsword, point flashing outward as he extended into a full lunge. The sword sank into Gear's chest, even as the man leaped back, withdrawing the lunge, twisting the weapon as he pulled it clear. A bellow thundered from Gear's throat. The Hound staggered back into the ruins of the bed, biting at the wound gushing blood from its side.

Hairlock screamed in rage and jumped forward, closing in on Gear.

Tattersail scythed one foot into the puppet's path, flinging him against the far wall.

Gear howled. A dark rift opened around him with the sound of tearing burlap. He whirled and plunged into the deepening shadow. The rent closed and was gone, leaving in its wake a rippling of cold air.

Astonished beyond her pain, Tattersail swung her attention to Captain Paran and the bloodied sword in his hands. 'How?' she gasped. 'How could you have pierced the Hound's magic? Your sword—'

The captain looked down at it. 'Just lucky, I suppose.'

'Oponn!' Hairlock hissed, as he regained his feet, and glared at Tattersail. 'Hood's Curse on the Fools! And you, woman, this I'll not forget. You will pay – I swear it!'

Tattersail looked away and sighed. A smile touched her lips as words uttered earlier now returned with new, grim meaning. 'You'll be too busy staying alive, Hairlock, to start on me. You've given Shadowthrone something to think about. And you'll live to regret his attention, puppet. Deny that if you dare.'

'I'm returning to my box,' Hairlock said, scrambling. 'Expect Tayschrenn here in minutes. You'll say nothing, Sorceress.' He clambered inside. 'Nothing.' The lid slammed shut.

Tattersail's smile broadened, the taste of blood in her mouth like an omen, a silent, visible warning to Hairlock of things to come – a warning she knew he couldn't see. That made the taste almost sweet.

She tried to move, but it seemed that a chill had come to her limbs. Within her mind visions floated, but walls of darkness closed in around them before they could register. She felt herself fading.

A man's voice spoke close by, urgent. 'What do you hear?'

She frowned, trying to concentrate. Then she smiled. 'A spinning coin. I hear a spinning coin.'

BOOK TWO

DARUJHISTAN

What windfall has brushed our senses?
This rocking thunderhead that scraped
the lake's placid waters
and spun a single day's shadows
like a wheel that rolled us
from dawn to dusk, while we
tottered our tender ways . . .

What windlass crackles dire warnings?
There in the gentle swells that tossed
a bobbing cork our way
with its fine magenta scent wafting
like a panoply of petals
that might be ashes
in twilight's crimson smear . . .

Rumour Born
Fisher (b.?}

CHAPTER FIVE

And if this man sees you in his dreams,
while you rock in the season's
brooding night
'neath a tree's stout branch,
and your shadow is hooded
above the knotted rope,
so will the winds of his passing
twitch your stiffened limbs
into some semblance of running . . .

Rumour Born
Fisher (b.?)

907th Year in the Third Millennium
The Season of Fanderay in the year of the Five Tusks
Two thousand years since the birth of Darujhistan, the city

In his dream the small round man found himself leaving the
city of Darujhistan through Two Ox Gate as he headed
towards the setting sun. The tattered tails of his faded red
waistcoat flapped in his haste. He had no idea how far he
would have to walk. Already his feet ached.

There were miseries in the world, and then there was *misery*. In times of conscience he held the world's concerns above his own. Fortunately, he reflected, such times were few, and this, he told himself, was not one of them.

'Alas, the very same dream propels these many-toed implements beneath these wobbly knees.' He sighed. 'Ever the same dream.' And so it was. He saw before him the sun riding the distant hilltop, a copper disc through woodsmoke haze. His feet carried him down the winding dirt street of Gadrobi Shantytown, the shacks and huts on either side crouching in the gathering gloom. Old men wrapped in the dingy yellow rags of lepers squatted over nearby cookfires, falling silent as he passed. Similarly clad women stood by the muddy well, pausing in their endless dunking of cats – a bemusing activity, its symbolism lost on the man as he hurried past.

He crossed Maiten River bridge, passed through the dwindling Gadrobi Herder camps, out on to the open road flanked by vineyard plantations. He lingered here, thinking of the wine these succulent grapes would produce. But dreams carried on with their own momentum, and the thought was but fleeting in its passage.

He knew his mind was in flight – fleeing the doomed city at his back, fleeing the dark, brooding smudge in the sky above it; but most of all, fleeing all that he knew and all that he was.

For some, the talent they possessed found its channel through a toss of knucklebones, the reading of heat fractures in scapulae, or the Fatid of the Deck of Dragons. For Kruppe, he had no need of any such affectations. The power of divination was in his head and he could not deny it, no matter how hard he tried. Within the walls of his skull rang the dirge of prophecy, and it echoed through his bones.

He muttered under his breath. 'Of course this is a dream, the flight of sleep. Perhaps, thinks Kruppe, he will in truth escape this time. None could call Kruppe a fool, after all. Fat with

172

sloth and neglect, yes; inclined to excesses, indeed, somewhat clumsy with a bowl of soup, most certainly. But not a fool. Such times are upon us when the wise man must choose. Is it not wisdom to conclude that other lives are of less importance than one's own? Of course, very wise. Yes, Kruppe is wise.'

He paused to catch his breath. The hills and the sun before him seemed no closer. Such were dreams like the hastening of youth into adulthood, a precipitous course one could never turn back on – but who mentioned youth? Or one youth in particular? 'Surely not wise Kruppe! His mind wanders – Kruppe excuses the pun magnanimously – racked by the misery of his soles, which are tired, nay, half worn out from this reckless pace. Blisters have already appeared, no doubt. The foot cries out for a warm, soapy balm. Its companion joins in the chorus. Ah! Such a litany! Such a wail of despair! Cease complaining, dear wings of flight. How far is the sun, anyway? Just beyond the hills, Kruppe is certain. No more than that, surely. Yes, as certain as an ever-spinning coin – but who spoke of coins? Kruppe proclaims his innocence!'

A breeze swept into his dream, down from the north carrying with it the smell of rain. Kruppe began fastening his threadbare coat. He drew in his belly in an effort to secure the last two buttons, but succeeded in clasping only one. 'Even in sleep,' he groaned, 'guilt makes its point.'

He blinked against the wind. 'Rain? But the year has just begun! Does it rain in the spring? Kruppe has never before concerned himself with such mundane matters. Perhaps this scent is no more than the lake's own breath. Yes, indeed. The question is settled.' He squinted at the dark ridge of clouds above Lake Azur.

'Must Kruppe run? Nay, where is his pride? His dignity? Not once have they shown their faces in Kruppe's dreams. Is there no shelter on yon road? Ah, Kruppe's feet are flailed, his soles bloodied shreds of throbbing flesh! What's this?'

173

Up ahead was a crossroads. A building squatted on a low rise just beyond. Candlelight bled from its shuttered windows.

Kruppe smiled. 'Of course, an inn. Far has the journey been, clear the need for a place of rest and relaxation for the weary traveller. Such as Kruppe, wizened adventurer with more than a few leagues under his belt, not to mention spanning it.' He hurried forward.

A broad, bare-limbed tree marked the crossroads. From one heavy branch something long and wrapped in burlap swung creaking in the wind. Kruppe spared it but the briefest glance. He came to the path and began his ascent.

'Ill judgement, pronounces Kruppe. Inns for the dusty journeyman should not sit atop hills. The curse of climbing is discovering how great the distance yet to climb. A word to the proprietor shall be necessary. Once sweet ale has soothed the throat, slabs of juicy red meat and broiled yams eased the gullet, and clean, anointed bandages clothed the feet. Such repairs must take precedence over flaws in planning such as Kruppe sees here.'

His monologue fell away, replaced by gasps as he struggled up the path. When he arrived at the door Kruppe was so winded that he did not even so much as look up, merely pushed against the weathered panel until it swung inward with a squeal of rusty hinges. 'Alas!' he cried, pausing to brush the sleeves of his coat. 'A foamy tankard for this . . .' His voice died as he surveyed the array of grimy faces turned to him. 'Methinks the business is poor,' he mumbled. The place was indeed an inn – or it had been, perhaps a century past. ''Tis rain in the night air,' he said, to the half-dozen beggars crouched around a thick tallow candle set on the earthen floor.

One of the fellows nodded. 'We will grant you audience, hapless one.' He waved at a straw mat. 'Be seated and entertain our presence.'

Kruppe raised an eyebrow. 'Kruppe is graced by your

invitation, sire.' He dipped his head, then strode forward. 'But, please, do not think he is bereft of contributions to this honoured gathering.' He sat down cross-legged, grunting with the effort, and faced the one who had spoken. 'He would break bread with you all.' From a sleeve he withdrew a small rye loaf. A bread knife appeared in his other hand. 'Known to friends and strangers alike is Kruppe, the man now seated before you. Inhabitant of yon glittering Darujhistan, the mystic jewel of Genabackis, the juicy grape ripe for picking.' He produced a chunk of goat cheese and smiled broadly at the faces before him. 'And this is his dream.'

'So it is,' the beggars' spokesman said, his lined face crinkling with amusement. 'It ever pleases us when we taste your particular flavour, Kruppe of Darujhistan. And always are we pleased at your travelling appetites.'

Kruppe laid down the rye loaf and cut slices. 'Kruppe has always considered you mere aspects of himself, a half-dozen Hungers among many, as it were. Yet, for all your needs, you would urge what of your master? That he turn back from his flight, of course. That one's own skull is too worthy a chamber for deception to reign – and yet Kruppe assures you from long experience that all deceit is born in the mind and there it is nurtured while virtues starve.'

The spokesman accepted a slice of bread and smiled. 'Perhaps we are your virtues, then.'

Kruppe paused to study the cheese in his hand. 'A thought Kruppe has not considered before now, mingling with the silent observation of mould on this cheese. But alas, the subject is in danger of being lost within the maze of such semantics. Nor can beggars be choosers when it comes to cheese. You have returned once again, and Kruppe knows why, as he has already explained with admirable equanimity.'

'The Coin spins, Kruppe, still spins.' The spokesman's face lost its humour.

Kruppe sighed. He handed the chunk of goat cheese to the man seated on his right. 'Kruppe hears it,' he conceded wearily. 'He cannot help but hear it. An endless ringing that sings in the head. And for all that Kruppe has seen, for all that he suspects to be, he is just Kruppe, a man who would challenge the gods in their own game.'

'Perhaps we are your Doubts,' the spokesman said, 'which you have never been afraid to face before, as you do now. Yet even we seek to turn you back, even we demand that you strive for the life of Darujhistan, for the life of your many friends, and for the life of the youth at whose feet the Coin shall fall.'

'It falls this very night,' Kruppe said. The six beggars nodded at this, though mostly they remained intent on the bread and cheese. 'Shall Kruppe accept this challenge, then? What are gods, after all, if not the perfect victims?' He smiled, raising his hands and fluttering his fingers. 'For Kruppe, whose sleight of hand is matched only by his sleight of mind? Perfect victims of confidence, claims Kruppe, ever blinded by arrogance, ever convinced of infallibility. Is it not a wonder that they have survived this long?'

The spokesman nodded and said, around a mouthful of cheese, 'Perhaps we are your Gifts, then. Wasting away, as it were.'

'Possibly,' Kruppe said, his eyes narrowing. 'Yet only one of you speaks.'

The beggar paused to swallow, then he laughed, his eyes dancing in the candlelight. 'Perhaps the others have yet to find their voice, Kruppe. They await only their master's command.'

'My,' Kruppe sighed, as he prepared to stand, 'but Kruppe is full of surprises.'

The spokesman looked up. 'You return to Darujhistan?'

'Of course,' Kruppe replied, gaining his feet with a heartfelt groan. 'He merely stepped out for a breath of night air, so much cleaner beyond the city's crumbling walls, don't you agree?

Kruppe must needs exercise to hone his already prodigious skills. A walk in his sleep. This night,' he said, hitching his thumbs in his belt, 'the Coin falls. Kruppe must take his place in the centre of things. He returns to his bed, the night still young.' His eyes travelled among the beggars. All seemed to have gained weight, a healthy robust colour to their upturned faces. Kruppe sighed with satisfaction. 'It has, pronounces Kruppe, been a pleasure, gentlemen. Next time, however, let us settle on an inn that is not on a hilltop. Agreed?'

The spokesman smiled. 'Ah, but, Kruppe, Gifts are not easily attained, nor are Virtues, nor are Doubts easily overcome, and Hungers are ever the impetus to climbing.'

Kruppe's eyes narrowed on the man. 'Kruppe is too clever by far,' he muttered.

He left their company and shut the creaking door softly behind him. Returning down the path he came to the crossroads and stopped in front of the burlap-wrapped figure swinging from the branch. Kruppe planted his fists on his hips and studied it. 'I know who you are,' he said jovially. 'The final aspect of Kruppe to complete this dream's array of those faces facing him which are Kruppe's own. Or so you would proclaim. You are Humility but, as everyone knows, Humility has no place in Kruppe's life, remember that. So here you will stay.' With that he moved his gaze to the great city lighting the eastern sky blue and green. 'Ah, this wondrous fiery gem that is Darujhistan is home to Kruppe. And that,' he added, as he began to walk, 'is as it should be.'

From the wharf sprawled along the shore of the lake, upward along the stepped tiers of the Gadrobi and Daru Districts, among the temple complexes and the Higher Estates, to the summit of Majesty Hill where gathers the city's Council, the rooftops of Darujhistan presented flat tops, arched gables, coned towers, belfries and platforms crowded in such chaotic

177

profusion as to leave all but the major streets for ever hidden from the sun.

The torches marking the more frequented alleyways were hollow shafts that gripped pumice stones with fingers of blackened iron. Fed through ancient pitted copper pipes, gas hissed balls of flame around the porous stones, an uneven fire that cast a blue and green light. The gas was drawn from great caverns beneath the city and channelled by massive valves. Attending these works were the Greyfaces, silent men and women who moved like spectres beneath the city's cobbled streets.

For nine hundred years the breath of gas had fed at least one of the city's districts. Though pipes had been sundered by raging tenement fires and gouts of flame reached hundreds of feet into the sky, the Greyfaces had held on, twisting the shackles and driving their invisible dragon to its knees.

Beneath the rooftops was an underworld forever bathed in a blue glow. Such light marked the major avenues and the oft-frequented, narrow and crooked thoroughways of the markets. In the city, however, over twenty thousand alleys, barely wide enough for a two-wheeled cart, remained in shadow broken only by the occasional torch-bearing citizen or the globed lanterns of the City Watch.

By day the rooftops were bright and hot beneath the sun, crowded with the fluttering flags of domestic life drying in the lake wind. By night, the stars and moon illuminated a world webbed with empty clothes-lines and the chaotic shadows they cast.

On this night a figure wove around the hemp ropes and through the faint shadows. Overhead, a sickle moon sliced its way between thin clouds like a god's scimitar. The figure wore soot-stained cloth wrapped snugly about its torso and limbs, and its face was similarly hidden, leaving only space enough for its eyes, which scanned the nearby rooftops. A black leather harness criss-crossed the figure's chest, bearing pockets and tight, stiff loops holding tools of the trade: coils of copper wire, iron files, three metal saws each wrapped in oiled parchment, root gum and a squared lump of tallow, a spool of fishing string, a thin-bladed dagger and a throwing knife both sheathed under the figure's left arm, pommels facing forward.

The tips of the thief's moccasins had been soaked in pitch. As he crossed the flat rooftop he was careful not to lower his full weight on his toes, leaving mostly intact the half-inch strip of sticky tar. He came to the building's edge and looked down. Three flights below crouched a small garden, faintly lit by four gas lamps set at each corner of a flagstoned patio that encircled a fountain. A purple glow clung to the foliage encroaching on the patio, and glimmered on the water trickling down a series of stone tiers to the fountain's shallow pool. On a bench beside the fountain sat a guard reclined in sleep, a spear across his knees.

The D'Arle estate was a popular topic among the higher circles of Darujhistan's nobility, specifically for the eligibility of the family's youngest daughter. Many had been the suitors, many the gifts of gems and baubles that now resided in the young maiden's bedroom.

While such stories were passed like the sweetest bread in the upper circles, few of the commonry paid attention when the tales trickled down into their company. But there were those who listened carefully indeed, possessive and mute with their thoughts yet oddly eager for details.

His gaze on the dozing house guard in the garden below, the mind of Crokus Younghand picked its way carefully through speculations of what was to come. The key lay in finding out which room among the estate's score of chambers belonged to the maiden. Crokus did not like guesswork, but he'd found that his thoughts, carried almost entirely on instinct, moved with their own logic when determining these things.

Top floor most assuredly for the youngest and fairest daughter of the D'Arles. And with a balcony overlooking the garden.

He turned his attention from the guard to the wall immediately beneath him. Three balconies, but only one, off to the left, was on the third floor. Crokus pulled back from the edge and slipped silently along the roof until he judged he was directly above the balcony, then he approached again and looked down.

Ten feet, at the most. On either side of the balcony rose ornately carved columns of painted wood. A half-moon arch spanned them an arm's length down, completing the fancy frame. With a final glance at the house guard, who had not moved, and whose spear did not seem in danger of clattering to the flagstones at any moment, Crokus slowly lowered himself down the wall.

His moccasins' pitch gripped the eaves with snug assurance. There were plenty of handholds, as the carver had cut deep into the hardwood, and sun, rain and wind had weathered the paint. He descended along one of the columns until his feet touched the balcony's handrail where it abutted the wall. A moment later he crouched on the glazed tiles in the shadow of a wrought-iron table and pillowed chair.

No light leaked between the shutters of the sliding door. Two soft steps brought him next to it. A moment's examination identified the style of the latch's lock. Crokus withdrew a fine-toothed saw and set to work. The sound the tool made was minimal, no more than the shivering of a locust's leg. A fine tool, rare and probably expensive. Crokus was fortunate in having an uncle who dabbled in alchemy and had need of such magically hardened tools when constructing his bizarre condensing and filtering mechanisms. Better yet, an absent-minded uncle prone to misplacing things.

Twenty minutes later the saw's teeth snipped the last

restraining bolt. He returned the tool to his harness, wiped the sweat from his hands, then nudged the door open.

Crokus poked his head into the room. In the grey dimness he saw a large four-poster bed a few feet to his left, its headboard against the outer wall. Mosquito netting descended around it, ending in piled heaps on the floor. From within came the even breaths of someone deep in sleep. The room was redolent of expensive perfume, something spicy and probably from Callows.

Immediately across from him were two doors, one ajar and leading into a bathing chamber; the other a formidable barrier of banded oak sporting an enormous lock. Against the wall to his right stood a clothes cupboard and a makeup stand over which stood three polished silver mirrors hinged together. The centre one rose flush on the wall, the outer two angled on to the tabletop to provide an infinity of admiring visages.

Crokus turned sideways and edged into the room. He rose slowly and stretched, relieving his muscles of the tension that had held them for the past half-hour. He swung his gaze to the makeup stand, then tiptoed towards it.

The D'Arle estate was third from the summit of Old K'rul's Avenue, which climbed the first of the inner city's hills to a circular court tangled with weeds and irregular, half-buried dolmens. Opposite the court rose K'rul Temple, its ancient stones latticed with cracks and entombed in moss.

The last monk of the Eldering God had died generations past. The square belfry that rose from the temple's inner court bore architectural stylings of a people long dead. Four rose marble posts marked the corners of the high platform, still holding aloft a peaked roof with sides that were scaled in green-stained bronze tiles.

The belfry overlooked a dozen flat roofs, of houses that belonged to gentry. One such structure crowded close to one of

181

the temple's rough-hewn walls, and across its roof lay the heavy shadow of the tower. On this roof crouched an assassin with blood on his hands.

Talo Krafar of Jurig Denatte's Clan drew breath in hissing gasps. Sweat trickled muddy streaks down his brow and droplets fell from his broad, crooked nose. His dark eyes were wide as he stared down at his hands, for the blood staining them was his own.

His mission this night had been as a Roamer, patrolling the city's rooftops which, except for the occasional thief, were the assassins' sole domain, the means by which they travelled the city for the most part undetected. The rooftops provided their routes on missions of unsanctioned political . . . activities or the continuation of a feud between two Houses, or the punishment for betrayal. The Council ruled by day under public scrutiny; the Guild ruled by night, unseen, leaving no witnesses. It had always been this way, since Darujhistan first rose on the shores of Lake Azur.

Talo had been crossing an innocuous rooftop when a crossbow quarrel had driven a hammer blow to his left shoulder. He was flung forward by the concussion, and for an unknown length of time stared dumbfounded at the cloud-wreathed sky overhead, wondering what had happened. Finally, as numbness slowly gave way to agony, he twisted on to his side. The quarrel had gone entirely through him. It lay on the tarred tiles a few feet away. He rolled until he was beside the bloodied bolt.

One glance had been enough to confirm that this was no thief's quarrel. It had come from a heavy weapon – an assassin's weapon. As this fact worked its way through the confused jumble of Talo's thoughts, he drew himself up to his knees, and then to his feet. An unsteady jog brought him to the building's edge.

Blood streamed from the wound as he climbed down to the unlit alley below. His moccasins resting finally on the slick, rubbish-littered cobblestones, he paused, forcing clarity into his head. An assassin war had begun this night. But which Clan Leader was fool enough to believe he or she could usurp Vorcan's mastery of the Guild? In any case, he would return to his clan's nest, if possible. With this in mind, he began to run.

He had dashed into the shadows of his third alley when ice trickled down his spine. Breath catching, Talo froze. The sensation creeping over him was unmistakable, as certain as instinct: he was being stalked. He glanced down at the blood-soaked front of his shirt and realized that there was no hope of outrunning his hunter. No doubt his stalker had seen him enter the alley and even now had a crossbow trained on its mouth at the far end. At least, that is how Talo would play it.

He'd have to turn the game round, set a trap. And for that he'd need the rooftops. Talo turned back to the alley-mouth he had just entered and studied the nearby buildings. Two streets to his right squatted the K'rul Temple. His gaze fixed on the dark edifice that was the belfry. *There.*

The climb left him close to unconsciousness, and he now crouched in the belfry's shadow one building away from the temple. His exertions had pumped blood from his shoulder in horrifying volume. He'd seen blood before, of course, but never so much of his own at one time. He wondered for the first time seriously if he would die. A numbness spread in his arms and legs, and he knew if he remained where he was any longer he might never leave. With a soft grunt he pushed himself upright. The jump down to the temple roof was only a matter of a few yards, but the impact jarred him to his knees.

Gasping, Talo drove thoughts of failure from his mind. All that was left was to climb down the temple's inner wall to the court, then ascend the belfry's spiral staircase. Two tasks. Two simple tasks. And, once within the belfry's shadows, he could command every nearby rooftop. And the stalker would come to him. Talo paused to check his own crossbow, which was strapped to his back, and the three quarrels sheathed on his left thigh.

He glared into the darkness around him. 'Whoever you are, you bastard,' he whispered, 'I want you.'

He began to crawl across the temple roof.

The lock on the jewel box had proved simple to pick. Ten minutes after entering the room Crokus had swept it clean. A small fortune's worth of gold, gem- and pearl-studded jewellery now resided in a small leather bag tied to his belt.

He squatted by the dressing-table and held in his hands his final prize. *This, I'll keep.* The item was a sky-blue silk turban with gold-braided tassels, no doubt intended for the upcoming Fête. He ended his long minute of admiration, tucked the turban under an arm, then rose. His gaze lingered on the bed across from him, and he moved closer.

The netting obscured the form half buried beneath soft blankets. Another step brought him to the bedframe's edge. From the waist up the girl was naked. An embarrassed flush rose in the thief's cheeks, but he did not look away. *Queen of Dreams, but she's lovely!* At seventeen years of age, Crokus had seen enough whores and dancers not to tremble agape at a woman's exposed virtues; even still his gaze lingered. Then, grimacing, he headed back to the balcony door. A moment later he was outside. He drew a deep breath of the cool night air to clear his head. In the blanket of darkness overhead a handful of stars shone sufficiently bright to pierce the gauze of clouds. Not clouds, but smoke, drifting across the lake from the north. The word of Pale's fall to the Malazan Empire had been on the tongues of everyone for the past two days.

And we're next.

His uncle had told him that the Council still frantically proclaimed neutrality, desperate in their efforts to separate the city from the now destroyed Free Cities alliance. But the Malazans didn't seem to be listening. *And why should they?* Uncle

Mammot had asked. *Darujhistan's army is a contemptible handful of noble sons who do nothing but strut back and forth on Whore Street, gripping their jewelled swords . . .*

Crokus climbed to the estate's roof and padded silently across its tiles. Another house, of equal height, was before him, its flat top less than six feet away. The thief paused at the edge and looked down to the alley thirty feet below, seeing only a pool of darkness, then he jumped to land softly on the next roof.

He began to cross it. Off to his left rose the stark silhouette of K'rul's belfry tower, gnarled like a bony fist thrust into the night sky. Crokus brought one hand down to the leather bag tied to his belt, probing with his fingers the knot and the condition of the drawstrings. Satisfied that all was secure, he checked the turban tucked beneath a strap of his harness. All was well. He continued his soundless way across the rooftop. A fine night indeed. Crokus smiled to himself.

Talo Krafar opened his eyes. Dazed and uncomprehending, he stared about himself. Where was he? Why did he feel so weak? Then memory returned, and a groan slipped from his lips. He had blacked out, leaning here against this marble pillar. But what had awoken him? Stiffening, the assassin pushed himself up on the dusty column and scanned the rooftops below. There! A figure moved across the flat top of a building less that fifty feet away.

Now, you bastard. Now. He raised his crossbow, anchoring one elbow against the pillar. He had already cocked his weapon, though he had no memory of having done so. At this distance there was no chance of missing. In seconds his stalker would be dead. Talo bared his teeth and took careful aim.

Crokus was half-way across the rooftop, one hand tracing the silk finery of the turban snug over his heart, when a coin

185

clattered loudly at his feet. Instinctively he pounced down and trapped it beneath both hands. Something hissed through the air immediately above his head, and he looked up, startled, then ducked again as a ceramic tile shattered twenty feet away.

He moaned with sudden realization. As he clambered to his feet one hand absently collected the coin and tucked it under his belt.

Talo cursed in disbelief. He lowered the crossbow and stared down at the figure, dumbfounded, until his instinct for danger asserted itself one last time. Whirling, he caught a blurred glimpse of a cloaked figure standing before him, arms raised. Then the arms flashed down and two long, grooved daggers slid into Talo's chest. With a final baffled grunt, the assassin died.

A grating sound reached Crokus's ears and he spun to face the belfry. A black shape tumbled from between the pillars and landed with a thump fifteen feet away. Moments later a crossbow clanged down beside it. Crokus looked up to see a silhouette framed between the pillars, glittering long-bladed knives in its hands. The figure seemed to be studying him.

'Oh, Mowri,' the thief prayed, then turned and ran.

In the K'rul belfry the killer's oddly shaped eyes watched the thief scamper towards the rooftop's far side. With a slight lifting of its head the killer sniffed the air, then frowned. A burst of power had just frayed the fabric of night, like a finger poking through rotted cloth. And, through the rent, something had come.

The thief reached the far edge and disappeared over it. The killer hissed a spell in a language older than the belfry and the temple, a language that had not been heard in this land for millennia, then sprang from the tower. Enwreathed in magic,

186

the killer's descent to the rooftop below was slow, controlled. The landing came as a light brush on the tiles.

A second figure appeared, its cloak spread like a black wing, from the above darkness to join the first. Then a third, also descending in silence, landed on the rooftop. They spoke briefly. The last to arrive muttered a command, then moved off. The remaining two exchanged a few last words, then set out on the thief's trail, the second one preparing its crossbow.

Ten minutes later Crokus leaned against the sloped roof of a merchant's house to regain his breath. He'd seen no one, heard nothing. Either the killer hadn't pursued or he had managed to lose him. Or her. In his mind returned his single vision of the figure as it stood in the belfry. No, unlikely that it could be a woman – too tall, perhaps six and a half feet, and thin.

A tremor ran through the young thief. What had he stumbled on? An assassin had almost skewered him, and then had himself been murdered. A Guild war? If so, it made the rooftops a risky place to be.

Warily, Crokus rose and looked about him.

A tile further along the roof clattered down the sloped side. Crokus whirled to see the killer dashing towards him. One look at the two daggers flashing in the air and the thief darted to the roof's edge and leaped out into darkness.

The building across from him was too distant, but Crokus had chosen his resting place on familiar territory. As he fell into the shadows he reached out grasping hands. The guidewire caught his arms near the elbows and he scrambled frantically for a secure grip, then hung dangling twenty feet above the alley.

While most of the clothes-lines spanning the city's streets were just thin, unreliable hemp, among them were wrapped wires. Placed by thieves generations past they were securely bolted to the walls. By day Monkey Road, as the thieves called

187

it, looked no different from any other line, festooned with undergarments and sheets. With the sun's setting, however, came its true purpose.

With hands burned raw Crokus made his way along the wire towards the far wall. He chanced to glance up then, and froze. On the roof's edge before him stood a second hunter, taking careful aim with a heavy, antique crossbow.

Crokus let go of the wire. A quarrel whizzed directly above his head as he fell. From behind and below a window shattered. His drop was cut short by the first of a series of clothes-lines, tugging his limbs and twitching him about before snapping. After what seemed an eternity of bone-wrenching jerks and the whip of cord slicing through his clothes and flaying his skin, Crokus struck the alley's cobblestones, straight-legged and leaning far forward. His knees buckled. He dipped a shoulder enough to earn a slightly cushioned roll, brought up short when his head struck a wall.

Dazed and groaning, Crokus pushed himself upright. He looked up. Through vision blurred with pain he saw a figure descending in seeming slow-motion immediately overhead. The thief's eyes widened. *Sorcery!*

He turned and staggered dizzily before managing a limping run down the alleyway. He reached the corner and, briefly lit by gaslight, hurried across a wide street then entered the mouth of another alley. Once in its shadow, Crokus stopped. Cautiously, he poked his head out from the wall's edge for a look. A quarrel struck the brick beside his face. He jumped back into the alley, spun and sprinted.

Above him Crokus heard the flapping of a cloak. A burning spasm in his left hip made him stumble. Another quarrel whipped past his shoulder and skidded on the cobblestones. The spasm passed as quickly as it had come and he staggered on. Ahead, at the alley-mouth, was the lit doorway of a tenement. An old woman sat on the stone steps puffing on a pipe. Her eyes glittered as she watched the thief approach. As Crokus bounded past her and up the steps she rapped the pipe against the sole of her shoe. Sparks rained on to the cobbles.

Crokus pushed open the door and plunged inside. He paused. A narrow, poorly lit hallway was before him, a staircase crowded with children at the far end. His eyes on the stairs, he jogged up the hall. From the curtained doorways on either side came a cacophony of noise: voices raised in argument, wailing babies, the clatter of cookware.

'Don't you people ever sleep?' Crokus shouted as he ran. The children on the stairs scampered out of his way and he took the warped steps two at a time. On the top floor he stopped at a door a third of the way down the hall, this one solid oak. He pushed it open and entered the room within.

An old man sitting behind a massive desk looked up briefly from his work, then resumed his frantic scrawl on a sheet of crinkled parchment. 'Evening, Crokus,' he said distractedly.

'And to you, Uncle,' Crokus gasped.

On Uncle Mammot's shoulder squatted a small winged monkey, whose glittering, half-mad gaze followed the young thief's dart across the room to the window opposite the door. Flinging open the shutters Crokus climbed up on to the sill. Below was a squalid, overgrown garden mostly lost in shadows. A lone, gnarled tree rose upward. He eyed the branches across from him, then gripped the window-frame and leaned back. He drew a deep breath, then propelled himself forward.

As he passed through the intervening gap he heard a surprised grunt come from directly above, then a wild scratching against stone. An instant later someone crashed down into the garden below. Cats shrieked and a voice groaned out a single pained curse.

Crokus clung to a bowing branch. He timed each bounce of the resilient wood then extended his legs as the branch pulled him up. His moccasins landed on a window-sill and held.

Grunting, he swung himself on to it and let go of the branch. He punched at the wooden shutters. They sprang inward and Crokus followed head first, down on to the floor and rolling to his feet.

He heard movement from another room in the apartment. Scrambling to his feet, he bolted for the hallway door, flung it open and slipped out just as a hoarse voice shouted a curse behind him. Crokus ran to the far end of the passage, where a ladder led to a hatch on the ceiling.

Soon he was on the roof. He crouched in the darkness and tried to catch his breath. The burning sensation returned to his hip. He must have damaged something in his fall from the guidewire. He reached down to massage the spot and found his fingers pressing something hard, round and hot. *The coin!* Crokus reached for it.

Just then he heard a sudden whistling sound, and chips of stone spattered him. Ducking, he saw a quarrel, its shaft split by the impact, bounce once on the rooftop then plummet over the edge, spinning wildly. A soft moan escaped his lips and he scrambled across the roof to the far side. Without pause he jumped. Ten feet down was an awning, sagged and stretched out of shape, on which he landed. The iron spars framing the canvas dipped but held. From there it was a quick climb down to the street.

Crokus jogged to the corner, where an old building squatted with yellow light bleeding through dirty windows. A wooden sign hung above the door, bearing the faded image of a bird dead on its back, feet jutting upward. The thief bounded up the steps and pushed open the door.

A rush of light and noise washed over him like balm. He slammed the door behind him and leaned against it. He closed his eyes, pulling the disguising cloth from his face and head, revealing shoulder-length black hair – now dripping with sweat – and regular features surrounding light blue eyes.

As he reached up to wipe his brow a mug was pushed into his hand. Crokus opened his eyes to see Sulty hurry by, carrying on one hand a tray loaded with pewter tankards. She glanced at him over her shoulder and grinned. 'Rough night, Crokus?'

He stared at her, then said, 'No, nothing special.' He raised the mug to his lips and drank deep.

Across the street from the ramshackle Phoenix Inn, a hunter stood at the roof's edge and studied the door through which the thief had just passed. The crossbow lay cradled in its arms.

The second hunter arrived, sheathing two long-knives as it came alongside the first.

'What happened to you?' the first hunter asked quietly, in its native tongue.

'Had an argument with a cat.'

The two were silent for a moment, then the first hunter sighed worriedly. 'All in all, too awry to be natural.'

The other agreed. 'You felt the parting too, then.'

'An Ascendant . . . meddled. Too cautious to show itself fully, however.'

'Unfortunate. It's been years since I last killed an Ascendant.'

They began to check their weapons. The first hunter loaded the crossbow and slipped four extra quarrels in its belt. The second hunter removed each long-knife and cleaned it carefully of sweat and grime.

They heard someone approach from behind, and turned to see their commander.

'He's in the inn,' the second hunter said.

'We'll leave no witnesses to this secret war with the Guild,' the first added.

The commander glanced at the door of the Phoenix Inn. Then, to the hunters, she said, 'No. The wagging tongue of a witness might be useful to our efforts.'

191

'The runt had help,' the first hunter said meaningfully.

The commander shook her head. 'We return to the fold.'

'Very well.'

The two hunters put away their weapons. The first glanced back at the inn and asked, 'Who protected him, do you think?'

The second hunter snarled. 'Someone with a sense of humour.'

CHAPTER SIX

There is a cabal breathing
deeper than the bellows
drawing up the emerald fires
beneath rain-glistened cobbles,
while you may hear the groaning
from the caverns below,
the whisper of sorcery
is less than the dying sigh
of a thief stumbling unwilling
into Darujhistan's secret web . . .

Cabal (fragment)
Puddle (b.1122?)

The splayed tip of her right wing brushed the scarred black rock as Crone climbed the whistling updraughts of Moon's Spawn. From the pocked caves and starlit ledges her restless brothers and sisters called out to her as she passed. 'Do we fly?' they asked. But Crone made no reply. Her glittering black eyes were fixed on heaven's vault. Her enormous wings beat a thundering refrain of taut, unrelenting power. She had no time for the nervous cackling of the younglings; no time for answering their simplistic needs with the wisdom her thousand years of life had earned her.

This night, Crone flew for her lord.

As she rose above the shattered peaks of the Moon's crest a high wind swept her wings, rasping dry and cold along her oily feathers. Around her, thin wisps of shredded smoke rode the currents of night air like lost spirits. Crone circled once, her sharp gaze catching the glimmer of the few remaining fires among the crags below, then she dipped a wing and sailed out on the wind's tide as it rolled northward to Lake Azur.

The featureless expanse of the Dwelling Plain was beneath her, the grass sweeping in grey waves unbroken by house or hill. Directly ahead lay the glittering jewelled cloak that was Darujhistan, casting into the sky a sapphire glow. As she neared the city her unnaturally acute vision detected, here and there among the estates crowding the upper tier, the aquamarine emanation of sorcery.

Crone cackled aloud. Magic was ambrosia to Great Ravens. They were drawn to it by the scent of blood and power, and within its aura their lifespans lengthened into centuries. Its musk had other effects as well. Crone cackled again. Her gaze fixed on one particular estate, around which glowed a profusion of protective sorcery. Her lord had imparted to her a thorough description of the magical signature she must find, and now she had found it. Crooking her wings, she sank gracefully towards the estate.

Inland from Gadrobi District's harbour the land rose in four tiers climbing eastward. Ramped cobblestone streets, worn to a polished mosaic, marked Gadrobi District's Trade Streets, five in all, which were the only routes through Marsh District and into the next tier, Lakefront District. Beyond Lakefront's crooked aisles twelve wooden gates opened on to Daru District, and from Daru another twelve gates – these ones

194

manned by the City Watch and barred by iron portcullis – connected the lower and upper cities.

On the fourth and highest tier brooded the estates of Darujhistan's nobility as well as its publicly known sorcerers. At the intersection of Old King's Walk and View Street rose a flat-topped hill on which sat Majesty Hall, where each day the Council gathered. A narrow park encircled the hill, with sand-strewn pathways winding among centuries-old acacias. At the park's entrance, near High Gallows Hill, stood a massive rough-hewn stone gate, the last-surviving remnant of the castle that once commanded Majesty Hill.

The days of kings had long since ended in Darujhistan. The gate, known as Despot's Barbican, stood stark and unadorned, its lattice of cracks a fading script of past tyranny.

In the shadow of the Barbican's single massive lintel stone stood two men. One, his shoulder against the pitted rock, wore a ringed hauberk and a boiled leather cap bearing the City Watch insignia. Scabbarded to his belt was a plain shortsword, its grip of wrapped leather worn smooth. A pike leaned against one shoulder. He was nearing the end of his midnight guard duty and patiently awaited the arrival of the man who would officially relieve him. The guard's eyes flicked on occasion to the second man, with whom he had shared this place many another night over the past year. The glances he cast at the well-dressed gentleman were surreptitious, empty of expression.

As with every other time Councilman Turban Orr came to the gate at this dead hour of night, the nobleman had scarcely deemed the guard worthy of notice; nor had he ever given an indication that he recognized the guard as being the same man each time.

Turban Orr seemed a man short on patience, forever pacing and fretting, pausing every now and then to adjust his jewelled burgundy cloak. The councilman's polished boots clicked as he

195

paced, throwing a soft echo under the Barbican. From the shadow the guard's gaze caught Orr's gloved hand where it rested on the silver pommel of a duelling sword, noting the index finger tapping in time with the boot clicks.

At the early part of his watch, long before the arrival of the councilman, the guard would walk slowly around the Barbican, reaching out on occasion to touch the ancient, grim stonework. Six years' worth of night watch at this gate had bred a close relationship between the man and the rough-cut basalt: he knew every crack, every chisel scar; he knew where the fittings had weakened, where time and the elements had squeezed mortar from between the stones then gnawed it to dust. And he also knew that its apparent weaknesses were but a deception. The Barbican, and all it stood for, patiently waited still, a spectre of the past, hungry to be born yet again.

And that, the guard had long ago vowed, he would never let it do – if such things were within his power. Despot's Barbican provided the man with every reason he needed to be what he was: Circle Breaker, a spy.

Both he and the councilman awaited the arrival of the other; the one who never failed to appear. Turban Orr would growl his usual complaint, disgusted with tardiness; then he would grasp the other's arm and they would walk side by side beneath the Barbican's brooding lintel stone. And, with eyes long accustomed to darkness, the guard would mark the other's face, burning it indelibly in the superb memory hidden behind expressionless, unmemorable features.

By the time the two Council members returned from their walk, the guard would have been relieved and well on his way to delivering a message according to his master's instructions. If Circle Breaker's luck held, he might survive the civil war into which Darujhistan, he felt, was about to plunge – and never mind the Malazan nemesis. One nightmare at a time, he often told himself, particularly on nights like these, when Despot's Barbican seemed to breathe its promise of resurrection with mocking certainty.

'As this may be in your interest,' High Alchemist Baruk read aloud from the parchment note in his plump hands. Always the same opening line, hinting of disquieting knowledge. An hour earlier his servant Roald had delivered the note, which, like all the others that had come to him over the past year, had been found tucked into one of the ornamental murder holes in the estate's rear postern gate.

Recognizing the pattern, Baruk had immediately read the missive then dispatched his messengers out into the city. Such news demanded action, and he was one of the few secret powers within Darujhistan capable of dealing with it.

Now he sat in a plush chair in his study, musing. His deceptively sleepy gaze flicked down again to the words on the parchment. 'Councilman Turban Orr walks in the garden with Councilman Feder. I remain known only as Circle Breaker, a servant of the Eel, whose interests continue to coincide with your own.' Once again Baruk felt temptation. With his talents it would be a small thing to discover the writer's identity – though not the Eel's, of course: that was an identity sought by many, all to no avail – but, as always, something held him back.

He shifted his bulk on the chair and sighed. 'Very well, Circle Breaker, I'll continue to honour you, though clearly you know more of me than I of you, and fortunate it is indeed that your master's interests coincide with my own. Still.' He frowned, thinking about the Eel, about the man's – or woman's – undisclosed interests. He knew enough to recognize that too many forces had come into play – a gathering of Ascendant powers was a fell thing. To continue to step unseen in defence of the city was becoming increasingly difficult. So, the question came yet again: Was this Eel using him as well?

Oddly enough, he did not feel too concerned about this possibility. So much vital information had been passed into his hands already.

He folded the parchment carefully and muttered a simple cantrip. The note vanished with a small plop of displaced air, joining the others in a safe place.

Baruk closed his eyes. Behind him the broad window shutters rattled in a gust of wind, then settled again. A moment later there came a sharp rap against the smoky glass. Baruk sat upright, his eyes startled open. A second rap, louder than the first, brought him round with a swift alacrity surprising for one of his girth. On his feet, he faced the window. Something crouched on the ledge, visible through the shutters only as a bulky black shape.

Baruk frowned. *Impossible*. Nothing could penetrate his magic barriers undetected. The alchemist gestured with one hand, and the shutters sprang open. Behind the glass waited a Great Raven. Its head snapped to view Baruk with one eye, then the other. It pushed boldly against the thin glass with its massive, ridged chest. The pane bulged, then shattered.

His Warren fully open, Baruk raised both hands, a savage spell on his lips.

'Don't waste your breath!' the Raven rasped, swelling its chest and ruffling its mangy feathers to rid itself of glass shards. It cocked its head. 'You've called your guards,' it observed. 'No need, Wizard.' A single hop brought the enormous bird on to the floor. 'I bring words you will value. Have you anything to eat?'

Baruk studied the creature. 'I'm not in the habit of inviting Great Ravens into my home,' he said. 'You are no disguised demon, either.'

'Of course not. I'm named Crone.' Her head bobbed mockingly. 'At your pleasure, Lord.'

Baruk hesitated, considering. After a moment he sighed and

198

said, 'Very well. I've returned my guards to their posts. My servant Roald comes with the leavings of supper, if that's agreeable to you.'

'Excellent!' Crone waddled across the floor to settle on the rug before the fireplace. 'There, Lord. Now, a calming crystal of wine, don't you think?'

'Who has sent you, Crone?' Baruk asked, walking over to the decanter on his desk. Normally he did not drink after sunset, for night was when he worked, but he had to acknowledge Crone's perceptiveness. A calming balm was exactly what he needed.

The Great Raven hesitated slightly before answering, 'The Lord of Moon's Spawn.'

Baruk paused in the filling of his glass. 'I see,' he said quietly, struggling to control his surging heart. He set the decanter down slowly and, with great concentration, raised the goblet to his lips. The liquid was cool on his tongue, and its passage down his throat indeed calmed him. 'Well, then,' he said, turning, 'what would your lord have of a peaceful alchemist?'

Crone's chipped beak opened in what Baruk realized was silent laughter. The bird fixed a single glittering eye on him. 'Your answer rode the very breath of your words, Lord. Peace. My lord wishes to speak with you. He wishes to come here, this very night. Within the hour.'

'And you're to await my answer.'

'Only if you decide quickly, Lord. I have things to do, after all. I'm more than a simple message-bearer. Those who know wisdom when they hear it hold me dear. I am Crone, eldest of the Moon's Great Ravens, whose eyes have looked upon a thousand years of human folly. Hence my tattered coat and broken beak as evidence of your indiscriminate destruction. I am but a winged witness to your eternal madness.'

In quiet mockery Baruk said, 'More than just a witness. It's well known how you and your kind feasted on the plain outside Pale's walls.'

199

'Yet we were not the first to feast on flesh and blood, Lord, lest you forget.'

Baruk turned away. 'Far be it for me to defend my species,' he muttered, more to himself than to Crone, whose words had stung him. His eyes fell on the shards of glass littering the floor. He voiced a mending spell and watched as they reassembled. 'I will speak with your lord, Crone.' He nodded as the glass pane rose from the floor and returned to the window-frame. 'Tell me, will he as easily disdain my wards as you did?'

'My lord is possessed of honour and courtesy,' Crone replied ambiguously. 'I shall call him, then?'

'Do so,' Baruk said, sipping his wine. 'An avenue will be provided for his passage.'

There came a knock at the door.

'Yes?'

Roald stepped inside. 'Someone is at the gate wishing to speak with you,' the white-haired servant said, setting down a plate heaped with roast pork.

Baruk glanced at Crone and raised an eyebrow.

The bird ruffled her feathers. 'Your guest is mundane, a restless personage whose thoughts are thick with greed and treachery. A demon crouches on his shoulder, named Ambition.'

'His name, Roald?' Baruk asked.

The servant hesitated, his soft eyes flicked uneasily at the bird now ambling towards the food.

Baruk laughed. 'My wise guest's counsel indicates she well knows the man's name. Speak on, Roald.'

'Councilman Turban Orr.'

'I would remain for this,' Crone said. 'If you would seek my counsel.'

'Please do, and, yes, I would,' the alchemist replied.

'I am no more than a pet dog,' the Great Raven crooned slyly, anticipating his next question. 'To the councilman's eyes, that is. My words a beast's whimper to his ears.' She speared a piece of meat and swallowed it quickly.

Baruk found himself beginning to like this mangy old witch of a bird. 'Bring the councilman to us, Roald.'

The servant departed.

Archaic torches lit an estate's high-walled garden with a flickering light that threw wavering shadows across the pavestones. As a nightwind swept in from the lake, rustling leaves, the shadows danced like imps. On the second floor of the building was a balcony overlooking the garden. Behind the curtained window, two figures moved.

Rallick Nom lay prone on the garden wall in a niche of darkness beneath the estate's gabled cornice. He studied the feminine silhouette with the patience of a snake. It was the fifth night in a row that he had occupied his hidden vantage-point. The Lady Simtal's lovers numbered as many, but he had identified two in particular worthy of attention. Both were city councilmen.

The glass door opened and a figure walked out on to the balcony. Rallick smiled as he recognized Councilman Lim. The assassin shifted position slightly, slipping one gloved hand under the stock of his crossbow, reaching up with the other to swing back the oiled crank. His eyes on the man leaning against the balcony railing across from him, Rallick carefully inserted a quarrel. A glance down at the bolt's iron head reassured him. The poison glittered wetly along the razor-sharp edges. Returning his attention to the balcony he saw that Lady Simtal had joined Lim.

No wonder there's no shortage of lovers for that one, Rallick thought, his eyes narrowing in study. Her black hair, now unpinned, flowed down sleek and shiny to the small of her back. She wore a gauze-thin nightdress and, with the lamps of the room behind her, her body's round curves were clearly visible.

As they spoke their voices carried to where Rallick lay hidden.

'Why the alchemist?' Lady Simtal was asking, evidently resuming a conversation begun inside. 'A fat old man smelling of sulphur and brimstone. Hardly suggestive of political power. Not even a council member, is he?'

Lim laughed softly. 'Your naïvety is a charm, Lady, a charm.'

Simtal pulled back from the railing and crossed her arms. 'Educate me, then.' Her words came sharp, tightly bridled.

Lim shrugged. 'We have naught but suspicions, Lady. But it is the wise wolf that follows every spoor, no matter how slight. The alchemist would have people think as you do. A doddering old fool.' Lim paused, as if in thought, perhaps weighing how much he should reveal. 'We have sources,' he continued cautiously, 'among the magery. They inform us of one certain fact heavy with implications. A good many of the wizards in the city fear the alchemist, and they name him by a title – that alone suggests a secret cabal of some sort. A gathering of sorcerers, Lady, is a fell thing.'

Lady Simtal had returned to the councilman's side. Both now leaned on the railing studying the dark garden below. The woman was silent for a time, then she said, 'He has Council ties?'

'If he has, the evidence is buried deep.' Lim flashed a grin. 'And if he hasn't, then that might change – this very night.'

Politics, Rallick snarled silently. *And power. The bitch spreads her legs to the Council, offering a vice few can ignore.* Rallick's hands twitched. He would kill this night. Not a contract: the Guild had no part in this. The vendetta was personal. She was gathering power around her, insulating herself, and Rallick thought he understood why. The ghosts of betrayal would not leave her alone.

Patience, he reminded himself, as he took aim. For the last two years the life of Lady Simtal had been one of indolence, the riches she had stolen had served to whet her every greed, and the prestige as sole owner of the estate had done much to grease the hinges of her bedroom door. The crime she'd committed had not been against Rallick but, unlike her victim, Rallick had no pride to halt vengeance.

Patience, Rallick repeated, his lips moving to the word as he sighted down the crossbow's length. A quality defined by its reward, and that reward was but moments away.

'A fine-looking hound,' Councilman Turban Orr said, as he handed Roald his cloak.

In the room Baruk was the only one capable of discerning the aura of illusion surrounding the black hunting dog lying curled on the rug before the fireplace. The alchemist smiled and gestured to a chair. 'Please be seated, Councilman.'

'I apologize for disturbing you so late at night,' Orr said, as he lowered himself into the plush chair. Baruk sat down opposite him, Crone between them. 'It's said,' Orr continued, 'that alchemy flowers best in deep darkness.'

'Hence you gambled on my being awake,' Baruk said. 'A well-placed wager, Councilman. Now, what would you have of me?'

Orr reached down to pat Crone's head.

Baruk looked away to keep himself from laughing.

'The Council votes in two days,' Orr said. 'With a proclamation of neutrality such as we seek, war with the Malazan Empire will be averted – so we believe, but there are those in the Council who do not. Pride has made them belligerent, unreasonable.'

'As it does us all,' murmured Baruk.

Orr leaned forward. 'The support of Darujhistan's sorcerers would do much to favour our cause,' he said.

'Careful,' Crone rumbled. 'This man now hunts in earnest.'

Orr glanced down at the dog.

203

'A bad leg,' Baruk said. 'Pay it no mind.' The alchemist leaned back in his chair and plucked at a loose thread on his robe. 'I admit to some confusion, Councilman. You appear to be assuming some things I cannot countenance.' Baruk spread his hands and met Orr's eyes. 'Darujhistan's sorcerers, for one. You could travel the Ten Worlds and not find a more spiteful, rabid collection of humanity. Oh, I don't suggest that they are all like this – there are those whose only interest, indeed, obsession, lies in the pursuit of their craft. Their noses have been buried in books so long they could not even tell you what century this is. The others find bickering their only true pleasure in life.'

A smile had come to Orr's thin lips as Baruk spoke. 'But,' he said with a cunning gleam in his dark eyes, 'there is one thing they all acknowledge.'

'Oh? What is that, Councilman?'

'Power. We're all aware of your eminence among the city's mages, Baruk. Your word alone would bring others.'

'I'm flattered that you would think so,' Baruk replied. 'Unfortunately, therein lies your second erroneous assumption. Even if I had such influence as you suggest,' Crone snorted and Baruk flicked a savage glare at her, then continued, 'which I do not, for what possible reason would I support such a wilfully ignorant position as yours? A proclamation of neutrality? Might as well whistle against the wind, Councilman. What purpose would it serve?'

Orr's smile had tightened. 'Surely, Lord,' he purred, 'you have no wish to share the same fate as the wizards of Pale?'

Baruk frowned. 'What do you mean?'

'Assassinated by an Empire Claw. Moon's Spawn was entirely on its own against the Empire.'

'Your information contradicts mine,' Baruk said stiffly, then cursed himself.

'Lean not too heavily on this one,' Crone said smugly. 'You are both wrong.'

Orr's eyebrows had risen at Baruk's words. 'Indeed? Perhaps it might profit us both to share our information?'

'Unlikely,' Baruk said. 'Throwing the threat of the Empire at me implies what? That if the proclamation is voted down, the city's sorcerers will all die at the Empire's hand. But if it wins, you're free to justify opening the gates to the Malazans in peaceful co-existence, and in such a scenario the city's magery lives on.'

'Astute, Lord,' Crone said.

Baruk studied the anger now visible beneath Orr's expression. 'Neutrality? How you've managed to twist that word. Your proclamation serves the first step towards total annexation, Councilman. Fortunate for you that I cast no weight, no vote, no influence.' Baruk rose. 'Roald will see you out.'

Turban Orr also rose. 'You've made a grave error,' he said. 'The proclamation's wording is not yet complete. It seems we would do well to remove any consideration regarding Darujhistan's magery.'

'Too bold,' Crone observed. 'Prod him and see what more comes forth.'

Baruk strode towards the window. 'One may only hope,' he said drily over a shoulder, 'that your vote fails to win the day.'

Orr's reply was hot and rushed. 'By my count we've reached a majority this very night, Alchemist. You could have provided the honey on the cream. Alas,' he sneered, 'we'll win by only one vote. But that will suffice.'

Baruk turned to face Orr as Roald quietly entered the room, bearing the councilman's cloak.

Crone stretched out on the rug. 'On this night of all nights,' she said, in mock dismay, 'to tempt myriad fates with such words.' The Great Raven cocked her head. Faintly, as from a great distance, she thought she could hear the spinning of a coin.

There was a tremble of power, coming from somewhere within the city, and Crone shivered.

Rallick Nom waited. No more indolence for the Lady Simtal. The end of such luxuries came this night. The two figures moved away from the railing and faced the glass door. Rallick's finger tightened on the trigger.

He froze. A whirring, spinning sound filled his head, whispering words that left him bathed in sudden sweat. All at once everything shifted, turned over in his mind. His plan for quick vengeance tumbled into disarray, and from the ruins arose something far more . . . elaborate.

All this had come between breaths. Rallick's gaze cleared. Lady Simtal and Councilman Lim stood at the door. The woman reached out to slide the panel to one side. Rallick swerved his crossbow an inch to the left, then squeezed the trigger. The blackened iron rib of the bow bucked with the release of tension. The quarrel sped outward, so fast as to be invisible until it hit home.

A figure on the balcony spun with the quarrel's impact, arms thrown out as it stumbled. The glass door shattered as the figure fell through it.

Lady Simtal screamed in horror.

Rallick waited no longer. Rolling on to his back he reached up and slid the crossbow into the narrow ledge between the cornice and the roof. Then he slipped down the outside of the wall, hung with his hands briefly as shouts of alarm filled the estate. A moment later he dropped, spinning as he fell, and landed cat-like in the alley.

The assassin straightened, adjusted his cloak, then calmly walked into the side-street, away from the estate. No more indolence for the Lady Simtal. But no quick demise, either. A very powerful, very well-respected member of the City Council had just been assassinated on her balcony. Lim's wife – now widow – would certainly have something to say about this. The first phase, Rallick told himself as he strode through Osserc's Gate and descended the wide ramp leading down into the Daru District, just the first phase, an opening gambit, a hint to Lady Simtal that a hunt has begun, with the eminent mistress herself as the quarry. *It won't be easy: the woman's no slouch in the intrigue game.*

'There'll be more blood,' he whispered aloud, as he turned a corner and approached the poorly lit entrance to the Phoenix Inn. 'But in the end she'll fall, and with that fall an old friend will rise.' As he neared the inn a figure stepped from the shadows of an adjacent alleyway. Rallick stopped. The figure gestured, then stepped back into the darkness.

Rallick followed. In the alley he waited for his eyes to adjust.

The man in front of him sighed. 'Your vendetta probably saved your life tonight,' he said, his tone bitter.

Rallick leaned against a wall and crossed his arms. 'Oh?'

Clan Leader Ocelot stepped close, his narrow, pitted face twisted into its habitual scowl. 'The night's been a shambles, Nom. You've heard nothing?'

'No.'

Ocelot's thin lips curled into a humourless smile. 'A war has begun on the rooftops. Someone is killing us. We lost five Roamers in less than an hour, meaning there's more than one killer out there.'

'Undoubtedly,' Rallick replied, fidgeting as the damp stones of the inn's wall reached through his cloak and touched his flesh with chill. As always, Guild affairs bored him.

Ocelot continued, 'We lost that bull of a man, Talo Krafar, and a Clan Leader.' The man snapped a glance over his shoulder as if expecting a sudden dagger to come flashing at his own back.

Despite his lack of interest Rallick's eyebrows lifted at this last bit of news. 'They must be good.'

'Good? All of our eye-witnesses are dead, goes the sour joke this night. They don't make mistakes, the bastards.'

'Everyone makes mistakes,' Rallick muttered. 'Has Vorcan gone out?'

Ocelot shook his head. 'Not yet. She's too busy recalling all the Clans.'

Rallick frowned, curious in spite of himself. 'Could this be a challenge to her Guild mastery? Perhaps an inside thing, a faction—'

'You think we're all fools, don't you, Nom? That was Vorcan's first suspicion. No, it's not internal. Whoever's killing our people is from outside the Guild, outside the city.'

To Rallick the answer seemed obvious suddenly, and he shrugged. 'An Empire Claw, then.'

Though his expression bore reluctance, Ocelot nevertheless acknowledged agreement. 'Likely,' he grated. 'They're supposed to be the best, aren't they? But why go after the Guild? You'd think they'd be taking out the nobles.'

'Are you asking me to guess the Empire's intentions, Ocelot?'

The Clan Leader blinked, then his scowl deepened. 'I came to warn you. And that's a favour, Nom. With you wrapped up in this vendetta thing, the Guild's not obliged to spread its wing over you. A favour.'

Rallick pushed himself from the wall and turned to the alley-mouth. 'A favour, Ocelot?' He laughed softly.

'We're setting a trap,' Ocelot said, moving to block Rallick's way. He jerked his scarred chin at the Phoenix Inn. 'Make yourself visible, and leave no doubt as to what you do for a living.'

Rallick's gaze on Ocelot held steady, impassive. 'Bait.'

'Just do it.'

Without replying, Rallick left the alley, climbed the steps and entered the Phoenix Inn.

'There is a shaping in the night,' Crone said, after Turban Orr had left. The air around her shimmered as she assumed her true shape.

Baruk strode to his map table, hands clasped behind his back to still the trembling that had seized them. 'You felt it too, then.' He paused, then sighed. 'All in all, these seem the busiest hours.'

'A convergence of power ever yields thus,' Crone said, as she rose to stretch her wings. 'The black winds gather, Alchemist. Beware their flaying breath.'

Baruk grunted. 'While you ride them, a harbinger of our tragic ills.'

Crone laughed. She waddled to the window. 'My master comes. I've other tasks before me.'

Baruk turned. 'Permit me,' he said, gesturing. The window swung clear.

Crone flapped up on to the sill. She swivelled her head round and cocked an eye at Baruk. 'I see twelve ships riding a deep harbour,' she said. 'Eleven stand tall in flames.'

Baruk stiffened. He had not anticipated a prophecy. Now he was afraid. 'And the twelfth?' he asked, his voice barely a whisper.

'On the wind a hailstorm of sparks fill the night sky. I see them spinning, spinning about the last vessel.' Crone paused. 'Still spinning.' Then she was gone.

Baruk's shoulders slumped. He turned back to the map on the table and studied the eleven once Free Cities that now bore the Empire flag. Only Darujhistan remained, the twelfth and last marked by a flag that was not burgundy and grey. 'The passing of freedom,' he murmured.

Suddenly the walls around him groaned, and Baruk gasped as an enormous weight seemed to press down on him. The blood pounded in his head, lancing him with pain. He gripped the edge of the map table to steady himself. The incandescent globes of light suspended from the ceiling dimmed, then flickered out. In the darkness the alchemist heard cracks sweeping down the walls, as if a giant's hand had descended on the building. All at once the pressure vanished. Baruk raised a shaking hand to his sweat-slicked brow.

A soft voice spoke behind him. 'Greetings, High Alchemist. I am the Lord of Moon's Spawn.'

Still facing the table, Baruk closed his eyes and nodded. 'The title isn't necessary,' he whispered. 'Please call me Baruk.'

'I'm at home in darkness,' the Lord said. 'Will this prove an inconvenience, Baruk?'

The alchemist muttered a spell. Before him the details of the map on the table took on distinction, emanating a cool blue glow. He faced the Lord and was startled to discover that the tall, cloaked figure reflected as little heat as the room's inanimate objects. Nevertheless, he was able to distinguish quite clearly the man's features. 'You're Tiste Andii,' he said.

The Lord bowed slightly. His angled, multihued eyes scanned the room. 'Have you any wine, Baruk?'

'Of course, Lord.' The alchemist walked over to his desk.

'My name, as best as it can be pronounced by humans, is Anomander Rake.' The Lord followed Baruk to the desk, his boots clicking on the polished marble floor.

Baruk poured wine, then turned to study Rake with some curiosity. He had heard that Tiste Andii warriors were fighting the Empire up north, commanded by a savage beast of a man named Caladan Brood. They had allied with the Crimson Guard and, together, the two forces were decimating the Malazans. So, there were Tiste Andii in Moon's Spawn, and the man standing before him was their lord.

This moment marked the first time Baruk had ever seen a Tiste Andii face to face. He was more than a little disturbed. Such remarkable eyes, he thought. One moment a deep hue of amber, cat-like and unnerving, the next grey and banded like a snake's – a fell rainbow of colours to match any mood. He wondered if they were capable of lying.

In the alchemist's library lay copies of the surviving tomes of *Gothos' Folly*, Jaghut writings from millennia past. In them Tiste Andii were mentioned here and there in an aura of fear, Baruk recalled. Gothos himself, a Jaghut wizard who had descended the deepest warrens of Elder Magic, had praised the gods of the time that the Tiste Andii were so few in number. And if anything, the mysterious black-skinned race had dwindled since then.

Anomander Rake's skin was jet-black, befitting Gothos' descriptions, but his mane flowed silver. He stood close to seven feet tall. His features were sharp, as if cut from onyx, a slight upward tilt to the large vertical-pupilled eyes.

A two-handed sword was strapped to Rake's broad back, its silver dragonskull pommel and archaic crosshilt jutting from a wooden scabbard fully six and a half feet long. From the weapon bled power, staining the air like black ink in a pool of water. As his gaze rested on it Baruk almost reeled, seeing, for a brief moment, a vast darkness yawning before him, cold as the heart of a glacier, from which came the stench of antiquity and a faint groaning sound. Baruk wrenched his eyes from the weapon, looked up to find Rake studying him from over one shoulder.

The Tiste Andii quirked a knowing smile, then handed Baruk one of the wine-filled goblets. 'Was Crone her usual melodramatic self?'

Baruk blinked, then could not help but grin.

Rake sipped his wine. 'She's never been modest in displaying her talents. Shall we sit?'

'Of course,' Baruk replied, relaxing in spite of his trepidation. From his years of study the alchemist knew that great power shaped different souls differently. Had Rake's been

211

twisted Baruk would have known immediately. But the Lord's control seemed absolute. That alone engendered awe. The man shaped his power, not the other way around. Such control was, well, *inhuman*. He suspected that this would not be the first insight he'd have regarding this warrior-mage that would leave him astonished and frightened.

'She threw everything she had at me,' Rake said suddenly. The Tiste Andii's eyes shone green as glacial ice.

Startled by the vehemence of that outburst, Baruk frowned. *She? Oh, the Empress, of course.*

'And even then,' Rake continued, 'she couldn't bring me down.'

The alchemist stiffened in his chair. 'Yet,' he said cautiously, 'you were driven back, battered and beaten. I can feel your power, Anomander Rake,' he added, grimacing. 'It pulses from you like waves. So I must ask: how is it you were defeated? I know something of the Empire's High Mage Tayschrenn. He has power but it's no match to yours. So again I ask, how?'

His gaze on the map table, Rake replied, 'I've committed my sorcerers and warriors to Brood's north campaign.' He turned a humourless grin on Baruk. 'Within my city are children, priests and three elderly, exceedingly bookish warlocks.'

City? There was a city within Moon's Spawn?

A dun tone had entered Rake's eyes. 'I cannot defend an entire Moon. I cannot be everywhere at once. And as for Tayschrenn, he didn't give a damn about the people around him. I thought to dissuade him, make the price too high . . .' He shook his head as if perplexed, then he looked to Baruk. 'To save the home of my people, I retreated.'

'Leaving Pale to fall—' Baruk shut his mouth, cursing his lack of tact.

But Rake merely shrugged. 'I didn't anticipate that I'd face a full assault. My presence alone had been keeping the Empire at bay for almost two years.'

212

'I've heard the Empress is short of patience,' murmured Baruk thoughtfully. His eyes narrowed, then he looked up. 'You have asked to meet with me, Anomander Rake, and so here we are. What is it you wish from me?'

'An alliance,' the Moon's lord answered.

'With me? Personally?'

'No games, Baruk.' Rake's voice was suddenly cold. 'I'm not fooled by that Council of idiots bickering at Majesty Hall. I know that it's you and your fellow mages who rule Darujhistan.' He rose and glared down with eyes of grey. 'I'll tell you this. For the Empress your city is the lone pearl on this continent of mud. She wants it and what she wants she usually gets.'

Baruk reached down and plucked at the frayed edge of his robe. 'I see,' he said, in a low voice. 'Pale had its wizards.'

Rake frowned. 'Indeed.'

'Yet,' Baruk continued, 'when the battle was begun in earnest, your first thought was not for the alliance you made with the city but for the well-being of your Moon.'

'Who told you this?' Rake demanded.

Baruk looked up and raised both hands. 'Some of those wizards managed to escape.'

'They're in the city?' Rake's eyes had gone black.

Seeing them, Baruk felt sweat break out beneath his clothes. 'Why?' he asked.

'I want their heads,' Rake replied casually. He refilled his goblet and took a sip.

An icy hand had slipped around Baruk's heart and was now tightening. His headache had increased tenfold in the last few seconds. 'Why?' he asked again, the word coming out almost as a gasp.

If the Tiste Andii knew of the alchemist's sudden discomfort he made no sign of it. 'Why?' He seemed to roll the word in his mouth like wine, a light smile touching his lips. 'When the

213

Moranth army came down from the mountains, and Tayschrenn rode at the head of his wizard cadre, and when word spread that an Empire Claw had infiltrated the city,' Rake's smile twisted into a snarl, 'the wizards of Pale fled.' He paused, as if reliving memories. 'I dispatched the Claw when they were but a dozen steps inside the walls.' He paused again, his face betraying a flash of regret. 'Had the city's wizards remained, the assault would have been repelled. Tayschrenn, it seemed, was preoccupied with ... *other* imperatives. He'd saturated his position – a hilltop – with defensive wards. Then he unleashed demons not against me but against some of his companions. That baffled me but, rather than allow such conjurings to wander at will, I expended vital power destroying them.' He sighed and said, 'I pulled the Moon back mere minutes from its destruction. I left it to drift south and went after those wizards.'

'After them?'

'I tracked down all but two.' Rake gazed at Baruk. 'I want those two, preferably alive, but their heads will suffice.'

'You killed those you found? How?'

'With my sword, of course.'

Baruk recoiled as if struck. 'Oh,' he whispered. 'Oh.'

'The alliance,' Rake said, before draining his goblet.

'I'll speak to the Cabal on this matter,' Baruk answered, rising shakily to his feet. 'Word of the decision will be sent to you soon.' He stared at the sword strapped to the Tiste Andii's back. 'Tell me, if you get those wizards alive, will you use *that* on them?'

Rake frowned. 'Of course.'

Turning away, Baruk closed his eyes. 'You'll have their heads, then.'

Behind him Rake laughed harshly. 'There's too much mercy in your heart, Alchemist.'

* * *

214

The pale light beyond the window signified the dawn. Within the Phoenix Inn only one table remained occupied. Around it sat four men, one asleep in his chair with his head lying in a pool of stale beer. He snored loudly. The others were playing cards, two red-eyed with exhaustion while the last one studied his hand and talked. And talked.

'And then there was the time I saved Rallick Nom's life, at the back of All Eve's Street. Four, no, *five* nefarious hoodlums had backed the boy to a wall. He was barely standing, was Rallick, gushing blood from a hundred knife wounds. Clear to me was the grim fact that it couldn't last much longer, that tussle. I come up on them six assassins from behind, old Kruppe with fire dancing on his fingertips – a magical spell of frightful violence. I uttered the cantrip in a single breath and lo! Six piles of ash at Rallick's feet. Six piles of ash aglitter with the coin from their wallets – hah! A worthy reward!'

Murillio leaned his long, elegant frame close to Crokus Younghand. 'Is this possible?' he whispered. 'For a turn to last as long as Kruppe's?'

Crokus grinned wearily at his friend. 'I don't mind, really. It's safe in here, and that's what counts for me.'

'Assassin's war, bosh!' Kruppe said, leaning back to mop his brow with a wilted silk handkerchief. 'Kruppe remains entirely unconvinced. Tell me, did you not see Rallick Nom in here earlier? Spoke long with Murillio here, the lad did. As calm as ever, was he not?'

Murillio grimaced. 'Nom gets like that every time he's just killed somebody. Lay down a card, dammit! I've early appointments to attend to.'

Crokus asked, 'So what was Rallick talking to you about?'

Murillio's answer was a mere shrug. He continued glaring at Kruppe.

The small man's pencil-thin eyebrows rose. 'Is it Kruppe's turn?'

Closing his eyes, Crokus slumped in his chair. He groaned. 'I saw three assassins on the rooftops, Kruppe. And the two that killed the third went after me, even though it's obvious I'm no assassin.'

'Well,' said Murillio, eyeing the young thief's tattered clothing and the cuts and scrapes on his face and hands, 'I'm inclined to believe you.'

'Fools! Kruppe sits at a table of fools.' Kruppe glanced down at the snoring man. 'And Coll here is the biggest of them all. But sadly gifted with self-knowledge. Hence his present state, from which many profane truths might be drawn. Appointments, Murillio? Kruppe didn't think the city's multitude of mistresses awoke so early in the day. After all, what might they see in their mirrors? Kruppe shivers at the thought.'

Crokus massaged the bruise hidden beneath his long, brown hair. He winced, then leaned forward. 'Come on, Kruppe,' he muttered. 'Play a card.'

'My turn?'

'Seems self-knowledge doesn't extend to whose turn it is,' Murillio commented drily.

Boots sounded on the stairs. The three turned to see Rallick Nom descending from the first floor. The tall, dark-skinned man looked rested. He wore his day cloak, a deep royal purple, clasped at the neck by a silver clamshell brooch. His black hair was freshly braided, framing his narrow, clean-shaven face. Rallick walked up to the table and reached down to grasp Coll's thinning hair. He raised the man's head from the pool of beer and bent forward to study Coll's blotched face. Then he gently set down the man's head, and pulled up a chair.

'Is this the same game as last night?'

'Of course,' Kruppe replied. 'Kruppe has these two men backed to the very wall, in danger of losing their very shirts! It's good to see you again, friend Rallick. The lad here,' Kruppe indicated Crokus with a limp hand, fingers fluttering, 'speaks

216

endlessly of murder above our heads. A veritable downpour of blood! Have you ever heard such nonsense, Rallick Kruppe's friend?'

Rallick shrugged. 'Another rumour. This city was built on rumours.'

Crokus scowled to himself. It seemed that no one was willing to answer questions this morning. He wondered yet again what the assassin and Murillio had been talking about earlier; hunched as they'd been over a dimly lit table in one corner of the room, Crokus had suspected some sort of conspiracy. Not that such a thing was unusual for them, though most times Kruppe was at its centre.

Murillio swung his gaze to the bar. 'Sulty!' he called out. 'You awake?'

There was a mumbled response from behind the wooden counter, then Sulty, her blonde hair dishevelled and plump face looking plumper, stood up. 'Yah,' she mumbled. 'What?'

'Breakfast for my friends here, if you please.' Murillio climbed to his feet and cast a critical, obviously disapproving eye over his clothing. The soft billowing shirt, dyed a bright green, now hung on his lanky frame, wilted and beer-stained. His fine tanned leather pantaloons were creased and patchy. Sighing, Murillio stepped away from the table. 'I must bathe and change. As for the game, I surrender consumed by hopelessness. Kruppe, I now believe, will never play his card, thus leaving us trapped in the unlikely world of his recollections and reminiscences, potentially for ever. Goodnight, one and all.' He and Rallick locked gazes, then Murillio gave a faint nod.

Crokus witnessed the exchange and his scowl deepened. He watched Murillio leave, then glanced at Rallick. The assassin sat staring down at Coll, his expression as unreadable as ever.

Sulty wandered into the kitchen, and a moment later the clanking of pots echoed into the room.

217

Crokus tossed his cards into the table's centre and leaned back, closing his eyes.

'Does the lad surrender as well?' Kruppe asked.

Crokus nodded.

'Hah, Kruppe remains undefeated.' He set down his cards and tucked in a napkin at his thick, jiggling neck.

In the thief's mind suspicions of intrigue ran wild. First the assassin's war, now Rallick and Murillio had something cooking. He sighed mentally and opened his eyes. His whole body ached from the night's adventures, but he knew he'd been lucky. He stared down at Coll without seeing him. The vision of those tall, black assassins returned to him and he shivered. Yet, for all the dangers hounding his back up on the rooftops this past night, he had to admit how exciting it'd all been. After slamming that door behind him and quaffing the beer Sulty had thrust into his hand, his whole body had trembled for an hour afterwards.

His gaze focused on Coll. Coll, Kruppe, Murillio and Rallick. What a strange group – a drunkard, an obese mage of dubious abilities, a dandified fop and a killer.

Still, they were his best friends. His parents had succumbed to the Winged Plague when he'd been four years old. Since then his uncle Mammot had raised him. The old scholar had done the best he could, but it hadn't been enough. Crokus found the street's shadows and moonless nights on rooftops far more exciting than his uncle's mouldy books.

Now, however, he felt very much alone. Kruppe's mask of blissful idiocy never dropped, not even for an instant – all through the years when Crokus had been apprenticed to the fat man in the art of thievery, he'd never seen Kruppe act otherwise. Coll's life seemed to involve the relentless avoidance of sobriety, for reasons unknown to Crokus – though he suspected that, once, Coll had been something more. And now Rallick and Murillio had counted him out of some new intrigue.

Into his thoughts came an image – the moonlit limbs of a sleeping maiden – and he angrily shook his head.

Sulty arrived with breakfast, husks of bread fried in butter, a chunk of goat cheese, a stem of local grapes and a pot of Callows bitter coffee. She served Crokus first and he muttered his thanks.

Kruppe's impatience grew while Sulty served Rallick. 'Such impertinence,' the man said, adjusting his coat's wide, stained sleeves. 'Kruppe is of a mind to cast a thousand horrible spells on rude Sulty.'

'Kruppe had better not,' Rallick said.

'Oh, no, of course not,' Kruppe amended, wiping his brow with his handkerchief. 'A wizard of my skills would never be-little himself on a mere scullion, after all.'

Sulty turned to him. 'Scullion?' She snatched a bread husk from the plate and slapped it down on Kruppe's head. 'Don't worry,' she said, as she walked back to the bar. 'With hair like yours nobody'd notice.'

Kruppe pulled the husk from his head. He was about to toss it down on the floor, then changed his mind. He licked his lips. 'Kruppe is magnanimous this morning,' he said, breaking into a wide smile and setting the bread down on his plate. He leaned forward and laced together his pudgy fingers. 'Kruppe wishes to begin his meal with some grapes, please.'

CHAPTER SEVEN

I see a man
crouched in a fire
who leaves me cold
and wondering what
he is doing here so boldly
crouched in my pyre . . .

Gadrobi Epitaph
Anonymous

This time, Kruppe's dream took him out through Marsh Gate, along South Road, then left on to Cutter Lake Road. Overhead the sky swirled a most unpleasant pattern of silver and pale green. 'All is in flux,' Kruppe gasped, his feet hurrying him along the dusty, barren road. 'The Coin has entered a child's possession, though he knows it not. Is it for Kruppe to walk this Monkey Road? Fortunate that Kruppe's perfectly round body is an example of perfect symmetry. One is not only born skilled at said balance, one must learn it through arduous practice. Of course, Kruppe is unique in never requiring practice – at anything.'

Off in the fields to his left, within a circle of young trees, a small fire cast a hazy red glow up among the budding branches. Kruppe's sharp eyes could make out a single figure seated there, seemingly holding its hands in the flames. 'Too many stones to turn underfoot,' he gasped, 'on this rocky, rutted road. Kruppe would try the ribbed earth, which is yet to green with the season's growth. Indeed, yon fire beckons.' He left the road and approached the circle of trees.

As he strode between two slim boles and stepped into the pool of light, the hooded figure turned slowly to study him, its face hidden in shadows despite the fire before it. Though it held its hands in the flame, they withstood the heat, the long, sinuous fingers spread wide.

'I would partake of this warmth,' Kruppe said, with a slight bow. 'So rare within Kruppe's dreams of late.'

'Strangers wander through them,' the figure said, in a thin, oddly accented voice. 'Such as I. Have you summoned me, then? It has been a long time since I walked on soil.'

Kruppe's brows rose. 'Summoned? Nay, not Kruppe who is also a victim of his dreams. Imagine, after all, that Kruppe sleeps even now beneath warm blankets secure in his humble room. Yet see me, stranger, for I am cold, nay, chilled.'

The other laughed softly and beckoned Kruppe to the fire. 'I seek sensation once again,' it said, 'but my hands feel nothing. To be worshipped is to share the supplicant's pain. I fear my followers are no more.'

Kruppe was silent. He did not like the sombre mood of this dream. He held his hands before the fire yet felt little heat. A chill ache had settled into his knees. Finally he looked over the flames to the hooded figure opposite him. 'Kruppe thinks you are an Elder God. Have you a name?'

'I am known as K'rul.'

Kruppe stiffened. His guess had been correct. The thought of an Elder God awakened and wandering through his dreams sent his thoughts scampering like frightened rabbits. 'How have you come to be here, K'rul?' he asked, a tremor in his voice. All at once this place seemed too hot. He pulled his handkerchief from his sleeve and mopped sweat from his brow.

K'rul considered before answering, and Kruppe heard doubt in his voice. 'Blood has been spilled behind the walls of this glowing city, Kruppe, upon stone once holy in my name. This – this is new to me. Once I reigned in the minds of many mortals, and they fed me well with blood and split bones. Long before the first towers of stone rose to mortal whims, I walked among hunters.' The hood tilted upward and Kruppe felt immortal eyes fixing upon him. 'Blood has been spilled again, but that alone is not enough. I believe I am here to await one who will be awakened. One I have known before, long ago.'

Kruppe digested this like sour bile. 'And what do you bring Kruppe?'

The Elder God rose abruptly. 'An ancient fire that will give you warmth in times of need,' he said. 'But I hold you to nothing. Seek the T'lan Imass who will lead the woman. They are the Awakeners. I must prepare for battle, I think. One I will lose.'

Kruppe's eyes widened with sudden comprehension. 'You are being used,' he breathed.

'Perhaps. If so, then the Child Gods have made a grave error. After all,' a ghastly smile seemed to come into his tone, 'I will lose a battle. But I will not die.' K'rul turned away from the fire then. His voice drifted back to Kruppe. 'Play on, mortal. Every god falls at a mortal's hands. Such is the only end to immortality.'

The Elder God's wistfulness was not lost on Kruppe. He suspected that a great truth had been revealed to him with those final words, a truth he was now given leave to use. 'And use it Kruppe shall,' he whispered.

The Elder God had left the pool of light, heading north-east across the fields. Kruppe stared at the fire. It licked the wood hungrily, but no ash was born, and though unfed since he'd arrived it did not dim. He shivered.

'In the hands of a child,' he muttered. 'This night, Kruppe is truly alone in the world. Alone.'

An hour before dawn Circle Breaker was relieved of his vigil at Despot's Barbican. This night none had come to rendezvous beneath the gate. Lightning played among the jagged peaks of the Tahlyn Mountains to the north as the man walked in solitude down the winding Charms of Anise Street in the Spice Quarter. Ahead and below glittered the Lakefront, the merchant trader ships from distant Callows, Elingarth and Kepler's Spite hunched dark and gloaming between gaslit stone piers.

A cool lake breeze carried to the man the smell of rain, though overhead the stars glistened with startling clarity. He had removed his tabard, folding it into a small leather satchel now slung on one shoulder. Only the plain shortsword strapped at his hip marked him as a soldier, yet a soldier without provenance.

He had divested himself of his official duties, and as he walked down towards the water, the years of service seemed to slough from his spirit. Bright were the memories of his child-hood at these docks, to which he had been ever drawn by the allure of the strange traders as they swung into their berths like weary and weathered heroes returned from some elemental war. In those days it was not uncommon to see the galleys of the Freemen Privateers ease into the bay, sleek and riding low with booty. They hailed from such mysterious ports as Filman Orras, Fort By a Half, Dead Man's Story and Exile; names that rang of adventure in the ears of a lad who had never seen his home city from outside its walls.

The man slowed as he reached the foot of the stone pier. The years between him and that lad marched through his mind, a possession of martial images growing ever grimmer. If he searched out the many crossroads he had come to in the past, he saw their skies storm-warped, the lands ragged and wind-torn. The forces of age and experience worked on them now, and whatever choices he had made then seemed fated and almost desperate.

Is it only the young who know desperation? he wondered, as he moved to sit on the pier's stone sea-wall. Before him rippled the bay's sooty waters. Twenty feet below, the rock-studded shore lay sheathed in darkness, the glitter of broken glass and crockery here and there winking like stars.

The man turned slightly to face the right. His gaze travelled the slope there as it climbed to the summit, on which loomed the squat bulk of Majesty Hall. *Never reach too far*. A simple lesson of life he had learned long ago on the burning deck of a corsair, its belly filling with the sea as it drifted outside the pinnacle fortifications of a city named Broken Jaw. Hubris, the scholars would call the fiery end of the Freemen Privateers.

Never reach too far. The man's eyes held on Majesty Hall. The deadlock that had come with the assassination of Councilman Lim still held within those walls. The Council raced aflurry in circles, more precious hours spent on eager speculation and gossip than on the matters of state. Turban Orr, his victory on the voting floor snatched from his hands in the last moment, now flung his hounds down every trail, seeking the spies he was convinced had infiltrated his nest. The councilman was no fool.

Overhead a flock of grey gulls swept lakeward, crying into the night-chilled air. He drew a breath, hunched his shoulders and pulled his gaze with an effort from Majesty Hill.

Too late to concern himself about reaching too far. Since the day the Eel's agent had come to him, the man's future was sealed; to some it would be called treason. And perhaps, in the end, it *was* treason. Who could say what lay in the Eel's mind?

224

Even his principal agent – the man's contact – professed ignorance of his master's plans.

His thoughts returned to Turban Orr. He'd set himself against a cunning man, a man of power. His only defence against Orr lay in anonymity. It wouldn't last.

He sat on the pier, awaiting the Eel's agent. And he would deliver into that man's hands a message for the Eel. How much would change with the delivery of that missive? Was it wrong for him to seek help, to threaten his frail anonymity – the solitude that gave him so much inner strength, that stiffened his own resolve? Yet, to match wits with Turban Orr – he did not think he could do it alone.

The man reached into his jerkin and withdrew the scroll. A crossroads marked where he now stood, he recognized that much. In answer to his ill-measured fear, he'd written the plea for help on this scroll.

It would be an easy thing to do, to surrender now. He hefted the frail parchment in his hands, feeling its slight weight, the vague oiliness of the coating, the rough weave of its tie-string. An easy, desperate thing to do.

The man lifted his head. The sky had begun to pale, the lake wind picking up the day's momentum. There would be rain, coming from the north as it often did at this time of year. A cleansing of the city, a freshening of its spice-laden breath. He slipped the string from the scroll and unfurled the parchment.

So easy.

With slow, deliberate movements, the man tore up the scroll. He let the ragged pieces drift down, scattering into the gloom of the lake's shadowed shore. The rising waves swept them outward to dot the turgid swells like flecks of ash.

Coming from somewhere in the back of his mind, he thought he heard a coin spinning. It seemed a sad sound.

A few minutes later he left the pier. The Eel's agent, out on

225

his morning stroll, would in passing note his contact's absence and simply continue on his way.

He made his way along the Lakefront Street with the summit of Majesty Hill dwindling behind him. As he passed, the first of the silk merchants appeared, laying out their wares on the wide paved walk. Among the silks the man recognized the dyed lavender twists and bolts of Illem, the pale yellows of Setta and Lest – two cities to the south-east he knew had been annexed by the Pannion Seer in the last month – and the heavy bold twists of Sarrokalle. A dwindled sampling: all trade from the north had ended under Malazan dominion.

He turned from the lake at the entry to the Scented Wood and headed into the city. Four streets ahead his single room waited on the second floor of a decaying tenement, grey and silent with the coming dawn, its thin, warped door latched and locked. In that room he allowed no place for memories; nothing to mark him in a wizard's eye or tell the sharp-witted spy-hunter details of his life. In that room, he remained anonymous even to himself.

The Lady Simtal paced. These last few days too much of her hard-won gold had been spent smoothing the waters. That damn bitch of Lim's had not let grief get in the way of her greed. Barely two days shrouded in black and then out on the courts hanging on that fop Murillio's arm, smug as a tart at a ball.

Simtal's pencilled brows knitted slightly. Murillio: that young man had a way of being seen. He might be worth cultivation, all things considered.

She stopped pacing and faced the man sprawled on her bed. 'So, you've learned nothing.' A hint of contempt had slipped into her tone and she wondered if he'd caught it.

Councilman Turban Orr, his heavily scarred forearm covering his eyes, did not move as he replied, 'I've told you all this.

There's no knowing where that poisoned quarrel came from, Simtal. Hell, poisoned! What assassin uses poison these days? Vorcan's got them so studded with magic everything else is obsolete.'

'You're digressing,' she said, satisfied that he'd missed the careless unveiling of her sentiments.

'It's like I said,' Orr continued. 'Lim was involved in more than one, uh, delicate venture. The assassination's probably unconnected with you. It could have been anyone's balcony, it just happened to be yours.'

Lady Simtal crossed her arms. 'I don't believe in co-incidence, Turban. Tell me, was it coincidence that his death broke your majority – the night before the vote?' She saw the man's cheek twitch and knew she'd stung him. She smiled and moved to the bed. She sat and ran a hand along his bared thigh. 'In any case, have you checked on him lately?'

'Him?'

Simtal scowled, withdrawing her hand and standing. 'My beloved dispossessed, you idiot.'

Turban Orr's mouth curved into a smug smile. 'I always keep a check on him for you, my dear. Nothing's changed in that area. He hasn't sobered up since you threw him out on his arse.' The man sat up and reached to the bedpost where his clothes hung. He began dressing.

Simtal whirled to him. 'What are you doing?' she demanded, her voice strident.

'What's it look like?' Turban pulled on his breeches. 'The debate rages on at Majesty Hall. My influence is required.'

'To do what? Bend yet another councilman to your will?'

He slipped on his silk shirt, still smiling. 'That, and other things.'

Simtal rolled her eyes. 'Oh, of course – the spy. I'd forgotten about him.'

'Personally,' Orr resumed, 'I believe the proclamation of

227

neutrality to the Malazans will go through – perhaps tomorrow or the next day.'

She laughed harshly. 'Neutrality! You're beginning to believe your own propaganda. What you want, Turban Orr, is power, the naked absolute power that comes with being a Malazan High Fist. You think this the first step to paving your road into the Empress's arms. At the city's expense, but you don't give a damn about that!'

Turban sneered up at Simtal. 'Stay out of politics, woman. Darujhistan's fall to the Empire is inevitable. Better a peaceful occupation than a violent one.'

'Peaceful? Are you blind to what happened to Pale's nobility? Oh, the ravens feasted on delicate flesh for days. This Empire devours noble blood.'

'What happened at Pale isn't as simple as you make it,' Turban said. 'There was a Moranth reckoning involved, a clause in the alliance writ. Such culling will not occur here – and what if it does? We could use it, as far as I'm concerned.' His grin returned. 'So much for your heart bleeding to the city's woes. All that interests you is you. Save the righteous citizen offal for your fawns, Simtal.' He adjusted his leggings.

Simtal stepped to the bedpost, reaching down to touch the silver pommel of Orr's duelling sword. 'You should kill him and be done with it,' she said.

'Back to him again?' The councilman laughed as he rose. 'Your brain works with all the subtlety of a malicious child.' He collected his sword and strapped it on. 'It's a wonder you wrested anything from that idiot husband of yours – you were so evenly matched in matters of cunning.'

'The easiest thing to break is a man's heart,' Simtal said, with a private smile. She lay down on the bed. Stretching her arms and arching her back, she said, 'What about Moon's Spawn? It's still just hanging there.'

Gazing down at her, his eyes travelling along her body, the

councilman replied distractedly, 'We've yet to work out a way to get a message up there. We've set up a tent in its shadow and stationed representatives in it, but that mysterious lord just ignores us.'

'Maybe he's dead,' Simtal said, relaxing with a sigh. 'Maybe the Moon's just sitting there because there's nobody left alive inside. Have you thought of that, dear Councilman?'

Turban Orr turned to the door. 'We have. I'll see you tonight?'

'I want him killed,' Simtal said.

The councilman reached for the latch. 'Maybe. I'll see you tonight?' he asked again.

'Maybe.'

Turban Orr's hand rested on the latch, then he opened the door and left the room.

Lying on her bed, Lady Simtal sighed. Her thoughts shifted to a certain dandy, whose loss to a certain widow would be a most delicious coup.

Murillio sipped spiced wine. 'The details are sketchy,' he said, making a face as the fiery alcohol stung his lips.

In the street below a brilliantly painted carriage clattered past, drawn by three white horses in black bridles. The man gripping the reins was robed in black and hooded. The horses tossed their heads, ears pinned back and eyes rolling, but the driver's broad, veined hands held them in check. On either side of the carriage walked middle-aged women. Bronze cups sat on their shaved heads from which unfurled wavering streams of scented smoke.

Murillio leaned against the railing and looked down upon the troupe. 'The bitch Fander's being carted out,' he said. 'Bloody grim rituals, if you ask me.' He sat back in the plush chair and smiled at his companion, raising the goblet. 'The Wolf Goddess of Winter dies her seasonal death, on a carpet of

229

white, no less. And in a week's time the Gedderone Fête fills the streets with flowers, soon to clog gutters and block drains throughout the city.'

The young woman across from him smiled, her eyes on her own goblet of wine, which she held in both hands like an offering. 'Which details were you referring to?' she asked, glancing up at him briefly.

'Details?'

She smiled faintly. 'The sketchy ones.'

'Oh.' Murillio waved one gloved hand dismissively. 'Lady Simtal's version held that Councilman Lim had come in person to acknowledge her formal invitation.'

'Invitation? Do you mean to the festive she's throwing on Gedderone's Eve?'

Murillio blinked. 'Of course. Surely your house has been invited?'

'Oh, yes. And you?'

'Alas, no,' Murillio said, smiling.

The woman fell silent, her eyelids lowering in thought.

Murillio glanced back to the street below. He waited. Such things, after all, moved of their own accord, and even he could not guess the pace or track of a woman's thoughts, especially when it had to do with sex. And this was most assuredly a play for favours – Murillio's best game, and he always played it through. Never disappoint them, that was the key. The closest-held secret is the one that never sours with age.

Few of the other tables on the balcony were occupied, the establishment's noble patrons preferring the scented airs of the dining room within. Murillio found comfort in the buzzing life of the streets, and he knew his guest did too – at least in this instance. With all the noise rising from below, their chances of being overheard were slight.

As his gaze wandered aimlessly along Morul's Street of Jewels, he stiffened slightly, eyes widening as they focused on a

230

figure standing in a doorway opposite him. He shifted in his seat, dropping his left hand past the stone railing, out of the woman's sight. Then he jerked it repeatedly, glaring down at the figure.

Rallick Nom's smile broadened. He stepped away from the doorway and strolled up the street, pausing to inspect an array of pearls laid out on an ebony table in front of a store. The proprietor took a nervous step forward then relaxed as Rallick moved on.

Murillio sighed, leaning back and taking a mouthful of liquor. *Idiot!* The man's face, his hands, his walk, his eyes, all said one thing: *killer.* Hell, even his wardrobe had all the warmth and vitality of an executioner's uniform.

When it came to subtlety Rallick Nom was sorely lacking. Which made this whole thing rather odd, that such a complex scheme could have been born from the assassin's rigidly geometric brain. Still, whatever its origins, it was pure genius.

'Do you dearly wish to attend, Murillio?' the woman asked.

Murillio smiled his warmest smile. He looked away. 'It's a large estate, isn't it?'

'Lady Simtal's? Indeed, fraught with rooms.' The woman dipped one dainty finger into the pungent, fiery liquid, then raised it to her lips, inserting it into her mouth as if in afterthought. She continued studying the goblet in her other hand. 'I would expect a good many of the servants' quarters, though lacking in the simplest needs of luxury, will remain empty for much of the night.'

No clearer invitation did Murillio require. Rallick's plan centred on this very moment, and its consequences. Still, adultery had one drawback. Murillio had no desire to meet this woman's husband on the duelling piste. He drove such disturbing thoughts away with another mouthful of wine. 'I would love to attend the Lady's festival, on one condition.' He looked up and locked gazes with the woman. 'That you will grace me

231

with your company that night – for an hour or two, that is.' His brow assumed a troubled furrow. 'I would not wish to impinge on your husband's claim on you, of course.' Which is exactly what he would be doing, and they both knew it.

'Of course,' the woman replied, suddenly coy. 'That would be unseemly. How many invitations do you require?'

'Two,' he said. 'Best that I be seen with a companion.'

'Yes, it's best.'

Murillio glanced down at his now empty goblet with a rueful expression. Then he sighed. 'Alas, I must be taking my leave.'

'I admire your self-discipline,' the woman said.

You won't on Gedderone's Eve, Murillio answered silently, as he rose from his chair. 'The Lady of Chance has graced me with this meeting of ours,' he said, bowing. 'Until the eve, Lady Orr.'

'Until then,' the councilman's wife answered, seeming already to lose interest in him. 'Goodbye.'

Murillio bowed again, then left the balcony. Among the crowded tables more than a few noblewomen's heavy-lidded eyes watched him leave.

Morul's Street of Jewels ended at Sickle Gate. Rallick felt the wide eyes of the two guards beside the ramp following him as he passed through the passage between the massive stones of the Third Tier Wall. Ocelot had told him to make it plain, and while Murillio was of the opinion that only a blind man could ever mistake him for anything other than a killer, Rallick had taken pains to achieve the obvious.

The guards did nothing, of course. Giving the appearance of being a murderer wasn't the same as being one in truth. The city's laws were strict in such things. He knew he might find himself being followed as he strode down the opulent streets of Higher Estates, but he'd leave them to it, making no effort to lose them. Darujhistan's nobles paid good money to loose spies on to the streets day after day. Might as well make them earn their bread.

Rallick had no sympathy for them. He did not, however, share the commoner's hatred for the nobility. Their constant airs, prickly honours and endless squabbles made for good business, after all.

When the Malazan Empire came that would end, he suspected. In the Empire, assassin guilds were illegal, and those of the trade who were deemed worthy were enlisted into the secret ranks of the Claw. As for those who weren't considered worthy, they simply disappeared. The nobles didn't fare much better, if the rumours from Pale held any truth. It would be a different world when the Empire came, and Rallick wasn't sure he wanted to be part of it.

Still, there were things left to achieve. He wondered if Murillio had succeeded in getting the invitations. Everything hinged on that. There'd been a long-drawn-out argument about it the night before. Murillio preferred widows. Adultery had never been his style. But Rallick had remained insistent, and finally Murillio had given in.

The assassin still wondered about his friend's reluctance. His first thought was that Murillio feared the possibility of a duel with Turban Orr. But Murillio was no slouch with a rapier. Rallick had practised with him in secluded places enough times to suspect that he was an Adept – and to that even Turban Orr could not make claim.

No, it wasn't fear that made Murillio shy from this part of the plan. It dawned on Rallick that there was a moral issue at stake. A whole new side of Murillio had revealed itself to Rallick then.

He was pondering the implications when his gaze found a familiar face among the street's crowd. He stopped and studied the surrounding buildings, and his eyes widened as he realized where his wanderings had taken him. His attention snapped back to the familiar figure appearing every few moments on the street's opposite side. The assassin's eyes narrowed thoughtfully.

Beneath the mid-morning's blue and silver hue, Crokus walked along Lakefront Street surrounded by the bedlam of merchants and shoppers. A dozen streets ahead rose the city hills beyond the Third Tier Wall. On the easternmost hill stood the K'rul belfry, its green-patched bronze scales glimmering in the sun's light.

To his mind the tower challenged Majesty Hall's bright mien, gazing over the estates and buildings crouched on the lower hills with its rheumed eyes and history-scarred face – a jaded cast to its mocking gleam.

Crokus shared something of the tower's imagined sardonic reserve for the pretence so rife in Majesty Hall, an emotion of his uncle's that had seeped into the lad over the years. Adding fuel to this fire was a healthy dose of youthful resentment towards anything that smacked of authority. And though he gave it little thought, these provided the primary impulses for his thieving activities. Yet he'd never before understood the most subtle and hurtful insult his thefts delivered – the invasion and violation of privacy. Again and again, in his dreamy wanderings both day and night, the vision of the young woman asleep in her bed returned to him.

Eventually Crokus grasped that the vision had everything to do with – *everything*. He'd come into her room, a place where the noble brats drooling at her heels couldn't enter, a place where she might talk to the ragged dolls of her childhood, when innocence didn't just mean a flower not yet plucked. Her sanctuary. And he'd despoiled it, he'd snatched from this young woman her most precious possession: her privacy.

No matter that she was the daughter of the D'Arles, that she was born to the pure blood – untainted by the Lady of Beggars' touch – that she would flow through life protected and shielded from the degradations of the real world. No matter any of these things. For Crokus, his crime against her was tantamount to rape. To have so boldly shattered her world . . .

His thoughts a storm of self-recrimination, the young thief turned up the Charms of Anise Street, pushing through the crowds.

In his mind the once-stalwart walls of righteous outrage were crumbling. The hated nobility had shown him a face that now haunted him with its beauty, and tugged him in a hundred unexpected directions. The sweet scents of the spice stores, wafting like perfume on the warming breeze, had unaccountably lodged a nameless emotion in his throat. The shouts of Daru children playing in the alleys brimmed his eyes with sentimental maundering.

Crokus strode through Clove Gate and entered Osserc Narrow. Directly ahead rose the ramp leading into Higher Estates. As he approached he had to move quickly to one side to avoid a large carriage coming up on him from behind. He didn't need to see the crest adorning the carriage's side panel to recognize its house. The horses snapped and kicked, surging forward heedless of anyone or anything in their path. Crokus paused to watch the carriage clatter up the ramp, people scattering to either side. From what he'd heard of Councilman Turban Orr, it seemed the duellist's horses matched his contempt for those he supposedly served.

By the time he reached the Orr estate the carriage had already passed through the outer gate. Four burly private guards had resumed their station to either side. The wall at their backs rose a full fifteen feet, topped with rusty iron cuttings set in sun-baked clay. Pumice torches lined the wall at ten-foot intervals. Crokus strolled past the gate, ignoring the guards. At the base the wall looked to be about four feet in breadth, the rough-hewn bricks a standard squared foot. He continued on along the street, then turned right to check the wall fronting the alley. A single service door, tarred oak banded in bronze, was set in this wall at the nearest corner.

And no guard. The shadows of the opposite estate draped a heavy cloak across the narrow aisle. Crokus entered the damp, musty darkness. He had travelled half the length of the alley when a hand closed around his mouth from behind and a dagger's sharp point pressed against his side. Crokus froze, then grunted as the hand pulled his face round. He found himself looking into familiar eyes.

Rallick Nom withdrew his dagger and stepped back, a severe frown marring his brow. Crokus gaped then licked his lips. 'Rallick, Beru's Heart, you scared me!'

'Good,' the assassin said. He came close. 'Listen carefully, Crokus. You'll not try Orr's estate. You'll not go near it again.'

The thief shrugged. 'It was just a thought, Nom.'

'Kill it,' Rallick said.

His lips thinning into a straight line, Crokus nodded. 'All right.' He turned and headed towards the strip of bright sunlight marking the next street. He felt Rallick's eyes on him until he stepped out on to Traitor's Track. He stopped. Off to his left climbed High Gallows Hill, its immaculate flowered slope a burst of colours surrounding the fifty-three Winding Steps. The five nooses above the platform swung slightly in the breeze, their shadows streaks of black reaching down the slope to the cobbles of the street. It had been a long time since the last High Criminal was hanged, while off in the Gadrobi District the Low Gallows' ropes were replaced weekly due to stretching. An odd contrast to mark these tense times.

Abruptly, he shook his head. Avoiding the turmoil of questions was too much of an effort. Had Nom followed him? No, a lesser likelihood than the assassin having marked Orr or someone in the estate for murder. A bold contract. He

236

wondered who had had the guts to offer it – a fellow noble, no doubt. But the courage of the contract's offering paled when compared to Rallick's accepting it.

In any case, the weight of the assassin's warning was enough to crush any idea of thieving Orr's estate – at least for now. Crokus jammed his hands into his pockets. As he walked, his thoughts lost in a maze of dead ends, he frowned with the realization that one of his hands, probing deep in the pocket, had closed around a coin.

He withdrew it. Yes, it was the coin he'd found on the night of the assassinations. He recalled its inexplicable appearance, clattering at his feet an instant before the assassin's crossbow quarrel whizzed past. Beneath the bright morning light Crokus now took the time to examine it. The first side he held up before him displayed the profile of a young man, with an amused expression, wearing some kind of floppy hat. Tiny rune-like lettering ran around the edge – a language the thief didn't recognize as it was so very different from the cursive Daru script with which he was familiar.

Crokus turned the coin. How odd! Another head, this one a woman's facing the other way. The etched script here was of a style different from the opposite side, a kind of left-slanting hatchwork. The woman looked young, with features similar to the man's; her expression held nothing of amusement, seeming to the thief's eyes cold and unyielding.

The metal was old, streaked here and there with raw copper and pitted around the faces with rough tin. The coin felt surprisingly heavy, though he concluded that its only worth lay in its uniqueness. He'd seen the coinage of Callows, Genabackis, Amat El and, once, the ridged bars of the Seguleh, but none had looked like this one.

Where had it fallen from? Had his clothing picked it up somewhere, or had he kicked it into motion while crossing the roof? Or had it been among the D'Arle maiden's treasure?

Crokus shrugged. In any case, its arrival had been timely.

By this time his walk had taken him to the East Gate. Just outside the city wall and along the road called Jatem's Worry, crouched the handful of sagging buildings named Worrytown: the thief's destination. The gate remained open during daylight hours, and a slow-plodding line of vegetable-carts crowded the narrow passage. Among them, he saw as he pushed his way along one edge, were the first wagonloads of refugees from Pale, those who'd managed to slip through the siege lines during the battle and had crossed the south Rhivi Plain and then through the Gadrobi Hills and finally on to Jatem's Worry. Scanning their faces he saw a fiery desperation dulled by exhaustion: they looked upon the city with a jaded eye towards its meagre defences, realizing that they'd bought only a short measure of time with their flight, yet too tired to care.

Disturbed by what he saw, Crokus hurried through the gate and approached Worrytown's largest structure, a rambling wooden tavern. Over the door hung a board on which had been painted, decades ago, a three-legged ram. To the thief's mind, the painting had nothing to do with the tavern's name, which was the Boar's Tears. The coin still in one hand, Crokus entered and paused just inside.

A few desultory faces turned to regard him briefly, then swung back to their cups. At a table in a gloomy corner opposite, Crokus saw a familiar figure, its hands raised above its head and gesticulating wildly. A grin tugged the thief's lips, and he strode forward.

'. . . and then did Kruppe sweep with motion so swift as to be unseen by any the king's crown and sceptre from the sarcophagus lid. Too many priests in this tomb, thinks Kruppe then, one less 'twould be a relief to all lest the dead king's musty breath shorten and so awaken his wraith. Many times afore this had Kruppe faced a wraith's wrath in some deep pit of D'rek, droning its list of life-crimes and bemoaning its need to devour my soul – harrah! Kruppe was ever too elusive for such sundry spirits and their knock-kneed chatter—'

Crokus laid a hand on Kruppe's damp shoulder, and the shiny round face swung up to observe him. 'Ah!' Kruppe exclaimed, waving a hand towards his lone companion at the table and explaining, 'An apprentice past comes to fawn in due fashion! Crokus, be seated by all means possible. Wench! Some more of your finest wine, haste!'

Crokus eyed the man seated opposite Kruppe. 'Seems you two might be busy right now.'

Hope flared in the man's expression and he rose quickly. 'Oh, no,' he exclaimed. 'By all means interrupt.' His eyes darted to Kruppe then back to Crokus. 'I must be leaving in any event, I assure you! Good day to you, Kruppe. Until some other time, then.' The man bobbed his head then departed.

'Precipitous creature,' Kruppe muttered, reaching for the mug of wine the man had left behind. 'Ah, look at this,' he said, frowning up at Crokus, 'nigh two-thirds full. A potential waste!' Kruppe drank it down in one swift gulp, then sighed. 'Said potential averted, Dessembrae be praised.'

Crokus sat. 'Was that man your trader contact?' he asked.

'Heavens, no.' Kruppe waved a hand. 'A poor refugee from Pale, wandering lost. Fortunate for him was Kruppe, whose brilliant insights have sent him—'

'Straight out the door,' Crokus finished, laughing.

Kruppe scowled.

The serving woman arrived with an earthen carafe of sour-smelling wine. Kruppe refilled the mugs. 'And now, wonders Kruppe, what would this expertly trained lad seek from this one-time master of all arts nefarious? Or have you triumphed yet again and come with booty atucked, seeking proper dispensation and the like?'

'Well, yes – I mean, no, not quite.' Crokus glanced around, then leaned forward. 'It's about last time,' he whispered. 'I knew you'd be out here to sell the stuff I brought you.'

Kruppe leaned forward to meet the lad, their faces inches apart. 'The D'Arle acquisition?' he whispered back, waggling his eyebrows.

'Exactly! Have you sold it off yet?'

Kruppe pulled a handkerchief from a sleeve and mopped his brow. 'What with all this talk of war, the traders' routes are all amiss. So, to answer your question, uhm, not quite yet, admits Kruppe—'

'Great!'

Kruppe started at the lad's shout, his eyes squeezing shut. When they opened again they were thin slits. 'Ah, Kruppe understands. The lad wishes their return to his possession so that he might seek higher recompense elsewhere?'

Crokus blinked. 'No, of course not. I mean, yes, I want it back. But I'm not planning on fencing it anywhere. That is, I'm still dealing with you on everything else. Only this one's special.' As he spoke Crokus felt heat rise to his face, and was thankful for the gloom. 'A special case, Kruppe.'

A broad smile broke on Kruppe's round face. 'Why, most certainly, then, lad. Shall I deliver said items to you this eve? Excellent, consider the matter closed. Pray, tell, what do you have in yon hand there?'

Crokus stared in confusion, then he glanced down at his hand. 'Oh, just a coin,' he explained, showing it to Kruppe. 'I picked it up the same night I thieved D'Arle's. Two-headed, see?'

'Indeed? May Kruppe examine the peculiar item more closely?'

Crokus obliged, then reached for the mug of wine. He leaned back. 'I was thinking of Orr's estate next,' he said casually, his eyes fixed on Kruppe.

'Mmm.' Kruppe turned the coin in his hand again and again. 'Poorest quality cast,' he muttered. 'Crooked stamping, too. Orr's estate, you say? Kruppe advises caution. The house is well protected. The metallurgist who foundried this should have been hanged, indeed, probably was, thinks Kruppe. Black copper, no less. Cheap tin, temperatures all too cool. Favour me, Crokus? Peruse the scene in the street from yon door. If you spy a red and green merchant's wagon wobbling into town, Kruppe would be much obliged for such information.'

Crokus rose and crossed the room to the door. Opening it he stepped outside and glanced around. Seeing no wagon in sight, the youth shrugged again and went back inside. He returned to the table. 'No merchant wagon.'

'Ah, well,' Kruppe said. He set down the coin on the table. 'Altogether worthless, judges wise Kruppe. You may part with it at your leisure.'

Crokus collected the coin and slipped it into his pocket. 'No, I'm keeping it. For good luck.'

Kruppe looked up, his eyes bright, but Crokus had his attention on the mug in his hands. The fat man glanced away, sighing. 'Kruppe must needs depart immediately, if this eve's rendezvous is to be propitious for all involved.'

Crokus drained his wine. 'We can head back together.'

'Excellent.' Kruppe rose, pausing to brush crumbs from his chest. 'Shall we be off, then?' He looked up to see Crokus frowning down at his hand. 'Has something smitten the lad?' he asked quickly.

Crokus started. He looked away guiltily, the colour rising in his face. 'No,' he mumbled. He glanced again at his hand. 'I must've picked up some wax somewhere,' he explained. He rubbed his hand on his leg and grinned sheepishly. 'Let's go.'

'It will be a fine day for a walk, pronounces Kruppe, who is wise in all things.'

White Gold's Round encircled an abandoned tower with a panoply of brightly dyed awnings. The goldsmith merchant shops, each with their own security guards loitering outside, faced out on the round street, the aisles between them narrow cracks leading to the tower's ruined compound.

The many tales of death and madness surrounding Hinter's Tower and its environs kept it empty and, uppermost in the minds of the goldsmiths, an unlikely approach to their precious stores.

As the afternoon waned towards dusk, the Round's crowds thinned and the private guards grew more wary. Iron grilles rattled into place over storefronts here and there, and among the few that remained open, torches were ignited.

Murillio entered the Round from the Third Tier Road, pausing every now and then to examine a shopkeeper's wares. Wrapped in a shimmering blue cloak from the Malle Waste, Murillio knew his ostentatious display of wealth would do much to allay suspicion.

He came to one shop in particular, framed on either side by unlit stores. The goldsmith, narrow-faced and pebble-nosed, leaned hawkishly on his counter, his weathered hands before him bearing tiny grey scars that looked like raven tracks on mud. One finger tapped a restless beat. Murillio approached, meeting the man's beetle eyes.

'Is this the shop of Krute of Talient?'

'I'm Krute,' the goldsmith grated sourly, as if disgruntled with his lot in life. 'Talient pearls, set in Bloodgold from the mines of Moap and Belt, none other to be found in all Darujhistan.' He leaned forward and spat past Murillio, who involuntarily stepped to one side.

'No customers this day?' he asked, pulling a handkerchief from his sleeve and touching his lips.

Krute's gaze tightened. 'Only one,' he said. 'Perused a cache of Goaliss gems, rare as dragon's milk and suckled from rock as grim. A hundred slaves lost to each stone prised from the angry veins.' Krute's shoulders jerked and his eyes darted. 'Out the back I keep them, lest temptation spatter the street with blood, and like.'

Murillio nodded. 'Sound practice. Did he purchase any?'

Krute grinned, revealing blackened stumps for teeth. 'One, but not the best. Come, I'll show you.' He went to the side door and opened it. 'Through here, then.'

Murillio entered the shop. Black curtains covered the walls, and the air was musty with old sweat. Krute led him into the back room, which if anything was more rank and stifling than the first. The goldsmith dropped the curtain between the two rooms and faced Murillio.

'Move quickly! I've laid out a horde of fool's gold and worthless stones on the counter out front. If any sharp-eyed customer marks them this hole will be finished.' He kicked at the back wall and a panel swung from its hinges. 'Crawl through, dammit, and tell Rallick that the Guild is not pleased with his generosity regarding our secrets. Go!'

Murillio fell to his knees and pushed his way through the portal, the earthen floor damp beneath his hands and staining his knees. He groaned his distaste as the door swung down behind him, then climbed to his feet. Before him rose Hinter's Tower, its mould-ridden stone walls glistening in the dying light. An overgrown cobbled pathway led up to the arched entrance bereft of a door and heavy with shadows. Of the chamber within Murillio saw only darkness.

Roots from the scraggy scrub oaks lining the path had pushed most of the cobbles up from the earth, making the way treacherous. After a cautious minute Murillio arrived at the doorway. He narrowed his gaze and tried to pierce the darkness. 'Rallick?' he hissed. 'Where the hell are you?'

A voice spoke behind him. 'You're late.'

Murillio spun, a long, thin duelling rapier in his left hand rasping from its sheath and sweeping low into guard position, a main-gauche appearing in his right hand as he dropped into

243

a defensive crouch, then relaxed. 'Dammit, Rallick!'

The assassin grunted in amusement, eyeing the rapier's razor-sharp tip, which had but a moment earlier hovered inches from his solar plexis. 'Good to see your reflexes have not dulled, friend. All that wine and those pastries seem not to have girdled you . . . much.'

Murillio resheathed his weapons. 'I expected to find you in the tower.'

Eyes widening, Rallick said, 'Are you mad? The place is haunted.'

'You mean that's not just a story you assassins made up to keep people away?'

Rallick turned and made his way to a lower terrace that had once overlooked the garden. White stone benches squatted in the wiry yellow grass like the stained bones of some gargantuan beast. Below the terrace, Murillio saw as he joined the assassin, sprawled a muddy, algae-filled pond. Frogs croaked and mosquitoes buzzed in the tepid air. 'Some nights,' Rallick said as he brushed dead leaves from one of the benches, 'wraiths crowd the entrance – you can walk right up to them, listen to their pleas and threats. They all want out.' He sat down.

Murillio remained standing, his gaze on the tower. 'What of Hinter himself? Does his wraith number among them?'

'No. The madman sleeps within, or so it's said. The wraiths are trapped in the sorcerer's nightmares – he holds on to them, and even Hood cannot draw them to his cold bosom. Do you wish to know where those wraiths have come from, Murillio?' Rallick grinned. 'Enter the tower, and you'll discover it first hand.'

Murillio had been about to go into the tower when Rallick had surprised him. 'Thanks for the warning,' he snapped sarcastically, gathering his cloak and sitting down.

Rallick waved the mosquitoes from his face. 'Well?'

'I have them,' Murillio said. 'Lady Orr's most trusted

hand-servant delivered them this afternoon.' He removed from inside his cloak a bamboo tube tied in blue ribbon. 'Two invitations to Lady Simtal's Fête, as promised.'

'Good.' The assassin looked quickly at his friend. 'You've not seen Kruppe's nose twitch?'

'Not yet. Ran into him this afternoon. Seems Crokus is making some bizarre demands. Of course,' Murillio added, scowling, 'who can tell when Kruppe's caught wind of something? In any case, I've seen nothing to suggest the slippery little gnome suspects we're up to anything.'

'What was that you said about Crokus making bizarre demands?'

'A peculiar thing, that,' Murillio mused. 'When I dropped by the Phoenix Inn this afternoon Kruppe was delivering to the lad the pickings from his last job. Now, surely Crokus hasn't abandoned Kruppe as his fence – we all would've caught wind of that.'

'That was from an estate, wasn't it? Whose?' Rallick asked.

'D'Arle's,' Murillio answered, then his eyebrows rose. 'Kiss of Gedderone! The D'Arle maiden! The ripe one with the cheeks – she's being shown at damn near every gathering, all the frilly lads leaving a trail for the mop-boys. Oh, my! Our young thief is perchance smitten, and now keeps her baubles for himself. Of all the hopeless dreams a boy could have, he's reached for the worst.'

'Maybe,' Rallick said quietly. 'Maybe not. A word to his uncle . . .'

Murillio's pained expression lifted. 'A nudge in the right direction? Yes, finally! Mammot will be pleased—'

'Patience,' Rallick interjected. 'Turning a thieving child into a man of standing and learning will require more work than a swooning heart will manage.'

Murillio frowned. 'Well, forgive me for being so excited at the prospect of saving the lad's life.'

Rallick's smile was soft. 'Never regret such pleasure,' he said.

Catching the assassin's tone, Murillio sighed, the sharp edges of his sarcasm sinking away. 'It's been many years since we had so many things of hope to strive for,' he said quietly.

'The path to one will be bloody,' Rallick said. 'Don't forget that. But, yes, it's been a long time. I wonder if Kruppe even remembers such days.'

Murillio snorted. 'Kruppe's memory is revised hourly. All that holds him together is fear of being discovered.'

Rallick's eyes darkened. 'Discovered?'

His friend seemed far away but then he collected himself and smiled. 'Oh, worn suspicions, no more. He's a slippery one, is Kruppe.'

Rallick chuckled at Murillio's mocking syntax. He studied the pond before them. 'Yes,' he agreed, after a time, 'he's the slippery one, all right.' He stood. 'Krute will be wanting to close up. The Round's asleep by now.'

'Right.'

The two men left the terrace, methane mists swirling around their legs. As they reached the path Murillio turned for a look at the tower's doorway, wondering if he could see the gibbering wraiths, but all he saw beneath the sagging arch was a wall of darkness. In some strange way he found that more disturbing than any horde of lost souls he might imagine.

Bright morning sunlight flowed in from the broad windows of Baruk's study, and a warm wind slipped into the room carrying the smells and noises from the street below. The alchemist, still dressed in his nightclothes, sat on a high stool at the map table. He held a brush in one hand, dipping it now and again into an ornate silver inkwell.

The red ink had been watered down. He painted wash on the map, covering the areas now held by the Malazan Empire. Fully one half of the map – the north half – was red. A small clear strip just south of Blackdog Forest marked Caladan Brood's forces, flanked on either side by two smaller patches indicating the Crimson Guard. The red wash surrounded these clear spots and extended down to engulf Pale, ending on the north edge of the Tahlyn Mountains.

The street noises had become quite loud, Baruk noted, as he leaned close to the map to paint the red tide's southern border. Construction work, he concluded, hearing the squeal of winches and a voice bellowing at passers-by. The sounds died away, then there came a loud *crack!* Baruk jumped, his right forearm jerking out and knocking over the inkwell. The red ink poured across his map.

Cursing, Baruk sat back. His eyes widened as he watched the spreading stain cover Darujhistan and continue south to Catlin. He stepped down from the stool, reaching for a cloth to wipe his hands, more than a little shaken by what could easily be taken as an omen. He walked across the chamber to the window, bent forward and looked down.

A crew of workers was busy tearing up the street directly below. Two burly men swung picks while three others formed a line passing the shattered cobblestones to a growing pile on the pavement. The foreman stood nearby, his back to a wagon, studying a parchment scroll.

Baruk frowned. 'Who's in charge of road maintenance?' he wondered aloud.

A soft knock diverted his attention. 'Yes?'

His servant, Roald, took a single step into the room. 'One of your agents has arrived, Lord.'

Baruk flicked a glance at the map table. 'Have him wait a moment, Roald.'

'Yes, Lord.' The servant stepped back and closed the door.

The alchemist walked over to the table and rolled up the ruined map. From the hallway came a loud voice followed by a

247

murmur. Baruk slid the map on to a shelf and turned in time to see the agent enter, on his trail a scowling Roald.

Waving at Roald to leave, Baruk gazed down at the gaudily dressed man. 'Good day, Kruppe.'

Roald stepped out and softly shut the door.

'More than good, Baruk, dear friend of Kruppe. Truly wonderful! Have you partaken of the morn's fresh air?'

Baruk glanced at the window. 'Unfortunately,' he said, 'the air outside my window has become rather dusty.'

Kruppe paused. His arms returned to his sides, then he reached into a sleeve and withdrew his handkerchief. He patted his brow. 'Ah, yes, the road workers. Kruppe passed them on his way in. A rather belligerent lot, thinks Kruppe. Indeed, rude, but hardly exceptional for such menial labourers.'

Baruk gestured to a chair.

With a beatific smile Kruppe sat. 'Such a hot day,' he said, eyeing the carafe of wine on the mantelpiece.

Ignoring this, Baruk strode to the window then turned his back to it. He studied the man, wondering if he would ever catch a glimpse of what lay beyond Kruppe's cherubic demeanour. 'What have you heard?' he asked softly.

'What has Kruppe heard? What *hasn't* Kruppe heard!'

Baruk raised an eyebrow. 'How about brevity?'

The man shifted in the chair and mopped his forehead. 'Such heat!' Seeing Baruk's expression harden, he continued, 'Now, as for news.' He leaned forward, his voice falling to a whisper. ''Tis muttered in corners in the bars, in dark doorways of dank streets, in the nefarious shadows of nocturnal night, in—'

'Get on with it!'

'Yes, of course. Well, Kruppe has caught wind of a rumour. An assassin's war, no less. The Guild is taking losses, 'tis said.'

Baruk turned back to the window, his eyes on the street below. 'And where do the thieves stand?'

248

'The rooftops are getting crowded. Throats are being slit. Profits have plummeted.'

'Where's Rallick?'

Kruppe blinked. 'He's disappeared,' he said. 'Kruppe has not seen him in days.'

'This assassin's war, it isn't internal?'

'No.'

'Has this new force been identified, then?'

'No.'

Baruk's gaze intensified. Below, the street workers seemed to spend more time arguing than working. An assassin's war could be trouble. Vorcan's Guild was strong, but the Empire was stronger, if indeed these newcomers were Claws. But something felt decidedly odd about the whole thing. In the past the Empress used such local guilds, often recruited from them. The alchemist could discern no purpose behind such a war, and that was even more disturbing to him than the war itself. Hearing a shuffling behind him, he remembered his agent. He turned and smiled. 'You can go now.'

Something flashed in Kruppe's eyes that startled Baruk. The fat man rose in a single fluid motion. 'Kruppe has more to tell, Master Baruk.'

Bemused, the alchemist nodded for Kruppe to continue.

'The tale is arduous and confused, alas,' he said, striding to join Baruk at the window. His handkerchief had disappeared. 'Kruppe can only surmise as best a man of innumerable talents may. In moments of leisure, during games of chance and the like. In the aura of the Twins an Adept may hear, see, smell, and touch things as insubstantial as the wind. A taste of Lady Luck, the bitter warning of the Lord's Laughter.' Kruppe's gaze snapped to the alchemist. 'Do you follow, Master?'

His eyes riveted on the man's round face, Baruk said quietly, 'You speak of Oponn.'

Kruppe looked back down at the street. 'Perhaps. Perhaps a

grim feint meant to mislead such as foolish Kruppe—'

Foolish? Baruk smiled inwardly. *Not this man.*

'– who can say?' Kruppe raised a hand, showing in his palm a flat disc of wax. 'An item,' he said softly, his eyes on the disc, 'that passes without provenance, pursued by many who thirst for its cold kiss, on which life and all that lay within life is often gambled. Alone, a beggar's crown. In great numbers, a king's folly. Weighted with ruin, yet blood washes from it beneath the lightest rain, and to the next no hint of its cost. It is as it is, says Kruppe, worthless but for those who insist otherwise.'

Baruk was holding his breath. His lungs burned, yet it was an effort to release them. Kruppe's words had drawn him into something – a place, hinting of vast stores of knowledge and the sure, unfailing, precise hand that had gathered it, marked it on parchment. A library, shelves of black wood in sharp relief, tomes bound to shiny leather, yellowed scrolls, a pitted, stained desk – Baruk felt he had but stolen a single glance into this chamber. Kruppe's mind, the secret place with its door locked to all but one. 'You speak,' Baruk said slowly, fighting to pull back into reality by focusing on the wax disc in Kruppe's hand, 'of a coin.'

Kruppe's hand snapped shut. He turned and set the disc down on the window-sill. 'Examine this semblance, Master Baruk. It marks both sides of a single coin.' The handkerchief reappeared and Kruppe stepped back, dabbing his brow. 'My, but it is hot, says Kruppe!'

'Help yourself to some wine,' Baruk murmured. As the man left his side the alchemist opened his Warren. He gestured and the wax disc rose into the air, slowly moving to hover before him at eye-level. He studied the imprint facing him. 'The Lady,' he muttered, nodding. The disc turned, revealing to him the Lord. The disc turned again, and Baruk's eyes widened as it began spinning. A whirring sound filled the back of his head.

He felt his Warren resisting a pressure that grew with the sound, then his source collapsed.

Faintly, as if from a great distance, he heard Kruppe speak. 'Even in this semblance, Master Baruk, blows the Twins' breath. No mage's Warren can withstand that wind.'

The disc still spun in the air in front of Baruk, a silver blur. A fine mist expanded around it. Hot droplets spattered his face and he stepped back. Blue fire flickered from the melting wax, the disc dwindling rapidly. A moment later it vanished, and the spinning sound and its accompanying pressure stopped abruptly.

The sudden silence filled Baruk's head with pain. He laid a trembling hand on the window-sill for support, then closed his eyes. 'Who carries the Coin, Kruppe?' His voice rasped from his constricted throat. 'Who?'

Kruppe once again stood at his side. 'A lad,' he answered casually. 'Known to Kruppe, assuredly so, as well as to your other agents, Murillio, Rallick and Coll.'

Baruk's eyes reopened. 'That can't be a coincidence,' he hissed, a desperate hope rising to struggle against the terror he felt. Oponn had entered the gambit, and in such reaches of power the life of a city and those within it meant nothing. He glared at Kruppe. 'Gather the group, then. All you've named. They've served my interests for a long time, and they must do so now, above all other concerns. Do you understand me?'

'Kruppe will convey your insistence. Rallick perchance is bound to Guild duties, while Coll, given purpose in life once again, might well steady his gaze and tread and take this mission to heart. Master Baruk? What is the mission, by the way?'

'Protect the Coinbearer. Watch him, mark whose face rests on him benign or foul. I must know if the Lady has him, or the Lord. And, Kruppe, for this, find Rallick. If the Lord claims the Coinbearer, the assassin's talents will be required.'

Kruppe blinked. 'Understood. Alas, may mercy smile upon young Crokus.'

'Crokus?' Baruk frowned. 'That's a name I know.'

Kruppe's face remained blank.

'Never mind. Very well, Kruppe.' He turned back to the window once again. 'Keep me informed.'

'As always, Baruk, Kruppe's friend.' The man bowed. 'And thank you for the wine, it was most delicious.'

Baruk heard the door open then close. He gazed down the street. He'd managed to clamp a hold on his fear. Oponn had a way of making ruins of the most finely wrought plans. Baruk despised that prospect of chance operating in his affairs. He could no longer rely on his ability to predict, to prepare contingencies, to work out every possibility and seek out the one best suited to his desires. *As the Coin spun, thus the city.*

Added to this the mysterious ways of the Empress. Baruk rubbed his brow. He'd have to instruct Roald to bring him some healing tea. His headache was reaching debilitating proportions. As he brought his hand down past his face his eyes caught a flash of red. He raised both palms into view. Red ink stained them. He leaned forward on the window-sill. Through a sparkling cloud of dust, Darujhistan's rooftops sprawled, and the harbour beyond. 'And you, Empress,' he whispered. 'I know you're here, somewhere. Your pawns move unseen as yet, but I will find them. Be sure of that, with or without Oponn's damned luck.'

BOOK THREE

THE MISSION

Marionettes dance afield
beneath masterly hands –
I stumble among them
crossed by the strings
in tangled two-step
and curse all these fools
in their mad pirouette –
I shall not live as they do
oh, no, leave me in my
circled dance –
these unbidden
twitchings you see
I swear on Hood's Grave
is artistry in motion

Sayings of the Fool
Theny Bule (b?)

CHAPTER EIGHT

He stepped down then
among women and men,
the sigil stripped
in her foul cleansing
there on the blood-soaked sand
spilled the lives
of Emperor and First Sword –
so tragic this treachery . . .
He was of the Old Guard,
commanding the honed edge
of Empire's fury,
and so in stepping down
but not away
he remained the remembrance
before her eyes, the curse
of conscience she would not stand.
A price was placed before him
that he glanced over in first passing
unknowing and so unprepared
in stepping down among women
and men, he found what
he'd surrendered and damned
its reawakening . . .

The Bridgeburners
Toc the Younger

A quarter-hour before dawn the sky held the colour of iron shot through with streaks of rust. Sergeant Whiskeyjack squatted on a dome of bedrock up from the pebble beach, gazing out over the misty calm surface of Lake Azur. Far to the south, on the lake's opposite shore, rose the faint glow of Darujhistan.

The mountain crossing of the night just past had been hell, the Quorl tossed about in the midst of three warring thunderheads. It was a miracle no one had been lost. The rain had since stopped, leaving the air cool and clammy.

He heard the sound of boots accompanied by a clicking noise behind him. Whiskeyjack turned and straightened. Kalam and a Black Moranth approached, picking their way through the mossy tumble of rocks at the base of the slope. Behind them rose the shadowed redwood forest, the patched trunks standing like bearded sentinels against the mountainside. The sergeant drew a deep breath of the chill morning air.

'Everything's fine,' Kalam said. 'The Green Moranth delivered as ordered, and more. Fiddler and Hedge are two happy sappers.'

Whiskeyjack raised an eyebrow. He turned to the Black Moranth. 'I thought your munitions were getting scarce.'

The creature's face remained in shadow beneath the hinged helmet. The words that came from it seemed born from a cavern, hollow and faintly echoing. 'Selectively, Bird That Steals. You are well known to us, Bridgeburner. You tread the enemy's shadow. From the Moranth, assistance will never be scarce.'

Surprised, Whiskeyjack looked away, the skin tightening around his eyes.

The Moranth continued. 'You asked of the fate of one of our kind. A warrior with but one arm, who fought at your side in the streets of Nathilog many years ago. He lives still.'

The sergeant took a deep breath of the sweet forest air. 'Thank you,' he said.

'We wish that the blood you next find on your hands is your enemy's, Bird That Steals.'

He frowned, then gave a brusque nod and turned his attention back to Kalam.

'What else?'

The assassin's face became expressionless. 'Quick Ben's ready,' he said.

'Good. Gather the others. I'll be laying out my plan.'

'*Your* plan, Sergeant?'

'Mine,' Whiskeyjack said firmly. 'The one devised by the Empress and her tacticians is being rejected, as of now. We're doing it my way. Get going, Corporal.'

Kalam saluted then left.

Whiskeyjack stepped down from the rock, his boots sinking into the moss. 'Tell me, Moranth, might a squadron of your Black be patrolling this area two weeks from now?'

The Moranth's head swivelled audibly towards the lake. 'Such unscheduled patrols are common. I expect to command one myself in two weeks' time.'

Whiskeyjack gazed steadily at the black-armoured warrior standing beside him. 'I'm not quite sure how to take that,' he said eventually.

The warrior faced him. 'We are not so unalike,' he said. 'In our eyes deeds have measure. We judge. We act upon our judgements. As in Pale, we match spirit with spirit.'

The sergeant frowned. 'What do you mean?'

'Eighteen thousand seven hundred and thirty-nine souls departed in the purge of Pale. One for each Moranth confirmed as a victim of Pale's history of enmity towards us. Spirit with spirit, Bird That Steals.'

Whiskeyjack found he had no response. The Moranth's next words shook him deeply.

'There are worms within your empire's flesh. But such degradation is natural in all bodies. Your people's infection is

257

not yet fatal. It can be scoured clean. The Moranth are skilled at such efforts.'

'How exactly,' Whiskeyjack paused, choosing his words carefully, 'do you intend this scouring?' He recalled the wagons piled with corpses winding out of Pale, and struggled against the ice tingling along his spine.

'Spirit with spirit,' the Moranth answered, returning his attention to the city on the south shore. 'We depart for now. You will find us here in two weeks' time, Bird That Steals.'

Whiskeyjack watched the Black Moranth walk away, pushing through the thicket surrounding the clearing where his riders waited. A moment later he heard the rapid thud of wings, then the Quorl rose above the trees. The Moranth circled once overhead, then turned north, slipping between the bearded boles and heading upslope.

The sergeant sat down on the bedrock again, his eyes on the ground as the members of his squad arrived, hunkering down around him. He remained silent, seeming unaware that he had company, his brow furrowed and jaw bunching as he ground his molars with a slow, steady precision.

'Sarge?' Fiddler said quietly.

Startled, Whiskeyjack looked up. He drew a deep breath. Everyone had gathered with the exception of Quick Ben. He'd leave Kalam to fill in the wizard later. 'All right. The original plan's been scrapped, since it was intended to get us all killed. I didn't like that part, so we'll do it my way and hopefully get out alive.'

'We ain't going to mine the city gates?' Fiddler asked, glancing at Hedge.

'No,' the sergeant answered. 'We'll put those Moranth munitions to better use. Two objectives, two teams. Kalam will lead one, and with him will be Quick Ben and . . .' he hesitated '. . . and Sorry. I'll lead the other team. The first task is to get into the city unnoticed. Out of uniform.'

He looked to Mallet. 'I take it the Green delivered?'

The healer nodded. 'It's a local make, all right. Eighteen-foot fisher, four oars, should get us across the lake easy enough. Even a couple of nets included.'

'So we'll do some fishing,' Whiskeyjack said. 'Coming into the harbour without a catch would look suspect. Anybody here ever fished?'

There was silence, then Sorry spoke up. 'I have, a long time ago.'

Whiskeyjack stared at her, then said, 'Right. Pick whoever you need for that.'

Sorry smiled mockingly.

Whiskeyjack pulled his gaze from hers with an oath under his breath. He eyed his two saboteurs. 'How much munitions?'

'Two crates,' Hedge replied, adjusting his leather cap. 'Cussers all the way down to Smokers.'

'We could cook a palace,' Fiddler added, shifting about excitedly.

'Good enough,' Whiskeyjack said. 'All right, everyone listen and pay attention, or we won't come out of this alive . . .'

In a secluded glade in the forest, Quick Ben poured white sand in a circle and sat down in its centre. He took five sharpened sticks and set them in a row before him, pushing them to various depths in the loam. The centre stick, the highest, rose about three feet; the ones on either side stood at two feet and the outer ones at a foot.

The wizard uncoiled a yard's length of thin gut string. He took one end and fashioned a scaled-down noose, which he tightened over the centre stick near the top. He ran the line to the left, looping it once over the next shaft, then crossed over to the right side and looped it again. He brought the string across to the far left stick, muttering a few words as he did so. He wrapped it twice and brought it over to the far right stick, where he tied a knot and cut the trailing string.

Quick Ben leaned back and folded his hands on his lap. A frown creased his brow. 'Hairlock!' An outer stick twitched, turned slightly, then fell still. 'Hairlock!' he barked again. All five shafts jerked. The centre one bent towards the wizard. The string tautened and a low-pitched hum emanated from it.

A cold wind swept across Quick Ben's face, stripping away the beads of sweat that had gathered in the last minute. A rushing sound filled his head, and he felt himself falling through dark caverns, their unseen walls ringing in his ears as if iron hammers clanged against the rock. Flashes of blinding silver light stung his eyes and the wind pulled at the skin and flesh of his face.

In some shielded part of his mind he retained a sense of distance, of control. Within this calm he could think, observe, analyse. 'Hairlock,' he whispered, 'you've gone too far. Too deep. This Warren has swallowed you and will never spit you out. You're losing control, Hairlock.' But these thoughts were for him alone; he knew the puppet was still distant.

He watched himself continue, spinning, whirling through the Caverns of Chaos. Hairlock was compelled to match him, only upward. Abruptly he found himself standing. Beneath his feet the black rock seemed to swirl, cracked here and there in its slow convolutions by bright, glowing red.

Looking around, he saw that he stood on a spar of rock, rising at an angle, its jagged apex a dozen feet in front of him. Turning, his gaze followed the spar as it sank down and out of sight, lost to billowing yellow clouds. A moment of vertigo gripped Quick Ben. He tottered, then, as he regained his balance he heard a chuckle behind him. He turned to see Hairlock perched atop the apex, his wooden body smeared and scorched, the doll's clothing ripped and frayed.

Quick Ben asked, 'This is the Spar of Andii, isn't it?'

Hairlock's round head bobbed. 'Half-way. Now you know

260

how far I have gone, wizard. To the very foot of the Warren, where power finds its first shape, and all is possible.'

'Just not very likely,' Quick Ben said, eyeing the marionette. 'How does it feel, standing in the middle of all that creation but unable to touch it, to use it? It's too alien, isn't it? It burns you with every reach.'

'I'll master it,' Hairlock hissed. 'You know nothing. Nothing.'

Quick Ben smiled. 'I've been here before, Hairlock.' He scanned the swirling gases around them, scudding on contrary winds. 'You've been lucky,' he said. 'Though they are few in number, there are creatures who call this realm home.' He paused and turned his smile on the puppet. 'They dislike intruders – have you seen what they do to them? What they leave behind?' The wizard's smile broadened at seeing Hairlock's involuntary jerk. 'So you have,' he said quietly.

'You are my protector,' Hairlock snapped. 'I'm bound to you, Wizard! The responsibility is yours, nor will I hide the fact if I am taken.'

'Bound to me, indeed.' Quick Ben lowered himself to his haunches. 'Good to hear your memory's come back. Tell me, how fares Tattersail?'

The puppet slumped, looking away. 'Her recovery is a difficult one.'

Quick Ben frowned. 'Recovery? From what?'

'The Hound Gear tracked me.' Hairlock shifted uneasily. 'There was a skirmish.'

A scowl grew on the wizard's face. 'And?'

The puppet shrugged. 'Gear fled, sorely wounded by a mundane sword in the hands of that captain of yours. Tayschrenn then arrived, but Tattersail had slipped into unconsciousness by then, so his search for answers was thwarted. But the fire of suspicion has been stoked beneath him. He sends out his servants, and they stalk the Warrens.

They hunt for signs of who and what I am. And why. Tayschrenn knows your squad is involved, he knows you're trying to save your own skins.' The puppet's mad gaze flickered. 'He wants you all dead, Wizard. And as for Tattersail, perhaps he hopes her fever will kill her so he won't have to – but there is much he'd lose if she died without his questioning her first. No doubt he'd seek out her soul, he'd pursue what she knows into Hood's own realm, but she'd know enough to be elusive.'

'Shut up for a minute,' Quick Ben ordered. 'Back to the beginning. You said Captain Paran stabbed Gear with his sword?'

Hairlock scowled. 'I did. A mortal weapon – it shouldn't have been possible. He may well have dealt the Hound a fatal wound.' The puppet paused, then growled, 'You've not told me everything, Wizard. There are gods involved in this. If you keep me in such ignorance I might well stumble into the path of one of them.' He spat. 'A slave to you is bad enough. Do you think you could challenge a god for mastery of me? I'd be taken, turned, perhaps even . . .' Hairlock unsheathed one of his small knives '. . . used against you.' He advanced a step, a dark glitter in his eyes.

Quick Ben raised an eyebrow. Inside, his heart lurched in his chest. Was it possible? Would he not have detected something? A flavour, a hint of immortal presence?

'One last thing, Wizard,' Hairlock murmured, taking another step. 'Tattersail's fever crested just this night past. She screamed something about a coin. A coin that had spun, but now it has fallen, it has bounced, it has entered someone's hand. You must tell me about this coin – I must have your thoughts, Wizard.' The puppet stopped suddenly and looked down at the knife in his hand. Hairlock hesitated, seeming confused, then sheathed the weapon and squatted. 'What's so important about a coin?' he growled. 'Nothing. The bitch raved – she was stronger than I had thought.'

Quick Ben froze. The puppet seemed to have forgotten that the wizard was present. The thoughts he now heard were Hairlock's own. He realized he was looking through the shattered window into the puppet's insane mind. And it was there that all the danger lay. The wizard held his breath as Hairlock continued, its eyes fixed on the clouds below.

'Gear should have killed her – would have, if not for that idiot captain. What irony, he now tends to her and puts his hand to his sword whenever I seek to come near. He knows I would snuff her life in an instant. But that sword. What god plays with this fool noble?' The puppet spoke on, but his words dwindled into inaudible mumbles.

Quick Ben waited, hoping for more, though what he'd already heard was enough to set his heart pounding. This mad creature was unpredictable, and all that held him in check was a tenuous control – the strings of power he'd attached to Hairlock's wooden body. But with this kind of madness came strength – enough strength to break those strings? The wizard was no longer as sure of his control as he had been.

Hairlock had fallen silent. His painted eyes still flickered with black flame – the leaking of Chaotic power. Quick Ben took a step forward.

'Pursue Tayschrenn's plans,' he commanded, then he kicked hard. The toe of his boot struck Hairlock's chest and sent the puppet spinning. Hairlock flew out over the edge, then fell downward. His outraged snarl dwindled as he disappeared into the yellow clouds.

Quick Ben drew a deep breath of the thick, stale air. He hoped that his abrupt dismissal had been enough to skew Hairlock's recollections of the past few minutes. Still, he felt those strings of control growing ever more taut. The more this Warren twisted Hairlock, the more power he would command.

The wizard knew what he'd have to do – Hairlock had given it to him, in fact. Still, Quick Ben wasn't looking forward to it.

The taste of sour bile rose into his mouth and he spat over the ledge. The air stank of sweat and it was a moment before he realized it was his own. He hissed a curse. 'Time to leave,' he muttered. He raised his arms.

The wind returned with a roar, and he felt his body flung up, up into the cavern above, then the next. As the caverns blurred by, a single word clung to his thoughts, a word that seemed to twist around the problem of Hairlock like a web.

Quick Ben smiled, but it was a smile responding to terror. And the word remained, *Gear*, and with that name the wizard's terror found a face.

Whiskeyjack rose amid silence. The expressions arrayed around him were sober, eyes downcast or fixed elsewhere, closed into some personal, private place where swam the heaviest thoughts. The lone exception was Sorry, who stared at the sergeant with bright, approving eyes. Whiskeyjack wondered who was doing the approving within those eyes – then he shook his head, angry that something of Quick Ben and Kalam's suspicions had slipped into his thoughts.

He glanced away, to see Quick Ben approaching. The wizard looked tired, an ashen tint to his face. Whiskeyjack's gaze snapped to Kalam.

The assassin nodded. 'Everyone, look alive,' he said. 'Load up the boat and get it ready.'

Mallet leading the way, the others headed down to the beach.

Waiting for Quick Ben to arrive, Kalam said, 'The squad looks beat, Sergeant. Fiddler, Trotts and Hedge moved enough dirt in those tunnels to bury the Empire's dead. I'm worried about them. Mallet – he seems to be holding together, so far . . . Still, whatever Sorry knows about fishing, I doubt any one of us could row their way out of a bathtub. And we're about to try crossing a lake damn near big as a sea?'

Whiskeyjack's jaw tightened, then he forced a casual shrug into his shoulders. 'You know damn well that any Warren opening anywhere near the city will likely be detected. No choice, Corporal. We row. Unless we can rig up a sail.'

Kalam grunted. 'Since when does the girl know about fishing?'

The sergeant sighed. 'I know. Came out of nowhere, didn't it?'

'Bloody convenient.'

Quick Ben reached the dome of rock. Both men fell silent at seeing his expression.

'I'm about to propose something you're going to hate,' the wizard said.

'Let's hear it,' Whiskeyjack replied, in a voice empty of feeling.

Ten minutes later the three men arrived on the slick pebbled beach, both Whiskeyjack and Kalam looking shaken. A dozen yards from the water's edge sat the fisher boat. Trotts was straining on the rope attached to the prow hook, gasping and moaning as he leaned forward with all his weight.

The rest of the squad stood in a clump off to one side, quietly discussing Trotts' futile efforts. Fiddler chanced to look up. Seeing Whiskeyjack marching towards them, he blanched.

'Trotts!' the sergeant bellowed.

The Barghast's face, woad tattoos stretched into illegibility, turned to Whiskeyjack with wide eyes.

'Let go of the rope, soldier.'

Kalam released an amused snort behind Whiskeyjack, who glared at the others. 'Now,' he said, his voice harsh, 'since one of you idiots convinced everyone else that loading all the equipment into the boat when it's still on shore was a good idea, you can all man the rope and drag it into the lake – not you, Trotts. You get inside, get comfortable, there at the stern.' Whiskeyjack paused. He studied Sorry's expressionless face.

265

'From Fiddler and Hedge I expect this, but I thought I put you in charge of setting things up.'

Sorry shrugged.

Whiskeyjack sighed. 'Can you rig us a sail?'

'There's no wind.'

'Well, maybe there will be!' Whiskeyjack said, exasperated.

'Yes,' Sorry answered. 'We have some canvas. We'll need a mast.'

'Take Fiddler and make one. Now, the rest of you, get this boat into the water.'

Trotts climbed inside and sat down at the stern. He stretched out his long legs and draped an arm over the splashboard. He bared his filed teeth in what might have been a smile.

Whiskeyjack turned to a grinning Kalam and Quick Ben. 'Well?' he demanded. 'What're you waiting for?'

The grins died.

CHAPTER NINE

Have you seen the one
who stands apart
cursed in a ritual
sealing his kind
beyond death the host
amassed and whirling
like a plague of pollen –
he stands apart
the First among all
ever veiled in time
yet outcast and alone
a T'lan Imass wandering
like a seed unfallen

Lay of Onos T'oolan
Toc the Younger

T oc the Younger leaned forward in his saddle and spat. It
was his third day out from Pale, and he longed for the
city's high walls around him. The Rhivi Plain stretched
out on all sides, cloaked in yellow grass that rippled in the
afternoon wind, but otherwise featureless.

He scratched the edges of the wound that had taken his left eye, and muttered under his breath. Something was wrong. He should have met her two days past. Nothing was going as planned these days. What with Captain Paran vanishing before even meeting Whiskeyjack and the story making the rounds about a Hound attacking the 2nd's last-surviving mage and leaving fourteen dead marines in its wake, he supposed he shouldn't be surprised that this rendezvous had gone awry as well.

Chaos seemed a sign of the times. Toc straightened and rose in his saddle. Though there was no true road as such on the Plain, merchant caravans had mapped a rough track running north–south along the western edge. Trade had since died out, but the passing of generations of wagons and horse trains had left its mark. The centre of the Plain was home to the Rhivi, those small brown-skinned people who moved with the herds in a seasonal cycle. Though not warlike, the Malazan Empire had forced their hand, and now they fought and scouted alongside Caladan Brood's Tiste Andii legions against the Empire.

Moranth reports placed the Rhivi far to the north and east, and Toc was thankful for that. He was feeling very alone out in this wasteland, yet loneliness was a lesser evil, all things considered.

Toc's single eye widened. It seemed he wasn't so alone, after all. Perhaps a league ahead ravens wheeled. The man cursed and loosened the scimitar sheathed at his hip. He fought the urge to push his horse into a gallop and settled for a quick trot.

As he neared he saw trampled grass off to one side of the trader's track. The cackling laughter of the ravens was the only sound to break the stillness. They had already begun feeding. Toc reined in his horse and sat unmoving in his saddle, hunched forward. None of the bodies he saw looked as if they were apt to start moving, and the ravens' preoccupied squabbling was good evidence that any survivors had long gone.

Still, he had a bad feeling about this. Something hung in the air, something between a smell and a taste.

He waited, for what he wasn't certain, but a reluctance to move gripped him. All at once he identified the strangeness he felt: magic. It had been unleashed here. 'I hate this,' he muttered, then dismounted.

The ravens gave him room, but not much. Ignoring their outraged shrieks he approached the bodies. They numbered twelve in all. Eight wore the uniforms of Malazan Marines – but these weren't average soldiers. His gaze narrowed on the silver sigils on their helmets. 'Jakatakan,' he said. Élites. They'd been cut to pieces.

He turned his attention to the remaining bodies and felt a tremor of fear run through him. No wonder the Jakatakan had taken such a beating. Toc strode to one of the bodies and crouched beside it. He knew something of the clan markings among the Barghast, how each hunter group was identified through their woad tattooing. The breath hissed between his teeth and he reached out to turn the savage's face towards him, then he nodded. These were Ilgres Clan. Before the Crimson Guard had enlisted them, their home territory had been fifteen hundred leagues to the east, among the mountains just south of the Porule. Slowly Toc rose. The Ilgres numbered among the strongest of those who had joined the Crimson Guard at Blackdog Forest, but that was four hundred leagues north. So what had brought them here?

The stench of spilled magic wafted across his face and he turned, his eye fixing on a body he hadn't noticed before. It lay beside scorched grass. 'So,' he said, 'my question's answered.' This band had been led by a Barghast shaman. Somehow, they'd stumbled on to a trail and this shaman had recognized it for what it was. Toc studied the shaman's body. Killed by a sword wound in the throat. The unleashing of sorcery had been the shaman's, but no magic had opposed him. And that was odd, particularly since it was the shaman who had died, rather than whomever he'd attacked.

Toc grunted. 'Well, she's said to be hell on mages.' He walked a slow circle around the kill site, and found the trail with little difficulty. Some of the Jakatakan had survived, and from the smaller set of boot-prints, so had their charge. And overlaying these tracks were half a dozen moccasin prints. The trail veered westerly from the trader's track, yet still led south.

Returning to his horse, Toc mounted and swung the animal around. He removed the short bow from its saddle holster and strung it, then nocked an arrow. There was no hope of coming up on the Barghast undetected. Out on this plain he'd be visible a long time before entering arrow-range – and that range had become much closer now that he'd lost an eye. So they'd be waiting for him, with those damn lances. But he knew he had no choice; he hoped only to take down one or two of them before they skewered him.

Toc spat again, then wrapped the reins around his left forearm and adjusted his grip on the bow. He gave the wide red scar crossing his face a vigorous, painful scratch, realizing that the maddening itch would return in moments anyway. 'Oh well,' he said, then drove his heels into the horse's flanks.

The lone hill that rose up before Adjunct Lorn was not a natural one. The tops of mostly buried stones encircled its base. She wondered what might be entombed within it, then dismissed her misgivings. If those standing stones were of the size she'd seen rising around the mysterious barrows outside Genabaris, this mound dated back millennia. She turned to the two exhausted marines stumbling in her wake. 'We'll make our stand here. You with the crossbow, I want you lying up top.'

The man ducked his head in answer and staggered to the mound's grassy summit. Both he and his comrade seemed almost relieved that she'd called a halt, though they knew their death was but minutes away.

Lorn eyed the other soldier. He'd taken a lance barb in his left shoulder and the blood still flowed profusely down the front of his breastplate. How he had stayed on his feet in the last hour was beyond Lorn's understanding. He looked upon her with eyes dulled by resignation, showing nothing of the pain he must be feeling.

'I'll hold your left,' he said, shifting his grip on the curved tulwar in his right hand.

Lorn unsheathed her own longsword and fixed her attention northwards. Only four of the six Barghast were visible, approaching slowly. 'We're being flanked,' she called out to her crossbowman. 'Take the one on your left.'

The soldier beside her grunted. 'My life need not be sheltered,' he said. 'We were charged with your protection, Adjunct—'

'Quiet,' Lorn commanded. 'The longer you stand the better protected I'll be,' she said.

The soldier grunted again.

The four Barghast were lingering now, just out of bowshot range. Two still carried their lances; the other two gripped short axes. Then a voice cried out far to Lorn's right and she whirled to see a lance speeding towards her, and behind it a charging Barghast.

Lorn brought her blade across her body and dropped into a crouch as she raised the weapon over her head. Her sword caught the lance's shaft and even as it did so she was turning, pulling her weapon to one side. The deflected lance sped past and cracked into the hillside off to her right.

Behind her she heard the crossbowman release a quarrel. As she spun back to the four charging Barghast there came a scream of pain from the other side of the mound. The soldier beside her seemed to have forgotten his wound, as he gripped his tulwar with both hands and planted his feet wide.

'Attend, Adjunct,' he said.

The Barghast off to the right cried out and she turned to see him spinning with the impact of a quarrel.

The four warriors before them were no more than thirty feet away. The two with lances now launched them. Lorn made no move, realizing almost immediately that the one aimed at her would fly wide. The soldier beside her dropped away to his left, but not enough to avoid the lance as it thudded into his right thigh. It struck with such force as to drive right through his leg and embed itself in the earth. The soldier was pinned, but his only response was a soft gasp, and he raised his sword to parry an axe swinging at his head.

In this time Lorn had already closed with the Barghast rushing at her. His axe was a shorter weapon, and she took advantage of this with a thrust before he came into his own range. He brought the copper-sheathed haft up to parry, but Lorn had already flicked her wrist, completing the feint and dipping under the axe. Her lunge buried the sword point in the Barghast's chest, slicing the leather armour as if it were cloth.

Her attack had committed her, and her sword was nearly wrenched from her hand as the savage toppled backwards. Off-balance, she staggered a step, expecting the crushing blow of an axe. But it did not arrive. Regaining her balance she spun round, to find her crossbowman, now wielding his tulwar, engaging the other Barghast. Lorn snapped her attention to see how her other guard fared.

Somehow, he still lived, though he faced two Barghast. He'd managed to drag the lance out of the earth, but the weapon's shaft remained in his leg. That he was able to move at all, much less defend himself, spoke eloquently of Jakatakan discipline and training.

Lorn rushed to engage the Barghast on the man's right, nearest her. Even as she did so, an axe slipped past the soldier's

272

guard and struck him across the chest. Scale snapped as the heavy weapon's edge ripped through armour. The soldier groaned and fell to one knee, blood spraying on to the ground.

Lorn was in no position to defend him and could only watch in horror as the axe swung again, this time striking the man in the head. The helmet collapsed inward and his neck broke. He toppled sideways, landing at Lorn's feet. Her forward momentum carried her right over him.

A curse broke from her lips as she sprawled, crashing into the Barghast in front of her. She tried to bring the point of her sword up behind him but he twisted lithely to one side and leaped away. Lorn took a wild swing at him, missing, even as she fell. She felt her shoulder dislocate as she hit the hard ground, and the sword dropped from her numbed hand.

Now, she thought, the only thing left to do is die. She rolled on to her back.

With a growl the Barghast was standing beside her, axe raised high.

Lorn was in a good position to see the skeletal hand bursting from the earth beneath the Barghast. It grasped an ankle. Bones snapped and the warrior screamed. Vaguely, as she watched, she wondered where the other two savages had gone. All sounds of fighting seemed to have stopped, but the ground rumbled with a growing, urgent thunder.

The Barghast stared down at the hand crushing his shin. He screamed again as the wide, rippled blade of a flint sword shot up between his legs. The axe left the warrior's hands as he frantically brought them down in an effort to deflect the sword, twisting to one side and kicking out with his free leg. It all came too late. The sword impaled him, jamming against his hipbone and lifting him from the ground. His dying shriek rose skyward.

Lorn climbed to her feet with difficulty, her right arm hanging useless at her side. She identified the thundering sound as the beat of hoofs, and turned in the direction from which they came. A Malazan. As that fact sank in, she swung her attention from the rider and looked around. Both her guards were dead, and arrows jutted from two Barghast bodies.

She took a shallow breath – all she could manage as pain spread across her chest – and gazed upon the creature that had risen from the earth. It was cloaked in rotting furs, and it stood over the warrior's body, one leg still clutched in its hand. The other hand gripped the sword, which had been pushed the length of the Barghast's body, the point emerging from his neck.

'I was expecting you days ago,' Lorn said, glaring at the figure.

It turned to regard her, its face hidden in shadow beneath the yellowed bone shelf of its helmet. The helmet, she saw, was the skull-cap of some horned beast, one horn broken off at its base.

The rider arrived behind her. 'Adjunct!' he called out, dismounting. He came to her side, bow still in his hand and arrow nocked. His lone eye glanced across Lorn and, seeming satisfied that her wound was not mortal, fixed on the massive but squat creature facing them. 'Hood's Breath, a T'lan Imass.'

Lorn continued glaring at the T'lan Imass. 'I knew you were about. It's the only thing that explains a Barghast shaman bringing himself and his hand-picked hunters into the area. He must have used a Warren to get here. So where *were* you?'

Toc the Younger stared at the Adjunct, amazed at her outburst. His gaze flicked back to the T'lan Imass. The last time he'd seen one was in Seven Cities, eight years past, and then it had been from a distance as the undead legions marched out into the western wastelands on some mission even the Empress could learn nothing about. At this close range, Toc eagerly studied the T'lan Imass. Not much left of it, he concluded. Despite the sorcery, three hundred thousand years had taken their toll. The skin that stretched across the squat man's robust bones was a shiny nut brown in colour, the texture of leather. Whatever flesh it had once covered had contracted to thin strips the consistency of oak roots – such muscles showed through torn patches here and there. The creature's face, what Toc could see of it, bore a heavy chinless jawbone, high cheeks and a pronounced brow ridge. The eye sockets were dark holes.

'I asked you a question,' Lorn grated. 'Where were you?'

The head creaked as the Imass looked down at its feet. 'Exploring,' it said quietly in a voice born of stones and dust.

Lorn demanded, 'Your name, T'lan?'

'Onos T'oolan, once of the Tarad Clan, of the Logros T'lan. I was birthed in the autumn of the Bleak Year, the ninth son to the Clan whetted as warrior in the Sixth Jaghut War—'

'Enough,' Lorn said. She sagged wearily and Toc moved to her side. Glancing up at him she scowled, 'You look grim.' Then a small smile came to her lips. 'But good to me.'

Toc grinned. 'First things first, Adjunct. A place for you to rest.' She did not protest as he guided her to a grassy knoll near the barrow and gently pushed her to her knees. He glanced back to see the T'lan Imass still standing where it had first emerged from the ground. It had turned, however, and seemed to be studying the barrow. 'We must make your arm immobile,' Toc said to the worn, weathered woman kneeling before him. 'I am named Toc the Younger,' he said, squatting down.

She raised her gaze at this. 'I knew your father,' she said. Her smile returned. 'Also a great bowman.'

He ducked his head in reply.

'He was a fine commander too,' Lorn continued, studying the ravaged youth who was now tending to her arm. 'The Empress has regretted his death—'

'Not dead for sure,' Toc interrupted, his tone tight and his single eye averted as he began removing the gauntlet from her hand. 'Disappeared.'

275

'Yes,' Lorn said softly. 'Disappeared since the Emperor's death.' She winced as he pulled away the gauntlet and tossed it aside.

'I'll need some strips of cloth,' he said, rising.

Lorn watched him stride to one of the Barghast bodies. She had not known who her Claw contact would be, only that he was the last left alive among Dujek's forces. She wondered why he had veered so sharply from his father's path. There was nothing pleasant, or proud, in being a Claw. Only efficiency and fear.

He took a knife to the body's tanned leather armour, slicing it back to reveal a rough woollen shirt, into which he cut. Then he returned to her side, a handful of long strips in one hand. 'I didn't know you had an Imass for company,' he said, as he crouched beside her again.

'They choose their own modes of travel,' Lorn said, a hint of anger in her voice. 'And come when they please. But yes, he's an integral player in my mission.' She fell silent, gritting her teeth in pain as Toc slipped the rude sling over her shoulder and under her arm.

'I have little good to report,' Toc said, and he told her of Paran's disappearance, and of Whiskeyjack and his squad departing without the captain in attendance. By the time he had finished he had adjusted the sling to his own satisfaction, and sat back on his haunches with a sigh.

'Damn,' Lorn hissed. 'Help me to my feet.'

After he'd done so, she wobbled a bit and gripped his shoulder to steady herself. Then she nodded. 'Get me my sword.'

Toc strode to the spot she'd indicated. After a brief search he found the longsword in the grass, and his eye thinned to a slit upon seeing the weapon's dusty red blade. He brought it to her, and said, 'An Otataral sword, Adjunct, the ore that kills magic.'

'And mages,' Lorn said, taking the weapon awkwardly in her left hand and sheathing it.

'I came upon the dead shaman,' Toc said.

'Well,' Lorn said, 'Otataral is no mystery to you of the Seven Cities, but few here know it, and I would keep it that way.'

'Understood.' Toc turned to regard the immobile Imass.

Lorn seemed to read his thought. 'Otataral cannot quench their magic – believe me, it's been tried. The Warrens of the Imass are similar to those of the Jaghut and the Forkrul Assail – Elder-, blood- and earthbound – that flint sword of his will never break, and it cuts through the finest iron as easily as it will flesh and bone.'

Toc shivered and spat. 'I'll not envy you your company, Adjunct.'

Lorn smiled. 'You'll be sharing it for the next few days, Toc the Younger. We've a long walk to Pale.'

'Six, seven days,' Toc said. 'I expected you to be mounted.'

Lorn's sigh was heartfelt. 'The Barghast shaman worked his talents on them. A disease took them all, even my stallion, which I brought with me through the Warren.' Her lined face softened momentarily, and Toc could feel her genuine sorrow.

It surprised him. All that he'd heard of the Adjunct had painted for him a picture of a cold-blooded monster, the gauntleted hand of death that could descend from anywhere at any time. Perhaps this side of her existed; he hoped he would not have to see it. Then again, he corrected himself, she'd not spared her soldiers a second glance. Toc spoke, 'You'll ride my mare, Adjunct. She's no warhorse, but she's quick and long on endurance.'

They walked to where he'd left his horse, and Lorn smiled. 'That's a Wickan breed, Toc the Younger,' she said, as she laid a hand on the mare's neck, 'so cease the modesty, else I lose trust in you. A fine animal.'

Toc helped her into the saddle. 'Do we leave the Imass where it is?' he asked.

Lorn nodded. 'He'll find his own way. Now, let's give this

mare the opportunity to prove herself. Wickan blood is said to smell of iron.' She reached down and offered her left arm. 'Mount up,' she said.

Toc barely managed to hide his shock. Share the saddle with the Adjunct of the Empire? The notion was so absurd that he came near to laughing. 'I can walk, Adjunct,' he said gruffly. 'With such little time to waste, you would be better to ride on, and ride hard. You'll see Pale's walls in three days. I can manage a jog at ten-hour stretches.'

'No, Toc the Younger.' Lorn's tone brooked no argument. 'I need you in Pale, and I need to hear all there is about the occupying legions, and Dujek, and Tayschrenn. Better to arrive a few days late than unprepared. Now, grasp my arm and let's be on with it.'

Toc complied.

As he sank into the saddle behind Lorn, his mare snorted and stepped quickly to one side. Both he and the Adjunct almost fell. They turned to see the T'lan Imass standing beside them. It raised its head to Lorn.

'The barrow has yielded a truth, Adjunct,' Onos T'oolan said.

Toc felt her stiffen. 'And that is?'

'We are upon the right path,' the T'lan Imass replied.

Something told Toc that the path the creature referred to had nothing to do with the trader's track leading south to Pale. He cast one final glance back at the barrow as Lorn silently swung the horse around, and then at Onos T'oolan. Neither seemed likely to unveil their secrets, but Lorn's reaction had raised the hairs on the back of his neck, and the itch around his lost eye roused itself. Toc muttered a curse under his breath and began to scratch.

'Something the matter, Toc the Younger?' Lorn asked, not turning.

He thought about his reply. He said, 'The price of being blind, Adjunct. Nothing more.'

278

*   *   *

Captain Paran paced in the narrow room. This was madness! All he knew was that he was being hidden, but the only answers to his questions would come from a bed-ridden sorceress locked in some strange fever, and a nasty puppet whose painted eyes seemed to fix on him with intense hatred.

Vague memories haunted him as well, the feel of slick, cold stones scraping beneath his fingernails at a moment when all his strength had poured from his body; and then the hazy vision of a massive dog – a Hound? – in the room, a dog that seemed to breathe death. It had been seeking to kill the woman, and he'd stopped it – somehow, he wasn't sure of the details.

A suspicion nagged him that the dog wasn't dead, that it would be back. The puppet ignored most of his questions, and when it did speak to him it was to voice dire threats. Apparently, though the Sorceress was ill, her presence alone – her continued existence – was all that kept Hairlock from fulfilling those threats.

Where was Whiskeyjack? Had the sergeant left without him? What would that do to Adjunct Lorn's plan?

He ceased pacing and turned a glare on the sorceress lying in the bed. Hairlock had told Paran that she'd somehow hidden him when Tayschrenn arrived, the High Mage having sensed the dog's presence. Paran had no memory of any of that, but he wondered how the woman could have managed anything after the beating she'd taken. Hairlock had scoffed that the sorceress hadn't even been aware of opening her Warren that one last time; that she'd done it all on instinct. Paran had the feeling that the marionette had been scared by that unveiling of power. Hairlock seemed most eager for the woman's death, but was either unable to achieve it himself or too frightened to try. The creature had muttered something about wards she'd raised about her person.

Yet Paran found nothing to impede his ministrations when

279

the fever had been at its worst. It had broken the previous night, and now Paran felt his impatience reaching some kind of threshold. The sorceress slept, but if she didn't awaken soon he'd take matters into his own hands – leave this hiding place, perhaps seek out Toc the Younger, provided he could avoid Tayschrenn or any officers on his way out of the building.

Paran's unseeing glare remained fixed on the sorceress, his thoughts racing. Slowly, a new awareness tickled the edges of his mind, and he abruptly blinked. The woman's eyes were open, and they studied him.

He took a half-step forward but was stopped dead by her first words.

'I heard the Coin drop, Captain.'

The blood drained from Paran's face. An echo flittered through his memory. 'A coin?' he asked, his voice barely a whisper. 'A spinning coin?' *The voices of gods, of dead men and women. Howls of Hounds – all pieces of my memory's torn tapestry.*

'Spins no longer,' the woman replied. She pushed herself into a sitting position. 'How much do you remember?'

'Scant,' the captain admitted, surprised at himself for telling the truth. 'The puppet will not even tell me your name,' he said.

'Tattersail. I've been, uh, in the company of Whiskeyjack and his squad.' A veil of caution seemed to slip over her sleepy gaze. 'I was to take care of you until your health returned.'

'I believe you did,' Paran said. 'And I returned the favour, which evens the scales, Sorceress.'

'So it does. Well, now what?'

Paran's eyes widened. 'You don't know?'

Tattersail shrugged.

'But this is ridiculous,' Paran exclaimed. 'I know nothing of what's happening here. I awaken to find a half-dead witch and a talking puppet for company, and of my new command

280

not a single sign. Have they left for Darujhistan already?'

'I can't give you much in the way of answers,' Tattersail murmured. 'All I can tell you is the sergeant wanted you alive, because he needs to know who tried to assassinate you. We'd all like to know, in fact.' She fell silent, expectant.

Paran studied her round, ghostly pale face. There was something about her that seemed to disregard her physical mundanity, overwhelmed it, in fact, so that the captain found himself responding in ways that surprised him. It was, he saw, a friendly face, and he couldn't recall the last time he'd experienced such a thing. It left him off-balance, with only Tattersail to steady him. And that made him feel as if he were descending a spiral, with the sorceress in the centre. Descending? Perhaps it was an ascent. He wasn't sure, and the uncertainty made him wary.

'I recall nothing of it,' he said. And that wasn't entirely a lie, though it felt like it with her heavy-lidded eyes steady upon him.

'I think,' Paran added, despite his misgivings, 'there were two of them. I recall a conversation, though I was dead. I think.'

'But you heard a spinning coin,' Tattersail said.

'Yes,' he answered, bewildered. *And more . . . I went to a place – yellow, infernal light, a chorus of moans, a death's head . . .*

Tattersail nodded to herself as if confirming a suspicion. 'A god intervened, Captain Paran. Returned the life to you. You might think it was on your behalf, but I'm afraid there wasn't any altruism involved. Are you following me?'

'I'm being used,' Paran stated flatly.

She raised an eyebrow. 'That doesn't bother you?'

Paran shrugged and turned away. 'It's nothing new,' he muttered.

'I see,' she said quietly. 'So Whiskeyjack was right, then. You're not just some new captain, you're something a lot more.'

281

'That's my concern,' Paran snapped, still avoiding her gaze. Then he faced her, his expression dark. 'And what's your role in all this? You took care of me. Why? Serving your god, are you?'

Tattersail barked a laugh. 'Not likely. Nor did I do much for you in any case. Oponn took care of that.'

Paran stiffened. 'Oponn?' *The Twins, sister and brother, the Twins of Chance. He who pushes, she who pulls. Have they been in my dreams? Voices, mention of my . . . sword.* He was still for a moment, then he strode over to the dresser. On it lay his sheathed sword. He laid a hand on the grip. 'I purchased this sword three years ago, though its first use came just a few nights past – against the dog.'

'You recall that?'

Something in Tattersail's voice brought him around. In her eyes he now saw fear. She made no attempt to hide it. He nodded. 'Yet I named the weapon the day I bought it.'

'The name?'

Paran's grin was ghastly. 'Chance.'

'The pattern has been long in the weaving,' Tattersail said, closing her eyes and sighing. 'Though I suspect even Oponn could not have imagined your blade tasting its first blood on a Hound of Shadow.'

Paran closed his eyes, then he sighed. 'The dog was a Hound.'

She looked at him and nodded. 'You've met Hairlock?'

'I have.'

'Beware him,' Tattersail said. 'It was his unleashing of a Warren of Chaos that left me fevered. If Warrens are indeed structured, then Hairlock's is diametrically opposed to mine. He's mad, Captain, and he vowed to kill you.'

Paran strapped on his sword. 'What's his role in all of this?'

'I'm not sure,' Tattersail said.

That sounded like a lie, but Paran let it pass. 'He was

coming in nightly to check on your progress,' he said. 'But I haven't seen him the past two nights.'

'How many days have I been out?'

'Six, I think. I'm no more certain of time's passage than you are, I'm afraid.' He strode to the door. 'All I know is, I can't just hide here for ever.'

'Wait!'

Paran smiled. 'Very well.' He faced her again. 'Tell me why shouldn't I leave?'

The sorceress hesitated, then spoke. 'I still need you here,' she said.

'Why?'

'It's not me that Hairlock's afraid of,' she answered, seeming to find the words difficult. 'It's you – your sword – that's kept me alive. He saw what you managed to do to the Hound.'

'Damn,' he hissed. Though essentially still a stranger to him, she'd reached through to him with her admission. He tried to fight the compassion welling up inside him. He told himself that his mission overrode all other concerns, that he'd repaid his debt to her, if ever there was one, that she hadn't given him all the reasons he suspected existed for his staying hidden, meaning she didn't trust him – he told himself all these things, but none of it was enough.

'If you go,' she said, 'Hairlock will kill me.'

'What of the wards about you?' he demanded, almost desperately. 'Hairlock said you've wards about you.'

Tattersail's smile was drawn. 'You think he'd just come right out and tell you how dangerous you really are? Wards?' She laughed. 'I've barely the strength to sit straight. If I attempted to open my Warren in this state the power would consume me, burn me to ashes. Hairlock wants you kept in the dark – about everything. The puppet lied.'

Even this rang like a half-truth in Paran's ears. But there was enough there that made sense, that gave reason to Hairlock's

283

hatred of him, and the puppet's obvious fear. The greater deceit would come from Hairlock, not Tattersail, or so he believed, though there was little to support that belief – only . . . at least Tattersail was human. He sighed. 'Sooner or later,' he said, unclipping his sword belt and returning it to the dresser, 'you and I will have to cut past all this misleading game-playing. Oponn or no, we've a common enemy.'

Tattersail sighed. 'Thank you. Captain Paran?'

He eyed her warily. 'What?'

She smiled. 'It is good to meet you.'

He scowled. She was at it again.

'This seems an unhappy army,' Lorn said, as they waited outside Pale's north gate. One of the guards had entered the city in search of another horse, while the remaining three stood muttering a short distance away.

Toc the Younger had dismounted. He moved close to his horse and said, 'It is, Adjunct. Very unhappy. Along with the dismantling of the Second and Sixth Armies came a shuffling of commands. Nobody's where they were before, right down to the greenest recruit. Squads split up everywhere. And now there's the rumour that the Bridgeburners are going to be retired.' He glanced over at the three marines, saw their hard eyes on him and the Adjunct. 'People around here don't like that,' he said quietly.

Lorn leaned back in her saddle. The pain in her shoulder had become a steady throb, and she was glad the journey was done – at least for the time being. They'd seen nothing of the T'lan Imass since the barrow, though she often sensed his presence, in the dusty wind, beneath the plain's cracked pan. While in the company of Toc the Younger she'd sensed the restless anger churning among the Malazan forces on this continent.

In Pale, ten thousand soldiers crowded the edge of revolt,

the spies among them brutally removed, awaiting only High Fist Dujek's word. And the High Mage Tayschrenn wasn't easing the situation by openly countermanding Dujek's instructions to his officers. Yet what troubled the Adjunct the most was this vague tale of a Hound of Shadow doing battle with the 2nd's last cadre mage – there was a mystery there, and she suspected it was vital. The rest could be dealt with, provided she took charge.

The Adjunct was eager for her meeting with Tayschrenn and this sorceress Tattersail – the name was familiar, tugging at memories that seemed born in her childhood. And around such evasive hints rustled a cloak of fear. But she was determined to deal with that when the time came.

The gate swung open. She looked up to see the marine with a warhorse, and they had company. Toc the Younger snapped a salute, the energy behind it making Lorn wonder at his loyalty. The Adjunct dismounted slowly, then nodded at High Fist Dujek.

The man seemed to have aged a dozen years since she'd last seen him, thirteen months ago in Genabaris. A small smile came to Lorn's mouth as the scene emerged in her mind: the High Fist a worn, weary one-armed man, the Empress's Adjunct, her sword arm in a sling, and Toc the Younger, last representative of the Claw on Genabackis, one-eyed and half his face scarred by fire. Here they were, representatives of three of the four Empire powers on the continent, and they all looked like hell.

Misreading her smile, Dujek grinned. 'Good to see you, too, Adjunct. I was overseeing the resupply when this guard brought word of your arrival.' His gaze grew thoughtful as he studied her, the grin fading. 'I'll find you a Denul healer, Adjunct.'

'Sorcery doesn't work on me, High Fist. It hasn't in a long time. A mundane healer is sufficient.' Her gaze narrowed on

Dujek. 'Assuming I'll have no need to unsheath my sword within the walls of Pale.'

'I make no guarantees, Adjunct,' Dujek said casually. 'Come, let us walk.'

Lorn turned to Toc the Younger. 'Thank you for the escort, soldier.'

Dujek laughed, his eyes bright on Toc. 'Unnecessary, Adjunct. I know who, and what, Toc the Younger is – as does virtually everyone else. If he's as good a Claw as he is a soldier, you'd do well to keep him alive.'

'Meaning?'

Dujek gestured that they walk. 'Meaning that his reputation as a soldier of the Second is the only thing preventing a knife across the throat. Meaning get him out of Pale.'

The Adjunct eyed Toc. 'I will see you later,' she said.

Joining Dujek, who had passed beneath the gate's massive arch, Lorn matched his pace as they entered the city. Soldiers crowded the streets, directing merchant wagons and the mobs of citizenry. Evidence of the rain of death still scarred many of the buildings, but labourers had been set to work under the direction of marines.

'The nobility are about to be culled,' Dujek said at her side. 'Tayschrenn wants it to be thorough, and public.'

'Empire policy,' Lorn replied stiffly. 'You're well aware of that, High Fist.'

Dujek glared at her. 'Nine out of ten nobles to hang, Adjunct? Children included?'

Lorn stared at him. 'That seems excessive.'

Dujek was silent for a time, leading her down the main avenue then heading uphill towards the Empire headquarters. Many faces turned to regard them stonily as they passed. It seemed Dujek's identity was known among Pale's citizens. Lorn tried to sense the atmosphere his presence created, but couldn't be certain if it was fear or respect, or both.

'My mission,' Lorn said, as they approached a three-storey stone building, its entrance blocked by a dozen watchful marines, 'will take me out of the city soon—'

'I don't want any details, Adjunct,' Dujek cut in. 'You do what you have to do and just stay out of my way.'

His tone was unthreatening, almost pleasant, but Lorn felt her muscles tense. This man was being pushed, and Tayschrenn was doing the pushing. What was the High Mage up to? The whole situation stank of incompetence.

'As I was saying,' Lorn continued, 'I won't be here long. When I am here, however,' and her voice hardened, 'I will make plain to the High Mage that his interference in the city's management will not be tolerated. If you need backing, you have it, Dujek.'

They stopped just outside the building's entrance, and the old man gazed steadily at her, as if weighing her sincerity. But when he spoke, his words surprised her. 'I can take care of my own problems, Adjunct. Do what you will, but I'm not asking for anything.'

'You'll permit the excessive culling of the nobility, then?'

Dujek's expression set into stubborn lines. 'Battle tactics can be applied in any situation, Adjunct. And the High Mage is no tactician.' He turned and led her up the steps. Two guards opened the doors, which looked new and were banded in bronze. The High Fist and the Adjunct entered.

They strode down a long, wide hallway marked by doors on either side every dozen feet or so. Marines stood guard before each one, hands on their weapons. It was clear to Lorn that the incident with the Hound had heightened wariness to an almost absurd degree. Then a thought struck her. 'High Fist, have there been attempts on your life?'

Dujek's grunt was amused. 'Four in the last week, Adjunct. You get used to it. All these marines here volunteered them-selves – they don't even listen to me any more. The last assassin was so badly chopped up I couldn't even make out if it was a man or a woman.'

'You've a lot of Seven Cities natives in your legions, High Fist?'

'Aye. Loyal to a fault when they want to be.'

Loyal to what, Lorn wondered, and to whom? Seven Cities recruits were being sent elsewhere these days. The Empress did not wish Dujek's soldiers to become aware that their homeland was on the brink of open rebellion. Such news might well tip the scales here on Genabackis, and that in turn would trigger Seven Cities itself. Both Lorn and the Empress were well aware how dangerous things had become, and they had to tread carefully indeed in their efforts to repair the damage. And it was now becoming obvious that Tayschrenn presented a major problem.

She realized that she needed Dujek's support more than he needed hers.

They arrived at the hall's end where stood massive double doors. The soldiers at either side saluted the High Fist then opened them. Beyond was a large chamber dominated by a hardwood table in its centre. Maps, scrolls, ink and paint jars crowded its surface. Dujek and Lorn entered and the doors were shut behind them.

'Tayschrenn has been informed of your arrival, but will be delayed somewhat,' Dujek said, sitting on the edge of the table. 'If you have questions regarding the recent events at Pale, ask them now.'

She knew he was giving her the opportunity to hear answers that didn't come from Tayschrenn. Though as to whose version of the truth she would accept was up to her. Lorn began to appreciate Dujek's comment about battle tactics. She strode to a nearby chair and settled slowly into its cushions. 'Very well, High Fist. Small matters first. Have you encountered any difficulty with the Moranth?'

288

Dujek scowled. 'Funny you should ask. They're getting pretty high-minded about some things. I had a hell of a time getting the Gold legions – their élite warriors – to fight Caladan Brood. Seems they consider him too honourable to treat as an enemy. The whole alliance was on shaky ground for a while there, but in the end they marched. Soon I'll send the Black to join them.'

Lorn nodded. 'Similar problems with the Green and the Blue in Genabaris,' she said, 'which explains why I came overland. The Empress suggests we make the most of the alliance, since it may not last.'

'We haven't much choice,' Dujek growled. 'How many legions will I have in the spring landing?'

Lorn hesitated, then said, 'Two. And a regiment of Wickan lancers. The Wickans and the Eleventh Legion will disembark at Nathilog. The Ninth will land in Nisst and join with the conscript forces – the Empress trusts the latter reinforcements will be sufficient to break the Crimson Guard at Fox Pass, thus opening Brood's flank.'

'Then the Empress is a fool,' Dujek said, his tone hard. 'The conscripts are next to useless, Adjunct, and by this time next year the Crimson Guard will have liberated Nisst, Treet, One Eye Cat, Porule, Garalt and—'

'I know the list.' Lorn rose abruptly. 'You'll receive two more legions next year, High Fist. That's it.'

Dujek thought for a time, his gaze on the map pegged to the table top. Lorn waited. She knew he was lost in reordering, re-evaluating his plans for next season's campaign, that he'd entered a world of matériel and divisions, in second-guessing Caladan Brood and the commander of the Crimson Guard, Prince K'azz. Finally he cleared his throat. 'Adjunct, is it possible to reverse the landings? The Eleventh and the Wickan lancers disembarking on the east coast, south of Apple. The Ninth on the west coast, to Tulips.'

Lorn strode to the table and studied the map. *Tulips? Why there?* That made no sense at all. 'The Empress would be curious as to your revised plans, High Fist.'

'Meaning "maybe".' Dujek rubbed the stubble on his jaw, then gave a sharp nod. 'All right, Adjunct. First, the conscripts will not hold Fox Pass. The Crimson Guard will be into the northlands by the time our reinforcements arrive. Much of that area is farmland, pasture. As we retreat, pulling the conscripts back to Nisst, we raze the countryside. No crops, no livestock. Whatever supplies K'azz will need he'll have to bring with him. Now, Adjunct, any army on the move, any army pursuing a routed army, is bound to leave its supply train behind, string it out in its haste to catch its enemy and deliver the killing blow. And that's where the Wickan lancers come in.'

The Wickan were born raiders, Lorn knew. In such countryside they'd be elusive, striking quickly and with deadly consequences. 'And the Eleventh? Where will they be in all this?'

'A third will be stationed in Nisst. The rest will be on the quick march – to Fox Pass.'

'While Caladan Brood remains south of Blackdog Forest? That doesn't make sense, High Fist.'

'You suggested using the Moranth for all it's worth, didn't you? Well, from Tulips the Moranth and their Quorl will be staging a massive lift.' Dujek's gaze narrowed as he studied the map. 'I want the Ninth south of Blackdog Swamp by the time I bring up my forces from here and place them south of Brood. A concerted push from the Gold and Black should push him right into our laps, while his allies, the Crimson Guard, are stuck on the wrong side of Fox Pass.'

'You intend to transport an entire legion by air?'

'Does the Empress want this war won in her lifetime or not?' He pushed himself away from the table and paced. 'Mind you,'

290

he said, as if struck by sudden doubts, 'it may all be academic. If I were Brood I'd . . .' His voice trailed away, and he faced the Adjunct. 'Will the transport orders be reversed?'

Lorn searched his face. Something told her that the High Fist had just made an intuitive leap, and it had to do with Caladan Brood, and that as far as Dujek was concerned, it was indeed now academic. She also realized that this was something he wouldn't share with her. She scanned the map again, trying to see what Dujek had seen. But it was hopeless, she was no tactician. Trying to guess Dujek's thoughts was hard enough; but to try the same with Caladan Brood was impossible. 'Your plan, although brash, is now officially accepted on behalf of the Empress. Your request will be fulfilled.'

Dujek nodded half-heartedly.

'One thing, High Fist, before Tayschrenn arrives. There was a Hound of Shadow here?'

'Yes,' the man said. 'I wasn't here at the time, but I saw the mess the beast left behind. If not for Tattersail it would've been far worse.'

Lorn saw a glint of horror in Dujek's eyes and into her mind returned the scene from the coast road west of Itko Kan, two years ago. 'I've seen the work of Hounds before,' she said, meeting his eyes.

In that moment of locked gazes they shared something profound. Then Dujek pulled his eyes away. 'This Tattersail,' Lorn said, to hide a pang of regret, 'must be a very capable sorceress.'

'The only cadre mage to have survived Tayschrenn's assault on Moon's Spawn,' Dujek replied.

'Indeed?' To Lorn, that revelation was even more remarkable. She wondered if Dujek suspected anything, but his next words put her at ease.

'She called it luck, on both counts, and she might be right.'

'Has she been a cadre mage for a long time?' Lorn asked.

'Ever since I took command. Perhaps eight, nine years.'

The familiarity of Tattersail's name returned to Lorn then, like a mailed fist clenching her heart. She found herself sitting down again, and Dujek had taken a step towards her, genuine concern in his eyes.

'Your injury needs attending to,' he said gruffly. 'I shouldn't have waited.'

'No, no, it's all right. Weariness, that's all.'

He studied her quizzically. 'Would you like some wine, Adjunct?'

She nodded. *Tattersail. Was it possible?* She would know when she saw the woman. She would know then. 'Nine years,' she murmured, 'the Mouse.'

'I beg your pardon?'

She looked up to find Dujek before her. He offered her a goblet of wine. 'Nothing,' she said, as she accepted it. 'Thank you.'

As the double doors swung open both turned. In strode Tayschrenn, his face dark with fury as he confronted Dujek.

'Damn you,' the High Mage grated. 'If you had a hand in this I'll find it, and that is a promise.'

Dujek raised an eyebrow. 'A hand in what, High Mage?' he asked coolly.

'I've just been to the Hall of Records. A fire? The place looks like the inside of an oven.'

Lorn rose and stepped between them. 'High Mage Tayschrenn,' she said, in a low, dangerous tone, 'perhaps you could tell me why this matter of some fire in some bureaucrat's chamber should override all other considerations?'

Tayschrenn blinked. 'I beg your pardon, Adjunct,' he said tightly, 'but within the Hall of Records were the city's census lists.' His dark eyes swung past her to fix on Dujek. 'Wherein all the names of Pale's nobility could be found.'

'Unfortunate,' the High Fist said. 'Have you begun an

292

investigation? My staff's services are, of course, entirely at your disposal.'

'Unnecessary, High Fist,' the wizard drawled sardonically. 'Why make all your other spies redundant?' Tayschrenn paused, then stepped back and bowed to Lorn. 'Greetings, Adjunct. I apologize for this ungracious-seeming reunion—'

'Save your apologies for later,' Lorn said levelly. She faced Dujek. 'Thank you for the wine and conversation,' she said, noting with satisfaction Tayschrenn's stiffening at that. 'I trust there'll be a formal dinner this evening?'

Dujek nodded. 'Of course, Adjunct.'

'Would you be so kind as to request Tattersail's attendance as well?' She felt yet another flinch come from the High Mage, and saw in Dujek's gaze a new respect as he looked upon her, as if acknowledging her own skills in this brand of tactics.

Tayschrenn interrupted. 'Adjunct, the sorceress has been ill as a result of her encounter with the Hound of Shadow,' he turned a smile on Dujek, 'which I'm sure has been described to you by the High Fist.'

Not well enough, Lorn thought ruefully, but let Tayschrenn imagine the worst. 'I'm interested in a wizard's evaluation of that event, High Mage,' she said.

'Which you shall have shortly.'

Dujek bowed. 'I will enquire as to Tattersail's health, Adjunct. If you will excuse me, then, I can be on my way.' He turned to Tayschrenn and gave a curt nod.

Tayschrenn watched the one-armed old man leave the room, then waited for the doors to close once again. 'Adjunct, this situation is—'

'Absurd,' Lorn finished hotly. 'Dammit, Tayschrenn, where's your sense? You've taken on the craftiest bastard the Empire military has ever had the privilege of possessing and he's eating you alive.' She spun to the table and refilled her goblet. 'And you deserve it.'

'Adjunct—'

She faced him. 'No. Listen, Tayschrenn. I speak directly from the Empress. She reluctantly approved your commandeering the assault on Moon's Spawn – but if she'd known you so thoroughly lacked subtlety, she would never have permitted it. Do you take everyone else for fools?'

'Dujek is just one man,' Tayschrenn said.

Lorn took a large mouthful of wine, then set down the goblet and rubbed her brow. 'Dujek's not the enemy,' she said wearily. 'Dujek's never been the enemy.'

Tayschrenn stepped forward. 'He was the Emperor's man, Adjunct.'

'Challenging that man's loyalty to the Empire is insulting, and it's that very insult that may well turn him. Dujek is not just one man. Right now he's ten thousand, and in a year's time he'll be twenty-five thousand. He doesn't yield when you push, does he? No, because he can't. He's got ten thousand soldiers behind him – and, believe me, when they get angry enough to push back, you'll not be able to withstand them. As for Dujek, he'll just end up being carried on the tide.'

'Then he is a traitor.'

'No. He's a man who cares for those he is responsible for and to. He's the best of the Empire. If he's forced to turn, Tayschrenn, then we're the traitors. Am I getting through?'

The High Mage's face was lined with a deep, disturbed frown. 'Yes, Adjunct,' he said quietly. 'You are.' He looked up. 'This task the Empress has commanded of me, it weighs heavily, Adjunct. These are not my strengths. It would do well if you dismissed me.'

Lorn gave that serious consideration. Mages by nature never commanded loyalty. Fear, yes, and the respect born of fear, but the one thing a mage found difficult to understand or cope with was loyalty. And yet there had been one mage, long ago, who had commanded loyalty – and that was the Emperor. She said, 'High Mage, we are all agreed on one thing. The old guard must disappear. All who stood with the Emperor and still cling to his memory will ever work against us, whether consciously or unconsciously. Dujek is an exception, and there is a handful of others like him. Those we must not lose. As for the others, they have to die. The risk lies in alerting them to that fact. If we're too open we may end up with an insurrection the size of which could destroy the Empire.'

'Apart from Dujek and Tattersail,' Tayschrenn said, 'we've cleaned out everyone else. As for Whiskeyjack and his squad, he's all yours, Adjunct.'

'With luck,' Lorn said, then frowned as the High Mage winced. 'What's the matter?'

He rose. 'I peruse my Deck of Dragons nightly,' he said. 'And I'm certain that Oponn has entered the world of mortal affairs. Tattersail's own reading did much to confirm my suspicions.'

Lorn looked at him sharply. 'She's an Adept?'

'Far more adept than I,' Tayschrenn admitted.

Lorn thought. 'What can you tell me of Oponn's involvement?'

'Darujhistan,' Tayschrenn replied.

Lorn closed her eyes. 'I was afraid you'd say that. We need Darujhistan – desperately. Its wealth, coming into our hands, would break this continent's back.'

'I know, Adjunct. But the matter is even worse than you realize. I also believe that, somehow, Whiskeyjack and Tattersail are in league with one another.'

'Any word of what happened to Captain Paran?'

'None. Someone is hiding him, or his body. I'm inclined to believe he's dead, Adjunct, but his soul has yet to pass through Hood's Gate and only a mage could prevent that.'

'Tattersail?'

The High Mage shrugged. 'Possibly. I would know more of this captain's role in all this.'

Lorn hesitated, then said, 'He was engaged in a long, arduous search.'

Tayschrenn growled, 'Perhaps he found whatever he was seeking.'

Lorn eyed him. 'Perhaps. Tell me, how good is Tattersail?'

'Good enough to be a High Mage,' Tayschrenn said. 'Good enough to survive a Hound's attack and to drive it away, though I would not think such a thing possible. Even I would have difficulty managing that.'

'Maybe she had help,' Lorn murmured.

'I hadn't thought of that.'

'Think on it now,' Lorn said. 'But before you do, the Empress requests that you continue your efforts, though not against Dujek. You're needed here as a conduit in case my mission goes wrong in Darujhistan. Do not involve yourself with managing the occupation of Pale. Further, you are to provide Dujek with details on Oponn's appearance. If a god has entered the fray, he has a right to know and to plan accordingly.'

'How can one plan anything with Oponn in the game?'

'Leave that to Dujek.' She studied his face. 'Do you have difficulty with any of these instructions?'

Tayschrenn smiled. 'In truth, Adjunct, I'm greatly relieved.'

Lorn nodded. 'Good. Now, I need a mundane healer and quarters.'

'Of course.' Tayschrenn strode to the doors, then paused and turned. 'Adjunct, I am glad you're here.'

'Thank you, High Mage.' After he left, Lorn sank into her chair and her mind travelled back nine years, to the sights and sounds experienced by a child, to a night, one particular night in the Mouse, when every nightmare a young girl's imagination could hold became real. She remembered blood, blood everywhere, and the empty faces of her mother, her father and older brother – faces numbed by the realization that they'd been

296

spared, that the blood wasn't their own. As the memories stalked once again through her mind, a name rode the winds, rustling in the air as if clawing through dead branches. Lorn's lips parted, and she whispered, 'Tattersail.'

The sorceress had found the strength to leave her bed. She now stood at the window, leaning with one hand against the frame for support, and looked down on a street crowded with military wagons. The systematic plunder that quartermasters called 'resupply' was well under way. The eviction of nobility and gentry from their familial estates for the stationing of the officer corps, of which she was one, had ended days ago, while the repairing of the outer walls, the refitting of sundered gates, and the clearing of 'Moon rain' continued apace.

She was glad she'd missed the river of corpses that must have filled the city streets during the initial phase of clean-up – wagon after wagon groaning beneath the weight of crushed bodies, white flesh seared by fire and slashed by sword, rat-gnawed and raven-pecked – men, women, and children. It was a scene she had witnessed before, and she had no wish ever to see it again.

Now, shock and terror had seeped down and out of sight. Scenes of normality reappeared as farmers and merchants emerged from hiding to meet the needs of occupiers and occupied alike. Malazan healers had swept the city, rooting out the birthing of plague and treating common ailments among all those they touched. No citizen would have been turned from their path. And sentiments began the long, perfectly planned swing.

Soon, Tattersail knew, there'd be the culling of the nobility, a scourge that would raise to the gallows the greediest, least-liked nobles. And the executions would be public. A tried and true procedure that swelled recruitment on a tide of base vengeance – with every hand stained by a righteous glee. A sword in such hands completed the conspiracy and included all players in the hunt for the next victim to the cause – the Empire's cause.

She'd seen it run its course in a hundred such cities. No matter how benign the original rulers, no matter how generous the nobility, the word of Empire, weighted by might, twisted the past into a tyranny of demons. A sad comment on humanity, a bitter lesson made foul by her own role in it.

In her mind returned the faces of the Bridgeburners, a strange counterpoint to the cynicism with which she viewed all around her. Whiskeyjack, a man pushed to the edge, or, rather, the edge creeping on him on all sides, a crumbling of beliefs, a failing of faiths, leaving as his last claim to humanity his squad, a shrinking handful of the only people that mattered any more. But he held on, and he pushed back – pushed back hard. She liked to think – no, she wanted to believe – he would win out in the end, that he'd live to see his world stripped of the Empire.

Quick Ben and Kalam, seeking to take the responsibility from their sergeant's shoulders. It was their only means of loving the man, though they'd never put it in such terms. In the others, barring Sorry, she saw the same, yet with them there was a desperation that she found endearing, a child-like yearning to relieve Whiskeyjack of everything their grim place had laid upon him.

She responded to them in a way deeper than she'd thought possible, from a core she'd long been convinced was burned out, the ashes scattered in silent lament – a core no mage could afford. Tattersail recognized the danger, but that only made it all the more alluring.

Sorry was another matter, and she found herself avoiding even thinking about that young woman.

And that left Paran. What to do about this captain? At the moment the man was in the room, seated on the bed behind her and oiling his sword, Chance. They'd not spoken much since she'd awakened four days ago. There was still too much distrust.

Perhaps it was that mystery, that uncertainty, that made them so attracted to one another. And the attraction was obvious: even now, with her back to the man, she sensed a taut thread between them. Whatever energy burned between them, it felt dangerous. Which made it exciting.

Tattersail sighed. Hairlock had appeared this very morning, eager and agitated about something. The puppet would not answer their queries, but the sorceress suspected that Hairlock had found a trail, and it seemed it might take the puppet out of Pale and on to Darujhistan.

That was not a happy thought.

She stiffened as the ward she'd placed outside her door was tripped. Tattersail whirled to Paran. 'A visitor,' she said.

He rose, Chance in his hands.

The sorceress waved her hand over him. 'You're no longer visible, Captain. Nor can anyone sense your presence. Make no sound, and wait here.' She strode into the outer room just as a soft knock sounded on the door.

She opened it to see a young marine standing in the hall-way. 'What is it?' she demanded.

The marine bowed. 'High Fist Dujek is enquiring as to your health, Sorceress.'

'Much better,' she said. 'That's kind of him. Now, if you'll—'

The marine interrupted diffidently. 'If you answered as you just have, I am to convey the High Fist's request that you attend a formal supper this evening in the main building.'

Tattersail cursed silently. She shouldn't have told the truth. Now, it was too late. A 'request' from her commander was not something that could be denied. 'Inform the High Fist that I will be honoured to share his company over supper.'

A thought struck her. 'May I ask who else will be present?'

'High Mage Tayschrenn, a messenger named Toc the Younger, and Adjunct Lorn.'

'Adjunct Lorn is here?'

'Arrived this morning, Sorceress.'

Oh, Hood's Breath. 'Convey my reply,' Tattersail said, struggling against a rising tide of fear. She shut the door, then heard the marine's boots hurrying down the hallway.

'What's wrong?' Paran asked, from the opposite doorway.

She faced him. 'Put that sword away, Captain.' She walked over to the dresser and began rummaging through the drawers. 'I'm to attend a dinner,' she said.

Paran approached. 'An official gathering.'

Tattersail nodded distractedly. 'With Adjunct Lorn there as well, as if Tayschrenn isn't bad enough.'

The Captain murmured, 'So she's finally arrived.'

Tattersail froze. She turned to him slowly. 'You've been expecting her, haven't you?'

Paran started and looked at her with frightened eyes.

She realized his mumbling hadn't been meant for her ears. 'Dammit,' she hissed. 'You're working for her!'

The captain's answer was clear as he spun round. She watched him vanish into the bedroom, her thoughts a storm of fury. The threads of conspiracy now thrummed in her mind. So, Quick Ben's suspicions had been accurate: a plan was afoot to kill the squad. Did that make her life at risk as well? She felt herself nearing a decision. What that decision was she wasn't sure, but there was a direction to her thoughts now, and it had the inevitable momentum of an avalanche.

The seventh bell was ringing from some distant tower as Toc the Younger passed into the Empire headquarters.

He showed his invitation to yet another grim-faced, intense guard, and was grudgingly allowed to continue on down the

300

main hall to the dining chamber. Unease churned in Toc's stomach. He knew the Adjunct was behind the request, but she could be as unpredictable and as manipulative as the rest. Beyond the doors he now approached might as well be a pit filled with vipers, all hungrily awaiting his arrival.

Toc wondered if he'd be able to keep anything down, and knowing the condition of his facial wound, he then wondered grimly if anyone else would be able to keep anything down. Among his fellow soldiers his scars were barely noticed: rare was the soldier in Dujek's army who did not carry a scar or three. Those few friends he had seemed simply thankful that he still lived.

In the Seven Cities, superstition held that loss of an eye was also the birth of inner sight. He'd been reminded of that belief at least a dozen times in the last couple of weeks. There had been no secret gift granted him in exchange for his eye. Flashes of searing light ripped through his mind every now and then, but he suspected that was no more than a memory of the last thing his eye had seen: fire.

And now he was about to sit among the loftiest company in the Empire, barring the Empress herself. Suddenly the wound was a thing of shame. He'd sit there as testament to the horrors of war – Toc stiffened just outside the dining room door. Was that why the Adjunct had invited him? He hesitated, then shrugged and entered.

Dujek, Tayschrenn and the Adjunct turned as one to regard him. Toc the Younger bowed.

'Thank you for coming,' Adjunct Lorn said. She stood with the two men near the largest of three fireplaces, in the wall opposite the entrance. 'Please, join us. We're now awaiting but one more guest.'

Toc strode to them, thankful for Dujek's grin. The High Fist set his crystal goblet down on the mantel and deliberately scratched the stump of his left arm.

'Bet it's driving you half crazed,' the old man said, his grin broadening.

'I scratch with both hands,' Toc said.

Dujek barked a laugh. 'Join us in a drink?'

'Thank you.' He noticed Lorn's appraisal as he accepted a goblet from Dujek. Taking the decanter from a nearby table, his glance crossed the High Mage, but Tayschrenn's attention was fixed on the roaring fire behind Lorn.

'Has your horse recovered?' the Adjunct asked.

Toc nodded as he filled his goblet. 'Doing handstands the last time I looked in on her,' he said.

Lorn smiled tentatively, as if unsure whether he was mocking her. 'I've explained your vital role in keeping me alive, Toc the Younger, how you loosed four arrows on the fly, and brought down four Barghast.'

He looked at her sharply. 'I didn't know I had the last two shots in me,' he said. He sipped wine, resisting the urge to scratch his wound.

Dujek grunted. 'Your father was also in the habit of surprising people. There's a man I miss.'

'I, too,' Toc replied, looking down.

The awkward silence that followed this exchange was mercifully broken by the arrival of the last guest. Toc turned with the others as the door swung open. He gazed at the woman standing in the entrance, then started. Was that Tattersail? He'd never seen her wearing anything but battle garb, and was now stunned. My, he thought wonderingly, she's not bad, if you like them big, that is. He half grinned.

Lorn's response to Tattersail's appearance had sounded much like a gasp, then she spoke. 'We have met before, though I doubt you'd remember.'

Tattersail blinked. 'I think I would have recalled that,' she said cautiously.

'I think not. I was but eleven years old at the time.'

302

'Then you must be mistaken. I'm rarely in the company of children.'

'They burned the Mouse Quarter a week after you swept through it, Tattersail.' Lorn's voice made everyone stiffen with its barely controlled rage. 'Those survivors, the ones you left behind, were resettled in Mock's Hole. And in those plague-ridden caverns my mother, my father and my brother died.'

The blood drained from Tattersail's round face.

Bewildered, Toc glanced at the others. Dujek's expression was masked, but there was a storm behind his eyes as he studied Lorn. On Tayschrenn's face, as he looked upon the sorceress, there dawned a sudden light.

'It was our first command,' Tattersail said quietly.

Toc saw Lorn trembling and held his breath. But when she spoke it was controlled, the words precise. 'An explanation is required.' She turned to High Fist Dujek. 'They were recruits, a cadre of mages. They were in Malaz City, awaiting their new commander, when the Master of the Claw issued an edict against sorcery. They were sent into the Old City – the Mouse – to cleanse it. They were –' her voice caught '– indiscriminate.' She swung her attention back to Tattersail. 'This woman was one of those mages. Sorceress, that night was my last with my family. I was given to the Claw the very next day. The news of my family's death was kept from me for years. Yet,' her words fell to a whisper, 'I well remember that night – the blood, the screams.'

Tattersail seemed unable to speak. The air in the room had grown thick, stifling. Finally the sorceress prised her gaze from the Adjunct and said to Dujek, 'High Fist, it was our first command. We lost control. I resigned from the officer corps the very next day and was posted with another Army.' She gathered herself. 'If it is the Adjunct's wish to convene a court, I offer no defence and will accept my execution as a just penalty.'

Lorn replied, 'That is acceptable.' She laid her left hand

303

upon her sword and prepared to withdraw it.

'No,' High Fist Dujek said. 'It is not acceptable.'

Lorn froze. She glared at the old man. 'You seem to forget my rank.'

'No, I haven't. Adjunct, if it is your will that those within the Empire who have committed crimes in the Emperor's name must be executed,' he stepped forward, 'then you must include me. Indeed, I believe High Mage Tayschrenn also has his share of horror committed on the Emperor's behalf. And, finally, there is the Empress herself to consider. Laseen, after all, commanded the Emperor's Claw – she created it, in fact. More, the Edict was hers, thankfully short-lived as it was.' He turned to Tattersail. 'I was there, Tattersail. Under Whiskeyjack's command I was sent down to rein you in, which I did.'

She shook her head. 'Whiskeyjack commanded?' Her eyes narrowed. 'This has the taste of a god's game.'

Dujek swung back to the Adjunct. 'The Empire has its history, and we each are in it.'

'In this,' Tayschrenn rasped, 'I must agree with the High Fist, Adjunct.'

'There's no need to have all this official,' Tattersail said, her eyes on Lorn. 'I hereby challenge you to a duel. On my behalf I shall employ all my magical skills in an effort to destroy you. You may defend with your sword, Adjunct.'

Toc took a step forward. He opened his mouth, then closed it again. He'd been about to tell Tattersail that Lorn carried an Otataral sword, that the duel would be grossly unfair, that she'd die within seconds, as the sword devoured her every spell. Then he saw that the sorceress knew all that.

Dujek rounded on Tattersail. 'Dammit, woman! Do you think everything hinges on how it's worded? Execution. Duel. None of it matters one whit! All that the Adjunct does, all that she says, is on behalf of Empress Laseen.' He spun to Lorn. 'You are here as Laseen's voice, as her will, Adjunct.'

Tayschrenn spoke softly, 'The woman named Lorn, the woman who once was a child, who once had a family,' he looked upon the Adjunct with anguish in his eyes, 'that woman does not exist. She ceased to exist the day she became the Adjunct.'

Lorn stared at the two men, her eyes wide.

Standing beside her, Toc watched those words battering her will, crushing the anger, shattering into dust every last vestige of identity. And from her eyes rose the icy, clinical repose of the Adjunct to the Empress. Toc felt his heart pounding hard against his chest. He'd just witnessed an execution. The woman named Lorn had risen from the turgid mists of the past, risen to right a wrong, to find justice and in that last act reclaim its life – and she had been denied. Not by the words of Dujek or Tayschrenn, but by the thing known as the Adjunct.

'Of course,' she said, removing her hand from her sword. 'Please enter, Sorceress Tattersail, and dine with us.'

The flat tone of her voice told Toc that her invitation had not cost anything – and this horrified him, shook him to his very core. A quick glance showed a similar response from Tayschrenn and Dujek, though the latter veiled it.

Tattersail looked positively ill, but she nodded shakily in answer to the Adjunct's invitation.

Toc found the decanter and a spare crystal goblet. He walked up to the sorceress. 'I am Toc the Younger,' he said, smiling, 'and you need a drink.' He poured the glass full and handed it to her. 'Often, when we camped on the march, I'd see you lugging that travelling wardrobe of yours around. Now I finally see what was in it. Sorceress, you're a sight for a sore eye.'

A look of gratitude entered Tattersail's gaze. She raised an eyebrow. 'I hadn't realized my travelling wardrobe garnered such attention.'

Toc grinned. 'I'm afraid you've provided a standing joke in

the Second. Anything surprising, be it an ambush or an unplanned skirmish – the enemy invariably came from your travelling wardrobe, Sorceress.'

Dujek guffawed behind him. 'I've often wondered where that phrase came from, and damn, I heard it a lot – even from my officers.'

The atmosphere in the room relaxed somewhat; though undercurrents of tension still swirled, they seemed to be between Tattersail and High Mage Tayschrenn. The sorceress turned her gaze upon Lorn whenever the Adjunct's attention was elsewhere, and Toc could see the compassion there, and his respect for her rose considerably. In her shoes, any look he gave Lorn would have been filled with fear. And whatever storm threatened between Tattersail and Tayschrenn seemed born of a difference in opinion coupled with suspicion; it didn't look personal.

Then again, Toc considered, Dujek's steady presence may have been providing the levelling influence. His father had spoken much of Dujek, of a man who never lost his touch with the powerless or the less powerful. In dealing with the former, he always made his own failings an easy recognition; and with the latter he had an unerring eye that cut away personal ambition with the precision of a surgeon removing septic flesh, leaving in its place someone who treated trust and honesty as givens.

Studying Dujek's easy, relaxed rapport with the others in attendance, including himself, and then with the servants who filed in bearing trays of food, it struck Toc that the man had not changed perceptibly from the one Toc the Elder had called friend. And that impressed Toc deeply, knowing as he did the pressures that burdened the High Fist.

As soon as everyone was seated and the first course presented, it was Adjunct Lorn who took command, however. Dujek relinquished it without a word or a gesture, evidently confident that the earlier incident was now over as far as the Adjunct was concerned.

Lorn addressed Tattersail in that uncanny, flat voice. 'Sorceress, permit me to compliment you on besting a Hound of Shadow, and on your timely recovery. I know that Tayschrenn has questioned you regarding this incident, but I would like to hear the tale from you directly.'

Tattersail set down her goblet and regarded her plate briefly before meeting the Adjunct's steady gaze. 'As the High Mage may have explained, it's now clear that the gods have entered the fray. Specifically, they've become involved with the Empire's plans for Darujhistan—'

Toc rose quickly. 'I believe,' he said, 'I should excuse myself now, as what will be discussed here exceeds—'

'Be seated, Toc the Younger,' Lorn commanded. 'You are the Claw representative here, and as such you are responsible for speaking on its behalf.'

'I am?'

'You are.'

Slowly, Toc sat.

'Please continue, Sorceress.'

Tattersail nodded. 'Oponn is central to this gambit. The Twin Jesters' opening move has created ripples – I'm sure the High Mage would agree with this – and thus attracted the attention of other gods.'

'Shadowthrone,' Lorn said. She looked to Tayschrenn.

The High Mage concurred. 'One could expect such a thing. I, however, have sensed nothing of Shadowthrone's attention upon us, even though I pursued that possibility vigorously after the Hound's attack.'

Lorn exhaled slowly. 'Sorceress, please go on.'

'The Hound's presence was triggered entirely by accident,' Tattersail said, flicking a glance at Tayschrenn. 'I was doing a reading from my Deck of Dragons, and came upon the card of the

Hound. As with all Adepts, I found the image animate to a certain extent. When I gave it my full concentration, it felt,' she cleared her throat, 'as if a portal opened, created entirely from the other side of that card – from High House Shadow itself.' She raised her hands and gazed steadily at the High Mage. 'Is this possible? The Shadow Realm is new among the Houses, its full power not yet expressed. Well, whatever happened – a portal, a rent – the Hound Gear appeared.'

'Then why,' Tayschrenn asked, 'did it appear in the street? Why not in your room?'

Tattersail smiled. 'I can speculate.'

'Please do,' the Adjunct said.

'I have wards about my room,' Tattersail said. 'The innermost of these are High Thyr.'

Tayschrenn started at that, clearly surprised.

'Such wards,' Tattersail continued, 'create a flux, a tide of power that surges and ebbs like a pulsing heart, one that is beating very fast. I suspect that these wards were sufficient to bounce the Hound away from my immediate area, since in its transitional state – half-way between its realm and ours – the Hound could not fully express its powers. Once it had arrived, however, it could, and it did.'

'How did you manage to fend off a Hound of Shadow?' Tayschrenn asked.

'Luck,' Tattersail replied, without hesitation. Her answer hung in the air, and it seemed to Toc that everyone had forgotten their meal.

'In other words,' Lorn said slowly, 'you believe that Oponn intervened.'

'I do.'

'Why?'

Tattersail barked a laugh. 'If I could work that out, Adjunct, I'd be a happy woman. As it is,' her humour fell away, 'it seems we're being used. The Empire itself has become a pawn.'

308

'Is there a way out?' Dujek asked, his words a growl that startled everyone.

Tattersail shrugged. 'If there is, it lies in Darujhistan, since that's where Oponn's gambit seems centred. Mind you, High Fist, drawing us into Darujhistan might well be what Oponn seeks to achieve.'

Toc sat back, absently scratching his wound. There was more to it, he suspected, though he could find no discernible source for his suspicion. He scratched harder. Tattersail could be glib when she wanted to be; her story had a straightforwardness to it. The best lies were the simple ones. Still, nobody else seemed unduly suspicious. The sorceress had shifted attention from her story to its implications for future action. She had everyone thinking past her, and the faster their thoughts raced, the further behind they left their doubts about her.

He watched her watching the others, and was the only one to notice the flash of triumph and relief in her eyes when Lorn spoke.

'Oponn is not the first god seeking to manipulate the Malazan Empire,' the Adjunct said. 'Others have failed, come away bloodied. It's unfortunate the lesson was lost on Oponn – and on Shadowthrone, for that matter.' She sighed deeply. 'Tattersail, whatever your differences with the High Mage, it is necessary, no, vital, that you work together in seeking to discover the details of Oponn's intervention. In the meantime, High Fist Dujek will continue preparing his legion to march, as well as solidifying our hold on Pale. For myself, I will be leaving the city shortly. Rest assured, my mission has goals identical to yours. Now, one last thing,' she turned to Toc, 'I wish to hear the Claw's evaluation of the words that have been exchanged here.'

He stared in surprise. He'd assumed the role she had expected of him without even realizing it. He sat straight and glanced at Tattersail. She now looked nervous, drawing her hands beneath the table. He waited until their gazes locked and held before he turned to the Adjunct.

'In so far as she knows it, the sorceress speaks the truth,' he said. 'Her speculations were genuine, although concerning the dynamics of magic I'm at a loss. Perhaps High Mage Tayschrenn could comment on that.'

Lorn seemed vaguely disappointed with Toc's evaluation, but she nodded anyway and said, 'Accepted, then. High Mage?'

Tayschrenn released a slow breath. 'Accurate,' he said. 'Speculation is sound.'

Toc refilled his goblet. The first course was removed almost untouched, but as the second course arrived everyone turned their full attention to it and conversation ceased. Toc ate slowly, avoiding Tattersail's eyes, though he sensed them upon him time and again. He wondered at his own actions: deceiving the Adjunct to the Empress, the High Mage and the High Fist all in one shot struck him as rash, if not suicidal. And his reasons for doing so were not entirely rational, which made it all the more distressing.

The 2nd had a long, bloody history. More times than Toc could count someone had come through for someone else whatever the odds. And, more often than not, it had been the mage cadre. He'd been there on the plain outside Pale, and he'd watched with a thousand others the cadre being torn apart, hopelessly outmatched. That kind of waste didn't sit well with the 2nd. And, though he was a Claw, the faces that surrounded him, the faces that looked upon him in hope, despair, and – at times – fatal resignation, those faces had been mirrors of his own, and they defied the Claw at every turn. The years in the Claw where feeling and caring had been systematically assailed, those years failed to withstand the day-in, day-out reality that was the 2nd Army.

310

This night, and with his words, Toc had given something back to Tattersail, not just for her but for the cadre. It didn't matter if she understood, and he knew she must be feeling bewildered by his actions; none of that mattered. What he'd done he'd done for himself.

He sat up. Now that's odd, he thought, my wound's stopped itching.

Feeling light-headed, Tattersail wobbled every now and then as she walked down the hall towards the door to her room. She knew it wasn't the wine. With her nerves as frayed as they were, that fine vintage had tasted like water, and had had as much effect.

Adjunct Lorn had raised in the sorceress memories she'd spent years burying. For Lorn, it had been a pivotal event. But for Tattersail, it had been just one nightmare among many. Still, it had pushed her where other crimes had not, and as a result she'd found herself attached to the 2nd Army – the Army she'd been sent to as a recruit, the closing of a circle, but in that time she had changed.

That attachment, those twenty-odd years of service, had this night saved her life. She knew that Toc the Younger had lied for her, and the look he had given her prior to stating his evaluation had been a message she'd understood. Though he had come to the 2nd as a Claw, as a spy, not even his years of training within that secret organization could withstand the new world in which he'd found himself.

Tattersail understood this all too clearly, for the same had happened to her. The sorceress in a cadre of mages who had entered the Mouse Quarter so long ago had cared naught for anyone but herself. Even her attempt to cut herself away from the horrors of which she'd been part had been born of a selfish desire to flee, to absolve her own conscience – but the Empire had denied her in this. An old soldier had come to her

311

the day after the slaughter in the Mouse Quarter. Old, nameless, a veteran sent to convince the sorceress that she was still needed. She well remembered his words. 'Should you ever outrun the guilt within your past, Sorceress, you will have outrun your soul. When it finds you again it will kill you.' And then, rather than deny her desperate needs absolutely, he'd sent her into a veteran army, the 5th, until the time came for her to return – to the 2nd, to a place under the command of Dujek Onearm. With that, she'd been given a second chance.

Tattersail came to her door and paused to sense the condition of her wards. All was well. Sighing, she entered her room, then leaned against the door as it closed behind her.

Captain Paran stepped out from the bedroom, his expression wary and somehow shy. 'Not under arrest? I'm surprised.'

'So am I,' she replied.

'Hairlock was here,' Paran said. 'He instructed me to give you a message.'

Tattersail studied the man's face, seeking a hint of what he was about to deliver. He avoided her gaze and remained standing near the doorway into the bedroom. 'Well?' she demanded.

Paran cleared his throat. 'First, he was, uh, excited. He knew of the Adjunct's arrival, and said she wasn't alone.'

'Not alone? Did he explain that?'

Paran shrugged. 'Said the dust walks around the Adjunct, the dirt shifts beneath her boots, and the wind whispers of frost and fire.' He raised his eyebrows. 'Does that explain anything? Damned if I know.'

Tattersail strode to her dresser. She began to remove the scant jewellery she'd donned for the dinner. 'I think it does,' she said slowly. 'Did he say anything else?'

'He did. He said that the Adjunct and her companion were leaving Pale soon, and that he intended to track them. Sorceress . . .'

312

She saw that Paran was struggling with something, as if fighting his every instinct. Tattersail laid one arm on the dresser and waited. When he met her gaze, her breath caught. 'You were about to say something,' she said, her voice low. Her heart was pounding all too fast, and she felt her body responding as if of its own accord. The look she'd seen in his eyes had been clear in its meaning.

'I know something of the Adjunct's mission,' he said. 'I was to be her contact in Darujhistan.'

Whatever had been building between them disintegrated as Tattersail's eyes went hard and anger darkened her face. 'She's going to Darujhistan, is she? And you and she were to oversee the long-awaited demise of the Bridgeburners. Together, you thought you'd be able to kill Whiskeyjack, to cut down his squad from within.'

'No!' Paran took a step forward, but when Tattersail shot out her hand, palm facing him, he froze. 'Wait,' he whispered. 'Before you do anything, just hear me out.'

Her Thyr Warren surged into her hand, eager for release. 'Why? Damn Oponn for letting you live!'

'Tattersail, please!'

She scowled. 'Speak.'

Paran stepped back and turned to a nearby chair. Hands held out at his sides, he sat down and looked up at her.

'Keep those hands there,' Tattersail commanded. 'Away from your sword.'

'This has been the Adjunct's personal mission, from the very start. Three years ago I was stationed in Itko Kan, Officers Corps. One day every available soldier was mustered out and marched to a section of the coast road.' Paran's hands had begun to shake, and the muscles of his jaw stood out. 'What we saw there, Tattersail, you would not believe.'

She recalled Quick Ben and Kalam's story. 'A massacre. A company of cavalry.'

313

Astonishment showed on Paran's face. 'How did you know?'

'Go on, Captain,' she grated.

'Adjunct Lorn arrived from the capital and took charge. She guessed that the massacre had been a ... a diversion. We began upon a trail. It was not a clear one, not at first. Sorceress, may I lower my arms?'

'Slowly. On the chair arms, Captain.'

He sighed gratefully and set down his trembling forearms as she'd instructed. 'Anyway, the Adjunct determined that a girl had been taken, possessed by a god.'

'Which god?'

Paran made a face. 'Come, now, if you know of the massacre, is it hard to guess? That company was killed by Shadow Hounds. Which god? Well, Shadowthrone comes to mind,' he said sarcastically. 'The Adjunct believes Shadowthrone was involved, but the god that possessed the girl was the Rope – I know of no other name for him – the Patron of Assassins, Shadowthrone's companion.'

Tattersail dropped her arm. She'd closed her Warren a minute earlier, since it had begun to push hard and she had feared she didn't have the strength to resist it much longer. 'You've found the girl,' she stated dully.

Paran sat forward. 'Yes!'

'Her name's Sorry.'

'You're aware of this,' Paran said, sinking back into the chair. 'Which means that Whiskeyjack is also aware, since who else could have told you?' He looked up into her eyes with a clouded expression. 'I'm now very confused.'

'You're not alone,' Tattersail said. 'So all this – your arrival, the Adjunct's – it was all a hunt for the girl?' She shook her head. 'That's not enough, it can't be enough, Captain.'

'It's all that I'm aware of, Tattersail.'

She studied him for a moment. 'I believe you. Tell me, what are the details of the Adjunct's mission?'

314

'I don't know,' Paran said, tossing up his hands. 'Somehow, I was the one she'd be able to find, so my being with the squad would bring her to the girl.'

'The Adjunct's talents are many,' Tattersail mused. 'Through the antithesis of sorcery, she might well possess the ability to have linked with you, especially if you've been in her company for the past two years.'

'Then why isn't she breaking down your door?'

Tattersail's eyes were on the jewellery scattered on the dresser. 'Oponn severed the link, Captain.'

'I dislike the thought of exchanging one set of shackles for another,' Paran grumbled.

'There's more to this,' Tattersail insisted, more to herself than to the captain. 'Lorn has a T'lan Imass with her.'

Paran jerked upright.

'Hairlock's snide hints,' she explained. 'I believe the mission was two-fold. Kill Sorry, yes, but also kill Whiskeyjack and his squad. The T'lan would not be involved if her plan concerned just you. Her Otataral sword is sufficient to destroy Sorry, and possibly kill the Rope as well, assuming that's who's possessing the girl.'

'I would not like to believe that,' Paran said. 'They are my command. My responsibility. The Adjunct would not betray me so—'

'Wouldn't she? Why not?'

The captain seemed at a loss to answer her, but there was a stubborn glower in his eyes.

Tattersail reached the decision she had sensed was coming, and it left her cold. 'Hairlock left too early. The puppet was eager, too eager to pursue the Adjunct and that T'lan Imass. He must have discovered something about them, about what they're up to.'

'Who is Hairlock's master?' Paran asked.

'Quick Ben, Whiskeyjack's mage.' She looked to him. 'He's

315

the best I've seen. Not the most powerful, mind you, but smart. Still, if the T'lan Imass comes on him unawares he won't stand a chance, and neither will the rest.' She paused, her eyes holding on the captain. 'I have to leave Pale,' she said abruptly.

Paran shot to his feet. 'Not alone.'

'Alone,' Tattersail insisted. 'I have to find Whiskeyjack, and if you're tagging along then Lorn will find him too.'

'I refuse to believe the Adjunct presents any risk to the sergeant,' Paran said. 'Tell me, can you succeed in killing Sorry? Even with Quick Ben's help?'

The sorceress hesitated. 'I'm not sure I want to,' she said slowly.

'What?'

'It has to be Whiskeyjack's decision, Captain. And I don't think I can give any good reason for convincing you of that. I just feel it's right.' She felt herself relying on instinct in this matter, but vowed to hold true to it.

'Even so,' Paran said, 'I can't remain hiding here, can I? What do I eat? The bedding?'

'I can get you out into the city,' Tattersail said. 'None will recognize you. Take a room in an inn and stay out of your uniform. If all goes well I'll be back in two weeks. You can wait that long, can't you, Captain?'

Paran stared. 'And what happens if I just walk out of here and introduce myself to Dujek Onearm?'

'The High Mage Tayschrenn would shred your brain with truth-seeking sorcery, Captain. You've Oponn's touch, and after tonight Oponn is now an official enemy of the Empire. And when Tayschrenn's done he'll leave you to die, which is preferable to the madness that would grip you if he kept you alive. He'll show that mercy, at least.' Tattersail anticipated Paran's thoughts. 'Dujek might well seek to protect you, but in this Tayschrenn outranks him. You've become a tool of Oponn, and for Dujek the safety of his soldiers takes precedence over his pleasure in frustrating Tayschrenn. So, in fact, he might not protect you at all. I'm sorry, Captain, but you're truly alone if you walk.'

'I'll be alone when you leave, too, Sorceress.'

'I know, but it won't be for ever.' She searched his eyes and felt compassion welling behind her own. 'Paran,' she said, 'it's not all bad. Despite all the distrust between us, I'm feeling things for you I haven't felt for anyone in – well, in some time.' She smiled sadly. 'I don't know what that's worth, Captain, but I'm glad I said it anyway.'

Paran gazed at her for a long minute, then said, 'Very well, Tattersail, I'll do as you ask. An inn? Do you have some local coin?'

'Easily acquired.' Her shoulders slumped. 'I'm sorry, but I'm exhausted.' As she turned to the bedroom her gaze fell on the dresser-top one last time. Amid a small pile of underclothing she saw her Deck of Dragons. It would be foolish not to do a reading, considering the decision she'd made.

Paran spoke close behind her. 'Tattersail, how thorough is your exhaustion?'

She felt the heat in his words triggering a smouldering fire beneath her stomach, and her gaze slid away from the Deck as she turned to face the captain. Though she voiced no reply to his question, her answer was clear. He took her hand, surprising her with such an innocent gesture. So young, she thought, and now he's leading me into the bedroom. She would have laughed if the act hadn't been so sweet.

False dawn played the eastern horizon as Adjunct Lorn guided her mount and packhorse out from Pale's East Gate. True to Dujek's words the guards were nowhere in sight, and the gate had been left open. She hoped the few sleepy eyes that had followed her through the streets had only mild curiosity behind them. In any case, she was dressed in simple, unadorned leather armour; her face was mostly hidden in the shadow cast by the plain bronze helmet's browguard. Even her horses were a local breed, sturdy and placid, much smaller than the Malazan warhorses with which she was most familiar, but a comforting ride none the less. It seemed unlikely that she would have attracted undue attention. More than one unemployed mercenary had left Pale since the Empire's arrival.

The south horizon was a jagged line of snow-capped mountains. The Tahlyn Mountains would remain on her right for some time, before the Rhivi Plain swept past them and became the Catlin Plain. Few farms broke the flatlands around her, and those that did crowded the city's own lands. The Rhivi people were not tolerant of such encroachments, and since every trade route that led to and from Pale crossed their traditional territory, those of the city wisely refrained from angering the Rhivi.

Ahead, as she walked her horses, the dawn showed its face with a streak of crimson. The rain had passed a few days back, and the sky overhead was silver-blue and clear, a few stars dwindling as light came to the world.

The day promised to be hot. The Adjunct loosened the leather thongs between her breasts, revealing the fine mail hauberk beneath. By midday she would reach the first wellspring, where she would replenish her supply of water. She ran a hand across the surface of one of the bladders strapped to her saddle. It came away wet with condensation. She passed her hand across her lips.

The voice that spoke beside her jolted her in the saddle and her mount snorted in fear and sidestepped.

'I will walk with you,' Onos T'oolan said, 'for a time.'

Lorn glared at the T'lan Imass. 'I would rather you announced your arrival,' she said tightly, 'from a distance.'

'As you wish.' Onos T'oolan sank into the ground like so much dust.

The Adjunct cursed. Then she saw him waiting a hundred

318

yards ahead of her, back-lit by the rising sun. The crimson sky seemed to have cast a red flame about the warrior. The effect jangled her nerves, as if she looked upon a scene that touched her deepest, oldest memories – memories that went beyond her own life. The T'lan Imass stood unmoving until she reached him, then fell into step beside her.

Lorn tightened her knees about the horse's shoulders and closed the reins until the mare settled down. 'Do you have to be so literal-minded, Tool?' she asked.

The desiccated warrior seemed to consider, then nodded. 'I accept that name. All of my history is dead. Existence begins anew, and with it shall be a new name. It is suitable.'

'Why were you selected to accompany me?' the Adjunct asked.

'In the lands west and north of Seven Cities, I alone among my clan survived the Twenty-eighth Jaghut War.'

Lorn's eyes widened. 'I thought those wars numbered twenty-seven,' she said quietly. 'When your legions left us after conquering Seven Cities, and you marched into the wastelands—'

'Our Bone Casters sensed an enclave of surviving Jaghut,' Tool said. 'Our commander Logros T'lan determined that we exterminate them. Thus we did.'

'Which explains your decimated numbers upon returning,' Lorn said. 'You could have explained your decision to the Empress. As it was, she was left without her most powerful army, and no knowledge of when it might return.'

'Return was not guaranteed, Adjunct,' Tool said.

Lorn stared at the tattered creature. 'I see.'

'The cessation of my clan's chieftain, Kig Aven, was accompanied by all my kin. Thus alone, I am unbound to Logro. Kig Aven's Bone Caster was Kilava Onass, who has been lost since long before the Emperor reawakened us.'

Lorn's mind raced. Among the Malazan Empire, the T'lan

319

Imass were also known as the Silent Host. She'd never known an Imass as loquacious as this Tool. Perhaps it had something to do with this 'unbounding'. Within the Imass, only Commander Logros ever spoke to humans on a regular basis. As for the *Bone Casters* – Imass shamans – they stayed out of sight. The only one that had ever appeared was one named Olar Ethil, who stood alongside the clan chieftain Eitholos Ilm during the battle of Kartool, which had seen an exchange of sorcery that made Moon's Spawn look like a child's cantrip.

In any case, she'd already learned more of the Imass from this brief conversation with Tool than was present in the Empire Annals. The Emperor had known more, much more, but making records of such knowledge had never been his style. That he had reawakened the Imass had been a theory argued among scholars for years. And now she knew it to be true. How many other secrets would this T'lan Imass reveal in casual conversation?

'Tool,' she said, 'had you ever met the Emperor personally?'

'I awakened before Galad Ketan and after Onak Shendok and, as with all the T'lan Imass, I knelt before the Emperor as he sat upon the First Throne.'

'The Emperor was alone?' Lorn asked.

'No. He was accompanied by the one named Dancer.'

'Damn,' she hissed. Dancer had died beside the Emperor. 'Where is this First Throne, Tool?'

The warrior was silent for a time, then it said, 'Upon the Emperor's death the Logros T'lan Imass gathered minds – a rare thing that was last done before the Diaspora – and a binding resulted. Adjunct, the answer to your question is within this binding. I cannot satisfy you. This holds for all Logros T'lan Imass and for all Kron T'lan Imass.'

'Who are the Kron?'

'They are coming,' Tool replied.

Sudden sweat sprang out on the Adjunct's brow. Logros'

320

legions, when they first arrived on the scene, numbered around nineteen thousand. They were believed now to number fourteen thousand, and the majority of those losses had come beyond the Empire's borders, in this last Jaghut War. Were another nineteen thousand Imass about to arrive? What had the Emperor unleashed?

'Tool,' she asked slowly, almost regretting her need to persist in questioning him, 'what is the significance of these Kron coming?'

'The Year of the Three Hundredth Millennium approaches,' the warrior replied.

'What happens then?'

'Adjunct, the Diaspora ends.'

The Great Raven called Crone rode the high winds above Rhivi Plain. The northern horizon was now a green-tinged curve, growing more substantial with every hour of flight. Weariness weighed down her wings, but the heaven's breath was a strong one. And more, nothing could assail her certainty that changes were coming to this world, and she drew again and again upon her vast reserves of magical power.

If ever there was a dire convergence of great forces, it was now, and in this place. The gods were descending to the mortal soil to do battle, shapings were being forged of flesh and bone, and the blood of sorcery now boiled with a madness born of inevitable momentum. Crone had never felt more alive.

With these unveiling of powers, heads had turned. And to one Crone flew in answer to a summons she was powerless to ignore. Lord Anomander Rake was not her only master, and for her this only made things more interesting. As for her own ambitions, she would keep them to herself. For now, knowledge was her power.

And if there was one secret more alluring than any other

she might covet, it was the mystery surrounding the half human warrior called Caladan Brood. Anticipation lifted Crone's wings with renewed strength.

Steadily, Blackdog Forest spread its verdant cloak over the north.

CHAPTER TEN

Kallor said: 'I walked this land when the T'lan
Imass were but children. I have commanded
armies a hundred thousand strong. I have spread
the fire of my wrath across entire continents, and
sat alone upon tall thrones. Do you grasp the
meaning of this?'
'Yes,' said Caladan Brood, 'you never learn.'

Conversations of War
(Second in Command
Kallor speaking with
Warlord Caladan Brood),
recorded by Outrider
Hurlochel, 6th Army

Vimkaros Inn stood just beyond Eltrosan Square in
the opal Quarter of Pale. That much Toc knew from
his wanderings through the city. But for the life of
him he could not think of anyone staying there whom he
knew. Yet the instructions for this mysterious meeting had
been clear.

He now approached the ostentatious structure warily. He
saw nothing suspicious. The square was crowded with the usual

gentry and merchant shops; of Malazan guards there were few. The culling of the nobility had done much to cloak Pale's atmosphere with a shocked stillness that hung about people like invisible yokes.

The past few days Toc had kept much to himself, carousing with his fellow soldiers when the mood took him, though those times seemed rarer these days. With the Adjunct gone, and Tattersail reported missing, Dujek and Tayschrenn were involved in mutually exclusive responsibilities. The High Fist was busy restructuring Pale, and his newly formed 5th Army; while the High Mage sought Tattersail, evidently without much success.

Toc suspected that the peace between the two men would not last. Since the dinner, he had stayed away from anything official, choosing to eat with his comrades rather than dine with the officers as was now his privilege as ranking Claw. The less noticed he made himself the better, as far as he was concerned.

He entered Vimkaros Inn and paused. Before him was a roofless courtyard with paths winding among a rich garden. Clearly, the inn had survived the siege unscathed. A wide central path led directly to a broad counter behind which stood a corpulent old man eating grapes. A few guests walked the side paths, moving among the plants and conversing in low tones.

The message had insisted he come dressed in local garb. Thus, Toc drew little attention as he strode to the counter.

The old man paused in his snacking and bowed with his head. 'At your service, sir,' he said, wiping his hands.

'I believe a table has been reserved in my name,' Toc said. 'I am Render Kan.'

The old man studied a wax tablet before him, then looked up with a smile. 'Of course. Follow me.'

324

A minute later Toc sat at a table on a balcony overlooking the garden court. His only company was a decanter of chilled Saltoan wine, which arrived when he did, and he now sipped from a goblet, his lone eye surveying the people in the garden below.

A servant arrived and bowed before him. 'Kind sir,' the man said, 'I am to deliver the following message. A gentleman will soon join you who has been out of his depth yet not aware of it. He is, now.'

Toc frowned. 'That's the message?'

'It is.'

'His own words?'

'And yours, sir.' The servant bowed again and departed.

Toc's frown deepened, then he sat forward, his every muscle tensing. He turned to the balcony's entrance in time to see Captain Paran stride through. He was dressed in the manner of the local gentry, unarmed, and looking quite fit. Toc rose, grinning.

'Not unduly shocked, I hope,' Paran said, as he arrived. They sat down and the captain poured himself some wine. 'Did the message prepare you?'

'Barely,' Toc replied. 'I'm not sure how to receive you, Captain. Is this according to the Adjunct's instructions?'

'She believes me dead,' Paran said, his brow wrinkling. 'And I was, for a time. Tell me, Toc the Younger, am I speaking to a Claw, or to a soldier of the Second?'

Toc's eye narrowed. 'That's a tough question.'

'Is it?' Paran asked, his gaze intense and unwavering.

Toc hesitated, then grinned again. 'Hood's Breath, no, it damn well isn't! All right, Captain, welcome to the defunct Second, then.'

Paran laughed, clearly relieved.

'Now what's all this about you being dead but not dead, Captain?'

Paran's humour vanished. He took a mouthful of wine and swallowed, looking away. 'An attempted assassination,' he explained, grimacing. 'I should have died, if not for Mallet and Tattersail.'

'What? Whiskeyjack's healer and the sorceress?'

Paran nodded. 'I've been recovering until recently in Tattersail's quarters. Whiskeyjack's instructions were to keep my existence secret for the time being. Toc,' he leaned forward, 'what do you know of the Adjunct's plans?'

Toc examined the garden below. Tattersail had known – she'd managed to keep it from everyone at the dinner. Remarkable. 'Now,' he said quietly, 'you ask questions of a Claw.'

'I do.'

'Where's Tattersail?' Toc swung his gaze to the captain and held the man's eyes.

The captain jerked his head. 'Very well. She travels overland – to Darujhistan. She knows a T'lan Imass accompanies the Adjunct, and she believes Lorn's plan includes killing Whiskeyjack and his squad. I do not agree. My role in the mission was to keep an eye on one member of the sergeant's squad, and that person was to be the only one to die. She gave me the command after three years of service to her – it's a reward, and I can't believe she would take it from me. There, that is what I know. Can you help me, Toc?'

'The Adjunct's mission,' Toc said, after releasing a long breath, 'as far as I'm aware of it, involves far more than just killing Sorry. The T'lan Imass is with her for something else. Captain,' Toc's expression was grim, 'the days of the Bridgeburners are numbered. Whiskeyjack's name is damn near sacred among Dujek's men. This is something of which I couldn't convince the Adjunct – in fact she seems to think the opposite – but if the sergeant and the Bridgeburners are eliminated, this army won't be pulled back in line, it will mutiny.

And the Malazan Empire will be up against High Fist Dujek with not a single commander who can match him. The Genabackan Campaign will disintegrate, and civil war may well sweep into the heart of the Empire.'

The blood had drained from Paran's face. 'I believe you,' he said. 'Very well, you've taken my doubts and made of them convictions. And they leave me with but one choice.'

'And that is?'

Paran turned the empty goblet in his hands. 'Darujhistan,' he said. 'With luck I'll catch Tattersail, and together we'll attempt to contact Whiskeyjack before the Adjunct does.' He glanced at Toc. 'Evidently the Adjunct can no longer sense my whereabouts. Tattersail forbade me to accompany her, arguing that Lorn would be able to detect me, but she also let slip that my "death" had severed the bonds between me and the Adjunct. I should have made the connection sooner, but she . . . distracted me.'

Into Toc's mind returned the memory of how she'd looked that evening, and he nodded knowingly. 'I'm sure she did.'

Paran sighed. 'Yes, well. In any case, I need at least three horses, and supplies. The Adjunct is proceeding on some kind of timetable. I know that much. So she's not travelling with much haste. I should catch up with Tattersail in a day or two, then together we can drive hard to the edge of the Tahlyn Mountains, skirt them and slip past the Adjunct.'

Toc had leaned back during Paran's elaboration of his plan, a half-smile on his lips. 'You'll need Wickan horses, Captain, since what you've described requires mounts superior to those the Adjunct's riding. Now, how do you plan to get past the city gates dressed as a local but leading Empire horses?'

Paran blinked.

Toc grinned. 'I've got your answer, Captain.' He spread his hands. 'I'll go with you. Leave the horses and supplies to me, and I guarantee we'll get out of the city unnoticed.'

'But—'

'Those are my conditions, Captain.'

Paran coughed. 'Very well. And now that I think on it, the company would be welcome.'

'Good,' Toc grunted. He reached for the decanter. 'Let's drink on the damn thing, then.'

The way was becoming more and more difficult, and Tattersail felt her first tremor of fear. She travelled a Warren of High Thyr and not even Tayschrenn possessed the ability to assail it, yet under attack it was. Not directly. The power that opposed her was pervasive, and it deadened her sorcery.

The Warren had become narrow, choked with obstacles. At times it shuddered around her, the dark walls to either side writhing as if under tremendous pressure. And within the tunnel she struggled to shape, the air stank of something she had difficulty identifying. There was a tinge of sour brimstone and a mustiness that reminded her of unearthed tombs. It seemed to drain the power from her with every breath she took.

She realized that she could not continue. She would have to enter the physical world and find rest. Once again she cursed her own carelessness. She had forgotten her Deck of Dragons. With them she would have known what to expect. She entertained once again the suspicion that an outside force had acted upon her, severing her from the Deck. The first distraction had come from Captain Paran, and while it had been pleasant, she reminded herself that Paran belonged to Oponn. After that, she'd experienced an unaccountable urgency to be on her way, so much so that she'd left everything behind.

Bereft of her Warren, she would find herself alone on the Rhivi Plain, without food, without even a bedroll. The mindless need for haste she'd experienced ran contrary to her every instinct. She was growing certain that it had been imposed upon her, that somehow she'd let her defences down, left herself exposed to such manipulations. And that returned her thoughts to Captain Paran, to the servant of Oponn's will.

Finally, she could go no further. She began to withdraw her strained power, collapsing the Warren layer by layer about her. The ground beneath her boots became solid, cloaked in spar yellow grass, and the air around her shifted into the dull lavender of dusk. A wind brushed her face smelling of soil. The horizon steadied itself on all sides – far off to her right the sun still bathed the Talhyn Mountains, the peaks glittering like gold – and immediately ahead rose an enormous silhouetted figure, turning to face her and voicing a surprised grunt.

Tattersail stepped back in alarm, and the voice that emerged from the figure pushed the air from her lungs in a whooshing breath of relief, then terror.

'Tattersail,' Bellurdan said sadly, 'Tayschrenn did not expect you'd manage to come this far. Thus, I was anticipating detecting you from a distance.' The Thelomen giant lifted his arms in an expansive, child-like shrug. At his feet was a familiar burlap sack, though the body within had shrunk since she'd last seen it.

'How has the High Mage managed to deny my Warren?' she asked. On the heels of her terror had come weariness, almost resignation.

'He could not do that,' Bellurdan answered. 'He simply anticipated that you would attempt to travel to Darujhistan, and as your Thyr Warren cannot function over water, he concluded you would take this path.'

'Then what happened with my Warren?'

Bellurdan grunted distastefully. 'The T'lan Imass who accompanies the Adjunct has created around them a dead space. Our sorcery is devoured by the warrior's Eldering powers. The effect is cumulative. If you were to open your Warren entirely, you would be consumed utterly, Tattersail.' The

Thelomen stepped forward. 'The High Mage has instructed me to arrest you and return you to him.'

'And if I resist?'

Bellurdan answered, in a tone filled with sorrow, 'Then I am to kill you.'

'I see.' Tattersail thought for a time. Her world seemed to have closed in now, her every memory irrelevant and discarded. Her heart pounded like a thundering drum in her chest. All that remained of her past, and her only true sense of her life, was regret – an unspecified, yet overwhelming regret. She looked up at the Thelomen, compassion brimming in her eyes. 'So where are this T'lan and the Adjunct, then?'

'Perhaps eight hours to the east. The Imass is not even aware of us. The time for conversation is ended, Tattersail. Will you accompany me?'

Her mouth dry, she said, 'I did not think you one to betray a long-standing friend.'

Bellurdan spread his hands wider and said, in a pained voice, 'I will never betray you, Tattersail. The High Mage commands both of us. How can there be betrayal?'

'Not that,' Tattersail replied quickly. 'I once asked if I could speak with you at length. Remember? You said yes, Bellurdan. Yet now you tell me conversation is ended. I had not imagined your word to be so worthless.'

In the dying light it was impossible to see the Thelomen's face, but the anguish in his tone was plain. 'I am sorry, Tattersail. You are correct. I gave you my word that we would speak again. Can we not do this while we return to Pale?'

'No,' Tattersail snapped. 'I wish it now.'

Bellurdan bowed his head. 'Very well.'

Tattersail forced the tension from her shoulders and neck. 'I have some questions,' she said. 'First, Tayschrenn sent you to Genabaris for a time, didn't he? You were searching through some scrolls for him?'

'Yes.'

'May I ask what were those scrolls?'

'Is it of vital significance now, Tattersail?'

'It is. The truth will help me in deciding whether to go with you, or die here.'

Bellurdan hesitated only a moment. 'Very well. Among the archives collected from the city's mages – all of whom were executed, as you know – were found some copied fragments of *Gothos' Folly*, an ancient Jaghut tome—'

'I know of it,' Tattersail interjected. 'Go on.'

'As a Thelomen, I possess Jaghut blood, though of course Gothos would deny it. The High Mage entrusted the examination of these writings to me. I was to seek out information concerning the burial of a Jaghut Tyrant, a burial that was in fact a prison.'

'Wait,' Tattersail said, shaking her head. 'The Jaghut had no government. What do you mean by a Tyrant?'

'One whose blood was poisoned by the ambition to rule over others. This Jaghut Tyrant enslaved the land around it – all living things – for close to three thousand years. The Imass of the time sought to destroy it, and failed. It was left to other Jaghut to attend to the sundering and imprisoning of the Tyrant – for such a creature was as abominable to them as it was to Imass.'

Tattersail's heart now hammered in her chest. 'Bellurdan.' She had to fight to push the words from her. 'Where was this Tyrant buried?'

'I concluded that the barrow lies south of here, in the Gadrobi Hills directly east of Darujhistan.'

'Oh, Queen of Dreams. Bellurdan, do you know what you've done?'

'I have done as I was commanded by our High Mage.'

'And that's why the T'lan Imass is with the Adjunct.'

'I don't understand what you are saying, Tattersail.'

'Dammit, you brainless ox!' she rasped. 'They plan to free the Tyrant! Lorn's sword – her Otataral sword—'

'No,' Bellurdan rumbled. 'They would not do such a thing. Rather, they seek to prevent someone else releasing it. Yes, that is more likely. It is the truth of things. Now, Tattersail, our conversation is done.'

'I can't go back,' the sorceress said. 'I must go on. Please, don't stop me.'

'We are to return to Pale,' Bellurdan said stubbornly. 'Your concern has been satisfied. Permit me to take you back so that I may continue seeking the proper burial place for Nightchill.'

There was no choice left in Tattersail's mind, but there had to be a way out. The conversation had bought her time, time to recover from the ordeal of travelling by Warren. Bellurdan's words returned to her: if she accessed her Thyr Warren now she would be consumed. Incinerated by the re-active influence of the T'lan Imass. Her eyes fell on the burlap sack beside the Thelomen and saw from it a faint gleam of sorcery. A spell. *My own spell.* She recalled now: a gesture of compassion, a spell of . . . preservation. *Is this my way out? Hood's Breath, is it even possible?* She thought of Hairlock, the journey from the dying body to a lifeless . . . vessel. *Shedenul, have mercy on us . . .*

The sorceress stepped back and opened her Warren. High Thyr magic blazed around her. She saw Bellurdan stagger back then steady himself. He screamed something, but she could not hear him. Then he charged at her.

She regretted the Thelomen's fatal courage as the fire blackened the world around her, even as she opened her arms and embraced him.

Lorn strode to Tool's side. The T'lan Imass faced west, and a tension swirled about him that she could almost see.

'What is it?' she asked, her eyes on the white fountain of fire rising above the horizon. 'I've never seen anything like that.'

'Nor I,' Tool replied. 'It is within the barrier I have cast around us.'

'But that's impossible,' the Adjunct snapped.

'Yes, impossible to last this long. Its source should have been consumed almost instantly. Yet . . .' The T'lan Imass fell silent.

There was no need for Tool to finish his sentence. The pillar of fire still raged in the night sky as it had for the past hour. The stars swam in the inky darkness around it, magic swirling in a frenzy as if from a bottomless well. On the wind was a smell that left Lorn slightly nauseous. 'Do you recognize the Warren, Tool?'

'Warrens, Adjunct. Tellann, Thyr, Denul, D'riss, Tennes, Thelomen Toblakai, Starvald Demelain . . .'

'Starvald Demelain, what in Hood's Name is that?'

'Elder.'

'I thought there were but three Elder Warrens, and that's not one of them.'

'Three? No, there were many, Adjunct, all born of one. Starvald Demelain.'

Lorn wrapped her cloak tighter about herself, eyes on the column of fire. 'Who could manage such a conjuring?'

'There was one . . . once. Of worshippers there are none left, so he is no more. I have no answer to your question, Adjunct.' The Imass staggered as the pillar bloomed outwards, then winked out. A distant thundering rumble reached them.

'Gone,' Lorn whispered.

'Destroyed,' Tool said. The warrior cocked his head. 'Strange, the source is indeed destroyed. But something has also been born. I sense it, a new presence.'

Lorn checked her sword. 'What is it?' she demanded.

Tool shrugged. 'New. It flees.'

Was this cause for worry? Lorn scowled and turned to the T'lan Imass, but he had already left her side, and was now

333

striding back to their campfire. The Adjunct glanced once more at the western horizon. There was a cloud, blotting out the stars. It looked huge. She shivered.

It was time to sleep. The Imass would stand guard, so she need not worry about surprise visitors. The day had been long, and she'd over-rationed her water; she felt weak, an unfamiliar sensation. Her scowl deepened as she walked to the camp. Tool, standing immobile beside the flames, reminded her of his arrival two days ago. The fiery glimmer that jumped along his withered flesh-and-bone helm once again triggered something primordial in her mind, and with it came a deep, unreasoning fear of darkness. She stepped close to the Imass. 'Fire is life,' she whispered, the phrase seeming to rise from the depths of instinct.

Tool nodded. 'Life is fire,' he said. 'With such words was born the First Empire. The Empire of Imass, the Empire of Humanity.' The warrior turned to the Adjunct. 'You've done well, my child.'

The grey pall of smoke hung unmoving over Blackdog Forest a dozen leagues north of her as Crone dipped her splayed tail and sank wearily towards the army encamped on the Rhivi Plain.

The tents marched outward like spokes from a central fortified hub where stood a large canopy, rippling in the morning breeze. Towards this centre the Great Raven descended. Her sharp gaze marked Rhivi plainsmen moving among the aisles. Off on the eastern rim fluttered the banners of the Catlin Horse, green and silver to mark the mercenary contingent of Caladan Brood's main army. By far the greatest proportion of soldiers, however, were Tiste Andii – Anomander Rake's people, dwellers of the city within Moon's Spawn – their tall, dark-clad forms moving like shadows between the tents.

Wheeled tracks led north to the forest fringes: supply routes to entrenchments once held by the Malazans and now marking

Brood's front lines. Rhivi-driven carts moved forward an end-less stream of supplies, while other wagons, laden with the dead and the wounded, entered the camp in a grim flow.

Crone cackled. Magic bled from the main tent and stained the dusty air with a heavy, turgid magenta, the colour of the D'riss Warren, earth magic. Her wings now felt light and held a youthful spring as she beat the air. 'Ahhh,' Crone sighed, 'magic.' Sweeping through the wards and traps, the Great Raven glided over the tent and thrummed rapidly as she dropped outside the entrance.

No guard barred the doorway, which had been left pulled back and tied to a support pole. Crone hopped inside.

With the exception of a small hanging at the far end, behind which squatted an army cot, no other divisions had been made within the tent. In the centre stood a massive table, its surface etched with the contours of the surrounding land. One man stood alone, leaning over it, his back to the doorway. An enormous iron hammer was slung across his broad back; despite its size and evident weight, it looked almost toy-like against that span of muscle and bone. Power rolled from him in musky waves.

'Delays, delays,' Crone muttered, as she flapped up to land on the tabletop.

Caladan Brood grunted distractedly.

'You sensed the storm of sorcery last night?' she asked.

'Sensed? We could see it. The Rhivi shamans seem some-what disturbed, but they have no answers. We'll discuss that later, Crone. Now I must think.'

Crone cocked her head at the map. 'The west flank falls back in total disarray. Who commands that Barghast mob?'

Brood asked, 'When did you fly within sight of them?'

'Two days past. I saw but a third of the original force left alive.'

Brood shook his head. 'Jorrick Sharplance, under him five

thousand Barghast and seven Blades of the Crimson Guard.'

'Sharplance?' Crone hissed laughter. 'Full of himself, is he?'

'He is, but the Barghast so named him. As I was saying, five legions of Gold Moranth dropped into his lap three days ago. Jorrick retreated under cover of night, and bled off two-thirds of his army east and west – his Barghast have a knack of disappearing where no cover seems possible. Yesterday his panicked mob did an about-face and met the Gold. His Barghast moved in as pincers. Two Moranth legions wiped out, the other three retreating to the forest with half their supplies scattered on the plain.'

Crone cocked her head again. 'Jorrick's plan?'

Brood inclined his head. 'He's Crimson Guard, though the Barghast call him their own. Young, thus fearless.'

The raven studied the map. 'And the east? How holds Fox Pass?'

'Well,' Brood said. 'Mostly Stannis conscripts on the other side – the Malazans are finding them a reluctant ally. We'll see the Crimson Guard's mettle in twelve months' time, when the next wave of Malazan marines disembark at Nisst.'

'Why not drive northward?' Crone asked. 'Prince K'azz could liberate the Free Cities over the winter.'

'The Prince and I agree on this,' Brood said. 'He stays where he is.'

'Why?' Crone demanded.

Brood grunted. 'Our tactics are our business.'

'Suspicious bastard,' Crone muttered. She hopped along the south edge of the map. 'Your underbelly remains for final grim scrutiny. Naught but Rhivi plainsmen between you and Pale. And now forces walk the plain that even the Rhivi know nothing of – yet you show little concern, warrior. Why is that, Crone wonders?'

'I have been in communication with Prince K'azz and his mages, and with the Barghast and Rhivi shamans. What was born on the plain last night belongs to no one. It is alone, and frightened. Even now the Rhivi have begun the search for it. Concerned? No, not by that. Still, there's much more going on in the south.' Brood straightened.

'Anomander is in the midst of it,' Crone purred. 'Plotting and counter-plotting, scattering broken glass in everyone's path. I've never seen him in a better mood.'

'Enough gossip. You have news for me?'

'Of course, Master.' Crone stretched her wings and sighed. She jabbed her beak at an itch, crunched a flea and gulped it down. 'I know who holds the Spinning Coin.'

'Who?'

'A youth whose bliss is ignorance. The Coin spins and turns a face to all those in his company. They've their own game, but it will converge with greater things, and so Oponn's thin threads reverberate in spheres otherwise immune to the Jesters' influence.'

'What does Rake know?'

'Of this, little. But you well know his dislike of Oponn. He would cut those threads given the opportunity.'

'Idiot,' Brood muttered. He thought for a time, unmoving, like a shaping of stone and iron, while Crone ambled back and forth across the Rhivi Plain, her long, black talons scattering the wooden regiment and division markers like dominoes.

'Without Oponn, Rake's power is presently unmatched,' Brood said. 'He hangs over Darujhistan like a beacon and the Empress is sure to send something against him. Such a battle would—'

'Level Darujhistan,' Crone chirped brightly. 'In flames numbering twelve, so fly the Free Cities, so much ash in the wind.'

'Rake's disdain for everything beneath him has left us stumbling and flat on our faces one time too many,' Brood said. He glanced at Crone and raised a hairless eyebrow. 'You're scattering my armies. Stop it.'

Crone stopped pacing and squatted. 'Once again,' she sighed, 'Caladan Brood the Great Warrior seeks the bloodless way. Rake gets that coin and he'll pull Oponn right in and spit the Lord and Lady on that lovely sword of his. Imagine the chaos that would ensue – a wonderful ripple that could topple gods and deluge realms.' She heard her own excitement and revelled in its blatancy. 'Such fun.'

'Quiet, bird,' Brood said. 'The Coin Bearer needs protection, now that Rake's recalled his mages.'

'But who is there to match the Tiste Andii?' Crone asked. 'Surely you don't intend to leave your campaign here?'

Brood bared his filed teeth in a nasty grin. 'Ha, caught you out, I think. Good. You need taking down a notch or two, Crone. You don't know everything. How does it feel?'

'I'll permit such torture from you, Brood,' Crone squawked, 'only because I respect your temper. Just don't push me too far. Tell me, who around here can match Rake's mages? This is something I must know. You and your secrets. How can I be a true servant to my master's wishes when he withholds vital information?'

'What do you know of the Crimson Guard?' Brood asked.

'Scant,' Crone replied. 'A company of mercenaries held in high regard among such kind, what of them?'

'Ask Rake's Tiste Andii for their assessment, crow.'

Crone's feathers arched indignantly. 'Crow? I'll not take such insults! I'm leaving. Returning to the Moon, there to devise such a list of foul names for Caladan Brood as to stain the realms!'

'Begone with you, then,' Brood said, smiling. 'You've done well.'

'If only Rake wasn't even more stingy than you,' Crone said, as she hopped towards the doorway, 'my spying skills would be used on you instead of on him.'

Brood spoke. 'One last thing, Crone.'

338

She stopped at the entrance and cocked her head.

The warrior's attention had returned to the map. 'When you find yourself over the Rhivi Plain far to the south, mark whatever powers you sense active there. But be careful, Crone. Something's brewing, and it stinks.'

Crone's cackle was her only reply, and then she was gone.

Brood stood over his map, thinking hard. He remained unmoving for close to twenty minutes, then he straightened. Stepping outside he searched the sky. Crone was nowhere in sight. He grunted and turned to survey the nearest tents. 'Kallor! Where are you?'

A tall grey man stepped around a tent and walked slowly up to Brood. 'The Gold have bogged down in the forest, Warlord,' he said in a gravelly voice, his ancient, lifeless eyes meeting Brood's. 'A storm comes down from the Laederon Heights. The Moranth's Quorls will be grounded for some time.'

Brood nodded. 'I'm leaving you in charge. Heading to Fox Pass.'

Kallor raised an eyebrow.

Brood stared at him, then said, 'Let's not get too excited. People will start thinking you're not as bored with all this as you make out to be. I'm meeting with Prince K'azz.'

A faint smile quirked Kallor's thin lips. 'What madness has Jorrick Sharplance perpetrated now?'

'None, so far as I'm aware,' Brood answered. 'Ease up on the lad, Kallor. He pulled off the last one. Remember, you were young once, too.'

The old warrior shrugged. 'Jorrick's last success belongs to the Lady of Luck if anything. It surely was not the product of genius.'

'I'll not argue you that one,' Brood said.

'May I ask, what is the reason for speaking with K'azz in person?'

Brood looked around. 'Where's that damn horse of mine, anyway?'

'Probably cowering,' Kallor said drily. 'Word is, his legs have become shorter and stubbier beneath your prodigious self. I remain unconvinced that such a thing is possible, but who can argue with a horse?'

'I need some of the Prince's men,' Brood said, heading off down an aisle. 'To be more precise,' he said, over his shoulder, 'I need the Crimson Guard's Sixth Blade.'

Watching Caladan Brood stride away, Kallor sighed. 'Rake again, is it, Warlord? You'd do better to follow my advice and destroy him. You will rue dismissing my advice, Brood.' His dull eyes followed Brood until he turned a corner and disappeared from sight. 'Consider that my last warning.'

The charred earth crunched under their horses' hoofs. The glance that Toc the Younger threw back over his shoulder was received with a grim nod from Captain Paran. They were nearing the source of last night's column of fire.

As Toc had promised, leaving the city had proved a simple matter; none accosted them, and the gates had been left ajar. Their horses were indeed Wickan-bred, lean and long-limbed; and though their ears flattened and eyes rolled they held to the discipline of their reins.

The still midday air was heavy with the stench of sulphur, and already a fine coat of ash covered the two riders and their horses. Overhead the sun was a bright copper orb. Toc stopped his mount and waited for the captain to arrive.

Paran wiped grimy sweat from his brow and adjusted his helmet. The camail felt heavy on his shoulders as he squinted ahead. They were heading towards the place where the pillar of fire had come from. The night just past had been one of deep fear for Paran: neither he nor Toc had ever witnessed such a conflagration of sorcery. Though they had camped leagues away they had felt the heat pouring from it. Now, as they approached, all Paran could feel was dread.

Neither he nor Toc spoke. Perhaps a hundred yards eastward rose something that looked like a misshapen tree stump, one gnarled, blackened branch reaching skyward. In a perfect circle around it the grassy sward was untouched for perhaps five yards. A dark smudge lay in this unburned area, slightly off to one side.

Paran nudged his mount forward and Toc followed after unslinging and stringing his bow. As Toc caught up with the captain, Paran saw that his companion had nocked an arrow.

The closer they approached the less like a tree the charred thing looked. The limb that reached out from it had familiar lines. Paran's gaze narrowed some more, then he cursed and spurred his horse. He closed the distance quickly, leaving behind a startled Toc.

Arriving, he dismounted and strode up to what he now saw were two bodies, one gigantic. Both had been burned beyond recognition, but Paran held no illusions as to who the other was. *All that come close to me, all that I care for . . .* 'Tattersail,' he whispered, then fell to his knees.

Toc joined him, but remained in the saddle, standing in the stirrups and scanning the horizon. A minute later he dismounted and walked a slow circle around the embracing bodies, stopping at the dark smudge they'd seen from a distance. He crouched to study it.

Paran raised his head and struggled to keep his eyes on the figures. The limb belonged to the giant. The fire that had consumed them both had blackened the arm for most of its length, but its hand was only slightly scorched. Paran stared at the grasping fingers and wondered what salvation the giant had reached for in its moment of death. *The freedom that is death, a freedom denied me. Damn the gods, damn them all.* Numbed, he was slow to realize that Toc called to him.

It was an effort to rise to his feet. He staggered to where Toc still crouched. On the ground before the man was a torn burlap sack.

'Tracks lead from this,' Toc said shakily, a strange expression on his face. He scratched vigorously at his scar, then rose. 'Heading north-east.'

Paran looked at his companion without comprehension. 'Tracks?'

'Small, like a child's. Only . . .'

'Only what?'

The man hugged himself. 'Those feet were mostly bones.' He met the captain's blank stare. 'As if the soles were gone, rotted or burned away – I don't know . . . Something horrible has happened here, Captain. I'm glad it's heading away, whatever it is.'

Paran turned back to the two entwined figures. He flinched. One hand reached up to touch his face. 'That's Tattersail,' he said, in a flat voice.

'I know. I'm sorry. The other one is the Thelomen High Mage Bellurdan. It has to be.' Toc looked down at the burlap sack. 'He took leave to come out here and bury Nightchill.' He added quietly, 'I don't think Nightchill needs burying any more.'

'Tayschrenn did this,' Paran said.

Something in the captain's voice brought Toc round.

'Tayschrenn. And the Adjunct. Tattersail was right. They would not have killed her otherwise. Only she didn't die easily, she never took the easy path in anything. Lorn's taken her from me, just like she's taken everything else.'

'Captain . . .'

Paran's hand unconsciously gripped the pommel of his sword. 'That heartless bitch has a lot coming to her, and I mean to deliver it.'

'Fine,' Toc growled. 'Just let's be smart about it.'

Paran glared at him. 'Let's get going, Toc the Younger.'

Toc glanced one last time into the north-east. This wasn't over, he told himself, shivering. He winced as a savage, painful

342

itch rose beneath his scar. Though he tried, he found he could not reach through to it. And a formless fire burned behind his empty eye-socket – something he had been experiencing often lately. Muttering, he strode to his horse and climbed into the saddle.

The captain had already swung his own mount and the trailing horse southward. The set of the man's back spoke volumes to Toc the Younger, and he wondered if he hadn't made a mistake in accompanying him. Then he shrugged. 'Well,' he said, to the two charred bodies, as he rode past, 'it's done, ain't it?'

The plain below lay sheathed in darkness. Looking to the west, Crone could still see the setting sun. She rode the highest winds, the air around her bitter cold. The Great Raven had left Caladan Brood's company two days ago. Since then, she'd detected no sign of life in the wastes below. Even the massive herds of Bhederin, which the Rhivi were in the habit of following, had disappeared.

At night, Crone's senses were limited, though it was in such darkness that she could best detect sorcery. As she winged ever southward she scanned the land far below with a hungry eye. Others among her brethren from Moon's Spawn regularly patrolled the plains in service to Anomander Rake. She'd yet to see one, but it was only a matter of time. When she did, she would ask them if they'd detected any source of magic recently.

Brood was not one to overreact. If something was happening down here that soured his palate, it could be momentous, and she wanted to know of it before anyone else.

Fire flashed in the sky ahead of her, perhaps a league distant. It flared briefly, tinged green and blue, then disappeared. Crone tensed. That had been sorcery, but of a kind she'd never known. As she swept into the area the air washed over her hot and wet, with a charnel stench that reminded her of – she cocked her head – burnt feathers.

343

A cry sounded ahead, angry and frightened. Crone opened her beak to reply, then shut it again. It had come from one of her kin, she was certain, but for some reason she felt the need to hold her tongue. Then another ball of fire flashed, this time close enough to Crone that she saw what it engulfed: a Great Raven.

Her breath hissed from her beak. In that brief instant of light she'd seen half a dozen more of her brethren wheeling in the sky ahead of her and to the west. She thrummed her wings and angled towards them.

When she could hear their panicked flapping about her on all sides, Crone called out, 'Children! Attend to Crone! The Great Mother has come!'

The ravens voiced relieved cries and closed in around her. They all shrieked at once in an effort to tell her what was happening, but Crone's angry hiss silenced them at once. 'I heard among you Hurtle's voice,' Crone said, 'did I not?'

One male swept near her. 'You did,' he replied. 'I am Hurtle.'

'I've just come from the north, Hurtle. Explain to me what has occurred.'

'Confusion,' Hurtle drawled sarcastically.

Crone cackled. She loved a good joke more than anyone. 'Indeed! Go on, lad!'

'Before dusk Kin Clip detected a flare of sorcery below her on the plain. It was odd, its feel, but clearly a Warren had just opened and something had issued on to the plain. Kin Clip spoke to me of this, then investigated. I shadowed her from above during the descent, and so saw what she saw. Crone, it has come to my mind that once again the art of soul-shifting has been exercised.'

'Eh?'

'Travelling on the ground and having just come from a Warren was a small puppet,' Hurtle explained, 'animate and possessing great power. When this puppet detected Clip he

344

gestured at her and she burst into flames. Since then, the creature has disappeared into its Warren, reappearing only to kill another of us.'

'Why do you remain?' Crone demanded.

Hurtle chuckled. 'We would determine its course, Crone. Thus far, it seems to travel southward.'

'Very well. Now that that's been confirmed, leave and take the others with you. Return to Moon's Spawn and report to our lord.'

'As you command, Crone.' Hurtle dipped a wing and slid off into darkness. His voice called out and was answered by a chorus.

Crone waited. She wanted to be certain that they had all departed the area before doing some investigating on her own. Was this puppet the thing birthed in the pillar of fire? It didn't seem likely. And what kind of sorcery did it employ that no Great Raven could absorb? There was an Eldering taste about this. Soul-shifting was no simple cantrip, and it had never been common among the wizards even when its techniques were known. Too many tales of madness born within the shifting.

Perhaps this puppet had survived from these times. Crone thought about that. Unlikely.

Magic bloomed on the plain below, then faded. A small magical force scampered from the spot, weaving as it ran. There, thought Crone, there lie the answers to my questions. Destroy my younglings, will you? Would you so easily disdain Crone?

She crooked her wings and dropped. The air whistled around her. She raised a penumbra of protective magic that encapsulated her just as the small figure ceased its march and looked up. Faintly, Crone heard a manic laugh rise up to meet her, then the puppet gestured.

The power that engulfed Crone was immense, far beyond anything she anticipated. Her defences held but she found herself buffeted, as if fists punched her from every direction.

345

She cried out in pain, spinning as she fell. It took all her strength and will to thrust out her battered wings and catch a rising current of air. She voiced an outraged, alarmed shriek as she climbed higher into the night sky. A glance down revealed that the puppet had returned once again to its Warren, for nothing magical was visible.

'Aye.' She sighed. 'What a price to pay for knowledge! Elder Warren indeed, the eldest of them all. Who plays with Chaos? Crone knows naught. All things are gathering, gathering here.' She found another stream of wind and angled south. This was something Anomander Rake must know of, never mind Caladan Brood's instructions that the Tiste Andii lord be kept ignorant of almost everything. Rake was good for more than Brood credited him. 'Destruction, for one.' Crone laughed. 'And death. Good at death!'

She picked up speed, so did not notice the dead smudge on the land below her, nor the woman camped in its centre. There was no magic there to speak of, in any case.

Adjunct Lorn squatted by her bedroll, her eyes scanning the night sky. 'Tool, was all that connected to what we witnessed two nights ago?'

The T'lan Imass shook his head. 'I think not, Adjunct. If anything, this concerns me more. It is sorcery, and it ignores the barrier I have set around us.'

'How?' she asked quietly.

'There is only one possibility, Adjunct. It is Eldering, a lost Warren of ages past, returned to us. Whoever its wielder might be, we must assume it tracks us, with purpose.'

Lorn straightened wearily, then stretched her back, feeling her vertebrae pop. 'Is its flavour Shadowthrone's?'

'No.'

'Then I will not assume it's tracking us, Tool.' She eyed her bedroll.

Tool faced the woman and watched in silence as she prepared to sleep. 'Adjunct,' he said, 'this hunter appears able to penetrate my defences, and thus it may open its Warren's portal directly behind us, once we are found.'

'I've no fear of magic,' Lorn muttered. 'Let me sleep.'

The T'lan Imass fell silent, but he continued staring down at the woman as the hours of night crawled on. Tool moved slightly as dawn lightened the east, then was still again.

Groaning, Lorn rolled on to her back as the sunlight reached her face. She opened her eyes and blinked rapidly, then froze. She slowly raised her head to find the T'lan Imass standing directly above her. And, hovering inches from her throat, was the tip of the warrior's flint sword.

'Success,' Tool said, 'demands discipline, Adjunct. Last night we witnessed an expression of Elder magic, choosing as its target ravens. Ravens, Adjunct, do not fly at night. You might think the combination of my abilities with yours ensures our safety. That is no guarantee, Adjunct.' The T'lan Imass withdrew his weapon and stepped to one side.

Lorn drew a shaky breath. 'A flaw,' she said, pausing to clear her throat before continuing, 'which I admit to, Tool. Thank you for alerting me to my growing complacency.' She sat up. 'Tell me, doesn't it strike you as odd that this supposedly empty Rhivi Plain should display so much activity?'

'Convergence,' Tool said. 'Power ever draws other power. It is not a complicated thought, yet it escaped us, the Imass.' The ancient warrior swung his head to the Adjunct. 'As it escapes their children. The Jaghut well understood the danger. Thus they avoided one another, abandoned each other to solitude, and left a civilization to crumble into dust. The Forkrul Assail understood as well, though they chose another path. What is odd, Adjunct, is that of these three founding peoples, it is the Imass whose legacy of ignorance survived the ages.'

Lorn stared at Tool. 'Was that an attempt at humour?' she asked.

The T'lan Imass adjusted his helmet. 'That depends on your mood, Adjunct.'

She climbed to her feet and strode to check her horses. 'You're getting stranger every day, Tool,' she said quietly, more to herself than to the Imass. Into her mind returned the first thing she had seen when she'd opened her eyes – that damned creature and his sword. How long had he stood like that? All night?

The Adjunct paused to test her shoulder tentatively. It was healing quickly. Perhaps the injury had not been as severe as she'd first thought.

As she saddled her horse she chanced to glance at Tool. The warrior stood staring at her. What kind of thoughts would occupy someone who'd lived through three hundred thousand years? Or did the Imass live? Before meeting Tool she had generally thought of them as undead, hence without a soul, the flesh alone animated by some external force. But now she wasn't so sure.

'Tell me, Tool, what dominates your thoughts?'

The Imass shrugged before replying. 'I think of futility, Adjunct.'

'Do all Imass think about futility?'

'No. Few think at all.'

'Why is that?'

The Imass leaned his head to one side and regarded her. 'Because, Adjunct, it is futile.'

'Let's get going, Tool. We're wasting time.'

'Yes, Adjunct.'

She climbed into the saddle, wondering how the Imass had meant that.

348

BOOK FOUR

ASSASSINS

I dreamed a coin
with shifting face –
so many youthful visages
so many costly dreams,
and it rolled and rang
'round the gilded rim
of a chalice
made for gems

Life of Dreams
Ilbares the Hag

CHAPTER ELEVEN

The night held close
as I wandered
my spirit unfooted
to either earth or stone
unravelled from tree
undriven by iron nail
but like the night itself
a thing of air
stripped of light
so I came upon them,
those masons who cut and carved
stone in the night
sighting by stars and battered hand.
'What of the sun?' asked I of them.
'Is not its cloak of revelation
the warmth of reason
in your shaping?'
And one among them answered,
'No soul can withstand
the sun's bones of light
and reason dims
when darkness falls –
so we shape barrows in the night

for you and your kin.'

'Forgive my interruption, then,' said I.

'The dead never interrupt,' said the mason,
'they but arrive.'

Pauper's Stone
Darujhistan

'Yet another night, yet another dream,' Kruppe moaned, 'with naught but a scant fire to keep this wanderer company.' He held his hands over the flickering, undying hearth that had been stoked by an Elder God. It seemed an odd gift, but he sensed a significance to it. 'Kruppe would understand this meaning, for rare and unwelcome is this frustration.'

The landscape around him was barren; even the ploughed earth was gone, with no sign of habitation in sight. He squatted by the lone fire in a tundra wasteland, and the air had the breath of rotting ice. To the north and to the east the horizon gleamed green, almost luminescent though no moon had risen to challenge the stars. Kruppe had never before seen such a thing, yet it was an image fashioned within his mind. 'Disturbing, indeed, proclaims Kruppe. Are these visions of instinct, then, unfurled in this dream for a purpose? Kruppe knows not, and would return to his warm bed this instant, were the choice his.'

He stared about at the lichen- and moss-covered ground, frowning at the strange bright colours born there. He'd heard tales of Redspire Plain, that land far to the north, beyond the Laederon Plateau. Is this what tundra looked like? He'd always pictured a bleak, colourless world. 'Yet peruse these stars overhead. They glisten with a youthful energy, nay, sparkle as if amused by the one who contemplates them. While the earth itself hints of vast blushes of red, orange and lavender.'

352

Kruppe rose as low thunder reached him from the west. In the distance moved a massive herd of brown-furred beasts. The steam of their breath gusted silver in the air above and behind them as they ran, turning as one this way and that but ever at a distance. He watched them for some time. When they came closest to him he saw the reddish streaks in their fur, and their horns, sweeping down then up and out. The land shook with their passage.

'Such is the life in this world, Kruppe wonders. Has he travelled back, then, to the very beginning of things?'

'You have,' said a deep voice behind him.

Kruppe turned. 'Ah, come to share my fire, of course.' He saw before him a squat figure, covered in the tanned hides of deer or some such similar animal. Antlers stretched out from a flat skull-cap on the man's head, grey and covered in fuzzy skin. Kruppe bowed. 'You see before you Kruppe, of Darujhistan.'

'I am Pran Chole of Cannig Tol's Clan among the Kron Tlan.' Pran stepped close and crouched before the fire. 'I am also the White Fox, Kruppe, wise in the ways of ice.' He glanced at Kruppe and smiled.

Pran's face was wide, the bones pronounced beneath smooth, gold skin. His eyes were barely visible between tight lids, but what Kruppe saw of them was a startling amber in colour. Pran reached out long, supple hands over the fire. 'Fire is life, and life is fire. The age of ice passes, Kruppe. Long have we lived here, hunting the great herds, gathering to war with the Jaghut in the southlands, birthing and dying with the ebb and flow of the frozen rivers.'

'Kruppe has travelled far, then.'

'To the beginning and to the end. My kind give way to your kind, Kruppe, though the wars do not cease. What we shall give to you is freedom from such wars. The Jaghut dwindle, ever retreat into forbidding places. The Forkrul Assail have vanished, though we never found need to fight them. And the

353

K'chain Che'Malle are no more – the ice spoke to them with words of death.' Pran's gaze swung back to the fire. 'Our hunting has brought death to the great herds, Kruppe. We are driven south, and this must not be. We are the Tlan, but soon the Gathering comes, and so shall be voiced the Rite of Imass and the Choosing of the Bone Casters, and then shall come the sundering of flesh, of time itself. With the Gathering shall be born the T'lan Imass, and the First Empire.'

'Why, Kruppe wonders, is he here?'

Pran Chole shrugged. 'I have come for I have been called. By whom, I know not. Perhaps it is the same with you.'

'But Kruppe is dreaming. This is Kruppe's dream.'

'Then I am honoured.' Pran straightened. 'One of your time comes. Perhaps this one possesses the answers we seek.'

Kruppe followed Pran's gaze to the south. He raised an eyebrow. 'If not mistaken, then Kruppe recognizes her as a Rhivi.'

The woman who approached was perhaps middle-aged, heavy with child. Her dark, round face bore features similar to Pran Chole's, though less pronounced. Fear shone in her eyes, yet there was a grim determination about her as well. She reached the fire and eyed the two men, most of her attention drawing to Pran Chole. 'Tlan,' she said, 'the Tellann Warren of the Imass of our time has birthed a child in a confluence of sorceries. Its soul wanders lost. Its flesh is an abomination. A shifting must take place.' She turned to Kruppe and swept back the thick woven robe she wore, revealing her swelled stomach. The bare, stretched skin had been recently traced in a tattoo. The image was that of a white-haired fox. 'The Elder God walks again, risen from blood spilled on consecrated stone. K'rul came in answer to the child's need and now aids us in our quest. He apologizes to you, Kruppe, for using the world within your dream, but no younger god can influence this place. Somehow you have made your soul immune to them.'

'The rewards of cynicism,' Kruppe said, bowing.

The woman smiled.

'I understand,' Pran Chole said. 'You would make of this child, born of Imass powers, a Soletaken.'

'Yes. It is the best we can manage, Tlan. A shapeshifter – which we too know as Soletaken – must be fashioned.'

Kruppe cleared his throat. 'Excuse Kruppe, please. But are we not missing someone vital to these plans?'

'She strides two worlds,' the Rhivi said. 'K'rul guides her now into yours. She is frightened still. It falls to you, Kruppe, to welcome her.'

Kruppe adjusted the sleeves of his faded, threadbare cloak. 'This should not prove difficult for one of Kruppe's charms.'

'Perhaps,' the Rhivi said, frowning. 'Her flesh is an abomination. You have been warned.'

Kruppe nodded affably, then looked around. 'Will any direction do?'

Pran Chole laughed.

'I suggest south,' the Rhivi said.

He shrugged and, with a bow to the two companions, he headed south. After a few minutes he glanced back, but the fire was nowhere in sight. He was alone in the chill night.

A full moon appeared on the eastern horizon, bathing the land in silver light. Ahead, the tundra rolled on as far as Kruppe could see, flat and featureless. Then he squinted. Something had just appeared, still distant, walking with seeming great difficulty. He watched it fall once, then climb back to its feet. Despite the luminescence, the figure looked black.

Kruppe moved forward. It had yet to see him, and he stopped when he was but thirty feet away. The Rhivi had been right. Kruppe produced his silk handkerchief and wiped the sweat that had sprung across his brow. The figure had been a woman once, tall, with long black hair. But that woman had been long dead. Her flesh had withered and assumed the hue of dark wood. Perhaps the most horrific aspect of her was her limbs, which had been roughly sewn back on to her body. 'Aye,' Kruppe whispered. This woman had been torn apart once.

The woman's head flew up and sightless eyes fixed upon Kruppe. She stopped, her mouth opening but no words coming forth.

Surreptitiously, Kruppe cast a spell upon himself, then looked at her yet again. He frowned. A spell had been woven about the woman, one of preservation. But something had happened to that spell, something had reshaped it. 'Lass!' Kruppe barked. 'I know you can hear me.' He didn't know, but decided to insist in any case. 'Your soul is trapped within a body that is not your own. It does not become you. I am named Kruppe, and I will lead you to succour. Come!' He spun round and began to walk. A moment later he heard a shuffling behind him, and smiled. 'Ah,' he whispered, 'Kruppe has charms indeed. But more, he can be harsh when necessary.'

The fire had returned, a beacon before them, and Kruppe saw the two figures awaiting them. The vestiges of the spell he had cast upon himself made the Tlan and the Rhivi blinding to his eyes, such was their power. Kruppe and the woman arrived.

Pran Chole stepped forward. 'Thank you, Kruppe.' He studied the woman and nodded slowly. 'Yes, I see the effects of the Imass upon her. But there is more.' He looked to the Rhivi. 'She was a mage once?'

The Rhivi moved close to the woman. 'Hear me, lost one. Your name is Tattersail, your sorcery is Thyr. The Warren flows within you now, it animates you, protects you.' She opened her robe once more. 'It is time to bring you back into the world.'

Tattersail stepped back in alarm.

'Within you is the past,' Pran said. 'My world. You know the present, and the Rhivi offers you to the future. In this place all is merged. The flesh you wear has upon it a spell of

356

preservation, and in your dying act you opened your Warren within the influence of Tellann. And now you wander within a mortal's dream. Kruppe is the vessel of change. Permit us to aid you.'

With a wordless cry Tattersail staggered into Pran's arms. The Rhivi quickly joined them.

'My,' Kruppe breathed, 'but Kruppe's dreams have taken a strange turn. While his own concerns are ever present, a haunting voice, once again he must set them aside.'

Suddenly K'rul stood beside him. 'Not so. It is not my way to use you without just recompense.'

Kruppe looked up at the Elder God. 'Kruppe asks for nothing. There is a gift in this, and I am glad to be part of its making.'

K'rul nodded. 'Nevertheless. Speak to me of your efforts.'

'Rallick and Murillio seek to right an old wrong,' Kruppe said, with a sigh. 'They think me ignorant of their schemes, but I shall turn such schemes to my purposes. Guilt rides this decision, but they are needed.'

'Understood. And the Coin Bearer?'

'Protection has been set in motion, though its final shaping is yet to come. I know that the Malazan Empire is present in Darujhistan, covertly for the moment. What they seek—'

'Is anything but clear, Kruppe. Even to them. Use this to your advantage when you find them. Allies might come from surprising quarters. I will tell you this: two now approach the city, one is a T'lan Imass, the other a bane to magic. Their purposes are destructive, but already forces are in play attending to them. Seek knowledge of them, but do not openly oppose them. They are dangerous. Power attracts power, Kruppe. Leave them to the consequences of their actions.'

Kruppe nodded. 'Kruppe is no fool, K'rul. He openly opposes no one, and he finds power a thing to be avoided at all costs.'

As they spoke the Rhivi woman had taken Tattersail in her

357

arms. Pran Chole squatted nearby, his eyes closed and his lips forming silent words. The Rhivi woman rocked the desiccated body in rhythmic motion, chanting softly. Water stained the Rhivi's thighs.

'Aye,' Kruppe whispered. 'She prepares to give birth in truth.'

Abruptly the Rhivi tossed away the body. It crumpled in a lifeless heap.

The Moon now hung immediately overhead, so bright that Kruppe found he could not look at it directly.

The Rhivi had assumed a squatting position, moving with the rhythm of labour, her face sheathed in sweat. Pran Chole remained immobile, though his body was racked in shivering bouts that twisted his face with pain. His eyes opened wide, glowing bright amber, and fixed on the Moon.

'Elder God,' Kruppe said quietly, 'how much will this Tattersail remember of her former life?'

'Unknown,' K'rul replied. 'Soul-shifting is a delicate thing. The woman was consumed in a conflagration. Her soul's first flight was carried on wings of pain and violence. More, she entered another ravaged body, bearing its own traumas. The child that is born will be like no other ever seen. Its life is a mystery, Kruppe.'

Kruppe grunted. 'Considering her parents, she will indeed be exceptional.' A thought came to him and he frowned. 'K'rul, what of the first child within the Rhivi?'

'There was none, Kruppe. The Rhivi woman was prepared in a manner unknown to any man.' He chuckled. 'Including myself.' He raised his head. 'This sorcery belongs to the Moon, Kruppe.'

They continued watching the labours of birth. To Kruppe it seemed they waited more hours in the darkness than any normal night could hold. The Moon remained overhead, as if it found its position to its liking – or, he reconsidered, as if it stood guard over them.

Then a small cry rose into the still air, and the Rhivi lifted in her arms a child furred in silver.

Even as Kruppe watched, the fur sloughed away. The Rhivi turned the child and placed her mouth against its belly. Her jaws bunched and the remaining length of umbilical cord fell away.

Pran Chole strode to stand beside Kruppe and the Elder God. The T'lan looked exhausted. 'The child drew from me power beyond my control,' he said softly.

As the Rhivi squatted again in afterbirth, holding the child against her chest, Kruppe's eyes widened. The mother's belly was smooth, the white fox tattoo was gone.

'I am saddened,' Pran said, 'that I may not return in twenty years to see the woman this child shall become.'

'You shall,' K'rul said in a low tone, 'but not as a T'lan. As a T'lan Imass Bone Caster.'

The breath hissed between Pran's teeth. 'How long?' he asked.

'Three hundred thousand years, Pran Chole of Cannig Tol's Clan.'

Kruppe laid a hand on Pran's arm. 'You've something to look forward to,' he said.

The T'lan stared at Kruppe a moment, then he threw back his head and roared with laughter.

The hours before Kruppe's dream had proved eventful, beginning with his meeting with Baruk that permitted the revelation of the Coin Bearer punctuated with the clever if slightly dramatic suspension of the coin's wax impression – a cantrip that had gone strangely awry.

But soon after the meeting, droplets of now-hardened wax pebbling the breast and arms of his coat, Kruppe paused just outside the alchemist's door. Roald was nowhere to be seen. 'Oh, my,' Kruppe breathed as he wiped sweat from his forehead. 'Why should Master Baruk find Crokus's name familiar? Ah, stupid Kruppe! Uncle Mammot, of course. Oh dear, that was close – all could well have been lost!' He continued on down the hall to the stairs.

For a time there, Oponn's power had waxed considerably. Kruppe smiled at his pun, but it was a distracted smile. He would do well to avoid such contacts. Power had a habit of triggering his own talents; already he felt the urgings of the Deck of Dragons within his head.

He hurried down the stairs and crossed the main hall to the doors. Roald was just entering, burdened beneath mundane supplies. Kruppe noted the dust covering the old man's clothing. 'Dear Roald, you look as if you've just weathered a sandstorm! Do you require Kruppe's assistance?'

'No,' Roald grunted. 'Thank you, Kruppe. I can manage. Will you be so kind as to close the doors on your way out?'

'Of course, kind Roald!' Kruppe patted the man's arm and strode out into the courtyard. The gates leading to the street had been left open, and beyond was a swirling cloud of dust. 'Ah, yes, the road repairs,' Kruppe muttered.

A headache had burgeoned behind his eyes, and the bright sun overhead wasn't helping matters any. He was half-way to the gates when he stopped. 'The doors! Kruppe has forgotten to close the doors!' He spun round and returned to the estate entrance, sighing as the doors closed with a satisfying click. As he turned away a second time someone shouted in the street beyond. There followed a loud crash, but this latter sound was lost on Kruppe.

With that bellowed curse a sorcerous storm roared into his head. He fell to his knees, then his head snapped up, eyes widening. 'That,' he whispered, 'was indeed a Malazan curse. Then why does House Shadow's image burn like fire in Kruppe's skull? Who now walks the streets of Darujhistan?' *A count of knots unending* . . . 'Mysteries solved, more mysteries created.'

The pain had passed. Kruppe climbed to his feet and brushed the dust from his clothing. 'Good that said affliction occurred beyond the eyes of suspicious beings, Kruppe notes with relief. All upon a promise made to friend Roald. Wise old friend Roald. Oponn's breath is this time welcome, though begrudgingly so.'

He strode to the gates and peered into the street. A cart filled with shattered cobbles had toppled. Two men argued incessantly as to whose fault it was while they righted the cart and proceeded to refill it. Kruppe studied them. They spoke well the Daru tongue, but to one who listened carefully there was the hint of an accent – an accent that did not belong. 'Oh, my,' Kruppe said, stepping back. He adjusted his coat, took a deep breath, then opened the gate and walked into the street.

The fat little man with the flopping sleeves walked from the house's gate and turned left. He seemed in a hurry.

Sergeant Whiskeyjack wiped the sweat from his brow with a scarred forearm, his eyes slits against the bright sunlight.

'That is the one, Sergeant,' Sorry said, beside him.

'Are you sure?'

'Yes, I'm sure.'

Whiskeyjack watched the man winding through the crowd. 'What's so important about him?' he asked.

'I admit,' Sorry replied, 'to some uncertainty as to his significance. But he is vital, Sergeant.'

Whiskeyjack chewed his lip, then turned to the wagon bed where a city map had been laid flat, its corners anchored down by chunks of rock. 'Who lives in that estate?'

'A man named Baruk,' Sorry answered. 'An alchemist.'

He scowled. How did she know that? 'Are you saying that fat little man is this Baruk?'

'No. He works for the alchemist. Not a servant. A spy, perhaps. His skills involve thievery, and he possesses . . . talent.'

Whiskeyjack looked up. 'A Seer?'

For some reason Sorry winced. The sergeant watched, bemused, as Sorry's face paled. Damn, he wondered, what on earth is going on with this girl?

'I believe so,' she said, her voice trembling.

Whiskeyjack straightened. 'All right. Follow him.'

She nodded shakily, then slipped into the crowd.

The sergeant rested his back against the wagon's side-wall. His expression soured as he studied his squad. Trotts was swinging his pick as if on a battlefield. Stones flew everywhere. Passers-by ducked, and cursed when ducking failed. Hedge and Fiddler crouched behind a wheelbarrow, flinching each time the Barghast's pick struck the street. Mallet stood a short distance away, directing pedestrians to the other pavement. He no longer bellowed at the people, having lost his voice arguing with an old man with a donkey wobbling under an enormous basket of firewood. The bundles now lay scattered across the street – the old man and the donkey nowhere to be seen – providing an effective barrier to wheeled vehicles.

All in all, Whiskeyjack concluded, everyone with him had assumed the role of heat-crazed street worker with a facility he found oddly disturbing.

Hedge and Fiddler had acquired the wagon, loaded down with cobbles, less than an hour after their midnight landing at a public dock on the Lakefront. Exactly how this had been accomplished, Whiskeyjack was afraid to ask. But it suited their plans perfectly. Something nagged at the back of Whiskeyjack's mind but he dismissed it. He was a soldier and a soldier followed orders. When the time came, there would be chaos at every major intersection of streets in the city.

'Planting mines ain't gonna be easy,' Fiddler had pointed out, 'so we do it right in front of everyone's nose. Road repair.'

Whiskeyjack shook his head. True to Fiddler's prediction, no one had yet questioned them. They continued ripping up

362

streets and replacing the old cobbles with Moranth munitions encased in fire-hardened clay. Was everything going to be so easy?

His thoughts returned to Sorry. *Not likely*. Quick Ben and Kalam had at last convinced him that their half of the mission was better off without her. She'd tagged along with his crew, eyes never still, but otherwise offering little in the way of assistance. He admitted to feeling some relief that he'd sent her off on that fat man's trail.

But what had pulled a seventeen-year-old girl into the world of war? He couldn't understand it – he couldn't get past her youthfulness, couldn't see beyond to the cold, murderous killer behind those dead eyes. As much as he told his squad that she was as human as any of them, the doubts grew with every question about her that he could not answer. He knew almost nothing about her. The revelation that she could manage a fishing boat had come from seemingly nowhere. And here in Darujhistan she'd hardly acted like a girl raised in a fishing village. There was a natural poise about her, a measure of assurance more common to the higher, educated classes. No matter where she was, she carried herself as if she belonged there.

Did that sound like a seventeen-year-old girl? No, but it seemed to match Quick Ben's assertions, and that galled him. How else to match her with that icy-cold woman torturing prisoners outside Nathilog? He could look at her and part of him would say: 'Young, not displeasing to the eye, a confidence that makes her magnetic.' While another part of his mind snapped shut. Young? He'd hear his own harsh, pained laugh. Oh, no, not this lass. She's *old*. She walked under a blood-red moon in the dawn of time, did this one. *Her face is the face of all that cannot be fathomed, and she's looking you in the eye, Whiskeyjack, and you'll never know what she's thinking.*

He could feel sweat drain down his face and neck. Nonsense. That part of his mind lost itself to its own terror. It

363

took the unknown and fashioned, in blind desperation, a visage it could recognize. Despair, he told himself, always demands a direction, a focus. Find the direction and the despair goes away.

Of course, it wasn't that easy. The despair he felt had no shape. It was not just Sorry, not just this endless war, not even the treachery from within the Empire. He had nowhere to look for answers, and he was tired of asking questions.

When he had looked upon Sorry at Greydog, the source of his horror lay in the unveiling of what he was becoming: a killer stripped of remorse, armoured in the cold iron of inhumanity, freed from the necessity to ask questions, to seek answers, to fashion a reasonable life like an island in a sea of slaughter.

In the empty eyes of this child, he'd seen the withering of his own soul. The reflection had been unblemished, with no imperfections to challenge the truth of what he saw.

The sweat running down his back beneath the jerkin felt hot against the chill that gripped him. Whiskeyjack lifted a trembling hand to his forehead. In the days and nights ahead, people would die by his command. He'd been thinking of that as the fruition of his careful, precise planning – success measured by the ratio of the enemy's dead to his own losses. The city – its busy, jostling multitudes unceasing in their lives small and large, cowardly and brave – no more than a game-board, and the game played solely for the benefit of others. He'd made his plans as if nothing of himself was at stake. And yet his friends might die – there, he'd finally called them what they were – and the friends of others might die, and sons, daughters, parents. The roll-call of shattered lives seemed unending.

Whiskeyjack pressed his back against the side-wall in an effort to steady his reeling mind. Desperately, he lifted his gaze from the street. He saw a man at a window on the second floor of the estate. The man was watching them, and his hands were bright red.

Shaken, the sergeant looked away. He bit into the side of his mouth until he felt a sharp stab of pain, then tasted blood. Concentrate, he told himself. Step back from that chasm. Concentrate, or you'll die. And not just you, but also your squad. They trust you to get them out of this. You've got to keep earning that trust. He drew a deep breath through his nostrils, then turned to one side and spat a mouthful of blood. He stared down at the red-slicked cobble. 'There,' he hissed. 'It's easy to look at it, isn't it?'

He heard footsteps and looked up to see Hedge and Fiddler arrive. Both men wore troubled expressions.

'You all right, Sarge?' Fiddler asked quietly. Behind the two saboteurs, Mallet approached, his gaze calculating and fixed on Whiskeyjack's white, sweat-soaked face.

The sergeant grimaced. 'We're behind schedule. How much longer?'

Their faces smeared with white dust and sweat, the two men looked at each other, then Hedge answered, 'Three hours.'

'We decided on seven mines,' Fiddler said. 'Four Sparkers, two Flamers and one Cusser.'

'Will that bring down some of these buildings?' Whiskeyjack asked, avoiding Mallet's eyes.

'Sure. No better way to block an intersection.' Fiddler grinned at his companion.

'You got one in particular you want dropped?' Hedge enquired.

'The estate behind you is an alchemist's.'

'Right,' Hedge said. 'That should light the sky all right.'

'You've got two and a half hours,' Whiskeyjack said. 'Then it's on to the Majesty Hill crossroads.'

Mallet stepped close. 'Another headache?' he asked softly.

Whiskeyjack closed his eyes, then gave a sharp nod.

The healer raised a hand and passed it over the sergeant's brow. 'Just easing it a little,' he said.

The sergeant grinned ruefully. 'This is getting old, Mallet. You're even using the same words.' A cool numbness flowed through his thoughts.

Mallet's face was drawn. He lowered his hand. 'When we have time I'll find the source, Whiskeyjack.'

'Right.' The sergeant smiled. 'When we have time.'

'Hope Kal and Quick are doing OK,' Mallet said, turning to watch the street traffic. 'You sent Sorry off?'

'Yes. We're on our own. They know where to find us, all three of them.' He glanced up at the estate window. The man with the red hands was still there, though now he was studying the distant rooftops. A cloud of dust rose between them, and Whiskeyjack returned his attention to the city map, where every major intersection, the barracks and Majesty Hill had been circled in red. 'Mallet?'

'Sarge?'

'Bit the inside of my cheek again.'

The healer stepped close, once more raising his hand.

Crokus Younghand strode south on Trallit's Walk. The first signs of the upcoming Gedderone Fête had appeared. Dyed banners hung from clothes-lines over the street, painted flowers and strips of bark framed doorways, and bushels of dried weeds had been tacked to walls at every crossing.

Outlanders already filled the streets, Gadrobi herders, Rhivi traders, Catlin weavers – a mob of sweaty, shouting, excited people. Animal smells mixed with human, making the narrower alleys so redolent as to be almost impassable, which in turn crowded the main thoroughfares even more.

In past years Crokus had revelled in the celebration, pushing through the midnight crowds and filling his own pockets by emptying those around him. During the Fête, worries of the

Malazan Empire's exploits in the far north disappeared for a time. His uncle always smiled at that, saying the turn of the season gave the efforts of humanity their proper perspective. 'The mewling, petty acts,' he'd say, 'of a short-lived and short-sighted species, Crokus, can do nothing to mar the Great Cycles of Life.'

As he walked home Mammot's words returned to him now. He had always looked upon his uncle as a wise, if slightly in-effectual, old man. Increasingly, however, he found himself troubled by Mammot's observations.

Celebrating Gedderone's Rite of Spring shouldn't be an excuse to avoid the pressures of reality. It wasn't just a harmless escape: it was a means of delaying the probable and making it inevitable. We could dance in the streets all year long, he scowled to himself, to a thousand Great Cycles, and with the same certainty reserved for the coming and going of seasons the Malazan Empire would march through our gates. They'd end the dance with the edge of a sword, being industrious, dis-ciplined people, impatient with useless expenditures of energy – grimly short-sighted.

He came to a tenement and, nodding at the pipe-smoking old woman sitting on the steps, went inside. The hallway was empty, the usual crowd of children no doubt outside playing in the streets, and a calming domestic murmur drifted out from behind closed doors. He climbed the creaking staircase to the first floor.

Outside Mammot's door the scholar's pet winged monkey hovered, scratching and pulling desperately at the latch. It ignored Crokus until he arrived to push it aside, then it squealed and flew in circles around his head.

'Being a pain again, eh?' Crokus said to the creature, waving a hand as it flew too close and ended up snarled in his hair. Tiny human-like hands gripped his scalp. 'All right, Moby,' he said, relenting, and opened the door.

Inside, Mammot was preparing herbal tea. Without turning he asked, 'Tea, Crokus? And as for that little monster who's probably riding your head, tell him I've had just about enough of him today.'

Moby sniffed indignantly and flapped over to the scholar's desk, where he landed with a belly-flop, scattering papers to the floor. He chirped.

Sighing, Mammot turned with the tray in his hands. His watery eyes fixed on Crokus. 'You look tired, lad.'

Crokus slumped into the less ragged of the two chairs occupying the room. 'Yes. Tired, and in a dark mood.'

'My tea will do its usual wonders,' Mammot said, smiling.

Crokus grunted, not looking up. 'Maybe. Maybe not.'

Mammot stepped forward and laid the tray on a small table between the chairs. He sat down with a soft groan. 'As you know, I possess few moral qualms about your chosen profession, Crokus, since I question rights of any kind, including ownership. Even privileges demand responsibility, as I've always said, and the privilege of ownership demands that the owner be responsible for protecting his or her claim. My only concern, of course, is for risks you must perforce take.' Mammot leaned forward and poured tea. 'Lad, a thief must be sure of one thing – his concentration. Distractions are dangerous.'

Crokus glanced up at his uncle. 'What have you been writing all these years?' he asked suddenly, gesturing at the desk.

Surprised, Mammot picked up his cup and sat back. 'Well! A genuine interest in education, then? Finally? As I've said before, Crokus, you possess the intelligence to go so far. And while I'm but a humble man of letters, my word will open to you many doors in the city. Indeed, even the City Council is not beyond your reach, if you would choose such a direction. Discipline, lad, the very same requirement you've mastered as a thief.'

A crafty expression glittered in Crokus's gaze as it held on Mammot. 'How long would it take,' he asked quietly, 'to become known in such circles?'

'Well,' said Mammot, 'it is the learning that matters, of course.'

'Of course.' In Crokus's mind, however, there rose the image of a sleeping maiden.

Mammot blew on his drink. 'With full-time studies, and your youthful eagerness, I would hazard a year, perhaps more, perhaps less. Is there a need for haste?'

'Just youthful eagerness, I suppose. In any case, you haven't answered me yet. What are you writing, Uncle?'

'Ah.' Mammot glanced at his desk, raising an eyebrow at Moby, who had opened an inkwell and was drinking from it. 'The history of Darujhistan,' he said. 'I am just beginning the fifth volume, which opens with the reign of Ektalm, second to last of the Tyrant Kings.'

Crokus blinked. 'Who?'

Smiling, Mammot sipped his tea. 'Usurper of Letastte and succeeded by his daughter, Sandenay, who brought on the Rising Time and with it the end of the age of tyrants.'

'Oh, right.'

'Crokus, if you're serious about all this, Darujhistan's history is where we'll begin in the lessons, but that doesn't mean starting at volume five. It means starting at the very beginning.'

Crokus nodded. 'Born on a rumour,' he said.

At the desk Moby squawked, then coughed. Mammot shot him a glance, then swung his attention back to Crokus, expression veiled as he replied, 'Yes, lad. Darujhistan was born on a rumour.' He hesitated. 'You've heard that saying elsewhere? Recently?'

'Someone mentioned it,' Crokus said casually. 'Can't recall who, though.' He could, in fact. It had been spoken by the assassin, Rallick Nom.

369

'Do you know what it means?'

Crokus shook his head.

Mammot leaned back. 'Drink your tea, my lad.' The old man paused, then began, 'In the Early Cycles in this Realm, three great peoples struggled for dominion, none of them human as we would know human. Bowing out early in the struggle were the Forkrul Assail, or the Krussail as they are now known. Not through weakness, but . . . well, disinterest. The remaining two peoples warred endlessly. Eventually one fell, for they were a race of individuals, battling as much among themselves as against their racial enemies. They were called the Jaghut, though the term has degenerated these days to Jhag, or Shurl. While losers in the war, they did not disappear entirely – it's said some Jaghut survive to this day, though, thankfully, not on Genabackis.

'So,' Mammot cupped his hands around his tea-cup, 'Darujhistan was born on a rumour. Among the indigenous Gadrobi hill tribes survived the legend that a Jaghut's barrow lay somewhere in the hills. Now, the Jaghut were possessors of great magic, creators of secret Warrens and items of power. Over time the Gadrobi legend made its way beyond the hills, into the Genabackan north and the Catlin south, to kingdoms since crumbled to dust in the east and west. In any case, searchers came to the hills, at first a trickle then hordes – entire tribes led by power-hungry shamans and warlocks. Every hillside was laced with trenches and bore-holes. From the camps and shanty-towns, from the thousands of treasure-seekers arriving each spring, a city was born.'

'Darujhistan,' Crokus said.

'Yes. The barrow was never found, and the rumour has long since dwindled – few are even aware of it these days, and those who are know better than to resume the search.'

'Why?'

Mammot frowned. 'Rarely does a Jaghut construction

370

appear in the hands of a human, but it has happened, and the consequences have inevitably been catastrophic.' The old man's frown deepened. 'The lesson is clear for those who would choose to recognize it.'

Crokus thought for a time. 'So the Krussail vanished, the Jhag were defeated. What happened to the third people, then? The ones who won? Why aren't they here instead of us?'

Mammot opened his mouth to reply, then stopped, reconsidering.

Crokus's eyes narrowed. He wondered what Mammot had been about to reveal, and why he'd chosen not to reveal it.

Mammot set down his cup. 'No one is certain what happened to them, Crokus, or how they became what they are today. They exist, sort of, and are known, to all who have faced the Malazan Empire, as the T'lan Imass.'

Sorry pushed through the crowd, struggling to keep the fat man within sight. It was not that he was difficult to follow, but the girl was struggling against a storm within her head, which had been triggered by a single word uttered by Sergeant Whiskeyjack.

Seer.

It had felt as if a dark, compacted thing in her brain had burst open with that word, and now warred against all that surrounded it. Though it had initially come upon her with a force that seemed almost overwhelming, she could now sense its waning. Whatever it fought was winning the battle. Yet, faintly, she thought she could hear the weeping of a child.

'I am Cotillion,' she heard herself murmur, 'Patron of Assassins, known to all as the Rope of Shadow.' The weeping grew fainter. 'The Seer is dead.'

A part of her mind cried out at that, while another asked, *What Seer?*

'I am within, yet apart. I stand at Shadowthrone's side, and he is named Ammanas and he is the Lord of Shadows. I am here as the hand of death.' Sorry smiled and nodded to herself, once again in control. Whatever had challenged that was now gone, once more buried deep inside. The luxury of weeping, of anger, of fear did not belong to her, had never belonged to her.

She drew a deep breath, and her senses narrowed to the task at hand. The fat little man was dangerous. The how and why of this remained to be answered, but every power hissed in alarm each time she caught a glimpse of him amid the crowds. And all that is dangerous, she told herself, must die.

Beneath the Second Tier Wall in the Lakefront, the market along Salt Walk was at its usual frenzied peak. The sour heat, building all day in the cluttered avenues and alleys, was at its height. Sweating, exhausted merchants screamed curses at competitors over the heads of customers. Fights broke out every few minutes in one or another area, the turgid jostle of the crowds pulling the contestants apart long before the arrival of ill-tempered guards.

Squatting on their grass mats, local Rhivi plainsmen called out in their nasal singsong endless descriptions of fine horse-flesh. At intersections, Gadrobi herders stood at tethering poles surrounded by braying goats and sheep, while others pushed wooden carts burdened with cheeses and clay jugs filled with fermented milk. Daru fishermen walked with spears of smoked fish bobbing above their heads streaming with buzzing flies. Catlin weavers sat behind waist-high fortresses comprised of bolts of brightly dyed cloth. Gredfalan farmers stood in their wagons selling the season's bitter fruits and sweet tubers. Woodsellers forced their ox-drawn wagons through the crowds, their children clinging to the stacked bundles of wood like monkeys. Dark-robed men and women from Callows sang out the clashing claims of their Thousand Sects of D'rek, each holding aloft their sect's particular icon.

Kruppe strode down the market street with a jaunty step, his arms waving about seemingly of their own accord. Such movement, however, was no mere affectation: it disguised the gesturing required for casting spells. As a thief, it appeared that Kruppe's tastes did not demand much. He stole food – fruit and sweets, mostly – and it was to such desires of the palate that he had honed his skills of magic.

As he walked, the chaotic dance of his arms was timed to catch apples flying from baskets, pastries leaping from trays, chocolate-covered cherries plucked from pans, all moving so swiftly as to be no more than blurs dodging bodies in their path. Inside the wide, flopping sleeves of his coat, pockets had been sewn, some large, some tiny. All that entered Kruppe's hands disappeared up his sleeves, tucked into appropriately sized pockets. He strode on, a connoisseur of edible delicacies of a hundred cultures, an expression of sated contentment on his round face.

Eventually, after a long, circuitous route, Kruppe arrived at the Phoenix Inn. He paused on the steps and chatted with a lone thug standing there, removing from a sleeve a glazed honeyball. Then, taking a bite from the sweetmeat, he pushed open the door and disappeared inside.

Half a block down the street, Sorry propped herself against the pitted wall of a tenement and crossed her arms. The fat little man was a wonder. She'd seen enough of his exquisite ballet to recognize him as an Adept. Yet she felt confused, for the mind behind the man's façade hinted at capacities far greater than those he'd shown. Confirmation that here indeed was a dangerous creature.

From where she stood she studied the inn. The man on the steps seemed to be screening everyone entering, but she couldn't detect any gesture that might indicate a thieves' cant. The conversations were brief, usually of mutual recognition.

Nevertheless she intended to enter the inn. It was the kind of place Whiskeyjack had sent Kalam and Quick Ben to find – a haunt of thieves, strong-arms and assassins. Why the sergeant wanted to find such a place was a detail that hadn't been shared with her. The wizard and Kalam had suspicions about her, and she sensed that their arguments were swaying Whiskeyjack. If they could, they'd keep her out of everything, but she didn't intend that to happen.

Pushing herself from the wall, Sorry crossed the street and approached the Phoenix Inn. Overhead, the afternoon had waned into a thick, heavy dusk, the smell of rain in the air. As she neared the front steps, the thug's attention focused on her. The man grinned. 'Following Kruppe around, eh?' He wagged his head. 'Girls shouldn't carry swords anyway. Hope you're not planning to go inside. With a sword? Uh, uh. Not unescorted, anyway.'

Sorry stepped back. She glanced up and down the street. The nearest pedestrian was over a street away, heading in the opposite direction. She closed her hands around the edges of her half-cloak and drew it around her waist. 'Let me pass,' she said quietly. How had that fat man spotted her?

The man leaned on the railing. 'All this is just begging for some kind of conversation, friendly-like,' he said. 'So how about you and me go back to the alley. You lay down your sword and I'll be gentle. Otherwise, things could get rough, and what would be the fun of—?'

Sorry's left hand darted out. A dagger flashed between them. The blade entered the man's right eye and then his brain. He jerked back over the rail and fell, landing with a heavy thud beside the steps. Sorry walked up to him and retrieved her dagger. She paused, adjusting the belt that carried her duelling sword, then checked the street. Seeing no one close enough to have noticed anything awry in the deepening gloom, she climbed the steps and entered the inn.

She was stopped before she'd taken her second step, coming face-to-face with a moaning boy hanging upside down. Two rough-looking women were taking turns to swing him back and forth. Every time he tried to reach up to the rope tied to his feet he earned a knock on the head. One of the women grinned at Sorry.

'Hey, now!' the woman said, grasping Sorry's arm as she walked by.

Sorry turned a cold eye on the woman. 'What?'

The woman leaned close, her breath a mist of beer as she whispered, 'You get in trouble, you just call for Irilta and Meese. That's us, right?'

'Thank you.'

Sorry resumed her walk. She'd already seen the fat little man – what had the thug called him? Kruppe. He'd seated himself at a table near the far wall, beneath the gallery. Through the crowded room Sorry saw a space open at the bar, where she might take position and observe. She pushed forward.

Since Kruppe evidently knew of her, she decided to make no effort in hiding her attention. Often, that was exactly the kind of pressure that cracked a man's will. In a war of patience, Sorry smiled inwardly, the mortal is ever at a disadvantage.

Crokus turned the corner and approached the Phoenix Inn. The course Mammot had set for him was intimidating, the education extending far beyond books, to the etiquette of court manners, the functions of various officials, blood-lines and particular quirks among certain dignitaries – but he'd vowed to himself he'd follow it through. His goal was one day to stand before that D'Arle maiden, awaiting a formal introduction.

Something in him mocked the image. There stands Crokus, the scholar, the sophisticated young promise, the thief. It was all too absurd. Yet it dogged him, steeled his resolve. He'd come to it one day soon. Until then, however, there were other matters to attend to, things that needed redressing.

As he came up to the inn's steps he saw a huddled shadow beneath the railing. Cautiously Crokus moved closer.

As Sorry reached the bar the door slammed open on the other side of the room. She turned with everyone else to see a young, black-haired man standing there.

'Someone's murdered Chert!' the man shouted. 'He's been knifed!'

Half a dozen patrons surged to the door, pushing past the young man and disappearing outside.

Sorry faced the bar again. Catching the barman's eye she said, 'Gredfalan ale, please, in a pewter tankard.'

The woman Irilta had called Meese appeared beside her, thumping two broad forearms on the bar as she leaned forward. 'Attend the lady, Scurve,' Meese growled. 'She got taste.'

Meese dipped her head close to Sorry's. 'Good taste all round. Chert was a pig.'

Sorry stiffened. Her hands slipped down beneath her cloak.

'Easy, girl,' Meese said, in a low tone. 'We ain't wagging tongues. Around here, y' take care of yourselves first, and I don't want no knife in my eye. We said we'd take care of you, didn't we?'

The ale arrived, as ordered. Sorry raised a hand and closed it on the tankard's handle. 'You don't want to take care of me, Meese,' she said quietly.

Another person arrived on Meese's other side. Glancing at him, Sorry saw that it was the black-haired youth, his face pale. 'Dammit, Meese,' he hissed, 'I'm having a really bad day.'

Meese chuckled and draped an arm over his shoulders. 'Scurve, serve us up a couple of them Gredfalan ales. Crokus here's earned Darujhistan's best.' Meese turned her head and bent close to Sorry again. 'Next time,' she whispered, 'you

376

don't want to show that kind of breeding. Not around here, anyway.'

Sorry frowned down at her drink. She'd been careless, ordering the city's best. Then she took a mouthful. 'That's fine,' she said. 'Fine indeed.'

Meese grinned, nudging Crokus. 'The lady likes it just fine.'

Crokus leaned forward, offering Sorry a weary but warm smile. From outside came the klaxon of the Guard.

Scurve served up the two ales.

Sorry watched Crokus's gaze move down her body, then stop. The youth's smile tightened, his face whitening even more than before. As the tankard was set before him, Crokus averted his eyes and reached for it.

'Pay up before you drink that, Crokus,' Scurve muttered. 'You're getting to be just as bad as Kruppe.'

Crokus reached into his pocket and pulled out a handful of coins. As he tried to count them some slipped between his fingers and bounced on the bar. Of the three that fell, two clattered briefly then stopped. The third coin spun, and continued spinning. Sorry's eyes swung to it, as did Scurve's and Meese's. Crokus reached for it, then hesitated. The coin was still spinning, its momentum unchanged.

Sorry stared at the coin, feeling echoes of power slam into her skull like ocean waves. From within, all at once, came an answering surge. Scurve shouted as the coin skidded across the bar, bounced once high into the air, then clattered to a stop directly in front of Crokus.

No one spoke. Beyond their small ring no one else had witnessed the event.

Crokus thrust his hand forward and collected the coin. 'Not this one,' he grated.

'Fine,' Scurve answered, in a similar, hoarse voice. He reached shaking hands to gather in the other coins Crokus had laid on the bar.

377

Beneath the counter, Sorry brushed her hand against her dagger's hilt and scabbard. It came away wet. So, Crokus had seen the blood. She would have to kill him. Only, her frown deepened, she knew she wouldn't.

'Crokus, my boy!' came a shout from under the gallery.

Meese sneered in that direction. 'The flopping fish himself,' she muttered. 'Kruppe calls, lad.'

Crokus snorted, having returned the coin to his pocket. He picked up his tankard. 'Later, Meese.'

So, she'd found Oponn's man – as easily as that. And he was connected to Kruppe, somehow. This was almost too simple. It made her suspicious.

'A likely lad,' Meese said. 'Me and Irilta, we look out for him, right?'

Sorry leaned against the bar, her eyes on the tankard in her hand. She'd have to play this very carefully. That burst of Shadow sorcery, responding to the Coin's influence, had been entirely instinctive. 'Right, Meese,' she said. 'No worries on that count. OK?'

Meese sighed. 'OK. Let's try for the cheap stuff now. Scurve? Daru beer, if you please. Earthenware, if you have it.'

Crouched against the Second Tier Wall on the Lakefront side was Quip's Bar, a common haunt of shipmen and fisher-hands. The bar's walls were cut sandstone, and over time the whole edifice had developed a backward lean, as if withdrawing from the front street. Quip's now sagged against the Second Tier Wall, as did the adjoining squatter shacks constructed mostly of driftwood and hull planks washed ashore from the occasional wreck out on Mole's Reef.

Dusk brought a light rain to Darujhistan, the mists crawling in from the water and on to the shore. Far out over the lake lightning flashed, but too distant for thunder to be heard.

378

Kalam emerged from Quip's Bar just as a local Greyface brought his burning pitch-stick to a nearby gas-light, having moments earlier opened the copper valves. The lamp ignited in a flash of blue flame that quickly evened out. Kalam paused outside the bar to watch the odd, grey-robed man continue on down the street. He squinted skyward, then moved up the street. He came to the last squatter shack, this one abutting a peculiar jag in the tier wall, and entered.

Quick Ben looked up from his cross-legged position in the centre of the dirt floor. 'Any luck?'

'No,' Kalam said. 'The Guild's gone to ground – why, I've no idea.' He went to the far wall and sat down on his bedroll. He leaned back against the ancient, pitted stone and eyed his comrade. 'You think maybe the City Council's moved to take out the local assassins?'

Quick Ben's gaze glittered in the gloom. 'You mean, anticipating we'd try to make contact?'

Kalam looked away. 'I doubt they're idiots. They must know it's the Malazan way. Offer the Guild a contract it can't refuse, then sit back and watch the rulers drop like headless flies. Whiskeyjack suggested the plan. Dujek OK'd it. Those two were talking the old Emperor's language there, Quick. The old man must be laughing in hell right now.'

The wizard shivered. 'An unpleasant image.'

Shrugging, Kalam continued, 'It's all academic, anyway, if we can't find a local assassin. Wherever they are, it's not in Lakefront District, I'd swear to that. The only name I picked up that's got mystery around it is someone named the Eel. Not an assassin, though. Something else.'

'Where next, then?' Quick Ben asked. 'Gadrobi District?'

'No. Just a bunch of farmers and herders there. Hell, the smell alone coming from that place is enough to cross it off the list. We'll try Daru, starting tomorrow.' Kalam hesitated. 'What about your side of things?'

Quick Ben bowed his head. When he answered it was a faint whisper. 'Almost ready.'

'Whiskeyjack nearly choked when he heard your proposal. So did I. You'll be walking into the viper's den, Quick. You sure it's necessary?'

'No.' Quick Ben looked up. 'Personally, I'd rather we just dropped everything and ran – away from it all, from the Empire, from Darujhistan, from war. But try convincing the sergeant to do that. He's loyal to an idea, and that's the hardest kind to turn.'

Kalam nodded. 'Honour, integrity, all that expensive crap.'

'Right. So we do it this way because it's the only way left to us. Hairlock's insanity has become a liability, but we can use him still, one last time. Power draws power, and with luck Hairlock's demise will do just that. The more Ascendants we can lure into the fray the better.'

'I always thought that was something to avoid, Quick.'

The wizard's smile was strained. 'Tell me about it. But right now the more confusion and chaos the better.'

'And if Tayschrenn catches wind?'

Quick Ben's smile broadened. 'Then we're dead all that much sooner. So it goes.'

Kalam barked a short, humourless laugh. 'So it goes.'

The wizard cocked his head. 'The sun's past the horizon. Time to start.'

'You want me out of here?' Kalam asked.

Quick Ben shook his head. 'No, I want you right where you are for this one. If I don't come back, take my body and burn it down to ash. Scatter the ash to the four winds, and curse my name with all your heart.'

Kalam was silent. Then he asked, in a growl, 'How long do I wait?'

'Dawn,' Quick Ben replied. 'You understand I would only ask this of my closest friend.'

'I understand. Now, get on with it, dammit.'

Quick Ben gestured. A ring of fire sprang from the earth, surrounding the wizard. He closed his eyes.

To Kalam, his friend seemed to deflate slightly, as if something essential to life had disappeared. Quick Ben's neck creaked as his chin sank down to his chest, his shoulders slumped, and a long breath escaped with a slow hiss. The ring of fire flared, then dimmed to a lapping glimmer on the earth.

Kalam shifted position, stretching out his legs and crossing his arms. In the gathering silence, he waited.

A pale Murillio returned to the table and sat down. 'Someone's disposing of the body,' he said, then shook his head. 'Whoever killed Chert was a professional with a real nasty streak. Right through the eye—'

'Enough!' Kruppe cried out, raising his hands. 'Kruppe happens to be eating, dear Murillio, and Kruppe also happens to have a delicate stomach.'

'Chert was a fool,' Murillio continued, ignoring Kruppe, 'but hardly the type to attract such viciousness.'

Crokus said nothing. He'd seen the blood on that dark-haired woman's dagger.

'Who can say?' Kruppe waggled his eyebrows. 'Perhaps he was witness to some horrific horror. Perhaps he was stamped out as a man crushes a cute mouse underfoot.'

Crokus glanced around. His eyes returned to the woman standing with Meese at the bar. Dressed in leather armour with a plain duelling sword strapped to her hip, she reminded him of the time he'd watched, as a young boy, a troop of mercenaries ride through the city. They had been the Crimson Guard, he recalled: five hundred men and women without a shiny buckle among them.

His gaze remained on the woman. Like a mercenary, a killer for whom killing had long since lost its horror.

What had Chert done to earn a knife in the eye?

Crokus looked away, in time to see Rallick Nom enter the bar. The assassin approached the table, seemingly unconscious of the locals moving from his path.

Coll intercepted him before he reached the table. The burly man slapped Rallick's back and leaned drunkenly against him. 'Nom, you old bastard!'

Rallick threw an arm around Coll's round shoulders and together they came to the table.

Kruppe looked up. 'Ho, my dear comrades! Kruppe invites you to join our familiar gathering.' Waving his arms at the two empty chairs, he rocked back in his seat. 'To bring you up to date on our dramatic doings, the lad Crokus has been staring dreamily into space while Murillio and Kruppe have discussed the latest natterings of the street rats.'

Coll remained standing, weaving unsteadily, a frown knitting his brows. Rallick sat down and reached for the pitcher of beer. 'What natterings are those?' the assassin asked casually.

'The rumour that we're now allied with Moon's Spawn,' Murillio said.

'Nonsense, of course,' Kruppe said. 'Have you seen anything to suggest such a thing?'

Murillio grinned. 'The Moon hasn't moved away, has it? Not only that, there's that Council tent stationed directly under it.'

Crokus spoke up. 'I heard from Uncle Mammot that the councilmen haven't had any luck getting a message to whoever's in Moon's Spawn.'

'Typical,' Murillio commented, his eyes narrowing briefly on Rallick.

'Who lives in there?' Crokus asked.

Coll tottered and threw both hands down on the table to steady himself. He thrust his red face at Crokus and bellowed, 'Five black dragons!'

382

* * *

Within the Warren of Chaos, Quick Ben knew of the innumerable shifting pathways that led to doors. Though he called them doors they were in fact barriers created where Warrens touched, a calcretion of energy as solid as basalt. Chaos touched on all realms with gnarled fingertips bleeding power, the doors hardened wounds in the flesh of other worlds, other avenues of magic.

The wizard had focused his talents on such doors. While within the Warren of Chaos, he had learned the ways of shaping their energy. He'd found means of altering the barriers, of sensing what lay beyond them. Each Warren of magic possessed a smell, each realm a texture, and though the pathways he took were never the same as those he'd taken before, he had mastered the means of finding those he sought.

He travelled now down one of those paths, a track of nothingness enclosed by the Warren's own accretions, twisting and fraught with contradictions. On one trail he'd will himself forward yet find himself moving back; he'd come to a sharp right turn, followed by another, then another, then yet another – all in the same direction.

He knew it was the power of his mind that opened the pathways, but they had their own laws – or perhaps they were his, yet unknown to him. Whatever the source of the shaping, it was madness defined.

He came at last to the door he sought. The barrier showed as nothing more than a dull, slate-grey stone. Hovering before it, Quick Ben whispered a command, and his spirit took the form of his own body. He stood a moment, mastering the disconnected tremble of his ghost-body, then stepped forward and laid hands on the door.

Its edges were hard and warm. Towards the centre it grew hot and soft to the touch. The surface slowly lost its opaqueness beneath the wizard's hands, becoming glassy like obsidian. Quick Ben closed his eyes.

He'd never before sought to pass through such a door. He was not even certain that it was possible. And if he survived into the beyond, was there any way to return? Past the mechanics of the one thing loomed his final, most difficult worry: he was about to attempt entry into a realm where he wasn't welcome.

Quick Ben opened his eyes. 'I am direction,' he said quietly. He leaned against the barrier. 'I am the power of will in a place that respects this, and only this.' He leaned harder. 'I am the Warren's touch. To chaos nothing is immune, nowhere is immune.' He felt the door begin to yield. He lashed out one hand behind him, fending off a growing pressure. 'Only I shall pass!' he hissed. Abruptly, with a strange thumping sound, he slipped through, energy flaring around his body.

The wizard staggered over rough, parched earth. He regained his balance and looked around. He stood on a barren plain, the horizon off to his left humped with low hills. Overhead spanned a sky the colour of quicksilver, a scatter of long, stringy clouds moving in unison and black as ink directly above.

Quick Ben sat down, folding his legs and clasping his hands in his lap. 'Shadowthrone,' he said, 'Lord of Shadows, I am come to your realm. Will you receive my presence as befits a peaceful visitor?'

From the hills came an answer: the howling of Hounds.

CHAPTER TWELVE

Walk with me
on Thieves' Road
hear its song
underfoot
how clear its
tone in misstep
as it sings
you in two

Apsalar's Cant
Drisbin (b. 1135)

K neading his brow, Kruppe sat reading in Mammot's study.

. . . and in the Calling Down to earth the God was Crippled, and so Chained in its place. In the Calling Down many lands were sundered by the God's Fists, and things were born and things were released. Chained and Crippled was this God

Kruppe glanced up from the ancient tome and rolled his

eyes. 'Brevity, Kruppe prays for brevity!' He returned to the faded handwritten script.

> and it bred caution in the unveiling of its powers. The Crippled God bred caution but not well enough, for the powers of the earth came to it in the end. Chained was the Crippled God, and so Chained was it destroyed. And upon this barren plain that imprisoned the Crippled God many gathered to the deed. Hood, grey wanderer of Death, was among the gathering, as was Dessembrae, then Hood's Warrior – though it was here and in this time that Dessembrae shattered the bonds Hood held upon him. Also among the gathering were

Kruppe groaned and flipped pages. The list seemed interminable, absurdly long. From this account he half expected to see his grandmother's name among those listed. Finally, after three pages, he found the names he sought.

> and among those that came from the vaulted heavens of silver, the Tiste Andii, dwellers of Darkness in the Place before Light, Black Dragons numbering five, and in their league sailed red-winged Silanah, said to dwell among the Tiste Andii in their Fang of Darkness descending from the vaulted heavens of silver

Kruppe nodded, muttering to himself. A descending Fang of Darkness – Moon's Spawn? Home to five Black Dragons and one Red Dragon? He shivered. How had Coll come upon this? True, the man hadn't always been a drunken lout, but even his past station, lofty as it was, hadn't been the scholarly kind.

Who, then, had spoken through the old man's wine-stained mouth?

'That,' Kruppe sighed to himself, 'shall have to wait its

answer. The significance, however, of Coll's bellowed claim lies in its evident truth, and as to how it pertains to the present situation.' He closed the book and rose to his feet. Behind him he heard footsteps.

'I've brought you herbal tea,' the old man said, as he entered the closet-sized room. 'Has *Alladart's Realm Compendium* been beneficial, Kruppe?'

'Beneficial indeed,' Kruppe said, gratefully accepting the earthenware mug. 'Kruppe has learned the value of modern language. Such long-lipped dribbles common to those ancient scholars are a curse Kruppe is thankful to find extinct in our time.'

'Ah, ha,' the old man said, coughing slightly and looking away. 'Well, do you mind if I ask what you were seeking?'

Kruppe glanced up, the corners of his eyes crinkling slightly. 'Not at all, Mammot. I thought to find mention of my grandmother's name.'

Mammot frowned, then nodded. 'I see. Well, I'll not enquire as to your luck, then.'

'Please, do not,' Kruppe said, eyes widening. 'Luck is such a dreadful companion these days, with all awry as all happens to be. But thank you for understanding Kruppe's need for circumspection.'

'Not at all,' Mammot said, waving one hand. 'I didn't mean to – well, yes, I did. Curiosity, you understand. The intellectual kind.'

Kruppe smiled beatifically and sipped tea.

'Well,' Mammot said, 'shall we return to the common room, then, and find respite before the hearth?'

They strode into the other chamber. Once seated, Kruppe stretched out his legs and leaned back. 'How has your writing been coming along?' he asked.

'Slow,' Mammot answered, 'as one would expect, of course.'

It seemed Mammot was working up to something, and so

Kruppe waited, idly wiggling his toes. A minute passed, then the old man cleared his throat and spoke. 'Kruppe, have you seen much of my dear nephew lately?'

Kruppe raised his eyebrows. 'Long ago,' he said, 'Kruppe made a promise to a man, the man being a concerned uncle to a young boy who found the streets an exciting playground. Aye, the lad dreamed of sword-fights and dark deeds committed in alleys on behalf of princesses in disguise, or some such thing—'

Mammot was nodding, his eyes closed.

'– and to such promises Kruppe has availed of himself thoroughly, for he, too, loved the boy. And as with any endeavour, survival is measured in ability, and so did Kruppe take the lad under his silken wing, with some success, yes?'

Mammot smiled, still nodding.

'And so, to answer the uncle's question. Indeed Kruppe has seen the lad.'

Mammot leaned forward and fixed Kruppe with an intense gaze. 'Have you seen anything odd in his actions? I mean, has he asked you any strange questions, made any requests?'

Kruppe's eyes narrowed. He paused to drink. 'Bluntly, yes. For one, he sought the return of a fine cache of jewellery he acquired recently, for personal reasons – as he said. Personal reasons. Kruppe wondered then and wonders now, but the lad's seeming sincerity, nay, focused intensity, struck Kruppe as laudable.'

'Agreed! Would you believe Crokus has now expressed an interest in formal education? I can't understand it. The boy's positively obsessed about something.'

'Perhaps, then, Kruppe should piece this together.'

'Thank you,' Mammot said, relieved. 'I would know where all this is coming from. So much ambition all at once, I fear it may soon burn itself out. If we can nourish it, however . . .'

'By all means,' Kruppe said. 'There is more to life than petty thievery, after all.'

Mammot grinned. 'Why, Kruppe, I'm surprised to hear that coming from you.'

'Such comments are better left between you and Kruppe. In any case, I believe Murillio knows something of all this. He intimated as much this evening while we dined at the Phoenix Inn.'

Mammot asked, 'Is Murillio well?'

Kruppe smiled. 'The net about the lad remains intact,' he said. 'For one, Rallick Nom has taken the responsibility seriously indeed. Mayhap he sees something of his own lost youth in Crokus. In truth, Rallick is a man whose true nature escapes Kruppe. Fiercely loyal for certain, and one who, as you well know, honours his debts with such vigour as to humble those around him. Excepting Kruppe, naturally. Yet is it blood that travels his veins? One must wonder, at times.'

A distant look had entered Mammot's face.

Kruppe tensed. The air smelled of magic. He leaned forward and studied the old man seated across from him. Someone was communicating with Mammot, and the Warren that now pulsed in the room was familiar to Kruppe.

He sat back and waited.

Eventually, Mammot got swiftly to his feet. 'I have some research to do,' he said distractedly. 'As for you, Kruppe, Master Baruk wishes to speak with you immediately.'

'I thought I sensed the alchemist's presence,' Kruppe said, rising with a soft grunt. 'Ah, the rigours of these fated nights ever urge us on. Until later, then, Mammot.'

'Goodbye,' the scholar said, a frown on his face as he crossed the room. He entered the small chamber where Kruppe had spent the past hour.

Kruppe adjusted the sleeves of his cloak. Whatever had happened, it had been enough to jar Mammot's etiquette, and that alone hinted at dire events. 'Well,' he murmured, 'best not keep Baruk waiting, then. At least,' he amended, as he headed for the door, 'not for too long. Decorum demands that Kruppe retain his sense of dignity. He shall walk fast, yes. But walk he shall, for Kruppe needs time to think, to plan, to scheme, to anticipate, to backtrack with some thoughts, to leap ahead with others, to do all the things necessary. First and foremost, Kruppe must discern the nature of the woman who followed him, and who killed Chert, and who noted that Crokus saw the blood on her weapon, and who marked Rallick Nom as an assassin with his very arrival. She might well provide the key to everything, and more, for the Coin did indeed turn its face upon her, if only for a moment. And that, thinks Kruppe, shall return to us all, for good or ill.' He stopped and looked around, blinking rapidly. 'At the very least,' he muttered, 'Kruppe should leave Mammot's room.' He glanced back at the chamber Mammot had entered. From within came the sounds of brittle pages being rapidly turned. Kruppe sighed in relief, then left.

Crone ruffled her singed feathers and hopped about in agitation. Where was that alchemist? She had a thousand things to attend to before the night was done, though in truth she couldn't think of any of them. Nevertheless, she disliked being kept waiting.

The door to the study opened and Baruk strode through, gathering a robe about his considerable bulk. 'My apologies, Crone, I was otherwise indisposed.'

Crone grunted. Sorcery trailed from the man in thick, pungent streams. 'My master, Lord Anomander Rake,' she said, without preamble, 'has commanded that I tell you what I told him of my adventures on the Rhivi Plain.'

Baruk came up to where the Great Raven paced on the map table. The alchemist frowned. 'You've been injured.'

'Pride, no more. Hearken then to my story.'

Baruk raised an eyebrow. The old witch's mood was dark. He fell silent and she began.

'A small wooden puppet approaches from the north, a creation of soul-shifting and sourced from a Warren of Chaos. Its power is immense, twisted, malign even to Great Ravens. It killed many of my kin as it slipped in and out of its Warren. It evidently took pleasure in such acts.' Crone snapped her beak in anger, then continued, 'It pursues a power I could not approach, and whatever this power, it strikes directly for the Gadrobi Hills – my lord and I are agreed in this. The power seeks something within those hills, yet we are not native to this land. Hence we bring this news to you, Alchemist. Two forces are converging on the Gadrobi Hills. My lord asks you why.'

Baruk's face had lost all its colour. He turned slowly and walked to a chair. Sitting down, he steepled his hands before his face and closed his eyes. 'The Malazan Empire seeks something it cannot hope to control, something buried within the Gadrobi Hills. Whether or not either force is capable of freeing that thing is another matter. Seeking is not the same as finding, and finding is not the same as succeeding.'

Crone hissed impatiently. 'Who is buried there, Alchemist?'

'A Jaghut Tyrant, imprisoned by the Jaghut themselves. Generations of scholars and sorcerers have sought to find this barrow. None managed to discover even so much as a clue.' Baruk looked up, his expression lined with worry. 'I know of one man, here in Darujhistan, who has gathered all the available knowledge concerning this burial place. I must confer with him. I can give your lord this, however. There lies a standing stone in the Gadrobi Hills – I know its location precisely. It is almost invisible, only its weathered top breaks the ground, perhaps a hand's span in height. The remaining twenty feet are beneath the earth. You will see the remnants of many pits and trenches that have been excavated around it – all fruitless. For while the stone marks the beginning point, it is not the entrance to the barrow.'

'Where, then, is this entrance?'

'That I will not tell you. Once I speak with my colleague, perhaps I can give you more details. Perhaps not. But the means by which the barrow is entered must remain a secret.'

'This avails us nothing! My lord—'

'Is extremely powerful,' Baruk cut in. 'His intentions are anything but clear, Crone, no matter that we are allied. What lies within that barrow can destroy a city – this city. That I will not allow to enter Rake's hands. You shall have the location of the standing stone, for it is there that the hunters must first go. I have one question to ask, Crone. This puppet, are you certain it pursues this other power?'

Crone bobbed her head. 'It tracks. It hides when necessary. You assume both powers are Malazan. Why?'

Baruk grunted. 'First, they want Darujhistan. They'll do anything to win it. They've had access to vast libraries among the lands they've conquered. The Jaghut barrow is no secret in and of itself. Second, you said both powers came down from the north. They can only be Malazan. Why one hides from the other is beyond me, though I wouldn't doubt that there are competing factions within the Empire – any political entity as large as that one is bound to be rife with discord. In any case, they pose a direct threat to Darujhistan and, by extension, to your lord's desires to prevent the Malazan Empire from conquering us. Assuming that the powers are Malazan seems warranted.'

Crone's displeasure was obvious. 'You will be kept informed of the activities on the Rhivi Plain. My lord must decide whether to intercept these powers before they reach the Gadrobi Hills.' She turned an angry eye on Baruk. 'He has received little assistance from his allies. I trust when we next speak that situation will be remedied.'

The alchemist shrugged. 'My first meeting with Anomander Rake has proved my only meeting with him. Assistance demands communication.' His tone hardened. 'Inform your lord that the present dissatisfaction exists with us as much as it does with him.'

'My lord has been busy with his side of things,' Crone muttered, flapping to the window-sill.

Baruk stared at the bird as she prepared to leave. 'Busy?' he asked darkly. 'In what way?'

'In due time, Alchemist,' Crone purred. A moment later she was gone.

Baruk cursed, and with an angry gesture returned the window to its place and slammed the shutters. Doing this through magic and from a distance was not as satisfying as it would have been had he done it physically. Grumbling, he rose and walked to the mantelpiece. As he poured himself some wine, he paused. Less than half an hour ago he'd conjured a demon. It was not an ambitious conjuring: he'd needed a spy, not a killer. Something told him he'd be calling upon far deadlier creatures in the near future. He scowled, then took a mouthful of wine. 'Mammot,' he whispered, as he opened his Warren, 'I need you.'

He smiled as a scene appeared in his head, of a small room and a stone hearth. Seated in the chair opposite his point of view was Kruppe. 'Good. I need you both.'

The Hound that approached Quick Ben was wide and heavy, its fur a pasty white. As it trotted up to the wizard, he saw that its eyes were also white. The creature possessed no pupils. It stopped a short distance away and sat.

Quick Ben bowed. 'You are the Hound called Blind,' he said, 'mate to Baran and mother of Gear. I come seeking no harm. I would speak with your master.'

He heard a growl beside him and froze. Slowly, he turned his head and looked down. Less than a foot from his right leg lay another Hound, mottled brown and tan, lean and scarred. Its eyes were fixed on Blind. 'Baran.' He nodded. Another growl answered Baran's, this one behind the wizard. He turned further to see, ten feet away, a third Hound, this one long, black and sleek. Its eyes, fixed on him, glowed red. 'And Shan,' he said quietly. He faced Blind again. 'Have you found your quarry, or are you my escort?'

Baran rose silently beside him, its shoulders level with his chest. Blind stood, then trotted off to the left. She stopped and looked back. Twin growls spurred Quick Ben after them.

The land around them changed slowly, details slipping into sourceless shadows and re-emerging subtly altered. On what the wizard thought of as the north horizon, a grey forest climbed a slope to what might have been a wall. This wall was in place of sky – maybe it *was* sky – but to Quick Ben it looked strangely close, even though the forest was leagues away. Glancing overhead did not help him confirm or refute his feeling that this realm was bordered by a magical wall, for it, too, seemed close, almost within reach. Yet black clouds rode winds above him, skewing his perceptions and making him dizzy.

Another Hound had joined their company. This one, a male, was dark grey, one of its eyes blue, the other yellow. Though it didn't come close, Quick Ben judged that it was the largest of those around him, and its movement hinted at deadly speed. He knew it as Doan, first born to the pack's leader, Rood, and its first mate, Pallick.

Doan trotted alongside Blind for a time, then, when they came to the crest of a low rise, he bolted forward. Reaching the crest, Quick Ben saw their destination. He sighed. Just as the image carved upon the altar within the temples dedicated to Shadowthrone, Shadowkeep rose from the plain like an enormous lump of black glass, fractured with curving planes, rippled in places, with some corners glistening white as if crushed. The largest surface facing them – a wall, he supposed

– was mottled and dull, as if it was a cortex, the weathered surface of obsidian.

There were no windows as such, but many of the slick surfaces looked semi-translucent and seemed to glow with an inner light. As far as Quick Ben could see, there was no door, no gate, no drawbridge.

They arrived, and the wizard exclaimed in surprise as Blind strode into the stone and disappeared. He hesitated, and Boran came as close to nudging him as Quick Ben allowed. He walked up to the mottled stone and held out his hands as he stepped into it. He felt nothing, passing through effortlessly to find himself in a hallway that could have been found in any mundane estate.

Barren of trappings, the corridor led straight forward for, perhaps, thirty feet and ended at double doors. Blind and Doan sat to either side of these doors, which now opened of their own accord.

Quick Ben entered the room beyond. The chamber was domed. Opposite him stood a simple obsidian throne on a slightly raised dais. The dull, cobbled floor bore no rugs, and the walls were bare except for torches spaced every ten feet. Quick Ben counted forty, but the light was fitful, seeming to struggle against encroaching shadows.

At first he thought the throne unoccupied, but as he approached he saw the figure seated there. It seemed composed of almost translucent shadows, vaguely human in form, but hooded, preventing even the glint of eyes. Still, Quick Ben could feel the god's attention fixed solely on him, and he barely repressed a shiver.

Shadowthrone spoke, his voice calm and clear. 'Shan tells me you know the names of my Hounds.'

Quick Ben stopped before the dais. He bowed. 'I was once an acolyte within your temple, Lord.'

The god was silent for a time, then he said, 'Is it wise to

395

admit such a thing, Wizard? Do I look kindly upon those who once served me but then abandoned my ways? Tell me. I would hear from you what my priests teach.'

'To begin upon the Path of Shadow and then to leave it is rewarded by the Rope.'

'Meaning?'

'I am marked for assassination by all who follow your ways, Lord.'

'Yet here you stand, Wizard.'

Quick Ben bowed again. 'I would strike a deal, Lord.'

The god giggled, then raised a hand. 'No, dear Shan. Strike naught.'

Quick Ben stiffened. The black Hound stepped around him, and ascended the dais. She lay down before her god and eyed the wizard blankly.

'Do you know why I just saved your life, Wizard?'

'I do, Lord.'

Shadowthrone leaned forward. 'Shan wants you to tell me.'

Quick Ben met the Hound's red stare. 'Shadowthrone loves deals.'

The god sighed and sank back. 'Acolyte, indeed. Well, then, Wizard, speak on, while you can.'

'I must begin with a question, Lord.'

'Ask it.'

'Does Gear still live?'

Shan's eyes flared and she half rose before the god's hand touched her head.

'Now that,' Shadowthrone said, 'is quite a question. You've managed something few, alas, have been able to do. Wizard, my curiosity is piqued. So, I answer you: yes, Gear survives. By all means, continue.'

'Lord, I would deliver into your hands the one who offended your Hound.'

'How? He belongs to Oponn.'

'Not him, Lord. But the one who led Gear to that chamber. The one who sought to take Gear's soul, and would have succeeded if not for Oponn's mortal tool.'

'In exchange for what?'

Quick Ben cursed inwardly. He could read nothing from the god's tone, and that made things even trickier than he'd expected. 'My life, Lord. I wish the Rope's reward lifted from me.'

'Anything else?'

'Yes.' He hesitated, then continued, 'I wish to choose the time and place, Lord. Otherwise, this one of whom I speak will escape your Hounds through its Warren of Chaos. Only I can prevent that. Thus, it must be part of the deal. All that you need do is have your Hounds ready. I will call upon you at the proper moment, providing you with the creature's precise location. The rest is up to your Hounds.'

'You've planned this well, Wizard,' Shadowthrone said. 'As of yet, I can think of no way to kill both the creature and you. I commend you. How then, do you intend to call upon me? Surely, you'll not once again enter my realm.'

'Lord, you will be contacted. I guarantee this, but I can say no more about it.'

'And if I were to lay my powers upon you now, Wizard? If I were to wring whatever lies hidden in that frail brain of yours, how would you prevent me?'

'To answer that, Lord, you must answer my proposal first.'

Shan growled and this time the god made no motion to still her.

Quick Ben went on hastily, 'Given that you will seek to betray me at every opportunity, given that you'll hunt for the weaknesses in my plan, given all this, I would have your word that you will complete your part of the deal if all else fails you, Lord. Give me that, and I will answer your last question.'

Shadowthrone was silent for a long minute. 'Ah well,' he

muttered. 'Your cunning is admirable, Wizard. I am astonished and, I must admit, delighted by this duel. My only regret is that you departed the Paths of Shadow – you would have risen far. Very well. You have my word. The Hounds will be ready. Now, why shouldn't I shred your brain here and now, Wizard?'

'Your answer, Lord, is in your very words.' Quick Ben raised his arms. 'I did indeed rise far, Shadowthrone, in service to you.' He opened his Warren. 'You'll not have me, Lord, because you can't.' Quick Ben whispered his word of recall, a word born of Chaos. Power burst around him, and he felt as if a giant hand had closed around him. As it pulled him back into his Warren, he heard Shadowthrone's scream of recognition.

'It is you! Delat! You shape-shifting bastard!'

Quick Ben smiled. He'd done it. He was out of reach. He'd done it – again.

Kruppe was ushered into Baruk's study with none of the delays he was so fond of confounding. Slightly disappointed, he took his seat and wiped his forehead with his handkerchief.

Baruk entered. 'You took your time getting here,' he growled. 'Well, never mind. Have you any news?'

Kruppe laid his handkerchief on his lap and began carefully to fold it. 'We continue to protect the Coin Bearer, as instructed. As for the presence of Malazan infiltrators, no luck.' It was a major lie, but necessary. 'I am to convey a message to you,' he continued, 'most unusual in its source. Indeed, strange in fact was its delivery to Kruppe.'

'Get on with it.'

Kruppe winced. Baruk was in a terrible mood. He sighed. 'A message to you personally, Master.' He completed folding his handkerchief and looked up. 'From the Eel.'

Baruk stiffened, then a scowl darkened his features. 'Why not?' he muttered. 'The man even knows who my agents are.' His gaze cleared and he watched Kruppe. 'I'm waiting,' he growled.

'Of course!' Kruppe shook loose his handkerchief and mopped his brow. '"Look to the streets to find those you seek." That, and no more. Delivered to Kruppe by the smallest child he'd ever seen—' He stopped and shook his head. No, such exaggeration would never do, not with Baruk's mood as foul as it appeared to be. 'A small child, in any case.'

Baruk stood glowering at the dying embers in the fireplace, his hands clasped behind his back, fingers twisting a large silver ring. 'Tell me, Kruppe,' he asked slowly, 'what do you know of this Eel?'

'Little, Kruppe admits. Man, woman? Unknown. Origins? A mystery. Designs? Perpetuating a status quo defined by aversion to tyranny. Or so it's said. Influence? Far-reaching, even if one discounts nine out of ten rumours associated with the Eel, his or her agents must number in the hundreds. All devoted to protecting Darujhistan. 'Tis said that Councilman Turban Orr is even now hunting them down, convinced they've ruined all his schemes. Mayhap they have, and for that we can all be relieved.'

Baruk seemed anything but relieved. Kruppe thought he could almost hear the man's teeth grinding. However, he turned to Kruppe and nodded. 'I have an assignment. For it, you will need to round up Murillio, Rallick and Coll. And take the Coin Bearer with you, just to keep him safe.'

Kruppe raised an eyebrow. 'Out of the city?'

'Yes. Paramount is the Coin Bearer – keep him beyond anyone's reach. As for your mission, you will observe. Nothing more. Do you understand me, Kruppe? Observe. To do anything else will be to risk the Coin Bearer falling into the wrong hands. While he is Oponn's tool, he also is the means by which another Ascendant can reach Oponn. The last thing we need is gods battling on the mortal plain.'

Kruppe cleared his throat. 'What are we to observe, Master?'

'I'm not sure, possibly a foreign work party, digging here and there.'

399

Kruppe started. 'As in . . . road repairs?'

The alchemist frowned. 'I will be sending you to the Gadrobi Hills. Remain there until either someone comes or I contact you with further instructions. If someone comes, Kruppe, you're to remain hidden. Avoid detection at all costs – use your Warren, if need be.'

'None shall find Kruppe and his worthy, loyal comrades,' Kruppe said, smiling and waggling his fingers.

'Good. That will be all, then.'

Surprised, Kruppe climbed to his feet. 'When are we to leave, Master?'

'Soon. I'll let you know at least a day beforehand. Is that sufficient time?'

'Yes, friend Baruk. Kruppe deems that more than enough time. Rallick appears temporarily indisposed, but with luck he shall be available.'

'Get him if you can. If the Coin Bearer's influence turns against us, the assassin is charged with killing the boy. Does he understand this?'

'We've discussed it,' Kruppe said.

Baruk inclined his head and fell silent.

Kruppe waited a moment, then quietly left.

Less than an hour after Quick Ben's soul had left the body seated on the hut's floor and journeyed into the Shadow Realm, it creaked back into life. Red-eyed with an exhaustion born of unrelenting tension, Kalam pushed himself to his feet and waited for his friend to come round.

The assassin laid his hands on his long-knives, just to be on the safe side. If Quick Ben had been taken, whatever controlled him might well announce its arrival by attacking anyone within range. Kalam held his breath.

The wizard's eyes opened, the glaze slipping away as awareness returned. He saw Kalam, and smiled.

The assassin released his breath. 'Done? Success?'

'Yes, on both counts. Hard to believe, isn't it?'

Kalam found he was grinning uncontrollably. He stepped forward and helped Quick Ben to stand. The wizard leaned heavily against him, also grinning.

'He realized who I was just as I left.' Quick Ben's grin broadened. 'You should have heard him scream.'

'Well, are you surprised? How many High Priests burn the robes of their vestment?'

'Not enough, if you ask me. Without temples and priests the gods' bloody meddling couldn't touch the mortal realm. Now, that would be paradise, right, friend?'

'Perhaps,' said a voice at the doorway. Both men turned to see Sorry standing within the entrance, her half-cloak drawn about her slim body. She was wet with rain, and only now did Kalam notice the water dripping through cracks all around them. The assassin stepped away from Quick Ben to free his hands. 'What are you doing here?' he demanded.

'You dream of paradise, Wizard? I wish I'd heard the entire conversation.'

'How did you find us?' Quick Ben asked.

Sorry stepped inside and pushed back her hood. 'I've found an assassin,' she said. 'I've marked him. He is in a place called the Phoenix Inn, in the Daru District. Are you interested?' she asked, dully eyeing both men.

'I want answers,' Kalam said, in a low voice.

Quick Ben backed to the far wall, to give the assassin room and to prepare his spells if need be – though he was in no real shape to manage his Warren at the moment. Nor, he noticed, did Kalam look up to a scrap, not that the assassin would allow that to stop him. Right now, he was at his most dangerous – that low tone had said it all.

Sorry held her dead eyes on Kalam. 'The sergeant has sent me to you—'

'A lie,' Kalam interjected softly. 'Whiskeyjack doesn't know where we are.'

'Very well. I sensed your power, Wizard. It has a notable signature.'

Quick Ben was stunned. 'But I established a shield around this place,' he said.

'Yes. I, too, was surprised, Wizard. Usually I cannot find you. It seems cracks appeared.'

Quick Ben thought about that. 'Cracks', he decided, wasn't the right word – but Sorry didn't know that. She'd sensed his whereabouts because she was what they'd suspected, a pawn of the Rope. The Shadow Realm had been linked, however briefly and however tenuously, to his flesh and blood. Yet none but a servant of Shadow possessed the necessary sensitivity to detect that link. The wizard moved to stand beside Kalam and laid a hand on the burly man's shoulder.

Kalam threw him a startled glare.

'She's right. Cracks appeared, Kalam. She's obviously a natural Talent in the ways of sorcery. Come on, friend, the girl's found what we've been looking for. Let's move on it.'

Sorry pulled up the hood around her head. 'I am not accompanying you,' she said. 'You'll know the man when you see him. I suspect it is his task to make his profession obvious. Perhaps the Guild is anticipating you. In any case, find the Phoenix Inn.'

'What the hell are you up to?' Kalam demanded.

'I will be completing an assignment for the sergeant.' She turned and left the hut.

Kalam's shoulders slumped and he let out a long breath.

'She's the one we thought her to be,' Quick Ben said quietly. 'So far, so good.'

'In other words,' the assassin growled, 'if I'd attacked her I'd be a dead man right now.'

'Exactly. We'll take her out, when the time's right. But for now we need her.'

Kalam nodded.

'Phoenix Inn?'

'Damn right. And when we get there the first thing I'm doing is buying a drink.'

Quick Ben smiled. 'Agreed.'

Rallick looked up as the heavy-set man entered the bar. His black skin marked him a southerner, which in itself was not unusual. What caught Rallick's attention, however, was the horn-handled, silver-pommelled long-knives tucked into the man's narrow belt. Those weapons were anything but southern, and stamped on the pommels was a cross-hatched pattern, recognizable to all within the trade as the mark of an assassin.

The man swaggered into the room as if he owned it, and none of the locals he shouldered aside seemed inclined to disagree with him. He reached the bar and ordered an ale.

Rallick studied the dregs in his own tankard. Obviously the man wanted to be marked, precisely by someone like Rallick Nom, a Guild assassin. So, who was the bait, then? This didn't fit.

Ocelot, his Clan Leader, was convinced, along with everyone else in the Guild, that Empire Claws had come into the city and now waged war against them. Rallick wasn't so sure. The man standing at the bar could as easily be Seven Cities as a traveller from Callows. He had the look of Malazan Empire about him. Was he Claw? If so, why show himself? Up until now the enemy hadn't left a single clue, or a single eye-witness, as to their identity. The brazenness he now observed either didn't fit, or marked a reversal of tactics. Had Vorcan's order to go to ground triggered it?

Alarm bells rang in Rallick's head. None of this felt right.

Murillio leaned close to him. 'Something wrong, friend?'

'Guild business,' Rallick replied. 'You thirsty?'

Murillio grinned. 'An offer I can't refuse.'

After a single, bemused glance at Coll's unconscious form, slumped in the chair, the assassin left the table. What *had* all that been about five black dragons? He made his way to the bar. As he pushed through the crowd, he gave one youth a hard elbow to the back. The boy gasped, then surreptitiously slipped towards the kitchen.

Rallick arrived, called Scurve over, then ordered another pitcher. Though he did not look the man's way, he knew he'd been marked by him. It was no more than a feeling, but one he'd learned to trust. He sighed as Scurve delivered the foaming pitcher. Well, he'd done what Ocelot had demanded of him, though he suspected his Clan Leader would be asking for more.

He returned to the table and conversed with Murillio for a time, plying his friend with the majority of the ale. Murillio sensed a growing tension around Rallick and took his cue. He drained the last of his drink and rose. 'Well,' he said, 'Kruppe's scurried off, Crokus too. And Coll's once again dead to the world. Rallick, I thank you for the ale. Time to find a warm bed. Until the morrow, then.'

Rallick remained seated for another five minutes, only once brushing gazes with the black man leaning against the bar. Then he rose and strode into the kitchen. The two cooks rolled their eyes at each other as he strode past. Rallick ignored them. He came to the door, which had been left ajar in hopes of a cooling draught. The alley beyond was wet, though the rain had passed. From a shadowed recess on the wall opposite the inn stepped a familiar figure.

Rallick walked up to Ocelot. 'It's done. Your man is the big black one nursing an ale. Two daggers, hatch-marked. He looks mean and not one I'd like to tussle with. He's all yours, Ocelot.'

The man's pocked face twisted. 'He's still inside? Good. Head back in. Make sure you've been noticed – damn sure, Nom.'

Rallick crossed his arms. 'I'm sure already,' he drawled.

'You're to draw him out, lead him into Tarlow's warehouse – into the loading grounds.' Ocelot sneered. 'Vorcan's orders, Nom. And when you head out, do it by the front door. No mistakes, nothing subtle.'

'The man's an assassin,' Rallick grated. 'If I'm not subtle he'll know it's a trap and crawl all over me in seconds flat.'

'You do as Vorcan wills, Nom. Now get back inside!'

Rallick stared at his commander, to make his disgust plain, then returned to the kitchen. The cooks grinned at him, but only for a moment. One look at Rallick's face was enough to kill any humour in the room. They bent to their tasks as if prodded by a landmaster.

Rallick entered the main room, then stopped dead in his tracks. 'Damn,' he muttered. The black man was gone. Now what? He shrugged. 'Front door it is.' He made his way through the crowd.

In an alley, on one side of which ran a high stone wall, Crokus leaned against the damp bricks of a merchant's house and gazed steadily at a window. It was on the third floor, beyond the wall, and behind its shuttered face was a room he knew intimately.

There'd been a light on inside for most of the two hours he'd stood below, but for the last fifteen minutes the room within had been dark. Numb with exhaustion and plagued with doubts, Crokus pulled his cloak tighter around him. He wondered what he was doing here, and not for the first time. All his resolve seemed to have drained into the gutters along with the rain.

Had it been the dark-haired woman in the Phoenix Inn? Had she rattled him that much? The blood on her dagger made

405

it obvious that she wouldn't hesitate to kill him just to keep her secret intact. Maybe it was the spinning coin that had him so confused. Nothing about that incident had been natural.

What was so wrong with his dream of being introduced to the D'Arle maiden? It had nothing to do with that killer woman in the bar.

'Nothing,' he mumbled, then scowled. Now he was talking aloud to himself.

A thought came to him that deepened his scowl. Everything had begun its mad unravelling the night he'd robbed the maiden. If only he hadn't paused, if only he hadn't looked upon her soft, round, lovely face.

A groan escaped him, and he shifted his feet. A high-born. That was the real problem, wasn't it?

It all seemed so stupid now, so absurd. How could he have convinced himself that such a thing as meeting her was possible? He shook himself. It didn't matter, he'd planned this, now it was time to do it.

'I don't believe this,' he muttered as he pushed himself from the wall and headed down the alley. His hand brushed the pouch tied to his waist. 'I'm about to put a maiden's ransom back.'

He came to the stone wall he'd been looking for, and began to climb. He drew a deep breath. *All right, let's get it done.*

The stone was wet, but he had enough determination in him to scale a mountain. He climbed on, and did not slip even so much as a single foothold.

CHAPTER THIRTEEN

> There's a spider here
> in this corner in that –
> her three eyes
> tiptoe in darkness,
> her eight legs
> track my spine,
> she mirrors and mocks
> my pacing.
>
> There's a spider here
> who knows all of me
> her web my history full writ.
> Somewhere in this strange place
> a spider waits
> for my panicked flight . . .
>
> *The Conspiracy*
> Blind Gallan (b.1078)

As soon as the Guild assassin left the room, Kalam drained the last of his beer, paid up, and ascended the staircase. From the gallery railing he studied the crowd below, then, seeing that no one paid him much attention, he strode down the hallway and entered the last room on the right.

He closed the door and locked it. Quick Ben was seated cross-legged on the floor, within a circle of melted blue wax. The wizard was hunched over, bare-chested, his eyes shut and droplets of sweat trickling down his face. Around him the air shimmered, as if glossed with lacquer.

Kalam walked around the wax circle to the bed. He took a leather satchel from a peg above the bedpost and set it down on the thin, straw-filled mattress. Peeling back the flap he removed the contents. A minute later he'd laid out the mechanisms for a goat's foot arbalest. The crossbow's metal parts had been blued, the narrow wooden stock soaked in pitch and dusted with black sand. Kalam slowly, quietly, assembled the weapon.

Quick Ben spoke behind him. 'Done. Whenever you're ready, friend.'

'The man left through the kitchen. But he'll be back,' Kalam said, rising with the arbalest in his hands. He attached a strap to it and slung the weapon over one shoulder. Then he faced the wizard. 'I'm ready.'

Quick Ben also stood, wiping his forehead with a sleeve. 'Two spells. You'll be able to float, control every descent. The other should give you the ability to see anything magical – well, almost anything. If there's a High Mage kicking around, we're out of luck.'

'And you?' Kalam asked, as he examined his quiver of bolts.

'You won't see me directly, just my aura,' Quick Ben replied with a grin, 'but I'll be with you all the way.'

'Well, hopefully this'll go smoothly. We make contact with the Guild, we offer the Empire's contract, they accept and remove for us every major threat in the city.' He shrugged into his black cloak and pulled up the hood.

408

'You sure we can't just go downstairs and walk right up to the man, lay it out?'

Kalam shook his head. 'Not how it's done. We've identified him, he's done the same with us. He's probably just made contact with his commander, and they'll arrange things to their liking. Our man should lead us now to the meet.'

'Won't it be an ambush we're walking into, then?'

The large man agreed. 'More or less. But they'll want to know what we want with them first. And once that's out, I doubt the Guild's master will be interested in killing us. You ready?'

Quick Ben raised a hand towards Kalam, then muttered briefly under his breath.

Kalam felt a lightness come into him, rising to his skin and emanating a cushion of cool air that enveloped his body. And before his eyes Quick Ben's figure formed a blue-green penumbra, concentrated at the wizard's long-fingered hands. 'I have them,' the assassin said, smiling, 'two old friends.'

Quick Ben sighed. 'Yes, here we are doing this all over again.' He met his friend's gaze. 'Hood's on our heels, Kal. I can feel his breath on my neck, these days.'

'You're not alone in that.' Kalam turned to the window. 'Sometimes,' he said drily, 'I have the feeling our Empire wants us dead.' He walked to the window, unlatched the shutters, then swung them inward and leaned both hands on the sill.

Quick Ben came up beside him and rested a hand on his shoulder. They gazed out at the darkness, a brief sharing of unease passing between them.

'We've seen too much,' Quick Ben said softly.

'Hood's Breath,' Kalam growled, 'what are we doing this for anyway?'

'Maybe if the Empire gets what it wants – Darujhistan – they'll let us slip away.'

'Sure, but who's going to convince the sergeant to walk out of the Empire?'

409

'We show him he hasn't got any choice.'

Kalam climbed on to the sill. 'Good thing I'm not a Claw any more. Just soldiers, right?'

Behind him Quick Ben touched his own chest and vanished. His disembodied voice held a note of wry amusement. 'Right. No more cloak-and-dagger games for old Kalam.'

The assassin pulled himself up, turning to face the wall then beginning his climb to the roof. 'Yeah, I've always hated it.'

Quick Ben's voice was beside him now. 'No more assassinations.'

'No more spying,' Kalam added, reaching for the roof's edge.

'No more disguising spells.'

Clambering on to the roof, Kalam lay still. 'No more daggers in the back,' he whispered, then sat up and scanned the nearby rooftops. He saw nothing; no unusual huddled shapes, no bright magical auras.

'Thank the gods,' came Quick Ben's whisper from above.

'Thank the gods,' Kalam echoed, then looked down over the roof's edge. Below a pool of light marked the inn entrance. 'You take the back door. I've got this one.'

'Right.'

Even as the wizard answered Kalam stiffened. 'There he is,' he hissed. 'You still with me?'

Quick Ben assented.

They watched the figure of Rallick Nom, now cloaked, crossing to the far side of the street and entering an alley.

'I'm on him,' Quick Ben said.

A blue-green glow rose around the wizard. He rose into the air and flew out swiftly across the street, slowing as he reached the alley. Kalam climbed to his feet and padded silently along the roof's edge. Reaching the corner, he glanced down to the rooftop of an adjacent building, then jumped.

He descended slowly, as if sinking through water, and landed without a sound. Off to his right, moving on a parallel path, was Quick Ben's magical aura. Kalam crossed the rooftop to the next building. Their man was heading for the harbour-front.

Kalam continued tracking Quick Ben's beacon, moving from one rooftop to the next, sometimes jumping down, at other times climbing. There was little subtlety about Kalam: where others used finesse he used the strength of his thick arms and legs. It made him an unlikely assassin, but he'd learned to use that to his advantage.

They now approached the harbour area, the buildings single-storeyed and large, the streets rarely lit except around the double-door entrances to warehouses, where the occasional private guard lingered. In the night air hung the taint of sewage and fish.

Finally, Quick Ben stopped, hovered over a warehouse courtyard, then hurried back to Kalam, who waited at the edge of a nearby two-storeyed clearing house. 'Looks like the place,' Quick Ben said, floating a few feet above Kalam. 'What now?'

'I want a good line of sight to that courtyard.'

'Follow me.'

Quick Ben led him to another building. Their man was now visible, crouching on the warehouse roof, attention down on the courtyard below.

'Kal, do you smell something bad about this?'

Kalam snorted. 'Hell, no, it's bloody roses out here. Take position, friend.'

'Right.'

Rallick Nom lay down on the rooftop, his head out over its edge. Below was the warehouse's courtyard, flat, grey and empty. Directly beneath him the shadows were impenetrable. Sweat trickled down Rallick's face.

From the shadow below came Ocelot's voice, 'He's got you in sight?'

411

'Yes.'

'And he's not moving?'

'No. Listen, I'm sure there's more than one of them. I would've known if he'd been trailing me, and no one was. It stinks of magery, Ocelot, and you know what I think about magery.'

'Dammit, Nom. If you'd just start using the stuff we give you, you'd rank among the best of us. But to Hood's Gate with that. We've got spotters, and unless there's a very good wizard around we'd pick up on any magic. Face it,' a note of malice entered Ocelot's voice, 'he's better than you. He tracked you all right. Solo.'

'What now?' Rallick asked.

Ocelot chuckled. 'We're closing the circle even as we speak. Your work's done, Nom. Tonight the assassins' war ends. In five minutes you can head home.'

High above the city a demon flapped on leathery wings, its green reptilian eyes surveying the rooftops below with a vision that detected magic as easily as it did heat. Though the demon was no larger than a dog, its power was immense, near par to the man who had summoned and chained it this very night. On the rooftops it saw two auras close together, one a man on whom spells had been cast, and the other a wizard, a very good wizard. In a ragged circle on other rooftops around these two, men and women moved inward, some betrayed by the heat of their bodies, others by items imbued with sorcery.

Until now the demon rode the high night winds bored and resentful of its master. A mere mission of observation, for one of such power! But now the demon felt a surge of bloodlust. If only its master had been weaker, so that it could break the bonds and descend to the rooftops, then there would have been slaughter.

The demon was musing on these thoughts, its eyes fixed on

412

the scene below, when a booted heel rammed into the back of its small, round head. The creature spun, tumbling, then twisted round to face its attacker, rage blazing in its skull.

A moment later it was fighting for its life. The figure that closed with the demon possessed a blinding magical aura. Grappling, the surging energies of both collided, enwrapped like tentacles. The demon struggled against the savage pain constricting it as the figure pressed its attack. A cold that burned filled the demon's skull, a cold alien in its breath of power, so alien that the demon could find no means of countering it.

The two fell slowly as they fought, duelling in absolute silence with forces invisible to the city's inhabitants below, while around them other figures descended towards the warehouse, cloaks spread like sails, crossbows crooked in their arms, hooded faces angled downward and hidden beneath black masks. There were eleven in all that passed the demon and its attacker. None of the others paid any attention, and with this realization the demon experienced an emotion it had never known before. Fear.

Its thoughts turning from battle to survival, the demon tore itself from its attacker's grasp. Loosing a high-pitched cry, it flapped upward.

The figure did not pursue, instead joining the others in their silent descent to the city.

As the twelve shrouded assassins dropped towards the circle of men and women below, one splitting off and angling above the circle's two targets, they took careful aim with their crossbows, and began a massacre.

Kalam stared down at the assassin lying supine on the roof below, wondering what to do next. Were they waiting for him to initiate contact? A low growl escaped him. Something was wrong. He could feel it like fever in his bones.

413

'Dammit, Quick. Let's get out of here!'

'Wait!' came Quick Ben's disembodied voice. 'Oh, damn,' he said softly then.

In front of Kalam two brightly glowing shapes dropped down on to the roof below, landing behind their mark.

'What the hell?'

Then he felt a slight tremor on the flat tiles beneath his hands. Kalam rolled on to his back, hearing a quarrel whiz past. Framed by his knees, a cloaked figure stood about thirty feet away. After missing with the quarrel the figure raced forward. Another landed behind the first one, near the roof's far edge.

Kalam scampered. He dropped down over the roof's edge.

Quick Ben floated above him. The spell of deflection he'd raised about himself was a High Order magery, and he was certain he remained unseen by these new assailants. He watched as the approaching figure slowed, then padded cautiously to the roof edge where Kalam had dropped from sight. Daggers gleaming in both gloved hands, this new assassin reached the edge and crouched. Quick Ben held his breath as the figure leaned forward.

Kalam hadn't gone far. He gripped the roof's gables. When the attacker's upper body came into view, blotting out the stars behind it, he surged upward on the strength of one arm, his other shooting up to close on the assassin's neck with a vice-like grip. Kalam jerked the assassin downward, at the same time bringing up his knee. The attacker's cloth-wrapped face met his knee with a crunch. Kalam, still gripping the gable with one hand, gave the now limp figure a shake, then sent the body spiralling down to the street below.

Gasping, he pulled himself back on to the roof. At the far end he saw the second assassin whirl around. Growling, Kalam surged to his feet and sprinted at the figure.

The unknown assassin stepped back as if startled, then brought a hand down and promptly vanished.

Kalam slid to a stop and stood crouched, both hands hanging at his sides.

'I see her,' Quick Ben whispered.

With a hiss Kalam spun in a full circle, then danced to one side, putting his back to the roof's edge. 'I don't.'

'She's putting energy into it,' Quick Ben said. 'I keep losing her. Wait, Kal.' The wizard fell silent.

Kalam's head snapped with every muted sound. His breath gusted in and out from his nostrils, his hands twitched. Wait. A low rumble came from his chest. Wait for what? A knife in his throat?

All at once the night exploded with sound and fire. The attacker burst into view immediately in front of Kalam, dagger flashing at his chest. Smoke and sparks rained from her but she moved as if unaffected. Kalam twisted to one side, trying to avoid the blade. The dagger tore through his shirt below his ribs, sinking deep into his flesh then ripping sideways. He felt a hot gush of blood as he drove a fist into the woman's solar plexus. She gasped, reeling back, threads of blood whipping from the dagger in her right hand. Kalam charged forward with a snarl. He closed and, ignoring the assassin's dagger, punched into her chest again. Ribs cracked. His other hand flat-palmed her forehead. The assassin sprawled backwards, landing with a thump on the roof. Her body stilled.

Kalam sank to one knee, drawing in gulps of air. 'Wait, you said, dammit! What the hell's wrong with you, Quick?' He pushed a knot of cloth into the wound below his ribcage. 'Quick?'

There was no reply. He tensed, then turned and scanned the lower rooftops. Bodies lay scattered here and there. The warehouse roof, where he'd seen two figures land behind their mark, was empty. Groaning softly, he sank down on to his knees.

With the woman's attack he'd heard something amid the

flashing fires. A boom, no, two booms, very close together. An exchange of magic. His breath caught. Was there a third assassin? A wizard? Quick Ben had damaged this one, but someone else had damaged Quick Ben. 'Oh, Hood,' he whispered, glaring about.

Rallick's first intimation of trouble was a sharp blow between his shoulder blades. The breath burst from his lungs, carrying with it the ability to move. His back throbbed, and he knew he'd been hit by a quarrel, but the Jazeraint armour under his shirt had withstood the impact – the quarrel's spiked head had pierced the iron but had been too spent to push further. Through the thumping pulse in his ears he caught a pair of footsteps approaching him from behind.

From the shadows below came Ocelot's voice, 'Nom? What's happening?'

Behind Rallick the footsteps stopped, and there came the soft clacking of a crossbow being cocked. Rallick's wind returned, the numbness receding from his body. His own weapon lay beside him, ready. He waited.

'Nom?'

A soft footfall sounded behind him and to the left. In one motion Rallick rolled on to his back, grasped his crossbow, sat up and fired. The assassin, less than fifteen feet away, was thrown back by the quarrel's impact, its weapon flying.

Rallick heaved himself to one side, only now seeing the second attacker well behind the first. The figure crouched and fired its crossbow. The quarrel caught Rallick's upper chest on the right, then ricocheted up past his head to disappear into the darkness. The blow left his right arm numb. He struggled to his feet, unsheathing his knife, the hooked blade a blue flicker in the night.

The assassin opposite him took a careful step forward, then backed away to the far edge and dropped over the side.

'Hood's Breath,' came Ocelot's voice beside Rallick. He turned but saw no one.

'He saw my magic,' Ocelot said. 'Good work on the first one, Nom. Maybe we can finally determine who these people are.'

'I don't think so,' Rallick said, his eyes on the motionless body. An incandescent shimmer now wreathed it.

As the body disappeared Ocelot cursed. 'Some kind of recall spell,' he said. Suddenly the Clan Master appeared in front of Rallick. His face twisted into a snarl as he glared about. 'We set the trap, we end up dead.'

Rallick did not reply. He reached over his shoulder, pulled out the quarrel and tossed it to one side. The trappers had become the trapped, that was true, but he felt certain that the man who'd followed him had nothing to do with these newcomers. He turned and gazed up at the roof where his follower had been stationed. Even as he watched there was a flash of red and yellow light and a double thunderclap, and in that instant Rallick saw a silhouetted figure at the roof's edge, defending itself from a frontal attack. The flash winked out leaving only darkness.

'Magery,' Ocelot whispered. 'High-power stuff, too. Come on, we're getting out of here.'

They left quickly, climbing down into the warehouse court.

Once she had marked them, Sorry could find the fat little man and the Coin Bearer effortlessly. Though she'd intended to trail this Kruppe after leaving Kalam and Quick Ben in the hut, something had drawn her instead to the boy. A suspicion, a sense that his actions were – at least for now – more important than Kruppe's meanderings.

The Coin Bearer was the last of Oponn's influence, and the god's most vital player in the game. Thus far, she'd done well in eliminating the other potential players – men like Captain Paran, who had been the Adjunct's aide and, by extension, a

417

servant to the Empress. And there had been that Claw Leader in Pale, the one she had garotted. On her path to the Bridgeburners, others had been removed as well, but only as necessary.

She knew that the boy would have to die, yet something within her seemed to be fighting that conclusion, and it was a part of her she could not recognize. She'd been taken, born a killer two years ago on a coastal road. The body she dwelt within was convenient, suitably unmarred by the events of a dramatic life – a young girl's body, a young girl whose mind was no match for the power that overwhelmed it, obliterated it.

But was it obliterated? What had the coin touched inside her? And whose voice was this that spoke with such power and determination in her head? It had come upon her before, when Whiskeyjack had uttered the word Seer.

She tried hard to remember any dealings she might have had with a seer in the last two years, but none came to mind.

She pulled her cloak tighter about her shoulders. Finding the boy had been easy, but as to what he was up to, that was another matter. On the surface it looked no more complicated than a simple theft. Crokus had stood in an alley studying a lighted window on the third floor of an estate, waiting until the light went out. Wrapped in unnatural shadows as she was, he had not seen her as he scaled the slick wall she leaned against. He climbed with impressive grace and skill.

After he'd gone she found another vantage-point, which allowed her full view of the room's balcony and sliding doors. This had meant entering the estate's garden. But there had been only one guard, patrolling the grounds. She'd killed him effortlessly and now stood beneath a tree with her eyes on the balcony.

Crokus had already reached it, had picked the lock and entered the room beyond. He was quite good, she had to admit. But what thief would then spend close to half an hour in the

418

chamber he was robbing? Half an hour and still counting. She'd heard no alarms, seen no lights spring to life behind any of the estate's other windows, nothing to indicate that anything had gone wrong. So what was Crokus doing in there?

Sorry stiffened. Sorcery had burgeoned in another part of Darujhistan, and its flavour was known to her. She hesitated, unable to decide. Leave the lad and investigate this new, deadly emanation? Or remain here until Crokus re-emerged or was discovered?

Then she saw something behind the balcony's sliding doors that ended her indecision.

Sweat ran down Crokus's face and he found he had repeatedly to wipe it from his eyes. He'd beaten the new triggers to get inside – the one on the balcony, the trip-wire at the latch – and now padded to the makeup table. Once there he froze, unable to move. *Idiot! What am I doing here?*

He listened to her soft, regular breathing behind him – *like the breath of a dragon* – he was certain he could feel it gusting against the back of his neck. Crokus looked up and scowled at his own reflection in the mirror. What was happening to him? If he didn't leave soon ... He began to remove his bag's contents. When he'd finished he glanced again at his own face – to see another behind it, a round, white face watching him from the bed.

The girl spoke. 'Since you're putting it all back, I'd prefer the proper arrangement. My makeup jar goes to the left of the mirror,' she said, in a whisper. 'The hairbrush goes to the right. Have you my earrings as well? Just leave them on the dresser.'

Crokus groaned. He'd even forgotten to cover his face. 'Don't try anything,' he growled. 'I've returned everything, and now I'll leave. Understand?'

The girl pulled her blankets about her and moved to the bed's end. 'Threats won't work, thief,' she said. 'All I need do

419

is scream and my father's Master Guardsman will be here in seconds. Would you cross your dagger with his shortsword?'

'No,' said Crokus. 'I'd put it to your throat instead. With you as a hostage, with you between me and the guard, will he swing his blade at me? Unlikely.'

The girl paled. 'As a thief, you'd lose a hand. But kidnapping a high-born, it'd be the high gallows for you.'

Crokus tried to shrug casually. He glanced at the balcony, gauging how fast he could be outside and then up on the roof. That new trip-wire was a nuisance.

'Stay where you are,' the girl commanded. 'I'm lighting a lantern.'

'Why?' Crokus demanded, fidgeting.

'To see you better,' she replied, and light bloomed in the room from the lantern in her lap.

He scowled. He hadn't noticed it there, so close at hand. She was ruining his plans even as he made them. 'What's the point in seeing me better?' he snarled. 'Just call your damn guards and have me arrested. Be done with it.' He pulled the silk turban from his shirt and dropped it on the tabletop. 'That's all of it,' he said.

The girl glanced at the turban and shrugged easily. 'That was to be part of my costume for the Fête,' she said. 'I've since found a nicer one.'

'What,' he hissed, 'do you want with me?'

Fear showed momentarily on her face at his desperate outburst, then she smiled. 'I wish to know why a thief who succeeded in stealing all my jewels should now be returning them. That isn't something thieves usually do.'

'With good reason,' he muttered, more to himself than to her. He stepped forward then stopped as she jerked back on to her bed, her eyes widening. Crokus raised a hand. 'Sorry, didn't mean to frighten you. Only . . . I want to see you better. That's all.'

'Why?'

He was at a loss for an answer to that. After all, he couldn't very well tell her he'd fallen madly in love with her. 'What's your name?' he blurted.

'Challice D'Arle. What's yours?'

Challice. 'Of course,' he said, rolling his eyes. 'You would be named something like that.' He glared at her. 'My name? None of your business. Thieves don't introduce themselves to their victims.'

Her eyebrows rose. 'Victim? But I'm no longer a victim, am I? You've settled that by returning. I'd think,' she said slyly, 'you're more or less obliged to tell me your name, considering what you're doing. And you must be the type who treats obligations seriously, no matter how strange they seem.'

Crokus frowned at that. What was she talking about? What did she know about how he looked at obligations? And why was she right? 'My name,' he sighed, defeated, 'is Crokus Younghand. And you're the daughter of the high born D'Arle who all those suitors are lining up to be introduced to. But one day you'll see me in that line, Challice, and only you will know where you last saw me. It'll be a formal introduction, and I'll bring a gift as is correct.' He stared at her, horrified by his own words.

Her wide eyes held his, emotion bright in them – emotion he'd no hope of understanding – then she burst out laughing. She immediately clapped a hand over her mouth, then jolted forward on the bed. 'You'd better go, Crokus. Someone will have heard me. Quickly, and beware the trip-wire!'

Crokus moved woodenly to the balcony's sliding doors. Her laughter had been the final punctuation to all his dreams. He felt dead inside, except for a cynic's chuckle that might have been his own, given the odd look she threw him. Her blankets had fallen down around her, and once again she was naked. It astonished him in a distant way that she hadn't even seemed to notice.

421

A voice came from beyond the door leading to the hallway, indistinct.

The girl hissed, 'Hurry, you fool!'

Alarm bells jangled in his head, awakening him. He had to move, and fast. Crokus stepped over the trip-wire and opened the door. He paused to glance back at her, and smiled as she clutched the blankets to her neck. Well, at least he'd won that much.

A knock sounded on the opposite door.

Crokus emerged on to the balcony and hitched himself up on to the railing. He looked down into the garden and almost fell. The guard was gone. In his place stood a woman – and, though she was cloaked, something about her triggered instant recognition. The woman from the bar, and she was looking right at him with dark eyes that burned him deep inside.

The door in the room opened and Crokus shook himself. *Damn that woman, anyway! Damn both of them!* He grasped the eaves above his head and swung lithely up and out of sight.

Kalam crouched motionless in the middle of the rooftop, a knife in each hand. Around him was silence, the night air tense and heavy. Long minutes passed. At times he convinced himself he was alone, that Quick Ben and the other wizard had left the roof; that they hunted each other in the sky overhead, or in the alleys and streets below, or on another roof. But then he'd hear something, a drawn breath, a scuff of cloth against leather, or a wisp of wind would brush his cheek on this windless night.

Then, before his eyes, the darkness was shattered. Two shapes appeared hovering over the rooftop. The assassin had found Quick Ben, attacking with a bolt of fire that seemed to stun the wizard, then swiftly closing the distance between himself and the dazed man.

Kalam surged forward to intercept. Quick Ben vanished then

422

reappeared immediately behind the assassin. The blue flash of power bursting from the wizard's hands struck the magic-wielding assassin full in the back. Clothes aflame, the man tumbled through the air.

Quick Ben whirled to Kalam. 'Come on! Get moving!'

Kalam ran, his friend flying beside him. As they reached the roof's edge he turned for a last look. The assassin mage had somehow snuffed the fire from his clothes and was regaining his balance. At the far edge two of his comrades appeared.

'Jump,' Quick Ben said. 'I'll stall them.'

'With what?' Kalam demanded, tottering on the edge.

In answer Quick Ben produced a small vial. He spun in the air and hurled it.

Kalam cursed, then jumped.

The vial struck the rooftop and shattered with a thin tinkle. Beyond, the three assassins paused. Quick Ben remained, his eyes on the white smoke rising from the glass shards. A figure took form within the smoke, growing in size. Its shape was almost insubstantial, the smoke stretching like threads in places, curling like wool in others. All that was visible within it was its eyes, two black slits, which it swung to Quick Ben.

'You,' it said, its voice that of a child, 'are not Master Tayschrenn.'

'That's right,' Quick Ben said, 'but I'm in his legion. Your service remains with the Empire.' He pointed across the roof. 'There are three who are the Empire's enemies, Demon. Tiste Andii, here to oppose the Malazan Empire.'

'My name is Pearl,' the Korvalah demon said softly, then turned to the three assassins, who had spread out along the far edge. 'They are not fleeing,' Pearl said, with a note of surprise.

Quick Ben wiped sweat from his forehead. He glanced down. Kalam was a vague shape waiting in the alley below. 'I know,' he said to Pearl. That observation had unnerved him as well. One of Tayschrenn's Korvalahrai could level a city if it so chose.

'They accept my challenge,' Pearl said, facing Quick Ben again. 'Should I pity them?'

'No,' he answered. 'Just kill them and be done with it.'

'Then I return to Master Tayschrenn.'

'Yes.'

'What is your name, Wizard?'

He hesitated, then said, 'Ben Adaephon Delat.'

'You are supposed to be dead,' Pearl said. 'Your name is so marked on the scrolls of those High Mages who fell to the Empire in Seven Cities.'

Quick Ben glanced up. 'Others are coming, Pearl. You are in for a fight.'

The demon lifted its gaze. Above them glowing figures descended, five in the first wave, one in the second. This last one radiated such power that Quick Ben shrank back, his blood chilled. The figure had something long and narrow strapped to its back.

'Ben Adaephon Delat,' Pearl said plaintively, 'see the last who comes. You send me to my death.'

'I know,' Quick Ben whispered.

'Flee, then. I will hold them enough to ensure your escape, no more.'

Quick Ben sank down past the roof.

Before he passed from sight Pearl spoke again. 'Ben Adaephon Delat, do you pity me?'

'Yes,' he replied softly, then pivoted and dropped down into darkness.

Rallick walked down the centre of the street. On either side of the wide corridor rose columns from which gas torches jutted, casting circles of blue light on to the wet cobblestones. The light rain had returned, coating everything in a slick sheen. To his right and beyond the resident houses lining that side of the street, the pale domes of the High Thalanti

424

on the hill glistened against the deep grey sky.

The temple was among the oldest structures in the city, its founding blocks over two thousand years old. The Thalanti monks had come, like so many others, carried on the wings of the rumour. Rallick knew less about the story than did Murillio and Coll. One of the Elder Peoples was believed to have been entombed among the hills, an individual of great wealth and power, that was the extent of his knowledge.

But it had been a rumour with many consequences. If not for the thousands of shafts sunk into the earth the caverns of gas would never have been found. And while many of those shafts had collapsed or had been forgotten over the centuries, still others remained, now connected by tunnels.

In one of the many chambers that honeycombed the ground beneath the temple waited Vorcan, Master of Assassins. Rallick imagined Ocelot making his descent, burdened with the news of disaster, and it brought a smile to his lean face. He'd never met Vorcan, but Ocelot suited those catacombs – just another of the city's rats rushing about beneath his feet.

One day, Rallick knew, he'd become a Clan Leader, he'd meet Vorcan face to face somewhere below. He wondered at how it would change him, and travelling down this path soured his thoughts with displeasure.

He had no option. Once, he thought, as he approached the block of the Phoenix Inn, long ago, there'd been choices he could have made that would have sent him on a different path. But those days were dead, and the future held only nights, a stretch of darkness that led down to the eternal dark. He would meet Vorcan, eventually, and he'd swear his life to the Guild Master, and that would be that, the closing of the final door.

And his sense of outrage at the injustices around him, the corruptions of the world, would wither in the unlit tunnels beneath Darujhistan. In the exactness of the methods of assassination, his final victim would be himself.

And this, more than anything, made his and Murillio's scheme the last act of humanity he'd ever make. Betrayal was the greatest of all crimes in Rallick's mind, for it took all that was human within a person and made it a thing of pain. In the face of that, murder itself was surcease: it was quick, and it ended the anguish and despair of a life without hope. If all went as planned, Lady Simtal and those men who'd conspired with her in the betrayal of her husband, Lord Coll, would die. Could that right the wrong, could it even the scales of retribution? No, but it might return to a man his life and his hope.

For himself, Rallick, such gifts had long since been lost, and he was not the kind of man to stir the ashes. No embers survived, no flame could be born anew. Life belonged to other people, and his only claim to it was his power to take it from them. Nor would he recognize hope if it came to him. Too much a stranger, too long a ghost.

As he neared the inn's entrance, Rallick saw Crokus approaching from down the street. He increased his pace. 'Crokus,' he called.

The boy flinched, then, seeing Rallick, he stopped and waited.

Rallick took his arm and steered him towards the alley without saying a word. Once in the shadows he tightened his grip, swung Crokus round and pulled him close. 'Listen to me,' he hissed, his face inches from the boy's own astonished visage, 'the Guild's best were slaughtered tonight. This isn't a game. You stay off the rooftops, do you understand me?'

Crokus nodded.

'And tell your uncle this. There's a Claw in the city.'

The boy's eyes widened.

'And,' Rallick continued, 'there's someone else. Someone coming down from the sky, killing everything in sight.'

'Uncle Mammot?'

'Just tell him. And now listen carefully, Crokus. What I'm

426

about to say is from me to you, one to one, understand?'

Crokus nodded again, his face pale.

'You stay on this path and you'll end up dead. I don't give a damn how exciting it all seems – what's excitement to you is desperation to others. Stop feeding off the city's lifeblood, lad. There's no hero's role in sucking others dry. Am I understood?'

'Yes,' Crokus whispered.

Rallick released the boy's arm and stepped back. 'Now, leave.' He shoved Crokus up the street, watched the boy stagger away and disappear around a corner. He drew a deep breath, surprised to find his hands trembling as he loosened his cloak's collar.

Murillio stepped from the shadows. 'I'm not sure it'll work, friend, but it was a good try.' He laid a hand on the assassin's shoulder. 'Master Baruk has a job for us. Kruppe insists we bring Crokus along.'

Rallick frowned. 'Along? Are we leaving Darujhistan, then?'

'Afraid so.'

'Go without me,' Rallick said. 'Tell Baruk I can't be found. Everything's at a critical juncture – our planning included.'

'Something else happening, Nom?'

'You heard the message I gave Crokus for his uncle?'

Murillio shook his head. 'I came late to your scene. Saw you dragging the lad into the alley.'

'Well,' Rallick said, 'let's go inside. It's been a night to make Hood smile, friend.'

Together, the two men strode from the alley. In the street outside the Phoenix Inn, dawn's light crept through the mists of the lingering rain.

In the centre of the rooftop lay a large patch of ash and bone that crackled faintly and cast out the occasional hissing spark. Anomander Rake slammed his sword into its sheath. 'I sent twelve of you,' he said, to the black-caped figure standing beside him, 'and I see but eight. What happened, Serrat?'

The Tiste Andii woman was clearly exhausted. 'We've been working hard, Lord.'

'Details,' Rake said abruptly.

Serrat sighed. 'Jekaral has a broken neck and three cracked ribs. Boruld's face is a mess, broken nose, broken cheekbone, broken jaw—'

'Who were they fighting?' Rake asked, turning to his lieutenant in exasperation. 'Has the Guild Master come out of hiding?'

'No, Lord. Both Jekaral and Boruld fell to a single man, not of the city's Guild.'

Rake's eyes flashed dangerously. 'Claw?'

'Possibly. He was accompanied by a High Mage. The one who gave us this Korvalah to play with.'

'It had the smell of Empire about it,' Rake muttered, his gaze on the smouldering patch that had begun to eat its way into the roof. 'One of Tayschrenn's conjurings, I should think.' A savage grin flashed. 'Pity to have disturbed his sleep this night.'

'Dashtal was struck by a poisoned quarrel,' Serrat said. 'One of the Guild's assassins managed that.' She hesitated. 'Lord. We were hard pressed in Brood's campaign. We're in need of rest. Mistakes were made this night. Some of the Guild slipped through our fingers and, had you not answered my request, we would have suffered more casualties destroying this demon.'

Rake placed his hands on his hips and surveyed the morning sky. After a moment he sighed. 'Ah, Serrat. Don't think me insensitive. But the Guild Master must be flushed. This Guild must be shut down.' He eyed his lieutenant. 'This Claw you encountered, do you think a meet was being established?'

'Not a meet,' Serrat answered. 'A trap.'

Rake nodded. 'Good.' He paused, his eyes matching Serrat's with a shade of violet. 'Return to Moon's Spawn, then. Have the High Priestess herself attend to Jekaral.'

428

Serrat bowed. 'Thank you, Lord.' She turned and gestured to the others.

'Oh,' Rake said, raising his voice to address his cadre of assassin-mages, 'one last thing. You've done well, exceptionally well. You've earned a rest. Three days and nights are yours to do with as you please.'

Serrat bowed again. 'We will mourn, Lord.'

'Mourn?'

'The poisoned quarrel killed Dashtal. The poison was the product of an alchemist, Lord. One of some ability. It contained paralt.'

'I see.'

'Will you return with us?'

'No.'

The lieutenant bowed a third time. As one, the eight Tiste Andii raised their hands, then vanished.

Rake glanced down at the sizzling patch just as it ate through the roof and fell into darkness. There came a faint crash from below. Lord Anomander Rake swung his gaze back to the sky, then sighed.

Sergeant Whiskeyjack rocked his chair on to its back two legs and anchored it against the crumbling wall. The small, dingy room reeked of urine and damp. Two single beds, wood-framed with burlap mattresses stuffed with straw, ran along the wall to his left. The three other rickety chairs had been pulled up around the lone table in the room's centre. Above the table hung an oil lantern, which shone down on Fiddler, Hedge and Mallet as they sat playing cards.

They'd done their work, finishing with the coming of dusk just outside Majesty Hall. Until the alliance with the Moranth, the Malazan saboteur had been nothing more than a glorified sapper, a digger of tunnels and breaker of city gates. Moranth alchemy had introduced to the Empire a variety of chemical

429

and powder explosives, most of which detonated when exposed to air. Applying a slow-working acid worm-holed the unfired clay shells. Sabotage had become an art, the precise equation of clay thickness and acid strength was tricky, and few survived to learn from their mistakes.

To Whiskeyjack's mind, Hedge and Fiddler were terrible soldiers. He had trouble recalling the last time they'd unsheathed their shortswords. Whatever discipline that had been part of their basic training had disintegrated through years in the field. Still, when it came to sabotage they had no equals.

Through hooded eyes Whiskeyjack studied the three men sitting at the table. It had been some minutes since any of them had made a move or said a word. One of Fiddler's new games, he decided, the man was forever inventing new ones, improvising the rules whenever they gave him an edge. Despite the endless arguments Fiddler was never short of players.

'And that's what boredom can do,' he said to himself. But, no, it was more than just boredom. Waiting gnawed, especially when it had to do with friends. Quick Ben and Kalam might be face down in some alley for all they knew. And that made it hard.

Whiskeyjack's gaze strayed to one of the beds, on which lay his armour and longsword. Rust stained the hauberk's tattered chain like old blood. The links were missing in some places, torn in others. In his bones and muscles the memory of that damage remained: every cut, every blow now haunted him with aches, greeting him each morning like old comrades. The sword, with its plain leather-wrapped grip and stub hilt, lay in its hide-over-wood scabbard, the belt and straps draped over the bedside.

That weapon had come to him after his first battle, found amid a field of dead. He'd still had the chalk of his father's quarry on his boots then, and a world's promise stretched out before him on the banners of Empire. The sword had come to him shiny, without even so much as a nick in its honed blade, and he had taken it as his own personal standard.

Whiskeyjack's gaze lost its focus. His mind had stepped into the grey, muddy tracks of his youth, where he walked the familiar path, lost and blinded by an unidentifiable sorrow.

The door flew open, carrying into the room a gust of steamy air and then Trotts. The Barghast's coal-dark eyes met the sergeant's.

Whiskeyjack stood quickly. He went to the bed and retrieved his sword. At the table the others remained intent on their card game, their only betrayal of anxiety a subtle shifting of chairs. Whiskeyjack pushed past Trotts and closed the door to a crack, through which he looked. Across the street, at the mouth of an alley, two figures crouched, the larger leaning heavily against the other. Whiskeyjack's breath hissed through his teeth. 'Mallet,' he said over his shoulder.

At the table the healer frowned at the two saboteurs, then carefully set down his cards.

The two figures in the alley crossed the street. Whiskeyjack's hand crept to grip his sword.

'Which?' Mallet asked, as he rearranged the blankets on one of the beds.

'Kalam,' the sergeant replied. The two men reached the door and he swung it wide to let them through, then shut it again. He beckoned at Trotts, who walked over to the curtained window, pulling back a corner to watch the street.

Kalam was pale, sagging against Quick Ben. The assassin's dark grey shirt was soaked with blood. Mallet moved to help the wizard and together they carried Kalam to the bed. As soon as the healer had him laid out, he waved Quick Ben away and began removing Kalam's shirt.

Quick Ben shook his head at Whiskeyjack and sat down in the chair Mallet had occupied. 'What's the game?' he asked,

431

picking up Mallet's cards and frowning as he studied them.

Neither Hedge nor Fiddler replied.

'No idea,' Whiskeyjack said, as he walked over to stand behind Mallet. 'They just sit and stare.'

Quick Ben grinned. 'Ah, a waiting game, right, Fid?' He leaned back comfortably and stretched out his legs.

Mallet glanced up at the sergeant. 'He'll be down for a while,' the healer said. 'The wound is clean, but he's lost a lot of blood.'

Crouching, Whiskeyjack studied the assassin's pallid face. Kalam's gaze remained sharp, focused on the sergeant. 'Well?' Whiskeyjack demanded. 'What happened?'

Quick Ben answered behind him. 'Had a bit of a mage duel out there.'

Kalam nodded in confirmation.

'And?' Whiskeyjack asked, straightening to glare at the wizard.

Quick Ben wilted slightly in his chair. 'It went sour. I had to release an Empire demon to get us out alive.'

Everyone in the room went still. At the window Trotts turned and made a tribal warding gesture, tracing the woad lines on his face.

Whiskeyjack's voice was soft. 'It's loose in the city?'

'No,' the wizard answered. 'It's dead.'

'*Who* did you run into?' Whiskeyjack bellowed, throwing up his hands.

'Not sure exactly,' Quick Ben said quietly. 'Whatever it was, it took care of the demon in less than a minute. I heard the death cry when we were only a block away. Assassin mages, Sergeant, coming down out of the sky. Seemed intent on wiping out the city's Guild.'

Whiskeyjack returned to his chair and dropped into it, the wood complaining beneath him. 'From the sky. Tiste Andii.'

'Yes,' Quick Ben muttered. 'We thought that. The sorcery

had that flavour. Old, dark and icy cold. Kurald Galain.'

'From what we saw,' Kalam added, 'they did a damn good job. No contact established, Sergeant. It was messy up there.'

'So the Moon's active here.' Whiskeyjack paused, then pounded his fist on the chair's arm. 'Worse, the Moon's lord is a move ahead of us. He reckoned we'd try to contact the Guild, so what does he do?'

'Takes out the Guild,' Kalam said. 'How's that for arrogance?'

'Whatever arrogance that lord has,' Whiskeyjack said, grimacing, 'he's earned it. I'll give him that. I wonder how good this city's Guild Master is – good enough to take on Tiste Andii? Unlikely.'

'And about the other thing,' Quick Ben said. 'It worked.'

The sergeant stared at the wizard for half a dozen seconds, then nodded.

'We also ran into Sorry,' Kalam said, wincing as Mallet pressed a hand on his wound. The healer muttered under his breath.

'Oh? I sent her after some fat man she thought was important. How come she ran into you two?'

Quick Ben's brows had risen. 'So she told the truth, then. We don't know how she found us, but she'd found the man we were looking for – and gave him to us.'

Mallet raised his hand. Where the wound had been there was now a pink scar. Kalam grunted his thanks and sat up.

Whiskeyjack tapped his fingers against the chair's arm. 'If we only knew who was running this damn city, we could try it ourselves.'

The assassin sniffed. 'If we start taking out Council members, maybe we'll flush out the real rulers.'

The sergeant frowned. 'Not bad,' he said, rising to his feet. 'Work on that. The Moon's lord knows we're here, now, with that demon popping up. We'll have to move fast.'

433

Fiddler spoke up. 'We could blow up Majesty Hall,' he said, smirking at Hedge.

'You've got enough munitions to manage that?' Whiskeyjack asked.

Fiddler's face fell. 'Well, uh, we've got enough to take out an estate, maybe. But if we pull up some of the mines we planted . . .'

Whiskeyjack sighed. 'This is getting absurd. No, we leave things as they are.' He watched the non-existent card game. It seemed to involve complete immobility. A stand-off. The sergeant's eyes narrowed. Were they trying to tell him something?

Orange and yellow hues lit the eastern horizon, casting a coppery sheen upon the city's bricks and cobbles. Apart from the dripping of water the streets were quiet, though the first emergings of citizenry were minutes away. Soon those farmers who had depleted their supplies of grains, fruits and root crops would take to their carts and wagons and depart the city. Merchant shops and stalls would open to catch the morning wave of shoppers.

Throughout Darujhistan the Greyfaces prepared to shut the valves feeding gas to the torches lining the major avenues. These figures moved in small groups, gathering at intersections then dispersing with the day's first bell.

Sorry watched Crokus wearily ascend a tenement's front steps. She stood half a block down the street, within shadows that seemed reluctant to disappear despite the growing light.

A short while earlier, she'd felt the Empire demon's death strike her almost physically, deep in her chest. Normally demons fled back to their realm once enough damage had been inflicted on them, enough to sever the links of summoning. But the Korvalah had not been simply cut down, or forcibly dismissed. There'd been a finality to its end that had left her

434

shaken. A death in truth. She still recalled its silent, despairing scream ringing in her head.

All the ambivalence surrounding the Coin Bearer was gone, driven away. She knew now she would kill him. It had to be done, and soon. All that remained before she could do so was the mystery of his actions. To what extent was Oponn using the boy?

She knew he'd seen her in the D'Arles' garden, just before he'd escaped to the estate's roof. Seeing the light come on behind the balcony's sliding doors had clinched her decision to continue following Crokus. The D'Arle family was powerful in Darujhistan. That the boy seemed to be involved in a clandestine love affair with the daughter was an outrageous proposition, yet what else could she conclude? So, the question remained: was Oponn working through the boy directly, insinuating a peculiar influence with the City Council? What powers of influence did this young maiden possess?

Only a matter of position, of possible scandal. Yet what was the political position of Councilman Estraysian D'Arle? Sorry realized that even though she'd learned much of Darujhistan's political arena she still did not know enough to second-guess Oponn's moves. Councilman D'Arle was Turban Orr's principal opposition on this proclamation-of-neutrality business – but what did that matter? The Malazan Empire could not care less. Unless the proclamation was no more than a feint. Was this Turban Orr seeking to lay the groundwork for an Empire-backed coup?

The answers to such questions would be slow in coming. She knew she'd have to exercise patience. Of course, patience was her finest quality. She'd hoped that showing herself to Crokus a second time, there in the garden, might trigger panic in the lad – or, at the very least, annoy Oponn if indeed the god's control was as direct as that.

Sorry had watched on, from the shadows she drew around

435

her, as the assassin named Rallick took the lad to task. She'd also lingered to catch the conversation between Rallick and Murillio. It seemed the boy had protectors, and an odd lot they were, assuming that the fat little man, Kruppe, was some kind of group leader. Hearing that they were to take Crokus out of the city on behalf of their 'master' made the whole situation even more intriguing.

She knew she'd have to make her move soon. The protection offered by Kruppe and this Murillio would not impede her much, she expected. Though Kruppe was certainly more than he seemed, violence hardly seemed his major skill.

She would kill Crokus, then, outside the city. As soon as she discovered the nature of their mission, and who their master was. As soon as everything had fallen into place.

Sergeant Whiskeyjack would have to wait a while longer for her return. Sorry smiled at that, knowing full well how relieved the whole squad would be that she was nowhere to be seen. As for that whole matter – the threat presented by Quick Ben and Kalam – well, everything in its own time.

Alchemist Baruk's savage migraine was ebbing. Whatever presence had been unleashed in the city was gone. He sat in his reading chair, pressing a cloth-wrapped chunk of ice against his forehead. It had been a conjuring. He felt certain of that. The emanations stank of demonry. But there'd been more. The moment before the presence vanished, Baruk had experienced a mental wrench that came close to driving him into unconsciousness.

He'd shared the creature's final death scream, his own shriek echoing down the hall and bringing his men-at-arms shouting to his bedroom door.

Baruk felt a wrongness, deep within him, as if his soul had been battered. For a single, brief second, he'd looked upon a world of absolute darkness, and from that darkness came

436

sounds, the creak of wooden wheels, the clank of chains, the groans of a thousand imprisoned souls. Then it was gone, and he found himself sitting in his chair, Roald kneeling at his side with a pail of ice from the cellar.

He now sat in his study, alone, and the ice pressed against his brow was warm compared to what he felt in his heart.

There was a knock at the door, and Roald entered, his face creased with worry. 'Lord, you have a visitor.'

'I have? At this hour?' He rose shakily to his feet. 'Who is it?'

'Lord Anomander Rake.' Roald hesitated. 'And . . . another.'

Frowning, Baruk waved a hand. 'Bring them in.'

'Yes, Lord.'

Rake entered, holding a dog-sized winged creature by the nape of its neck. The creature twisted and hissed, then turned pleading eyes to Baruk.

'This thing was following me here,' Rake said. 'Yours?'

Startled, Baruk managed a nod.

'I thought as much,' Rake said, releasing the demon to flap across the room and land at the alchemist's slippered feet.

Baruk gazed down on it. The demon was trembling.

Rake strode to a chair and sat, stretching out his long legs. 'A busy night,' he said.

Baruk gestured and the demon vanished with a faint popping sound. 'Indeed,' he said, his voice hard. 'My servant was on a mission. I had no idea it would involve you.' He went to stand before the Tiste Andii. 'Why were you in the middle of an assassin war?'

'Why not?' Rake answered. 'I started it.'

'What?'

He smiled up at Baruk. 'You don't know the Empress as well as I do, Baruk.'

'Please explain.' Colour had risen in the alchemist's face.

Rake looked away. 'Tell me this, Baruk,' he said, turning to meet the alchemist's gaze, 'who in this city is most likely to be aware of your secret council? And who might benefit the most from your removal? And, most importantly, who in this city is capable of killing you?'

Baruk did not answer immediately. He walked slowly to the table, where a newly painted map had been laid out. He leaned over it, hands resting on the edge. 'You suspect the Empress might seek out Vorcan,' he said. 'A contract to offer.'

'On you and the rest of the High Mages,' Rake said, behind him. 'The Empress has sent a Claw here, not so much to worry your city's defences, but to establish contact with the Master Assassin. I wasn't entirely certain that I was right in this, but I meant to prevent that contact.'

Baruk's eyes remained on the map's red wash. 'So you sent your own assassins to wipe out her Guild. To flush her out.' He faced Rake. 'And then what? Kill her? All on the basis of some suspicion of yours?'

'This night,' Rake said calmly, 'we prevented the Claw from making that contact. Your demon's report will confirm this. Besides, you aren't suggesting that the death of Vorcan and the decimation of the city's assassins is a bad thing, are you?'

'I fear I am.' Baruk was pacing, struggling against a growing sense of outrage. 'I may not know the Empress as well as you, Rake,' he said, gritting his teeth, 'but I do know this city – far better than you ever will.' He glared at the Tiste Andii. 'To you, Darujhistan is just another battleground for your private war with the Empress. You don't give a damn about how this city survives – how it has managed to survive three thousand years.'

Rake shrugged. 'Enlighten me.'

'The City Council has its function, a vital one. They are the city's machine. True, Majesty Hall is a place of pettiness, corruption, endless bickering but, despite all that, it's also a place where things get done.'

438

'What's that got to do with Vorcan and her gang of killers?'

Baruk grimaced. 'Like any burdened wagon, the wheels require grease. Without the option of assassination the noble families would have long since destroyed themselves, taking the city with them, through civil war. Secondly, the Guild's efficiency provides a measure of control on vendettas, arguments and so forth. It is the guaranteed option of bloodshed, and bloodshed is messy. Usually too messy for the nobility's sensibilities.'

'Curious,' Rake said. 'Nevertheless, don't you think that Vorcan would listen very carefully indeed to an offer from the Empress? After all, Laseen has the precedent of handing over the rule of a conquered city to an assassin. In fact, at least a third of her present High Fists come from that profession.'

'You are missing the point!' Baruk's face was dark. 'You did not consult us, and that cannot be tolerated.'

'*You* haven't answered me,' Rake retorted, in a voice quiet and cold. 'Would Vorcan take the contract? Could she manage it? Is she that good, Baruk?'

The alchemist turned away. 'I don't know. That's my answer, to all three questions.'

Rake stared hard at Baruk. 'If you were indeed nothing more than an alchemist, I might believe you.'

Baruk's smile was wry. 'Why would you think me anything but?'

Now it was Rake's turn to smile. 'There are few who would argue with me without flinching. I am unused to be addressed as an equal.'

'There are many paths to Ascendancy, some more subtle than others.' Baruk walked over to the mantel above the fireplace, took a carafe, then went to the shelf behind his desk and retrieved two crystal goblets. 'She's a High Mage. We all have magical defences, but against her . . .' He filled the goblets with wine.

439

Rake joined the alchemist. He accepted the glass and raised it between them. 'I apologize for not informing you. In truth, the thought hadn't crossed my mind as being especially important. Until tonight, I was acting on a theory, nothing more. I didn't consider the ripples a grounded Guild might cause.'

Baruk sipped his wine. 'Anomander Rake, tell me something. There was a presence in our city tonight – a conjuring.'

'One of Tayschrenn's Korvalah demons,' Rake answered. 'Released by a Claw wizard.' He took a mouthful of the tart liquid, let it roll for a moment, then swallowed with satisfaction. 'It's gone.'

'Gone?' Baruk asked quietly. 'Where?'

'Out of Tayschrenn's reach,' Rake said, a tight smile on his lips. 'Out of anyone's reach.'

'Your sword,' Baruk said, repressing a shiver as the memory of that closing vision returned to him. The creak of wheels, the clank of chains, the groans of a thousand lost souls. And darkness.

'Oh, yes,' Rake said, refilling his goblet. 'I received the two Pale wizards' heads. As you promised. I admire your efficiency, Baruk. Did they protest?'

Baruk paled. 'I explained to them the options,' he said quietly. 'No, they didn't protest.'

Rake's soft laugh chilled the blood in Baruk's veins.

At the distant sound Kruppe rose. The small fire flickered steadily before him, but its heat seemed less. 'Ah,' he sighed, 'Kruppe's hands are near numb, yet his ears are as sharp as ever. Listen to this faint sound in the very nether regions of his present dream. Does he know its source?'

'Perhaps,' K'rul said beside him.

Startled, Kruppe turned, his eyebrows rising. 'Kruppe thought you long gone, Eldering One. None the less, he is thankful for your company.'

440

The hooded god nodded. 'All is well with the child Tattersail. The Rhivi protect her, and she grows swiftly, as is the nature of Soletaken. A powerful warlord now shelters her.'

'Good,' Kruppe said, smiling. The noises in the distance drew his attention again. He stared out into the darkness, seeing nothing.

'Tell me, Kruppe,' K'rul said, 'what do you hear?'

'The passing of a great wagon or some such thing,' he replied, with a frown. 'I hear its wheels, and chains, and the groaning of slaves.'

'Its name is Dragnipur,' K'rul said. 'And it is a sword.'

Kruppe's frown deepened. 'How can a wagon and slaves be a sword?'

'Forged in darkness, it chains souls to the world that existed before the coming of light. Kruppe, its wielder is among you.'

In Kruppe's mind his Deck of Dragons rose. He saw the image of half man, half dragon – the Knight of High House Darkness, also known as the Son of Darkness. The man held aloft a black sword trailing smoky chains. 'The Knight is in Darujhistan?' he asked, fighting a shiver of fear.

'In Darujhistan,' K'rul replied. 'Around Darujhistan. Above Darujhistan. His presence is a lodestone to power, and great is the danger.' The Elder God faced Kruppe. 'He is in league with Master Baruk and the T'orrud Cabal – Darujhistan's secret rulers have found a two-edged ally. Dragnipur tasted a demon's soul this night, Kruppe, in your city. It is never thirsty for long, and it will feed on more blood before this is done.'

'Can anyone withstand it?' Kruppe asked.

K'rul shrugged. 'None could when it was first forged, but that was long ago, before even my time. I cannot answer for the present. I have one other piece of information, Kruppe, a small piece, I'm afraid.'

'Kruppe hearkens.'

'The journey Master Baruk is sending you on to the Gadrobi

Hills. Elder magic brews anew, after so long. It is Tellann – of the Imass – but what it touches is Omtose Phellack – Jaghut Elder magic. Kruppe, stay out of their way. Especially guard the Coin Bearer. What is about to come is a danger as grave as the Knight and his sword, and as ancient. Step carefully, Kruppe.'

'Kruppe always steps carefully, Eldering One.'

BOOK FIVE

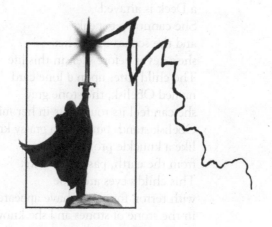

THE GADROBI
HILLS

Beyond these thin hide walls
a child sits, before her on worn silk
a Deck is arrayed.
She cannot yet speak
and the scenes before her
she's never before seen in this life.
The child gazes upon a lone card
named Obelisk, the stone grey
she can feel its roughness in her mind.
Obelisk stands buried in a grassy knoll
like a knuckle protruded
from the earth, past and future.
This child's eyes are wide
with terror, for cracks have appeared
in the stone of stones and she knows
the shattering is begun.

Silverfox
Outrider Hurlochel,
6th Army

CHAPTER FOURTEEN

> I saw them on the shores
> the deepening pits of their gaze
> vowed immortal war
> against the sighing calm
> of Jaghut seas . . .
>
> *Gothos' Folly*
> Gothos (b.?)

907th Year in the Third Millennium
The Season of Fanderay in the Year of the Five Tusks
By Malazan reckoning, 1163rd Year of Burn's Sleep
T'lan Imass reckoning, The Year of Gathering, Tellann Arise

As the days passed, Adjunct Lorn felt a sharpness return to her mind, the exhaustion and depression fading away. The thought that she could allow herself to slip into carelessness so easily had left her shaken, and that was not a feeling with which she was familiar. She did not know how to deal with it, and this kept her unbalanced, not quite sure of her own efficacy.

As the Gadrobi Hills appeared, first to the south and then

to the west as well, she sensed a desperate urgency to regain her confidence. The mission approached a vital juncture. Success with the Jaghut barrow would almost ensure success with everything else.

Since this dawn she'd ridden hard, pushing to keep her schedule intact after travelling so slowly in the first few days. Both horses were in need of rest, so she now walked ahead of them, the reins tucked through her belt. And beside her walked Tool.

Though the Imass spoke often, at her prodding, of many fascinating things, he denied her efforts regarding matters important to the Empire, and to Laseen's continued power. All seemed to return to the vows he had taken at the last Gathering. For the Imass, something was coming to a head. She wondered if it was somehow connected with freeing this Jaghut Tyrant. And that was a disturbing thought.

Still, she would not permit any ambivalence to threaten the mission. In this she was Laseen's arm, and it was directed not of Lorn's own accord but by the Empress. Dujek and Tayschrenn had well reminded her of that truth. Thus, she played no role in all this – not as the woman named Lorn. How could she be held responsible for anything?

'In my years among humans,' Tool said, beside her, 'I have come to recollect the passing of emotions in body and expressions. Adjunct, you have worn a frown the past two days. Is this significant?'

'No,' she snapped. 'It isn't.' Purging her thoughts of personal feelings had never been so difficult as it was now – was this a lasting effect of Oponn's meddling? Perhaps Tool could rid her of it. 'Tool,' she said, 'what is significant, as you put it, is that I don't know enough about what we're doing. We are seeking a standing stone, the barrow's marker. Well, assuming it can be found, why was it not so long ago? Why could not three thousand years of hunting find this barrow?'

446

'We will find the standing stone,' Tool replied calmly. 'It marks the barrow in truth, but the barrow is not there.'

The Adjunct scowled. *More riddles.* 'Explain.'

The Imass was silent for a minute, then he said, 'I am born of an Elder Warren, Adjunct, known as Tellann. It is more than a source of magic, it is also a time.'

'Are you suggesting that the barrow exists in a different time? Is that how you plan to reach it – by using your Tellann Warren?'

'No, there is no parallel time any different from the one we know. That time is gone, past. It is more a matter of . . . flavour. Adjunct, may I continue?'

Lorn's mouth thinned into a straight line.

'The Jaghut who entombed the Tyrant were born of a different Elder Warren. But the term "Elder" is relative only to the existing Warrens of this age. The Jaghut Omtose Phellack is not "Elder" when compared to Tellann. They are the same, of the same *flavour*. Do you understand thus far, Adjunct?'

'Patronizing bastard,' she muttered to herself. 'Yes, Tool.'

The Imass nodded, his bones creaking. 'The barrow has not been found before, precisely because it is Omtose Phellack. It lies within a Warren now lost to the world. Yet, I am Tellann. My Warren touches Omtose Phellack. I can reach it, Adjunct. Any T'lan Imass could. I was chosen because I am without a Clan. I am alone in every way.'

'Why should that be important?' Lorn asked, her stomach twisting.

Tool looked at her. 'Adjunct. What we seek to accomplish is the freeing of a Jaghut Tyrant. Such a being, should it escape our control, or defy our predictions, is capable of destroying this continent. It can enslave all living upon it, and it would do so if permitted. If, instead of me, Logros had selected a Bone Caster; and if the Tyrant was freed, that Bone Caster would become enslaved. A Jaghut Tyrant is dangerous alone. A

Jaghut Tyrant with an Imass Bone Caster at its side is unstoppable. They would challenge the gods, and they would kill most of them. Also, I am without a Clan, thus my enslavement – should that event befall – would not enslave blood kin.'

Lorn stared at the Imass. What were the Empress and Tayschrenn thinking of? How could they hope to control this thing? 'You are saying, Tool, that you're expendable.'

'Yes, Adjunct.'

And so, she realized, am I. 'What,' she asked, 'will stop the Tyrant? How do we control it?'

'We don't, Adjunct. That is the gamble we take.'

'And what does that mean?'

Tool shrugged, an audible lifting and dropping of bones beneath the rotted furs. 'The Lord of Moon's Spawn, Adjunct. He will have no choice but to intervene.'

'He's capable of stopping the Tyrant?'

'Yes, Adjunct. He is, although it will cost him dearly, weaken him. More, he is capable of delivering the single punishment that a Jaghut Tyrant fears most.' A faint gleam of light rose in Tool's eye sockets as the Imass stared at Lorn. 'Enslavement, Adjunct.'

Lorn stopped in her tracks. 'You mean the Moon's lord will have the Tyrant working on his side?'

'No, Adjunct. The enslavement is by the lord's hand, but it is beyond him as well. You see, the Empress knows who the lord is, and what he possesses.'

Lorn nodded. 'He's Tiste Andii, and a High Mage.'

A rasp of laughter came from Tool. 'Adjunct, he is Anomander Rake, the Son of Darkness. Bearer of Dragnipur.'

Lorn frowned.

Tool seemed to have noticed her confusion, for the Imass elaborated. 'Dragnipur is a sword, born of the Age before Light. And Darkness, Adjunct, is the Goddess of the Tiste Andii.'

448

A few minutes later, Lorn found her voice. 'The Empress,' she said quietly, 'knows how to pick her enemies.'

And then Tool hit her with another stunning revelation. 'I am sure,' the Imass said, 'the Tiste Andii regret their coming to this world.'

'They *came* to this world? From where? How? Why?'

'The Tiste Andii were of Kurald Galain, the Warren of Darkness. Kurald Galain stood alone, untouched. The Goddess, their mother, knew loneliness . . .' Tool hesitated. 'There is probably little truth in this story, Adjunct.'

'Go on,' Lorn said quietly. 'Please.'

'In her loneliness, the Goddess sought something outside herself. Thus was born Light. Her children the Tiste Andii saw this as a betrayal. They rejected her. Some hold they were cast out, others that they departed their mother's embrace by choice. While Tiste Andii mages still use the Warren of Kurald Galain they are no longer *of* it. And some have embraced another Warren, that of Starvald Demelain.'

'The First Warren.'

Tool nodded.

'Whose Warren did Starvald Demelain belong to?'

'It was the home of Dragons, Adjunct.'

Murillio turned in his saddle and brought the mule to a halt on the dusty road. He glanced ahead. Kruppe and Crokus had already reached the Worry Crossroads. He patted his brow with the soft satin of his burnous, then looked back again. Coll leaned hunched over in his saddle, losing the rest of his breakfast.

Murillio sighed. It was a wonder to see the man sober, but that he'd insisted on accompanying them bordered on miraculous. Murillio wondered if Coll suspected anything of Rallick's plans – but no, he would've brought a fist down on his and Rallick's head in short order if he'd so much as caught a hint of what they were doing.

449

It had been Coll's pride that had got him into his present mess, and drink did nothing to diminish it. To the contrary, in fact. Coll had even donned his brigandine armour, replete with arm and leg greaves. A bastard sword hung at the large man's hip and, with his mail coif and helmet, he looked every inch a noble knight. The only exception was the green tinge to his rounded face. He was also the only one of them to have found a horse instead of these damned mules Kruppe had scrounged.

Coll straightened in his saddle and smiled wanly at Murillio, then spurred his horse alongside. They resumed the journey without a word, nudging their mounts into a canter until they'd caught up with the others.

As usual, Kruppe was pontificating. 'No more than a handful of days, assures Kruppe, wizened traveller of the wastes beyond glittering Darujhistan. No reason to be so glum, lad. Consider this a mighty adventure.'

Crokus looked to Murillio and threw up his hands. 'Adventure? I don't even know what we're doing out here! Won't anybody tell me anything? I can't believe I agreed to this!'

Murillio grinned at the boy. 'Come now, Crokus. How many times have you expressed curiosity about our constant travels outside the city? Well, here we are – all your questions are about to find answers.'

Crokus hunched down in his saddle. 'You told me you all worked as agents for some merchant. What merchant? I don't see any merchant. And where's our horses? How come Coll's the only one with a horse? How come nobody gave me a sword or something? Why—?'

'All right!' Murillio laughed, holding up a hand. 'Enough, please! We *are* agents for a merchant,' he explained. 'But it's rather unusual merchandise we're acquiring.'

'A rather unusual merchant as well, Kruppe adds with a warm smile. Lad, we are agents seeking information on behalf of our employer, who is none other than High Alchemist Baruk!'

Crokus stared at Kruppe. 'Baruk! And he can't afford to give us horses?'

Kruppe cleared his throat. 'Ah, yes. Well. There was something of a misunderstanding between worthy, honest Kruppe and a conniving, deceitful stabler. None the less, Kruppe received full recompense, thus saving our kind master eleven silver coins.'

'Which he'll never see,' Murillio muttered.

Kruppe went on, 'As for a sword, lad, what on earth for? Ignore blustery, pallid Coll there, with all his sweaty trappings of war. A mere affectation of his. And Murillio's rapier is no more than an ornamental trifle, though no doubt he would claim that the jewels and emeralds studding said item's hilt are towards achieving fine balance or some such martial detail.' Kruppe smiled beatifically at Murillio. 'Nay, lad, the true masters at acquiring information need no such clumsy pieces of metal; indeed, we disdain them.'

'OK,' Crokus grumbled, 'what kind of information are we looking for, then?'

'All that yon ravens overhead can see,' Kruppe said, waving a hand in the air. 'Other travellers, other efforts within the Gadrobi Hills, all grist for Master Baruk's mill of news. We observe without being observed. We learn while remaining a mystery to all. We ascend to the—'

'Will you shut up?' Coll moaned. 'Who brought the waterskins?'

Smiling, Murillio removed a clay jug webbed in twine from his saddlehorn and handed it to Coll.

'A sponge,' Kruppe said, 'squeezed beneath the burden of armour. See the man down our precious water, see it immediately reappear salty and grimy on his weathered skin. What yon poisons have leaked forth? Kruppe shudders at the thought.'

Coll ignored him, handing the jug to Crokus. 'Buck up, lad,' he said. 'You're getting paid, and damn well. With luck there'll

451

be no trouble. Believe me, in this kind of work, excitement is the last thing we're looking for. Still,' he glared at Murillio, 'I'd feel a whole lot better if Rallick were with us.'

Crokus bristled. 'And I'm an unworthy stand-in, right? You think I don't know that, Coll? You think—?'

'Don't tell me what I think,' Coll rumbled. 'I never said you were a stand-in, Crokus. You're a thief, and those kinds of skill come in a lot handier than anything I could manage. The same for Murillio. And as for Kruppe, well, his talents extend no further than his stomach and whatever he wants jammed in it. You and Rallick share a lot more than you think, and that's why you're the most qualified man here.'

'Barring the necessary brains, of course,' Kruppe said, 'which is my true skill – though one such as Coll would never understand such abilities, alien as they are to him.'

Coll leaned towards Crokus. 'You're wondering why I'm wearing all this armour,' he whispered loudly. 'It's because Kruppe's in charge. When Kruppe's in charge I don't feel safe unless I'm prepared for war. If it comes to that, lad, I'll get us out alive.' He leaned back and stared straight ahead. 'I've done it before. Right, Kruppe?'

'Absurd accusations.' Kruppe sniffed.

'So,' Crokus said, 'what are we supposed to be on the lookout for?'

'We'll know it when we see it,' Murillio said. He nodded towards the hills rising to the east. 'Up there.'

Crokus was silent for a time, then his eyes narrowed. 'The Gadrobi Hills. Are we looking for a rumour, Murillio?'

Murillio stiffened, but it was Kruppe who replied, 'Indeed, lad. Rumours upon rumours. I applaud your cunning conclusion. Now, where is that water jug? Kruppe's thirst has become intense.'

Sorry's departure through Jammit's Gate was casual, unhurried. Tracking the Coin Bearer was simple, and did not require that

452

the boy remain within her range of vision. She sensed Crokus and Kruppe, in the company of two others, on the road a league beyond Worrytown. They did not seem to be in any kind of rush.

Whatever mission they were on, that it concerned the welfare of Darujhistan was plain. Thinking on it, Sorry was sure that the men within that group were spies and, in all likelihood, able ones. The dandy, Murillio, could move through noble-born circles with an ease coupled with a desirable coyness – the perfect combination for a spy. Rallick, though he did not accompany them on this mission, was the eyes and ears within the Assassins' Guild, thus covering another power base. Kruppe's world was that of the thieves and lower classes, whence rumours sprang to life like weeds in muddy soil. The third man was clearly a military man, no doubt serving as the group's sword arm.

On a mundane level, then, an adequate group to protect the Coin Bearer, though insufficient to prevent her killing him – especially with the assassin left behind.

Yet something nagged within Sorry's mind, a vague suspicion that the group was heading into danger – a danger that threatened her as well. Once beyond Worrytown she picked up her pace. As soon as she found herself alone on the road, she opened her Warren of Shadow and slipped into its swift tracks.

The Adjunct could find nothing to set apart the hill they approached. Its grass-cloaked summit was dwarfed by those around it. A half dozen scraggly, wind-twisted scrub oaks climbed one side amid a scree of broken boulders. The summit flattened out into a rough circle, rock pushing through here and there.

Overhead wheeled ravens, so high as to be no more than specks against the muggy grey sky. Lorn watched Tool striding ahead of her, the Imass choosing an unwavering path towards the hill's base. She slumped in her saddle, feeling defeated by the world around her. The midday heat sapped her strength, and the sluggishness reached through to her thoughts – not Oponn's doing, she knew. This was the pervasive dread clinging to the air, the sense that what they were doing was wrong, terribly wrong.

To fling this Jaghut Tyrant into the hands of the Empire's enemy, to trust this Tiste Andii Anomander Rake to destroy it, yet at great cost to himself – thus opening the way for Malazan sorceries in turn to kill the Son of Darkness – now seemed precipitous, absurd in its ambitions.

Tool came to the base of the hill and waited for the Adjunct to arrive. Lorn saw, at Tool's hide-wrapped feet, a grey rock jutting perhaps ten inches from the earth.

'Adjunct,' the Imass said, 'this is the barrow marker we seek.'

She raised an eyebrow. 'There's hardly any soil cover here at all,' she said. 'Are you suggesting this standing stone has eroded down to its present size?'

'The stone has not eroded,' Tool answered. 'It has stood here since before the sheets of ice came to cover this land. It stood here when the Rhivi Plain was an inland sea, long before the waters withdrew to what is now Lake Azur. Adjunct, the stone is in fact taller than both of us combined, and what you think to be bedrock is shale.'

Lorn was surprised at the hint of anger in Tool's voice. She dismounted and set to hobbling the horses. 'How long do we stay here, then?'

'Until this evening passes. With tomorrow's dawn I will open the way, Adjunct.'

Faintly from above came the cries of ravens. Lorn lifted her head and gazed at the specks wheeling high over them. They'd been with them for days. Was that unusual? She didn't know. Shrugging, she unsaddled the horses.

The Imass remained motionless, his gaze seeming fixed on the stone marker.

Lorn went about preparing her camp. Among the scrub oaks she found wood for a small cooking fire. It was dry, weathered and likely to yield little smoke. Though she did not anticipate company, caution had become her habit. Before dusk arrived she found a nearby hill higher than those around it, and ascended to its summit. From this position she commanded a view that encompassed leagues on all sides. The hills continued their roll southward, sinking to steppes to the south-east. Due east of them stretched Catlin Plain, empty of life as far as she could see.

Lorn turned to the north. The forest they had travelled round a few days ago was still visible, a dark line thickening as it swept westward to the Tahlyn Mountains. She sat down and waited for night to fall. It was then that she'd be able to spot any campfires.

Even as night fell, the heat remained oppressive. Lorn walked around the hill's summit to stretch her legs. She found evidence of past excavations, scars that dug into the shale. And evidence of the Gadrobi herders remained, from as far back as when they fashioned stone tools. Against the south side of the hill the ground had been carved out, not in search of a barrow but as a stone quarry. It appeared that beneath the shale was flint, chocolate brown, sharp-edged and crusted in white chalk.

Curious, Lorn investigated further, scrambling down into the cavity. Stone flakes carpeted the pit's base. She crouched and picked up a piece of flint. It was the tip of a spear point, expertly shaped.

The echo of this technology was found in Tool's chalcedony sword. She needed no further proof of the Imass's assertions. Humans had indeed come from them, had indeed inherited a world.

Empire was a part of them, a legacy flowing like blood through human muscle, bone and brain. But such a thing could easily be seen as a curse. Were they destined one day to become human versions of the T'lan Imass? Was war all there was? Would they bow to it in immortal servitude, no more than deliverers of death?

Lorn sat down in the quarry and leaned against the chiselled, weathered stone. The Imass had conducted a war of extermination lasting hundreds of thousands of years. Who or what had the Jaghut been? According to Tool, they'd abandoned the concept of government, and turned their backs on empires, on armies, on the cycles of rise and fall, fire and rebirth. They'd walked alone, disdainful of their own kind, dismissive of community, of purposes greater than themselves.

They would not, she realized, have started a war.

'Oh, Laseen,' she murmured, tears welling in her eyes, 'I know why we fear this Jaghut Tyrant. Because he became human, he became like us, he enslaved, he destroyed, and he did it better than we could.' She lowered her head into her hands. 'That's why we fear.'

She fell silent then, letting the tears roll down her cheeks, seep between her fingers, trickle along her wrists. Who wept from her eyes? she wondered. Was it Lorn, or Laseen? Or was it for our kind? What did it matter? Such tears had been shed before, and would be again – by others like her and yet unlike her. And the winds would dry them all.

Captain Paran glanced at his companion. 'You've got a theory about all this?' he asked.

Toc the Younger scratched his scar. 'Damned if I know, Captain.' He stared down at the black, burned, crusted raven lying on the ground in front of them. 'I've been counting, though. That's the eleventh roasted bird in the last three hours. And, unless they're covering the Rhivi Plain like some bloody carpet, it seems we're on somebody's trail.'

Paran grunted, then kicked his horse forward.

Toc followed. 'And it's a nasty somebody,' he continued.

'Those ravens look like they was blasted from the inside out. Hell, even the flies avoid them.'

'In other words,' Paran grated, 'sorcery.'

Toc squinted at the hills south of them. They'd found a woodcutter's trail through the Tahlyn Forest, shaving days off their journey. As soon as they'd returned to the Rhivi traders' track, however, they'd found the ravens, and also the signs of two horses and one moccasined man on foot. This latter group of tracks was only a few days old.

'Can't understand why the Adjunct and that Imass are moving so slowly,' Toc muttered, repeating words he'd uttered a dozen times since the day's beginning. 'You think she doesn't know something's trailing her?'

'She's an arrogant woman,' Paran said, his free hand gripping his sword. 'And with that Imass with her, why should she worry?'

'Power draws power,' Toc said, scratching again at his scar. The motion triggered yet another flash of light in his head, but it was changing. At times he thought he could almost see images, scenes within the light. 'Damn Seven Cities' superstitions, anyway,' he growled, under his breath.

Paran looked at him oddly. 'You say something?'

'No.' Toc hunched down in his saddle. The captain had been pushing them hard. His obsession was running them down; even with the extra mount, the horses were near finished. And a thought nagged Toc. What would happen when they caught up with the Adjunct? Obviously, Paran intended to catch Lorn and the Imass, spurred by vengeance that overwhelmed his previous intentions. With Lorn dead or her plans awry, Paran's command would be safe. He could join Whiskeyjack and the squad at leisure. Assuming they still lived, of course.

Toc could think of a thousand flaws in the Captain's plans. First and foremost was the T'lan Imass. Was Paran's sword its match? In the past, sorcery had been flung at the Imass warriors

457

with a frenzy born of desperation. Nothing had worked. The only way to destroy an Imass was to chop it to pieces. Toc didn't think the captain's weapon, god-touched as it was, could do the job, but there was no convincing Paran of anything these days.

They came upon another raven, its feathers fluttering in the wind, its entrails swollen by the sun and bright red like cherries. Toc rubbed his scar again, and almost fell from the saddle as an image, clear and precise, burgeoned in his head. He saw a small shape, moving so fast as to be but a blur. Horses screamed, and a massive tear opened up in the air. He jolted, as if something large and heavy had struck him, and the tear yawned, swirling darkness beyond. Toc heard his own horse scream. Then it was gone, and he found himself gripping the hinged horn of his saddle with all his strength.

Paran rode ahead, apparently noticing nothing, his back straight and his gaze fixed southward. One hand played lightly on the sword's pommel.

Toc shook himself, leaned to one side and spat. What had he just seen? That tear – how could the air itself be torn like that? The answer came to him. *A Warren, an opening Warren could do that.* He spurred his horse alongside Paran's.

'Captain, we're heading into an ambush.'

Paran's head snapped around. His eyes glittered. 'Then prepare yourself.'

Toc opened his mouth to protest, but he shut it without speaking. What was the use? He strung his bow and loosened the scimitar in its scabbard, then set an arrow against the bowstring. He glanced over at Paran, who had unsheathed his sword and laid it across his thighs. 'It'll come by Warren, Captain.'

Paran found no need to question Toc's certitude. He almost looked eager.

Toc studied the sword, Chance. The dull, hazy light played along the polished blade like water. Somehow it, too, looked eager to Toc's eye.

CHAPTER FIFTEEN

> 'Tis bloody stirrups when the Jaghut
> ride their souls, a thund'rous charge
> without surcease,
> the hard knots within thud
> drumming fierce the flow of ice
> a certain promise . . .
> 'tis the Jaghut warring the dusk
> on a field of broken stones . . .
>
> *Jaghut*
> Fisher (b.?)

Quick Ben sat in the hut, his back to the ancient stone tier Wall. Before him rose the five sticks that linked him with Hairlock. The string connecting the sticks was taut. Across from the wizard, near the hide-covered entrance, sat Trotts.

Kalam had still not recovered enough to accompany Quick Ben, or to guard him as Trotts now did. The wizard had known the Barghast warrior for years, he'd fought alongside him in more battles than he cared to recall, and more than once one of them had saved the other's skin. And yet Quick Ben realized he really knew very little about Trotts. The one thing he did know, however, comforted him. The Barghast was a savage, brutal fighter, as capable with his throwing axes as he was with the longsword he now cradled in his lap. And he was fearless in the face of sorcery, secure in the fetishes tied into his braids, and in the woad tattoos inscribed by the hand of his clan's shaman.

Considering what might fall into their laps, those protections could come in handy.

The Barghast stared at the wizard with flat, expressionless eyes, unwavering in the dim light.

Quick Ben shook out the kinks in his hands, then bent forward to study the array of tied sticks. 'Hairlock's crouching inside his Warren,' he said. 'Not moving. Seems to be waiting.' He sat back and withdrew his dagger, which he jammed point first into the packed earth. 'So we wait, too. And watch.'

Trotts asked, 'Watch what?'

'Never mind.' Quick Ben sighed. 'You have that scrap of bedroll?'

Trotts removed from a sleeve a torn piece of cloth. He came forward, giving the sticks more room than was necessary, and pushed the scrap into the wizard's hand.

Quick Ben set it down on his left. He muttered a few words and passed his hand over it. 'Resume your seat,' he said. 'And keep your weapon ready in case things go bad.'

He closed his eyes then, reaching into his Warren. Before him an image formed that made him jerk with surprise. 'What,' he whispered, 'is Hairlock doing on Rhivi Plain?'

Paran could feel nothing but the white fire of vengeance, filling his mind, coruscating through his body. Oponn had chosen to use him. Now he would use Oponn, the Twins' power, that horrifying edge of destruction that came with Ascendancy. And like the gods, he could be cold-blooded in that use, even if it meant pulling Oponn kicking and screaming on to this plain to face whatever lay ahead.

A hiss of warning that might have been his conscience reached through to him. Toc the Younger was his friend, perhaps the only friend he had. Unprotected by any god, his chance of surviving what was coming was slim. Would there be another death to lay at his feet? Paran pushed aside the possibility. He was here to answer for Tattersail's murder. The Adjunct had taught him the value of being singleminded. *But what did Tattersail teach you?*

'If things get too hot,' he said, 'pull out, Toc. Ride for Darujhistan. Find Whiskeyjack.'

The scout nodded.

'If I go down—'

'I heard you, Captain.'

'Good.'

Silence fell between them, the only sounds remaining the thump of hoofs and the hot west wind that blew like sand whispering across stone.

Vague anticipations crowded Paran's head. Was the Adjunct waiting for them? If she recognized him and Toc, she'd have no reason to attack them. For all she knew, the captain had been killed. And Toc was a Claw. There'd be no ambush. The Adjunct would simply step out into the open and hail him, no doubt shocked by his appearance but hardly suspicious.

And when she came close, Chance would sing. It would be done, and if necessary they'd deal with the Imass afterwards. He hoped that the Imass would simply leave with the mission's collapse. Without the Adjunct, everything would fall through.

At least, so he hoped. Chance might be a gifted sword, but the T'lan Imass were Elder creations, born of sorceries that made Oponn less than a child.

Paran's grip on the sword's handle was tight. His hand ached, and he could feel sweat between his fingers. Chance felt

461

no different from any other weapon. Should he be expecting something more? He couldn't recall much of the time he'd last used it, against the Hound. But if there was power in the weapon, should he not be able to sense it? As it was, Chance felt cold, as if he clutched a shard of ice that refused to melt in his grip. If anything, Chance felt awkward, as if he was a novice and held it wrongly.

What had triggered this sudden crumpling of confidence? *Pulling an Ascendant into the fray . . . how precisely do I do that? Of course, if Oponn's as eager as last time . . .* Maybe it was no more than just the tension that came with waiting for something to happen. Was Toc mistaken? He turned to the man beside him and opened his mouth to speak.

A loud, manic cackle stopped him. Paran pulled savagely on the reins. His horse screamed and reared. The air seemed to rip and a cold wind gusted against them. The captain raised his sword and cursed. The horse screamed again, this time in pain. It crumpled beneath him, as if its bones had been turned to dust. Paran sprawled, the sword flying from his hand as the ground rose up to meet him. The horse's fall had the sound of a bag filled with rocks and lamp oil, landing beside him and rolling over his legs.

Toc's bowstring twanged and an arrow shattered against something hard.

Paran pushed himself on to his side and looked up.

The puppet Hairlock floated above the ground twenty feet ahead. A second arrow struck as the captain watched, also shattering.

Hairlock laughed again, swinging his mad stare to Toc. He gestured.

Paran cried out, twisting to see Toc thrown from his mount. The Claw cartwheeled through the air. A jagged tear opened in the air in front of him. Paran shouted a second time in helpless horror as Toc the Younger plunged into that tear and

462

disappeared into swirling mists. The rent closed with a snap, leaving no sign of Paran's companion.

Hairlock descended slowly to the ground. The puppet paused to adjust his tattered clothing, then strode towards Paran.

'I thought it might be you,' Hairlock sniggered. 'Isn't vengeance sweeter than honey, eh, Captain? Your death will be long, protracted and very, very painful. Imagine my pleasure at seeing you like this!'

Paran pushed with his legs. The horse's body fell back, freeing him. He scrambled to his feet and dived for his sword, grasping it while rolling, then regained his feet.

Hairlock watched in evident amusement and began to advance. 'That weapon is not for me, Captain. It'll not even cut me. So,' the puppet came on, 'wail away.'

Paran raised the weapon, a wave of despair coming over him.

Hairlock stopped and cocked his head. He whirled to face the north.

'Impossible!' the puppet snarled.

Now Paran caught what Hairlock had already heard: the howling of Hounds.

In the hut Quick Ben had watched the ambush, dumbfounded. What was Paran doing? Where was Tattersail? 'Hood's Path,' he'd whispered angrily, 'talk about losing track!' In any case, it had all happened too fast for him to prevent the loss of the one-eyed man accompanying the captain.

His eyes flew open and he snatched the scrap of cloth. 'Sorry,' he hissed. 'Sorry! Hear me, woman! I know you. I know who you are. Cotillion, Patron of Assassins, the Rope, I call upon you!'

He felt a presence enter his mind, followed by a man's voice. 'Well done, Quick Ben.'

The wizard said, 'I have a message for you, Rope. For Shadowthrone.' He felt a heightened tension in his head. 'A deal's been struck. Your lord's Hounds hunger for vengeance. I haven't time to explain it all now – leave that to Shadowthrone. I am about to give to you the location of the one Shadowthrone seeks.'

He heard wry amusement in the Rope's voice. 'I provide the link, correct? The means by which you stay alive in all this. I congratulate you, Quick Ben. Few mortals have ever succeeded in avoiding my lord's inclination to double-cross. It seems you have outwitted him. Very well, convey to me this location. Shadowthrone will receive it immediately.'

Quick Ben cast forth Hairlock's precise position on the Rhivi Plain. He only hoped the Hounds would arrive in time. He had a lot of questions for Paran, and wanted the captain to reach them alive but he had to admit that the chances of that were slight.

All that remained for the wizard now was to prevent the puppet's escape. He smiled again. That was something he looked forward to.

Onos T'oolan had squatted before the standing stone since dawn. In the hours since, Lorn had wandered the nearby hills, at war with herself. She now knew with a certainty that what they were doing was wrong, that its consequences went far beyond the petty efforts of a mundane Empire.

The T'lan Imass worked in the span of millennia, their purposes their own. Yet their endless war had become her endless war. Laseen's Empire was a shadow of the First Empire. The difference lay in that the Imass conducted genocide against another species. Malaz killed its own. Humanity had not climbed up since the dark age of the Imass: it had spiralled down.

The sun stood high overhead. She had last looked upon

Tool an hour past. The warrior had not moved an inch. Lorn climbed yet another hill, already a quarter-mile distant from the standing stone. She hoped to catch a glimpse of Lake Azur, to the west.

She came to the hill's summit and found herself not thirty feet from four mounted travellers. It was hard to determine who was more surprised, but the Adjunct moved first, her sword rasping into her hands as she sprang to close the distance.

Two were essentially unarmed, a boy and a short fat man. They and one other, a gaudily dressed man now unsheathing a duelling rapier, rode mules. But it was the last man who held Lorn's attention. Fully armoured astride a horse, he was the first to react to her charge. Bellowing, he spurred his mount past the others and unsheathed a bastard sword.

Lorn smiled as the fat man attempted to open a Warren and failed. Her Otataral blade steamed briefly before a cold wash of air poured from it. The fat man, his eyes widening, reeled back in his saddle and promptly rolled over the mule's rump, landing heavily in the dust. The boy leaped down from his own mount and paused, unsure whether to aid the fat man or remove the dagger from his belt. As the armoured man rode past him, he reached his decision and ran to where the fat man had fallen. The one with the rapier had also dismounted and approached in the warrior's wake.

Lorn's eyes caught all this between blinks. Then the warrior was upon her, swinging his bastard sword one-handed down towards her head.

The Adjunct didn't bother to parry. Instead, she dodged in front of the horse to come up on the man from his left, away from his sword arm. The horse reared. Lorn darted past, slicing her blade across the man's thigh, above the plate armour. The Otataral edge sliced through chain links, leather and flesh with equal ease.

465

The warrior grunted and clapped a mailed hand to the spurting wound even as the horse threw him from the saddle.

Ignoring him, Lorn engaged the duellist, attempting to beat his thin blade aside and close to bring the edge of her weapon into play. But the man was good, deftly disengaging her attempted beat. The sword's swing unbalanced her before she could slow its momentum preparatory to an upper-cut, and in this moment the duellist extended his rapier.

She cursed as her forward motion brought her on to the blade's tip. The point pushed through the links of her hauberk and entered her left shoulder. Pain lanced like fire up her arm. Angered by the wound, she swung her sword savagely at the man's head. The flat of the blade caught him flush on the forehead and he sprawled back like a limp doll.

Lorn cast a quick glance to where the warrior still struggled to stop the blood gushing from his leg, then whirled to face the last two men. The boy stood before the fat man, who lay unconscious. Though his face was pale, he held a thin-bladed dagger in his left hand and a larger knife in the other. His eyes were hard as he stared at her.

The thought crossed Lorn's mind, belatedly, that she need not have attacked these men. She wore mercenary garb, and the T'lan Imass was not even within sight. Words might have achieved the same results, and she'd never liked shedding blood. Well, it was too late for that now. She advanced slowly.

'We meant no harm,' the boy said in Daru. 'Leave us be.'

Lorn hesitated. The suggestion surprised her. Why not? She straightened. 'Agreed,' she answered in the same language. 'Patch up your friends and steer clear.'

'We'll head back to Darujhistan,' the boy said, looking equally surprised. 'We'll camp here and recover, leave in the morning.'

The Adjunct stepped back. 'Do that, and you'll stay alive. Try anything else, and I'll kill you all. Understood?'

466

The boy nodded.

Lorn backed away, angling to the north. She'd head that way for a time, then swing round to the east and come back down to where Tool was. She had no idea what had brought these men out into the hills, but didn't suspect it had anything to do with her, or even the barrow. As she increased the distance between herself and the hill, she saw the boy rush over to the warrior. In any case, she concluded, there wasn't much left of that group to cause her worry. The duellist wasn't dead, but he'd awake to a headache. As for the warrior, it was touch and go. She'd seen a lot of blood come from him. The fat man might have broken his neck, and as a mage he was harmless in her vicinity. That left the boy, and since when had she had cause to fear a boy?

Lorn quickened her pace.

After the startling communication from Quick Ben, Sorry had contacted Shadowthrone. The Lord of Shadows had fumed briefly, and after informing the Rope that Ben Adeaphon Delat had been a high priest of Shadow, Sorry found herself sharing Shadowthrone's anger. The man would pay for his many deceits.

Shadowthrone's Hounds had indeed been ready, and she was sure that even now they closed the hunt.

As she resumed her journey through her Warren she met with increasing resistance, a strange pressure with every step she took eastward. Finally, she relented and emerged into the Gadrobi Hills. It was midday, and half a mile ahead rode the Coin Bearer's party. She closed the gap swiftly until she was no more than a hundred yards behind them, gathering shadows about her as she went – though even this proved increasingly difficult. And that could mean only one thing: a T'lan Imass was nearby.

To what, and to whom, was the Coin Bearer riding? Had she

miscalculated entirely? Were they agents for the Malazan Empire? That possibility ran contrary to Oponn's influence, but she had trouble arriving at any other conclusion.

This, she told herself, would prove an interesting day.

The party was fifty yards ahead, making their way up a hillside. They reached the summit and disappeared briefly from her view. She quickened her pace, only to hear sounds of fighting on the hilltop – a fight in which Otataral was unveiled.

A flash of rage ran through her. Memory was attached to Otataral, a very personal memory. Cautiously she sought a vantage point at the hill's crest.

The exchange had been short, and the Coin Bearer's party looked near wiped out. In fact, only the Coin Bearer still stood, facing a tall, lithe woman wielding an Otataral blade.

Sorry recognized Adjunct Lorn. On a mission, no doubt, for her dear Empress, a mission that included a T'lan Imass, still out of sight but close. She caught their conversation. If the boy's group weren't agents for the Empire then perhaps their master in Darujhistan had sensed the presence of the Imass out here, and had sent them to investigate.

She would discover the nature of the Adjunct's mission later. Right now, however, it was time to kill the Coin Bearer. And the near proximity of the Imass made success all the more certain. Even Oponn's powers could not overcome the influence of a Tellann Warren. Murdering the boy would be easy. Sorry waited, then smiled as Adjunct Lorn withdrew, heading north.

In minutes, the Coin of Oponn would be in her hands. And this day, a god might die.

As soon as Lorn was sufficiently distant Crokus ran to the warrior. Sorry rose slowly into a crouch, then moved forward in silence, her garotte in her hands.

The Hounds howled again, their eager cries closing in from all sides. Hairlock crouched, indecisive. Then the puppet faced the captain. 'You'll have to wait a little longer to die, Captain. I've no intention of allowing things to be rushed. No, I wish to linger over your demise.'

Chance sweaty in his hands, Paran shrugged. To his own surprise, it made little difference to him. If the Hounds arrived to find Hairlock gone, they'd probably take out their frustration on him, and that would be that. 'You'll come to regret the opportunity, Hairlock. Whether this sword's magic is meant for you or not, I was looking forward to chopping you into kindling. Is your magic a match for my hatred? It would have been nice to find out.'

'Oh, sudden bravery! What do you know of hatred, Captain? When I return I'll show you precisely what hatred can achieve.' The wooden figure gestured and a dozen feet away another tear opened in the air, this one exuding a fetid stench. 'Stubborn mutts,' Hairlock muttered. 'Until later, Captain,' and he scurried for the rent.

In the hut, Quick Ben's grin turned savage. He jerked the dagger free with his right hand and, in a single, fluid motion, sliced the taut strings connecting the sticks.

'Goodbye, Hairlock,' he hissed.

Paran's eyes widened as the puppet flopped on to his stomach. A moment later Hairlock let loose a shriek.

The captain's eyes narrowed. 'Looks like somebody cut your strings, Hairlock,' he said.

The Hounds were close. In moments they'd be all over them.

'Your life, Captain!' Hairlock cried. 'Fling me into the Warren and your life is yours, I swear it!'

Paran leaned on his sword and made no reply.

'Pawn of Oponn,' Hairlock snarled, 'I would spit on you if I could! Spit on your soul!'

The earth rumbled, and at once massive shapes moved around Paran, silently closing in on the immobile marionette. Paran recognized Gear, the Hound he'd wounded. He felt the sword in his hands answer that challenge with an eager tremor that reached into his arms. Gear's head swung in his direction as it passed, and Paran saw a promise in its eyes. The captain smiled. *If anything draws Oponn out, it will be the fight to come.*

Hairlock shrieked one last time, and then the Hounds were upon him.

A large shadow passed across the hill and Paran looked up to see a Great Raven swooping over them. The bird cawed hungrily. 'Too bad,' Paran said to it, 'I doubt its remains would be palatable.'

Three Hounds began fighting over the splintered wood – all that was left of Hairlock. The remaining four, led by Gear, now turned to Paran.

The captain raised his sword and dropped into a combative crouch. 'Come on, then. Through me to the god using me, just once let the tool turn in the Twins' hands. Come on, Hounds, let us soak this ground with blood.'

The creatures fanned out into a half-circle, Gear in the centre.

Paran's smile broadened. *Come to me, Gear. I'm tired of being used and death doesn't seem so frightening any more. Let's be done with it.*

Something heavy pressed down on him, as if a hand had reached down from the sky and tried to drive him into the earth. The Hounds flinched. Paran staggered, unable to breathe, a sudden darkness closing around the edges of his vision. The ground groaned beneath him, the yellowed grasses of the plain lying flat. Then the pressure lifted and chilled air flooded back into his lungs. Sensing a presence, the captain whirled.

'Step aside,' a tall, black-skinned, white-haired man said, as

470

he pushed past to confront the Hounds. Paran almost dropped his sword. A Tiste Andii?

The man wore a massive two-handed sword strapped to his back. He stood before the Hounds, making no move towards the weapon. All seven had now arrayed themselves before them, but they shifted restlessly, warily eyeing the newcomer.

The Tiste Andii glanced at Paran. 'Whatever you've done to draw the attention of gods, it was unwise,' he said, in Malazan.

'It seems I never learn,' Paran replied.

The Tiste Andii smiled. 'Then we are much alike, mortal.'

Mortal?

The Hounds paced back and forth, growling and snapping the air. The Tiste Andii watched them, then spoke. 'Enough meddling. I see you, Rood,' he said to one Hound, mangy brown, scarred and yellow-eyed. 'Take your kin and leave. Tell Shadowthrone I won't tolerate his interference. My battle with Malaz is my own. Darujhistan is not for him.'

Rood was the only Hound not growling. Its glowing eyes bore steadily into the Tiste Andii's.

'You have heard my warning, Rood.'

Paran watched as the Tiste Andii cocked his head. Slowly he returned his attention to the captain. 'Gear wishes you dead.'

'It's the price I pay for showing mercy.'

The Tiste Andii raised an eyebrow.

Paran shrugged. 'See the scar he carries?'

'That was your mistake, mortal. You must finish what you set out to do.'

'Next time. What happens now?'

'For the moment, mortal, they find the thought of killing me more desirable than that of killing you.'

'And what are their chances?'

471

'The answer to that is evident in how long they've been hesitating, wouldn't you think, mortal?'

The Hounds attacked faster than anything Paran could have imagined. His heart lurched as a flurry of motion closed in around the other man. As the captain stepped back an invisible fist of darkness exploded behind his eyes, a snapping of massive chains, the groan of huge wooden wheels. He squeezed shut his eyes against the staggering pain, then forced them open again to see that the fight was over. The Tiste Andii had his sword in his hands, its black blade slick with blood – blood that boiled and swiftly became ash. Two Hounds lay unmoving, one to either side of him. A wayward wind drew a wintry breath across the scene with a sound like a gasp, shivering the grasses.

Paran saw that one Hound had been nearly decapitated, while the other had been sliced across its broad chest – it did not look like a killing wound, but the creature's eyes, one blue the other yellow, stared sightlessly skyward.

Rood yelped and the others backed away.

Paran tasted blood in his mouth. He spat, then raised a hand to find blood trickling from his ears. The pain in his head was ebbing. He looked up just as the Tiste Andii's head came round to face him. Seeing death in the man's eyes, Paran stepped back and half raised his sword, though the effort took all his strength. He watched, uncomprehending, as the Tiste Andii shook his head. 'For a moment I thought . . . No, I see nothing now . . .'

Paran blinked stinging tears from his eyes, then wiped his cheeks. He started on seeing that the stain of those tears on his forearm was pink. 'You just killed two Hounds of Shadow.'

'The others withdrew.'

'Who are you?'

The Tiste Andii did not answer, his attention once more on the Hounds.

472

Behind them a cloud of shadow was forming in the air, deepening and thickening in its centre. A moment later it dissipated, and a black, shrouded, translucent figure stood in its place, hands tucked into its sleeves. Shadows commanded whatever face lay hidden beneath the hood.

The Tiste Andii lowered his sword's point to the ground. 'They were warned, Shadowthrone. I want one thing understood. You may prove my match here, especially if your Rope is about. But I promise you, it will be messy, and there are those who will avenge me. Your existence, Shadowthrone, could become uncomfortable. Now, I've yet to lose my temper. Withdraw your Realm's influence from the proceedings, and I will leave it at that.'

'I am not involved,' Shadowthrone said quietly. 'My Hounds found the quarry I sought. The hunt is over.' The god's head tilted to observe the two dead creatures. 'Over for all time, for Doan and Ganrod.' Shadowthrone looked up. 'There is no release for them?'

'None. Nor for any who would pursue vengeance.'

A sigh issued from the hooded darkness of the god's face. 'Ah, well. As I said, I am not involved. However, the Rope is.'

'Recall him,' the Tiste Andii commanded. 'Now.'

'He will be severely displeased, Anomander Rake. His plans extend far beyond Darujhistan, seeking to reach the Malazan throne itself.'

Anomander Rake . . . Paran recalled Tattersail's convictions after scrying her Deck of Dragons. *The Knight of High House Dark, the Son of Darkness, the lord with the black sword and its deadly chains. Ruler of Moon's Spawn, or so she thought. She saw this coming. This very moment, the clash between Shadow and Dark, the blood spilled* . . .

'I fight my own battles,' Rake growled. 'And I'd rather deal with Laseen on the Malazan throne than with a servant of Shadow. Recall him.'

473

'One last point,' Shadowthrone said, a giggle escaping him, 'I am not responsible for whatever actions the Rope might take against you.'

A smile entered Rake's tone. 'Convince him of the wise course, Shadowthrone. I have no patience for your games. If I am pushed, by either you, your Hounds, or by the Rope, I'll make no distinction. I will assail the Shadow Realm, and you are invited to try to stop me.'

'You lack all subtlety,' the god said, sighing. 'Very well.' He paused and shadows swirled around him. 'He has been recalled. Forcibly extracted, as it were. The field is yours once again, Anomander Rake. The Malazan Empire is all yours, as is Oponn,' Shadowthrone added.

'Oponn?' Rake's head turned slowly, and the captain once again looked into eyes of deep, cold blue. Paran's spirits sank. The Tiste Andii's gaze fell to the sword, then again to Shadowthrone. 'Begone,' Rake said. 'The matter is ended.'

Shadowthrone dipped his head. 'For now.' The god raised his hands and shadows gathered around him. The surviving Hounds closed in, leaving their dead kin where they lay. The shadows thickened, became opaque, entirely hiding those within. When they dispersed, the lord and his Hounds were gone.

Paran eyed the Tiste Andii who now faced him. After a moment the captain shrugged.

Rake's brows rose. 'That's it?' he asked. 'That's the extent of your comments? Do I speak with Oponn directly? I thought I sensed a presence before, but when I looked more carefully . . . nothing.' Rake shifted grip on his sword, the point rising. 'Do you hide within, Oponn?'

'Not as far as I'm aware,' Paran replied. 'Apparently Oponn saved my life or, rather, brought me back to life. I've no idea why, but I've been told that I've become Oponn's tool.'

'You are journeying to Darujhistan?'

Paran nodded.

'May I approach?' Rake asked, sheathing his sword.

'Why not?'

The Tiste Andii strode up to him and laid a hand against his chest. Paran felt nothing untoward. Rake stepped back. 'Oponn may have been within you in the past, but it seems the Twins have hastily withdrawn. I see their signs, but no god controls you now, mortal.' He hesitated. 'Their treatment of you was ... unkind. If Caladan Brood was here he could heal that ... You're no longer Oponn's tool.' The Tiste's eyes remained blue, but they'd lightened to the colour of the sky. 'But your sword is.'

There was a squawk nearby and both turned to see a Great Raven alight on one of the Hound's bodies. It plucked out an eye and gobbled it down. Paran fought back a wave of nausea. The huge battered bird hopped towards them.

'This man's sword, Master,' the raven said, 'is not Oponn's only tool, I'm afraid.'

Paran shook his head, his only surprise the realization that nothing surprised him any more. He sheathed his sword.

'Speak on, Crone,' Rake commanded.

The raven cocked its head at Paran. 'Here, Master?'

Rake frowned. 'Perhaps not.' He faced the captain again. 'Hold on to that weapon until your luck turns. When that happens, and if you're still alive, break it or give it to your worst enemy.' A grin crossed his features. 'Thus far, it seems your luck holds.'

Paran hesitated. 'I'm free to go?'

Lord Anomander Rake nodded.

The captain looked around, then strode off in search of the surviving horses.

Minutes later, the shock came to Paran, driving him to his knees. Toc was gone. He'd dragged the man with him in his relentless, mindless pursuit across the plain. He looked up, eyes unseeing. He'd called Hairlock his enemy. He'd proclaimed Lorn's death his final goal. As if these two things would answer the anguish within him, would heal the pain of loss. *But the demon is within me.*

Oponn had been unkind . . . What had Rake meant? *Have any of these thoughts been my own? Look at me – my every move seems a desperate search for someone to blame, always someone else. I've made being a tool of a god an excuse, a justification for not thinking, for simply reacting. And others have died for it.*

Rake had also said, 'Finish what you start.' He would have to deal with his own demons later. There could be no turning back. But it had been wrong to think that what he planned would end the pain within him. Adding Lorn's blood to his stained hands would not achieve what he sought.

Paran rose, collected the reins of the surviving horses. He led the beasts back to the scene of the fight. The Tiste Andii had vanished, but the Hounds remained, motionless dark humps in the yellow grass. He dropped the reins and approached one. The slice across its chest still leaked blood. Crouching, Paran reached out, ran his fingers along the animal's hide. *See what the desire for murder gets you? Hood's Breath, but you were a beautiful beast.* His fingertips brushed blood. The captain recoiled at the contact, but it was too late. Something rippled up his arm, swept through him. He fell back into darkness, the sound of chains rattling taut.

Paran found himself walking and he was not alone. Through the gloom he could make out figures on all sides, each shackled with long iron chains, leaning forward as if pulling at an immense weight. The ground underfoot was barren, lifeless. Overhead there was nothing but darkness. Beneath the constant creak of the chains was a heavier sound that Paran could feel through the soles of his boots. Alone unchained, he fell back towards the source of that sound, passing chained figures, many of them not human. A shape appeared, hulking,

476

pitching. A wagon, impossibly huge, its wooden wheels taller than a man. Driven by an insatiable desire to discover what it carried, Paran moved closer.

A chain ripped across his chest, throwing him from his feet. An ear-piercing howl sounded directly above him. Claws gouged his left arm, pinning it to the ground. A chain rippled under his back. He struggled as a cold wet nose and savage teeth pushed under his chin. The jaws opened, slipped around his neck, then tightened.

Paran lay perfectly still, waiting for the fatal clenching of those jaws. Instead, they pulled away. He found himself staring up into the Hound's eyes, one blue, one brown. A massive collar of iron circled its neck. The beast lunged away. The chain under him snapped taut, flinging Paran into the air. He felt more than heard the wagon groan sideways, even as he landed sprawling into the path of one of the wooden wheels.

A hand grasped the collar of his cloak and dragged him clear. The captain scrambled to his feet.

A voice beside him spoke. 'Any man who has earned mercy from Hounds and walks here unchained is a man worth talking to. Walk with me.'

The shadow of a cowl hid the stranger's features. The man was big, dressed in rags. After releasing Paran he resumed straining on his chain. 'Never before,' he grunted, 'has this prison been so tested.' He hissed as the wagon lurched yet again to the Hounds' frantic attempts to escape. 'I fear this will overturn.'

'And if it does?'

The face swung to him briefly and in the darkness Paran saw the flash of teeth. 'The pulling will get harder.'

'Where are we?'

'The Warren within the Sword. Did not Dragnipur take your life, too?'

'If it had, would I not be chained as well?'

477

'True enough. What then are you doing here?'

'I don't know,' Paran admitted. 'I saw the Hounds killed by Rake's sword. Then I touched the blood of one of the slain beasts.'

'That explains their confusion. They thought you one of their own ... at first. You were wise to submit to that Hound's challenge.'

'Too frightened to move, you mean.'

The stranger laughed. 'Even so.'

'What is your name?'

'Names are meaningless. Rake killed me. Long ago. That is enough.'

Paran fell silent. *Eternity, chained here, forever pulling. And I ask for the man's name. Would any apology suffice?*

The wagon bucked savagely, earth ripped from under its wheels. Figures fell, wailing. The Hounds howled their fury.

'Gethol's Breath,' the stranger gasped. 'Will they never cease?'

'I don't think they will,' Paran said. 'Can those chains be broken?'

'No. None have managed it yet, that is, and there are dragons among us. But these Hounds ...' He sighed. 'It is astonishing, but already I long for the peace their arrival has shattered.'

'Perhaps I can help.'

The stranger barked a laugh. 'By all means, try.'

Paran moved away, heading towards the Hounds. He had no plan in mind. *But I alone am unchained.* The thought stopped him and he smiled. *Unchained. No one's tool.* He continued on, wondering. He passed figures straining step by step, some silent, some muttering in madness. None raised its head to glance as he passed. The sound of bestial gasping reached him.

'Hounds!' Para called. 'I would help!'

After a time, they appeared from the gloom. Blood sheathed

478

their shoulders and chests, the flesh torn and mangled by the collars. The Hounds trembled, muscles jumping along their flanks. Their eyes, level with Paran's own, met his with such numbed, helpless misery that his heart lurched. He reached out to the odd-eyed one. 'I would examine your collars, your chains, seeking a flaw.'

The beast walked alongside him – they were ever moving forward, the wagon unceasing in its roll. Paran bent close, running his hands on the collar, seeking a join. There was none. Where the chain attached, the link and the collar seemed of one solid piece. Though he knew little of smithing, he believed this attachment would prove the weakest element and should already show signs of strain. But his fingertips told him otherwise. The iron was not even scratched.

Paran ran his hand along the chain, leaving the Hound's side. He paused noticing the other beast watching his every move, then continued on. From the animal to the wagon, over seventy armspans of length, he ran his hands from link to link, seeking a change in the feel of the iron, seeking heat, gouges. *Nothing.* He arrived alongside the wagon. The wheel he walked behind was solid wood, a span in width, nicked and gouged but otherwise featureless. The wall of the bed was twenty or more feet high. The slatted sideboards of withered, bone-grey wood showed spaces a finger's width between. Paran flinched back on seeing skeletal fingers crowding the cracks, wriggling helplessly.

The wagon's frame beneath the sideboards drew his attention. Here the wood was black, glistening with pitch. Chain-ends entered it, countless in number, sinking seamlessly into the wood. Under his touch the frame seemed solid, yet it was as if the chain links passed through it – whatever held them, then, was beyond the wagon's frame. Paran drew a deep breath of the cool, stale air, then ducked under the bed.

The frame's beam was a dozen spans thick, condensation

dripping down from its pitched underside in endless rain. At the inside edge Paran found once again the chains, continuing on further under the wagon. Grasping one, he followed it inward. The links grew colder as did the air around him. Before long he was forced to release the chain, his hands burned by the cold. The rain from the underside of the wagon came down as slivers of ice. Two paces ahead, the chains converged, swallowed by a suspended pool of absolute darkness. Cold poured from it in pulsing waves. Paran could get no closer.

He hissed in frustration as he scrambled along opposite the dark hole, wondering what to do next. Even if he managed to break a chain, he had no idea which ones belonged to the Hounds. As for the others ... Anomander Rake seemed a creature of clear – if cold – justice. To break a chain could unleash ancient horrors upon the realms of the living. Even the stranger he'd spoken with could once have been a Tyrant, a horrible dominator.

Paran unsheathed Chance. As the blade leaped free of the scabbard it bucked wildly in his hands. The captain grinned even as tremors of terror reached through his hands from the sword. 'Oponn! Dear Twins, I call on you! *Now!*'

The air groaned. Paran stumbled over someone, who loosed a stream of curses. Sheathing his sword, he reached down, hand closing on brocaded cloth. He pulled the god to his feet. 'Why you?' Paran demanded. 'I wanted your sister.'

'Madness, mortal!' the male Twin snapped. 'To call me here! So close to the Queen of Darkness – *here, within a god-slaying sword!*'

Paran shook him. Filled with a mindless, bestial rage, the captain *shook* the god. He heard the Hounds howl, and fought back a sudden desire to join his voice to their cries.

The Twin, terror in his bright eyes, clawed at Paran. 'What – what are you doing?'

Paran stopped, his attention drawn to two chains that had gone slack. 'They're coming.'

The wagon seemed to leap upward, rocked as it had never been before. The thunder of the impact filled the air, wood and ice cascading down.

'They have your scent, Twin.'

The god shrieked, battered his fists into Paran's face, scratching, kicking, but the captain held on. 'Not the luck that pulls.' He spat blood. 'The luck . . . that pushes—'

The wagon was hammered again, its wheels bucking into the air to come down with a splintering, echoing concussion. Paran had no time to wonder at the savage strength that coursed through him, a strength sufficient to hold down a god gripped in panic. He simply held on.

'Please!' the Twin begged. 'Anything! Just ask it! Anything within my powers.'

'The Hounds' chains,' Paran said. 'Break them.'

'I – I cannot!'

The wagon shuddered sickeningly, distant wood splintering. Paran dragged the Twin a pace as it rolled forward again. 'Think of a way,' he said. 'Or the Hounds will have you.'

'I – I cannot be sure, Paran.'

'What? You can't be sure of what?'

The Twin gestured towards the blackness. 'In there. The chains are held in place within it – within the Warren of Darkness, within Kurald Galain. Should they enter . . . I do not know – I cannot be certain, but the chains may disappear.'

'How can they enter?'

'They could be leaving one nightmare only to enter another.'

'It cannot be worse, Twin. I asked you, how?'

'Bait.'

'What?'

The Twin smiled shakily. 'As you said, they're coming. But,

481

Paran, you must release me. By all means, hold me before the portal, but please, at the last moment . . .'

'I release my hold on you.'

The god nodded.

'Very well.'

The Hounds struck the wagon again, and this time they broke through. Clutching the Twin, Paran spun round to see the beasts charging out of the gloom. His captive shrieked.

The Hounds leaped.

Paran released the god, dropping flat to the ground as the Hounds passed through the air above. The Twin vanished. The Hounds flashed past, disappeared into the portal in silence, and were gone.

Paran rolled to his feet, even as darkness reached out for him, not with the cold of oblivion but with a breath like warm, sighing wind.

He opened his eyes to find himself on his hands and knees on the plain's yellowed grass, beside a flattened, blood-smeared patch where the body of a Hound had once lain. Insects buzzed close by. His head aching, Paran climbed to his feet. The other Hound's body was gone as well. What had he done? And why? Of all the things that the Twin could have offered him . . . *Tattersail . . . Toc the Younger . . .* Then again, to pluck a soul back through Hood's Gate was not likely within Oponn's power to achieve. Had he freed the Hounds? He realized he would probably never know.

He staggered over to the horses. At least, for a short time there, he had been unchained. He had been free, and what he had done he had done by his own choice. *My own choice.*

He looked to the south. *Darujhistan and the Adjunct await me. Finish what you started, Paran. Finish it once and for all.*

'Damn inconvenient,' Coll growled as Crokus completed tying the bandage. 'She was good,' he added. 'She knew exactly what to do. I'd say she'd been trained. Sort of fits, since she was dressed like a mercenary.'

'I still don't understand,' Crokus said, sitting back on his haunches. He glanced at Murillio and Kruppe. Both remained unconscious. 'Why did she attack us? And why didn't she kill me?'

Coll did not reply. He sat glaring at his horse, which stood a dozen feet away, quietly cropping grass. He'd already voiced a dozen foul curses at the beast, and Crokus suspected that their relationship had been, as Kruppe would put it, irretrievably compromised.

'What's this?' Coll grunted.

Crokus realized that the man was looking past the horse, a frown deepening the lines of his forehead.

The boy turned, then let out a wild shout, springing backwards and snatching at his daggers. His boot caught a stone and he sprawled. He jumped to his feet, one blade freed and in his hand. 'It's her!' he yelled. 'The woman from the bar! She's a killer, Coll.'

'Easy, lad,' Coll said. 'She looks anything but dangerous, despite that sword on her hip. Hell,' he added, pushing himself straighter, 'if anything, she looks completely lost.'

Crokus stared at the woman, who stood at the summit's edge. 'Hood's Breath,' he muttered. Coll was right. He'd never seen anyone look so bewildered, so utterly at a loss. She was looking at them, tensed as if ready to flee. All the poise, the deadly confidence she'd possessed in the Phoenix Inn was gone, as if it had never been. Crokus sheathed his dagger.

'So,' he asked, 'what do we do now, Coll?'

'The wounded man shrugged. 'Ease the girl's mind, I guess. From the looks of it, she needs some help.'

'But she killed Chert,' Crokus stated. 'I saw the blood on her knife.'

Coll squinted at the girl. 'I don't doubt you, boy, but

this girl doesn't look capable of killing anyone.'

'You think I can't see that?' Crokus said. 'I'm just telling you what I saw. I know it doesn't make any sense!'

Coll sighed. 'Anyway, she still needs our help. So go and get her, Crokus.'

The boy threw up his hands. 'How do I do that?'

'Damned if I know,' Coll replied, grinning. 'Try flirting.'

Crokus threw the man a disgusted look, then he walked cautiously towards the girl. She tensed and backed a step. 'Careful!' Crokus cried, pointing at the summit's crest behind her.

The girl saw that she stood at the very edge of a steep slope. Oddly enough, this seemed to relax her. She moved a few steps closer to Crokus, her wide eyes searching his.

'That's right,' Crokus murmured. 'Everything's fine. Do you understand?' He pointed at his mouth and made talking motions.

Coll groaned.

The girl surprised them both by replying in Daru, 'I understand you,' she said haltingly. 'More now. You're not Malazan, you're not speaking Malazan. But I understand you.' She frowned. 'How?'

'Malazan, huh?' Coll said. 'Where are you from, girl?'

She thought for a moment. 'Itko Kan,' she said.

'What the hell?' Coll laughed. 'What storm blew you here?'

Realization flooded her eyes. 'Where's my father? What happened to the nets? I bought the twine, and there was that Seer – Riggalai the Seer, the wax-witch. I remember her – she died!' The girl fell to her knees. 'She died. And then—'

Coll's expression was severe, thoughtful. 'And then?'

'I don't remember,' the girl whispered, looking down at her hands. 'I don't remember anything more.' She began to cry.

'Gedderone's thousand teats,' Coll cursed quietly, waving Crokus to his side. 'Listen carefully, lad. Don't wait for us. Take

484

this girl to your uncle. Take her to Mammot, and quickly.'

Crokus scowled. 'Why? I can't just leave you here, Coll. Who knows when Murillio and Kruppe will come around? What if that mercenary comes back?'

'What if she does?' Coll asked pointedly.

Crokus flushed and looked away.

'Murillio's a tough bastard, despite the perfume,' Coll said. 'He'll be up and dancing in no time. Take the girl to your uncle, lad. Do as I say.'

'You still haven't told me why,' Crokus said.

'It's a hunch, no more.' Coll reached up and gripped the boy's shoulder. 'This girl's been possessed. I think. Someone, something, brought her here, to Darujhistan, and on to our trail. The truth is somewhere in her head, Crokus, and it could be vital. Your uncle knows the right people, they can help her, lad. Now, saddle up my horse. I'll wait here for our friends to wake. Hell, I can't walk anyway. I shouldn't move for at least a couple of days. Kruppe and Murillio will handle things here. Go!'

Crokus eyed the weeping girl. Then he said. 'All right, Coll. We'll go back, me and her.'

'Good,' Coll grunted. 'Now, lay me out a bedroll and some food. Then ride on out of here, and if that damn horse of mine has a heart attack outside the city gates, even better. Hop to it, lad.'

CHAPTER SIXTEEN

Dessembrae knows the sorrows
in our souls.
He walks at the side of each mortal
a vessel of regret on the fires
of vengeance.
Dessembrae knows the sorrows
and would now share them with us all.

The Lord of Tragedy
Holy Book prayer
(Canon of Kassal)

The puncture wound in Lorn's left shoulder was not deep. Without magical aid, however, the risk of infection was a cause for concern. She returned to the camp to find Tool still positioned where he had been since dawn.

Ignoring the Imass, the Adjunct found her collection of herbs in her saddle bag. She sat down and leaned back against the saddle, then set to treating the wound.

It had been a foolish, unnecessary attack. Too many things had happened recently, too many ideas, too much of the woman Lorn interfering with her functions and duties as

Adjunct to the Empress. She was making mistakes that she would not have made a year ago.

Tool had given her more to think about than she could handle. The words the Imass had thrown at her feet, as if in afterthought, had reached into and grasped something deep within her and now would not let go. Emotions seeped into the Adjunct, clouding the world around her. She'd abandoned sorrow long ago, along with regret. Compassion was anathema to the Adjunct. Yet now all these feelings swept through her in tides pulling her every which way. She found herself clinging to the title of Adjunct, and what it meant, as if it was a lifeline to sanity, to stability and control.

She completed cleaning the wound as best she could, then prepared a poultice. *Control.* The word rebounded in her thoughts, clipped, hard and sure. What was the heart of Empire, if not control? What shaped Empress Laseen's every act, her every thought? And what had been at the heart of the very first Empire – the great wars that shaped the T'lan Imass to this day?

She sighed and looked down at the dirt beneath her. But that was no more than we all sought, she told herself. From a young girl bringing twine home to her father, to the immortal power that had seized her for its own use. *Through the gamut of life we struggled for control, for a means to fashion the world around us, an eternal, hopeless hunt for the privilege of being able to predict the shape of our lives.*

The Imass, and his three-hundred-thousand-year-old words, had given to Lorn a sense of futility. And it worked on her, it threatened to overwhelm her.

She'd given the boy his life, surprising both him and herself. Lorn smiled ruefully. Prediction had become a privilege now lost to her. Never mind the outside world, she could not even guess her own actions, or the course of her thoughts.

Was this the true nature of emotion? she wondered. The

great defier of logic, of control – the whims of being human. What lay ahead?

'Adjunct.'

Startled, Lorn looked up to see Tool standing over her. Frost covered the warrior, steaming in the heat.

'You have been wounded.'

'A skirmish,' she said gruffly, almost embarrassed. 'It's over now.' She pressed the poultice against the wound then wrapped cloth around her shoulder. It was an awkward effort, since she could use only one hand.

Tool knelt beside her. 'I will assist you, Adjunct.'

Surprised, Lorn studied the warrior's death's face. But his next words wiped out any thought of the Imass revealing compassion.

'We have little time, Adjunct. The opening awaits us.'

An expressionless mask settled over her face. She jerked a nod as Tool finished, his withered, shredded hands – the nails blunt, polished brown and curved – deftly tying a knot with the strips of cloth. 'Help me to my feet,' she commanded.

The marker had been shattered, she saw, as the Imass guided her forward. Apart from this, however, all looked unchanged. 'Where is this opening?' she asked.

Tool halted before the broken stones. 'I will lead, Adjunct. Follow closely behind me. When we are within the tomb, unsheath your sword. The deadening effect will be minimal, yet it will slow the Jaghut's return to consciousness. Enough for us to complete our efforts.'

Lorn drew a deep breath. She shrugged off her doubts. There was no turning back now. Had there ever been such a chance? The question, she realized, was a moot one: the course had been chosen for her. 'Very well,' she said. 'Lead on, Tool.'

The Imass spread out his arms to the sides. The hillside before them blurred, as if a curtain of wind-blown sand rose before it. A churning wind roiled through this strange mist. Tool stepped forward.

Following, Lorn at first recoiled at the stench that wafted into her, a stench of air poisoned by centuries of pulsing sorcery, countless wards dispersed by Tool's Tellann powers. She pushed ahead, her eyes fixing on the Imass's broad, tattered back.

They entered the hillside. A rough corridor, leading into darkness, appeared before them. Frost limned the stacked boulders forming the walls and ceiling. As they went further, the air grew bitter cold, stripped of scents, and thick green and white ropes of ice tracked the walls. The floor, which had been frozen, packed earth, became slabs of stone, slick with ice.

Numbness seeped into Lorn's extremities and her face. She saw her breath curl in a white stream, drawn inward to the darkness beyond. The corridor narrowed and she saw strange symbols painted on and within the ice streaking the walls, dull red ochre in colour. These markings brushed something deep inside her – she almost recognized them, but as soon as she concentrated on doing so, the sensation of familiarity vanished.

Tool spoke. 'My people have visited here before,' he said, pausing to look at the Adjunct over one shoulder. 'They added their own wards to those of the Jaghut who imprisoned this Tyrant.'

Lorn was irritated. 'What of it?'

The Imass stared at her in silence, then replied, dully, 'Adjunct, I believe I know the name of this Jaghut Tyrant. I am now beset by doubts. It should not be freed. Yet, like you, I am compelled.'

Lorn's breath caught.

'Adjunct,' Tool continued, 'I acknowledge the ambivalence you have been feeling. I share it. When this is done, I shall leave.'

489

She was confused. 'Leave?'

Tool nodded. 'Within this tomb, and with what we will do, my vows are ended. They will bind me no longer. Such is the residual power of this sleeping Jaghut. And for that, I am thankful.'

'Why are you telling me this?'

'Adjunct, you are welcome to accompany me.'

Lorn opened her mouth, but could think of no immediate reply so shut it again.

'I ask that you consider my offer, Adjunct. I shall journey in search of an answer, and I shall find it.'

Answer? To what? she wanted to ask. Yet something stopped her, a surge of fear that said to her: You don't want to know. Remain ignorant in this. 'Let's get on with it,' she grated.

Tool resumed his march into the darkness.

After a minute Lorn asked, 'How much time is this going to take?'

'Time?' There was amusement in his voice. 'Within this barrow, Adjunct, time does not exist. The Jaghut who imprisoned their kin brought an age of ice to this land, the barrow's final seal. Adjunct, a half-league of ice stands over this burial chamber – still. We have come to a time and place before the faltering of the Jaghut ice, before the coming of the great inland sea known to the Imass as Jhagra Til, before the passing of countless ages—'

'And when we return?' Lorn interrupted. 'How much time will have passed?'

'I cannot say, Adjunct.' The Imass paused and turned back to her, his eye sockets glimmering with a sourceless light. 'I have never done this before.'

Despite the hardened leather armour, the feel of a woman pressing against Crokus's back had brought to his face more sweat than the afternoon heat could account for. Yet it was a mix of feelings that had his heart thumping against his chest. On the one hand was the bald fact that here was a girl of nearly his age, and an attractive one at that, with surprisingly strong arms wrapped around his waist and her warm, moist breath on his neck. On the other hand, this woman had murdered a man, and the only reason he could think of her arriving on the scene back there in the hills was that she'd been planning to kill him, too. So he found himself too tense to enjoy sharing the saddle with her.

They had said little to each other since leaving Coll. In another day, Crokus knew, Darujhistan's walls would come into view. He wondered if she'd remember it. And then a voice spoke in his head that sounded like Coll's: *'Why don't you ask the girl, idiot?'* Crokus scowled.

She spoke first. 'Is Itko Kan far from here?'

He thought about laughing, but something – an instinct – stopped him. Tread softly, he told himself. 'I've never heard of such a place,' he said. 'It's in the Malazan Empire?'

'Yes. We aren't in the Empire?'

Crokus growled, 'Not yet.' Then his shoulders slumped. 'We're on a continent called Genabackis. The Malazans came from the seas both east and west. They now control all the Free Cities to the north, as well as the Nathilog Confederacy.'

'Oh,' the girl replied weakly. 'You're at war with the Empire, then.'

'More or less, though you'd never know it as far as Darujhistan is concerned.'

'Is that the name of the town you live in?'

'Town? Darujhistan's a city. It's the biggest, richest city in all the land.'

There was awe and excitement in her reply. 'A city. I've never been to a city. Your name is Crokus, isn't it?'

'How did you know that?'

'That's what your soldier friend called you.'

491

'Oh, of course.' Why did the fact that she'd known his name send his heart lurching?

'Aren't you going to ask me my name?' the woman asked quietly.

'You can remember it?'

'No,' she admitted. 'That's strange, isn't it?'

He heard pathos in that reply, and something melted inside – making him even angrier. 'Well, I can't very well help you in that, can I?'

The woman seemed to withdraw behind him, and her arms loosened their grip. 'No.'

Abruptly his anger fell away. Crokus was ready to scream at the chaos in his head. Instead he shifted in the saddle, forcing her to clutch him tightly. Ah, he smirked, that's better. Then his eyes widened. *What am I saying?*

'Crokus?'

'What?'

'Give me a Darujhistan name. Pick one. Pick your favourite.'

'Challice,' he responded immediately. 'No, wait! You can't be Challice. I already know a Challice. You've got to be someone else.'

'Is she your girlfriend?'

'No!' he snapped. He pulled at the reins and they stopped. Crokus clawed at his hair, then threw a leg over and dropped to the ground. He pulled the reins over the horse's head. 'I want to walk,' he said.

'Yes,' she said. 'I would like to, too.'

'Well, maybe I want to run!'

She stepped round to face him, her expression troubled. 'Run? From me, Crokus?'

He saw things falling into ruins behind her eyes – what were those things? He felt a desperate need to know, but asking straight out was clearly impossible. Why it was impossible he

492

couldn't say. It just was. He looked down at the ground and kicked at a rock. 'No,' he mumbled. 'I didn't mean that. Sorry.'

Her eyes widened. 'That was my name!' she gasped. 'That was my name, Crokus – you just said my name!'

'What?' He frowned. 'Sorry?'

'Yes!' She looked away. 'Only, it wasn't always my name. I don't think. No. It wasn't the name my father gave me.'

'Can you remember that one?'

She shook her head and ran a hand through her long, dark hair.

Crokus started walking, and the girl fell into step beside him. The road wound down through the low hills. In an hour they'd reach the Catlin Bridge. The panic that had filled him was subsiding, perhaps having burned itself out. He felt relaxed, and that surprised him, since he couldn't recall the last time he'd felt relaxed in a female's company.

They walked in silence for a time. Ahead, the sun sank down in a golden blaze, shimmering along a blue and green line on the horizon beyond the hills. Crokus pointed to the glistening line. 'That's Lake Azur. Darujhistan lies on its south shore.'

'Haven't you thought of a name for me yet?' the woman asked.

'The only name that comes to mind,' Crokus said sheepishly, 'is my matron's.'

The girl glanced at him. 'Your mother's?'

Crokus laughed. 'No, not that kind of matron. I meant the Lady of Thieves, Apsalar. Only, it's not good to take that kind of name, since she's a goddess. What about Salar?'

Her nose wrinkled. 'No, I like Apsalar. Make it Apsalar.'

'But I just said—'

'That's the name I want,' the girl insisted, her face darkening.

Uh-oh, Crokus thought. Better not press this one. 'All right.' He sighed.

493

'So you're a thief.'

'What's wrong with that?'

Apsalar grinned. 'Given my new name, nothing. Nothing at all, Crokus. When do we camp?'

He blanched. He hadn't thought about that. 'Maybe we should just push on,' he said warily, not meeting her eyes.

'I'm tired. Why don't we camp at this Catlin Bridge?'

'Well, I've only got the one bedroll. You can have it. I'll stand watch.'

'All night? What's there to watch out for?'

Crokus rounded on her. 'Why all these questions?' he demanded hotly. 'It's dangerous out here! Didn't you see Coll's wound? And how do we know the garrison's still there?'

'What garrison?'

Crokus cursed himself. He averted his gaze. 'The garrison on the other side of the bridge,' he said. 'But it's a long bridge—'

'Oh, come on, Crokus!' Apsalar laughed and drove her elbow into his ribs. 'We'll share the bedroll. I don't mind, so long as you keep your hands to yourself.'

Rubbing his ribs, Crokus could only stare at her.

Cursing, Kruppe glared over his shoulder at Murillio. 'Damnation! Can't you urge that beast any faster?'

The mule was living up to its reputation, refusing anything but a plodding walk. Murillio grinned sheepishly. 'What's the big hurry, Kruppe? The boy can take care of himself.'

'It was Master Baruk's explicit command that we guard him, and guard him we must!'

Murillio's eyes narrowed. 'So you keep saying,' he muttered. 'Is this some favour on Mammot's behalf? Has the boy's uncle got all worried all of a sudden? Why's Baruk so interested in Crokus? You convey the alchemist's orders, Kruppe, but you don't explain them.'

Kruppe reined in his mount. 'Oh, very well,' he said.

494

'Mutiny in the ranks forces Kruppe's sly hand. Oponn has chosen Crokus, for whatever purposes the devious deity may devise. Baruk would have us keep an eye on the lad and, more, prevent any other powers from finding him.'

Murillio rubbed the bruise on his forehead and winced. 'Damn you.' He sighed. 'You should've explained all this from the start, Kruppe. Does Rallick know?'

'Of course not,' Kruppe replied tartly. 'He's too busy, after all, unable to extricate himself from his various responsibilities. Hence,' Kruppe's expression turned crafty, 'the assassin's absence on this journey. But why, pray tell, is Kruppe informing Murillio of such things? Clearly, Murillio knows more of Rallick's doings than poor, ignorant Kruppe.'

Murillio's look was blank. 'What do you mean?'

Kruppe sniggered, then kicked his mule into motion once again.

Murillio followed.

'And as for our present mission,' Kruppe continued blithely, 'what seems a vast failure, particularly on Coll's part, is in truth an astonishing success. Master Baruk must be made aware of the nefarious activities afoot in the Gadrobi Hills.'

'Success? What are you talking about?'

Kruppe waved a hand. 'Dear man, though I was conscious but a moment during the fracas, clear it was that this woman warrior possessed an Otataral sword. Which means, as any child might guess, she's Malazan.'

Murillio hissed slowly between his teeth. 'And we left Coll back there? Are you insane, Kruppe?'

'He'll mend enough to follow us shortly,' Kruppe said. 'The need for haste overwhelms all other considerations.'

'Except cheap deals with a certain stabler,' Murillio growled. 'So, there's some Malazan in the Gadrobi Hills. What's she up to? And don't try telling me you don't know. If you didn't suspect something we wouldn't be in such a hurry.'

495

'Suspicions, indeed.' Kruppe nodded, his shoulders hunching. 'Recall Crokus uttering that perceptive comment as we left the crossroads? Hunting a rumour, or some such thing?'

'Wait a minute.' Murillio groaned. 'Not that barrow legend again? There's not a—'

Kruppe held up a finger and cut in smoothly, 'What we believe is irrelevant, Murillio. The fact remains that the Malazans are seeking the truth of that rumour. And both Kruppe and Master Baruk suspect, being of equal intelligence, that they might well discover it. Hence this mission, my fluttery friend.' He waggled his brows. 'Otataral in the hands of a swordmaster of the Empire. A T'lan Imass lurking in the vicinity—'

'What?' Murillio exploded, his eyes wide. He made to turn his mule around, but the beast complained and planted its hoofs. He struggled with it, cursing. 'Coll's all cut up and he's got a Malazan killer out there and an Imass! You've lost your mind, Kruppe!'

'But, dear Murillio,' Kruppe crooned, 'Kruppe would have thought you eager, nay, desperate to return to Darujhistan as quickly as possible!'

That stopped the man. He rounded on Kruppe, face darkening. 'Come on,' he gritted, 'out with it, then.'

Kruppe's brows rose. 'Out with what?'

'You've been hinting about something, poking me with it. So if you think you know something about whatever, let's hear it. Otherwise, we turn round right now and head back to Coll.' Seeing Kruppe's eyes dart, Murillio grinned. 'Hah, you thought to distract me, didn't you? Well, it's not going to work.'

Kruppe raised his hands palm up. 'No matter whose brain was responsible for your scheme to return Coll to his rightful title, Kruppe can do naught but eagerly applaud!'

Murillio's jaw dropped. *How in Hood's name did Kruppe . . . ?*

The man continued, 'But all that is inconsequential when

faced with the fact of Crokus, and the grave danger he is presently in. More, if this young girl was indeed possessed, as Coll suspects, the risks are frightening to behold! Was she the only hunter for the lad's frail, unprotected life? What of the thousand gods and demons who would eagerly confound Oponn at the first opportunity? Thus, would Murillio, friend of long standing with Crokus, so callously abandon the child to the fates? Is Murillio a man to succumb to panic, to what-ifs, to a host of imagined nightmares slinking about within the shadows of his overwrought imagination—?'

'All right!' Murillio barked. 'Now hold your tongue and let's ride.'

Kruppe gave a brusque nod at this wise remark.

An hour later, as dusk clambered up the hillsides and ever westward to the dying sun, Murillio started and threw Kruppe a furious glare that was lost in the gloom. 'Damn him,' he whispered, 'I said I wasn't about to let him distract me. So what's the first thing he does? Distract me.'

'Murillio murmurs something?' Kruppe asked.

Murillio massaged his forehead. 'I'm having dizzy spells,' he said. 'Let's find a camp. Crokus and the girl won't make it to the city before tomorrow anyway. I doubt he's in any danger on the road, and we'll find him easily enough before tomorrow's sunset. They should be fine in the daytime – hell, they'll be with Mammot, right?'

'Kruppe admits to his own weariness. Indeed, a camp should be found, and Murillio can construct a small fire, perhaps, and so prepare dinner while Kruppe ponders vital thoughts and such.'

'Fine.' Murillio sighed. 'Just fine.'

It came to Captain Paran a couple days after his encounter with the Tiste Andii and the events within the lord's sword that Rake had not suspected him to be a Malazan soldier. Or

497

he'd be dead. Oversights blessed him, it seemed. His assassin in Pale should have checked twice – and now the Son of Darkness, snatching him from the jaws of the Hounds, had in turn let him walk free. Was there a pattern to this? It had Oponn's flavour, yet Paran didn't doubt Rake's assertion.

Then did his luck indeed lie in his sword? And had these mercies of fortune marked pivotal moments – moments that would come back to haunt those who'd spared him? For his own well-being, he hoped not.

His was no longer the Empire's road. He'd walked that path of blood and treachery for too long. Never again. What lay before him, then, was the singular effort to save the lives of Whiskeyjack and the squad. If he managed that, he would not begrudge his own death as a consequence.

Some things went beyond a single man's life, and maybe justice existed outside the minds of humanity, beyond even the hungry eyes of gods and goddesses, a thing shining and pure and final. Some philosophers he'd read during his schooling in the Malazan capital, Unta, had asserted what seemed to him then an absurd position. Morality was not relative, they claimed, nor even existing solely in the realm of the human condition. No, they proclaimed morality as an imperative of all life, a natural law that was neither the brutal acts of beasts nor the lofty ambitions of humanity, but something other, something unassailable.

Just another hunt for certainty. Paran scowled and stiffened in his saddle, his eyes fixed on the trader track winding before him through low, rounded hills. He recalled discussing this with Adjunct Lorn, at a time when neither had been compelled by the outside world. Just another hunt for certainty, she'd said, in a voice brittle and cynical, putting an end to the discussion as clearly as if she'd driven a knife into the wine-stained table between them.

For such words to have come from a woman no older than

him, Paran suspected then, as he did now, that her particular view had been no more than an easy, lazy mimicry of Empress Laseen's. But Laseen had a right to it and Lorn did not. At least, in Paran's mind. If anyone had a right to world-weary cynicism, it was the Empress of the Malazan Empire.

Truly had the Adjunct made herself Laseen's extension. But at what cost? He'd seen the young woman behind the mask just once – as they'd looked out over a road carpeted with dead soldiers then proceeded to pick their way through them. The pale, frightened girl that was Lorn had shown herself in a single frail moment. He couldn't remember what had triggered the return of the mask – likely it had been something he'd said, something he'd tossed off in his own guise as a hardened soldier.

Paran sighed deeply. *Too many regrets. Lost chances – and with each one passing the less human we all became, and the deeper into the nightmare of power we all sank.*

Was his life irretrievable? He wished he had an answer to that question.

Movement in the south caught his attention, and with it he became aware of a rumbling sound, rising up from the earth around him. He rose in the saddle. A wall of dust curled over the ridge of land directly ahead. He swung his mount westward and nudged it into a trot. Moments later he reined in. The curtains of dust hung in that direction as well. Cursing, he spurred to the crest of a nearby rise. Dust. Dust on all sides. *A storm? No, the thunder is too regular.* He rode down to the plain below and reined in again, wondering what to do. The dust wall rose, cresting the hill he faced. The deep rumbling grew. Paran squinted into the dust. Dark, massive shapes moved there, spreading out to either side, sweeping down on his position. In moments he was surrounded.

Bhederin. He'd heard tales of the huge shaggy creatures, moving across the inner plains in herds half a million strong.

499

On all sides, Paran could see nothing but the humped reddish-brown, dust-caked backs of the beasts. There was nowhere he could lead his horse, no place of safety within sight. Paran leaned back in his saddle and waited.

Something flashed to his left, tawny and low to the ground. The captain half turned, just as something heavy hammered him from the right and clung, dragging him from the saddle. Cursing, Paran thumped heavily in the dust, grappling with wiry limbs, ragged black hair. He drove his knee up, connecting with a solid stomach. His attacker rolled to one side, gasping. Paran scrambled to his feet, found himself facing a youth in tanned hides. The boy sprang to close with the captain once again.

Paran sidestepped and clouted the boy on the side of the head. His attacker sprawled unconscious.

Piercing cries were sounding on all sides. The Bhederin were parting, moving away. Figures emerged, closing on Paran's position. Rhivi. Sworn enemies to the Empire, allied in the north with Caladan Brood and the Crimson Guard.

Two warriors came to the unconscious boy's side; each took an arm and dragged him off.

The herd had come to a stop.

Another warrior approached, striding boldly up to Paran. His dust-streaked face was stitched with dyed threads, black and red, from high on the cheeks down to the jawline then up and around the mouth. A Bhederin hide rode the broad line of his shoulders. Stopping less than an arm's length in front of Paran, the warrior reached out and closed his hand on the grip of Chance. Paran struck away the hand. The Rhivi smiled, stepped back and loosed a high-pitched, ululating cry.

Figures rose on the backs of the surrounding Bhederin, lances balanced in one hand as they crouched on the shaggy backs. The huge animals beneath the warriors ignored them as if they were but tick-birds.

The two Rhivi who had taken the boy away now returned, joining the stitch-faced warrior, who said something to the one on his left. This man moved forward. Before Paran could react, he surged into motion, throwing a leg behind the captain then driving his shoulder into Paran's chest.

The warrior fell on top of him. A knife blade slid against the line of Paran's jaw, sliced through the helmet strap. The iron skullcap was pulled away and fingers snagged a handful of his hair. Dragging the warrior with him, Paran pushed himself upright. He'd had enough. Death was one thing, death without dignity quite another. As the Rhivi's hand twisted, pulling his head up, the captain reached between the warrior's legs and found his own handful. He yanked hard.

The warrior shrieked, releasing Paran's hair. A knife appeared again, flashing at the captain's face. He ducked to one side, his free hand snapping up to grasp the wrist, pushing away the knife. He squeezed once more with his other hand. The Rhivi shrieked again, then Paran let go, twisted round and drove his armoured elbow into the man's face.

Blood spattered like rain in the dust. The warrior reeled back, crumpled to the ground.

A lance haft hammered a glancing blow along Paran's temple. He spun round with the impact. A second lance struck him in the hip, hard as a kick from a horse, numbing his leg. Something pinned his left foot to the ground.

Paran unsheathed Chance. The weapon was almost knocked from his hand with a ringing, pealing sound. He swung it upward and it was struck again. Half blinded with pain, sweat and dust, Paran reared upright, shifting to a two-handed grip and drawing Chance down to a centre guard position. The sword's blade was struck a third time, but he retained his grip.

There was silence. Gasping, blinking, Paran raised his head, looked around.

Rhivi surrounded him, but none moved. Their dark eyes were wide.

Paran flicked his gaze to his weapon, glared back up and around at the warriors, then his eyes returned to Chance. And stayed there.

Three iron lanceheads sprouted from the blade like leaves, each point split and jammed, the hafts shattered and gone, leaving only white wood jutting out from the sockets.

He looked down at his pinned foot. A lance had struck, through his boot, but the wide blade of the head was turned, its flat side pressing against his foot. Splintered wood surrounded him. Paran glanced at his hip, saw no wound. A jagged tear marred the leather of Chance's scabbard.

The Rhivi warrior with the smashed face lay motionless a few feet from where Paran stood. The captain saw that his mount and the packhorses were untouched and had not moved. The other Rhivi had pulled back. The encirclement now divided as a small figure approached.

A girl, perhaps no more than five years old. The warriors moved aside from her as if in awe, or fear, possibly both. She wore antelope skins tied with cord at the waist, and nothing on her feet.

There was something familiar about her, a way of walking, her stance as she stopped before him – something in her heavy-lidded eyes – that made Paran frown uneasily.

The girl stopped to regard him, her small round face slowly coming to mirror Paran's own frown. She raised one hand, as if reaching for him, then dropped it. The captain found he could not pull away his eyes from her. *Child, do I know you?*

As the silence between them lengthened, an old woman came up behind the girl, rested a wrinkled hand on her shoulder. Looking worn, almost exasperated, the old woman studied the captain. The girl beside her said something, the quick lilting language of the Rhivi, surprisingly low-pitched for

502

one so young. The old woman crossed her arms. The girl spoke again, insistently.

The old woman addressed Paran in Daru, 'Five lances claimed you as our enemy.' She paused. 'Five lances were wrong.'

'You've plenty more,' Paran said.

'So we have, and the god favouring your sword has no followers here.'

'So finish it,' Paran growled. 'I'm tired of the game.'

The girl spoke, a tone of command that rang like iron on stone.

The old woman turned in obvious surprise.

The girl continued, her words now evidently explanatory. The old woman listened, then swung her dark, glittering gaze back to the captain. 'You are Malazan, and Malazans have chosen to be the enemies of the Rhivi. Is this choice yours as well? And know this: I will recognize a lie when I hear it.'

'I am Malazan by birth,' Paran said. 'I have no interest in calling the Rhivi my enemy. I would rather have no enemies at all.'

The old woman blinked. 'She offers you words to ease your grief, soldier.'

'Meaning?'

'You are to live.'

Paran did not quite trust this turn of events. 'What words has she for me? I've never seen her before.'

'Nor has she seen you before. Yet you know each other.'

'No, we don't.'

The old woman's eyes hardened. 'Will you hear her words or not? She offers you a gift. Will you throw it back in her face?'

Profoundly uneasy, he said. 'No, I suppose not.'

'The child says you need not grieve. The woman you know has not passed through the Arching Trees of Death. Her journey was beyond the lands you can see, beyond those of the

503

spirit that all mortals sense. And now she has returned. You must be patient, soldier. You will meet again, so this child promises.'

'Which woman?' Paran demanded, his heart pounding.

'The one you thought dead.'

He looked again at the girl. The familiarity returned like a blow to his chest. He staggered back a step. 'Not possible,' he whispered.

The girl withdrew, dust swirling. She vanished.

'Wait!'

Another cry sounded. The herd lurched into motion, closing in, obscuring the Rhivi. In moments all Paran could see were the backs of the giant beasts, shuffling past. He thought to push among them, but knew it would bring him only death.

'Wait!' the captain shouted again, but the sound of hundreds – thousands – of hoofs on the plain drowned his efforts.

Tattersail!

It was fully an hour before the Bhederin herd's tail end appeared. As the last of the beasts strolled past the captain, he looked around. The wind rolled the dust cloud eastward, over the sloping, humped hills.

Paran climbed into the saddle, swung his mount southward once again. The hills of Gadrobi rose before him. *Tattersail, what did you do?* He recalled Toc noting the trail of small prints leading from the scorched pillar that had been all that was left of Bellurdan and Tattersail. *Hood's Breath, did you plan such a thing? And why the Rhivi? Reborn, already a child of five, maybe six – are you even mortal any more, woman? Have you ascended? You've found yourself a people, a strange, primitive people – to what end? And when we next meet, how old will you appear to be then?*

He thought again about the Rhivi. They'd been driving the herd north, a herd big enough to feed . . . *an army on the march.*

Caladan Brood – he's on his way to Pale. That is something I don't think Dujek's prepared for. Old Onearm's in trouble.

He had another two hours of riding before sunset. Beyond the Gadrobi Hills was Lake Azur, and the city of Darujhistan. And within the city, Whiskeyjack and his squad. *And in that squad, a young woman I've been preparing to meet for three years. The god possessing her – is he even my enemy any more?*

The question arrived unbidden, turning his heart cold. *Gods, what a journey this has been, and here I had thought to travel this plain unnoticed. A foolish thought. Scholars and mages write endlessly of fell convergences – it seems I am a walking convergence, a lodestone to draw Ascendants. To their peril, it seems. My sword Chance answered those five lances, despite my treatment of one of the Twins. How to explain that? The truth is, my cause has become my own. Not the Adjunct's, not the Empire's. I said I'd rather have no enemies at all – and the old woman saw those as true words. And so, it seems, they are.*

Endless surprises, Ganoes Paran. Ride on, see what comes.

The track climbed a hillside and the captain spurred his horse up the slope. Reaching the summit, he yanked hard on the reins. The horse snorted indignantly and swung her head round, eyes rolling. But Paran's attention was elsewhere. He leaned back in the saddle and loosened his sword.

A heavily armoured man struggled to his feet beside a small campfire. Beyond him was a hobbled mule. The man tottered, his weight on one leg, and unsheathed a bastard sword, which he then leaned on as he regarded the captain.

Paran nudged his mount forward, scanning the immediate area. It seemed that the warrior was alone. He brought his horse to a halt with thirty feet between them.

The man spoke in Daru. 'I'm in no shape for a fight, but if you want one it's yours.'

Once again Paran found himself thankful for the Adjunct's

insistence that he be thoroughly schooled: his reply was as fluent as this native's. 'No. I've lost the taste for it.' He waited, leaning forward in the saddle, then grinned at the mule. 'Is that beast a War Mule?'

The man barked a laugh. 'I'm sure it thinks it is,' he said, relaxing. 'I've food to spare, traveller, if you're of a mind.'

The captain dismounted and approached. 'My name's Paran,' he said. He sat down by the fire.

The other followed suit, the fire between them. 'Coll,' he grunted, stretching out a bandaged leg. 'You down from the north?'

'Genabaris, initially. Spent some time in Pale, recently.'

Coll's brows rose at that. 'You've the look of a mercenary,' he said, 'though likely an officer. I heard it was pretty bad up there.'

'I arrived a little late,' Paran admitted. 'Saw lots of rubble and lots of dead, so I'm inclined to believe the stories.' He hesitated, then said, 'There was a rumour in Pale that Moon's Spawn is now over Darujhistan.'

Coll grunted, tossing a handful of sticks on to the fire. 'So it is,' he said. He gestured at a battered pot tucked against the coals. 'That's stew, if you're hungry. Help yourself.'

Paran realized he was famished. He accepted Coll's offer gratefully. As he ate, using a wooden spoon the man loaned him, he thought to ask about that leg wound. But then he recalled his Claw training. When you play a soldier, you play it to the hilt. Nobody talks about what's obvious. Something staring you in the eye, you look around it and grumble about the weather. Anything important will come out in its own time. Soldiers have nothing to look forward to, making patience an easy virtue, and sometimes it's not just a virtue, but a contest of indifference. So Paran emptied the pot, while Coll waited in casual silence, poking at the fire and adding the occasional stick from an enormous pile behind him –

where the wood had come from was anybody's guess.

Finally, Paran wiped his mouth with his sleeve and scrubbed the spoon as clean as he could manage without water. He sat back then, and belched.

Coll spoke. 'You heading into Darujhistan, then?'

'I am. And you?'

'Should be able to manage it in another day or so, though I can't say I'm looking forward to riding into the city on the back of a mule.'

Paran looked westward. 'Well,' he said, squinting, 'sun's about down. Mind if I share this camp for the night?'

'By all means.'

The captain rose and attended to his horses. He thought about delaying a day to let this man mend some more, then lending him a horse. If he rode into the city in the company of a local, there'd be advantages – someone to direct him, perhaps even give him a place to stay for a day or two. Not only that, but he might learn something in the meantime. Would another day matter? Possibly, but it looked worth it. He hobbled the Wickan horses near the mule, then carried his saddle back to the fire.

'Been thinking about your problem,' Paran said, as he dropped the saddle and sat with his back against it. 'I'll ride in with you. You can use my pack horse.'

Coll's eyes were alert. 'A generous offer.'

Seeing the man's suspicion, Paran smiled. 'The horses could use the extra day's rest, for one. Second, I've never before been to Darujhistan, so in exchange for my so-called generosity I'd like to plague you with endless questions in the next two days. After that, I get my horse back and you're on your way, and if anyone's come out ahead, it's me.'

'Better warn you now, Paran, I'm not much of a talker.'

'I'll take the risk.'

Coll considered for a time. 'Hell,' he said, 'I'd be mad not to

507

accept, wouldn't I? You don't look the type to stick me in the back. I don't know your real story, Paran. If that's something you want to keep to yourself, that's your business. That won't stop me from asking questions, though. It's up to you whether you lie or not.'

'I think that goes both ways, doesn't it?' Paran responded. 'Well, you want my story straight? Fine, here it is, Coll. I'm a deserter from the Malazan Army, ranked as captain. I also did a lot of work with the Claw, and looking back on it that's where the trouble started. Anyway, it's done.' *Oh, yes, and one more thing: people who get close to me usually end up dead.*

Coll was silent, his eyes glittering in the firelight and fixed on the man opposite him. Then he puffed his cheeks and blew out a loud breath of air. 'Truth as bald as that makes a challenge, don't it?' He stared into the fire, then leaned back on his elbows and lifted his face to the stars now appearing overhead. 'I was once a noble in Darujhistan, the last son of a long-lined, powerful family. I was set for an arranged marriage but I fell in love with another woman – a hungry, ambitious woman, though I was blind to that.' He smiled wryly. 'She was a whore, in fact, only where most whores I've met are pretty down-to-earth, she was as twisted a soul as you could imagine.'

He passed a hand across his eyes. 'Anyway, I refuted my obligations and broke off the arranged marriage. It killed my father, I think, when I married Aystal – that was the whore's name, though she's changed it since.' He laughed harshly at the night sky. 'Didn't take her long. I'm still not sure how she managed the details, how many men she took to bed to buy their influence, or how they did it. All I know is I woke up one day and found myself stripped of title, stripped even of my family name. The estate was hers, the money was hers, it was all hers, and her need for me had ended.'

The flames licked the dry wood between them. Paran said nothing. He sensed that more was to come from the man opposite him, and that Coll was struggling with it.

'But that wasn't the worst betrayal, Paran,' he said at length, meeting the captain's eyes. 'Oh, no. That came when I walked away from it. I could've fought her. I might even have won.' His jaw tautened – the only hint of anguish that escaped his self-control – then he continued, in a flat, empty voice, 'Acquaintances I'd known for decades looked right through me. To everyone I was dead. They chose not to hear me. They just walked past, or didn't even come to the gates of their estates when I called on them. I was dead, Paran, even the city's records claimed it. And so I agreed with them. I walked away. Disappeared. It's one thing to have your friends mourn your passing in your face. But it's another to betray your own life, Paran. But, as you said, it's done.'

The captain looked away, squinting into the darkness. What's this human urge, he wondered, that brings us to such devastation? 'The games of the high born,' he said quietly, 'span the world. I was born a noble, like you, Coll. But in Malaz we'd met our match in the old Emperor. He crushed us at every turn until we cowered like whipped dogs. Cowered for years. But it was only an issue of power, wasn't it?' he said, more to himself than to the man who shared the fire. 'There are no lessons worthy enough for a noble to heed. I look back on my years within that twisted, hungry company – I look back on that life now, Coll, and I see it wasn't a life at all.' He was silent for a time, then a slow smile curved his mouth and his gaze swung to Coll. 'Since I walked away from the Malazan Empire, and severed once and for all the dubious privileges of my noble blood, damn, I've never felt so alive. It was never a life before, only the palest shadow of what I've now found. Is that a truth most of us are too frightened to face?'

Coll grunted. 'I'm not the sharpest man you'll meet, Paran, and your thoughts are running a touch too deep for me. But if I understand you right, you're sitting there looking at a chopped-up old fool of a man and you're telling him he's alive. Right now. As alive as can be. And whatever he betrayed back then, it wasn't life, was it?'

'You tell me, Coll.'

The man grimaced and ran a hand through his thinning hair. 'The thing is, I want it back. I want it all back.'

Paran burst out laughing, and continued to laugh until sharp pains cramped his stomach.

Coll sat watching him, then a low, rumbling chuckle rose from his chest. He reached back, retrieved a handful of sticks and tossed them into the fire, one at a time. 'Well, dammit, Paran,' he said, amused lines crinkling around his eyes, 'you've come out of the blue like a god-sent bolt of lightning. And I appreciate it. I appreciate it more than you'll ever know.'

Paran wiped tears from his eyes. 'Hood's Breath,' he said. 'Just one War Mule talking to another, right?'

'I guess so, Paran. Now, if you'll look in that pack of mine, you'll find a jug of Worrytown wine. Its vintage is about a week.'

The captain rose. 'Meaning?'

'Meaning it's running out of time.'

BOOK SIX

THE CITY
OF
BLUE FIRE

Rumours like tattered flags
wind-snapped and echoing
in the streets below
told the tale of the days upon us . . .
'Twas said an eel had slipped ashore
or not one but a thousand
under a jagged moon that might be dead,
'twas whispered that a claw scraped slow
on the city's cobbles, even as a dragon
was seen sailing high silver and black in the nightsky.
'Twas heard, they say, a demon's death cry
on the rooftops on a night of blood, even
as the master's hundred hands lost
a hundred daggers to the dark,
and 'twas rumoured then, a lady
masked highborn had offered to unbidden guests
a fête to remember . . .

Rumour Born
Fisher (b.?)

CHAPTER SEVENTEEN

Few can see
the dark hand
holding aloft
the splinter, or
the notched chains
fated to be heard
before death's rattle,
but hark the wheel
of minions and victims
who moan the
lord's name
in the dark heart
of Moon's Spawn . . .

Silverfox
Outrider Hurlochel,
6th Army

As Rallick Nom approached the Phoenix Inn from the alleyway, a large, beefy woman stepped out from a shadowed niche and confronted him. He raised an eyebrow. 'You want something, Meese?'

'Never mind what I want.' She grinned invitingly. 'You've known about that for years. Anyway, I come to tell ya something, Nom. So relax.'

He crossed his arms and waited.

Meese glanced back up the alley, then hunched close to the assassin. 'There's someone in the bar. Been asking for ya. By name.'

Startled, Rallick straightened. 'What's he look like?' he asked casually.

'Like a soldier outa uniform,' Meese replied. 'Never seen him around before. So what do ya think, Nom?'

He looked away. 'Nothing. Where's he sitting?'

Meese grinned again. 'At Kruppe's table. Home ground. Now ain't that fine?'

Rallick stepped past the woman and headed towards the inn. As she moved to follow he held out his hand. 'A minute between us, Meese,' he said, without turning. 'Where's Irilta?'

'Inside,' she said, behind him. 'Good luck, Nom.'

'Luck's never free,' Rallick muttered, as he turned the corner and climbed the steps.

He stood still just within the door and surveyed the crowd. A few strangers, not enough to cause him concern, however. His gaze slid across to a man sitting at Kruppe's table. He almost had to take a second look, so nondescript was he. Then Rallick strode straight for him, the crowd parting as he went – something he'd never noticed before. Amused, he held his eyes on the stranger until he was noticed. They locked gazes, though the man made no move other than to take a sip from his tankard then set it down carefully on the table.

Rallick pulled out a chair and dragged it opposite. 'I'm Rallick Nom.'

There was something solid about this person, a kind of assurance that was calming. Rallick felt himself relaxing in spite of his habitual caution. The man's first words changed that, however.

'The Eel has a message for you,' he said quietly. 'Direct, by word of mouth only. Before I deliver it, though, I'm to give you some background – as only I can.' He paused to drink from the tankard, then resumed. 'Now, Turban Orr has hired another dozen hunters. What are they hunting? Well, me, for one. Your problem is that he's going to be harder to reach. The Eel approves of your efforts concerning Lady Simtal. Coll's return is desired by all who value integrity and honour within the Council. If you require anything, ask now and it's yours.'

Rallick's eyes had hardened. 'Never knew Murillio had such a big mouth,' he said.

The man shook his head. 'Your compatriot has revealed nothing. Nor have you. It is the Eel's business. Now, what do you require?'

'Nothing.'

'Good.' The stranger nodded, as if he'd expected that reply and was pleased. 'Incidentally, Turban Orr's efforts to pass the proclamation have been . . . impeded. Indefinitely. The Eel wishes to thank you for your unwitting role in that. Nevertheless, the councilman explores other options. He has been watched closely. Hence our fortunate discovery that is at the heart of the Eel's message to you. Last night, beneath Despot's Barbican, Turban Orr met with a representative of the Assassins' Guild – how he managed that was quite a feat, considering how difficult your comrades have been to find. In any case, a contract was tendered by Turban Orr.' The man waited for the shock to wear off Rallick's face, then continued. 'Tendered by Turban Orr, as I said, but not on his own behalf. Rather, Lady Simtal has decided that Coll's death should be a fact in the real world as it is on paper.'

'Who?' Rallick rasped. 'Who was the contact?'

'I'm coming to that. First, it was accepted, for the payment

515

was substantial. They are aware that Coll is presently outside Darujhistan. They simply await his return.'

'The assassin's name.'

'Ocelot.' The man rose. 'The Eel wishes you success in all your ventures, Rallick Nom. Thus the message ends. Good evening.' He turned to leave.

'Wait.'

'Yes?'

'Thank you,' Rallick said.

The stranger smiled, then left.

The assassin took the man's seat, and leaned against the wall. He waved at Sulty, who had a pitcher of ale and a tankard waiting. She hurried over. Behind her strode, at a more leisurely pace, Irilta and Meese. They sat down without preamble, each with her own tankard.

'Everybody's still breathing,' Irilta said, raising her drink. 'And here's t' that.'

Meese lifted hers as well and the two women drank deep. Then Meese bent forward. 'Any word of Kruppe and the boy?'

Rallick shook his head. 'I may not be here when they come back,' he said. 'Tell Murillio to go ahead if I don't show, and if other ... events occur. And, if that happens, tell him our man's eyes are open.' Rallick filled his tankard and drained it immediately. Then he rose. 'Don't wish me luck,' he said.

'How about success?' Meese asked, a worried expression on her broad face.

Rallick jerked his head in a nod. Then he left the inn.

Anomander Rake was hiding something. Baruk was certain of it as he stared moodily into the fireplace. In his right hand was a goblet of goat's milk, and in his left a large fragment of Daru flatbread. Why had the Tiste Andii permitted the Imass to enter the barrow? He'd asked that question already of the Lord sitting beside him, but an answer didn't seem forthcoming.

516

Instead, all the alchemist got from Rake was that irritating smugness. Baruk took a bite from the flatbread, the crack loud between them.

Rake stretched out his legs and sighed. 'An odd hour to dine,' he said.

'All my hours have been odd, lately,' Baruk said, around the bread. He drank a mouthful of milk.

'I'd no idea that both the Shadow Lord and Oponn had become involved in affairs,' Rake said.

Baruk felt the Lord's eyes on him, but he remained staring at the fire. 'I had an intimation of Oponn,' he said. 'But nothing definite.'

Rake snorted in reply.

Baruk downed some more milk. 'You hold your hunches close to your chest. I do the same.'

'This avails us nothing,' Rake snapped.

The alchemist turned in his chair to face the Tiste Andii. 'Your ravens watched that woman and the T'lan Imass enter the barrow. Do you still believe they will fail?'

'Do you?' Rake retorted. 'I seem to recall that that was your position on the matter, Baruk. As far as I was and am concerned, I don't much care whether they succeed or not. Either way, there'll be a fight. I suspect you'd imagined there would be a way to avoid one. Obviously, your intelligence concerning the Malazan Empire is sorely lacking. Laseen knows only one thing, and that's force. She'll ignore power until it's unveiled, and then she'll hit you with everything at her disposal.'

'And you just wait for it to happen?' Baruk scowled. 'That's how cities are destroyed. That's how thousands of people die. Does any of that matter to you, Anomander Rake? So long as you win in the end?'

A tight smile played on the Lord's thin lips. 'An accurate assessment, Baruk. In this case, however, Laseen wants Darujhistan intact. I mean to prevent that. But destroying the

517

city to defy her would be too easy. I could have managed that weeks ago. No, I want Darujhistan to remain as it is. Yet out of Laseen's reach. That, Alchemist, is victory.' His grey eyes were on Baruk. 'I would not have sought an alliance with you otherwise.'

The alchemist frowned. 'Unless you plan treachery.'

Rake was silent for a time, studying his hands clasped on his lap. 'Baruk,' he said softly, 'as any commander of long standing knows, treachery breeds its own. Once committed, whether against an enemy or an ally, it becomes a legitimate choice for everyone in your command, from the lowest private seeking promotion, to your personal aides, bodyguards and officers. My people know of our alliance with you, Alchemist. If I were to betray it, I would not long remain the Lord of Moon's Spawn. And rightly so.'

Baruk smiled. 'And who could challenge your power, Rake?'

'Caladan Brood, for one,' Rake replied immediately. 'And then there's my four assassin mages. Even Silanah, the dweller within the Moon's caverns, might take it upon herself to exact judgement on me. I can think of others, Baruk, many others.'

'So fear holds you in check, Son of Darkness?'

Rake scowled. 'That title is held by those fools who think me worthy of worship. I dislike it, Baruk, and would not hear it again from you. Does fear hold me in check? No. As powerful as fear is, it is no match for what compels me. Duty.' The Lord's eyes had shifted into a dun tone as they remained fixed on his hands, which he now turned palms up. 'You have a duty to your city, Baruk. It drives you, shapes you. I'm no stranger to such a thing. Within Moon's Spawn are the last of the Tiste Andii on this world. We are dying, Alchemist. No cause seems great enough to return to my people the zest for life. I try, but inspiration has never been a great talent of mine. Even this Malazan Empire could not make us rise to defend ourselves – until we ran out of places to run to.

'We still die on this continent. Better that it be by the sword.' He let his hands slip from his lap. 'Imagine your spirit dying while your body lives on. Not for ten years, not for fifty. But a body that lives on for fifteen, twenty thousand years.'

Rake rose swiftly. He looked down upon a silent Baruk, and smiled a smile that launched a dagger of pain into the alchemist's heart. 'Thus duty holds me, yet a duty that is in itself hollow. Is it enough to preserve the Tiste Andii? Simply preserve them? Do I raise Moon's Spawn into the heavens, where we live on, beyond any risk, any threat? What, then, will I be preserving? A history, a particular point of view.' He shrugged. 'The history is done, Baruk, and the Tiste Andii point of view is one of disinterest, stoicism and quiet, empty despair. Are these gifts to the world worthy of preservation? I think not.'

Baruk had no immediate response. What Anomander Rake had described was almost beyond comprehension, yet its anguished cry reached through to the alchemist. 'And yet,' he said, 'here you are. Allied with the Empire's victims. Do you stand alone in this, Anomander Rake? Do your people approve?'

'They care not,' Rake said. 'They accept my commands. They follow me. They serve Caladan Brood when I ask them to. And they die in the mud and forests of a land that is not their own, in a war not their own, for a people who are terrified of them.'

Baruk sat forward. 'Then why? Why do you do all this?'

A harsh laugh was Rake's response. After a moment, however, his bitter amusement fell away and he said, 'Is an honourable cause worth anything these days? Does it matter that we've borrowed it? We fight as well as any man. We die alongside them. Mercenaries of the spirit. And even that is a coin we scarcely value. Why? It doesn't matter why. But we never betray our allies.

519

'I know you are worried that I did nothing to prevent the T'lan Imass from entering the barrow. I believe the Jaghut Tyrant will be freed, Baruk. But better now, with me here beside you, than at some other time when the Jaghut has no one capable of opposing him. We'll take this legend and carve the life from it, Alchemist, and never again will the threat haunt you.'

Baruk stared at the Tiste Andii. 'Are you that certain you'll be able to destroy the Jaghut?'

'No. But when it is finished with us, it will have been much reduced. Then it falls to others – to your Cabal, in fact. There's no certainty in this, Baruk. That seems a fact particularly galling to you humans. You'd better learn to accept it. We may well be able to destroy the Jaghut Tyrant, but even this will serve Laseen's plans.'

The alchemist was bemused. 'I don't understand.'

Rake grinned. 'When we are finished with it, *we* will have been much reduced. And then will come the powers of the Malazan Empire. So, you see, either way she wins. If anything has her worried, it's your T'orrud Cabal, Baruk. Of your abilities she knows nothing. Which is why her agents seek this Vorcan. The Guild Master accepting the contract will solve the problem you represent.'

'Yet,' Baruk mused, 'there are other factors involved.'

'Oponn,' Rake stated. 'That is a danger to everyone involved. Do you think Oponn cares for a mortal city? For its people? It is the nexus of power that matters to Oponn, the whirlwind where games get nasty. Will immortal blood be spilled? That's the question the gods are eager to have answered.'

Baruk stared down at his goblet of goat's milk. 'Well, at least we've avoided that so far.' He took a sip.

'Wrong,' Rake said. 'Forcing Shadowthrone out of the game marked the first spilling of immortal blood.'

Baruk almost choked on the milk. He set down the goblet and stared up at the Tiste Andii. 'Whose?'

'Two Hounds died by my sword. Knocked Shadowthrone somewhat off-balance, I believe.'

Baruk leaned back and closed his eyes. 'Then the stakes have risen,' he said.

'As far as Moon's Spawn, Alchemist.' Rake returned to his chair and sat, once again stretching his legs out to the fire's warmth. 'Now, what more can you tell me about this Jaghut Tyrant? I recall you said you wished to consult an authority.'

Baruk opened his eyes and tossed the flatbread into the fire. 'There's a problem there, Rake. I'm hoping you can help explain what's happened. Please,' he said, rising, 'follow me.'

Grunting, Rake climbed back to his feet. This night he'd not worn his sword. To Baruk the Lord's broad back looked incomplete, but he was thankful for the weapon's absence.

He led Rake from the room and down the central stairs to the lower chambers. The first of these subterranean rooms held a narrow cot, and on the cot lay an old man. Baruk indicated him. 'As you see, he appears to be sleeping. He is named Mammot.'

Rake raised an eyebrow. 'The historian?'

'Also a High Priest of D'rek.'

'That explains the cynicism in his writings,' Rake said, grinning. 'The Worm of Autumn breeds an unhappy lot.'

Baruk was surprised that this Tiste Andii had read Mammot's *Histories* but, then, why not? A life spanning twenty thousand years necessitated hobbies, he supposed.

'So,' Rake said, striding to the bed, 'this Mammot sleeps a deep sleep. What triggered it?' He crouched before the old man.

Baruk joined him. 'That is the odd part. I admit to knowing little of earth magic. D'riss is a Warren I've never explored. I called on Mammot, as I indicated to you, and upon his arrival

I asked him to tell me all he knew of the Jaghut Tyrant and the barrow. He promptly sat down and closed his eyes. They've yet to open, and he's not uttered a single word since.'

Rake straightened. 'He took your request seriously, I see.'

'What do you mean?'

'As you guessed, he opened his D'riss Warren. He sought to answer your question by rather, shall we say, direct means. And now something's trapped him.'

'He travelled by Warren to the Jaghut Tyrant's barrow? The old fool!'

'Into a concentration of Tellann sorcery, not to mention Jaghut Omtose Phellack. On top of all that, a woman with an Otataral sword.' Rake crossed his arms. 'He'll not come round until both the T'lan Imass and the Otataral have left the barrow. And even then, if he's not quick, the awakening Jaghut might take him.'

A chill burgeoned in Baruk's bones. 'Take, as in possession?'

Rake nodded, his expression grim. 'A High Priest, is he? The Jaghut would find him very useful. Not to mention the access Mammot provides to D'rek. Do you know, Baruk, if this Tyrant's capable of enslaving a goddess?'

'I don't know,' Baruk whispered, sweat trickling down his round face as he stared at Mammot's recumbent form. 'Dessembrae fend,' he added.

The old woman sitting on the tenement steps squinted at the late afternoon sky while she tamped dried Italbe leaves into her steatite pipe. On the wooden steps beside her was a small covered bronze brazier. Thin kindling sticks jutted from holes around the bowl. The old woman withdrew one and set it to her pipe, then tossed it into the street.

The man walking down the opposite side of the street caught the signal and ran a hand through his hair. Circle Breaker felt near to panic. This taking to the streets was far too risky. Turban Orr's hunters were close to him – he could feel it with dread certainty. Sooner or later, the councilman would recall his many meetings beneath Despot's Barbican, and the guard who'd been stationed there every time. This brazen showing of himself compromised everything.

He turned a corner, passing beyond the old woman's sight, and continued for three blocks until he came opposite the Phoenix Inn. Two women lounged by the door, laughing at some joke between them.

Circle Breaker tucked his thumbs into his sword-belt and angled the scabbard out to the side. Its bronze-capped end scraped against the stone wall beside him. Then he withdrew his hands and continued on his way towards Lakefront. *Well, it's done.* All that remained for him was one final contact, possibly redundant, but he would follow the Eel's orders. Things were coming to a head. He did not expect to live much longer, but he'd do what he must until that time. What more could be asked of him?

At the entrance of the Phoenix Inn, Meese nudged Irilta. 'That's it,' she muttered. 'You do the back-up this time. Usual pattern.'

Irilta scowled, then nodded. 'Head off, then.'

Meese descended the steps and turned up the street. She reversed the route taken by Circle Breaker until she reached the tenement. She saw the old woman still sitting there, lazily watching passers-by. As Meese passed through her line of vision, the old woman removed the pipe from her mouth and tapped it against the heel of her shoe. Sparks rained on to the cobbles.

That was the signal. Meese came to the corner of the block, then turned right and entered the alley running the building's length. A door opened for her a third of the way down and she strode into a dimly lit room with an open door beyond.

Someone hid behind the first door but she did not acknowledge that someone's presence. She passed through the second, inner door and found herself in a hallway. From there it was a quick jog up the stairs.

Apsalar – or Sorry, as she had been known before – hadn't been much impressed by her first sight of Darujhistan. For some reason, despite her excitement and anticipation, it had all seemed too familiar.

Disappointed, Crokus had wasted no time in taking her to his uncle's home once they'd stabled Coll's horse. The journey to the city, and then through its crowded streets, had been, for Crokus, a continual storm of confusion. This woman seemed to have a knack for catching him off-guard, and all he desired now was to throw her into someone else's lap and be done with it.

Yet, if that was truly the case, why did he feel so miserable about it?

Crokus left Mammot's library and returned to the outer room. Moby chirped and stuck out its red tongue at him from Mammot's desk. Ignoring the creature, Crokus stood before Apsalar, who'd seated herself in the better of the two chairs – his chair, of course. 'I don't understand. From the looks of it, he's been gone for a couple of days at least.'

'So? Is that so unusual?' Apsalar asked casually.

'It is,' he grumbled. 'Did you feed Moby as I asked?'

She nodded. 'The grapes?'

'Yes.' He placed his hands on his hips. 'Strange. Maybe Rallick knows something about it.'

'Who's Rallick?'

'An assassin friend,' Crokus replied distractedly.

Apsalar shot to her feet, her eyes wide.

'What's wrong?' Crokus asked, stepping close. The girl looked positively terrified. He glared around, half expecting to see some demon rise out of the floor or the cupboard, but the room was unchanged – a little messier than usual, though. Moby's fault, he assumed.

'I'm not sure,' she said, relaxing with an effort. 'It was as if I was about to remember something. But it never came.'

'Oh,' Crokus said. 'Well, we could—'

A knock sounded on the door.

Crokus brightened, walking over to it. 'Oh, he probably lost his keys or something,' he said.

'It was unlocked,' Apsalar pointed out.

Crokus opened the door. 'Meese! What're you—?'

'Quiet!' the big woman hissed, pushing past him and shutting the door. Her gaze fell on Apsalar and her eyes widened. Then she turned back to Crokus. 'Good I found you, lad! You've seen no one since getting back?'

'Why, no. That's just it—'

'A stabler,' Apsalar said, frowning up at Meese. 'Have we met?'

'She's lost her memory,' Crokus explained. 'But, yes, we stabled Coll's horse.'

'Why?' Meese demanded, then as Crokus was about to elaborate she went on, 'Never mind. The stabler shouldn't prove a problem. Well, we're in luck!'

'Dammit, Meese,' Crokus said. 'What's going on?'

She met his eyes. 'That D'Arle guard you killed the other night. The one in the garden. They've got your name and description, lad. Don't ask me how. But the D'Arles are talking high gallows when you're caught.'

The blood left Crokus's face. Then his head jerked to Apsalar. He opened his mouth, then shut it again. No, she truly didn't remember. But it must have been her. He collapsed into Mammot's chair.

'We've got to hide you, lad,' Meese said. 'Both of you, I guess. But don't you worry, Crokus, me and Irilta, we'll take care of you till something can be worked out.'

'I don't believe this,' he whispered, staring at the wall opposite him. 'She betrayed me, damn her!'

Meese looked questioningly at Apsalar, who said, 'It's a guess, but I'd say a girl named Challice.'

Meese closed her eyes briefly. 'Challice D'Arle, the court's honey these days.' Compassion softened her face as she looked down on Crokus. 'Oh, lad. That's the way of it, then.'

He jerked in the seat and glared up at her. 'It isn't any more.'

Meese grinned. 'Right. For now,' she said, arms folded over her chest, 'we just sit tight till night, then it's the rooftops for us. Don't worry, we'll handle things, lad.'

Apsalar rose. 'My name's Apsalar,' she said. 'Pleased to meet you, Meese. And thank you for helping Crokus.'

'Apsalar, huh? Well,' her grin broadened, 'guess the rooftops will be no problem for you, then.'

'None,' she replied, knowing somehow that she was right in this.

'Good enough,' Meese said. 'Now, how about we find something to drink?'

'Meese,' Crokus asked, 'do you know where my uncle might have gone?'

'Can't help you there, lad. No idea.'

She wasn't sure about the old woman on the steps, but the one immediately below, tucked into a shadowed niche and steadily watching the tenement building – that one would have to be taken care of. It seemed that this Coin Bearer had protection.

Serrat was not unduly concerned. Next to her lord, Anomander Rake, she ranked the deadliest among the Tiste Andii of Moon's Spawn. Finding this boy-servant of Oponn's had not proved difficult. Once her lord had given her the necessary details, Oponn's magical signature had been easy to find. It helped that she'd encountered it before – and from this very boy – on the rooftops two weeks past. Her agents had chased the Coin Bearer that night, abandoning him once he'd entered the Phoenix Inn – but only at her command. If she'd suspected then what she now knew, Oponn's presence would have ended that very night.

Ill luck, Serrat smiled to herself, taking a more comfortable position on the rooftop. They'd move at night, she suspected. As for the woman hiding below, she'd have to be removed. Indeed, with a spell of blurring and enough in the way of shadows, she might as easily take the woman's place.

There'd be no suspicion from the other woman, then, the one presently inside with the Coin Bearer. Serrat nodded. Yes, that would be how she'd play it.

But for now, she'd wait. Patience ever rewards.

'Well,' Murillio said, as he scanned the crowd, 'they're not here. Which means they're with Mammot.'

Kruppe drew a deep breath of the sweaty, smoky air. 'Ah, civilization. Kruppe believes your assessment is accurate, friend. If so, then we might as well rest here, drinking and supping for an hour or two.' With that, he strode into the Phoenix Inn.

A few old hands, seated at Kruppe's table, gathered their tankards and pitcher and left, murmuring apologies and grinning among themselves. Kruppe gave them a gracious nod and settled with a loud sigh into his usual chair. Murillio paused at the bar and spoke with Scurve, then he joined Kruppe.

Brushing dust from his shirt, Murillio frowned distractedly at his road-weary condition. 'I look forward to a bath,' he said. 'Apparently Scurve saw Rallick in here earlier, talking with some stranger. Since then, nobody's seen him.'

Kruppe waved an uninterested hand. 'Kind Sulty arrives,' he announced. A moment later a pitcher of ale stood on the table. Kruppe wiped his tankard with his silk handkerchief, then filled it with the foaming brew.

527

'Weren't we supposed to report to Baruk?' Murillio asked, his eyes on his friend.

'All in due time,' Kruppe said. 'First, we must recover from our ordeals. What if Kruppe were to lose his voice in very midsentence of said report? What would avail Baruk of that?' He raised his tankard and drank deep.

Murillio drummed the fingers of one hand restlessly on the table, his eyes constantly scanning the crowd. Then he straightened in his seat. He filled his tankard. 'So now that you know what Rallick and I are up to,' he said, 'what do you plan to do about it?'

Kruppe's eyebrows lifted. 'Kruppe? Why, nothing but good, of course. Timely assistance, and such. No need for blatant fretting, friend Murillio. By all means proceed as planned. Think of wise Kruppe as no more than a kindly chaperon.'

'Hood's Breath,' Murillio groaned, eyes rolling. 'We were doing fine without your help. The best thing you could do for us is stay out of our way. Don't get involved.'

'And abandon my friends to the fates? Nonsense!'

Murillio finished his ale and rose. 'I'm going home,' he said. 'You can make the report to Baruk in a week's time for all I care. And when Rallick finds out you know all about our plans, well, Kruppe, I'd hate to be in your boots.'

Kruppe waved dismissively. 'See Sulty yon? Upon her tray is Kruppe's supper. Rallick Nom's nasty daggers and nastier temper pale to insignificance before such repast as now approaches. Goodnight to you, then, Murillio. Until the morrow.'

Murillio stared down at him, then grumbled, 'Goodnight, Kruppe.'

He left the bar through the kitchen door. As soon as he stepped into the back alley a figure accosted him from across the way. Murillio frowned. 'That you, Rallick?'

'No,' the shadowed figure said. 'Fear me not, Murillio. I

have a message to you from the Eel. Call me Circle Breaker.'
The man strode closer. 'The message concerns Councilman
Turban Orr . . .'

Rallick moved from rooftop to rooftop in the darkness. The
need for absolute silence slowed his hunt considerably. There'd
be no conversation with Ocelot. Rallick expected he'd have
but one shot at the man. If he missed his chance, his Clan
Leader's sorcery would prove the deciding factor. *Unless . . .*

Rallick paused and checked his pouch. Years back, the
alchemist Baruk had rewarded him for work well done with a
small bag of reddish dust. Baruk had explained its magic-
deadening properties, but Rallick resisted placing his trust in
the powder. Had its potency survived the years? Was it a match
for Ocelot's powers? There was no telling.

He crossed a high rooftop, skirting the edge of a dome. Off
to his right and below was the city's eastern wall. The faint
glow of Worrytown rose beyond it. The assassin suspected that
Ocelot would await Coll's arrival at Worry Gate, hiding within
crossbow range. Better to kill the man before he entered the
city.

This limited the possibilities considerably. Lines of sight
were few, and K'rul Hill was the best of them. Still, Ocelot
might well have used sorcery already, and lie hidden from
mundane eyes. Rallick might stumble right over him.

He reached the north side of the dome's skirt. Before him
rose the K'rul Temple. From the belfry, there'd be a clean shot
just as Coll entered the gate. Rallick removed the pouch from
his bag. Whatever the dust covered, Baruk had said, would be
impervious to magic. More, it had an area effect. The assassin
scowled. How much of an area? And did it wear off? Most
importantly, Baruk had said – and Rallick remembered this
clearly – do not let it touch your skin. Poison? he'd asked. 'No,'
the alchemist had replied. 'The powder changes some people.

There is no predicting such changes, however. Best not to take the chance, Rallick.'

Sweat trickled down his face. Finding Ocelot was already a slim chance. Coll's death would ruin everything and, more, it would strip from Rallick his last claim ... to what? *To humanity*. The price of failure had become very high. 'Justice,' he hissed angrily. 'It has to mean something. It has to!'

Rallick untied the pouch. He dipped into it and scraped out a handful of the powder. He rubbed it between his fingers. It felt like rust. 'That's it?' he wondered. Maybe it had deteriorated. Shrugging, he began to massage it into his skin, starting with his face. 'What changes?' he muttered. 'I don't feel any changes.'

Reaching under his clothing as much as was possible, Rallick used up the last of the powder. The pouch itself was stained on the inside. He turned it inside out, then stuffed it into his belt. Now, he grimaced, the hunt continues. Somewhere out there an assassin waited, eyes fixed on Jammit's Worry Road. 'I'll find you, Ocelot,' he whispered, his eyes fixed on K'rul's belfry tower. 'And magic or no magic, you won't hear me, you won't even feel my breath on your neck until it's too late. I swear it.'

He began his ascent.

CHAPTER EIGHTEEN

This blue city
hides under its cloak
a hidden hand
that holds like stone
a blade envenomed
by the eight limbed Paralt –
the sting brings death
in the span of grief
that marks a final breath –
so this hand defies
sorcery's web
and trembles the gossamer strand
of a spider's deadly threat.
This hand beneath
the blue city's cloak
drives home Power's
gentle balance.

The Conspiracy
Blind Gallan (b.1078)

531

S ergeant Whiskeyjack strode to the bedside. 'You sure you're up to it?' he asked Kalam.

The assassin, sitting with his back against the wall, glanced up from honing his long knives. 'Not much choice, is there?' He returned to his sharpening.

Whiskeyjack's expression was drawn and haggard from lack of sleep. He looked across the small room to where Quick Ben crouched in a corner. A fragment of bedroll was clutched in the wizard's hands, and his eyes were closed.

At the table, Fiddler and Hedge had dismantled their massive arbalest. They now sat cleaning and examining each piece. They were looking at a fight ahead of them.

Whiskeyjack shared their conviction. Each hour that passed brought their many hunters that much closer. Of those it was the Tiste Andii he feared the most. His squad was good, but not that good.

By the window was Trotts, leaning against the wall with his burly arms crossed. And against one wall slept Mallet, his snores loud in the room.

The sergeant returned his attention to Kalam. 'It's a long shot, isn't it?'

The assassin nodded. 'No reason for the man to keep showing himself. They got burned the last time.' He shrugged. 'I'll try the inn again. If anything, someone will mark me and the Guild will come. If I can get a word in before they kill me, there's a chance. It's not much . . .'

'. . . but it'll have to do,' Whiskeyjack finished. 'You've got tomorrow. If we draw a blank,' he looked over to Fiddler and Hedge and found their eyes on him, 'we detonate the intersections. Do damage, hurt them.'

The two saboteurs grinned their anticipation.

Quick Ben's loud hiss of frustration brought everyone round. The wizard's eyes had opened. He tossed the torn cloth contemptuously on to the floor. 'No good, Sergeant,' he said. 'Can't find Sorry anywhere.'

Kalam rumbled a curse and thrust his weapons into their scabbards.

'So, what does that mean?' Whiskeyjack asked the wizard.

'Most likely,' Quick Ben said, 'she's dead.' He gestured at the cloth. 'With that, there's no way the Rope could hide from me. Not while still possessing Sorry.'

'Maybe once you told him you'd figured him out,' Fiddler said, 'he tossed in his coins and quit the game.'

Quick Ben made a face. 'The Rope isn't scared of us, Fiddler. Come back to earth. If anything, he'd be coming down on us. Shadowthrone must've told him by now who I am or, rather, who I once was. It's not the Rope's business, but Shadowthrone might insist. Gods don't like being cheated. Especially being cheated twice.' He climbed to his feet and stretched the kinks from his back. He met Whiskeyjack's gaze. 'I don't understand this, Sergeant. I'm stumped.'

'Do we abandon her?' Whiskeyjack asked.

Quick Ben nodded. 'Might as well.' He paused, then stepped forward. 'We were all wishing we were wrong about her,' he said, 'but what Sorry did had nothing to do with being human. And, as far as I'm concerned, I'm glad of that.'

'I'd hate to think,' Kalam said, from the bed, 'that evil was real, that it existed with a face as plain as the next man's. I know, Whiskeyjack, you've got your reasons for wanting it that way.'

Quick Ben moved closer to the sergeant, his gaze softening. 'Keeps you sane every time you order somebody to die,' he said. 'We all know about that, Sergeant. And we'd be the last to suggest there's some other way that maybe you haven't thought of yet.'

'Well, I'm glad to hear it,' Whiskeyjack growled. He surveyed everyone in the room, seeing that Mallet was awake and watching him. 'Anybody else got something to say?'

'I have,' Fiddler said, then ducked at the sergeant's glower. 'Well, you asked, didn't you?'

'Out with it, then.'

Fiddler straightened in his chair and cleared his throat. Hedge poked him in the ribs as he was about to begin. After a menacing scowl, he tried again. 'It's like this, Sergeant. We've seen a hell of a lot of our friends die, right? And maybe we didn't have to give the orders, so maybe you think it's easier for us. But I don't think so. You see, to us those people were living, breathing. They were friends. When they die, it hurts. But you go around telling yourself that the only way to keep from going mad is to take all that away from them, so you don't have to think about it, so you don't have to feel anything when they die. But, damn, when you take away everybody else's humanity, you take away your own. And that'll drive you mad as sure as anything. It's that hurt we feel that makes us keep going, Sergeant. And maybe we're not getting anywhere, but at least we're not running away from anything.'

There was silence in the room. Then Hedge punched Fiddler in the arm. 'I'll be damned! You got a brain in there, after all. I guess I been wrong about you all these years.'

'Yeah, right,' Fiddler said, rolling his eyes at Mallet, 'and who is it who's burned his hair off so many times he's gotta wear some ugly leather cap all the time, hey?'

Mallet laughed, but the tension remained and everyone's gaze swung back to fix on their sergeant. Slowly, Whiskeyjack studied each man in his squad. He saw the caring in their eyes, the open offer to the friendship he'd spent years suppressing. All that time pushing them away, pushing everyone away, and the stubborn bastards just kept on coming back.

So Sorry hadn't been human. His conviction that all she'd done was within the possibilities of humanity now seemed to rest on uncertain ground. But it did not collapse. He'd seen too much in his life. There'd be no sudden faith in his view of human history, no burgeoning optimism to chase away all the demonic memories of the hells he'd lived through.

Still, there came a time when some denials lost their function, when the world's relentless battering at him made his foolishness obvious even to himself. He was, finally, and after all these years, among friends. That was a hard admission and he realized he was already impatient with it. 'All right,' he growled, 'enough with the flapping lips. We've got work to do. Corporal?'

'Sergeant?' Kalam replied.

'Get yourself ready. You've got the daylight hours to re-establish contact with the Assassins' Guild. Meanwhile, I want everyone else to lay out their weapons and give them a good cleaning. Repairs to armour. There'll be an inspection, and if I find a single damn thing I don't like, there'll be hell coming down. Understood?'

'We hear ya,' Mallet said, grinning.

Despite their slow pace, Coll's wound had opened half a dozen times since they'd begun the journey. He'd found a way of sitting in his saddle, leaning to one side and taking most of the weight on his uninjured leg, and since this morning the wound had yet to reopen. The awkward position brought pains and cramps to the rest of him, however.

Paran knew a foul mood when he saw one. Though it was clear to both of them that a bond had formed between them, comfortable and unfettered by pretences, they'd exchanged but scant words as the ravages of Coll's wound continued to take its toll.

Coll's entire left leg, from the hip where the sword had done its damage down to the foot, was a uniform sun-darkened brown colour. Clots of drying blood gathered in the joints of his upper leg plates and knee guard. As the thigh swelled, they were forced to slice the leather padding beneath the plate.

535

Succour had been denied them at the Catlin Bridge garrison, since the lone surgeon stationed there had been sleeping off one of his 'bad nights'. Clean bandages had been donated, though, and it was these – already soaked through – that now covered the wound.

There was little traffic on Jammit's Worry despite the city's walls being within sight. The flood of refugees from the north had since ended, and those who would gather for the Gedderone Festival had already done so.

As they approached the edge of Worrytown, Coll raised himself from the semi-conscious state he'd been in for the last few hours. His face was deathly white. 'Is this Worry Gate?' he asked dully.

'I believe so,' Paran said, since they were on the road sharing that strange name. 'Will we be permitted to pass within?' he asked. 'Will the guards call for a surgeon?'

Coll shook his head. 'Take me on through. Phoenix Inn. Take me to the Phoenix Inn.' His head sagged again.

'Very well, Coll.' He'd be surprised if the guards permitted it, and he'd need a story to tell them, though Coll had said nothing of how he'd been wounded. 'I hope,' he muttered, 'there's someone in this Phoenix Inn with a healer's touch.' The man looked bad. Paran fixed his gaze on the city's gates. He'd already seen enough to understand why the Empress wanted it so avidly. 'Darujhistan.' He sighed. 'My, but you are a wonder, aren't you?'

Rallick nudged himself another inch upward. His limbs trembled with exhaustion. If not for the morning shadows on this side of the belfry, he'd have been spotted long ago. As it was, he would not remain hidden much longer.

Taking the stairs would have been suicide in the darkness. Ocelot would have set alarms all along the way – the man was no fool at covering the approaches to his position.

If he was up there, Rallick reminded himself. If not, Coll was in trouble. There was no telling if his friend had arrived at the gates yet, and the silence from the top of the belfry could mean anything. He paused to rest and glanced up. Ten feet to go, the most critical ones yet. He was so tired it was all he could do simply to retain the handholds. The silent approach was now beyond him. His only advantage lay in that Ocelot's concentration would be eastward, while he now climbed the west side of the tower.

He drew some deep breaths, then reached for another handhold.

Passers-by stopped to watch Paran and Coll move slowly through Worrytown towards the gate. Ignoring them, and the questions they asked, the captain focused his attention on the two guards at the gate itself. They'd spotted him and Coll, and now stood waiting.

Reaching the gate, Paran motioned that they would pass through. One guard nodded while the other walked alongside the captain's horse. 'Your friend needs a surgeon,' he said. 'If you wait just inside we can have one here in five minutes.'

Paran refused the offer. 'We need to find the Phoenix Inn. I'm from the north, never been here before. The man said the Phoenix Inn, so that's where I'm going to take him.'

The guard was dubious. 'Be surprised if he'd make it that far. But if that's what you want, the least we can do is give you an escort.'

As they emerged from the gate's shadow the other guard cried out in surprise.

Paran held his breath as the man stepped close to Coll. 'I know him,' he said. 'He's Coll Jhamin, of House Jhamin. I served under him. What happened?'

'I thought Coll died a few years back,' the other guard said.

537

'Screw the writs,' his companion snapped. 'I know what I know, Vildron. This is Coll, all right.'

'He wants to go to the Phoenix Inn,' Paran told the man. 'That's the last thing he said to me.'

The man nodded. 'Let's do it right, though.' He turned to the other guard. 'I'll take the grief if there's any, Vildron. Get me the wagon – it's still hitched up from this morning, right?' The guard smiled up at Paran. 'Thanks for getting him here. Some of us in the city still got eyes, and damn what the high-brows whisper. We'll put him in the back of the wagon – less jarring that way.'

Paran relaxed. 'Thanks, soldier.' He looked past the man, eager to see what he could of the city now that the wall was behind him. Immediately before them rose a humped hill, its sides overgrown with weeds and gnarled trees. On its summit squatted a temple of some kind, abandoned long ago, from which a square-sided tower rose, capped by a bronze-tiled roof. As his eyes reached the belfry's open-sided platform, he saw a flash of movement. He squinted.

Rallick raised his head cautiously over the platform's edge. He almost gasped aloud. The belfry was empty. Then he remembered Ocelot's sorcery. Holding his breath, he strained one last time with leaden arms, drawing himself flat on to the platform. As soon as he moved to gather in his feet, the barren stone of the platform shimmered and he saw Ocelot lying before him, crossbow cocked, taking aim at something below.

Rallick unsheathed his knives and moved all at once. But his exhaustion gave him away, his boots scuffing the stone.

Ocelot spun on to his back, weapon swinging to fix on Rallick. The Clan Leader's face twisted into a mask of rage and fear. He wasted no time with words and immediately released the quarrel set in his crossbow.

Rallick tensed for the impact that he was certain would

538

throw him across the platform and possibly over the edge. A flash of red before his chest blinded him momentarily, but no impact came. Blinking, Rallick looked down. The quarrel had vanished. The truth came to him in an instant. The quarrel had been magic, created by sorcery to fly unimpeded, but Baruk's rusty powder had worked. Even as this thought burst into his head, he propelled himself forward.

Ocelot swore and dropped the crossbow. As he reached for his knife, Rallick landed on him. A loud grunt sounded from the Clan Leader, his eyes squeezing shut in pain.

Rallick drove the dagger in his right hand against Ocelot's chest. The weapon scraped across mail beneath the cloth shirt. Damn, the man had learned something from that other night – and this was Rallick's own precaution, come to defy him now. The blade in his left hand he angled upward, under Ocelot's right arm. The weapon's point cut into flesh, then continued on into the man's armpit.

Rallick saw, inches from his face, the dagger's tip emerge from the cloth covering Ocelot's right shoulder, followed by a bloom of blood. He heard a knife skitter across the flagstones.

Teeth bared, Ocelot snapped his left hand up to the back of Rallick's neck, finding his braid. He gave it a savage yank, twisting Rallick's head around. Then he tried to sink his teeth into Rallick's neck.

Ocelot gasped as Rallick jammed a knee into his crotch. He tightened his hold on the braid again, this time near its knotted end.

Rallick heard the snick of metal and attempted desperately to roll to his right. Wounded as Ocelot's right arm was, it struck his body with enough force to drive the wedged wrist-blade through the chain links and into his chest. A dull fire blossomed from the wound. Ocelot jerked the blade free and, still holding Rallick's braid, drew back for another stab.

Rallick brought up his right arm and, in a single sweeping

motion, sliced through his braid. Freed, he pushed himself on to that side, withdrawing the knife in his left hand as he did so. Ocelot slashed wildly at his face, missing by inches.

With all the remaining strength in his left arm, Rallick slammed his knife into Ocelot's stomach. Links snapped and the blade sank to its hilt. The Clan Leader's body doubled up, curling around the embedded weapon. Gasping, Rallick lurched forward and hammered the other dagger into Ocelot's forehead.

Rallick lay unmoving for a time, wondering at the absence of pain. The plan would fall to Murillio now. Coll would be avenged. Murillio could handle it – he had no choice.

Ocelot's body seemed to grow heavier on him despite the blood leaking from it. 'I'd always believed I was this man's match,' he muttered. He pushed himself from the still-twitching body and rolled on to his back in the centre of the platform. He'd hoped to see sky, to look one last time on its bright, depthless blue. Instead, he found himself looking at the underside of the belfry's roof, its ancient stone arch crowded with nesting bats. This detail fixed itself in his head as he felt the blood stream from his chest. He thought he could see beady eyes glittering down at him.

After seeing no other sign of movement on the belfry, Paran's gaze swung to the avenue on his left. Vildron approached, seated on a wagon drawn by two horses. The guard waiting beside Coll's horse said, 'Give me a hand here, will you? Let's get the old man down.'

Paran dismounted and hurried to help him. He glanced at Coll's face. Though still hunched on the saddle, he was unconscious. How much longer could he last? If that was me, Paran realized, I'd be dead by now. 'After all this,' he growled as they dragged Coll from the saddle, 'you'd damn well better live.'

* * *

Groaning, Serrat rolled on to her back. The sun beat down hot against her eyelids as the scattered fragments of her memory gathered. The Tiste Andii had been about to make her move on the woman in the alley below. With that one dead, the Coin Bearer's protectors would number but one. And when they left the tenement block under cover of darkness, they'd walk right into the trap she'd set.

The assassin-mage opened her eyes to a mid-morning sun overhead. Her daggers, which she'd held in her hands as she crouched at the rooftop's edge, now lay on the pebbled surface beside her, neatly placed side by side. A thick, dull ache throbbed in the back of her skull. She probed the wound, wincing, then sat up.

The world spun, then settled. Serrat was bewildered and angry. She'd been blind-sided, and whoever had done it was good, good enough to sneak up on a Tiste Andii assassin-mage. And that was worrying, since they'd yet to meet such a match in Darujhistan, with the exception of those two Claw on the night of the ambush. But if it had been the Claw, she'd be dead now.

Instead, the arrangements looked to have been designed more with embarrassment in mind than anything else. Leaving her here in broad daylight, weapons beside her, hinted of a subtle and cunning sense of humour. Oponn? Possibly, though gods rarely acted so directly, preferring unwitting agents culled from among the mortal masses.

One certainty rose from the mystery, however, and that was that she'd lost her opportunity to kill the Coin Bearer – at least, for another day. Next time, she vowed, as she climbed to her feet and accessed her Kurald Galain Warren, her secret foes would find her ready for them.

The air around her shimmered with sorcery. When it settled, Serrat was gone.

541

* * *

Motes of dust drifted through the dead, hot air of the Phoenix Inn's attic. The slanting ceiling rose from five feet along the east wall to seven feet along the west wall. Sunlight streamed in from windows at each end of the long and narrow room.

Both Crokus and Apsalar slept, though at opposite ends of the room. Sitting on a crate beside the trap-door, Meese cleaned her nails with a sliver of wood. Leaving Mallet's tenement and making their way across the rooftops to this hiding place had proved an easy task. Too easy, in fact. Irilta reported that no one on the streets had followed them. And the rooftops themselves had been empty of life. It was as if a path free of obstruction had been made for them.

More of the Eel's brilliance at work? Meese grunted softly. Maybe. More likely Meese was putting too much weight on the instinctive unease that travelled like an elusive itch along her spine. Even now she felt hidden eyes upon them, and that, she told herself, glaring around the musty attic, was impossible.

There came a soft knock at the trap-door. The door swung up and Irilta appeared. 'Meese?' she whispered loudly.

'Breathing down your neck,' Meese rumbled, tossing the wood sliver on to the oily floor. 'Tell Scurve this place is a fire waiting to happen.'

Irilta grunted as she pulled herself into the room. She shut the trap-door and wiped the dust from her hands. 'Getting strange downstairs,' she said. 'City wagon rolls up and off comes a guard and some other fellow carrying Coll between them. The old fool's near-dead from a sword cut. They put him in Kruppe's room a floor down. Sulty's run off to find a cutter, but it don't look good. Not good at all.'

Meese squinted in the dusty air, her gaze fixing on Crokus where he still slept. 'What's the other one look like?' she asked.

Irilta grinned. 'Good enough for a roll on the mat, I'd say. Said he found Coll on Jammit's Worry, bleeding all over the

542

place. Coll woke up long enough to tell him to ride here. The guy's downstairs in the bar right now, eating enough for three men.'

Meese grunted. 'Foreigner?'

Irilta strode to the window facing the street. 'Speaks Daru like he was born to it. But he said he'd come down from the north. Pale, Genabaris before that. He's got the soldier about him, I'd say.'

'Any word from the Eel yet?'

'We keep the lad here for now.'

'And the girl?'

'The same.'

Meese sighed loudly. 'Crokus ain't gonna like being cooped up here.'

Irilta glared over at Crokus's sleeping form. *Was the lad truly asleep?* 'No choice. Got word that there's a couple of guardsmen waiting at Mammot's place – too late, of course, but they've got damn close.' Irilta rubbed dust from the window and leaned forward. 'Sometimes I swear I see someone, or maybe something. Then I blink and it's gone.'

'Know what you mean.' Bones creaking, Meese pushed herself to her feet. 'I think even the Eel's beginning to sweat.' She chuckled. 'Life's heating up, friend. Rolling times ahead.'

Irilta nodded grimly. 'Roll on, roll on.'

Captain Paran refilled his tankard for the third time. Was this what that Tiste Andii had meant about his luck turning? Since coming to this land he'd found three friends – something wholly unexpected and new to him, precious, in fact. But the Tattersail he knew was dead, and in her place . . . *a child.* Toc was dead. And now it looked like Coll would join that list.

He ran a finger through a pool of spilled beer on the table, creating a river leading to a crack between two planks, then watched as the beer drained down and out of sight. He felt a

543

spreading wetness on his right shin but ignored it as his eyes focused on the crack. The wood had been bolted down, joining the thick planks to an equally robust frame of legs.

What had Rake said? Paran rose and unclipped his sword belt. He laid it on the table, then withdrew Chance.

The few regulars in the bar fell silent and turned to watch him. Behind the counter, Scurve reached for his club.

The captain noticed none of this. With the sword in his right hand, he set the point into the crack and brought the weapon vertical. Working it back and forth, he managed to drive it close to half its length between the planks. Then he sat down again and reached for his beer.

Everyone relaxed, and spoke among themselves in shared confusion.

Paran swallowed a mouthful of beer, frowning at Chance. What had Rake said? When your luck turns, break the sword. Or give it to your worst enemy. He doubted Oponn would accept it, however. And that meant breaking it. The sword had been with him for a long time. He'd used it in battle only once, and that had been against the Hound.

Faintly, he heard the words of one of his childhood tutors. The man's lined face rose into his thoughts to accompany the voice. 'Those whom the gods choose, 'tis said, they first separate from other mortals – by treachery, by stripping from you your spirit's lifeblood. The gods will take all your loved ones, one by one, to their death. And, as you harden, as you become what they seek, the gods smile and nod. Each company you shun brings you closer to them. 'Tis the shaping of a tool, son, the prod and pull, and the final succour they offer you is to end your loneliness – the very isolation they helped you create.' *Never get noticed, boy.*

Had the shaping begun? Paran scowled. Was he responsible for taking Coll's life? The mere brush of friendship between them – enough to seal the man's doom? 'Oponn,' he whispered, 'you've a lot to answer for, and answer for it you shall.'

He set down the tankard and rose. Then he reached for the sword.

Climbing the steps of the Phoenix Inn, Kalam paused. Damn, there it was again, this feeling that unseen eyes were fixed on him. The sensation, born of his Claw training, had struck him four times in quick succession since he'd come within sight of this bar. Heeding such warnings was what kept him alive, and yet he felt no malice in that unwanted attention – rather, it had the feel of amused curiosity, as if whoever watched him knew full well who and what he was, yet seemed unconcerned.

He shook himself, then entered the bar. As soon as he took his first step into the heavy, stagnant atmosphere, Kalam knew that something was wrong. He shut the door behind him, waited for his eyes to adjust to the gloom. He heard breathing, the light scuff of furniture and clank of tankards coming to rest on tabletops. So, there were people here. Then why the silence?

As the grey confines of the bar grew defined, he saw that its denizens had turned their backs to him and were watching a man standing behind his table at the far end of the room. The lantern light reflected dully from a sword thrust through the table, and the man had closed one hand around its grip. He seemed oblivious to every one else in the bar.

Kalam took a half-dozen steps, coming to the near end of the counter. His dark eyes remained on the man with the sword, and a frown deepened the lines on his broad, flat forehead. The assassin stopped. Was it a trick of this damn light? he wondered. 'No,' he said, startling the innkeeper behind the counter, 'it isn't.' He pushed himself back from the counter, ran his eyes over the others in the chamber – all locals. He'd have to take the risk.

A band of tension tightened around Kalam's neck and

shoulders as he strode directly for the man, who looked to be but moments away from snapping his sword's blade. The assassin plucked an empty chair from a table in his path and slammed it down one-handed opposite the man. Startled eyes fixed on Kalam.

'Your god-given luck's holding, Captain,' the assassin rumbled, in low, close tones. 'Sit down.'

His expression confused and frightened, Paran released his grip on the weapon and sank back into his seat.

Kalam followed suit and leaned forward over the table. 'What's all this drama anyway?' he asked, in a whisper.

The captain frowned. 'Who are you?'

Behind them conversations resumed, loud with rattled nerves.

'Ain't you guessed?' Kalam wagged his head. 'Corporal Kalam, Ninth Squad, Bridgeburners. The last time I saw you, you was recovering from two fatal knife wounds—'

Paran's hands shot out and gripped Kalam's shirt. The assassin was too surprised to react, and the captain's words confused him all the more. 'Is your squad's healer still alive, Corporal?'

'What? Alive? Yeah, sure, why not? What's—?'

'Shut up,' Paran snapped. 'Just listen, soldier. Bring him here. Now! No questions. I'm giving you a direct order, Corporal.' He released his grip on the assassin's shirt. 'Now, move!'

Kalam almost saluted, but caught himself in time. 'As you command, sir,' he whispered.

Paran glared at the corporal's back until the man disappeared through the front door. Then he surged to his feet. 'Innkeeper!' he called, stepping around the table. 'The black man will be showing up in a few minutes with company. Send them up to Coll's room on the double. Understood?'

Scurve nodded.

Paran strode to the stairs. As he reached them he glanced back at the sword. 'And nobody touch that sword,' he ordered, swinging a glare across everyone in the room. Nobody seemed inclined to challenge him. With a sharp, satisfied nod, the captain ascended the stairs.

On the first floor, he strode down the hallway to the last room on the right. He entered without knocking to find Sulty and a local surgeon sitting at the room's lone table. Coll's blanket-covered form lay unmoving on the bed.

The surgeon rose. 'It's no good,' he said, in a thin, reedy voice. 'The infection's too far along.'

Paran asked, 'Is he still breathing?'

'Aye,' the surgeon replied. 'But it won't be for much longer. If the wound had been further down on his leg, I might have been able to cut it off. Even then, I'm afraid the poison's spread through all of him. I'm sorry, sir.'

'Leave,' Paran snapped.

The surgeon bowed and prepared to depart.

'What do I owe you for the services?' the captain asked, remembering.

The surgeon frowned over at Sulty. 'Why, nothing, sir. I failed.' He left the room, shutting the door behind him.

Sulty joined the captain at the bedside. She wiped her face as she looked down on Coll, but said nothing. A few minutes later she, too, left the room, unable to remain any longer.

Paran found a stool and pulled it over to the bed. He sat and leaned his forearms on his knees. He was not sure how long he sat there, staring down at the straw-littered floor, but the door slamming open behind him brought him to his feet.

A bearded man stood in the doorway, his slate-grey eyes hard and cold.

'Are you Mallet?' Paran demanded.

The man shook his head and strode inside. Behind him

547

appeared Kalam and another man. The latter's gaze found Coll, and he walked quickly to the bed.

'I'm Sergeant Whiskeyjack,' the bearded man said quietly. 'Pardon my directness, sir, but what the hell are you doing here?'

Ignoring the question, Paran joined the healer. Mallet laid a hand over the crusted bandages. He glared up at the captain. 'Can't you smell the rot? He's gone.' Mallet frowned and leaned forward. 'No, wait ... Damn, I don't believe it.' The healer took a spoon-shaped blade from his pouch and removed the bandages. Then he began to dig into the wound with the blade. 'Shedenul's Mercy, someone's stuffed this with herbs!' He drove his fingers into the wound.

Coll jerked and moaned.

Mallet grinned. 'Hah, that got you going, did it? Good.' He probed deeper. 'This cut's half-way through the bone,' he breathed in amazement. 'Those damn herbs have poisoned his marrow. Who the hell treated this?' he asked, looking accusingly at Paran.

'I don't know,' Paran said.

'All right,' Mallet said, removing his hand and wiping it on the blankets. 'Move back, everybody. Give me some room. A minute later, Captain, and this man would've been striding through Hood's Gate.' He pressed his hand down on Coll's chest and closed his eyes. 'And be glad I'm as good as I am.'

'Now, Captain?'

Paran walked over to the table and motioned for the sergeant to join him. 'First, has Adjunct Lorn contacted you yet?'

Whiskeyjack's blank look was sufficient answer.

'Good, I'm in time, then.' Paran glanced up at Kalam, who had stationed himself behind the sergeant. 'You've been set up. The plan was to take the city, yes, but also to make certain you were all killed in the process.'

548

Whiskeyjack held up a hand. 'A moment, sir. You and Tattersail worked this out?'

Paran closed his eyes briefly. 'She's ... dead. Chasing Hairlock out on the Rhivi Plain. Tayschrenn got to her. It was also her intent to find you and tell you all that I'm telling you. I'm afraid I won't be her equal as your ally once the Adjunct shows up, but at least I can prepare you somewhat.'

Kalam spoke. 'I don't like the idea of Oponn's pawn supposedly helping us.'

Paran nodded. 'I have it on good authority that I'm not Oponn's. That sword downstairs is, though. Your squad wizard should be able to confirm this.'

'The Adjunct's plan,' Whiskeyjack reminded him, the fingers of one hand tapping slowly on the tabletop.

'She'll have no trouble finding you. She has a talent in that area. But I fear she's not the major threat. There's a T'lan Imass with her. Maybe her mission is simply to lead him to you, then he'll handle the rest.'

Kalam cursed and began pacing behind the sergeant's chair.

Whiskeyjack reached a decision. 'The satchel, Corporal.'

The assassin frowned, then picked up the sergeant's standard-issue supply satchel left beside the door. He returned and set it down on the tabletop.

Whiskeyjack released the straps and pulled out an object wrapped in burgundy silk. He removed the cloth, revealing twin yellowed bones of a human forearm. The elbow-end's ball joints were bound together with verdigrised copper wire; the wrist ends were wrapped as well, but as a misshapen knife grip, beyond which jutted a serrated blade.

'What is it?' the captain asked. 'I've never seen its like before.'

'Be surprised if you had,' Whiskeyjack said. 'Back in the days of the Emperor, the inner ring of military commanders each possessed one of these, the booty of a looted K'Chain

Che'Malle tomb.' He grasped the bones with both hands. 'It was the source of much of our success, Captain.' He rose and drove the point into the table.

A flash of white light erupted from the bones, then contracted to a swirl spinning thread-like between them. Paran heard a voice he knew.

'I was getting worried, Whiskeyjack,' High Fist Dujek growled.

'Unavoidable,' the sergeant replied, frowning at Paran. 'We've had little to report . . . until now. But I need to know the situation in Pale, High Fist.'

'You want an update before you spill the bad news, eh? Fair enough,' Dujek said. 'Tayschrenn's stumbling in circles. He was last happy when Bellurdan was killed along with Tattersail. Two more of the Old Guard gone in one fell swoop. Since then, all he's got is questions. What game is Oponn playing? Was there truly a clash between the Knight of Darkness and Shadowthrone? Did a soul-shifted puppet kidnap, torture then murder a Claw officer in Nathilog and what truths were revealed by the poor man?'

'We were not aware that Hairlock had done that, High Fist.'

'I believe you, Whiskeyjack. In any case, enough of the Empress's plans *have* been discovered and, indeed, she seems convinced that the dismantling of my army will pull me back under her wing, in time to saddle me with the command of the Seven Cities' garrisons and put a bloody stop to the rebellion that's brewing. She seriously miscalculated there – if only she'd paid attention to Toc the Younger's reports. Well . . . Laseen's intentions now seem to be riding on Adjunct Lorn and Onos T'oolan. They've reached the Jaghut barrow, Whiskeyjack.'

Mallet joined them and met Kalam's stunned gaze. Clearly, even they'd had no idea that their sergeant was so well informed. Suspicion dawned in the assassin's eyes, and Paran nodded to himself. It was happening, after all.

550

Dujek continued, 'The Moranth Black are ready to march, but it's only for show, and to get them out of the city. So, what are we looking at, friend? The balance of the world is with you, in Darujhistan. If Lorn and Onos T'oolan succeed in unleashing the Tyrant on the city, you can be certain that you and your squad are intended to be on the casualty list. Closer to home, here's what you want: we're ready to move. Tayschrenn himself will trigger events when he announces the disbanding of the Bridgeburners – the blind idiot. Now, I'm waiting.'

'High Fist,' Whiskeyjack began, 'Captain Paran's made it. He's sitting across from me right now. His story is that Oponn's working through his sword, not him.' He met the captain's eyes. 'I believe him.'

Dujek spoke. 'Captain?'

'Yes, High Fist?'

'Was Toc any help?'

Paran winced. 'He gave his life for this, High Fist. The puppet Hairlock ambushed us, tossed Toc into a – a rent or something.'

There was silence, then Dujek said, his voice hoarse, 'I'm sorry to hear that, Captain. More than you know. His father . . . Well, enough of that. Go on, Whiskeyjack.'

'No success yet in contacting the local Assassins' Guild, High Fist. We've mined the intersections, though. I'll be explaining everything to my men tonight. The question remains what to do about Captain Paran.'

'Understood,' Dujek replied. 'Captain Paran?'

'Sir?'

'Have you come to any conclusions?'

Paran glanced at Whiskeyjack. 'Yes, sir. I think so.'

'So? What choice will you make, Captain?'

He ran a hand through his hair and leaned back in the chair. 'High Fist,' he said slowly, 'Tayschrenn killed Tattersail.' *And failed, but that is a secret I will keep to myself.* 'The Adjunct's plan included betraying her word to me, and probably killing me in the process. But, I admit, that's secondary to what Tayschrenn did.' Looking up, he met Whiskeyjack's steady gaze. 'Tattersail took care of me, and I her after that Hound. It . . .' he hesitated '. . . it meant something, High Fist.' He straightened. 'So, I gather you intend to defy the Empress. But what then? Do we challenge the Empire's hundred legions with ten thousand men? Do we proclaim an independent kingdom and wait for Laseen to make an example of us? I need more details, High Fist, before I decide whether I join you. Because, sir, I want vengeance.'

Dujek responded, 'The Empress loses Genabackis, Captain. We've got the support for that. By the time the Malazan Marines arrive to reinforce the campaign, it'll already be over. The Crimson Guard won't even let them disembark. Expect Nathilog to rise up and Genabaris to follow. The Moranth alliance is about to lose its punch – though I'm afraid I can't give you the details on that.

'My plans, Captain? They might not make sense, because I don't have time to explain. But we're readying ourselves to take on a new player in the game – someone completely outside all of this, and that someone is damn nasty. He is called the Pannion Seer, who even now prepares his armies for a holy war. You want vengeance? Leave Tayschrenn to enemies closer to home. As for Lorn, she's all yours, if you can manage it. I can't offer you anything more, Captain. You can say no. Nobody will kill you for that.'

Paran stared at his hands. 'I want to know when High Mage Tayschrenn gets what he deserves.'

'Agreed.'

'Very well, High Fist. As far as this present situation is concerned, however, I'd rather Sergeant Whiskeyjack remained in command.'

Dujek asked, a grin in his voice, 'Whiskeyjack?'

'Accepted,' the sergeant answered. He smiled at Paran. 'Welcome aboard, Captain.'

'Enough?' Dujek asked.

'We'll speak again after it's all done,' Whiskeyjack said. 'Until then, High Fist, success.'

'Success, Whiskeyjack.'

The threads of light faded. As soon as they were gone Kalam rounded on his sergeant. 'You old bastard! Fiddler told me Dujek wouldn't hear any talk of revolt! Not only that, the High Fist told you to walk after this mission!'

Whiskeyjack shrugged, removing the strange contraption from the table. 'Things change, Corporal. When Dujek got the Adjunct's word on next year's reinforcements, it became obvious that someone was ensuring that the Genabackan Campaign would end in disaster. Now, even Dujek won't tolerate that. Obviously, plans would have to be revised.' He faced Paran, his eyes hardening. 'I'm sorry, Captain, but Lorn has to live.'

'But the High Fist—'

Whiskeyjack shook his head. 'She's on her way into the city, assuming that she and the Imass succeed in freeing the Jaghut. The Tyrant will need a reason to come to Darujhistan, and we can only assume that, somehow, Lorn will be that reason. She will find us, Captain. Once that happens, we'll decide what's to be done with her, depending on what she tells us. If you challenge her openly, she will kill you. If necessary, she *will* have to die, but her demise will be subtle. Do you have problems with any of this?'

Paran released a long breath. 'Can you at least explain why you went ahead and mined the city?'

'In a moment,' Whiskeyjack said, rising. 'First,' he said, 'who's the wounded man?'

'Not wounded any more,' Mallet said, grinning at Paran. 'Just sleeping.'

Paran also rose. 'In that case, I'll also explain everything. Just let me go downstairs and retrieve my sword.' At the door he paused and turned to Whiskeyjack. 'One more thing. Where's your recruit, Sorry?'

Kalam answered, 'Missing. We know what she is, Captain. Do you?'

'Yes.' *But she may not be what she once was, assuming Shadowthrone didn't lie.* He thought to relate that part of his story, then dismissed the notion. He couldn't be sure, after all. Better to wait and see.

The burial chamber proved to be a small, nondescript beehive tomb, the low dome constructed of roughly dressed stones. The passageway leading to it was narrow and less than four feet high, sloping slightly downwards. The chamber's floor was of packed earth and in its centre rose a circular wall of stones, capped by a single, massive lintel stone. Frost-crusted objects lay on this flat surface.

Tool swung to the Adjunct. 'The object you seek is called a Finnest. Within it is stored the Jaghut Tyrant's powers. It is perhaps best described as a self-contained Omtose Phellack Warren. He will discover it is missing once fully awakened, and will unerringly hunt it down.'

Lorn blew on her numb hands, then slowly approached the lintel stone. 'And while it's in my possession?' she asked.

'Your Otataral sword will deaden its aura. Not completely. The Finnest should not remain in your hands for long, Adjunct.'

She scanned the objects scattered on the stone surface. The Imass joined her. Lorn picked up a scabbarded knife, then discarded it. In this Tool could not help her. She had to rely upon her own senses, honed by the strange, unpredictable effects of the Otataral. A mirror set in an antler caught her eye. The mica surface was latticed in a web of frost, yet it seemed to glimmer with a light of its own. She reached for it, then hesitated. Beside it, almost lost among the crystalline frost, was a small, round object. It lay upon a flap of hide. Lorn frowned, then picked it up.

As its ice coating melted, she saw that it was not perfectly round. She polished the blackened surface and studied it closely.

'I believe it is an acorn,' Tool said.

Lorn nodded. 'And it's the Finnest.' Her gaze fell to the capped mound of rocks. 'What an odd choice.'

The Imass shrugged in a clatter of bones. 'The Jaghut are odd people.'

'Tool, they weren't very war-like, were they? I mean, before your kind sought to destroy them.'

The Imass was slow to reply. 'Even then,' he said at last. 'The key lay in making them angry, for then they destroyed indiscriminately, including their own.'

Lorn shut her eyes briefly. She pocketed the Finnest. 'Let's get out of here.'

'Yes, Adjunct. Even now the Jaghut Tyrant stirs.'

555

CHAPTER NINETEEN

> But someone died here
> alas. Who drinks
> of this now and then
> and stirs the ashes
> of thine own pyre?
> Maker of Paths, you
> were never so thirsty
> in youth . . .
>
> *Old Temple*
> Sivyn Stor
> (b.1022)

'This isn't right, Meese,' Crokus said, as he rubbed the sleep from his eyes. 'We can't just hide in here for ever.'

Apsalar said, from the window, 'It's almost dark.'

Meese crouched once again to check the trap-door's lock. 'We're moving you again, after the twelfth bell. Irilta's down below, getting details.'

'Who's giving these orders?' Crokus demanded. 'Have you found Uncle Mammot yet?'

'Relax, lad.' Meese straightened. 'No, we ain't found your uncle. And the orders come from your protectors. I won't answer any questions about who they are, Crokus, so save your breath.'

Apsalar shifted position by the window to take in Meese. 'Your friend's been a long time,' she said. 'Do you think something's happened?'

Meese looked away. This girl was sharp. Of course, Meese had known that the first time they'd met, and old Chert had found out the hard way. 'Not sure,' she admitted. She bent to unlock the trap-door. 'You both stay put,' she ordered, glaring at Crokus. 'I ain't going to be happy if you do something stupid. Understand?'

The boy looked glum, his arms crossed. He watched as Meese opened the trap-door and climbed down the ladder.

'Close this up after me,' she said, from below, 'and lock it. Wait to hear from either me or Irilta, got it?'

'Yes.' Crokus strode to the square hole in the floor and stared down at Meese. 'We got it,' he said, grasping the door and swinging it shut. Then he locked it.

'Crokus,' Apsalar asked, 'why did you kill a guard?'

This was their first time alone since entering the city. Crokus glanced away. 'It was an accident. I don't want to talk about it.' He crossed the room to the back window. 'All these people trying to protect me,' he said. 'Makes me uneasy. There's more going on than just an order for my arrest. Hood's Breath, the Thieves' Guild takes care of such things, that's why they get ten per cent of every job I do. No, none of it makes sense, Apsalar. And,' he said, as he unlatched the window, 'I'm sick of everybody telling me what to do.'

She came to his side. 'Are we leaving, then?'

'Damn right. It's already dusk so we'll take the rooftops.' He pulled and the window swung inward.

'Where?'

Crokus grinned. 'I've got a great hiding-place in mind. Nobody will find us, not even my protectors. Once there, I can do what I want.'

Apsalar's brown eyes searched his face. 'What do you want to do?' she asked softly.

He looked away, concentrating on propping up the window. 'I want to talk to Challice D'Arle,' he said. 'Face to face.'

'She betrayed you, didn't she?'

'Never mind that. Are you staying here?'

'No,' she said, surprised. 'I'm coming with you, Crokus.'

The power of her Warren bristled on her body. Serrat scanned the area one more time, still seeing and sensing nothing. She was certain she was alone. The Tiste Andii tensed as the window in the attic beneath her creaked inward on rusty hinges. Knowing herself to be invisible, she leaned forward.

The lad's head popped out. He glanced at the alley below, the opposite rooftops and those to either side, then he looked up. His gaze passed right through Serrat, and she smiled.

It hadn't taken long to find him again. His only company, she could sense, was a young woman whose aura was harmless, astonishingly innocent. The other two women no longer occupied the attic. Excellent. It would be that much easier. She stepped back as the Coin Bearer climbed through the window.

A moment later he scrambled on to the sloping rooftop.

Serrat decided that she would waste no time. Even as the Coin Bearer pushed himself to his feet, she sprang forward.

Her charge met an invisible hand, driving into her chest with bone-jarring force. It pushed her back through the air, giving a final shove that sent her cartwheeling beyond the roof's edge. Her spells of invisibility and flight remained with her, even when she rebounded off a brick chimney, dazed and drifting.

558

Apsalar appeared on the roof's edge. Crokus crouched before her, daggers in hand and glaring all around him. 'What's wrong?' she whispered, frightened.

Slowly, Crokus relaxed and turned a rueful grin her way. 'Just nerves,' he said. 'Thought I saw something, felt a wind. Looked like ... Well, never mind.' He looked around again. 'There's nothing here. Come on, then.'

'Where's this new hiding-place of yours?' Apsalar asked, as she gained the rooftop.

He faced east and pointed to the shadowed hills rising on the other side of the wall. 'Up there,' he said. 'Right under their very noses.'

Murillio clasped on his sword-belt. The longer he waited for Rallick to arrive the more certain he was that Ocelot had killed his friend. The only question that remained was whether Coll still lived. Maybe Rallick had done enough, wounded Ocelot sufficiently to prevent the Clan Master from completing the contract. *I can hope, anyway.*

They'd know at the Phoenix Inn, and each minute that passed made his Spartan room seem smaller, more cramped. If Coll lived, Murillio vowed to attempt Rallick's role in the plan. He checked his rapier. It'd been years since his last duel, and Turban Orr was said to be the city's best. His chances looked poor.

He collected his cape and fastened the collar around his neck. And who was this Circle Breaker with all the devastating news? How did this Eel justify involving himself or herself in their schemes? Murillio's eyes narrowed. Was it possible? That little round runt of a man?

He pulled on his doeskin gloves, muttering under his breath.

A scrape at the door caught his attention. A heavy sigh of relief escaped him. 'Rallick, you old bastard,' he said, as he opened the door. For an instant he thought the hallway empty, then his gaze fell to the floor. The assassin lay there, his clothing soaked through with blood, looking up at him with a weak grin.

'Sorry I'm late,' he said. 'My legs keep giving out.'

Cursing, Murillio helped Rallick into the room and on to the bed. He returned to the door, checked the hallway, then shut and set the lock.

Rallick pushed himself upright against the headboard. 'Orr offered a contract on Coll—'

'I know, I know,' Murillio said, as he approached. He knelt beside the bed. 'Let's see to your wound.'

'I need to take off my armour first,' Rallick said. 'Ocelot stuck me one. Then I killed him. Coll's still alive as far as I know. What day is this?'

'The same day,' Murillio said, as he helped his friend remove his mail hauberk. 'We're still on schedule, though from all this blood it looks like you won't be duelling Orr at Simtal's Fête. I'll handle that.'

'Stupid idea.' Rallick groaned. 'You'll just get killed and Turban Orr will walk away, still Lady Simtal's backer and still powerful enough to prevent Coll's claim to rights.'

Murillio made no reply to that. He peeled back the leather padding to expose the wound. 'What's with all this blood on you?' he demanded. 'There's nothing here but a week-old scar.'

'Huh?' Rallick probed the place where Ocelot's wrist-blade had stabbed him. It felt mildly tender, itchy at the edges. 'I'll be damned,' he muttered. 'Anyway, get me a washcloth, so I can clean all this rust off.'

Murillio sat back on his haunches, clearly confused. 'What rust?'

'The stuff on my face,' Rallick said, scowling at his friend.

Murillio leaned close.

'Baruk's magic-deadening powder!' the assassin snapped. 'How the hell do you think I managed to kill Ocelot?'

'Your face is clean, Rallick,' Murillio said. 'You're welcome to the washcloth. We'll get all that dried blood off you in any case.'

'Give me a mirror first,' Rallick said.

Murillio found one and stood watching Rallick study his own pallid reflection, which bore a deep frown. He observed drily, 'Well, that expression confirms it for me.'

'Confirms what?' the assassin asked, in a dangerous tone.

'That you're you, Rallick.' Murillio squared his shoulders. 'Rest here for a while. You've lost a lot of blood. I'm off to find the Eel and tell him a thing or two.'

'You know who the Eel is?'

He strode to the door. 'I've got a hunch. If you can walk, try locking this door behind me, will you?'

Kruppe mopped his brow with his limp, sodden handkerchief. 'Kruppe has uttered every single detail at least a thousand times, Master Baruk,' he complained. 'Will this ordeal never end? Look at yon window. A whole day in Kruppe's life has passed!'

The alchemist sat frowning down at his slippers, occasionally wiggling his toes, as the minutes passed. It was as if he'd forgotten Kruppe's presence in the room, and it had been this way for the past hour, no matter how much Kruppe talked.

'Master Baruk,' Kruppe tried again, 'may your loyal servant leave? He's not yet recovered from his horrific journey in the eastern wastelands. Simple fare, of roast mutton, potatoes, fried onions and carrots, mussels in garlic butter, dates, cheese, smoked slipper minnows and a carafe of wine, now occupies Kruppe's mind to the exclusion of all else. Such as he has been reduced, his world contracting apace with his stomach—'

Baruk spoke. 'For the past year,' he said slowly, 'an agent of

561

the Eel's, known to me as Circle Breaker, has been providing me with vital information regarding the City Council.'

Kruppe's mouth shut with an audible click.

'It lies within my powers, of course, to identify this Circle Breaker at my leisure. I have a score of missives written in his own hand – the parchment alone suffices.' Baruk's eyes lifted to fix on the mantelpiece. 'I am considering doing so,' he said. 'I must speak with this Eel. We've reached a critical juncture in the life of Darujhistan, and I must know the Eel's purposes. We could work in close alliance, sharing all we know, and perhaps we can save the life of this city. Perhaps.'

Kruppe cleared his throat and wiped his brow again. He carefully folded the handkerchief on his lap, then stuffed it into a sleeve. 'If you wish to convey such a message,' he said quietly, 'Kruppe can oblige Master Baruk.'

Baruk's gaze dropped calmly to Kruppe. 'Thank you. How soon the reply?'

'By this evening,' Kruppe said.

'Excellent. I admit to resisting my own decision to compromise this Circle Breaker. The means you offer seem the best. You may go now, Kruppe.'

Kruppe's head bobbed. He rose. 'Until tonight, then, Master Baruk.'

Coll slept while the men in the room continued their discussion. Mallet said that the man might well sleep for days, Hood's Gate having been as close as it was.

Paran felt frustrated. Something was missing from Whiskeyjack's explanations. The saboteurs had gone ahead with planting the mines, and even now it was Whiskeyjack's plan to detonate them. More, the efforts to contact the Assassins' Guild remained with the purpose of offering a contract on Darujhistan's true rulers. These facts hardly complemented this idea of a full-scale, continent-wide revolt.

If anything, wouldn't Dujek be seeking local alliances?

As the sergeant went on, more and more of what the man said gathered in the captain's mind, and he sensed a pattern emerging. He broke his hour-long silence and addressed Whiskeyjack. 'You still intend to cripple Darujhistan. And I keep thinking about that, and now I think I've worked out why.' He studied Whiskeyjack's blank expression. 'What you seek is to crack this city wide open. Chaos in the streets, a headless government. Everybody who matters shows up and they kill each other. What does that leave?' Paran leaned forward, his eyes hard. 'Dujek's got an army ten thousand strong, about to become outlaws of the Empire. Maintaining ten thousand soldiers is an expensive business. Housing them is even tougher. Dujek knows Pale's days are numbered. Caladan Brood's on the march down the Rhivi Plain right now. Are the Moranth about to pull out of the alliance? Maybe make a move of their own? Tayschrenn's in Pale – maybe old Onearm can handle him, maybe not. How am I so far, Sergeant?'

Whiskeyjack glanced over at Kalam, then shrugged. 'Go on,' he said to Paran.

'Darujhistan's filled with panic. No one knows anything. In marches Dujek, rebel army at his heels. He'll set things aright. Wealth beyond measure falls into his lap – and he'll need all of it if he's to oppose what the Empress sends after him. So, the city gets conquered after all. Fancy that.' He sat back.

'Not bad,' Whiskeyjack admitted, grinning at the surprise on the faces of Mallet and Kalam. 'With one piece missing. Something,' he eyed Paran, 'that might relieve the captain's sense of betrayal, if not his outrage.'

Paran's smile was cold. 'Surprise me.'

'All right, Captain. We don't give a damn if the Empress wants to come after us. She won't have much to do it with, since Seven Cities is days away from reclaiming its independence. It's coming down, Captain. On all sides. So why do we maintain our army? Look to the south. Something's growing there, so ugly it makes the Imass look like kittens. When I say we're in trouble, I don't mean just Genabackis, I mean the world. We're all in for a fight, Captain. And that's why we need Darujhistan.'

'What's to the south?' Paran asked sceptically.

Kalam answered, his words a breath of fear, 'The Pannion Seer. So the rumours are true, then. The Seer's proclaimed a holy war. The genocide's begun.'

Whiskeyjack got to his feet. 'Explain it to the man,' he said to Kalam. 'That Guild still needs contacting, if possible. Hood knows, we've made a show of ourselves at this bar. Might be what's needed, though.' He looked to Paran. 'Captain, I don't think Adjunct Lorn should know you're alive, do you?'

'No.'

'Can you stay here until I call for you?'

Paran glanced at Kalam, then nodded.

'Good. Mallet, let's move.'

'We've lost at least two days,' Lorn pronounced, thankful for the day's lingering heat. 'These are thirsty horses.'

Tool stood near the shattered barrow marker, watching the Adjunct ready her horses for the journey into Darujhistan. 'How fares your wound, Adjunct?' he asked.

'Mostly healed,' she replied. 'Otataral has that effect on me.'

'My task is finished,' the Imass said. 'If it becomes your desire to accompany me after you have completed your mission, I will be found here for the next ten days. I wish to observe this Jaghut Tyrant – though it will not see me, nor will I interfere. My thoughts of success are with you, Adjunct.'

Lorn climbed on to her horse and stared down at the Imass. 'Fare well in your search, Onos T'oolan.'

'That name is past. I am now Tool.'

564

She grinned, then gathered the reins and kicked her mount forward, the packhorse trailing on its lead. Once the Finnest was out of her hands, she would focus her talents on discovering this Coin Bearer. Until now she had not allowed herself to think about Oponn. She had had too many other, more immediate concerns, like Sorry.

A strong sense of regret filled her at the loss of Captain Paran. That man would have made her task much easier, possibly even enjoyable. Though he'd been a dour man, getting grimmer by the minute, she had to admit that she had been attracted to him. There might have been something there.

'Well,' she sighed, as she urged her horse up a hillside, 'dying's never in anybody's plans.'

Tool's estimation gave her two days at the most. Then the Jaghut would be fully awake, and free of the barrow. The Finnest would have to be securely in place long before then. She looked forward to her meeting with Sorry, and instinctively brushed a hand against her sword's pommel. To kill a servant of Shadow, perhaps the Rope himself. The Empress's pleasure at that would be immense.

She realized that the doubts that had plagued her, borne on those dark wings of knowledge, now lay quiescent. An effect of her time in the barrow? More likely this acorn in her pocket. Or perhaps she'd moved unconsciously beyond them. *When the time for action comes, all doubts must be discarded.* An old Claw tenet. She knew herself well, and she knew how to control all that was within her. Years of training, discipline, loyalty and duty. The virtues of a soldier.

She was ready for the mission, and with this realization the weight on her shoulders vanished. She urged her mount into a gallop.

Crokus craned his head and squinted into the darkness above. 'Right to the top,' he said. 'We can see the whole city from there.'

Apsalar eyed the stairs dubiously. 'It's awfully dark,' she said. 'Are you sure this tower is abandoned? I mean, my father told me stories about ghosts, undead monsters, and they always lived in ruined places.' She looked around with wide eyes. 'Places just like this one.'

Crokus groaned. 'The god K'rul's been dead for thousands of years,' he said. 'Besides, no one ever comes here, so what would all those monsters do with all that spare time? What would they eat? Tell me that! Stupid stories.' He walked to the foot of the spiral staircase. 'Come on, the view's worth it.'

She watched Crokus climb upward and hurried to follow before he disappeared from sight. What at first seemed to be impenetrable darkness slowly faded to grey, and Apsalar was surprised to find herself able to discern even the minutest details. The first things she noticed were the soot-stained paintings on the wall to their left. Each stone panel was as wide as a single step, rising half a dozen feet in a jagged procession that mimicked the stairs. 'Crokus,' she whispered, 'there's a story painted on this wall.'

Crokus snorted. 'Don't be ridiculous! You can't even see your hand in front of your face in here.'

I can't?

He continued, 'Wait till you get up top. Those clouds we saw should have cleared the moon by now.'

'There's something wet on these steps,' Apsalar said.

'Run off from up top,' he explained, exasperated.

'No, it isn't,' she insisted. 'It's thick, and sticky.'

Crokus stopped above her. 'Look, will you be quiet for a minute? We're almost there.'

They emerged on to a platform bathed in the moon's silver glow. Near one of the low walls Crokus saw a heap of cloth. 'What's that?' he wondered. 'Looks like somebody's been camping up here.'

Apsalar stifled a gasp. 'That's a dead man!'

566

'What?' Crokus hissed. 'Not another one!' He rushed to the huddled figure and crouched beside it. 'Blessed Mowri, somebody's stabbed him in the head.'

'There's a crossbow over here.'

He grunted. 'An assassin. I saw one just like this killed here last week. There's an assassin war going on. Just like I told Kruppe and Murillio.'

'Look at the moon,' Apsalar breathed, from the far side of the platform.

Crokus shivered. She was still a cold one, at times. 'Which one?' he asked, rising.

'The shining one, of course.'

Feeling contrary, Crokus studied Moon's Spawn instead. A faint reddish glow suffused it – something he'd not seen before. A worm of fear squirmed in his stomach. Then his eyes widened. Five massive winged shapes seemed to sweep down the Moon's face, angling north-east. He blinked, and they were gone.

'Do you see its oceans?' Apsalar asked.

'What?' He turned.

'Its oceans. Grallin's Sea. That's the big one. The Lord of the Deep Waters living there is named Grallin. He tends vast, beautiful underwater gardens. Grallin will come down to us, one day, to our world. And he'll gather his chosen and take them to his world. And we'll live in those gardens, warmed by the deep fires, and our children will swim like dolphins, and we'll be happy since there won't be any more wars, and no empires, and no swords and shields. Oh, Crokus, it'll be wonderful, won't it?'

Her profile was in silhouette. He stared at her. 'Of course,' he said quietly. 'Why not?' And then that question repeated itself in his head for an entirely different reason. Why not?

BOOK SEVEN

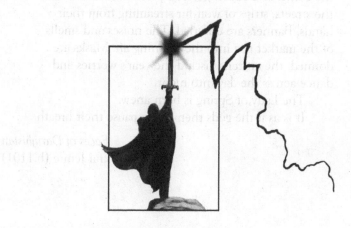

THE FÊTE

The Flaying of Fander, She-Wolf of Winter, marks the Dawn of Gedderone. The priestesses race down the streets, strips of wolf-fur streaming from their hands. Banners are unfurled. The noises and smells of the market rise into the morning air. Masks are donned, the citizens discard the year's worries and dance across the day into night.

The Lady of Spring is born anew.

It is as if the gods themselves pause their breath . . .

Faces of Darujhistan
Maskral Jemre (b.1101)

CHAPTER TWENTY

> It is said that the matron's
> blood like ice brought forth into this
> world a birthing of dragons
> and this flowing river of fate
> brought light into dark and dark into light,
> unveiling at last in cold, cold eyes
> the children of chaos . . .
>
> *T'matha's Children*
> Heboric

Murillio wondered again at Rallick's healed wound. He'd already concluded that whatever magic-deadening powder of Baruk's the assassin had used had been responsible for the healing. Nevertheless, much blood had been lost, and Rallick would need time to recover – time they didn't have. Was the assassin capable of killing Orr now?

In answer to his own question, Murillio laid a hand on the rapier at his side. He strode down the empty street, cleaving the low-lying mists that swirled like incandescent cloaks in the gaslight. Dawn was still two hours away. As was the Daru custom, the new year's celebrations would begin with sunrise, lasting through the day and well into the night.

He walked through a silent city, as if he were the last of the living yet to flee the past year's turmoil, and now shared the world with ghosts tolled among the year's dead. The Five Tusks had slipped behind in the ancient cycle, and taking its place was the Year of the Moon's Tears. Murillio mused on such obscure, arcane titles. A massive stone disc in Majesty Hall marked the Cycle of the Age, naming each year in accordance with its mysterious moving mechanisms.

As a child, he'd thought the wheel magical in how it spun slowly as the year rolled by, coming into the new year aligned precisely with the dawn whether there was cloud in the sky or not. Mammot had since explained to him that the wheel was in fact a machine. It had been a gift to Darujhistan over a thousand years ago, by a man named Icarium. It was Mammot's belief that Icarium had Jaghut blood. By all accounts he'd ridden a Jaghut horse, and a Trell strode at his side – clear evidence, Mammot asserted, to add to the wonder of the wheel itself, for the Jaghut were known to have been skilled at such creations.

Murillio wondered at the significance of the names each year bore. The close association of the Five Tusks with Moon's Tears held prophecy, according to the Seers. The Boar Tennerock's tusks were named Hate, Love, Laughter, War and Tears. Which Tusk would prove dominant in the year? The new year's name provided the answer. Murillio shrugged. He viewed such astrology with a sceptical eye. How could a man of a thousand years ago – Jaghut or otherwise – have predicted such things?

Still, he admitted to more than a few qualms. The arrival of Moon's Spawn threw the new year's title into a different light, and he knew that the local scholars – particularly those who moved in the noble circles – had become an agitated and short-tempered lot. Quite unlike their usual patronizing selves.

Murillio turned a corner on his approach to the Phoenix Inn, and collided with a short, fat man in a red coat. Both grunted, and three large boxes that the man had been carrying fell between them, spilling out their contents.

'Aye, why, Murillio! Such fortune as Kruppe is known for! Thus does your search end, here in this dank, dark street where even the rats shun the shadow. What? Is something the matter, friend Murillio?'

He stared down at the objects on the cobbles at his feet. Slowly, Murillio asked, 'What are these for, Kruppe?'

Kruppe stepped forward and frowned down at the three expertly carved masks. 'Gifts, friend Murillio, of course. For you and Rallick Nom. After all,' he looked up with a beatific smile, 'the Lady Simtal's Fête demands the finest in workmanship, the subtlest of design perfectly mated with ironic intent. Don't you think Kruppe's taste is sufficiently expensive? Do you fear embarrassment?'

'You'll not distract me this time,' Murillio growled. 'First of all, there are three masks here, not two.'

'Indeed!' Kruppe replied, bending down to pick one up. He brushed spatters of mud from the painted face. 'This is Kruppe's own. Well chosen, Kruppe pronounces with certain aplomb.'

Murillio's eyes hardened. 'You're not coming, Kruppe.'

'Well, of course Kruppe will attend! Do you think Lady Simtal would ever show herself if her long-time acquaintance, Kruppe the First, was not in attendance? Why, she'd wither with shame!'

'Dammit, you've never even met Simtal!'

'Not relevant to Kruppe's argument, friend Murillio. Kruppe has been acquainted with Simtal's existence for many years. Such association is made better, nay, pristine, for the fact that she has not met Kruppe, nor Kruppe her. And, in final argument designed to end all discussion, here,' he pulled from his sleeve a parchment scroll tied in blue silk ribbon, 'Kruppe's invitation, signed by the Lady herself.'

Murillio made a grab for it but Kruppe replaced it deftly in his sleeve.

'Rallick will kill you,' Murillio said levelly.

'Nonsense.' Kruppe placed the mask over his face. 'How will the lad ever recognize Kruppe?'

Murillio studied the man's round body, the faded red waistcoat, gathered cuffs, and the short oily curls atop his head. 'Never mind.' He sighed.

'Excellent,' Kruppe said. 'Now, please accept these two masks, gifts from your friend Kruppe. A trip is saved, and Baruk need not wait any longer for a secret message that must not be mentioned.' He replaced his mask in its box, then spun round to study the eastern skyline. 'Off to yon alchemist's abode, then. Good evening, friend—'

'Wait a minute,' Murillio said, grasping Kruppe's arm and turning him round. 'Have you seen Coll?'

'Why, of course. The man sleeps a deep, recovering sleep from his ordeals. 'Twas healed magically, Sulty said. By some stranger, yet. Coll himself was brought in by yet a second stranger, who found a third stranger, who in turn brought a fifth stranger in the company of the stranger who healed Coll. And so it goes, friend Murillio. Strange doings, indeed. Now, Kruppe must be off. Goodbye, friend—'

'Not yet,' Murillio snarled. He glanced around. The street was still empty. He leaned close. 'I've worked some things out, Kruppe. Circle Breaker contacting me put everything into order in my mind. I know who you are.'

'Aaai!' Kruppe cried, withdrawing. 'I'll not deny it, then! It's true, Murillio, Kruppe is Lady Simtal connivingly disguised.'

'Not this time! No distractions. You're the Eel, Kruppe. All this blubbering, sweaty meek-mouse stuff is just an act, isn't it? You've got half this city in your pocket, Eel.'

Eyes wide, Kruppe snatched the handkerchief from his sleeve and mopped his brow. He wrung sweat from it, droplets spattering on the cobbles, then a veritable torrent splashed on to the stones.

Murillio barked a laugh. 'No more magical cantrips, Kruppe. I've known you a long time, remember? I've seen you cast spells. You've got everybody fooled, but not me. I'm not telling, though. You don't have to worry about that.' He smiled. 'Then again, if you don't come out with it here and now, I might get annoyed.'

Sighing, Kruppe returned the handkerchief to his sleeve. 'Annoyance is uncalled for,' he said, waving a hand and fluttering his fingers.

Murillio blinked, suddenly dizzy. He rubbed his forehead and frowned. What had they just been talking about? It couldn't have been important. 'Thanks for the masks, friend. They'll come in handy, I'm sure.' His frown deepened. What a confusing thing to say! He wasn't even angry that Kruppe had figured things out; nor that the fat little man would attend the Fête. How odd! 'Good that Coll's all right, isn't it? Well,' he mumbled, 'I'd better head back to check on Rallick.'

Smiling, Kruppe nodded. 'Until the Fête, then, fare you well, Murillio, Kruppe's finest and dearest friend.'

'Goodnight,' Murillio replied, turning to retrace his steps. He lacked sleep. All these late nights were taking their toll. That was the problem. 'Of course,' he muttered, then began to walk.

His features darkening, Baruk studied the Tiste Andii lounging in the chair across from him. 'I don't think it's a very good idea, Rake.'

The Lord raised an eyebrow. 'As I understand such things, the event includes the wearing of disguises,' he said, with a slight smile. 'Do you fear I lack taste?'

'I've no doubt your attire will be suitable,' Baruk snapped. 'Particularly if you choose the costume of a Tiste Andii warlord. It's the Council that worries me. They're not all fools.'

'I would be surprised if they were,' Rake said. 'Indeed, I would have you point out the cunning ones. I don't imagine you will refute my suspicion that there are those within the Council seeking to pave the way for the Empress – for a price, of course. Power comes to mind. Nobles delving in merchant trades no doubt drool at the prospect of Empire trade. Am I far off the mark, Baruk?'

'No,' the alchemist admitted sourly. 'But we have that under control.'

'Ah, yes,' Rake said. 'This brings to mind my other reason for wishing to attend this Lady Simtal's Fête. As you said, the city's power will be there. I assume this includes such mages as are in your T'orrud Cabal?'

'Some will attend,' Baruk conceded. 'But I must tell you, Anomander Rake, your débâcles with the Assassins' Guild has made a good number of them rue our alliance. They'll not appreciate your presence in the least.'

Rake's smile returned. 'To the extent that they will reveal their community to cunning Council members? I think not.' He rose in a fluid motion. 'No, I would like to attend this Fête. My own people hold little to such social affairs. There are times when I grow weary of their dour preoccupations.'

Baruk's gaze focused on the Tiste Andii. 'You suspect a convergence, don't you? A fell gathering of powers, like iron filings to a lodestone.'

'With so much power gathered in one place,' Rake admitted, 'it's likely. I'd rather be on hand in such circumstances.' His eyes held Baruk's, their colour flowing from dun green to amber. 'Also, if this event is as publicly known as you suggest, then the Empire's agents within the city will know of it.

Should they wish to cut out Darujhistan's heart, they'll have no better opportunity.'

Baruk barely repressed a shiver. 'Extra guards have been hired, of course. If an Empire Claw should strike, they will find their hands full with the T'orrud mages besides.' He thought for a time, then nodded wearily. 'Very well, Rake. Simtal will accept you as my guest. You will wear an effective disguise?'

'Naturally.'

Baruk climbed to his feet and strode to the window. Beyond the sky had begun to pale. 'And so it begins,' he whispered.

Rake joined him. 'What begins?'

'The new year,' the alchemist replied. 'Past is the Five Tusks. The dawn you see marks the birth of the Year of the Moon's Tears.'

Lord Anomander Rake stiffened.

Baruk noticed. 'Indeed. An unusual coincidence, though I would put little weight upon it. The titles were devised over a millennium ago, by a visitor to these lands.'

When Rake spoke his voice was a ravaged whisper. 'Icarium's gifts. I recognize the style. Five Tusks, Moon's Tears – the Wheel is his, correct?'

Eyes wide, Baruk hissed his surprise between his teeth. A dozen questions struggled to be uttered first, but the Lord continued. 'In the future, I'd suggest you heed Icarium's gifts – all of them. A thousand years is not so long a time, Alchemist. Not so long a time. Icarium last visited me eight hundred years ago, in the company of the Trell Mappo, and Osric – or Osserc, as the local worshippers call him.' Rake smiled bitterly. 'Osric and I argued, as I recall, and it was all Brood could do to keep us apart. It was an old argument . . .' His almond eyes shaded into grey. He fell silent, lost in memories.

There came a knock at the door and both turned to see Roald enter and bow.

'Master Baruk, Mammot has awakened and appears

577

refreshed. More, your agent Kruppe has delivered a verbal message. He extends his regret that he cannot deliver it to you in person. Do you wish to receive it now?'

'Yes,' Baruk said.

Roald bowed again. 'The Eel will contact you the eve of this day. At Lady Simtal's Fête. The Eel further finds the prospect of shared information and co-operation intriguing. That is all.'

Baruk brightened. 'Excellent.'

'Shall I bring Mammot to you, Master?'

'If he's able.'

'He is. A moment, then.' Roald left.

The alchemist smiled. 'As I said,' he laughed, 'everyone will be there, and in this case, *everyone* is an appropriate term.' His smile broadened at Rake's blank look. 'The Eel, Lord. Darujhistan's master-spy, a figure without a face.'

'A masked face,' the Tiste Andii reminded him.

'If my suspicions are correct,' Baruk said, 'the mask won't help the Eel one bit.'

The door opened again and there stood Mammot, looking fit and full of energy. He nodded to Baruk. 'Withdrawal proved easier than I'd imagined,' he said, without preamble. His bright gaze fixed on Anomander Rake and he smiled, then bowed. 'Greetings, Lord. I've looked forward to this meeting ever since Baruk brought to us the offer of alliance.'

Rake glanced at Baruk and raised an eyebrow.

The alchemist said, 'Mammot numbers among the T'orrud Cabal.' He faced the old man again. 'We were deeply worried, friend, given the Elder mageries at play around the barrow.'

'I was snared for a time,' Mammot admitted, 'but at the extreme edges of the Omtose Phellack influence. Quiescent regard proved the correct course, as the one stirring within did not sense me.'

'How much time do we have?' Baruk asked tightly.

'Two, perhaps three days. Even for a Jaghut Tyrant, it is an effort to make the return journey to life.' Mammot's eyes fell upon the mantelpiece. 'Ah, your carafe of wine awaits as is usual. Excellent.' He strode over to the fireplace. 'Have you word of my nephew, by any chance?'

Baruk frowned. 'No, should I have? The last time I met the child was, what, five years ago?'

'Mmm,' Mammot said, raising his freshly filled goblet and taking a mouthful. 'Well, Crokus has grown somewhat since then, I assure you. I hope the lad's all right. He was—'

Baruk threw up a hand and staggered a step forward. 'What?' he demanded in sudden fear. 'What's his name? Crokus? Crokus!' The alchemist rapped his forehead. 'Oh, what a fool I've been!'

Mammot's face crinkled into a wise smile. 'Oh, you mean the matter of the Coin Bearer, do you?'

Shock registered in Baruk's face. 'You knew?'

Standing to one side, his charcoal-grey eyes fixed intently on Mammot, Rake said, in a strangely flat tone, 'Mammot, forgive me for interrupting. Will you be attending Lady Simtal's Fête?'

The old man nodded easily. 'Of course.'

'Very good,' Rake said, with something like anticipation. He pulled his leather gloves from his belt. 'We'll speak then.'

Baruk had no time to think about Rake's sudden departure. It was his first mistake of the day.

A woman with a shaved head and long flowing robes ran shrieking from the gates, a shred of brown fur streaming from one hand. Adjunct Lorn stepped back to let the priestess pass. She watched as the woman plunged into the crowd behind her. The festival had spilled out beyond Darujhistan's walls, and Worrytown's main street was a streaming mob she'd spent the last half-hour pushing through on her way to the gates.

Absently she rubbed the rapier wound in her shoulder. Her

journey into the barrow seemed to have slowed the healing, and an ache had settled inside the puncture, cold as the ice in the barrow's tunnel. Eyeing the two guards stationed at the gate, she approached warily.

Only one seemed to pay her any attention, and this man spared her but the briefest glance before returning his attention to the Worrytown mob. Lorn entered the city unremarked, simply one more traveller come to attend the spring festival.

Immediately within the gates the avenue split around the base of a squat hill, on which crouched a half-ruined temple and tower. Off to her right rose another hill, evidently a garden, given the wide steps ascending to the summit, covered in trees, and the many fetishes and banners tied to branches and the gas-lamps.

Lorn's sense of those she sought was strong, unerring. Once past the hills, she could see an inner wall. Sergeant Whiskeyjack and his squad were somewhere beyond it, in the lower city. Lorn strode through the surging crowds, one hand hitched in her sword belt, the other massaging the puffed red flesh around her wound.

The guard at Worry Gate pushed himself from the wall he had been leaning against and paced a slow circle on the cobblestones. He paused to adjust his peaked helmet, loosening the strap a notch.

The other guard, an older man, bandy-legged and short, approached. 'Those fools out there making you uneasy?' he asked with a grin more gaps than teeth.

The first man glanced through the gateway. 'Had a near-riot here a couple of years back,' he said.

'I was there,' the old man said, hawking on to the stones. 'We had to pull the hoods off our polearms, draw some blood. That sent them packing, and I don't think the lesson's gone on them. I wouldn't worry much. This ain't your regular duty, is it?'

'No, just filling in time for a friend.'

'That's the way of it, isn't it? What's your usual round?'

'Midnight till the third bell, Despot's Barbican,' Circle Breaker replied. He adjusted his helmet again, hoping the unseen friendly eyes had marked his signal. That woman who had passed through a few minutes ago had matched the Eel's description perfectly. Circle Breaker knew he wasn't mistaken.

She'd looked the warrior, dressed as a mercenary and trying to hide the blood-stains of a wound on her shoulder. His searching glance had been but momentary. Years of practice, however, made it sufficient. He'd caught everything the Eel's messenger had told him to look for.

'That's a hell of a watch,' the old man said beside him, turning to squint up at Despot's Park. 'And you were here t' meet the dawn.' He wagged his head. 'The bastards got us working too hard these days, what with the city infiltrated with Empire spies and the like.'

'It doesn't get any better,' Circle Breaker agreed.

'I'm here for another three hours, and you think they give me some time to join my wife and kids in the festival?' The old man spat again. 'No way. Old Berrute's off to stand around watching other people having fun in some bloody estate.'

Circle Breaker held his breath, then sighed. 'Lady Simtal's Fête, I suppose.'

'Damn right. Bloody Councilmen chuffing around with all their stinking airs. And me with sore feet and all, standing like a statue.'

This was a bit of luck, Circle Breaker smiled to himself. His companion's next station was precisely what the Eel had wanted for Circle Breaker. Better yet, the old man was complaining about it. 'They need those statues,' he said. 'Keeps them secure.' He stepped close to Berrute. 'Didn't you tell the sergeant about your bad feet?'

581

'What's the point?' Berrute complained. 'He just delivered them orders, he didn't come up with them.'

Circle Breaker looked up the street, as if considering something, then he laid a hand on the other's shoulder and met his gaze. 'Look, I don't have any family. For me, today's just another day. I'll stand in for you, Berrute. Next time I want some time off, though, I'll come calling.'

Genuine relief lit the old man's eyes. 'Nerruse bless you,' he said, grinning again. 'It's a deal, friend. Hey, I don't even know your name!'

Circle Breaker smiled, then told him.

With most of the revelry out in the streets, the interior of Quip's Bar was all but deserted. Adjunct Lorn paused inside the doorway and waited for her eyes to adjust to the gloom. A few desultory voices drifted out to her, mingling with the clatter of wooden cards.

She entered the low-ceilinged chamber. A dishevelled old woman watched her dully from behind the counter. Against the far wall was a table at which sat three men. Copper coins glittered in the lamplight, amid pools of spilled beer on the tabletop. The men held cards in their hands.

The man with his back against the wall, wearing a scorched leather cap, looked up to meet Lorn's eyes. He gestured to an empty chair. 'Have a seat, Adjunct,' he said. 'Join in the game.'

Lorn blinked, then hid her shock with a shrug. 'I don't gamble,' she said, lowering herself into the rickety chair.

The man examined his cards. 'Not what I meant,' he said.

The one seated on her left muttered, 'Meant a different game, did Hedge.'

She turned to regard him. Skinny, short, with massive wrists. 'And what's your name, soldier?' she asked quietly.

'Fiddler. The guy losing his coins is Mallet. We've been expecting you.'

'So I gather,' Lorn said drily, leaning back. 'Your intelligence impresses me, gentlemen. Is the sergeant nearby?'

'Making the rounds,' Fiddler said. 'Should be by in ten minutes or so. We've got the back room in this rat trap. Right up against the Tier wall.'

Hedge added, 'Me and Fid dug through that damn wall, seven bloody feet thick at its base. An abandoned house on the Daru side.' He grinned. 'It's our back door.'

'So you're the saboteurs. And Mallet? A healer, correct?'

Mallet nodded, still contemplating his cards. 'C'mon, Fiddler,' he said, 'it's your game. Let's hear the next rule.'

Fiddler sat forward. 'Knight of House Dark is the wild card,' he said. 'That's the opening suit, too. Unless you're holding the Virgin of Death. If you get her you can open with half ante and double up if you win the round.'

Mallet slapped down the Virgin of Death. He tossed a single copper coin into the centre of the table. 'Let's run it through, then.'

Fiddler dealt the man another card. 'We ante up now, Hedge, two coppers apiece and High Hell come the Herald of Death.'

Lorn watched the bizarre game proceed. These men were using a Deck of Dragons. Astonishing. The man Fiddler was inventing the rules as they went along, and yet she watched the cards merge into a pattern on the tabletop. Her brows knitted thoughtfully.

'You got the Hound on the run,' Fiddler said, pointing at the latest card placed on the table by Mallet. 'Knight of Dark's close, I can feel it.'

'But what about this damned Virgin of Death?' groused the healer.

'She's had her teeth pulled. Take a look, the Rope's right outa the picture, ain't he?' Fiddler laid another card. 'And there's the Dragon bastard himself, sword all smoking and

583

black as a moonless night. That's what's got the Hound scampering.'

'Wait a minute,' Hedge cried, ramming down a card atop the Knight of Dark. 'You said the Captain of Light's rising, right?'

Fiddler concentrated on the pattern. 'He's right, Mallet. We pay over two coppers each automatically. That Captain's already dancing on the Knight's shadow—'

'Excuse me,' Lorn said loudly. The three men looked at her. 'Are you a Talent, Fiddler? Should you be using this deck?'

Fiddler scowled. 'It ain't your business, Adjunct. We been playing for years, nobody's tossed a dagger our way. You want in, just say so. Here, I'll give you your first card.'

Before she could protest he placed a card before her, face up. She stared down at it.

'Now, ain't that odd?' Fiddler remarked. 'Throne, inverted. You owe us all ten gold each – a year's pay for all of us, hell of a coincidence.'

Hedge snorted loudly. 'Also happens to be the Empire Guilt Coin paid to our kin once we're confirmed dead. Thanks a lot, Fid.'

'Take the coin and shut up,' Fiddler snapped. 'We ain't dead yet.'

'I'm still holding a card,' Mallet said.

Fiddler rolled his eyes. 'So let's see the damn thing, then.'

The healer set the card down.

'Orb.' Fiddler laughed. 'True sight and judgement closes this game, wouldn't you know it?'

Lorn sensed a presence at her back. She turned slowly to find a bearded man behind her. His flat grey eyes held hers. 'I'm Whiskeyjack,' he said softly. 'Good morning, Adjunct, and welcome to Darujhistan.' He found a nearby chair and pulled it to the table, sitting down beside Hedge. 'You'll want a report, right? Well, we're still trying to contact the Assassin's Guild.

584

All the mining's done, ready for the order. One squad member lost thus far. In other words, we've been damn lucky. There are Tiste Andii in the city, hunting us.'

'Who have you lost, Sergeant?' Lorn asked.

'The recruit. Sorry was her name.'

'Dead?'

'Been missing for a few days now.'

Lorn clenched her teeth to bite back a curse. 'So you don't know if she's dead?'

'No. Is there a problem, Adjunct? She was just a recruit. Even if she'd been nabbed by the guard, there's scant little she could tell them. Besides, we've heard no such news. More likely some thugs scrubbed her in some back alley – we've been scurrying down a lot of rat-holes trying to find these local assassins.' He shrugged. 'It's a risk you live with, that's all.'

'Sorry was a spy,' Lorn explained. 'A very good one, Sergeant. You can be certain that no thug killed her. No, she's not dead. She's hiding, because she knew I'd come looking for her. I've been on her trail for three years. I want her.'

'If we'd had a hint of all this,' Whiskeyjack said tightly, 'it could've been arranged, Adjunct. But you kept it to yourself, and that makes you on your own now.' His eyes hardened on her. 'Whether we contact the Guild or not, we detonate the mines before tomorrow's dawn, and then we're out of here.'

Lorn drew herself up. 'I am Adjunct to the Empress, Sergeant. As of now this mission is under my direction. You will take orders from me. All this independent crap is over, understand?' For a moment she almost thought she saw a flash of triumph in the man's eyes. A second look revealed it to be no more than the expected anger.

'Understood, Adjunct,' Whiskeyjack replied curtly. 'What are your orders?'

'I am serious in this, Sergeant,' she warned. 'And I don't care how angry this makes you. Now, I suggest we retire to more private surroundings.' She rose. 'Your men can remain here.'

Whiskeyjack stood. 'Of course, Adjunct. We have the back room. If you will follow me.'

Lorn reached down to the bed's top blanket. 'There is blood here, Sergeant.' She turned to regard the man as he closed the door.

He faced her. 'One of my men had a brush with a Tiste Andii assassin-mage. He'll recover.'

'Highly unlikely, Sergeant. The Tiste Andii are all with Caladan Brood in the north.' Her eyes widened in disbelief. 'You don't mean to suggest that the Lord of Moon's Spawn himself has left his fortress? To do what? Hunt down Malazan spies? Don't be absurd.'

Whiskeyjack scowled. 'Corporal Kalam and my squad mage had a rooftop engagement with at least half a dozen Tiste Andii. That my men survived makes it highly unlikely that the Moon's lord was anywhere in the vicinity, doesn't it, Adjunct? Put it together. The Moon stations itself just south of the city. Its lord strikes an alliance with Darujhistan's rulers, and their first task is to wipe out the local Assassins' Guild. Why? To prevent people like us from contacting them and offering a contract. And, so far, it's worked.'

Lorn thought for a time, then she said, 'So if the Guild cannot be contacted, why not do the assassinations yourselves? Your Corporal Kalam ranked among the best in the Claw before his . . . his falling out. Why not take out the city's rulers?'

The man folded his arms across his chest and leaned against the wall beside the door. 'We've been considering that, Adjunct. And we're a step ahead of you. Right now, one of my men is negotiating for us to work as private strong-arms for a highbrow Fête this evening. Everybody who's anybody is

586

supposed to attend – Council members, High Mages, the works. My saboteurs have enough left-over munitions to make it a party this city will have a hard time forgetting.'

Lorn struggled against a growing sense of frustration. As much as she'd intended to take command of things, it seemed that this Whiskeyjack had been doing just fine up until now, given the circumstances. She suspected she could not have done things any better, though she still doubted the story about the Tiste Andii. 'Why on earth,' she asked finally, 'would an estate hire a bunch of strangers as guards?'

'Oh, there'll be city soldiers there as well. But none of them is a Barghast.' Whiskeyjack smiled cynically. 'Titillation factor, Adjunct. It's what makes the nobility drool. Look there, a big tattooed barbarian glowering down at them. Exciting, yes?' He shrugged. 'It's a risk, but one worth taking. Unless, of course, you have a better idea, Adjunct?'

She heard the challenge in his tone. Had she thought about it, she would have realized long before now that her title and power would not intimidate this man. He'd stood at Dassem Ultor's side, arguing tactics with the Sword of the Empire in the midst of battle. And it seemed that demotion to sergeant had failed to break this man – that much she'd gathered from the Bridgeburners' reputation at Pale. He would not hesitate to challenge her every command if he found reason to do so. 'Your plan is sound,' she said. 'Tell me the name of this estate.'

'Some woman named Lady Simtal. I don't know the family name, but everybody seems to know her. Said to be a real looker, with influence in the Council.'

'Very well,' Lorn said, adjusting her cloak. 'I'll return in two hours, Sergeant. There are other matters I must attend to. Be certain that all is ready – detonation procedures included. If you don't get hired, we'll have to find another way of being at that fête.' She strode to the door.

'Adjunct?'

587

She turned.

Whiskeyjack walked to the back wall and pulled aside a tattered hanging. 'This tunnel emerges into another house. From it you can enter the Daru District.'

'Unnecessary.' Lorn was irritated by his condescending tone.

As soon as she was gone Quick Ben scrambled from the tunnel. 'Dammit, Sergeant,' he muttered. 'You almost had her walking in on me!'

'No chance,' Whiskeyjack observed. 'In fact, I made certain she wouldn't use it. Anything from Kalam?'

Quick Ben paced the small room. 'Not yet. But he's about to run out of patience.' He turned to the sergeant. 'So? Do you think she was fooled?'

'Fooled?' Whiskeyjack laughed. 'She was reeling.'

'Paran said she was going to drop something off,' Quick Ben said. 'Did she?'

'Not yet.'

'It's getting tight, Sergeant. Damn tight.'

The other door opened and Trotts entered, his filed teeth exposed in something between a smile and a grimace.

'Success?' Whiskeyjack asked.

Trotts nodded.

As the afternoon waned Crokus and Apsalar waited atop the tower's platform. Every now and then they peered over the edge to watch the festivities. There was a taste of mania among the crowds below, as if they danced on the rim of desperation. In spite of the season's rejoicing, the shadow of the Malazan Empire hung over all. Indeed, with Moon's Spawn immediately to the south, Darujhistan's place between the two forces was obvious to everyone.

'Somehow,' Crokus muttered, as he watched the crowds moving down the streets like churning rivers, 'Darujhistan seems smaller. Almost insignificant.'

'It looks huge to me,' Apsalar said. 'It's one of the biggest cities I've ever seen,' she said. 'As big as Unta, I think.'

He stared at her. She'd been saying strange things lately, which did not seem right coming from a fishergirl from a small coastal village. 'Unta. That's the Empire capital, isn't it?'

She frowned, which made her look older. 'Yes. Only I've never been there.'

'Well, how could you know how big it is, then?'

'I'm not sure, Crokus.'

Possession, Coll had said. Two sets of memory warred in the woman, and the war was getting worse. He wondered if Mammot had shown up yet. For a moment he came near to regretting their escape from Meese and Irilta. But then his thoughts turned to what was to come. He sat down on the platform and propped himself against the low wall. He stared at the assassin's body across from him. The blood that had been spilled had blackened under the hot sun. A trail of droplets crossed the floor to the stairs. Clearly, this assassin's killer had himself been wounded. Yet Crokus did not feel in danger, up here, although he wasn't sure why.

For an abandoned belfry tower, this place had witnessed a lot of drama lately.

'Are we waiting for night?' Apsalar asked.

Crokus nodded.

'Then we find this Challice?'

'That's right. The D'Arles will be at Lady Simtal's Fête, I'm sure of it. The estate has an enormous garden, almost a forest. It goes right up to the back wall. Getting in should be easy.'

'Won't you be noticed once you join the guests, though?'

'I'll be dressed as a thief. Everybody will be wearing costumes. Besides, there'll be hundreds of people there. It might take an hour or two, but I'll find her.'

'And then?'

'I'll think of something,' Crokus said.

589

Apsalar stretched out her legs on the paving stones and crossed her arms. 'And I'm supposed to hide in the bushes, huh?'

He shrugged. 'Maybe Uncle Mammot will be there,' he said. 'Then everything will be all right.'

'Why?'

'Because that's what Coll said,' Crokus shot back, exasperated. Was he supposed to tell her she'd been possessed for who knew how long? 'We'll work out a way to get you home,' he explained. 'That's what you want, right?'

She nodded slowly, as if no longer certain of that. 'I miss my father,' she said.

To Crokus, Apsalar sounded as though she was trying to convince herself. He'd looked at her when they'd arrived, thinking, Why not? And he had to admit to himself now that her company wasn't bad. Except for all the questions, of course. Mind, what if he'd been in her situation, waking up thousands of leagues from home? It'd be terrifying. Would he have held up as well as she seemed to be doing?

'I'm feeling all right,' she said, watching him. 'It's as if something inside is keeping things together. I can't explain it any better, but it's like a smooth, black stone. Solid and warm, and whenever I start getting scared it takes me inside. And then everything's fine again.' She added, 'I'm sorry. I didn't mean to push you away.'

'Never mind,' he said.

Within the shadows of the stairwell, Serrat studied the two figures out on the platform. Enough was enough. She'd opened her Kurald Galain Warren into a defensive layering of wards around her. No more of these invisible enemies. If they wanted her, they'd have to show themselves. And then she'd kill them. And as for the Coin Bearer and the girl, where could they hope to escape to, up here on this tower?

She unsheathed her daggers and prepared for her attack. A dozen wards protected her back, all along the staircase. An approach from there was impossible.

Two sharp points touched her flesh, one under her chin and the other beneath her left shoulder blade. The Tiste Andii froze. And then she heard a voice close to her ear – a voice she recognized.

'Give Rake this warning, Serrat. He'll only get one, and the same for you. The Coin Bearer shall not be harmed. The games are done. Try this again and you'll die.'

'You bastard!' she exploded. 'My lord's anger—'

'Will be in vain. We both know who sends this message, don't we? And, as Rake well knows, he's not as far away as he once was.' The point beneath her chin moved away to allow her to nod, then returned. 'Good. Deliver the message, then, and hope we don't meet again.'

'This will not be forgotten,' Serrat promised, shaking with rage.

A low chuckle answered her. 'Compliments of the Prince, Serrat. Take it up with our mutual friend.'

The daggers left her flesh. Serrat exhaled a long breath, then sheathed her weapons. She snapped a Kurald Galain spell and vanished.

Crokus jumped at a faint plopping sound from the stairwell. He laid his hands on his knives, tensing.

'What's wrong?' Apsalar said.

'Shhh. Wait.' He felt his heart pound hard against his chest. 'I'm ducking at shadows,' he said, sitting back. 'Well, we're off soon, anyway.'

It was an age of wind, sweeping across the grass plains beneath a pewter sky, a wind whose thirst assailed all life, mindless, un-relenting like a beast that did not know itself.

591

Struggling in his mother's wake, it was Raest's first lesson in power. In the hunt for domination that would shape his life, he saw the many ways of the wind – its subtle sculpting of stone over hundreds and then thousands of years, and its raging gales that flattened forests – and found closest to his heart the violent power of the wind's banshee fury.

Raest's mother had been the first to flee his deliberate shaping of power. She'd denied him to his face, proclaiming the Sundering of Blood and thus cutting him free. That the ritual had broken her he disregarded. It was unimportant. He who would dominate must learn early that those resisting his command should be destroyed. Failure was her price, not his.

While the Jaghut feared community, pronouncing society to be the birthplace of tyranny – of the flesh and the spirit – and citing their own bloody history as proof, Raest discovered a hunger for it. The power he commanded insisted upon subjects. Strength was ever relative, and he could not dominate without the company of the dominated.

At first he sought to subjugate other Jaghut, but more often than not they either escaped him or he was forced to kill them. Such contests held only momentary satisfaction. Raest gathered beasts around him, bending nature to his will. But nature withered and died in bondage, and so found an escape he could not control. In his anger he laid waste to the land, driving into extinction countless species. The earth resisted him, and its power was immense. Yet it was directionless and could not overwhelm Raest in its ageless tide. His was a focused power, precise in its destruction and pervasive in its effect.

Then into his path came the first of the Imass, creatures who struggled against his will, defying slavery and yet living on. Creatures of boundless, pitiful hope. For Raest, he had found in them the glory of domination, for with each Imass that broke he took another. Their link with nature was minimal, for the Imass themselves played the game of tyranny over their lands. They could not defeat him.

He fashioned an empire of sorts, bereft of cities yet plagued with the endless dramas of society, its pathetic victories and inevitable failures. The community of enslaved Imass thrived in this quagmire of pettiness. They even managed to convince themselves that they possessed freedom, a will of their own that could shape destiny. They elected champions. They tore down their champions once failure draped its shroud over them. They ran in endless circles and called it growth, emergence, knowledge. While over them all, a presence invisible to their eyes, Raest flexed his will. His greatest joy came when his slaves proclaimed him god – though they knew him not – and constructed temples to serve him and organized priesthoods whose activities mimicked Raest's tyranny with such cosmic irony that the Jaghut could only shake his head.

It should have been an empire to last for millennia, and its day of dying should have been by his own hand, when he at last tired of it. Raest had never imagined that other Jaghut would find his activities abhorrent, that they would risk themselves and their own power on behalf of these short-lived, small-minded Imass. Yet what astonished Raest more than anything else was that when the Jaghut came they came in numbers, in community. A community whose sole purpose of existence was to destroy his empire, to imprison him.

He had been unprepared.

The lesson was learned, and no matter what the world had become since that time, Raest was ready for it. His limbs creaked at first, throbbing with dull aches bridged by sharp pangs. The effort of digging himself from the frozen earth had incapacitated him for a time, but finally he felt ready to walk the tunnel that opened out into a new land.

Preparation. Already he'd initiated his first moves. He sensed that others had come to him, had freed the path of Omtose

593

Phellack wards and seals. Perhaps his worshippers remained, fanatics who had sought his release for generations, and even now awaited him beyond the barrow.

The missing Finnest would be his first priority. Much of his power had been stored within the seed, stripped from him and stored there by the Jaghut betrayers. It had not been carried far, and there was nothing that could prevent his recovering it. Omtose Phellack no longer existed in the land above – he could feel its absence like an airless void. Nothing could oppose him now.

Preparation. Raest's withered, cracked face twisted into a savage grin, his lower tusks splitting desiccated skin. The powerful must gather other power, subjugate it to their own will, then direct it unerringly. His moves had already begun.

He sloshed through the slush now covering the barrow's muddy floor. Before him rose the slanted wall that marked the tomb's barrier. Beyond the lime-streaked earth waited a world to be enslaved. Raest gestured and the barrier exploded outward. Bright sunlight flared in the clouds of steam rolling around him, and he felt waves of cold, ancient air sweeping past him.

The Jaghut Tyrant walked into the light.

The Great Raven Crone rode the hot streams of wind high above the Gadrobi Hills. The burst of power that launched tons of earth and rocks a hundred feet into the sky elicited a cackle from her. She dipped a wing, eyes on the white pillar of steam, and banked towards it.

This, she laughed to herself, should prove interesting.

A wash of air pounded down on to her. Shrieking her outrage, Crone twisted and slid along the shunting wind. Massive shadows flowed over her. Her anger was swept away on a surge of excitement. Head craning, she beat the air with her wings and climbed again. In matters such as these, a proper point of view was essential. Crone climbed higher still, then cocked her head and looked down. By the light of the sun scales flashed iridescent from five ridged backs, but of the five one shone like fire. Sorcerous power bled in ripples from the web of their spread wings. The dragons sailed silent over the landscape, closing on the billowing dust-cloud above the Jaghut tomb. Crone's black eyes fixed on the dragon that blazed red.

'*Silanah!*' she screamed, laughing. '*Dragnipurake t'na Draconiaes! Eleint, eleint!*' The day of the Tiste Andii had come.

Raest emerged into rich afternoon sunlight. Yellow-grassed hills rose in weathered humps in every direction but the one he faced. To the east behind a thinning curtain of drifting dust stretched an empty plain.

The Jaghut Tyrant grunted. Not so different after all. He raised his arms, feeling wind slide along his cabled muscles. He drew a breath, tasting the life-rich air. He quested lightly with his power and exulted in the waves of fear that answered it – answers that came from the mindless life beneath his feet or hiding in the grasses around him. But of higher life, higher concentrations of power, he sensed nothing. Raest drove his senses down into the ground, seeking what dwelt there. Earth and bedrock, the sluggish molten darkness beneath, down, down to find the sleeping goddess – young as far as the Jaghut Tyrant was concerned. 'Shall I wake you?' he whispered. 'Not yet. But I shall make you bleed.' His right hand closed into a fist.

He speared the goddess with pain, driving a fissure through the bedrock, feeling the gush of her blood, enough to make her stir but not awaken.

The line of hills to the north lifted skyward. Magma sprayed into the air amid a rising pillar of smoke, rock and ash. The earth shuddered even as the sound of the eruption swept over Raest in a fierce, hot wind. The Jaghut Tyrant smiled.

He studied the shattered ridge and breathed the heavy, sulphurous air, then turned about and strode west towards the highest hill in that direction. His Finnest lay beyond it, perhaps three days' walk. He considered opening his Warren, then decided to wait until he reached the hill's summit. From that vantage point, he could better judge the Finnest's location.

Half-way up the slope he heard distant laughter. Raest stiffened just as the day darkened suddenly around him. On the sward before him he saw five enormous shadows sweeping up the slope, then beyond the hill's summit. The sunlight returned. The Jaghut Tyrant looked into the sky above him.

Five dragons banked in perfect formation, their heads dipping to watch him as they glided back in his direction. '*Estideein eleint*,' he whispered, in his Jaghut tongue. Four were black, barbed in silver along the wings and flying two to either side of the fifth dragon, this one red and twice as large as the others. 'Silanah red-wings,' Raest muttered, eyes narrowing. 'Elder-born and true-blooded Tiam, you lead Soletaken, whose blood is alien to this world. I feel you all!' He raised fists to the sky. 'Colder than the ice born of Jaghut hands, as dark as blindness – I feel you!'

He lowered his arms. 'Harass me not, *eleint*. I cannot enslave you, but I will destroy you. Know that. I will drive you to the ground, each and all, and with my own hands I shall tear your hearts from your chests.' His eyes narrowed on the four black dragons. 'Soletaken. You would challenge me at the command of another. You would battle with me for no reason of your own. Ah, but if I were to command you I would not throw your lives away so carelessly. I would cherish you, Soletaken, I would give you causes worth believing in, show you the true rewards of power.' Raest scowled, as their derision swept through his mind. 'So be it.'

The dragons passed low overhead in silence, banking once

again and disappearing behind the hills to the south. Raest spread his arms wide and unleashed his Warren. His flesh split as power flowed into him. His arms shed skin like ash. He both felt and heard hills crack all around him, the snapping of stone, the sundering of crags. To all sides the horizons blurred as dust curtained skyward. He faced south. *'This is my power! Come to me!'*

A long minute passed. He frowned at the hills before him, then cried out and whirled to his right just as Silanah and the four black dragons, all less than ten feet above the ground, plunged over the summit of the hill he'd been climbing.

Raest screamed at the whirlwind of power battering him, his shrunken eyes locked on Silanah's blank, empty, deadly gaze – eyes as large as the Jaghut's head – as it bore down upon him with the speed of a springing viper. The red dragon's jaws opened wide and Raest found himself staring down the beast's throat.

He screamed a second time and released his power all at once.

The air detonated as the Warrens collided. Jagged shards of rock ripped in all directions. Starvald Demelain and Kurald Galain warred with Omtose Phellack in a savage maelstrom of will. Grasses, earth and rock withered to fine ash on all sides, and within the vortex stood Raest, his power roaring from him. Lashes of sorcery from the dragons lanced into his body, boring through his withered flesh.

The Jaghut Tyrant flayed his power like a scythe. Blood spattered the ground, sprayed in gouts. The dragons shrieked.

A wave of incandescent fire struck Raest from the right, solid as a battering fist. Howling, he was thrown through the air, landing in a bank of powdery ash. Silanah's fire raced over him, blackening what was left of his flesh. The Tyrant clambered upright, his body jerking uncontrollably as sorcery gouted from his right hand.

The ground shook as Raest's power hammered Silanah down, driving the dragon skidding and tumbling across the slope. The Tyrant's exultant roar was cut short as talons the length of a forearm crunched into him from behind. A second clawed foot joined the first, snapping through the bones of Raest's chest as if they were twigs. More talons flexed around him as a second dragon sought grip.

The Tyrant twisted helplessly as the claws lifted him into the air and started ripping his body apart. He dislocated his own shoulder in reaching round to dig his fingers into a sleek scaled shin. At the contact, Omtose Phellack surged into the dragon's leg, shattering bone, boiling blood. Raest laughed as the claws spasmed loose and he was flung away. More bones snapped as he struck the ground, but it did not matter. His power was absolute, the vessel that carried it had little relevance. If need be, the Tyrant would find other bodies, bodies in the thousands.

He climbed once more to his feet. 'Now,' he whispered, 'I deliver death.'

CHAPTER TWENTY-ONE

> The flowering of light from darkness
> brought into my sight there on the field
> a host of dragons caught
> like a crest of wind before the eternal flame.
> I saw the ages in their eyes
> a worldly map inscribed
> in each whirled scale on their hides.
> Their sorcery bled from them
> like the breathing of stars
> and I knew then
> that dragons had come among us . . .
>
> *Anomandaris*
> Fisher (b.?)

Shadows crowded the garden's undergrowth. Adjunct Lorn rose from her crouch and brushed the dirt from her hands. 'Find an acorn.' She smiled to herself. 'Plant it.'

Somewhere beyond the heavily wooded garden, servants shouted at each other as they scrambled about making last-minute arrangements. She hitched her cloak's tail into her belt and quietly slipped among the boles of vine-wrapped trees. A moment later the back wall came into view.

An alley lay beyond, narrow and choked with the leaves and fallen branches from the gardens rising above the walls on its either side. Her route in – and now out – was a thing of ease. She scaled the rough-stoned wall, grasping vines when necessary, then slid over the top.

She landed with a soft crunch of twigs and dry leaves, within shadows as deep as those in the garden. She adjusted her cloak, then walked to one end of the alley where she leaned against a corner, crossed her arms and smiled at the crowds passing to and fro on the street before her.

Two tasks left to perform, then she would leave this city. One of those tasks, however, might prove impossible. She sensed nothing of Sorry's presence. Perhaps the woman was indeed dead. Under the circumstances it was the only explanation.

She watched the sea of people, its tide of faces swirling past. The latent madness there made her uneasy, especially with the city's guards maintaining an aloof distance. She wondered at the taint of terror in that multitude of faces, and how almost every face seemed familiar.

Darujhistan blurred in her mind, becoming a hundred other cities, each rising out of her past as if on parade. Joy and fear, agony and laughter – the expressions merged into one, the sounds coming to her no different from each other. She could distinguish nothing, the faces becoming expressionless, the sounds a roar of history without meaning.

Lorn passed a hand over her eyes, then staggered back a step and reeled into the alley's shadows behind her. She slid down one wall into a sagging crouch. *A celebration of insignificance. Is that all we are in the end? Listen to them!* In a few hours the city's intersections would explode. Hundreds would die instantly, thousands to follow. Amid the rubble of shattered cobbles and toppled buildings would be these faces, locked in expressions somewhere between joy and terror. And from the dying would come sounds, hopeless cries that dwindled in the passing of pain.

She'd seen them all before, those faces. She knew them all, knew the sound of their voices, sounds mired in human emotions, sounds clear and pure with thought, and sounds wavering in that chasm between the two. Is this, she wondered, my legacy? *And one day I'll be just one more of those faces, frozen in death and wonder.*

Lorn shook her head, but it was a wan effort. She realized, with sudden comprehension, that she was breaking down. The Adjunct was cracking, its armour crumbling and the lustre gone from its marbled grandeur. A title as meaningless as the woman bearing it. The Empress – just another face she'd seen somewhere before, a mask behind which someone hid from mortality.

'No use hiding,' she whispered, frowning down at the dead leaves and branches around her. 'No use.'

A few minutes later she pushed herself upright once again. She brushed the dirt meticulously from her cloak. One task remained within her abilities. Find the Coin Bearer. Kill him, and take Oponn's Coin. Make the god pay for its intrusion in Empire affairs – the Empress and Tayschrenn would see to that.

The task demanded concentration, fixing her senses upon one particular signature. It would be her last act, she knew. But she would succeed. Death at the hands of failure was unthinkable. Lorn turned to the street. Dusk crept from the ground and engulfed the crowds. Far off to the east thunder sounded, yet the air was dry, with no hint of rain. She checked her weapons. 'The Adjunct's mission,' she said quietly, 'is almost done.'

She entered the street and disappeared into the mob.

Kruppe rose from his table at the Phoenix Inn and attempted to fasten the last button on his waistcoat. Failing, he let his stomach relax once again and let loose a weary sigh. Well, at least the coat had been cleaned. He adjusted the cuffs of his new shirt, then walked out of the mostly empty bar.

He'd spent the last hour seated at his table, to all outward appearances musing on nothing of great importance, though in his head a pattern formed, born of his Talent, and it disturbed him greatly. Meese and Irilta losing Crokus and the girl brought everything into focus – as with most unwitting servants of the gods, once the game was done so was the servant's life. The Coin might be gambled in a single contest, but to have it floating around indefinitely was far too dangerous. No, Crokus would find his luck abandoning him when he needed it most, and it would cost the lad his life.

'No, no,' Kruppe had murmured over his tankard. 'Kruppe can't permit that.' Yet the pattern of success remained elusive. He felt certain he had covered all the potential threats regarding the lad or, rather, someone was doing a good job of protecting Crokus – that much the pattern showed him. He experienced a nagging suspicion that the 'someone' wasn't himself, or any of his agents. And he'd just have to trust in its integrity.

Circle Breaker had come through yet again, and Kruppe was still confident that Turban Orr's hunt for the man would prove fruitless. The Eel knew how to protect his own. In fact, Circle Breaker was due for retirement – for the man's own safety – and Kruppe intended to deliver the good news this very night, at Lady Simtal's Fête. Circle Breaker deserved no less after all these years.

The pattern also told him something he already knew: his cover was blown. The spell he had cast on Murillio wouldn't last much longer, nor was it required to. Kruppe had wanted his freedom unimpeded this day. After that, well, things would fall as they would fall – and the same applied for his meeting with Baruk.

If anything gave Kruppe pause, it was the pattern's abrupt ending. Beyond tonight, the future was blank. Clearly, a crux had been reached, and it would turn, he knew, at Lady Simtal's Fête.

Kruppe now entered the Higher Estates District, with a generous nod at the lone guard stationed near the ramp. The man scowled, but otherwise made no comment. The Fête was set to begin in thirty minutes, and Kruppe planned on being one of the first to arrive. His mouth watered at the thought of all those pastries, fresh and dripping with warm, sweet liquids. He removed his mask from inside his coat and smiled at it. Perhaps, among all those attending, High Alchemist Baruk alone would appreciate the irony of this moulded visage. Ah, well, he sighed. One is more than enough, given who that one is. After all, is Kruppe greedy?

His stomach rumbled in answer.

Crokus strained his eyes towards the darkening east. Something like lightning flashed every now and then beyond the hills, each one closer than the last. But the thunder's rumble, which had begun early that afternoon and still continued, sounded somehow wrong, its timbre unlike the normal bass that rolled through the earth. It seemed almost brittle. The clouds that had appeared over the hill earlier had been an eerie ochre colour, sickly, and those clouds now approached the city.

'When are we leaving?' Apsalar asked, leaning on the wall beside him.

Crokus shook himself. 'Now. It's dark enough.'

'Crokus? What will you do if Challice D'Arle betrays you a second time?'

He could barely see her face in the gloom. Had she meant that to cut? It was hard to tell from her voice. 'She won't,' he said, telling himself that he believed it. 'Trust me,' and he turned towards the stairwell.

'I do,' she said simply.

Crokus winced. Why did she make things seem so easy for her? Hood's Breath, *he* wouldn't trust him. Of course, he didn't know Challice very well. They'd only had that one, confusing conversation. What if she called the guards? Well, he'd make sure Apsalar got away safely. He paused and grasped her arm. 'Listen,' his own voice sounded unduly harsh, but he pushed on, 'if something goes wrong, go to the Phoenix Inn. Right? Find Meese, Irilta, or my friends Kruppe and Murillio. Tell them what happened.'

'All right, Crokus.'

'Good.' He released her arm. 'Wish we had a lantern,' he said, as he stepped into the darkness, one hand reaching before him.

'Why?' Apsalar asked, slipping past him. She took his hand and led him down. 'I can see. Don't let go of my hand.'

That might be a hard thing to do even if he'd desired it, he realized. Still, there were a lot of rough calluses on that small hand. He let them remind him of what this woman was capable of doing, though the effort embarrassed him in some vague way.

Eyes wide, yet seeing nothing, Crokus allowed himself to be guided down the stairs.

The captain of Simtal's House Guard viewed Whiskeyjack and his men with obvious distaste. 'I thought you were all Barghast.' He stepped up to Trotts and jabbed a finger into the warrior's massive chest. 'You led me to believe you were all like you, Niganga.'

A low, menacing growl emerged from Trotts, and the captain stepped back, one hand reaching for his short sword.

'Captain,' Whiskeyjack said, 'if we were all Barghast—'

The man's narrow face swung to him with a scowl.

'– you'd never be able to afford us,' the sergeant finished

604

with a tight smile. He glanced at Trotts. *Niganga? Hood's Breath!* 'Niganga is my second-in-command, Captain. Now, how would you like us positioned?'

'Just beyond the fountain,' he said. 'Your backs will be to the garden, which has, ah, run wild of late. We don't want any guests getting lost in there, so you gently steer them back. Understood? And when I say gently I mean it. You're to salute anyone who talks to you, and if there's an argument direct them to me, Captain Stillis. I'll be making the rounds, but any one of the house guard can find me.'

Whiskeyjack nodded. 'Understood, sir.' He turned to survey his squad. Fiddler and Hedge stood behind Trotts, both looking eager. Past them Mallet and Quick Ben stood on the edge of the street, heads bent together in conversation. The sergeant frowned at them, noticing how his wizard winced with every boom of thunder to the east.

Captain Stillis marched off after giving them directions through the estate's rooms out to the terrace and garden beyond. Whiskeyjack waited for the man to leave his line of sight, then he strode to Quick Ben and Mallet. 'What's wrong?' he asked.

Quick Ben looked frightened.

Mallet said, 'That thunder and lightning, Sergeant? Well, it ain't no storm. Paran's story is looking real.'

'Meaning we have little time,' Whiskeyjack said. 'Wonder why the Adjunct didn't show up – you think she's melting her boots getting away from here?'

Mallet shrugged.

'Don't you get it?' Quick Ben said shakily. He took a couple of deep breaths, then continued, 'That creature out there is in a fight. We're talking major sorceries, only it's getting closer, which means that it's winning. And that means—'

'We're in trouble,' Whiskeyjack finished. 'All right, we go as planned for now. Come on, we've been assigned right where

605

we want to be. Quick Ben, you sure Kalam and Paran can find us?'

The wizard moaned. 'Directions delivered, Sergeant.'

'Good. Let's move, then. Through the house and eyes forward.'

'He looks like he's going to sleep for days,' Kalam said, straightening beside Coll's bed and facing the captain.

Paran rubbed his red-shot eyes. 'She must have given them something,' he insisted wearily, 'even if they didn't see it.'

Kalam wagged his head. 'I've told you, sir, she didn't. Everyone was on the look-out for something like that. The squad's still clean. Now, we'd better get moving.'

Paran climbed to his feet with an effort. He was exhausted, and he knew he was just an added burden. 'She'll turn up at this estate, then,' he insisted, strapping on his sword.

'Well,' Kalam said, as he walked to the door, 'that's where you and me come in, right? She shows up and we take her out – just like you've wanted to do all along.'

'Right now,' Paran said, joining the assassin, 'the shape I'm in will make my role in the fight a short one. Consider me the surprise factor, the one thing she won't be expecting, the one thing that'll stop her for a second.' He looked into the man's dark eyes. 'Make that second count, Corporal.'

Kalam grinned. 'I hear you, sir.'

They left Coll still snoring contentedly and went down to the bar's main floor. As they passed along the counter, Scurve looked at them warily.

Kalam released an exasperated curse and, in a surge of motion, reached out and grasped him by the shirt. He pulled the squealing innkeeper half-way across the counter until their faces were inches apart. 'I'm sick of waiting,' the assassin growled. 'You get this message to this city's Master of the Assassins. I don't care how. Just do it, and do it fast. Here's the

606

message: the biggest contract offer of the Master's life will be waiting at the back wall of Lady Simtal's estate. Tonight. If the Guild Master's worthy of that name then maybe – just maybe – it's not too big for the Guild to handle. Deliver that message, even if you have to shout it from the rooftops, or I'm coming back here with killing in mind.'

Paran stared at his corporal, too tired to be amazed. 'We're wasting time,' he drawled.

Kalam tightened his grip and glared into Scurve's eyes. 'We'd better not be,' he growled. He released the man by gently lowering him on to the counter-top. Then he tossed a handful of silver coins beside Scurve. 'For your troubles,' he said.

Paran gestured and the assassin nodded. They left the Phoenix Inn.

'Still following orders, Corporal?'

Kalam grunted. 'We were instructed to make the offer in the name of the Empress, Captain. If the contract's accepted and the assassinations are done, then Laseen will have to pay up, whether we've been outlawed or not.'

'A gutted city for Dujek and his army to occupy, with the Empress paying for it. She'll choke on that, Kalam.'

He grinned. 'That's her problem, not mine.'

In the street, the Greyfaces moved through the noisy crowd like silent spectres, lighting the gas-lamps with long-poled sparkers. Some people, brazen with drink, hugged the figures and blessed them. The Greyfaces, hooded and anonymous, simply bowed in reply and continued on their way once freed.

Kalam stared at them, his brows knitting.

'Something the matter, Corporal?' Paran asked.

'Just something nagging me. Can't pin it down. Only, it's got to do with those Greyfaces.'

The captain shrugged. 'They keep the lanterns lit. Shall we make our way, then?'

Kalam sighed. 'Might as well, sir.'

The black lacquered carriage, drawn by two dun stallions, moved slowly through the press. A dozen feet ahead marched a brace of Baruk's own house guards, driving a wedge down the street's centre, using their wrapped weapons when shouts and curses failed.

In the plush confines of the carriage the outside roar surged and ebbed like a distant tide, muted by the alchemist's sound-deadening spells. He sat with his chin lowered on his chest, his eyes – hidden in the shadow of his brow and half-shut – study-ing the Tiste Andii seated across from him. Rake had said nothing since his return to the estate just minutes before their planned departure.

Baruk's head throbbed. Sorcery shook the hills to the east, sending waves of concussion that struck every mage within range like mailed fists. He well knew its source. The barrow dweller approached, its every step contested by Anomander Rake's Tiste Andii. It seemed that Mammot's prediction had been too generous. They didn't have days, they had hours.

Yet, despite the warring Warrens, despite the fact that the Jaghut Tyrant's power was superior to Rake's mages' – that the barrow dweller came on, relentless, unstoppable, a growing storm of Omtose Phellack sorcery – the Lord of Moon's Spawn sat at ease on the padded couch, legs stretched out before him and gloved hands folded in his lap. The mask lying on the velvet at his side was exquisite, if ghastly. In better times Baruk might have been amused, appreciative of its workmanship, but right now when he regarded it his lone response was suspicion. A secret was locked in that mask, something that bespoke the man who would wear it. But the secret eluded Baruk.

Turban Orr adjusted his hawk mask and paused just before the wide steps leading to the estate's main doors. He heard another carriage arrive at the gates and turned. From the doorway at his back came the shuffle of footsteps.

Lady Simtal spoke behind him. 'I would rather you'd permitted one of my servants to inform me of your arrival, Councilman. Allow me the privilege of escorting you into the main chamber.' She slipped her arm through his.

'A moment,' he muttered, eyes on the figure now emerging from the carriage. 'It's the alchemist's carriage,' he said, 'but that's hardly Baruk, now, is it?'

Lady Simtal looked. 'Trake unleashed!' she gasped. 'Who would that be?'

'Baruk's guest,' Orr said drily.

Her grip bit into his arm. 'I'm aware of his privilege, Councilman. Tell me, have you seen this one before?'

The man shrugged. 'He's masked. How could I tell?'

'How many men do you know, Turban, who are seven feet tall and wear two-handed swords strapped to their backs?' She squinted. 'That white hair, do you think it's part of the mask?'

The councilman did not reply. He watched as Baruk emerged behind the stranger. The alchemist's mask was a conservative silver-inlaid half-shield that no more than covered his eyes. An obvious statement denying duplicity. Turban Orr grunted, knowing well that his suspicions about the alchemist's influence and power were accurate. His eyes returned to the stranger. His mask was that of a black dragon, lacquered with fine silver-traced highlights; somehow the dragon's expression seemed . . . sly.

'Well?' Lady Simtal demanded. 'Are we going to linger out here all night? And where's your dear wife, anyway?'

'Ill,' he said distractedly. He smiled at her. 'Shall we introduce ourselves to the alchemist's guest? And have I complimented you yet on your attire?'

'You haven't,' she said.

'A black panther suits you, Lady.'

609

'But of course it does,' she replied testily, as Baruk and his guest strode down the paved walk towards them. She disengaged her arm and stepped forward. 'Good evening, Alchemist Baruk. Welcome,' she added to the black-dragon-masked man. 'An astonishing presentation. Have we met?'

'Good evening, Lady Simtal,' Baruk said, bowing. 'Councilman Turban Orr. Permit me to introduce,' he hesitated, but the Tiste Andii had been firm on this, 'Lord Anomander Rake, a visitor to Darujhistan.' The alchemist waited to see if the councilman would recognize the name.

Turban Orr bowed formally. 'On behalf of the City Council, welcome, Lord Anomander Rake.'

Baruk sighed. Anomander Rake, a name known by poets and scholars, but not, it appeared, by councilmen.

Orr continued, 'As a lord, I assume you hold title to land?' He almost stepped back as the dragon's visage swung to regard him. Deep blue eyes fixed on his.

'Land? Yes, Councilman, I hold title. However, my title is honorary, presented to me by my people.' Rake looked past Orr's shoulder to the room beyond the wide doorway. 'It seems, Lady, that the evening is well under way.'

'Indeed.' She laughed. 'Come, join in the festivities.'

Baruk breathed another relieved sigh.

Murillio had to admit that Kruppe's choice of mask suited him perfectly. He found himself grinning behind his feather-decked peacock mask in spite of his trepidation. He stood near the opened doorway leading out to the patio and garden, a goblet of light wine in one hand, the other hitched in his belt.

Rallick leaned against the wall beside him, arms crossed. His mask was that of a Catlin tiger, idealized to mimic the god Trake's image. Murillio knew the assassin let the wall bear his weight out of exhaustion rather than from a lazy slouch. He wondered yet again if matters would fall to him. The assassin

610

stiffened suddenly, eyes on the entrance across from them.

Murillio craned to see past the crowd. There, the hawk. He murmured, 'That's Turban Orr all right. Who's he with?'

'Simtal,' Rallick growled. 'And Baruk, and some monster of a man wearing a dragon's mask – and armed.'

'Baruk?' Murillio laughed nervously. 'Let's hope he doesn't recognize us. It wouldn't take him a second to put everything together.'

'It doesn't matter,' Rallick said. 'He won't stop us.'

'Maybe you're right.' Then Murillio almost dropped his glass. 'Hood's Weary Feet!'

Rallick hissed between his teeth. 'Dammit! Look at him! He's heading straight for them!'

Lady Simtal and Turban Orr excused themselves, leaving Baruk and Rake momentarily alone in the middle of the chamber. People moved around them, some nodding deferentially at Baruk but all keeping their distance. A crowd gathered around Simtal where she stood at the foot of the winding staircase, eager with questions regarding Anomander Rake.

A figure approached Baruk and his companion. Short, round, wearing a faded red waistcoat, both hands clutching pastries, the man wore a cherub's mask, its open red-lipped mouth smeared with cake icing and crumbs. His route to them met with one obstacle after another as he negotiated his way across the room, excusing himself at every turn and twist.

Rake noticed the newcomer, for he said, 'Seems eager, doesn't he?'

Baruk chuckled. 'He's worked for me,' he said. 'And I've worked for him as well. Anomander Rake, behold the one they call the Eel. Darujhistan's master-spy.'

'Do you jest?'

'No.'

611

Kruppe arrived, his chest heaving. 'Master Baruk!' he said breathlessly. 'What a surprise to find you here.' The cherub face swung over and up to Rake. 'The hair is an exquisite touch, sir. Exquisite. I am named Kruppe, sir. Kruppe the First.' He raised a pastry to his mouth and jammed it in.

'This is Lord Anomander Rake, Kruppe.'

Kruppe nodded vigorously, then swallowed audibly. 'Of course! Why, then, you must be quite used to such a lofty stance, sir. Kruppe envies those who can look down upon everyone else.'

'It is easy to fool oneself,' Rake answered, 'into viewing those beneath one as small and insignificant. The risks of oversight, you might say.'

'Kruppe might well say, assuming the pun was intended. But who would disagree that the dragon's lot is ever beyond the ken of mere humankind? Kruppe can only guess at the thrill of flight, the wail of high winds, the rabbits scurrying below as one's shadow brushes their limited awareness.'

'My dear Kruppe,' Baruk sighed, 'it is but a mask.'

'Such is the irony of life,' Kruppe proclaimed, raising one pastry-filled hand over his head, 'that one learns to distrust the obvious, surrendering instead to insidious suspicion and confused conclusion. But, lo, is Kruppe deceived? Can an eel swim? Hurrah, these seeming muddy waters are home to Kruppe, and his eyes are wide with wonder!' He bowed with a flourish, spattering bits of cake over Rake and Baruk, then marched off, still talking. 'A survey of the kitchen is in order, Kruppe suspects . . .'

'An eel indeed,' Rake said, in an amused tone. 'He is a lesson to us all, is he not?'

'Agreed,' Baruk muttered, shoulders slumping. 'I need a drink. Let me get you one. Excuse me.'

Turban Orr stood with his back to the wall and surveyed the

crowded room. He was finding it difficult to relax. The last week had been exhausting. He still awaited confirmation from the Assassins' Guild that Coll was dead. It wasn't like them to take so long to complete a contract, and sticking a knife into a drunk shouldn't have been too difficult.

His hunt for the spy in his organizations had reached a dead end, but he remained convinced that such a man – or woman – existed. Again and again, and especially since Lim's assassination, he'd found his moves in the Council blocked by countermoves, too unfocused for him to point a finger at any one person. But the proclamation was dead in the water.

He'd come to that conclusion this morning. And he'd acted. Even now his most trusted and capable messenger rode the trader's track, probably passing through the Gadrobi Hills and that thunderstorm at this very moment, on his way to Pale. To the Empire. Turban Orr knew the Malazans were on the way. No one in Darujhistan could stop them. And the Moon's lord had been defeated once, at Pale. Why would it be any different this time around? No, the time had come to ensure that his own position would survive the Empire's occupation. Or, better yet, an even higher rank to reward his vital support.

His eyes fell casually on a guard stationed to one side of the spiral staircase. The man looked familiar somehow – not his face, but the way he stood, the set of the shoulders. Was the man's usual station at Majesty Hall? No, the uniform was that of a regular, while Majesty Hall was the domain of the Élites. Turban Orr's frown deepened behind the hawk mask. Then the guard adjusted his helmet strap, and Turban Orr gasped. He leaned back against the wall, overcome by trembling. Despot's Barbican! All those nights, night after night – for years – that guard had witnessed his midnight meetings with his allies and agents. There stood his spy.

He straightened, closing one hand over the pommel of his duelling sword. He'd leave no room for questions, and damn

613

Simtal's sensibilities – and damn this party. He wanted his vengeance to be swift and immediate. He'd let no one stop him. His eyes fixing on the unsuspecting guard, Turban Orr stepped forward.

He collided with a hard shoulder and staggered back. A large man in a tiger mask turned to him. Orr waited for an apology, but received only silence. He moved to step past the man.

The stranger's arm intercepted him. Turban Orr cursed as a gloved hand poured wine down his chest. 'Idiot!' he snapped. 'I am Councilman Turban Orr! Out of my way.'

'I know who you are,' the man said quietly.

Orr jabbed a finger into the man's chest. 'Keep that mask on, so I'll know who to look for later.'

'I didn't even notice your mask,' the man said, his voice cold and flat. 'Fooled by the nose, I suppose.'

The councilman's eyes narrowed. 'Eager to die, are you?' he grated. 'I will oblige you.' His hand twitched on his sword's pommel. 'In a few minutes. Right now I have—'

'I wait on no man,' Rallick Nom said. 'And certainly not for some thin-lipped prancer pretending to manhood. If you've the belly for a duel, make it now or stop wasting time with all this talk.'

Shaking, Turban Orr took a step back and faced the man directly. 'What's your name?' he demanded hoarsely.

'You are not fit to hear it, Councilman.'

Turban Orr raised his hands and whirled to the crowd. 'Hear me, guests! Unexpected entertainment for you all!' Conversation died and everyone faced the councilman. He continued, 'A fool has challenged my honour, friends. And since when has Turban Orr permitted such an insult?'

'A duel!' someone cried excitedly. Voices rose.

Orr pointed at Rallick Nom. 'This man, so bold as to wear Trake's face, will be dead shortly. Look upon him now, friends, as he looks upon you – and know that he is all but dead already.'

'Stop babbling,' Rallick drawled.

The councilman pulled the mask from his face, revealing a tight grin. 'If I could kill you a thousand times,' he said, 'it would not be enough to satisfy me. I must settle with you but once.'

Rallick removed his mask and tossed it on to the carpeted stairs. He looked upon Turban Orr with flat, dark eyes. 'Done breaking wind, Councilman?'

'Unmasked and still a stranger,' Orr said, scowling. 'So be it. Find yourself a second.' A thought struck him, and he turned back to the crowd, searching it. Towards the back he saw the mask he sought, that of a wolf. His choosing of a second could well have political benefits, assuming the man accepted. And, in this crowd, he'd be a fool to deny Orr. 'For myself,' he said loudly, 'I would be honoured if Councilman Estraysian D'Arle act as my second.'

The wolf started. Beside him stood two women, one no more than a girl. D'Arle's wife was dressed as a veiled woman of Callows, while the girl had selected – outrageously – the minimal garb of a Barghast warmaiden. Both wife and daughter spoke to Estraysian. He stepped forward. 'The honour is mine,' he rumbled, completing the ritual acceptance.

Turban Orr felt a surge of triumph. To have his most powerful enemy in the Council at his side for this duel would send a message mixed enough to panic half the Council members present. Pleased at his coup, he faced his nameless opponent again. 'And your second?'

Silence fell over the room.

'I haven't much time,' Lady Simtal said in a low voice. 'After all, as the hostess for this fête . . .'

'It's your duty,' murmured the man before her, 'to satisfy your

615

guests.' He reached forth and brushed the hair from her forehead. 'Which is something I'm certain you can do, and do well.'

She smiled and walked to the door. She locked its latch, then spun to face the man again. 'Perhaps half an hour,' she said.

The man strode to the bed and tossed down his leather gloves. 'I'm confident,' he said, 'that those thirty minutes will be satisfying indeed, each more than the last.'

Lady Simtal joined him beside the bed. 'I suppose,' she whispered, as she slipped her arms around the man's neck and drew his face down to her lips, 'that you've no choice now but to tell the Widow Lim the sad news.' She touched her lips to his, then ran her tongue along the line of his jaw.

'Mmm? What sad news is that?'

'Oh, that you've found yourself a more worthy lover, of course.' Her tongue reached into his ear. Abruptly she pulled back and met his eyes searchingly. 'Do you hear that?' she asked.

He brought his arms around her and drew her closer. 'Hear what?'

'That's just it,' she said. 'It's suddenly quiet downstairs. I'd better—'

'They're in the garden, no doubt,' the man said reassuringly. 'The minutes are passing, Lady.'

She hesitated, then made the mistake of letting him press his body against hers. Lady Simtal's eyes widened in near-alarm. Her breathing changed. 'So,' she gasped, 'what are we doing still dressed?'

'Good question,' Murillio growled, pulling both of them on to the bed.

In the silence following Turban Orr's question, Baruk found himself preparing to step forward. Knowing well what that

616

would reveal, he felt compelled nevertheless. Rallick Nom was here to right a dreadful wrong. More, the man was a friend, closer to the alchemist than Kruppe or Murillio – and, in spite of his profession, a man of integrity. And Turban Orr was Lady Simtal's last link to real power. If Rallick killed the man, she'd fall.

Coll's return to the Council was something Baruk and his fellow T'orrud mages greatly desired. And Turban Orr's death would be a relief. More was riding on this duel than Rallick imagined. The alchemist adjusted his robe and drew a deep breath.

A large hand closed on his upper arm and, before Baruk could react, Lord Anomander Rake stepped forward. 'I offer my services as second,' he said loudly. He met Rallick's eyes.

The assassin betrayed nothing, not once looking at Baruk. He answered Rake's offer with a nod.

'Perhaps,' Turban Orr sneered, 'the two strangers know each other.'

'We've never met,' Rake said. 'However, I find myself instinctively sharing his distaste for your endless talk, Councilman. Thus I seek to avoid a Council debate on who will be this man's second. Shall we proceed?'

Turban Orr led the way out to the terrace, Estraysian D'Arle behind him. As Baruk turned to follow he felt a familiar contact of energies at his side. He swung his head and recoiled. 'Good gods, Mammot! Where did you get that hideous mask?'

The old man's eyes held his briefly then shied away. 'An accurate rendition of Jaghut features, I believe,' he said softly. 'Though I think the tusks are a little short.'

Baruk shook himself. 'Have you managed to find your nephew yet?'

'No,' Mammot replied. 'I am deeply worried by that.'

'Well,' the alchemist grunted as they walked outside, 'let's hope that Oponn's luck holds for the lad.'

617

'Of course,' Mammot murmured.

Whiskeyjack's eyes widened as a crowd of excited guests poured out from the main chamber and gathered on the terrace.

Fiddler scurried to his side. 'It's a duel, Sergeant. The guy with the wine stain on his shirt is one of them, a councilman named Orr. Nobody knows who the other man is. He's over there with that big man in the dragon mask.'

The sergeant had been leaning, arms crossed, against one of the marble pillars encircling the fountain, but at seeing the tall dragon-masked figure he came near to toppling into the fountain behind him. 'Hood's Balls!' he cursed. 'Recognize that long silver hair, Fid?'

The saboteur frowned.

'Moon's Spawn,' Whiskeyjack breathed. 'That's the mage, the Lord who stood on that portal and battled Tayschrenn.' He reeled off an impressive list of curses, then added, 'And he's not human.'

Fiddler groaned. 'Tiste Andii. The bastard's found us. We've had it.'

'Shut up.' Whiskeyjack was recovering from his shock. 'Line everybody up the way that Captain Stillis wanted us. Backs to the woods and hands on weapons. Move!'

Fiddler scrambled. The sergeant watched the saboteur round up his men. Where the hell were Kalam and Paran anyway? He caught Quick Ben's eye and gestured the mage over.

'Fid explained it,' Quick Ben said, leaning close. 'I may not be much use, Sergeant. That barrow-dweller's unleashing waves of nasty stuff. My head feels ready to explode.' He grinned wanly. 'And look around. You can pick out all the mages by the sick looks on their faces. If we all accessed our Warrens, we'd be fine.'

'Then why don't you?'

The wizard grimaced. 'That Jaghut would fix on us as if we were a beacon of fire. And he'd take the weaker ones – even from this distance, he'd take them. And then there'd be hell to pay.'

Whiskeyjack watched the guests create a space on the terrace, lining up on either side. 'Check with Hedge and Fiddler,' he ordered, eyes lingering on the Tiste Andii. 'Make sure they've got something handy, in case it all comes apart. This estate's got to burn then, hot and long. We'll need the diversion to set off the intersection mines. Give me the nod telling me they're up to it.'

'Right.' Quick Ben moved off.

Whiskeyjack grunted in surprise as a young man stepped round him, dressed as a thief, complete with face mask.

'Excuse me,' the man muttered, as he walked into the crowd.

The sergeant stared after him, then glanced back at the garden. How the hell had that lad got past them in the first place? He could've sworn they'd sealed off the woods. He loosened his sword surreptitiously in its sheath.

Crokus had no idea what kind of costume Challice D'Arle would be wearing, and he was resigned to a long hunt. He'd left Apsalar at the garden's back wall, and now felt guilty. Still, she'd seemed to take it well – though in a way that made him feel even worse. Why did she have to be so nice about things?

He spared barely a thought about the crowd's strange formation, looking as he was for a head somewhere at chest level to everyone else. As it turned out, that proved unnecessary, for Challice D'Arle's costume was no disguise.

Crokus found himself between two burly house guards. Across from him, twenty feet away with no one to block his view, stood Challice and an older woman Crokus took to be her mother. Their attention was held unerringly on a tall, severe-looking man standing at one end of the cleared space and speaking with another man, who was strapping on a duelling glove. It slowly dawned on the thief that a duel was but moments away.

Squeezing between the two guards, Crokus craned his neck to find the other duellist. At first he thought him the giant with the dragon mask and two-handed sword. Then his gaze found the man. Rallick Nom. His eyes snapped back to the first duellist. Familiar. He nudged the guard on his left. 'Is that Councilman Turban Orr?'

'It is, sir,' the guard replied, an odd tightness in his tone.

Crokus glanced up to see the man's face wet with sweat, trickling down from under his peaked helmet. Strange. 'So, where's Lady Simtal?' he asked casually.

'Nowhere in sight,' the guard answered, with obvious relief. 'Otherwise she'd stop this.'

Crokus nodded at that. 'Well,' he said, 'Rallick will win.'

The guard's gaze was on him, the eyes hard and piercing. 'You know the man?'

'Well—'

Someone tapped his back and he turned to find a cherub's face smiling mindlessly at him. 'Why, Crokus lad! What an inventive costume you're wearing!'

'Kruppe?'

'Well guessed!' Kruppe replied. The painted wooden face swung to the guard. 'Oh, kind sir, I have a written message for you.' Kruppe placed a scroll into the man's hand. 'Compliments of a long-time secret admirer.'

Crokus grinned. These guards had all the luck when it came to noble ladies.

Circle Breaker accepted the scroll and slid from it the silk tie.

More than once he had sensed Turban Orr's eyes on him. First in the central chamber, when it looked as if the

620

councilman might accost him directly, and now, while others argued over who should referee the duel.

Circle Breaker prayed Rallick would kill Turban Orr. He felt his own fear racing through his body, and it was with trembling hands that he read the Eel's message.

The time has come for Circle Breaker to retire from active duty. The circle is mended, loyal friend. Though you have never seen the Eel, you have been his most trusted hand, and you have earned your rest. Think not that the Eel simply discards you now. Such is not the Eel's way. The sigil at the bottom of this parchment will provide you passage to the city of Dhavran, where loyal servants of the Eel have prepared your arrival by purchasing an estate and a legitimate title on your behalf. You enter a different world soon, with its own games.

Trust your new servants, friend, in this and all other concerns.

Proceed, this very night, to the Dhavran trader's pier in Lakefront. You seek the river longboat named Enskalader. Show the sigil to any crewman aboard – all are servants of the Eel. The time has come, Circle Breaker. The circle is mended. Fare you well.

Baruk threw up his hands in exasperation. 'Enough of this!' he bellowed. 'I will referee this duel, and accept all responsibility. Judgement of victory is mine. Accepted by both parties?'

Turban Orr nodded. Even better than Estraysian being his second. Baruk's proclaiming him victor in the duel would be a coup in its own right. 'I accept.'

'As do I,' Rallick said, his short cloak drawn about his body.

A sudden wind thrashed the treetops in the garden, sweeping down from the east. Thunder boomed from this side of the hills. A number of onlookers seemed to flinch. Turban Orr grinned, stepping into the cleared area. Leaves skirled past, clattering like tiny bones. 'Before it rains,' he said.

His allies in the crowd laughed at this. 'Of course,' Orr continued, 'it might prove more entertaining to draw things out. A wound here, a wound there. Shall I cut him to pieces slowly?' He feigned dismay at the chorus of eager assent. 'Too eager for blood, friends! Must the ladies dance on slick flagstones once darkness falls? We must consider our host . . .' And where *was* Simtal? His imagination conjured an image in answer and he frowned. 'No indeed,' he said coldly, 'it shall be quick.'

The councilman unsheathed his sword and fastened his glove's leather straps to the ornate grip behind the bell guard. He scanned the faces of his audience, even now seeking some betrayal of expression – he had friends who were enemies, enemies who would be friends, the game would continue beyond this moment, but it could prove a telling moment. He would recall every face later, and study it at his leisure.

Turban Orr assumed his stance. His opponent stood ten feet away, both hands hidden beneath his cloak. He looked at ease, almost bored. 'What's this?' Orr demanded. 'Where is your weapon?'

'I'm ready,' Rallick replied.

Baruk placed himself equidistant between the two duellists, slightly off to one side. His face was pale, as if he had fallen ill. 'Comments from the seconds?' he asked faintly.

Rake made no reply.

Estraysian D'Arle cleared his throat. 'I hereby make it known that I oppose this duel as facile and trite.' He stared at Turban Orr. 'I find the councilman's life irrelevant in the best of times. Should he die,' the tall man looked over to Rallick, 'there will be no vengeance pact from the House of D'Arle. You, sir, are freed of that.'

622

Rallick bowed.

Turban Orr's smile tightened. The bastard would pay for that, he vowed. He lowered himself into a crouch, ready to launch an attack as soon as the duel began.

Baruk said, 'You have been heard, Estraysian D'Arle.' The alchemist raised a handkerchief before him, then released it.

Turban Orr jumped forward and lunged in a single, fluid motion, so fast he'd fully extended his weapon before the handkerchief struck the paving stones. He saw his opponent's left hand dart under his blade, then twist up and outward, a short, curved knife flashing in its grip. The parry was a blur, yet Orr caught it and deftly disengaged, driving his point low and towards the man's mid-section. He had no time even to notice the second knife, as Rallick turned his body sideways, the blade in his right hand guiding Turban Orr's sword past him. The assassin stepped in then, his left hand moving in a high swing that buried its blade in the councilman's neck. Rallick followed this by driving his other knife into Orr's chest.

The councilman staggered to one side, his sword clanging on the stones as he clutched at the gushing wound in his neck. The motion was reflex, for he was already dead from the wound in his heart. He toppled.

Rallick stepped back, weapons once again hidden beneath his cloak. 'A thousand other deaths,' he whispered, so low that only Baruk and Rake heard him, 'would not have satisfied me. But I'll settle for this one.'

Baruk stepped close and made to speak, but then, at a gesture from Rake, he turned to see Estraysian D'Arle approaching.

The councilman's heavy eyes held Rallick. 'I might suspect,' he said, 'given your style, that we have witnessed an assassination. Of course, not even the Guild of Assassins is brash enough to commit public murder. Therefore I've no choice but to keep such suspicions to myself. And leave it at that.

623

Good evening, gentlemen.' He whirled and strode away.

'I think,' Rake said, his masked face swinging to the assassin, 'that that was a rather uneven match.'

A rush of people closed in around Turban Orr's body. Voices shouted in dismay.

Baruk studied the cool satisfaction on Rallick's face. 'It's done, Rallick. Go home.'

A large, rounded woman in a bright green, gold-trimmed robe joined them. Unmasked, she smiled broadly at Baruk. 'Greetings,' she said. 'Interesting times, yes?' A personal servant stood at her side, bearing a padded tray on which squatted a water-pipe.

Rallick stepped back with a slight bow, then left.

Baruk sighed. 'Greetings, Derudan. Permit me to introduce Lord Anomander Rake. Lord, the witch Derudan.'

'Forgive the mask,' Rake said to her. 'It is best that it remain on, however.'

Smoke streamed down from Derudan's nose. 'My compatriots share my growing unease, yes? We feel the approaching storm, and while Baruk continues to reassure us, still the misgivings, yes?'

'Should it prove necessary,' Rake said, 'I will attend to the matter personally. I do not believe, however, that our greatest threat is the one beyond the city's walls. A suspicion, Witch, no more.'

'I think,' Baruk said tentatively, 'that we would like to hear these suspicions of yours, Rake.'

The Tiste Andii hesitated, then shook his head. 'Unwise. The matter is presently too sensitive to be broached. I shall remain here for now, however.'

Derudan waved dismissively at Baruk's angry growl. 'True, the T'orrud Cabal is unused to feeling helpless, yes? True also, dangers abound, and any might prove a feint, a diversion, yes? Cunning is the Empress. For myself, I affirm the trust between

624

us, Lord.' She smiled at Baruk. 'We must speak, you and I, Alchemist,' she said, linking arms with him.

Rake bowed to the woman. 'A pleasure meeting you, Witch.' He watched the witch and the alchemist walk away, the servant scurrying at Derudan's heel.

Kruppe intercepted a servant burdened with delicious-looking savouries. Taking two handfuls at random, he turned back to resume his conversation with Crokus. He stopped. The lad was nowhere in sight.

The crowd milled about on the terrace, some upset although the majority appeared simply confused. Where was Lady Simtal? they asked. Some, grinning, changed the question to: Who's she with? Already a new wave of anticipation rose among the nobles. They circled like vultures, waiting for their faltering hostess.

Smiling beatifically behind the cherub mask, Kruppe raised his eyes slowly to the balcony overlooking the patio, in time to see a figure appear as a dark, feminine silhouette behind the shutters. He licked sticky sugar from his fingers, smacking his lips. 'There are times, Kruppe murmurs, when celibacy born of sad deprivation becomes a boon, nay, a source of great relief. Dear Murillio, prepare for a storm.'

Simtal pushed apart two slats of the shutters and looked down. 'You were right,' she said. 'They have indeed retired to the terrace. Odd, with that storm coming. I should get dressed.' She returned to the bed and began to collect her clothing, which lay scattered all around it. 'And what about you, Murillio?' she asked. 'Don't you think your companion below is wondering where you are, dear lover?'

Murillio swung his legs over the bedside and pulled on his tights. 'I think not,' he said.

Simtal shot him a curious look. 'Who did you come with?'

'Just a friend,' he answered, buttoning his shirt. 'I doubt you'd recognize the name.'

At that moment the door's lock snapped and the door itself slammed inward.

Dressed only in her underclothes, Simtal loosed a startled cry. Her eyes flashed at the tall, cloaked man standing in the doorway. 'How dare you enter my bedroom? Leave at once, or I'll call—'

'Both guards patrolling this hallway have departed, Lady,' Rallick Nom said, stepping into the room and closing the door behind him. The assassin glanced at Murillio. 'Get dressed,' he snapped.

'Departed?' Simtal moved to place the bed between herself and Rallick.

'Their loyalty has been purchased,' the assassin said. 'The lesson shouldn't be lost on you.'

'I need only scream and others will come.'

'But you haven't,' Rallick grinned, 'because you're curious.'

'You don't dare harm me,' Simtal said, straightening. 'Turban Orr will hunt you down.'

The assassin took another step forward. 'I'm here only to talk, Lady Simtal,' he said. 'You won't be harmed, no matter what you deserve.'

'Deserve? I've done nothing – I don't even know you.'

'Neither did Councilman Lim,' Rallick said quietly. 'And tonight the same could be said for Turban Orr. Both men paid for their ignorance, alas. Fortunate that you missed the duel, Lady. It was unpleasant, but necessary.' His eyes hardened on the pale woman. 'Allow me to explain. Turban Orr's offer of contract to the Assassins' Guild is now officially cancelled. Coll lives, and now his return to this house is assured. You're done with, Lady Simtal. Turban Orr is dead.'

He turned and walked from the room, closing the door behind him.

Murillio rose slowly. He looked into Simtal's eyes, seeing there a growing terror. Undermined by the stripping away of her links to power, her once secure defences collapsed. He watched as she seemed physically to contract, her shoulders drawing inward, her hands clasped at her stomach, knees bending. Then he could look no longer. The Lady Simtal was gone, and he dared not study too closely the creature in her place.

He unsheathed his ornamental dagger and tossed it on the bed. Without another word or gesture, he left the room, knowing with certainty that he would have been the last man to see her alive.

Out in the hallway he paused. 'Mowri,' he said softly. 'I'm not cut out for this.' Planning to reach this point was one thing; having now reached it was another. He hadn't considered how he'd feel. Justice got in the way of that, a white fire he'd had no reason to look behind, or push aside. Justice had seduced him and he wondered what he had just lost, he wondered at the death he felt spreading within him. The regret following in that death's wake, so unanswerable it was, threatened to overwhelm him. 'Mowri,' he whispered a second time, as close to praying as he'd ever been, 'I think I'm now lost. Am I lost?'

Crokus edged round a marble pillar, his eyes on the rather short Barghast warmaiden sitting on the fountain's rim. Damn those guards at the wood's edge, anyway. He was a thief, wasn't he? Besides, they all looked pretty distracted.

He waited for his opportunity, and when it came he darted for the shadows between the first line of trees. No shout of alarm or call to halt sounded behind him. Slipping into the darkness, Crokus turned and crouched. Yes, she still sat there, facing in his direction.

He drew a deep breath, then stood straight, a pebble in one hand. Eyeing the guards, he waited. Half a minute later he

627

found his chance. He stepped forward and flung the pebble into the fountain.

Challice D'Arle jumped, then looked round as she wiped droplets of water from her painted face.

His heart sank as her gaze passed over him, then her head whipped back.

Crokus gestured desperately. This was it, this was when he'd find out where she stood as far as he was concerned. He held his breath and gestured again.

With a backward glance towards the patio, Challice rose and ran to him.

As she came close she squinted at him. 'Gorlas? Is that you? I've been waiting all night!'

Crokus froze. Then, without thinking, he lunged forward and clasped a hand over her mouth, his other arm encircling her waist. Challice squealed, trying to bite his palm, and struggled against him, but he dragged her into the darkness of the garden. Now what? he wondered.

Circle Breaker leaned against the marble pillar just inside the estate's main chamber. Behind him guests milled around Turban Orr's body, arguing loudly and voicing empty threats. The air hung heavy over the garden, smelling of blood.

He wiped at his eyes, trying to calm his heart. *It's over. Queen of Dreams, I'm done. I can rest now. Finally rest.* He straightened slowly, taking a deep breath, adjusted his sword belt and glanced around. Captain Stillis was nowhere in sight, and the chamber was almost empty except for a knot of servants outside the kitchen entrance. Lady Simtal was still missing, and confusion now seeped into the void of her absence.

Circle Breaker looked one last time at the guests in the garden, then he made his way to the doors. As he passed a long table on which sat the remnants of pastries and puddings, he heard faint snoring. Another step forward brought him to the table's end and into view the small round man seated in a plush antique chair. The smeared cherub mask hid the man's face, but Circle Breaker could see the closed eyes, and the nasal drone that matched the rise and fall of his chest was loud and steady.

The guardsman hesitated. Then, shaking his head, he moved on. Beyond the gates now within sight waited the streets of Darujhistan, and freedom. Now that he'd begun his first steps on that path, he would let nothing deter him.

I've done my part. Just another nameless stranger who couldn't run from the face of tyranny. Dear Hood, take the man's shrivelled soul – his dreams are over, ended by an assassin's whim. As for my own soul, well, you shall have to wait a while longer.

He passed through the gates, welcoming at last the smile that came unbidden to his mouth.

CHAPTER TWENTY-TWO

Ravens! Great Ravens!
Your damning cawls deride
histories sweeping beneath
your blackened wings –

> Shatter the day
> O flags of night,
> rend with shadows
> this innocent light

Ravens! Great Ravens!
Your drumming clouds arrive
swoop'd sudden sheer,
hissing travails
from no place
t' the other –

> Shatter the day,
> O flags of night,
> rend with shadows
> this innocent light

Ravens! Great Ravens!
Your beaks clatter open
disgorging the sweat

630

of straining dismay
the clack of bones
promised this day –

I've seen the sheen
of your eyes the laughter
that rimes the living
your passing but an illusion –
we stop, we stare
we curse your cold winds
in knowing your flight's path
wheeling you round us
again, oh, for ever again!

Ravens
Collitt (b.978)

R aest had driven two of the black dragons from the battle.
The remaining two now circled high overhead while
Silanah Redwings sped down and out of sight beyond
the hill. She was hurting, the Jaghut Tyrant knew, the power of
her immense lifeforce bleeding away.

'And now,' he said, through tattered lips, 'she will die.' Raest's
flesh had been torn away, ravaged by the virulent power of the
dragons, power that burst from their jaws like breath of fire. His
brittle, yellowed bones were splintered, crushed and shattered.
All that kept him upright and moving was his Omtose Phellack
Warren.

Once the Finnest was in his hands, he would make his body
anew, filling it with the vigour of health. And he was near his
goal. One last ridge of hills and the city's walls would be
visible, its fortifications all that stood between Raest and his
greater powers.

The battle had laid waste to the hills, incinerating

everything in the deadly clash of Warrens. And Raest had driven back the dragons. He'd listened to their cries of pain. Laughing, he'd flung dense clouds of earth and stone skyward to blind them. He ignited the air in the path of their flight. He filled clouds with fire. It was, he felt, good to be alive again.

As he walked, he continued to devastate the land around him. A single jerk of his head had shattered a stone bridge spanning a wide, shallow river. There had been a guardhouse there, and soldiers with iron weapons – odd creatures, taller than Imass, yet he sensed that they could be easily enslaved. These particular men, however, he destroyed lest they distract him in his battle with the dragons. He'd met another man, similarly clad and riding a horse. He killed both man and beast, irritated at their intrusion.

Wreathed in the crackling fire of his sorcery, Raest ascended the side of the hill behind which Silanah had disappeared minutes earlier. Anticipating another ambush, the Jaghut Tyrant gathered his power, fists clenching. Yet he reached the crest unmolested. Had she fled? He craned skyward. No, the two black dragons remained, and between them a Great Raven.

Raest crossed the hill's summit and stopped when the valley beyond came into view. Silanah waited there, her red pebbled skin streaked with black, wet burns across her heaving chest. Wings folded, she watched him from her position at the base of the valley, where a stream wound a tortured cut through the earth, its jagged path choked with bramble.

The Jaghut Tyrant laughed harshly. Here she would die. The far side of the valley was a low ridge, and beyond, glowing in the darkness, was the city that held his Finnest. Raest paused at seeing it. Even the great Jaghut cities of the early times were dwarfed by comparison. And what of its strange blue and green light, fighting the darkness with such steady, unfaltering determination?

There were mysteries here. He was eager to discover them. 'Silanah!' he cried. '*Eleint!* I give you your life! Flee now, Silanah. I show mercy but once. Hear me, *eleint!*'

The red dragon regarded him steadily, her multi-faceted eyes glowing like beacons. She did not move, nor did she reply.

Raest strode towards her, surprised to find her Warren gone. Was this surrender, then? He laughed a second time.

As he neared, the sky above him changed, filling with a sourceless mercurial glow. The city beyond vanished, replaced by wind-whipped mudflats. The distant jagged line of mountains loomed massive, uncarved by rivers of ice, bright and savage with youth. Raest's steps slowed. *This is an Elder vision, a vision before even the Jaghut. Who has lured me here?*

'Oh, my, oh, my . . .'

The Tyrant's gaze snapped down to find a mortal standing before him. Raest cocked a withered brow at the man's peculiar clothing, the coat tattered and faded red with large, food-stained cuffs, the baggy shimmering pantaloons dyed an astonishing pink, and the broad black leather boots covering his small feet. The man withdrew a cloth and patted the sweat from his brow. 'Dear sir,' he wheezed, 'you've not aged well at all!'

'There is Imass within you,' Raest rasped. 'Even the language you speak echoes their guttural throats. Have you come forth to grovel at my feet? Are you my first acolyte, then, eager for my rewards?'

'Alas,' the man replied, 'you are mistaken, sir. Kruppe – this humble, weak mortal who stands before you – bows to no man, be he Jaghut or god. Such are the nuances of this new age that you are felled by indifference, made insignificant in your mighty struggles by lowly Kruppe into whose dream you have ignobly stumbled. Kruppe stands before you so that you may gaze upon his benign countenance in the last moments before your demise. Magnanimous of Kruppe, all things considered.'

633

Raest laughed. 'I have walked in the dreams of mortals before. You believe you are the master here, but you are mistaken.' The Tyrant's hand shot out, virulent power erupting from it. The sorcery engulfed Kruppe, blazing darkly, then faded, leaving not even a remnant of the man.

A voice spoke to Raest's left: 'Rude, Kruppe proclaims. Disappointing, this precipitateness.'

The Jaghut swung around, eyes narrowing. 'What game is this?'

The man smiled. 'Why, Kruppe's game, of course.'

A sound behind Raest alerted him, but too late. He spun – even as a massive flint sword crunched through his left shoulder, tearing a path that snapped ribs, sliced through sternum and spine. The blow dragged the Tyrant down and to one side. Raest sprawled, pieces of his body striking the ground around him. He stared up at the T'lan Imass.

Kruppe's shadow moved over Raest's face and the Tyrant met the mortal man's watery eyes.

'He is Clanless, of course. Unbound and beyond binding, yet the ancient call commands him still – to his dismay. Imagine his surprise at being found out. Onos T'oolan, Sword of the First Empire, is once more called upon by the blood that once warmed his limbs, his heart, his life of so very long ago.'

The T'lan Imass spoke. 'You have strange dreams, mortal.'

'Kruppe possesses many surprises, even unto himself.'

'I sense,' Onos T'oolan continued, 'a Bone Caster's hand in this summoning.'

'Indeed. Pran Chole of Kig Aven's clan of the Kron T'lan Imass, I believe he called himself.'

Raest raised himself from the ground, drawing his sorcery around his body to hold its shattered parts in place. 'No T'lan Imass can withstand me,' he hissed.

'A dubious claim,' Kruppe said. 'Even so, he is joined in this endeavour.'

634

The Jaghut Tyrant straightened to see a tall, black-shrouded figure emerge from the streambed. He cocked his head as the apparition approached. 'You remind me of Hood. Is the Death Wanderer still alive?' He scowled. 'But, no. I sense nothing from you. You do not exist.'

'Perhaps,' the figure replied, in a deep, soft tone that hinted of regret. 'If so,' he continued, 'then neither do you. We are both of the past, Jaghut.' The figure halted fifteen feet away from Raest and swung his hooded head in the dragon's direction. 'Her master awaits your arrival, Jaghut, but he waits in vain and for this you should thank us. He would deliver a kind of death from which there is no escape, even by such a creature as you.' The head turned, and the darkness within the hood once again regarded the Tyrant. 'Here, within a mortal's dream, we bring an end to your existence.'

Raest grunted. 'In this age there are none who can defeat me.'

The figure laughed, a low rumble. 'You are a fool, Raest. In this age even a mortal can kill you. The tide of enslavement has reversed itself. It is now we gods who are the slaves, and the mortals our masters – though they know it not.'

'You are a god, then?' Raest's scowl deepened. 'You are a child to me if so.'

'I was once a god,' the figure replied. 'Worshipped as K'rul, and my aspect was the Obilisk. I am the Maker of Paths – do you find significance in that ancient title?'

Raest took a step back, raising his desiccated hands. 'Impossible,' he breathed. 'You passed into the Realms of Chaos – returned to the place of your birth – you are among us no more—'

'As I said, things have changed,' K'rul said quietly. 'You have a choice, Raest. Onos T'oolan can destroy you. You have no understanding of what his title of Sword signifies – he is without equal in this world. You can fall ignobly beneath the blade of an Imass, or you can accompany me – for in one thing we are the same, you and I. Our time has passed, and the Gates of Chaos await us. What choice do you make?'

'I make neither, Eldering One.' With a soft, hollow laugh, Raest's battered, withered body collapsed.

K'rul cocked his head. 'He's found another body.'

Kruppe pulled out his handkerchief. 'Oh, my,' he said.

Kalam gestured sharply and Paran ducked down. The captain's mouth was dry. There was something very wrong with this garden. He wondered if it was simply the exhaustion he felt. The garden's air itself rubbed his senses raw. He thought he could see the darkness pulse, and the smell of decay had thickened to a stench.

Kalam reached for his knives. Paran tensed, unable to see anything beyond the assassin. Too many trees, not enough light. Somewhere ahead flickered gas-lamps, and people were gathered on the terrace. But civilization seemed a thousand leagues away. Here, the captain felt as if he was within a primordial presence, breathing slowly and heavily on all sides.

Kalam gestured that Paran remain where he was, then slipped into the shadows to their right. Crouching low, the captain edged forward to where the assassin had been standing moments earlier. There looked to be a glade, or clearing, just ahead. He couldn't be certain, however, nor could he see anything amiss. Yet his feeling of wrongness now ached in his skull. He took another step. Something occupied the glade's centre, blockish, like a dressed stone, or an altar, and before it stood a small woman, almost wraith-like in the darkness. Her back was to Paran.

One moment she stood alone, the next Kalam rose behind her, knives glimmering in his hands. He drew back his arms.

The woman moved in a blur, one elbow driving backwards into the assassin's stomach. She twisted round and drove her

636

knee into the man's crotch. A shout burst from Kalam as he reeled back a step, then fell to the ground with a heavy thump.

Paran's sword was in his hand. He dashed into the clearing.

The woman saw him and voiced a surprised, frightened yelp. 'No!' she cried. 'Please!'

The captain stopped at that girlish voice. Kalam sat up. He groaned, then said, 'Dammit, Sorry. Wasn't expecting you. We figured you were dead, girl.'

The woman eyed Paran warily as he approached cautiously. 'I should know you, shouldn't I?' she asked Kalam. Then, as Paran came closer, she raised a frightened hand between them and stepped back. 'I – I killed you!' With a soft moan she fell to her knees. 'Your blood was on my hands. I remember it!'

A fire of rage flared in Paran. He raised his sword and moved to stand over her.

'Wait!' Kalam hissed. 'Wait, Captain. Something's not right here.'

With great difficulty, the assassin climbed to his feet, then prepared to sit down on the stone block.

'Don't!' the girl gasped. 'Can't you feel it?'

'I can,' Paran growled. He lowered his weapon. 'Don't touch that thing, Corporal.'

Kalam stepped away. 'Thought it was just me,' he muttered.

'It's not stone at all,' the woman said, her face free of the anguish that had twisted it a moment before. 'It's wood.' She rose and faced Kalam. 'And it's growing.'

A suspicion came to Paran. 'Girl, do you remember me? Do you know who I am?'

She frowned at him, then shook her head. 'I know Kalam,' she said. 'He's an old friend, I think.'

The assassin choked on something, then coughed loudly, wagging his head.

The woman pointed at the wooden block. 'See? It's growing again.'

637

Both men looked. A haze blurred the block's edges, swelling and shifting, then vanished, yet it was clear to Paran that the thing was now bigger.

'It has roots,' the woman added.

Paran shook himself. 'Corporal? Remain here with the girl. I won't be long.' He sheathed his sword and left the glade. After winding through the undergrowth for a minute, he came to its edge and looked out on a terrace crowded with guests. A low-walled fountain rose from the paving stones to his left, encircled by marble pillars spaced about a yard apart.

The captain saw that Whiskeyjack and the squad had arrayed themselves in a rough line a dozen feet from the garden's edge, facing the terrace. They looked tense. Paran found a dead branch and snapped it in half.

At the sound all six men turned. The captain pointed at Whiskeyjack and Mallet, then stepped back between the trees. The sergeant whispered something to Quick Ben. Then he collected the healer and they came over.

Paran pulled Whiskeyjack close. 'Kalam's found Sorry, and something else besides,' he said. 'The girl's not all there, Sergeant, and I don't think it's an act. One minute she remembers killing me, the next she doesn't. And she's got it into her head right now that Kalam's an old friend.'

Mallet grunted.

After a brief glance back at the party, Whiskeyjack asked, 'So what's this "something else"?'

'I'm not sure, but it's ugly.'

'All right.' The sergeant sighed. 'Go with the captain, Mallet. Take a look at Sorry. Any contact from the Assassins' Guild yet?' he asked Paran.

'No.'

'Then we move soon,' Whiskeyjack said. 'We let Fiddler and Hedge loose. Bring Kalam when you come back, Mallet. We need to talk.'

638

Rallick found his path unobstructed as he moved across the central chamber towards the front doors. Faces turned to him and conversations fell away, rising again as he passed. A bone-deep weariness gripped the assassin, more than could be accounted for by the blood lost to a wound already healed. The malaise gripping him was emotional.

He paused at seeing Kruppe rising from a chair, mask dangling from one plump hand. The man's face was sheathed in sweat and there was fear in his eyes.

'You've a right to be terrified,' Rallick said, approaching him. 'If I'd known you'd be here—'

'Silence!' Kruppe snapped. 'Kruppe must think!'

The assassin scowled but said nothing. He'd never before seen Kruppe without his usual affable façade, and the sight of him so perturbed made Rallick profoundly uneasy.

'Be on your way, friend,' Kruppe said then, his voice sounding strange. 'Your destiny awaits you. More, it seems this new world is well prepared for one such as Raest, no matter what flesh he wears.'

Rallick's scowl deepened. *The man sounds drunk.* He sighed, then turned away, his mind returning once again to what had been achieved this night. He continued on his way, leaving Kruppe behind. What now? he wondered. So much had gone into reaching this moment. The sharp focus of his thoughts seemed dulled now by success. Never the crusader, Rallick's obsession to right the wrong had been, in a sense, no more than the assassin assuming the role Coll himself should have taken. He'd played the instrument of Coll's will, relying on a faith that the man's own will would return.

And if it didn't? His scowl deepening, Rallick crushed that question before it could lead his thought in search of an answer. As Baruk had said, the time had come to go home.

As he passed a silver-masked woman touched his arm.

Startled by the contact, he turned to look at her. Long brown hair surrounded the featureless mask, its eyehole slits revealing nothing of what lay behind it. The woman stepped close. 'I've been curious,' she said quietly, 'for some time. However, I see now I should have observed you personally, Rallick Nom. Ocelot's death could have been avoided.'

The assassin's gaze darkened. 'Vorcan.'

Her head tilted in a fraction of a nod.

'Ocelot was a fool,' Rallick snapped. 'If Orr's contract was sanctioned by the Guild, I await punishment.'

She did not reply.

Rallick waited calmly.

'You're a man of few words, Rallick Nom.'

His answer was silence.

Vorcan laughed softly. 'You say you await punishment, as if already resigned to your own death.' Her gaze shifted from him towards the crowded terrace. 'Councilman Turban Orr possessed protective magic, yet it availed him naught. Curious.' She seemed to be considering something, then she nodded. 'Your skills are required, Rallick Nom. Accompany me.'

He blinked, then, as she strode towards the garden at the rear of the house, he followed.

Crokus held one hand over Challice's mouth as he lay atop her. With his other he removed his thief's mask. Her eyes widened in recognition. 'If you scream,' Crokus warned in a harsh voice, 'you'll regret it.'

He'd managed to drag her perhaps ten yards into the undergrowth before she tripped him. They'd thrashed about, but he'd won the battle.

'I just want to talk to you,' Crokus said. 'I won't hurt you, Challice, I swear it. Unless you try something, of course. Now, I'm going to remove my hand. Please don't scream.' He tried to read the expression in her eyes, but all he

640

saw was fear. Ashamed, he raised his hand.

She didn't scream, and a moment later Crokus found himself wishing she had. 'Damn you, thief! When my father catches you he'll have you skinned alive! That's if Gorlas doesn't find you first. You try anything with me and he'll have you boiled, slowly—'

Crokus jammed his hand over her mouth again. Skinned? Boiled? 'Who's Gorlas?' he demanded, glaring. 'Some amateur chef? So you did betray me!'

She stared up at him.

He lifted his hand again.

'I didn't betray you,' she said. 'What are you talking about?'

'That murdered house guard. I never did it, but—'

'Of course you didn't. Father hired a Seer. A woman killed that guard, a servant of the Rope's. The Seer was terrified and didn't even stay to be paid! Now get off me, thief.'

He let her go and sat back on the ground. He stared into the trees. 'You didn't betray me? What about Meese? The guards at Uncle Mammot's? The big hunt?'

Challice climbed to her feet and brushed dead leaves from her hide cloak. 'What are you babbling about? I have to get back. Gorlas will be looking for me. He's the first son of House Tholius, in training to be a master duellist. If he sees you with me, there'll be real trouble.'

He looked up at her blankly. 'Wait!' He sprang to his feet. 'Listen, Challice! Forget this Gorlas idiot. Within the year my uncle will introduce us formally. Mammot is a famous writer.'

Challice rolled her eyes. 'Get your feet back on the ground. A writer? Some old man with ink-stained hands who walks into walls – has his house power? Influence? House Tholius has power, influence, everything required. Besides, Gorlas loves me.'

'But I—' He stopped, looking away. Did he? No. Did that matter, though? What did he want from her, anyway?

'What do you want from me, anyway?' Challice demanded.

He studied his feet. Then he met her eyes. 'Company?' he asked diffidently. 'Friendship? What am I saying? I'm a thief! I rob women like you!'

'That's right,' she snapped. 'So why pretend otherwise?' Her expression softened. 'Crokus, I won't betray you. It will be our secret.'

For the briefest of moments he felt like a child being stroked and consoled by a kindly matron, and he found himself enjoying it.

'Before you,' she added, smiling, 'I'd never met a real thief from the streets.'

His enjoyment ended in a surge of anger. 'Hood's Breath, no,' he sneered. 'Real? You don't know what's real, Challice. You've never had blood on your hands. You've never seen a man die. But that's the way it should be, isn't it? Leave the dirt to us, we're used to it.'

'I saw a man die tonight,' Challice said quietly. 'I never want to again. If that's what "real" means, then I don't want it. It's all yours, Crokus. Goodbye.' She turned and walked away.

Crokus stared at her back, her braided hair, as her words rang in his head.

Suddenly exhausted, he turned to the garden. He hoped Apsalar had remained where he'd left her. The last thing he wanted now was to have to track her down. He slipped into the shadows.

Mallet recoiled with his first step into the glade. Paran gripped his arm. Their eyes met.

The healer shook his head. 'I'll not approach any closer, sir. Whatever lives there is anathema to my Denul Warren. And it ... it senses me ... with hunger.' He wiped sweat from his brow, drew a shaky breath. 'Best bring the girl to me here.'

Paran released his arm and darted into the clearing. The

block of wood was now the size of a table, veined in thick, twisting roots and pocked on its sides with rough squared holes. The earth around it looked soaked in blood. 'Corporal,' he whispered, chilled. 'Send the girl over to Mallet.'

Kalam laid a hand on her shoulder. 'It's all right, lass,' he said, in the tone of a kindly uncle, 'you go on, now. We'll join you shortly.'

'Yes,' she smiled, and moved to where the healer stood at the glade's edge.

Kalam rubbed his bristly jaw, eyes following her. 'Never seen Sorry smile before,' he said, as Paran arrived. 'And that's a shame.'

They stood and watched as Mallet spoke quietly to the girl, then stepped forward and laid a hand on her forehead.

Paran cocked his head. 'The storm's stopped,' he said.

'Yeah. Hope it means what we'd like it to mean.'

'Someone's stopped it. I share your hope, Corporal.' For the captain however, it was a small hope. Something was building. He sighed. 'It's not even the twelfth bell yet. Hard to believe.'

'Long night ahead of us,' the assassin said, making it clear that he, too, found himself sorely lacking in optimism. He grunted. Mallet had voiced an amazed cry that reached them. The healer drew back his hand and waved at Paran and Kalam. 'You go,' the assassin said.

The captain frowned at the black man, confused. Then he went over to where the healer and Sorry waited. The girl's eyes were closed, and she seemed in a trance.

Mallet was direct. 'The possession's gone,' he said.

'Guessed as much,' Paran replied, eyeing the girl.

'There's more to it, though,' the healer continued. 'She's got someone else inside her, sir.'

Paran's brows rose.

'Someone who was there all along. How it survived the Rope's presence is beyond me. And now I've got a choice.'

643

'Explain.'

Mallet crouched, found a twig and began to scratch aimless patterns in the dirt. 'That someone's been protecting the girl's mind, acting like an alchemist's filter. In the last two years, Sorry's done things that would drive her insane if she'd remembered any of it. That presence is fighting those memories right now, but it needs help, because it isn't as strong as it once was. It's dying.'

Paran squatted beside the man. 'You're thinking of offering that help, then?'

'Not sure. You see, sir, I don't know its plans. Don't know what it's up to, can't read the pattern it's trying to make. So let's say I help it, only what it wants is absolute control? Then the girl's possessed all over again.'

'So you think the presence was protecting Sorry from the Rope, only so it could now jump in and take over?'

'Put it that way,' Mallet said, 'and it doesn't make sense. What gets me, though, is why else would that presence commit itself so thoroughly? Its body, its flesh is gone. If it lets go of the girl it's got nowhere to go, sir. Now, maybe it's a loved one, a relative or something like that. A person who was willing to sacrifice herself absolutely. That's a possibility.'

'Herself? It's a woman?'

'It was. Damned if I know what it is now. All I get from it is sadness.' The healer met Paran's eyes. 'It's the saddest thing I've ever known, sir.'

Paran studied the man's face briefly, then he rose. 'I'm not going to give you an order on what to do, Healer.'

'But?'

'But, for what it's worth, I say do it. Give it what it needs so it can do what it wants to do.'

Mallet puffed out his cheeks, then tossed down the twig and straightened. 'My instinct, too, sir. Thanks.'

Kalam spoke loudly from the glade. 'Far enough. Show yourselves.'

644

The two men spun around to see Kalam looking into the woods to their left. Paran grasped Mallet's arm and pulled him into the shadows. The healer dragged Sorry with them.

Two figures entered the glade, a woman and a man.

Crokus snaked closer through the vines and mulch of the forest floor. For an off-limits garden, this was a busy tangle of wood. The voices he'd heard in his search for Apsalar now revealed themselves as two men and one silver-masked woman. All three were looking at an odd, blurry tree stump in the centre of the glade. Slowly Crokus let out a breath. One of the men was Rallick Nom.

'There is ill in this,' the woman said, stepping back. 'A hunger.'

The large black-skinned man at her side grunted. 'Wouldn't argue with you on that, Guild Master. Whatever it is, it ain't Malazan.'

The thief's eyes widened. *Malazan spies? Guild Master? Vorcan!* Seemingly impervious to the strangeness around her, the woman now turned to Rallick. 'How does it affect you, Rallick?'

'It doesn't,' he said.

'Approach it, then.'

The assassin shrugged and walked up to the writhing, knotted block. Its blurred movement stopped.

Vorcan relaxed. 'You seem to damage its efforts, Rallick. Curious.'

The man grunted. 'Otataral dust.'

'What?'

'I rubbed it into my skin.'

Vorcan stared.

The other man's eyes narrowed on Rallick. 'I remember you, Assassin. Our quarry when we first sought to make contact. The night of the ambush from above.'

Rallick nodded.

'Well,' the Malazan continued, 'I'm surprised you survived.'

'He is a man of many surprises,' Vorcan said. 'Very well, Corporal Kalam of the Bridgeburners, your request for an audience reached me and I have granted it. Before we begin, however, I would appreciate it if the rest of your party were to join us.' She turned to the trees on her right.

Crokus's head was already reeling – Bridgeburners! – but it felt moments away from bursting when he saw two men emerge from the shadows, with Apsalar between them. She looked drugged, and her eyes were closed.

One of the men said, 'Guild Master, I am Captain Paran of the Ninth Squad.' He drew a deep breath, then continued, 'In this matter, however, Kalam speaks for the Empire.'

Vorcan turned back to the black man. 'Then the audience is begun.'

'We both know, Guild Master, that the City Council is not Darujhistan's true power base. And since you're not, either, we've concluded that the city's mages operate covertly, keeping the status quo intact being their overriding interest. Whoever they are, they're good at hiding themselves. Now, we might just decide to kill every mage in Darujhistan, but that would take too long, and it might prove messy. Instead, Guild Master, the Malazan Empire has issued a contract on Darujhistan's true rulers. One hundred thousand gold jakatas. Each. More, the Empress offers the mantle of the city's control, accompanied with the title High First and all the privileges that come with it.' He crossed his arms.

Vorcan was silent, then she said, 'Empress Laseen is willing to pay nine hundred thousand jakatas to me?'

'If that's the number. Yes,' Kalam agreed.

'The T'orrud Cabal is a powerful force, Corporal. But before I answer, I would know of the creature who approaches from the east.' Her face tightened fractionally. 'Five dragons opposed it for a time, presumably hailing from Moon's Spawn. I assume that Master Baruk and his Cabal have sealed an agreement with the Son of Darkness.'

Kalam looked stunned, then recovered quickly. 'Guild Master, the approaching force was not of our making. We'd welcome its destruction at the hands of the Son of Darkness. As for your hidden question, I would assume that the alliance between the Tiste Andii and the Cabal will become void with the death of the cabal's members. We're not asking you to try to kill the Lord of Moon's Spawn.'

Paran cleared his throat. 'Guild Master, Moon's Spawn and the Malazan Empire have clashed before. The pattern indicates that the Son of Darkness is likely to retreat rather than stand against us alone.'

'Accurate,' Vorcan agreed. 'Corporal Kalam, I have no wish to waste the lives of my assassins on such an effort. Only an assassin who is a High Mage could hope to succeed. Therefore, I accept the contract. I will conduct the assassinations. Now, as to the matter of payment . . .'

'Delivered by Warren upon completion of the contract,' Kalam said. 'You may know this already, Guild Master, but the Empress was once an assassin. She abides by the rules of conduct. The gold shall be paid. The title and rule of Darujhistan given without hesitation.'

'Accepted, Corporal Kalam.' Vorcan turned to Rallick. 'I begin immediately. Rallick Nom, the task I now give you is vital. I have considered your strange ability to negate the growth of this . . . ill thing. My instincts are such: it must not be permitted to continue growing. You will remain here, thus holding it in stasis.'

'For how long?' he growled.

'Until my return. At that time I will test its defences. Oh, and one more thing: Ocelot's actions were not sanctioned by the Guild. Executing him fulfilled the Guild's judgement as to

647

fit punishment. Thank you, Rallick Nom. The Guild is pleased.'

Rallick walked over to the strange stump and sat down on it.

'Until later,' Vorcan said, and strode from the glade.

Crokus watched as the three Malazan spies gathered for a whispered discussion. Then one of the men grasped Apsalar's arm and gently guided her into the woods, making for the rear wall. The remaining two, Captain Paran and Corporal Kalam, glanced over at Rallick.

The assassin's head was in his hands, his elbows on his thighs, staring gloomily at the ground.

Kalam hissed a sigh through his teeth and shook his head. A moment later both men left, in the direction of the terrace.

Crokus hesitated, a part of him wanting to rush into the glade and confront Rallick. *Assassinate the mages! Hand Darujhistan to the Malazans?* How could the man allow such a thing to happen? He did not move, however, a fear growing inside him that he, in truth, knew nothing of this man. Would the assassin listen to him? Or would he answer Crokus with a knife in the throat? Crokus didn't feel like taking the chance.

In the last minute Rallick had not moved. Then he rose, turned directly to where Crokus lay hidden.

The thief groaned.

Rallick beckoned.

Slowly, Crokus approached.

'You hide well,' Rallick said. 'And you were lucky Vorcan kept her mask on – she couldn't see much out of it. You heard, then?'

Crokus nodded, his eyes drawn to what he'd called a tree stump in spite of himself. It looked more like a small wooden house. The pocks on its sides could well have been windows. Unlike Vorcan, he sensed not hunger but a kind of urgency, almost frustration.

'Before you condemn me, listen carefully, Crokus.'

The thief dragged his attention from the wooden block. 'I'm listening.'

'Baruk may yet be at the party. You must find him, tell him exactly what's happened. Tell him Vorcan is a High Mage – and she'll kill them all unless they gather to defend each other.' The assassin reached out a hand to Crokus's shoulder. The boy flinched, his eyes wary. 'And if Baruk has gone home, find Mammot. I saw him here not long ago. He wears the mask of a tusked beast.'

'Uncle Mammot? But he's—'

'He's a High Priest of D'riss, Crokus, and a member of the T'orrud Cabal. Now, hurry. There's no time to waste.'

'You mean you're going to stay here, Rallick? Just sit there on that . . . that stump?'

The assassin's grip tightened. 'Vorcan spoke true, lad. Whatever this thing is, it seems I can hold it in check. Baruk needs to know of this conjuring. I trust his senses more than I do Vorcan's, but for now I will obey her in this.'

For a moment Crokus resisted, his thoughts on Apsalar. They'd done something to her, he was certain – and if they'd harmed her, he'd make them pay. But . . . Uncle Mammot? Vorcan was planning to kill his uncle? The thief's eyes hardened as he looked up at Rallick. 'Consider it done,' he said.

At that instant, a roar of rage and agony, coming from the terrace, shook the trees. The block of wood behind them responded with a burst of bright yellow fire, its roots writhing and swelling like groping fingers.

Rallick pushed Crokus hard then whirled and dived on to the block. The yellow fire winked out and cracks opened in the earth, spreading in all directions. 'Go!' yelled Rallick.

The thief, his heart hammering, turned and sprinted for Lady Simtal's estate.

* * *

Baruk's hand snapped out and yanked savagely on the bell cord. Above him, he heard the wagoner cry out. The carriage skidded to a halt. 'Something's happened,' he hissed to Rake. 'We left too early, dammit!' He moved on the seat to the window and opened its shutters.

'A moment, Alchemist,' Rake said levelly, his brows knitted and his head cocked as if listening for something. 'The Tyrant,' he pronounced. 'But he is weakened, and enough mages remain to deal with him.' He opened his mouth to add something, then shut it again. His eyes deepened to azure as he studied the alchemist. 'Baruk,' he said quietly, 'return to your estate. Prepare for the Empire's next move – we'll not have long to wait.'

Baruk stared at the Tiste Andii. 'Tell me what's happening,' he said angrily. 'Will you challenge the Tyrant or not?'

Rake tossed his mask on to the floor between them and clasped the collar of his cloak. 'If it proves necessary, I shall.'

Fists pounded on the carriage and voices shouted good-naturedly. The crowds around them pushed in on all sides, rocking the carriage. The festival approached the Twelfth Bell, the Hour of Ascension as the Lady of Spring took to the sky in the coming of the moon.

Rake continued, 'In the meantime the city's streets must be cleared,' he said. 'I imagine it's your desire to minimize the loss of life.'

'And this is all you give me, Rake?' Baruk gestured sharply. 'Clear the streets? How in Hood's name do we manage that? There are three hundred thousand people in Darujhistan, and they're *all* in the streets!'

The Tiste Andii opened the door beside him. 'Then leave that to me. I need to find a high vantage-point, Alchemist. Suggestions?'

Baruk's frustration was so great that he had to fight the

desire to defy Anomander Rake. 'K'rul's Belfry,' he said. 'A square tower near Worry Gate.'

Rake stepped out of the carriage. 'We'll speak again at your estate, Alchemist,' he said, leaning back inside. 'You and your fellow mages must prepare yourselves.' He faced the crowds, pausing for a moment as if smelling the air. 'How far to this belfry?'

'Three hundred paces – surely you don't mean to go on foot?'

'I do. I am not yet ready to unveil my Warren.'

'But how—?' Baruk fell silent, as Anomander Rake provided the answer to his question.

Standing head and shoulders above the jostling crowds, he unsheathed his sword. 'If you value your souls,' the Son of Darkness bellowed, 'make way!' Raised high, the sword groaned awake, chains of smoke writhing from the blade. A terrible sound as of wheels creaking filled the air and behind it arose a chorus of moaning filled with hopelessness. Before Lord Anomander Rake the crowd in the street shrank back, all thoughts of festivity swept away.

'Gods forfend!' Baruk whispered.

It had begun innocently enough. Quick Ben and Whiskeyjack stood together near the fountain. Servants scurried as, despite the night's bloodshed and the hostess's absence, the party's energy burgeoned anew as the twelfth bell approached. They were joined by Captain Paran.

'We have met with the Guild Master,' he said. 'She has accepted the contract.'

Whiskeyjack grunted. 'Where would we all be without greed?'

'I just noticed something,' Quick Ben said. 'My headache's gone. I'm tempted to access my Warren, Sergeant. See what I can see.'

Whiskeyjack thought briefly. 'Go ahead.'

Quick Ben stepped back into the shadow of a marble pillar.

Before them, an old man wearing a ghastly mask drifted towards Whiskeyjack's line of men. Then a large, buxom woman with a water-pipe approached the old man. Her servant followed half a step behind. Trailing smoke as she walked, she called to the old man.

The next moment the night was shattered as a wave of energy flowed like a stream of water between Whiskeyjack and Paran, striking the old man in the chest. The sergeant's sword was in his hand as he turned to find his wizard, magic swirling from him, pushing him to one side and racing for the woman. 'No!' Quick Ben screamed. 'Stay away from him!'

Paran, too, had unsheathed his sword in his hand, the blade keening as if filled with terror. He sprinted forward.

A bestial roar of rage shook the air as the old man, his mask torn away, whirled. His burning eyes found the woman and he flung a hand towards her. The surge of power that streamed from him was as grey as slate, crackling in the air.

Whiskeyjack, frozen, watched in disbelief as Quick Ben's body hurled into the woman's. Both collided with the servant and all three went down in a heap. The writhing stream of energy cut a swath through the stunned crowd, incinerating everyone it touched. Where men and women had stood a moment earlier there was nothing but white ash. The attack branched out, ripping through everything in sight. Trees disintegrated, stone and marble exploded in clouds of dust. People died, some with parts of their body simply gone, blood spraying in black flecks as they crumpled. A lance of energy shot wildly skyward, flashing in the night sky within a heavy cloud. Another struck the estate with a rattling boom. A third snaked towards Paran as he closed the gap between him and the old man. The power struck the sword, and it and Paran vanished.

The sergeant took a half-step forward, then something hard

and massive struck a glancing blow to his shoulder. He was spun round, his right knee buckling inward as he fell.

He felt the snap of bone, then the meaty tearing of flesh and skin as his weight bore him down. His sword clanged. Agony lancing through him, he rolled to free his pinned leg, and came up against a toppled pillar.

An instant later hands grasped his cloak. 'I got you!' Fiddler grunted.

Whiskeyjack bellowed in pain as the saboteur dragged him across the paving-stones. Then darkness swept in around him and he knew no more.

Quick Ben found himself buried beneath flesh, and for a second he could not breathe. Then the woman's hands pressed down on his shoulders and she pushed herself off him. She shouted at the old man.

'Mammot! *Anikaleth araest!*'

Quick Ben's eyes widened as he sensed the wave of power rise through her body. The air suddenly smelled of deep forest loam.

'*Araest!*' she yelled, and the power burst from her in a virulent pulse.

Quick Ben heard Mammot's scream of pain.

'Attend, Wizard!' the woman said. 'He is Jaghut-possessed.'

'I know,' he growled, rolling on to his stomach then climbing to his hands and knees. A quick glance showed Mammot on the ground, waving a feeble hand. The wizard's gaze flicked to where Whiskeyjack had been. The pillars around the fountain had toppled, and the sergeant was nowhere in sight. In fact, he realized, none of the squad was visible. On the terrace crumpled bodies lay in grotesque piles, none moving. Everyone else had fled.

'Mammot recovers,' the woman said desperately. 'I have nothing left, Wizard. You must do something now, yes?'

He stared at her.

Paran stumbled, slid across greasy clay and rolled up against a bank of tufted reeds. A storm racked the sky above him. He scrambled to his feet, the sword Chance hot and moaning in his hand. A calm shallow lake stretched out on his left, ending in a distant ridge of faintly luminescent green. To his right the marshes continued out to the horizon. The air was cool, sweet with decay.

Paran sighed shakily. He studied the storm overhead. Jagged arcs of lightning warred with each other, the clouds dark and twisting as if in agony. A concussion sounded to his right and he spun. A thousand paces away, something had appeared. The captain squinted. It rose above the marsh grasses like an animated tree, gnarled and black, pulling at the roots that gripped it and flinging them aside. Another figure appeared, danced lithely around it, a brown-bladed jagged sword in its hands. This figure was clearly in retreat, as the gnarled man-shape lashed at it with miasmic waves of power. They were approaching Paran's position.

He heard bubbling, sucking sounds behind him and turned. 'Hood's Breath!'

A house was rising out of the lake. Swamp grass and mud slid from its battered stone walls. A huge stone doorway gaped black, hissing with steam. The second level of the structure looked misshapen, scarred, the cut stones melted away here and there, revealing a skeletal wooden frame.

Another explosion drew his attention back to the fighters. They were much closer now, and Paran could see the figure with the two-handed sword clearly. A T'lan Imass. Despite its awesome skill with the chalcedony weapon in its hands it was being driven back. Its attacker was a tall, lean creature with flesh like oak. Two gleaming tusks rose from its lower jaw, and it was shrieking with rage. It struck the T'lan Imass again, flinging the warrior fifteen paces, to roll through the muck and come to rest almost at Paran's feet.

The captain found himself staring down into depthless eyes.

'The Azath is not yet ready, mortal,' the T'lan Imass said. 'Too young, not yet of strength to imprison that which called it into being – the Finnest. When the Tyrant fled, I sought out its power.' It tried to rise, failed. 'Defend the Azath, the Finnest seeks to destroy it.'

Paran looked up to see the apparition stalking towards him. *Defend?* Against that? The choice was taken from him. The Finnest roared and a sizzling wave of power rolled towards him. He swung Chance into its path.

The blade slid through the energy. Unaffected, the power swept over, then into Paran. Blinded, he screamed as bitter cold lanced through him, shattering his thoughts, his sense of self. An invisible hand closed around his soul. *Mine!* The word rang in his head, triumphant and filled with savage glee. *You are mine!*

Paran dropped Chance, fell to his knees. The grip on his soul was absolute. He could only obey. Fragments of awareness reached through. *A tool, nothing more. All I have done, all I have survived, to reach but this.*

Deep within him he heard a sound, repeating again and again, growing louder. A *howl*. The chill of his blood that had seamlessly filled every part of his body began to break apart. Flashes of heat, bestial and defiant, ripped through the cold. He threw back his head, the howling reaching his throat. As it broke loose, the Finnest staggered back.

Blood of a Hound! Blood no one can enslave – Paran launched himself at the Finnest. His muscles filled with pain as overwhelming strength flowed into them. *You dare!* He struck the creature, driving it to the ground, battering its oak flesh with his fists, sinking his teeth into the bark of its face. The Finnest tried to push him away, and failed. It screamed, flailing its limbs. Paran began ripping it methodically to pieces.

A hand closed on the collar of his cloak, pulled him from the tattered body. Frenzied, Paran tried to twist round, to rend the creature holding him. The T'lan Imass shook him. 'Cease!'

The captain blinked.

'Cease! You cannot destroy the Finnest. But you have held it. Long enough. The Azath will take it now. Do you understand?'

Paran sagged, the fires within him ebbing. Glancing down at the Finnest, he saw roots and fibrous tendrils rising from the wet earth to wrap themselves around the battered apparition and begin to pull their captive down into the cloying mud. In a moment, the Finnest was gone.

The T'lan Imass released Paran and stepped back. It regarded him steadily for a long moment.

Paran spat blood and splinters from his mouth, wiped his lips with the back of a hand. He bent down and retrieved Chance. 'Damned luck turned,' he mumbled, sheathing the weapon. 'Do you have something to say, Imass?'

'You are a long way from home, mortal.'

Paran reappeared a moment later, staggering half-blind across the terrace, then collapsing in a heap. Quick Ben scowled. *What in Hood's Breath happened to him?*

A Jaghut curse escaped Mammot, fierce as if ripped from the soul. The old man regained his feet, trembling with rage. Then his hooded eyes were on the wizard.

'*Awaken the Seven within me!*' Quick Ben roared, then shrieked as seven Warrens opened within him. His agonized scream rode the cascading waves of power as they swept across the terrace.

The Jaghut Possessed threw up his arms before his face as the waves struck. Mammot's body withered beneath the clambering, frenzied attack. Flesh was ripped away, fires lancing, boring holes through him. He was driven to his knees, a vortex swirling like madness around him. Mammot howled, raising a fist that was nothing but charred bone. The fist spasmed and one of Quick Ben's Warrens slammed shut. The fist jerked again.

Quick Ben sagged. 'I'm done.'

Derudan grabbed a handful of the wizard's cloak. 'Wizard! Listen to me!'

Another Warren was driven away. Quick Ben shook his head. 'I'm done.'

'Listen! That man – the one over there – what's he doing?'

Quick Ben looked up. 'Hood's Breath!' he yelled, in sudden terror. A dozen paces away crouched Hedge, only his head and shoulders showing behind a bench. The saboteur's eyes shone with a manic glaze that the wizard recognized, and a large, bulky arbalest was in his hands, pointed directly at Mammot.

A wordless, wailing scream came from Hedge.

The wizard shouted and dived for the woman a second time. As he flew through the air, he heard the *thock* of the saboteur's crossbow. Quick Ben closed his eyes before colliding once again with the woman.

Crone flew tight circles over the plain where the Jaghut Tyrant had been. He had reached to within fifty paces of Silanah, then vanished. Not a flight through a Warren, but a vanishing more complete, more absolute and all the more fascinating for that.

It had been a glorious night, a battle worthy of remembrance, and its end proved no end at all. 'Delicious mystery,' she cackled. Crone knew her presence was demanded elsewhere, but she was reluctant to leave. 'Such terrible energies I have witnessed.' She laughed. 'I mock the waste, the sheer foolishness! Ah, and now all that remains is questions, questions!'

She craned her head upward. Her lord's two Tiste Andii

Soletaken remained overhead. No one wanted to leave before the truth of the Jaghut Tyrant's fate was revealed. They'd earned the right to witness it, though Crone was beginning to suspect such answers would never come.

Silanah loosed a keening cry, then rose from the ground, the Warren that birthed her flight a strong, pungent exhalation. The red dragon's head swung westward, and she voiced a second cry.

With a mad flap of wings, Crone brought her descent under control, then skirted the tattered ground. She climbed skyward again, and saw what Silanah had seen. Crone shrieked in joy and anticipation – and surprise. 'And now it comes! It comes!'

As he shut his eyes, Quick Ben collapsed the last of his Warrens. The woman's arms closed around him as he struck her. She grunted loudly and collapsed beneath his momentum.

The detonation snatched the air from his lungs. The stones under them jumped and a flash of fire and flying masonry filled their world to the exclusion of all else. Then everything was still.

Quick Ben sat up. He looked to where Mammot had been standing. The paving stones were gone, and a wide, deep, steaming hole now yawned near the shattered fountain. The old man was nowhere in sight.

'Dear wizard,' the woman murmured beneath him. 'We live?'

Quick Ben glanced down at her. 'You'd closed your Warren. Very clever.'

'Closed, yes, but not by choice. Why clever?'

'Moranth munitions are mundane weapons, Witch. Opened Warrens draw their explosive force. That Tyrant is dead. Obliterated.'

And then Hedge was beside them, his leather cap half blown away and flash-burns covering one side of his face. 'You all right?' he gasped.

The wizard reached out and cuffed the man. 'You idiot! How many times have I—?'

'He's dead, ain't he?' Hedge retorted, hurt. 'Just a smouldering hole in the ground – best way to deal with mages right?'

They saw Captain Paran rise shakily from the rubble-strewn terrace. He scanned the scene, his gaze finding the wizard. 'Where is Whiskeyjack?' he demanded.

'In the woods,' Hedge answered.

Paran stumbled in that direction.

'Big help he was,' Hedge muttered.

'Quick!'

The wizard turned to see Kalam approach. The assassin paused as he skirted the edge of the crater, then he said. 'Something's moving down there.'

Paling, Quick Ben rose, then helped the witch to her feet.

They approached the crater. 'Impossible,' the wizard breathed. A man-shaped form had coalesced at the base of the pit. 'We're dead. Or worse.'

Thrashing from the garden drew their attention. The three froze as strangely blurred roots broke free of the undergrowth and snaked hungrily towards the crater.

The Jaghut Possessed straightened, spreading grey, swirling arms.

The roots closed around the creature. It shrieked in sudden terror. '*Azath edieirmarn! No! You've taken my Finnest – but leave me! Please!*' Tendrils clambered in a frenzy, entwining its limbs. The Omtose Phellack power writhed in a panicked effort to escape, to no avail. The roots pulled the apparition down, then dragged it screaming into the garden.

'*Azath?*' Quick Ben whispered. 'Here?'

'None, I would swear,' Derudan said, her face white. 'It's said they arise—'

'Where unchained power threatens life,' the wizard finished.

'I know where it is,' Kalam said. 'Quick Ben, will that Jaghut escape?'

'No.'

'So we're done with it. What of the Azath?'

Quick Ben hugged himself. 'Leave it, Kalam.'

'I must leave,' Derudan said hastily. 'Again, my gratitude for twice saving my life.'

They watched her rush away.

Fiddler joined them, looking distracted. 'Mallet's tending to the sergeant,' he said, closing the straps on a bulky bag he carried. 'We're off, then.' He nudged Hedge. 'Got a city to blow.'

'Whiskeyjack's hurt?' Quick Ben asked.

'Broken leg,' Fiddler answered. 'Pretty bad.'

At a surprised cry from Derudan, who had gone to the opposite side of the fountain, they all turned. She'd walked on to a black-clad youth, who must have been crouching behind the fountain's stone wall. Darting like a rabbit, the boy leaped the fountain and raced towards the estate.

'What do you think he heard?' Fiddler wondered.

'Nothing that would mean much to him,' said Quick Ben, recalling their conversation. 'You and Hedge going to do the deed?'

'Sky high.' Fiddler grinned.

The two saboteurs checked their equipment one last time, then turned to the patio.

Meanwhile, Kalam stood glowering into the pit. Ancient copper water-pipes streamed water down its ragged sides. For some reason a memory of the Greyfaces flashed into his head. The assassin crouched, seeing one pipe that leaked no water. He sniffed the air, then lay flat on the ground and reached down to lay his hand over the pipe's broken end. 'Osserc,' he breathed.

He rolled and gained his feet, then asked Quick Ben,

'Where are they?'

The wizard's expression was blank. 'Who?'

Kalam roared, 'The saboteurs, dammit!'

'Just left,' Quick Ben replied, bemused. 'Through the estate.'

'To the back wall, soldier,' the assassin snapped. 'Find the others – Paran's taken command. Tell him to pull out. Find a place I know. I'll meet you there.'

'Where are you going?'

'After the saboteurs.' Kalam wiped sweat from his face. 'Pull out the city map when you can, Quick Ben.' The assassin's eyes were tight with fear. 'Check the legend on it. We've planted mines at every major intersection. It's the main valves – don't you see?' He waved an arm. 'The Greyfaces! The gas, Quick Ben!'

Kalam whirled and crossed the patio. A moment later he disappeared into the estate house.

Quick Ben stared after him. The gas? His eyes widened. 'We'll all go sky high,' he whispered. 'The whole damn city!'

CHAPTER TWENTY-THREE

It was said
she turned the blade on herself then
to steal the magic
of life.

Call to Shadow (IX. ii)
Felisin (b.1146)

Exhausted, Paran made his way through the undergrowth. He ducked beneath a tree into shadow – and the world shifted.

Jaws closed on his left shoulder, teeth grinding through chain, and lifted him from the ground. A surge of unseen muscle flung him through the air. He landed heavily, rolled to his knees and looked up in time to see the Hound close once again. Paran's left arm was numb; he reached vainly for his sword as the Hound opened its maw and closed it around his chest. Mail popped, flesh tore and blood sprayed as the Hound lifted Paran once again.

The captain hung in the giant beast's mouth. He felt Chance slide free of its scabbard, its weight pulling it away from his twitching hand. The Hound shook him. Blood spattered the ground. Then it dropped him and stepped back, looking almost baffled. It whined, began to pace back and forth, eyes darting again and again to the captain.

Pain surged through Paran in growing waves; his limbs shook uncontrollably, he could barely draw breath.

'It seems Rood must find someone to blame,' a voice said. Paran blinked, opened his eyes to see a black-cowled man standing above him. 'But he was premature, and for that I apologize. Evidently, some old scores need settling between you and the Hounds.' The man frowned at Rood. 'More, something has confused him about you . . . Kinship? Now, how could that be?'

'You were the one,' Paran said, as numbness spread through him, 'the one who possessed the girl—'

The man faced the captain. 'Yes, I am Cotillion. Shadowthrone regrets leaving you outside Hood's Gates – at the cost of two Hounds. Do you realize that those precious creatures had lived for a thousand years? Do you realize that no man – mortal or Ascendant – has ever before killed a Hound?'

Did I save their souls? Wouldn't telling that story matter? No, too much like begging. Paran glanced at Rood. *Kinship?* 'What do you want from me?' he asked Cotillion. 'My death? Leave me here, then, it's almost done.'

'You should have left us to our work, Captain, since you now hate the Empress so.'

'What you did to the girl—'

'What I did was merciful. I used her, yes, but she knew it not. Can the same be said for you? Tell me, is knowing you're being used better than not knowing?'

Paran said nothing.

'I can release to the girl all those memories, if you like. The memories of what I did, what she did, when I possessed her . . .'

'No.'

Cotillion nodded.

663

Paran could feel the pain returning and it surprised him. He'd lost so much blood that he'd expected to be fading from consciousness by now. Instead, the pain was back, incessant, throbbing amid unbearable itching. He coughed. 'Now what?'

'Now?' Cotillion seemed surprised. 'Now I start again.'

'Another girl like her?'

'No, the plan was flawed.'

'You stole her life!'

Cotillion's dark eyes hardened. 'Now she has it back. I see you still carry Chance, so the same cannot be said for you.'

Paran turned his head, found the weapon an arm's length away. 'When my luck turns,' he muttered. *And turn it did.* He found he could move his left arm, and the pain in his chest seemed less insistent than it had.

Cotillion laughed drily at Paran's words. 'It will be too late then, Captain. You gamble that the Lady continues to look kindly on you. You've surrendered whatever wisdom you may have once possessed. Such is the power of the Twins.'

'I am healing,' Paran said.

'So you are. As I said, Rood was premature.'

The captain slowly, cautiously, sat up. His chain armour was in shreds, but beneath he could see the red flame of newly healed flesh. 'I – I don't understand you, Cotillion, or Shadowthrone.'

'You are not alone in that. Now, as to Chance . . .'

Paran looked down at the weapon. 'It's yours, if you want it.'

'Ah.' Cotillion smiled, stepping over to pick it up. 'I'd suspected a change of heart, Captain. The world is so complex, isn't it? Tell me, do you pity the ones who used you?'

Paran closed his eyes. A terrible burden seemed to drain from him. He recalled the Finnest's grip on his soul. He glanced up at the Hound. In Rood's eyes he saw something almost . . . soft. 'No.'

'Wisdom returns quickly,' Cotillion said, 'once the bond is

severed. I will return you now, Captain, with this one last warning: try not to be noticed. And when next you see a Hound, run.'

The air swirled into darkness around Paran. He blinked, saw the trees of the estate garden rising before him. *I wonder, will I run from it . . . or with it?*

'Captain?' It was Mallet's voice. 'Where in Hood's Name are you?'

Paran sat up. 'Not in Hood's Name, Mallet. I'm here, in the shadows.'

The healer scrambled to his side. 'We've got trouble everywhere. You look—'

'Deal with it,' the captain barked, climbing to his feet.

Mallet stared at Paran. 'Hood's Breath, you look chewed to pieces . . . sir.'

'I'm going after Lorn. If we all live through this we will meet at the Phoenix Inn. Understood?'

Mallet blinked. 'Yes, sir.'

Paran turned to leave.

'Captain?'

'What?'

'Don't treat her kindly, sir.'

Paran moved off.

The images remained with Crokus, brutally sharp. They returned again and again even as he tried to move away from them, his thoughts driven by panic and desperation.

Uncle Mammot was dead. In the youth's head a distant, steady voice told him that the man who had borne Mammot's face was not the man he'd known all his life, and that what had been . . . claimed by the roots was something else, something horrific. The voice repeated this, and he heard its clear statement rising and falling beneath the storm of what he had seen with his own eyes: the images that would not leave him.

The central chamber of Lady Simtal's estate was abandoned, the fête's trappings scattered about on the floor amid puddles and smears of blood. The dead and those whom Mammot had hurt had been carried away by the guards; the servants had all fled.

Crokus raced across the room to the open front doors. Beyond, torchlight cast a hissing blue glow down on to the walkway's paved stones and the gates, which had been left ajar. The thief leaped down the steps and hurried for the gate. He slowed as he approached it, for something was wrong in the street.

Like Simtal's main floor, the street was empty, littered with pennants, banners and fetishes. Eddies of dry wind whipped tatters of cloth and reed paper about in dancing circles. The air felt heavy and close.

Crokus emerged on to the street. In either direction, as far as he could see, not a single reveller was visible, and a thick silence hung over all. The wind curled round him, first from one direction, then from another, as if seeking escape. A charnel smell filled the air.

Mammot's death returned to him. He felt utterly alone, yet Rallick's words urged him on. Days ago, the assassin had closed angry hands on the thief's shirt, pulling him close – and he'd called Crokus a drinker of the city's blood. He wanted to refute that, especially now. Darujhistan mattered. It was his home, and it mattered.

He turned in the direction of Baruk's estate. At least, with the streets empty, this wouldn't take long. He began to run.

The gusting wind beat against him, whipping his hair into his face. Darkness hung low above the street's gas lamps. Crokus skidded to a halt on a corner. He'd heard something. Cocking his head, he held his breath and listened. There, again. Birds – hundreds of them from the sound, murmuring, talking, clucking. And amid the charnel smell he now detected the reek of birds' nests. Crokus frowned, thinking. Then he looked directly overhead.

A shout broke from his lips and he ducked instinctively. Above him, blotting out the night sky's stars, was a ceiling of jagged black stone, hanging so low as to seem inches from the highest buildings. He stared up at it, then pulled away his gaze as a wave of dizziness spun through him. The ceiling was revolving slowly. In its pocks, shelves and crags he'd seen the restless motion of nesting ravens, oily blots against the grainy background.

Moon's Spawn had arrived, to clear the streets, to silence the festival of rebirth. What could it mean? Crokus didn't know, but Baruk would. Of course.

The thief resumed his run, his moccasins a whisper on the cobbles.

Kruppe took an expansive breath, his eyes bright as he surveyed the hastily abandoned leavings in the kitchen. 'Always the way of things.' He sighed, patting his stomach. 'Ever and anon, Kruppe's dreams come true. Granted, the pattern still finds shape, but Kruppe senses that all is well with the world, symbolized by the vision of bounty now arrayed before his renewed appetites. Rigours of the flesh demand replenishment, after all.'

He drew another satisfied breath of the steamy air. 'We must needs await, at the end, the spin of a coin. In the meantime, of course, wondrous food beckons.'

In an alley facing the gates of Lady Simtal's estate, Adjunct Lorn had watched the Coin Bearer appear, and a slow, satisfied smile spread over her lips. Finding the boy had been one thing, but she'd had no desire to enter the garden where she'd buried the Finnest.

Minutes earlier she'd sensed the death of the Jaghut Tyrant.

667

Had the Lord of Moon's Spawn been drawn into the battle? She hoped so. It had been her hope that the Jaghut would reach the city, perhaps even retrieve the Finnest, thus challenging the Son of Darkness as an equal. In retrospect, however, she realized that the Lord would never have permitted that.

Which meant that Whiskeyjack still lived. Well, there'd be another time for that, once the city was in the hands of the Empress and Tayschrenn. Perhaps then they'd find no need to disguise their efforts: they could make the arrest a public spectacle. With this coup even Dujek could not challenge them.

She'd watched the Coin Bearer race down the street, seeming not even to have noticed Moon's Spawn hanging so close overhead. A moment later, she followed. With the Coin in her hands, the Empress would bring Oponn to its knees.

Like a drowning voice, deep within her mind, came a question heavy with dismay and despair: What of your doubts? What of the woman who'd once challenged Tayschrenn, in Pale? Has so much changed? Has so much been destroyed?

The Adjunct shook her head, dispelling the plaintive cries. She was the arm of the Empress. The woman called Lorn was dead, had been dead for years, and would remain forever dead. And now the Adjunct moved through these hollow shadows, in a city cowering in fear. The Adjunct was a weapon. Its edge could bite deep, or it could snap, break. She might once have called the latter 'death'. Now, it was no more than the misfortune of war, a flaw in the weapon's design.

She paused and hid against a wall as the Coin Bearer stopped on a corner and realized for the first time what hovered above him. She considered attacking now, while he was so confused, possibly terrified. But then he continued on.

The Adjunct crouched down. Time for Tayschrenn's gambit. Hopefully the Jaghut Tyrant had managed to inflict damage upon the Moon's lord. She removed a small flask from her shirt and held the patinated glass up to the shine of gaslight. The contents swirled like trapped smoke as she gave it a shake.

She rose and threw it across the street. The flask struck a stone wall and shattered. Glowing red smoke curled upward, slowly taking shape.

The Adjunct spoke: 'You know your task, Lord of the Galayn. Succeed, and freedom will be yours.'

She unsheathed her sword and closed her eyes briefly, locating the Coin Bearer in her mind. He was fast, but she was faster. The Adjunct smiled again. Now, the Coin would be hers.

When she moved, it was as a blur, quicker than any eye could follow, even that of a Galayn lord loose on the material plane.

In his study, Baruk cradled his head in his hands. Mammot's death had come like a knife to his own heart, and he still felt its stabbing pain. He was alone in the chamber, having dismissed Roald earlier.

Rake had suspected. He'd refused to speak of it, considering it too sensitive a matter. The alchemist had wearily to admit that the Tiste Andii had been correct. Would he even have believed Rake? Undoubtedly, the power possessing Mammot had shielded itself, defying detection. Rake had anticipated Baruk's anger at such a suggestion, and had, wisely and with compassion, chosen to say nothing.

And now Mammot was dead, even as was the Jaghut Tyrant. Had it been Rake who had killed his old friend? If so, he hadn't used his sword, yet another mercy granted both Mammot and Baruk – the alchemist had sensed, if anything, a kind of relief in Mammot's death cry.

A soft cough at the door alerted him. Baruk rose swiftly and turned. His brows rose. 'Witch Derudan!'

Her face was pale, her smile wan. 'I thought of you, upon Mammot's end. I am here, so. Alas,' she said, as she strode to a chair by the fireplace and set her water-pipe down on the floor beside it, 'my servant has taken the rest of the evening off.' She removed the ash-cup and tapped its contents into the unlit hearth. 'Such mundane exertions,' she said, sighing.

At first, Baruk resented her intrusion. He preferred to mourn alone. But as he watched her, the supple grace of her movements, his thoughts changed. Her Warren was Tennes, ancient and bound to the cycles of seasons; and among the handful of deities she could call upon was Tennerock, the Boar of Five Tusks. Derudan's greatest power – the one she shared, in any case – was the Tusk named Love. He chastised himself. Slow had the realization come that she was bringing him a gift.

Derudan replaced the ash-cup and packed it with leaves. She closed a hand around it, and the contents glowed with sudden heat. A moment later the witch sat heavily in the chair. She drew deeply on the mouthpiece.

Baruk strode to the other chair. 'Rake believes it isn't yet over,' he said, sitting.

She nodded. 'I was witness to Mammot's end, yes? He was opposed by myself . . . and a most remarkable wizard. The flesh that was Mammot was destroyed by a Moranth incendiary. The Jaghut spirit survived but was taken . . . by an Azath.' Her heavy-lidded eyes appraised him.

'Azath? Here, in Darujhistan?'

'Indeed, such mysterious conjurings, known for their hunger for mages, will impose upon our efforts . . . a certain caution, yes?'

'Where has it arisen?'

'In the garden of Simtal's estate. Did I not also mention a Moranth incendiary? Lady Simtal's Fête had some unusual guests, yes?'

'Malazans?'

'Twice my life saved – the wizard of whom I spoke, who commands within him seven Warrens—'

'*Seven?*' Baruk said, flinching. 'Hood's Breath, is that even possible?'

'If they mean ill, it shall fall to the Son of Darkness to meet the challenge.'

Both stiffened as power surged into life somewhere nearby. The alchemist was on his feet, fists clenched. 'A demon is unleashed,' he hissed.

'I feel it as well,' Derudan said, her face white. 'Of great power.'

'A Demon Lord.' Baruk nodded. '*This* is what Rake awaited.'

Derudan's eyes widened and she pulled on her mouthpiece before asking, 'Is he capable of defeating such a creature? Son of Darkness he is, but feel this creature's power, yes?'

'I don't know,' Baruk said quietly. 'If not, then the city is doomed.'

At that point there came another blow, followed by another. The witch and the alchemist stared at each other in recognition. Two of their Cabal had just died violent deaths.

'Paral,' she whispered in fear.

'And Tholas,' Baruk said. 'It's begun, and damn Rake for being so right.'

She looked at him blankly.

Baruk grimaced. 'Vorcan.'

Standing on the stained, pitted bronze tiles of the belfry's roof, Anomander Rake's head snapped around. His eyes deepened to black. The wind clawed at his long, silver hair and his grey cloak, its moan hollow and lost. He raised his gaze momentarily to Moon's Spawn as it moved west. He could feel its pain, as if the wounds it had received at Pale were somehow echoed in his own body. A flash of regret crossed his lean features.

Air buffeted him and he heard the heavy flap of wings. Rake

671

smiled. 'Silanah,' he said softly, knowing she would hear him. The red dragon slipped between two towers and banked, returning to his position. 'I know you sense the Demon Lord's presence, Silanah. You would help me in this. I know, I know.' He shook his head. 'Return to Moon's Spawn, dear friend. This battle is mine. Yours is done. But know this: if I fail, you may seek to avenge my death.'

Silanah swept overhead and loosed a thin wail.

'Go home,' Rake whispered.

The red dragon cried again, then swung westward and rose through the night air.

He sensed a presence at his side and turned to find a tall, hooded man sharing his view of the city below. 'Unwise,' Rake murmured, 'to appear unannounced.'

The man sighed. 'The stones beneath your feet, Lord, are newly sanctified. I am reborn.'

'There is no place in the world for an Eldering god,' Rake said. 'Take my word for it.'

K'rul nodded. 'I know. I anticipated returning to the Realms of Chaos, with a Jaghut Tyrant for company. Alas, he evaded me.'

'And found imprisonment elsewhere.'

'I am relieved.'

The two were silent for a long minute, then K'rul sighed. 'I am lost. In this world. In this time.'

Rake grunted. 'You are not alone with those sentiments, Eldering One.'

'Do I follow in your steps, Lord? Do I seek out new battles, new games to play in the company of Ascendants? Are you rewarded in spirit for your efforts?'

'Sometimes,' Rake said quietly. 'But mostly, no, I am not.'

The hooded face turned to the Tiste Andii. 'Then why?'

'I know no other way of living.'

'I have no means of assisting you this night, Anomander

672

Rake. I am manifest in this sanctified place, and manifest in a lone mortal's dreams, but nowhere else.'

'I will do my best, then,' Rake said, 'to avoid damaging your temple.'

K'rul bowed, then vanished.

Alone once again, Rake turned his attention to the street below. An apparition arrived. It paused to sniff the air, then began changing – *veering*. A Lord of the Galayn, and a Soletaken.

'Well,' the Lord of Moon's Spawn growled, 'so am I.' The Tiste Andii spread his arms wide, then rose upward. Kurald Galain sorcery swirled around him, blending his clothing, his massive sword, drawing all inward to the shape he now climbed towards. The veering was smooth, eloquent, as jet-black wings unfolded from his shoulders. Flesh and bone surged in size, changed in shape.

As he flew higher, eyes fixed on the stars, Anomander Rake became a black dragon, silver-maned and dwarfing even Silanah. His eyes gleamed silver, the vertical slits of the pupils dilating. His breath gusted in heavy grunts, the snap of his wings loud amid the deep groan of muscle on bone. His chest swelled to draw in the cold, dry air, and power filled his being.

Rake climbed ever higher, slipping through a stray cloud that scudded in darkness over the city. When he finally tilted his wings forward and caressed the surface of a wayward wind, he looked down on a city that glimmered like a mottled copper coin at the bottom of a pellucid pond.

Sorcery flared occasionally, centred mostly in the Estate District, and Rake sensed death within those emanations. He considered the message delivered by Serrat, courtesy of a foul mage he'd thought a thousand leagues away. Was the sorcery the work of these unwelcome intruders? He rumbled in frustration – he would deal with them later. Before him now was a battle. The Empress and her Empire had challenged him again

673

and again, wilful in the desire to test his strength. Each time he'd withdrawn, unwilling to commit himself. *Very well, Empress, my patience is at an end.*

The membrane of his wings tautened, the joints creaking, as he grunted a straining breath. He hung almost motionless for a second studying the great city beneath him. Then, tucking in his wings, Anomander Rake, the Son of Darkness and Lord of Moon's Spawn, plummeted.

Kalam knew the pattern of detonation the saboteurs would follow. He skirted one side of the street as he ran. So what if Moon's Spawn hung over them as if ready to descend on the city and crush the life from it like a god's heel – Fiddler and Hedge wouldn't give a damn. They had a job to do.

The assassin cursed every stubborn bone in their heads. Why didn't they run away like normal, sane people? He came to a corner and crossed the intersection diagonally. Ahead, at the far end of the street, rose Majesty Hill. As he reached the corner he almost collided with the two saboteurs. Fiddler darted to one side of him, Hedge to the other, running as if not even recognizing him, terror plain on their faces.

Kalam reached back and with each hand grasped a cloak's hood. Then he grunted in pain as the two men jerked him backward and off his feet. 'Damn you bastards!' he yelled. 'Hold it!'

'It's Kal!' Hedge yelled.

Kalam twisted around to find a rusty shortsword inches from his face, with Fiddler's white face and wide eyes immediately behind it. 'Put that piece of junk away,' the assassin snapped. 'You want to give me an infection?'

'We're getting out of here!' Hedge hissed. 'Forget the damn mines! Forget everything!'

Still gripping their cloaks, Kalam shook them both. 'Calm down. What's happened?'

674

Fiddler moaned and pointed up the street.

Turning, Kalam stiffened.

A twelve-foot-tall creature shambled down the middle of the road, hunched shoulders wrapped in a glittering cape with a high cowl. A two-bladed axe was slung in its wide dragon-hide belt, its handle as long as Kalam was tall. The creature's wide, squat face held two slitted eyes.

'Oh, Hood's Gates and back,' the assassin muttered. 'That's Tayschrenn's precious lord.' He pushed the two saboteurs around the corner. 'Get moving. Back to Simtal's estate.' Neither objected, and moments later were running as fast as they could down the street. Kalam crouched at the corner and waited for the Galayn lord to come into view. When it did, he blanched. 'Soletaken.'

The Galayn was assuming a form better suited to wholesale destruction. The dun-brown dragon paused, its wingtips brushing the buildings on either side. Its rumble trembled the cobbles.

Kalam watched as the creature tensed its limbs, then rose upward on a wave of power. The darkness swallowed it. 'Hood's Breath,' he said. 'Now things are going to get messy.' He whirled and ran to catch up with the saboteurs.

The Coin Bearer came to a street lined with walled estates. He slowed his pace, studying each structure he passed.

The time had come, the Adjunct knew. Before the boy had a chance to get inside one of those places, where he might find protection. She adjusted her grip on the sword, padding in silence not fifteen feet behind him.

She drew a long, deep breath, then surged forward, sword's point extended.

At the sharp, ringing clang of metal immediately behind him, Crokus dived forward. He dipped a shoulder and rolled, regaining his feet. He cried out in shock. The woman who had attacked Coll in the hills was in a whirlwind exchange with a tall, round-shouldered man with two scimitars.

The thief's jaw dropped as he watched the fight. As good as the woman had shown herself against Coll, she was now being driven back as a flurry of attacks swept around her. They both moved so quickly that Crokus could not even see the parries, or the blades themselves, but as he watched, he saw the blossoming of wounds on the woman – her arms, legs, chest. Her expression held complete disbelief.

Then a voice chuckled beside him, 'He's good, ain't he?'

Crokus whirled to see a tall, thin man, wearing a grey and crimson longcoat, his hands in its pockets. He swung a narrow hatchet face to the thief and grinned. 'You headin' somewhere, boy? Somewhere safe?'

Crokus nodded numbly.

The man's grin widened. 'I'll escort you, then. And don't worry, you're covered from the roofs, too. Cowl's up there, damn his snakeskin hide. But he's a powerful mage, anyway. Serrat was furious, I hear. Let's walk, then.'

Crokus let the man take his arm and lead him away from the duel. The thief cast a glance over his shoulder. The woman was trying to disengage now, her left arm hanging useless and glistening in the gaslight. Her opponent continued pressing, silent as a ghost.

'Don't worry,' the man beside him said, pulling him along. 'That's Corporal Blues. He lives for this stuff.'

'C-Corporal?'

'We've been covering your back, Coin Bearer.' The man's other hand reached up to his collar, which he turned back to reveal a brooch. 'The name's Fingers, Sixth Blade, Crimson Guard. You're being protected, boy, compliments of Prince K'azz and Caladan Brood.'

Crokus stared, then he scowled. 'Coin Bearer? What's

676

that mean? I think you've got the wrong person.'

Fingers laughed drily. 'We figured you was walking blind and dumb, boy. The only explanation. You've got other people trying to protect you, too, you know. There's a coin in your pocket, probably two-headed, right?' He grinned at the thief's stunned expression. 'It's Oponn's own. You've been serving a god and you didn't even know it! How's your luck been, lately?' He laughed again.

Crokus stopped at a gate.

'This is the place, then?' Fingers asked, glancing at the estate rising behind the compound wall. 'Well, there's a powerful mage living in there, ain't there? Well,' he released the thief's arm, 'you should be safe enough inside. Good luck, boy, and I mean that. But listen,' Fingers' eyes hardened, 'if your luck goes sour, you dump that coin, y' hear?'

Confusion flickered across Crokus's face. 'Thank you, sir.'

'Our pleasure,' Fingers said, as he placed his hands in his pockets again. 'Get a move on, then.'

The Adjunct broke away, taking a cut across her right shoulder blade as she did so. She ran, blood spraying with the effort, and the man did not pursue.

What a fool she'd been! Thinking that the Coin Bearer wasn't protected! But who was that man? Never before had she faced such a swordsman, and the most appalling thing was that he had fought without the aid of sorcery. For once, her Otataral blade and her skill had not been enough.

She staggered, half blind, down the street, then wheeled round a corner. Out of the corner of her eye she saw a flash of movement. The Adjunct threw her back to a wall and raised her sword again.

A large woman stood before her, regarding her quizzically. 'Looks to me,' she drawled, 'like you're already done.'

'Leave me be,' Lorn gasped.

677

'Can't do it,' Meese said. 'We been on you since Circle Breaker picked you up at the gate. The Eel says you've got some things t' pay for, lady. And we're here to collect.'

As soon as the woman said that, the Adjunct sensed another presence, immediately on her left. She cried out as she tried to spin into a defensive crouch, and in the cry was an overwhelming sense of frustration and despair. *What a waste!* she cursed. *No, not like this!*

Even as that thought thundered through her head, both women attacked. She parried the blade coming at her from the left, but could only watch in horror as the woman who'd spoken revealed two blades, both driving for her chest.

The Adjunct screamed in rage as the weapons punched into her. Her sword clanged and bounded as it struck the cobbles. Hands groping, Lorn slid down the wall. 'Who?' she managed, a blind need behind the word. *'Who?'*

One of the women bent low over her. 'What's that?'

Anguish filled Lorn's face, the corners of her mouth drooping as her eyes closed. 'Who?' she asked again. 'Who is this Eel?'

'Let's go, Meese,' the woman said, ignoring the body at her feet.

Paran found her sprawled on the grimy cobbles of an alley-mouth. Something had drawn him to her unerringly, a final closing of the mysterious link between them. Her sword was beside her, the grip slick with blood, its edges gouged and nicked. The captain crouched beside her.

'You made it a hard fight,' he whispered, 'for what that is worth.'

He watched her eyes flicker open. She stared up at him as recognition arrived. 'Captain. Ganoes.'

'Adjunct.'

'They have killed me.'

678

'Who?'

She managed a stained smile. 'I don't know. Two women. Looked like ... thieves. Thugs. Do you see ... the irony, Ganoes Paran?'

Thin-lipped, he nodded.

'No ... glorious end ... for the Adjunct. If you'd come ... a few minutes sooner ...'

The captain said nothing. He watched the life leave Lorn, feeling nothing. *Ill luck, knowing me, Adjunct. I'm sorry for that.* Then he collected the Otataral sword and slipped it into his scabbard.

Above him two voices spoke in unison. 'You gave him our sword.'

He straightened to find himself facing Oponn. 'The Rope took it from me, to be more precise.'

The Twins could not conceal their fear. They looked upon Paran with something akin to pleading. 'Cotillion spared you,' the sister said, 'the Hounds spared you. Why?'

Paran shrugged. 'Do you blame the knife, or the hand wielding it?'

'Shadowthrone never plays fair,' the brother whined, hugging himself.

'You and Cotillion both used mortals,' the captain said, baring his teeth, 'and paid for it. What do you want from me? Sympathy? Help?'

'That Otataral blade—' the sister said.

'Will not be used to do your dirty work,' Paran finished. 'You'd best flee, Oponn. I imagine even now Cotillion has given Shadowthrone the sword Chance, and the two are putting their heads together to plan how best to use it.'

The Twin Jesters flinched.

Paran laid a hand over the sword's sticky grip. 'Now. Else I return Cotillion's favour.'

The gods vanished.

The captain drew a deep breath. He turned once again to Lorn.

Her armour removed, she proved light in his arms.

The air roared around Anomander Rake as he plummeted, but he made no other sound, his Warren drawn in tight around him. Below, now sweeping lazy circles over Darujhistan, was the dun dragon – Rake's equal in size, with the power to match.

But it was a fool, hunting for him in the streets below.

Rake carefully spread his wings, angling towards the Galayn lord. His hind limbs reached down, talons spreading. He drew in the air around him, preparing for a burst of power. He was Kurald Galain, Tiste Andii, and darkness was his home.

The Galayn lord was immediately beneath him now, growing larger with incredible speed. Rake opened his mouth, head snapping back as he bit into a wall of air. This sound brought the dun dragon's gaze upward, but it was already too late.

CHAPTER TWENTY-FOUR

> I am the House
> imprisoning in my birth
> demonic hearts,
> so locked in each chamber
> some trembling enraged
> antiquity.
> And these roots of stone
> spread the deepest cracks
> in parched ground
> holding for ever the dream
> of fruit, ah, pilgrims
> come to my door
> and starve . . .
>
> *Azath (ii.iii)*
> Adaephon (b.?)

The compound beyond the gate was empty. Crokus ran across it, wondering if he was too late. He bounded up the steps and reached for the door latch. A burst of energy flung him backwards.

Dazed, the thief found himself sitting on the paving stones

before the steps, his flesh tingling. At the door a deep crimson glow slowly faded. A ward. 'Hood!' he hissed, climbing to his feet. He'd run into barriers like these before, in the Higher Estates. There was no way to get through them.

Cursing again, Crokus whirled and raced to the gate. He emerged on to the street and looked around, seeing no one. If those Crimson Guard still protected him, they weren't showing themselves.

There was a slight chance that the garden entrance to Baruk's estate was unguarded by magic – a very slight chance. He ran down the street and turned into the first alley to his right. There'd be a wall to scale, but he did not consider that much of an obstacle.

He came to the alley's end and skidded to a halt on the street beyond. The wall was high, he saw. He'd need a running start. Crokus trotted across the street, trying to catch his breath. What was the point of all this? Couldn't Baruk take care of himself, after all? Wasn't he a High Mage, and hadn't even Fingers commented on the alchemist's sorcerous defences?

He hesitated, scowling at the wall opposite him.

At that moment a piercing, earth-shaking scream was loosed directly above the street. Crokus threw himself against the wall behind him as an enormous shape descended into the gaslight. Filling the street, it struck the ground less than twenty yards to the thief's left. He was thrown from his feet by the impact. Stones shattered.

He ducked beneath the hail of bricks and cobbles, then, as the scatter of rubble diminished, he jumped to his feet.

A dragon, its wings tattered and streaked with blood, slowly regained its feet in the street, wagging its massive wedge-shaped head from side to side. Along its brown flanks, scales had been torn away, revealing deep puncture wounds. Its neck and shoulders glistened with blood.

Crokus saw that the wall beyond it – Baruk's – had been obliterated, opening the garden to his view. Snapped tree trunks rose amid steaming earth. A raised patio marked the approach of the estate's back entrance. Two toppled statues lay in pieces before the doors.

The dragon looked stunned. Crokus tensed. Now was the time to move. Almost disbelieving his own temerity, the thief darted into the street behind the creature, hoping to reach the cover of the garden. His gaze remained on the dragon as he ran, his thoughts on the coin of luck in his pocket.

Then, before his eyes, the creature's shape changed, drawing into itself in a shimmering haze. Crokus slowed, then stopped, unable to pull away his attention. His heart hammered against his ribs, as if seeking escape. Each drawn breath was a painful gasp. His luck, he told himself in terror, had just ended.

The shimmering faded, and a giant man-shaped apparition now stood on the street, cloaked and cowled.

Crokus tried to will himself to move, but his body refused to obey. He stared, eyes widening, as the demon turned to him. It snarled and removed an enormous axe from its belt. Hefting the weapon, it spoke in a deep, soft voice. 'What reason to continue this?' it asked reasonably. 'The Empress permits your escape, Lord. Once again she grants you mercy. Accept it, and leave.'

'Good idea,' the thief whispered. Then he frowned, for the demon's attention, he now saw, was directed past him.

A man spoke behind him. 'We run no further, Galayn.'

A hand fell on the thief's shoulder, breaking the spell of immobility. Crokus ducked and spun to one side, then looked up into shifting, indigo eyes set in a black, narrow face.

'Flee, mortal,' the silver-haired man said, drawing a two-handed sword from the scabbard slung between his shoulder-blades. The black weapon seemed almost invisible, as if it swallowed all light that found it.

'You were at the fête!' Crokus blurted.

The man's eyes flickered, as if seeing him for the first time. 'Coin Bearer,' he said, with a wry smile, 'fear not. Brood has convinced me to spare you, at least for the moment. Begone, child.' His gaze returned to the Galayn lord. 'This will be a close thing.'

'I know that weapon,' the demon snarled. 'Dragnipurake. And I smell the reek of Tiama in you, Lord. There is more of her in you than Tiste Andii blood.'

Crokus backed against what remained of Baruk's wall.

The Galayn lord grinned, revealing long, curved canines. 'The Empress would reward your services, Lord. You've only to say yes, and this battle can be avoided.'

Anomander Rake stepped forward. 'Attend, Galayn.'

With a roar the demon attacked, axe whistling through the air and streaming blue flames.

Rake whirled his sword in a circle, catching the axe and adding to its momentum. As the double-blades swept past, the Tiste Andii stepped in close, sword drawn back, pommel against his left hip. In a blur of motion he extended the blade. The demon ducked and, releasing one hand from the axe haft, reached for Rake's throat. The Tiste Andii twisted his right shoulder and caught the blow.

Thrown backwards, Rake landed heavily on the cobbles.

The demon pounced, flaming weapon above its head.

Rake regained his feet in time to catch the axe with his sword. The clash of weapons sent a jolt through the air and ground. The demon's axe flared bright white, cascading light like liquid. Rake's sword was swallowed in darkness, devouring the lashing waves of light that struck it.

The flagstones beneath Crokus's feet tilted sickeningly, as if the stones themselves had turned to soft clay. Overhead the stars swam wildly. Gripped by nausea, Crokus fell to his knees.

Rake began to launch attacks, savage swings of his black

weapon. At first the demon held its ground, delivering fierce ripostes, then staggered back a step, then another. Relentless, Rake pressed his attack. *'To the Mother's regret,'* he grated between blows, *'was Light granted birth. To her dismay . . . she saw too late . . . its corruption. Galayn . . . you are the unintended victim . . . to punishment . . . long overdue.'*

The demon reeled beneath the blows, desperately parrying every attack, no longer counter-attacking. The light bleeding from the axe flickered, dimmed, flared fitfully as darkness closed in around the blade. Shrieking, the demon launched itself at Rake. As it descended over the Tiste Andii, Crokus saw a streak of black burst from the demon's back, slicing through the cloak. The axe flew from the creature's hands, its fire dying as it clattered on the ground.

Squealing in horror, the demon clawed at the sword impaling it. Black smoke spread in swift tendrils from the weapon, engulfing the demon. The smoke twisted, became chains, drawing taut. The Galayn screamed in earnest.

Rake regained his feet and pushed the sword through the demon's chest until the hilt jammed against bone. The demon sank to its knees, its black eyes locking with Rake's own.

The swimming stars settled, the flagstones beneath the thief became solid once again, though warped and twisted. Crokus swallowed bile, his eyes fixed on the demon. It seemed to collapse in on itself, the chains of black smoke ever tightening, pulling the creature into the sword. It toppled backwards and Rake drove the weapon's point into the cobbled street, pinning the demon. Then the Tiste Andii leaned heavily on the hilt, and Crokus now noticed the blood-soaked cloth surrounding Rake's shoulder, where the demon's hand had struck. Wearily, the Tiste Andii swung his gaze to the thief.

'Move quickly,' he rasped. 'The alchemist is in danger. I cannot protect him now. Hurry, Coin Bearer.'

Crokus whirled and ran.

* * *

The death of Travale, third in the Cabal, still echoed in their thoughts. The witch Derudan had inscribed an ash circle on the floor in the centre of the chamber. With Baruk's help, she placed the two plush chairs within it, and now sat, smoking steadily, her dark eyes following the alchemist as he paced.

Baruk found himself reluctant to enter the protective circle. While they would be safe there, surrounded by High Tennes sorcery, they would not be able to counter-attack, should Vorcan arrive. More, some things could penetrate the defences of magic. Otataral, that strange rust-like ore from the Tanno Hills of Seven Cities, immediately came to mind. It was unlikely that Vorcan would possess such material, given that she was a High Mage, yet still Baruk felt reluctant to place himself in a position where he could not use his Warren against the assassin.

'Those of the Cabal,' Derudan said slowly, 'who are now dead, yes? Stubborn, convinced of their own invincibility. No doubt they paced restless steps, awaiting the assassin's imminent arrival.'

Baruk paused to reply, but was interrupted by a loud, in-human scream from outside. This was followed immediately by a concussion that rattled the walls. The alchemist made a move towards the door.

'Wait!' Derudan called from the circle. 'Appease not this curiosity, Baruk, for Vorcan will surely take advantage, yes?'

'A ward was shattered,' Baruk said. 'My defences are breached.'

'More the reason for caution,' Derudan admonished. 'Friend, I plead with you, join me here.'

'Very well,' Baruk sighed, moving towards her. A gust of air brushed the left side of his face. Derudan cried out a warning even as the alchemist turned.

Vorcan, her gloved hands glowing red, surged towards

Baruk. He raised his arms, knowing full well that he would be too late. At that moment, however, another figure appeared, emerging from darkness to intercept the Master Assassin with a flurry of blows. Vorcan reeled back, then lashed out with a hand, catching her attacker a glancing blow.

An agonized shriek rang through the chamber. Baruk stared, only now realizing that his protector was a Tiste Andii woman. He stepped aside lithely as she flew past him to strike the floor then the wall, where she lay unmoving. The alchemist pulled his gaze back to Vorcan, seeing that one of her hands no longer glowed.

He gestured, and virulent sorcery erupted from his arm, arcing yellow lightning. Vorcan hissed a counter-spell and the lightning was swallowed by a red haze before her that dimmed quickly, then disappeared. She advanced.

Vaguely, Baruk heard the witch Derudan shouting at him. Yet it was the Mistress of the Assassins' death-filled eyes that held him. The ease with which she'd dispelled his power made it clear that she was his master in sorcery. All he could do now, he understood with clarity, was await his death.

But Baruk heard a grunt behind him, then Vorcan gasped. The hilt of a dagger protruded from the assassin's chest. Frowning, she reached for it, then pulled it out and tossed it aside.

'All . . .' the alchemist heard the Tiste Andii woman gasp from the floor behind him '. . . all I can do. My apologies, Lord.'

Derudan appeared behind Vorcan. As she raised her hands and began an incantation, Vorcan whirled and something sped from her hand. The witch grunted, then crumpled.

Anguish flooded Baruk. With a wordless roar he launched himself at Vorcan. She laughed and ducked to one side, throwing out her glowing hand. The alchemist twisted, off-balance, narrowly avoiding the killing touch, then staggered past. He

687

heard her laughter again, as she moved in behind him.

A dozen feet in front of Baruk was the door. The alchemist's eyes widened to find it open. A youth crouched there, holding blockish objects in each hand.

Expecting at any moment to feel Vorcan's touch, Baruk threw himself forward. He saw the boy straighten at the same time and thrust forward first his right arm, then his left. As the alchemist fell towards the floor, two bricks flew over him. He heard them strike the woman behind him, one making a crunching sound, the other crackling. A flash of red accompanied the crackle.

As he struck the floor, the breath was hammered from Baruk's lungs. Agonized seconds passed as he struggled to draw air into his tortured chest. He rolled on to his back. Vorcan, he saw, lay motionless almost against his feet. The boy's face came into view, streaked with sweat, brow furrowed with concern.

'Alchemist Baruk?' he asked.

The man nodded.

The boy sighed, then grinned. 'You're alive. Good. Rallick sent me to warn you.'

Baruk sat up. 'The witch,' he said hoarsely. He pointed. 'Tend to her, please.'

He felt his strength returning as he watched the boy crouch beside Derudan.

'She's breathing,' Crokus announced. 'There's some kind of knife in her, looks like it's covered in sap.' He reached down to touch it.

'No!' Baruk shouted.

Crokus jumped back in alarm.

'Poison,' the alchemist said, climbing to his feet. 'Help me to her, quickly.' A moment later he knelt beside Derudan. A quick glance at the sap-like substance coating the blade confirmed his suspicion. 'White paralt,' he said.

'That's a spider, isn't it?'

Baruk laid a hand on Derudan. 'Your knowledge surprises me, boy,' he said. 'Fortunately, she's in the home of the one man who possesses its antidote.' He muttered something and a phial appeared in his hand.

'Rallick said there was no antidote to white paralt.'

'It's not something I'm likely to announce.' Baruk unstoppered the phial and poured the contents down the witch's throat, triggering a coughing fit. As Derudan's breathing became even, Baruk leaned back and eyed Crokus. 'You seem well acquainted with Rallick. What's your name?'

'Crokus. Mammot was my uncle, sir. I saw him die.'

Derudan's eyelids flickered, then opened. She smiled lazily. 'What I see pleases me,' she said weakly. 'Yes?'

Baruk returned the smile. 'Yes, my friend. But I make no claim for defeating Vorcan. That falls to Crokus, nephew of Mammot.'

Derudan's gaze swung to the youth. 'Ah, the one I came near to treading on earlier this evening.' The amusement left her expression. 'I am sorry for Mammot, child.'

'So am I,' he replied.

Baruk rose and turned. He hissed a vehement curse. Vorcan's body was gone. 'She's fled.' He hurried over to the Tiste Andii woman, he bent down and examined her. She was dead. 'I will soon know your name,' he whispered, 'and I will remember it.'

'I have to go!' Crokus announced.

Baruk wondered at the sudden panic in the boy's face.

'I mean,' Crokus continued, 'if everything's over here, that is.'

'I believe it is,' the alchemist answered. 'I thank you, Crokus, for your skill at throwing bricks.'

The boy went to the door. He paused, then tossed a coin into the air. He caught it, and grinned tightly. 'Just lucky, I suppose.' Then he was gone.

689

Captain Paran crouched beside Coll's bed. 'Still asleep,' he said, rising and facing Whiskeyjack. 'Go ahead.'

Kalam and the two saboteurs had arrived minutes earlier. So far, the sergeant mused, no losses, though the captain's armour had taken a beating and the look in his face when he'd entered the room with Lorn's body in his arms warned Whiskeyjack away from probing Paran's state of mind too deeply. The Adjunct's body now occupied a second bed, motionless and pale, a strange ironic smile curving her bloodless lips.

The sergeant studied everyone in the small room, the faces he knew so well all watching him, waiting. His gaze held on Sorry, or Apsalar as she now called herself. Whatever Mallet had done to her, she was a changed woman from the one he'd known. Less, and somehow more as well. Even Mallet was unsure of what he'd done. Certain memories, skills had been freed, and with them a brutal knowledge. The pain was there in the woman's eyes, a pain layered in years of horror – yet it seemed that she had it under control, that she'd found a way, a strength, to live with what she'd been. Her only words upon meeting him had been: 'I wish to return home, Sergeant.'

He had no objection, though he wondered how she planned to cross two continents and the ocean between them. Whiskeyjack reached for the wrapped forearm bones lying on the table. 'Yes, sir,' he said, in answer to Paran's command.

The hot sweaty air in the room thickened with tension. Whiskeyjack hesitated. There'd been a battle in Darujhistan's streets, and Quick Ben had confirmed the Galayn lord's death. In fact, the black wizard seemed still in shock. The sergeant sighed under his breath and massaged his newly healed leg, then drove the forearm's blade into the tabletop.

Contact was immediate. High Fist Dujek's gravelly voice filled the room. 'About time, Whiskeyjack! Don't bother telling me about the Galayn lord – Tayschrenn's in a coma or something. Everyone in Headquarters heard his scream. So Anomander Rake took out the beast. What else?'

Whiskeyjack glanced at Paran, who nodded deferentially. 'Adjunct Lorn's gambit failed,' the sergeant said. 'She's dead. We have her body with us. The intersections remain mined – we're not detonating them, High Fist, since they're likely to open the gas caverns beneath the city and turn us all into ash. So.' He drew a deep breath, feeling a twinge from his leg – Mallet had done what he could, and that'd been a lot, but some damage remained, and it made him feel fragile. 'So,' he repeated softly, 'we're pulling out, High Fist.'

Dujek was silent, then he grunted. 'Problems, Whiskeyjack. One, we're about to lose Pale. As I suspected, Caladan Brood left the Crimson Guard to handle things up north, and marched down here with his Tiste Andii. He's also got Rhivi with him, and Jorrick's Barghast, who've just finished chewing up Gold Moranth. Two, it gets worse.' The High Fist swallowed audibly. 'Seven Cities is maybe a week away from open rebellion. The Empress knows it. Some Claw from Genabaris arrived half an hour ago, looking for Tayschrenn. My people got to him first. Whiskeyjack, he was carrying a handwritten message from the Empress to Tayschrenn. I've just been outlawed by the Empire. It's official, and Tayschrenn was to have effected my arrest and execution. We're on our own, friend.'

The room was silent. Whiskeyjack closed his eyes briefly. 'Understood, High Fist. So, when do you march?'

'Seems the Black Moranth are with us – don't ask why. Anyway, I have a parley at dawn tomorrow with Caladan Brood and Kallor. That will decide matters, I suspect. Either he lets us walk, or he kills us taking Pale. Everything's riding on what he knows about the Pannion Seer.'

Whiskeyjack said, 'We're rendezvousing with some Black Moranth in a couple of days, High Fist. Makes me wonder how much they'd guessed when that arrangement was made. Anyway, they'll take us to you, wherever you are.'

'No,' Dujek replied. 'We may be under siege here. The Black will drop you off on the Catlin Plain. Their orders are clear on this, but you're welcome to try overruling them.'

The sergeant grimaced. Not likely. 'Catlin Plain it is. Just means it'll take us longer to get to you, sir.'

The glow surrounding the bones flickered briefly and they heard an echoing thump. Fiddler chuckled. Dujek had just pounded a fist on the table at his end of the conversation.

Whiskeyjack shot the saboteur a ferocious look.

'Captain Paran?' Dujek bellowed.

'Here, High Fist,' Paran replied, stepping forward.

'What I'm about to say is to Whiskeyjack, but I want you to hear it, Captain.'

'I'm listening.'

'Sergeant, if you want to be in my army, you'd better get used to the new order. First, I'm placing the Bridgeburners under Captain Paran's command. Second, you're not a sergeant any more, Whiskeyjack. You are my second-in-command, and that means responsibilities. I don't want you anywhere near Pale. And you know I'm right, dammit. Captain Paran?'

'Yes?'

'Whiskeyjack's squad has earned the right to walk. Understood? If any of them elect to rejoin the Bridgeburners, fine. But I don't want any recriminations if they decide otherwise. I trust that's clear.'

'Yes, High Fist.'

'And with Whiskeyjack between commissions,' Dujek continued inexorably, 'he's just coming along for the ride, if you follow me, Captain.'

Paran grinned. 'I do.'

'Now, the Black Moranth will know the story by the time they pick you up, so go with them.'

'Yes, High Fist.'

Dujek growled, 'Questions, Whiskeyjack?'

'No,' the grizzled veteran answered glumly.

'All right. Hopefully, we'll talk later.'

The bones' glow died.

Captain Paran rounded on the soldiers. He studied each face. *They were to have been my command. I could not have done better anywhere.* 'Very well,' he said gruffly. 'Who is ready to be outlawed and counted among Dujek's rebels?'

Trotts was the first to rise, his teeth bared. He was followed by Quick Ben, Hedge and Mallet.

There was a shocked silence, then Kalam nodded at Fiddler and cleared his throat. 'We're with you, only we're not going with you. Me and Fiddler, that is.'

'Can you explain that?' Paran asked quietly.

Apsalar spoke up, surprising everyone. 'They'll find that hard to do, Captain. And, I admit, I'm not sure what they're up to, but they're coming with me. Back to the Empire. Home.'

With an uneasy shrug, Fiddler rose and faced Whiskeyjack. 'We feel we owe it to her, sir,' he said. He looked to the captain. 'And we're settled on it, sir. But we're coming back, if we can.'

Bemused, Whiskeyjack pushed himself painfully to his feet. As he turned to face Paran, he froze. Behind the captain, Coll sat upright on the bed. 'Um,' Whiskeyjack said, gesturing.

Tension burgeoned in the room once again as everyone swung to Coll. Paran stepped forward in genuine relief.

'Coll! I'm—' He stopped abruptly, then said tonelessly, 'You've been awake for some time, I see.'

Coll's eyes flicked to the bones stuck in the tabletop, then returned to Paran. 'Heard it all,' he said. 'So tell me, Paran, do you soldiers need any help getting out of Darujhistan?'

Rallick stood in the darkness beneath the trees at the edge of the glade. It seemed that his magic-deadening powers had proved insufficient after all. He'd been driven from his seat by what had felt like a giant hand – a god's hand, sure and powerful and unyielding. He'd watched in astonishment as a maze of roots clambered swiftly across the clearing, headed towards the terrace. He'd heard a shriek, then the roots returned, wrapped around a man-shaped . . . apparition, which the roots pulled unceremoniously into the earth.

Rallick had been filled suddenly with near-euphoria. He knew with unaccountable certainty, that what grew here was right, and just.

It was new, young. Even now, as he continued watching it, he saw trembles of shaping ripple beneath its angular, geometric surfaces. What had been no more than a tree stump less than an hour ago was now a house. A massive door lay half buried in shadows beneath an arching branch. Vines barred shuttered windows. A balcony hung above and to the left of the door, festooned with leaves and creepers. It led into a kind of tower, turreted above the second storey and shingled to a gnarled peak. Another tower marked the house's front right flank, this one stockier and windowless, its roof flat with jagged merlons lining the edge. He suspected that this roof was a platform, with access through a trap-door of some kind.

The glade around the structure had changed, too, becoming mounded here and there as if the house's yard was a burial ground. Young, scraggly trees ringed each oblong mound, each growing as if an invisible wind twisted them away from the humped, grassy earth. The roots had dragged the apparition into one such mound.

It felt right, and just. These two words echoed in the assassin's head, with an appeal that wrapped calm around his heart. He almost imagined he felt an affinity with this child-house – as if it knew of him and accepted him.

He knew the house to be empty. Another sourceless certainty.

Rallick continued watching, as the lines of the house grew firm, sharply defined. A musty smell pervaded the area, as of freshly turned earth. The assassin felt at peace.

A moment later he heard thrashing behind him, and whirled to see Vorcan stagger through the undergrowth. Her face was covered in blood from a gash to her brow, and she nearly collapsed into Rallick's arms.

'Tiste Andii,' she gasped. 'After me. Hunting. They seek to avenge a murder!'

Rallick looked past her, and his eyes, long accustomed to the surrounding darkness, detected silent movement among the trees, closing in. He hesitated, gripping the now unconscious woman in his arms. Then he bent down, threw Vorcan over one shoulder, turned and ran towards the house.

He knew that the door would open for him, and it did. Beyond was a dark antechamber and an archway leading into a hallway running from side to side. A gust of warm, sweet air flowed over Rallick, and he entered without pause.

Korlat, blood-kin to Serrat, slowed as she approached the strange house. The door had closed behind their quarry. She came to the edge of the clearing, then squatted on her haunches. Her fellow hunters gathered slowly around her.

Horult hissed angrily, then said, 'Have you summoned our lord, Korlat?'

The woman shook her head. 'I know of such creations from old,' she said. 'The Deadhouse of Malaz City, the Odhanhouse of Seven Cities . . . *Azath edieimarn*, Pillars of Innocence – this door will not open to us.'

'Yet it opened to them,' Horult said.

'There is precedence. The Azath choose their own. It was so with the Deadhouse. Two men were chosen: one who would be Emperor, the other who would accompany him. Kellanved and Dancer.'

'I sense its power,' Orfantal whispered. 'Our lord could destroy it, now, while it's still young.'

'Yes,' agreed Korlat. 'He could.' She was silent a moment, then she rose. 'I am blood-kin to the fallen,' she said.

'You are blood-kin,' the others intoned.

'The quest for vengeance is ended,' Korlat said, the lines around her almond-shaped eyes tightening. 'Our lord will not be summoned. Leave him to his recovery. The Azath will not be touched, for it is new, a child.' Her eyes, soft brown, slowly regarded those of her companions. 'The Queen of Darkness spoke thus of Light when it was first born: "It is new, and what is new is innocent, and what is innocent is precious. Observe this child of wonder, and know respect."'

Orfantal scowled. 'Thus did Light survive, and so was Darkness destroyed, the purity vanquished – and now you would have us flawed as our Queen was flawed. Light became corrupted and destroyed our world, Korlat, or have you forgotten?'

Korlat's smile was a sad one. 'Cherish such flaws, dear sister, for our Queen's was hope, and so is mine. Now we must leave.'

Kruppe's expression was benign as he watched Crokus approach, clearly exhausted by this night of endless running. He nudged Murillio and fluttered his fingers in the young thief's direction. 'The lad returns with undue haste, yet I fear such sad tidings as Kruppe must bring.'

'He's had a rough night all around,' Murillio commented. He leaned against the gate's support wall outside the Simtal Estate. The streets remained empty, the citizens shocked numb with the night's horrors.

Kruppe gestured at Moon's Spawn, now a league to the west, well beyond the city's walls. 'A remarkable contraption, that. However, Kruppe is pleased that it has chosen to depart. Imagine, even the stars blotted out, leaving naught but dread in this world.'

'I need a drink,' Murillio muttered.

'Excellent idea,' Kruppe said. 'Shall we await the lad, however?'

The wait was not long. Crokus recognized them and slowed his frantic run. 'Apsalar's been kidnapped by the Empire!' he shouted. 'I need help!' He wobbled to a halt before Murillio. 'And Rallick's still in the garden—'

'Tut, tut,' Kruppe said. 'Easy, lad. Apsalar's location is known to Kruppe. As for Rallick, well . . .' He faced the street and waved his arms expansively. 'Breathe the night air, Crokus! A new year has begun! Come, let us walk, the three of us, masters of Darujhistan!' He linked arms with his comrades and pulled them forward.

Murillio sighed. 'Rallick's missing,' he explained. 'There's some kind of extraordinary house in Coll's garden now.'

'Ah, so much unveiled in that single statement!' Kruppe leaned against Crokus. 'While, no doubt, the lad's secret, over-riding concern at the moment regards the fate of a fair young maiden, whose life was saved at the last moment by a nobleson named Gorlas, of all things. Saved, Kruppe says, from a ton of masonry shrugged off a wall. 'Twas heroic, indeed. The lass near-swooned with satisfaction.'

'What are you talking about?' Crokus demanded. 'Who was saved?'

Murillio snorted. 'I think, dear Kruppe, Master of Darujhistan, you've got the wrong fair maiden in mind.'

'She's not fair, anyway,' Crokus asserted.

Kruppe's chest swelled slightly. 'You need but ask the gods, lad, and they'll tell that life itself isn't fair. Now, are you interested in how Lady Simtal's estate has just this night become Coll's estate? Or is your mind so thoroughly enamoured of this new love of yours that even the fates of your dearest friends – Kruppe included – yield such lack of interest?'

Crokus bridled. 'Of course I'm interested!'

'Then the story begins, as always, with Kruppe . . .'

Murillio groaned. 'Thus spake the Eel.'

EPILOGUE

I have seen a rumour born
swathed in snug mystery
left lying under the sun
in the hills of the Gadrobi

where the sheep have scattered
on wolf-laden winds
and the shepherds have fled
a whispering of sands

and it blinked in the glare
a heart hardened into stone
whilst the shadow of the Gates of Nowhere
crept 'cross the drifting dust of home

I have seen this rumour born
a hundred thousand hunters of the heart
in a city bathed in blue light . . .

Rumour Born (I. i-iv)
Fisher (b.?)

699

The sun lit the morning mists into a shield of white over the lake. Down on the beach a fisher-boat rocked in the freshening waves. Unmoored, it was moments before pulling free of the pebbles.

Mallet helped Whiskeyjack to a dome of rock above the beach, where they sat. The healer's gaze hesitated on the figure of Quick Ben, standing with shoulders hunched and staring across the lake. He followed the wizard's gaze. Moon's Spawn hung low on the horizon, a gold cast to its ravaged basalt. Mallet grunted. 'It's heading south. I wonder what that means?'

Whiskeyjack squinted against the glare. He began to massage his temples.

'More headaches?' Mallet asked.

'Not so bad, lately,' the grizzled man said.

'It's the leg that worries me,' the healer muttered. 'I need to work on it some more, and you need to stay off it awhile.'

Whiskeyjack grinned. 'As soon as there's time,' he said.

Mallet sighed. 'We'll work on it then.'

From the forested slope behind them Hedge called, 'They're coming in!'

The healer helped Whiskeyjack stand. 'Hell,' he whispered. 'It could've been a lot worse, right, Sergeant?'

Whiskeyjack glared across the lake. 'Three lost ain't that bad, considering.'

A pained expression crossed Mallet's face. He said nothing.

'Let's move,' Whiskeyjack growled. 'Captain Paran hates tardiness. And maybe the Moranth have good news. Be a change, wouldn't it?'

From the beach, Quick Ben watched Mallet supporting his sergeant up the slope. Was it time? he wondered. To stay alive in this business, no one could afford to let up. The best plans work inside other plans, and when it's right to feint, feint big. Keeping the other hand hidden is the hard part.

The wizard felt a stab of regret. No, it wasn't time. Give the

700

old man a chance to rest. He forced himself into motion. He wouldn't let himself look back – never a good idea. The scheme was hatched.

'Whiskeyjack's going to howl when he hears this one,' he whispered to himself.

Captain Paran listened to the others on the beach below, but made no move to join them. *Not yet.* His brush with Ascendants seemed to have left him with a new sensitivity – or perhaps it was the Otataral sword scabbarded at his side. But he could sense her, now, already in her adolescence, plump as he knew she'd be, smiling with her heavy-lidded eyes deceptively sleepy as she studied the morning sky.

I will come to you, he promised her. *When this Pannion Seer and his cursed holy war is crushed, I will come to you then, Tattersail.*

I know.

He stiffened. That voice in his head had not been his own. Or had it? He waited, waited for more. *Tattersail?* Only silence answered him. *Ah, my imagination, nothing more. To think you would call up enough of your old life, to find the feelings you once held for me, find them and feel them once again. I am a fool.*

He rose from his crouch at Lorn's graveside – a mound of rocks – and brushed twigs and orange pine needles from his clothing. *Look at me now. Agent for the Adjunct once, now a soldier. Finally, a soldier.* Smiling, he made his way down to his squad.

Then I shall await the coming of a soldier.

Paran stopped in his tracks, then, smiling, continued on. 'Now that,' he whispered, 'was not my imagination.'

The tradecraft hugged the southern shore, making for Dhavran and the river mouth. Kalam leaned on the gunwale, his gaze sweeping the north horizon's ragged, snow-capped mountains.

Near him stood another passenger, hardly memorable and disinclined to talk.

The only voices reaching the assassin came from Apsalar and Crokus. They sounded excited, each revolving around the other in a subtle dance that was yet to find its accompanying words. A slow, half smile quirked Kalam's mouth. It'd been a long time since he'd heard such innocence.

A moment later, Crokus appeared beside him, his uncle's demon familiar clutching his shoulder. 'Coll says that the Empire's capital, Unta, is as big as Darujhistan. Is it?'

Kalam shrugged. 'Maybe. A lot uglier. I don't expect we'll have a chance to visit it, though. Itko Kan lies on the south coast, while Unta is on Kartool Bay, the north-east coast. Miss Darujhistan already?'

An expression of regret came over Crokus's face. He stared down into the waves. 'Just some people there,' he said.

The assassin grunted. 'Know how you feel, Crokus. Hell, look at Fiddler back there, mooning away as if somebody had cut off one of his arms and one of his legs.'

'Apsalar still can't believe you'd go to all this trouble for her. She doesn't remember being much liked in your squad.'

'Wasn't her, though, was it? This woman here is a fishergirl from some two-copper village. And she's a long way from home.'

'She's more than that,' Crokus muttered. He had a coin in his hand and was playing with it absently.

Kalam threw the boy a sharp look. 'Really,' he said, deadpan.

Crokus nodded affably. He held up the coin and examined the face on it. 'Do you believe in luck, Kalam?'

'No,' the assassin growled.

Crokus grinned happily. 'Me neither.' He flipped the coin into the air.

They watched it plummet into the sea, flash once, then vanish beneath the waves.

From near the bow, Circle Breaker slowly nodded to himself. The Eel would be delighted with the news, not to mention greatly relieved. Then he returned his attention to the west, and wondered what it would be like, no longer anonymous to the world.

This ends the first tale
of the
Malazan
Book of the Fallen

GLOSSARY

Titles and Groups

First Sword of Empire: Malazan and T'lan Imass, a title
denoting an Imperial champion

Fist: a military governor in the Malazan Empire

High Fist: a commander of armies in a Malazan Campaign

Kron T'lan Imass: the name of the clans under the
command of Kron

Logros T'lan Imass: the name of the clans under the
command of Logros

The Bridgeburners: a legendary élite division in the Malaz
2nd Army

The Crimson Guard: a famous mercenary company
commanded by a deposed prince

The Pannion Seer: a mysterious prophet ruling the lands
south of Darujhistan

The Warlord: the name for Caladan Brood

The Claw: the covert organization of the Malazan Empire

Peoples (human and non-human)

Barghast (non-human): pastoral nomadic warrior society
Daru: cultural group sharing citizenry in cities in northern Genabackis
Gadrobi: indigenous cultural group in central Genabackis
Genabarii: cultural group (and language) in north-west Genabackis
Forkrul Assail (non-human): extinct mythical people (one of the Four Founding Races)
Jaghut (non-human): extinct mythical people (one of the Four Founding Races)
K'Chain Che'Malle (non-human): extinct mythical people (one of the Four Founding Races)
Moranth (non-human): highly regimented civilization centred in Cloud Forest
Rhivi: pastoral nomadic society in central plains of Genabackis
T'lan Imass: one of the Four Founding Races, now immortal
Tiste Andii (non-human): an Elder Race
Trell (non-human): pastoral nomadic warrior society in transition to sedentarianism

Ascendants

Apsalar, Lady of Thieves
Beru, Lord of Storms
Burn, Lady of the Earth, the Sleeping Goddess
Caladan Brood, the Warlord
Cotillion/The Rope (the Assassin of High House Shadow)
Dessembrae, Lord of Tragedy
D'rek, the Worm of Autumn (sometimes the Queen of Disease, *see* Poliel)

Fanderay, She-Wolf of Winter
Fener, the Boar (*see also* Tennerock)
Gedderone, Lady of Spring and Rebirth
Great Ravens, ravens sustained by magic
Hood (King of High House Death)
Jhess, Queen of Weaving
Kallor, the High King
K'rul, Elder God
Mowri, Lady of Beggars, Slaves and Serfs
Nerruse, Lady of Calm Seas and Fair Wind
Oponn, Twin Jesters of Chance
Osserc, Lord of the Sky
Poliel, Mistress of Pestilence
Queen of Dreams (Queen of High House Life)
Shadowthrone/Ammanas (King of High House Shadow)
Shedenul/Soliel, Lady of Health
Soliel, Mistress of Healing
Tennerock/Fener, the Boar of Five Tusks
The Crippled God, King of Chains
The Hounds (of High House Shadow)
Togg (*see* Fanderay), the Wolf of Winter
Trake/Treach, the Tiger of Summer and Battle
Son of Darkness/Moon's Lord/Anomander Rake (Knight of High House Dark)
Treach, First Hero

The world of sorcery

The Warrens (the Paths – those Warrens accessible to humans)

Denul: the Path of Healing
D'riss: the Path of Stone
Hood's Path: the Path of Death
Meanas: the Path of Shadow and Illusion
Ruse: the Path of the Sea
Rashan: the Path of Darkness
Serc: the Path of the Sky
Tennes: the Path of the Land
Thyr: the Path of Light

The Elder Warrens

Kurald Galain: the Tiste Andii Warren of Darkness
Tellann: the T'lan Imass Warren
Omtose Phellack: the Jaghut Warren
Starvald Demelain: the Tiam Warren, the First Warren

The Deck of Dragons – The Fatid (and associated Ascendants)

High House Life
King
Queen (Queen of Dreams)
Champion
Priest
Herald
Soldier
Weaver
Mason
Virgin

High House Death
King (Hood)
Queen
Knight (once Dassem Ultor)
Magi
Herald
Soldier
Spinner
Mason
Virgin

High House Light
King
Queen
Champion
Priest
Captain
Soldier
Seamstress
Builder
Maiden

High House Dark
King
Queen
Knight (Son of Darkness)
Magi
Captain
Soldier
Weaver
Mason
Wife

High House Shadow
King (Shadowthrone/Ammanas)
Queen
Assassin (the Rope/Cotillion)
Magi
Hound

Unaligned
Oponn (the Jesters of Chance)
Obilisk (Burn)
Crown
Sceptre
Orb
Throne

Bonecaster: a shaman of the T'lan Imass
Chance: a sword dedicated to Oponn
D'ivers: a higher order of shape-shifting
Dragnipur: a sword used by Anomander Rake
Finnest: an object used as a repository of power by a Jaghut
Otataral: a magic-negating reddish ore mined from the
Tanno Hills, Seven Cities
Soletaken: an order of shape-shifting
The T'orrud Cabal: the Cabal of Darujhistan
The Tyrant Kings: the ancient rulers of Darujhistan
Warrens of Chaos: the miasmic paths between the Warrens

Place Names

Apple	A Genabackan Free City
Blackdog Forest	On the continent of Genabackis, large boreal forest on shield bedrock, site of major battles between the

	Malazan Empire and the armies of Caladan Brood and the Crimson Guard during the First Campaigns
Cloud Forest	Home of the Moranth, situated on the north-west coast of Genabackis
Darujhistan	Legendary city on Genabackis, largest and most influential of the Free Cities, situated on the south shore of Lake Azur and peopled mainly by Daru and Gadrobi populations; the only known city to use natural gas as an energy source
Dhavran	A city west of Darujhistan
Free Cities	Mercantile alliance of city-states in northern Genabackis, all but one of which has since been conquered by the Malazan Empire
Gadrobi Hills	Hill range east of Darujhistan, sparsely inhabited at present although once the homeland of the Gadrobi people
Garalt	A Genabackan Free City
Genabaris	Large Malazan-held city on north-west coast of Genabackis and principal debarkation point during the campaigns
Gerrom	A small rural town in Itko Kan
Greydog	A Genabackan city
Itko Kan	Province on the continent of Quon Tali, within the Malazan Empire
Kan	The capital city of Itko Kan
Laederon Plateau	Northern tundra of Genabackis
Lest	City-state to the east of Darujhistan
Malaz City	Island city and home of the founding

	Emperor of the Malazan Empire
Malazan Empire	An empire originating on Malaz Island off the coast of the Quon Tali continent. The original founder was the Emperor Kellanved and his cohort Dancer, both of whom were assassinated by Laseen, the present Empress. The Empire spans Quon Tali, the subcontinent of Falar, Seven Cities, and the coasts of north Genabackis Additional forays include the continents of Stratem and Korel
Meningalle Ocean	Genabackan name for Seeker's Deep
Mock's Hold	A Keep overlooking Malaz City where the Emperor and Dancer were assassinated
Moon's Spawn	A floating mountain of black basalt inside which is a city, home of the Son of Darkness and the Tiste Andii
Moranth Mountains	The mountain range encircling Cloud Forest
Mott	A Genabackan city
Mouse Quarter	An ill-fated district in Malaz City
Nathilog	Malazan-held city in north-west Genabackis
Nisst	A Genabackan Free City
One Eye Cat	A Genabackan Free City
Pale	Free City on Genabackis, recently conquered by the Malazan Empire
Pannion Domin	Emerging empire in south-east Genabackis, ruled by the Pannion Seer
Porule	A Genabackan Free City
Quon Tali	Home continent of the Malazan Empire

711

Rhivi Plain	Central plain, north Genabackis
Seeker's Deep	Malazan name for Meningalle Ocean
Setta	City on eastern coast of Genabackis
Tahlyn Mountains	Mountain range on north side of Lake Azur
Tulips	A Genabackan Free City
Unta	Capital of the Malazan Empire, on Quon Tali

Darujhistan and environs

Despot's Barbican: an ancient edifice and remnant of the Age of Tyrants

Hinter's Tower: an abandoned sorcerer's tower in the Noble District

Jammit's Worry: the east road

K'rul's Belfry/Temple: an abandoned temple in the Noble District

Phoenix Inn: a popular haunt in the Daru District

Quip's Bar: a ramshackle bar in the Lakefront District

The Estates (the Houses)

The Old Palace (Majesty Hall): present site of the Council

Worrytown: the slum outside the wall on Jammit's Worry

Author's preface from the 2007
paperback edition

There is no point in beginning something without ambition. In so many aspects of my life I have held to that notion, and it has led to more than one fiery crash through the years. I still recall, with some bitterness, the response Cam (Ian C. Esslemont) and I received when flogging our co-written feature film and television scripts: 'Wonderful! Unique! Very funny, very dark . . . but here in Canada, well, we just can't budget for this stuff. Good luck.' In many ways, it was what followed by way of advice that proved the most crushing. 'Try something . . . simpler. Something like everything else out there. Something less . . . *ambitious*.'

We'd walk out of meetings frustrated, despondent, baffled. Did we really hear an invitation to mediocrity? Sure sounded like it.

Well, screw that.

Gardens of the Moon. Just to muse on that title resurrects all those notions of ambition, all that youthful ferocity that seemed to drive me headlong against a wall time and again. The need to *push*. Defy convention. Go for the throat.

I like to think I was entirely aware of what I was doing back then. That my vision was crystal clear and that I was actually standing there, ready to spit in the face of the genre, even as I reveled in it (for how could I not? As much as I railed against the tropes, I loved reading the stuff). Now, I'm not so sure. It's easy to ride on instinct in the moment, only to look back later and attribute cogent mindfulness to everything that worked (while ignoring everything that didn't). Too easy.

In the years and many novels since, certain facts have made themselves plain. Beginning with *Gardens of the Moon*, readers will either hate my stuff or love it. There's no in-between. Naturally, I'd rather everybody loved it, but I understand why this will never be the case. These are not lazy books. You can't float through, you just can't. Even more problematic, the first novel begins halfway through a seeming marathon – you either hit the ground running and stay on your feet or you're toast.

When challenged with writing this preface, I did consider for a time using it as a means of gentling the blow, of easing the shock of being dropped from a great height into very deep water, right there on page one of *Gardens of the Moon*. Some background, some history, some setting of the stage. I've since mostly rejected the idea. Dammit, I don't recall Frank Herbert doing anything like that with *Dune*, and if any novel out there was a direct inspiration in terms of structure, that was the one. I'm writing a history and fictional or not, history has no real beginning point; even the rise and fall of civilizations are far more muddled on the front and back ends than many people might think.

714

Gardens of the Moon's bare bones first saw life in a role-playing game. Its first draught was as a feature film co-written by the two creators of the Malazan world, myself and Ian C. Esslemont; a script that languished for lack of interest ('we don't do fantasy films because they suck. It's a dead genre. It involves costumes and costume dramas are as dead as Westerns' – all this before a whole slew of production companies shoved that truism in their faces, all this long before *Lord of the Rings* hit the big screen).

And that was just it. We were there. We had the goods, we knew that Adult Epic Fantasy was film's last unexplored genre – we didn't count *Willow*, which only earned merit in our eyes for the crossroads scene; the rest of the stuff was for kids through and through. And all the other films coming out in that genre were either B flicks or egregiously flawed in our eyes (gods, what could have been done with *Conan*!). We wanted a Fantasy version of *The Lion in Winter*, the one with O'Toole and Hepburn. Or *The Three Musketeers* adaptation with Michael York, Oliver Reed, Raquel Welch, Richard Chamberlain, etc, just add magic, mates. Our favourite television production was Dennis Potter's *The Singing Detective*, the original one with Gambon and Malahyde. We wanted sophisticated shit, you see. We were pushing Fantasy in that sizzling, scintillating context of jaw-dropping admiration. We were, in other words, as ambitious as hell.

Probably, too, we weren't ready. We didn't quite have the stuff. Thinking past our abilities, trapped in the lack of experience. The curse of the young.

When life took Cam in one direction and me in another, we both carried with us the notes for an entire created world. Constructed through hours upon hours of gaming. We had an enormous history all worked out – the raw material for twenty novels, twice as many films. And we each had copies of a script nobody wanted. The Malazan world was there in hundreds of hand-drawn maps, in pages upon pages of raw notes, in GURPS (Steve Jackson's Generic Universal Role Playing System – an alternative to AD&D) character sheets, building floor-plans, sketches, you name it.

The decision to begin writing the history of the Malazan world began a few years later. I would convert the script into a novel. Cam would write a related novel entitled *Return of the Crimson Guard* (and now, all these years later, and fresh on the heels of his *Night of Knives*, Cam's first epic, *Return*, is going to be published). As works of fiction, authorship would belong to the actual writer, the person putting word after word onto the page. For *Gardens*, the conversion meant almost starting from scratch. The script was three acts all set in Darujhistan. The main events were the assassin war on the rooftops and the grand, explosive finale of the fete. There was virtually nothing else. No back story, no context, no real introduction of characters. It was, in fact, more *Raiders of the Lost Ark* than *The Lion in Winter*.

Ambition never goes away. It may shuffle off, grumbling, feet dragging, only to slide across into something else – usually the next project. It doesn't take 'no' for an answer.

In writing *Gardens*, I quickly discovered that 'back story' was going to be a problem no matter how far back I went. And I realized that, unless I spoon-fed my potential readers (something I refused to do, having railed often enough at writers of fantasy epics treating us readers as if we were idiots), unless I 'simplified', unless I slipped down into the well-worn tracks of what's gone before, I was going to leave readers floundering. And not just readers, but editors, publishers, agents . . .

But, you know, as a reader, as a fan, I never minded floundering – at least for a little while, and sometimes for a long while. So long as other stuff carried me along, I was fine. Don't forget, I worshipped Dennis Potter. I was a fan of DeLillo's *The*

716

Names and Eco's *Foucault's Pendulum*. The reader I had in mind was one who could and would carry the extra weight – the questions not yet answered, the mysteries, the uncertain alliances.

History has proved this out, I think. Readers either bail on the series somewhere in the first third of *Gardens of the Moon*, or they're still sharing the ride to this day, seven going on eight books later.

I have been asked, would I have done it any differently in hindsight? And I honestly don't have an answer to that. Oh, there are elements of style that I'd change here and there, but . . . fundamentally, I'm just not sure what else I could have done. I am not and never will be a writer happy to deliver exposition that serves no other function than telling the reader about back story, history, or whatever. If my exposition doesn't have multiple functions – and I do mean multiple – then I'm not satisfied. Turns out, the more functions in it, the more complicated it gets, the more likely it will quietly shift into misdirection, into sleight of hand, and all the back story elements, while possibly there, end up buried and buried deep.

This was fast-paced writing, but it was also, bizarrely and in ways I still can't quite figure, *dense* writing. So, *Gardens* invites you to read rip-roaringly fast. But the author advises: you'd best not succumb to the temptation.

Here we are, years later now. Should I apologize for that bipolar invitation? To what extent did I shoot myself in the foot with the kind of introduction to the Malazan world as delivered in *Gardens of the Moon*? And has this novel left me dancing on one foot ever since? Maybe. And sometimes, on midnight afternoons, I ask myself: what if I'd picked up that fat wooden ladle, and slopped the whole mess down the reader's

717

throat, as some (highly successful) Fantasy writers do and have done? Would I now see my sales ranking in the bestseller's lists? Now hold on – am I suggesting that those ultra popular Fantasy writers have found their success in writing down to their readers? Hardly. Well, not all of them. But then, consider it from my point of view. It took eight years and a move to the UK for *Gardens of the Moon* to find a publisher. It took four more years before a US deal was finalized. The complaint? 'Too complicated, too many characters. Too . . . ambitious.'

I could take the fish-eyed retrospective angle here and say how *Gardens* marked a departure from the usual tropes of the genre, and any departure is likely to meet resistance; but my ego's not that big. It never felt like a departure. Glen Cook's *Dread Empire* and *Black Company* novels had already broken the new ground, but I'd read all those and, wanting more, I pretty much had to write them myself (and Cam felt the same). And while my style of writing did not permit imitation (he's a terse one, is Cook), I could certainly strive for the same tone of dispirited, wry cynicism, the same ambivalence and a similar sense of atmosphere. Maybe I was aware of the swing away from Good versus Evil, but that just seemed a by-product of growing up – the real world's not like that, why persist in making Fantasy worlds so fundamentally disconnected with reality?

Well, I don't know. It's exhausting just thinking about it.

Gardens is what it is. I have no plans on revision. I don't even know where I'd start.

Better, I think, to offer the readers a quick decision on this series – right there in the first third of the first novel, than to tease them on for five or six books before they turn away in disgust, disinterest or whatever. Maybe, from a marketing position, the latter is preferred – at least in the short term. But, thank God, my publishers know a false economy when they see one.

Gardens of the Moon is an invitation, then. Stay with it, and come along for the ride. I can only promise that I have done my best to entertain. Curses and cheers, laughter and tears, it's all in here.

One last word to all you nascent writers out there. Ambition is not a dirty word. Piss on compromise. Go for the throat. Write with balls, write with eggs. Sure, it's a harder journey but take it from me, it's well worth it.

Cheers,
Steven Erikson
Victoria, British Columbia
December 2007

STEVEN ERIKSON

THE MALAZAN BOOK OF THE FALLEN

The epic, genre-defining series

'Homeric in scope and vision . . . a story that never
fails to thrill and entertain . . . a saga that lives up
to its name, both intellectually and in its dramatic,
visually rich and lavish storytelling'
SF SITE

GARDENS OF THE MOON
Bled dry by interminable warfare, infighting and
confrontations with Anomander Rake and his Tiste
Andii, the Malazan Empire simmers with discontent.
Sinister forces gather as the gods themselves
prepare to play their hand . . .

DEADHOUSE GATES
In the Holy Desert Raraku, a long prophesied uprising
has begun and an untried commander battles to save
the lives of thirty thousand refugees. War and betrayal,
intrigue and roiling magic collide as destinies
are shaped and legends born . . .

MEMORIES OF ICE

The ravaged continent of Genabackis has given birth to a terrifying new empire: the Pannion Domin. But something more malign threatens this world. The Warrens are poisoned and rumours abound that the Crippled God is unchained and intent on revenge . . .

HOUSE OF CHAINS

In Northern Genabackis, a raiding party of tribal warriors descends from the mountains into the southern lands. For one among them – Karsa Orlong – it is the beginning of an extraordinary destiny . . .

MIDNIGHT TIDES

After decades of internecine warfare, the tribes of the Tiste Edur have united under the Warlock King. But ancient forces are awakening and the impending struggle is but a pale reflection of a far more profound, primal battle . . .

THE BONEHUNTERS

The prospect of laying siege to the ancient fortress of Y'Ghatan makes the Malaz 14th army uneasy, however this is but a sideshow. The Crippled God has been granted a place in the pantheon – a schism threatens and mortal blood will be spilled . . .

REAPER'S GALE

The Letherii Empire is in turmoil. And the Edur fleet draws ever closer. Warriors, gods and wanderers converge. Soon there will be a reckoning – and it will be on an unimaginable scale . . .

TOLL THE HOUNDS

The Lord of Death stands at the beginning of a conspiracy that will shake the cosmos, but at its end there waits another. For Anomander Rake, Son of Darkness, has come to right an ancient and terrible wrong . . .

DUST OF DREAMS

On Letherii, the exiled Malazan army prepares to march into the Wastelands to fight for an unknown cause against an enemy it has never seen. As others gather to confront their destinies, they all face a dread power that none can comprehend . . .

THE CRIPPLED GOD

The Bonehunters are marching to an unknown fate; in Kurald Galain, they await the coming of the dread Tiste Liosan; the Forkrul Assail wish to cleanse the world; the Elder Gods, too, are seeking to return. And to do so, they will free a force of utter devastation from her eternal prison . . .

'Nobody does it better than Erikson . . .
the best fantasy series around'
SFFWORLD